ANGELS AFTER MAN

RAFAEL NICOLÁS

Copyright © 2025 by rafael nicolás

ISBN: 979-8-9923251-3-3

eISBN: 979-8-9923251-4-0

Cover Illustration by Hyde Angelus

Dust Jacket Illustration by Andie Lugtu

Cover Designs by Alex Patrascu

Part I and Part II illustrations by Gustave Doré

All rights reserved.

No part of this book may be reproduced in any form or by any electronic or mechanical means, including information storage and retrieval systems, without written permission from the author, except for the use of brief quotations in a book review.

At times, I worry that this has all really been just for me. I can only hope it's been for someone else too.

PREFACE

This book contains the following: graphic violence, death (including of elders and minors), societal oppression, body horror, disease, sexism, racism, colorism, classism, imperialism, narcotic and human trafficking, homophobia with use of non-censored slurs, transphobia, bigotry, sexual content, non-graphic sexual violence, graphic trauma regarding sexual violence, pregnancy of non-woman character, military violence, issues of sexual consent, depictions of war and starvation, non-graphic emotional and physical and sexual child abuse and neglect, substance abuse, suicide, mental instability, self-harm, abusive romantic relationships.

All parts contain this content. All parts must be read.

DRAMATIS PERSONAE

God — God the Father, the Lord, our Creator
Satan — the devil, Lucifer, the fallen angel

HUMANS

Tadeo — a boy from a border town
Joana — a girl from a border town
Dante — a boy from a town in the south
Lupina (Guadalupe) — a girl from a border town
Father Toño — a priest from a border town

Metatron — Enoch

ARCHANGELS

Michael — the chief prince, angel of strength, angel of God
Raphael — angel of healing
Uriel — the oldest angel
Gabriel — God's messenger

DRAMATIS PERSONAE

OTHER ANGELS

Dina — the youngest angel
Phanuel — angel of forgiveness, friend of Michael

WATCHERS

Azazel — angel of body painting
Samyaza — lesser angel of healing
Baraqiel — angel of light
Kokabiel — angel of stars
Danel — angel of the sun
Armoni — angel of virtue

DEMONS

Baal — duke, fallen angel of flight
Asmodeus — duke, fallen angel of friendship
Rosier — fallen angel of fruit
Mammon — fallen angel of gold
Moloch — fallen angel of gift-giving
Gemory — fallen angel
Ara — fallen angel

Blessed are the dead

— REVELATION 14:13 (NIV)

PART I
NEW HEAVEN

CHAPTER 1

From blood, there came fire. Nazarene man, God, the Son of God — find him feeding the flames. Through a wound in his palm from a coarse hand drill, his red tears wept, then whipped hot unto themselves. Cracks like those that rip open the Earth, like the breaking of bones. Kneeling was as frail on him as the flutters of oranges, yellows, whites that bloomed bright over a desert-baked, middle-aging face. The shades of Hell, see, cast over the Son of God, the Nazarene man, with a shadow cast behind himself in the shape of death. A misplaced past; what will happen has already happened. Above, the mother moon is shattered into silver pieces to trade for a kiss. But never was it the silver that rewarded the crucifixion. Death was death's reward, and it was a kiss for a kiss. From God, the Son of God, ancient eyes opening in a manger. Incarnation to know to be wretched.

Silence, Nazarene man. Watch the bygone approach, enshrouded in veil and robe, a sentenced stranger without shape. The damned one spoke serpentine, asking if it had been forty days, forty mornings and nights, that they had spent here in silence, in starving. With each footstep, the Nazarene never stirred to the sound of marches between his own nor to each hiss between his prayers. Yet, prayer is pleading; what Son of God implores for his

Father to listen? The carpentry in his blood must have boiled; it believed love must be beat and sawed and nailed to be built. In the temple, the child had touched the wood of a wall, and he had breathed in the dust and hacked it out. No breath of life, see. The Lord's sighs into the mouths of man were absent in the teeth of a Nazarene boy. Hear his mother. She chased her lost son, and she had not found him but an ingrown body of grandeur dreams.

Son of God? You are no Son of God. Pre-determined mad man. Had the Nazarene come to the desert to die from the drought drying the skin of his tongue, or to collapse from the pulses of heat in his divine skull? Or had he come to drown in his animal sweat and find purpose there? Hours past, the man had searched in the sea of sand for all the drowned of an earlier apocalypse. Fingers had bore holes in the ground like those that would tear into hands and feet, pressed to wood the Nazarene man knew the scrape of before his own God-given, mother-ridden name.

First, the devil took a stone and threw it at the man's feet. He said, If you are the Son of God, turn this stone into bread.

But, Satan, it is written: Man shall not live on bread alone.

Then, the mocking devil said, If you are the Son of God, throw yourself from the high temple. It is written that He will command His angels concerning you, and they will lift you up into their hands, so that you will not strike a foot against a stone.

It is written: Do not put the Lord your God to the test.

Thus the devil brought God, the Son of God, with him to see all the kingdoms of the world and answered, All this I will give you, if you bow down and worship me.

It is written that the Nazarene man will die to the crucifix, and it is written that God is alone. He will walk with twelve alone, and he will break bread alone. He was born alone, and he will carry the bleeding of whips and a cross on his back alone. God, the Son of God, will be worshiped alone.

The devil has and will watch God die in tortured agony. In wretchedness. His final miracle.

The Lord will say: Lord, why have you forsaken me? The Lord will say: Lord, to you, I hand over my spirit. The Lord will say, It is finished. I have done it. Write this for they are His final words. I have found purpose through death and only death. It is only through suffering that I have found meaning to being here.

God is dead; He has killed Himself. It is only like this that He could save us.

CHAPTER 2

At the center of Heaven, the archangel Michael was burned at the stake. For minutes, his screams engulfed him and all the angels who'd gathered to watch his silhouette disappear into the trinity of flamed colors ripping at his brown skin, scratching to peel it away before the fires seeped into exposing muscle. As if an angel made of wax, the prince melted. As if he were a candle, thick blood rushed into his mouth, gurgling his cries in pain. Darkness scaled along his body where smoke trickled upwards, but it would not stop. His feet were buried in the Fountain of Life, in her waters, and Michael's burns would stitch closed only for the fire to skin him raw again. He burned, and he healed; bound to the fountain, Michael's suffering never ended and never began.

It was a man, in Heaven, who announced his sin with spindly hands still clutching the rope he'd ceremoniously confined the strongest angel of all with. He was ancient, with colorless hair, wrinkles that shrouded his features — the dark eyes, a stout body beneath a white robe, and new jewels that God had gifted. The man, Enoch the Elder, proclaimed: "The Lord commanded for your chief prince to pay penance." Enoch's marks of age seemed finer now, better carved, more purposefully placed along the sagging muscle of his arms, and they now marked him distinct among thousands of perfectly youthful angels gathered in Heaven, watching with oval-ed eyes or facing away with deep grimaces. "For when he returned to Heaven—" Enoch had to shout over the continual screams of Michael "—your prince came before God and asked for a home for the damned souls of man, where Satan and his followers may hold authority. The Lord, in His mercy, granted the devil his wish but the archangel a punishment — for acting as a messenger for the devil, for being his angel." He was stepping away from the Fountain of Life, and the angels nearby stumbled back as if Enoch were Satan himself. "And for having sullied his body," pure venom in his voice, "with that of the devil — your prince must know penance."

Among all the others, Dina watched, fingers interlocked, barely peering over the shoulders of two tall angels standing before him. And like all the others, his breath hitched. 'Sullied?' The old man, this strange man, who'd arrived in Heaven claiming to be like them, an angel himself. 'Michael sullied by the devil?' The youngest — or was he the second youngest now that this man was here? — looked all about, seeking an answer, hoping someone would ask the question that he wouldn't dare. Others anxiously shifted in the crowd, avoiding gazes or, like Dina, searching for guidance, perhaps from an archangel. But they were absent, all except for Michael.

Enoch spoke once more: "Your prince sullied his body, his body that is God's temple, as all your bodies are temples to God. He was tempted by Satan. He fell into sins of the flesh with the devil. Even your most holy prince betrayed our Lord, Creator. The greatest of God's elect could not be faithful." He took another step, and he spread his arms, offering himself to them. "Let it be known that there is no angel pure of sin, then. All angels are tainted. All angels carry the original sin of the first war." Dina's heart thudded against his chest, and he gripped nervously at his tunic's front, dipped his head, wishing his lace veil would slip down his face to shield his twitching expression and the frightened burn in his eyes. "Those you called the Watchers have proven to Heaven that the devil corrupted even those among you who thought yourselves so holy.

And, because of this, the Lord has said, as He once did: angel will serve man."

Dina's gaze flickered to Michael, to his writhing body — a mere shadow in the tongues of flames. Uneasily, Dina's nails picked at the joints of fingers. He watched. He listened to the gurgles of agony. 'Michael.' It couldn't be true. 'I was the one who revealed to Noah that a Flood would do away with sin.' How could Michael be tempted? Were all angels truly corrupted? Were all angels sinners before God — whether they had even committed a sin or not? Had it been Satan's forbidden fruit, the forbidden knowledge of evil, of sin, of flesh; had it been knowledge alone that condemned them?

"It will be man who inherits Heaven," said Enoch as Dina clenched his eyes shut, trying to swallow a hiccup now of worry and confusion. Where were his friends? Azazel? Armoni? What had Michael and the angels really done to the Watchers? "Man will be the new angels, and man will judge the original angels to see who will serve and who will be cast down." Finally, he proclaimed: "I will be known as Metatron, the first man to live in Heaven. I will sit at the left side of God. Know this for they are His words. The Lord's words."

Over the pain of their chief prince, the angels affirmed, "Amen."

But it was only for seven days that Michael burned, hardly a blink of an eye, and he didn't scream for much longer than Metatron's announcement. Only silence sounded from him after the first three days, even if the fire didn't appear to lose its intensity — or so it is said. Dina himself couldn't handle the sight, and he refused to visit the center of the city for all the time that Michael was tortured, refused to even step outside Uriel's home, even tried not to peer out the sparse windows. Yet, he saw the tortured archangel each time he shut his eyes, and he found himself without appetite for these days, as well. Hiding couldn't save Dina for long, however, for he lived in the house of an archangel, and one day, the prince Uriel returned from the unexplained absence since the stake burning began, bringing with him all the horror that Dina had been trying to avoid.

The front door, suddenly, violently, was thrown open with such a loud screech that Dina — laying on his stomach, sleeping, on the divan — startled awake.

"Seven days," came the voice of Uriel, in conversation, "of penance and burning? Is that really what the Lord commanded or your own whims?"

"Uriel," came the voice of Metatron, "step aside."

"Leave," replied Uriel as Dina hastily climbed off the cushions, stumbling onto bare feet, just in time to see the prince walk into the wide sitting area before the endless library. When Dina saw the old man-angel following behind, he flinched. "This is no place for you, Enoch." Uriel's brows were furrowed, a scowl pulling at his mouth while his hands curled into fists. "You will not touch the library."

But the man, Metatron, stopped, far from the archway leading into the labyrinth of books. His eyes landed on Dina, curiously, then he asked, "Who is this angel?" to Uriel.

Right past the young angel, Uriel halted his steps, facing away, towards the library. "No one."

"You told me that this house was yours alone," Metatron said. "Did you lie, archangel?"

"I don't sin," Uriel replied promptly. "That is Dina. He cleans my house and has no house of his own. Raphael told you of the chaos in Heaven when we heard what the Watchers had done, didn't he?" Metatron was quiet, and so Uriel sighed harshly. "The angels who sinned during our war were blamed and attacked, thrown from their homes. The Lord ordered me to take in this one, though He gave me no reason as to why. Dina is the one who spoke to your great-grandchild Noah." Metatron asked why. "Gabriel hesitated when God ordered His message to be given, and I suppose He wanted to show that even an insignificant angel could easily replace him."

Metatron laughed. "Is that so? So it is not only Michael's affinity for sins of the flesh, nor your lies, that have created God's dissatisfaction with His archangels? It is doubt."

"I told you that I don't lie," Uriel said, twisting around to show Metatron a glower. "Days that Raphael and I have spent before the Lord, trying to convince Him that your pride is like that of the devil. But it must be that He knows you will ruin yourself, that you will fall, and that you will bring the fate of man with you." Lower, he added: "You will not touch the library I have curated. All of Heaven's wisdom is here, and you will not corrupt it. It's the meeting of man and angel knowledges that flooded your Earth. Leave this place. Return to God if you so claim to be at His left side. Fly as high as you can, Metatron, so that you will burn to dust when you fall back to the Earth you belong."

"You will be the one to fall when us men judge you." But Metatron was turning on his heel, and as he did, he said, "I will be back, Uriel. The library will hold the history of man, whether you will be here to read it or not." His departure was quiet, his steps slow as he returned to the entrance that was just out of sight of the seating space with its three divans, its short tables, one of which held a scroll that Dina had been mindlessly skimming hours ago.

The young angel hesitated, then timidly raised his face to the tall Uriel, whose expression was hot stone, eyes so sharp in rage that Dina feared staring too long would cut him. "Uriel," he called softly. "Has Michael really been freed from the penance?"

"Start cleaning out the eastern side of the library," Uriel commanded, instead of answering, before he exhaled through his nose, face flickering with something akin to fear but too angry. "Metatron will return with God's blessing. I'm certain of it. Clean out the eastern side and then keep your mouth shut when he speaks to you. Do you hear me?" Dina nodded aggressively and tried to scurry behind as Uriel stepped into the library, began making his way across it. "Michael has ruined the last good will that us angels had with God. We will all pay the price." Dina looked back, as if Metatron followed, or as if Michael followed. He kept wondering of Michael, if it had really been seven days only, if God had been kind enough to be satisfied with that. "All of us will suffer because of the damned Michael, because of Satan, because of the Watchers."

Suffer? Dina didn't think so. For the rest of his life, he didn't think so.

The next time Metatron arrived, he did come proclaiming God's approval, and he'd come with tablets already, histories of humanity and genealogies that only he, the one man in Heaven, could inspect for accuracy. Uriel, this time, didn't resist when Metatron went to organize what he'd brought while Dina stood behind the prince's back, clutching a broom to keep his hands from trembling. An old friend, Armoni, had taught him to clean, had told Dina, 'It will always make you feel better. Even the worst of sadness isn't as terrible as it could be if you're in a spotless room.'

'I confess,' Dina thought, 'to not understand your anger, Uriel.' When Metatron snapped at Dina to help chase away the dust from some of the limestone shelves, Dina tried a pleasant smile, and he did as told even if he could feel Uriel's flared, angry look."Yes, Metatron," the young angel said obediently and dealt with the dust.

He simply couldn't understand why Uriel was furious, but he supposed that he was a sinner, and this was no different than how he'd been treated before. Half of Heaven lamented that they were ruined now, but Dina had been ruined by sin for most of his years. And thus, when Metatron left, then returned with more scrolls, Dina met him amicably, and he aided him. Each time Metatron brought more human wisdom, Uriel argued, but Dina never did. The young angel didn't even yelp when Metatron slapped him for dropping a stone tablet.

Time went on like this, and eventually, Dina no longer woke up cold, alone in Uriel's spare room, frightened to half-death from the image of Michael burning. If he tried to recall it specifically, the memory would return in horrific vividness, but it was merely one of many violences that Dina had seen by now. Heaven lived on forever, regardless.

Metatron, however, preached change, and Dina, one day, noticed that the materials being wheeled into the library were growing more divergent from all those that came before. Suddenly — wooden boards, thicker pages, a thick covering that could have been skin. That was odd; it'd only been a thousand or two thousand years since Metatron had risen; that seemed too quick for Earth to change to Dina. Distantly, he heard Uriel always arguing with Metatron, claiming that infesting the library with the scripture of living humans was a step too far. But — 'This is beautiful?' — Dina busied himself tracing the illustrations he found in the new manuscripts, the shape of humans, then animals, then all the flora. What a lovely place Earth seemed.

More books, more stories. More charming illustrations of humanity. With each day, Dina buried his face deeper into parchment and leather and tales; he hardly noticed what Metatron and Uriel were yelling about.

Dina heard something of a Christ. A man who was killed, as many of them are. And then Metatron said that man will all rise to Heaven, soon. Blink of an eye, and then Metatron said that not yet. Dina paid no mind, entranced by the stories he tried to decipher from illustrations because he couldn't read the human scripts. Some more blinks of eyes. Time passing. A century, then half of another one. Metatron called it the end times. Uriel ignored him. The end is near, but not too near. Dina waited.

It wasn't until a moment like any other that Heaven, like Earth, finally changed too — one instance in which Dina had accidentally dropped a thick book while dusting, then been struck hard across the face by Metatron and shoved into the half-cleaned tall shelves. "Forgive me," Dina replied instantly, the movement of his jaw numbing. "I didn't mean to—" There was no confusion, no indignation. Another violent memory for a body that held onto little else.

"This is the third time in the last few days," snarled Metatron. "How could I believe you? What has you so distracted?"

Blinking a few times, still leaning on the shelf he'd just landed against, Dina replied, "I can't be sure, but it won't happen again. I'll be more careful when I clean." He tried smiling through the ache of a forming bruise but Metatron took a sudden step forward, slammed his hand down on one of the limestone shelves. Every folded, rolled, engraved piece of wisdom there rattled, on every level, climbing so high they'd reach Heaven if they weren't all already there — but none dared fall for him, this man.

Metatron snapped, "Stop causing trouble." 'Don't you ever miss being a man, Metatron? I would. If I had been human once, I think I would miss it.' "Do you hear me?"

Golden, silver — the taste of blood in Dina's mouth as he nodded and lowered his body to pick up the book he'd dropped. "I will be good." He was already stepping away, reeling in a breath. "And I'll leave you now." Metatron visibly clenched his teeth, but he was moving, as well, turning back on the youngest angel, heading off.

To escape the labyrinth, one had to take as many left turns as they could, then a right turn when they approached the most modernly bound books, standing upright with their spines flaunted at each passerby. Dina often traced the titles he couldn't read, and he would have done it now were it not for the book he hugged to his chest — one of his favorites. Not far from here, the illustrated collections were, of which this large book actually belonged. Both Enoch and Uriel didn't care much for that section, crinkling their noses at the illustration of princes and their princesses, whereas Dina would often stare at them, purposefully trying to keep his mind empty, to not let a single thought form about the loving touches in the fairytales. There was also, often, art of winged people in Dina's favorite books.

'Fairies,' Uriel had called them once. Afterward, Dina had pointed at another illustration, and Uriel had answered, 'Eros.' And when Dina had opened a third book and held the woodblock-print before Uriel's fiery eyes, there had been a pause, then a hint of amusement in his deep, cold voice, 'That's Gabriel. The human's Gabriel.'

Some stray bookcases trailed toward a circular space that had once been part of a wider dining area but was now a mere carpet and plush velvet chair before a fireplace built into the wall. On the hearth, there were dying, dancing flames — and Dina remembered Michael — then he drifted his gaze to see the angel sat upon the chair with a blanket over his lap. Uriel, staring straight at the fire, in silence, hair covered by the hood of his onyx-black robe, speckled with tiny white specs, stars.

"Uriel?" Dina shuffled his feet closer. "There you are, brother. You didn't come earlier to eat..."

Without looking at him, Uriel replied, "I heard Enoch shouting at you." 'Metatron,' Dina wanted to correct him, but he simply frowned instead. "He's right that you've been more careless lately."

"Oh, it's my fault for thinking too much," Dina reassured, moving closer, lowering to settle on the ground right by Uriel's legs. "I was going to put my book away in its proper place, but I'd really like to sit here with you for a minute first. I hope that's alright with you." He turned his head up at him, blinking silver eyes. "Are you well?" Silence responded, but Dina didn't mind, flickering his gaze back toward the flames, searching for familiar shapes.

Then, a slow exhale, and Uriel said, "The humans are likely to come soon to Heaven. A lot of them." Leaning back into the chair, there was a high-pitched creak between the crackles of the fireplace. "The world is going to end soon. The Lord has told me."

Dina jumped, then laughed a little. "Is that so? That's exciting. We should continue building homes for them." He cracked open the enormous book in his hands. "I can't wait to see families here. I love children." He'd never seen a real one of course, but on the page he turned to, there was a sketch of a cherub.

Uriel murmured, "We don't age in Heaven. Will the humans who come here as children grow old or will they remain that way forever?" Dina flipped to another section of his book to see the reclining figure of a woman. "Maybe they'll be stunted." When the archangel paused, Dina lifted his head again and noticed Uriel's hard stare. "You're not even a little frightened... are you?"

"What's there to be frightened about?" asked the youngest angel.

"You don't see, at all, how they'll displace us? How they don't belong in Heaven?" Uriel leaned over the armrest, hovering his face not far from Dina's own. "Each one of them will be a new Enoch, a pile of flesh masquerading as one of us. It's as if you immediately forget each time that old man mistreats you. When Heaven is invaded by humans, and we're all suffering under their hands, will you ignore all of that too, Dina?"

Unsure, Dina said, "I don't think it'll be so bad, and I trust Enoch. God wouldn't let him live among us if he weren't wise." He barely suppressed the urge, as he often did, to reach and touch the archangel's hand. "I'm sure the Lord keeps us in mind."

The archangel paused. "You don't have the faintest idea of how wicked the humans are. All you read are fairytales and children's stories. You can't tell fantasy from truth. When they rise to Heaven, they will bring war back to us."

"But Metatron said," Dina argued softly, "that God will only bring the humans who are good here. All their wickedness will be washed away." 'Metatron spoke of another baptism.' Dina didn't really know what baptism was, of course, but he knew it meant a great deal to the man-turned-angel.

"There are no good humans," Uriel grunted, then leaned back against his chair again. "But if we're to believe they'll all transfigure into angels, which supposedly Enoch has, then that wouldn't be much better. We will all suffer. The humans will ascend into Heaven, and we will fall." Quieter, he added, "And we have sown the seeds of our own destruction."

A deep, deep frown tugged on Dina's lips, as he turned to his book once more. "I hope that doesn't happen," he said simply. "I hope the humans will be very kind."

There was, yet again, a moment of silence, but a hand eventually lowered itself onto Dina's hair, covered by the same lace veil he'd worn for many, many centuries. "I don't know why I tell you this." In his chest, Dina's heart had stuttered in confusion, in joy at Uriel's gentle touch. "You never understand."

"I'm sorry."

"Don't be." The prince shifted again, but not significantly, perhaps just crossing his legs. "You were made this way. We're all designed."

Dina wanted to lean into the touch, but he knew Uriel would jolt away from affection, maybe snarl at him; it had happened each time the young angel had tried to simply embrace him. "I wish I'd been made a little less like this," Dina said off-handedly. "But I also like living here with you." Dina's thinking made him smile again, then lift his body up to look over the armrest and at Uriel's sullen face. "You should talk to me more."

Furrowing his brows, Uriel nearly scoffed, but he didn't remove his hand from Dina's head. "About what? I've told you plenty of things already. Too many things. Haven't you been listening to me just now?"

"But there's a lot you haven't told me either." Dina waved a hand in the direction of the books.

"Such as?" Uriel prodded, his tone a little fonder than it ever was.

"Such as…" Dina glanced at the mouth into the labyrinth, thinking of the day that he knocked the archangel's most precious scrolls to the ground, then fallen to his knees and hurriedly pulled them all into his arms, but the prince of wisdom had appeared instantly, then shouted at him.

'It was the first time you'd ever screamed at me. You were always upset with me, but had never raised your voice, so I began to cry. Right in front of you, I started sniffling and rubbing both my eyes. It only made you angrier, but as you bent to pick up your writing, your hand lingered over the sketch of a star in between the calligraphy. You weren't very good at art, often ordered other angels to illustrate your manuscripts, but you could very well draw suns. Wiping at a tear, I stared at the star with you, and I said that all of your favorite scrolls have stars. You didn't answer me. I said that I knew this because I drop things so often. You said that, one day, I will break something of yours, and you will break me.'

The archangel's hand began to drift away like a lonesome twig swept by flood.

Dina whispered, "Why do you have this library?" It was Uriel's home; he slept in a dark room far from the exit and far from Dina's own bedroom. "I noticed that all the oldest writings in here are about the stars." 'You don't like that I've noticed, but Metatron has noticed too.'

"To remember," Uriel replied simply, "histories and dreams. Eternal life means eternal memories."

"What is there to remember," Dina asked, "about the stars?"

The question lingered, as the young angel had thought it would, but not as long as expected. Uriel, oddly, chuckled, and said, "Many angels before you have asked. One angel, Danel, when we were building the city, tried to meet the stars and find out everything about them to impress me. Many angels have tried to impress me." He listed a few names, some known and some unknown. "Lucifer, too, once followed after me, and I avoided him. And there was... Kokabiel. Angel of stars."

"I remember him... He was very strange."

"I hated him." Dina was saddened again — an angel should never hate — but Uriel continued, "He knew every detail of what came before somehow. When I told him to explain himself to me, he laughed in my face."

At this, the young angel raised a brow. "What is it that came before?" To Dina, the devil had come before, and all of Heaven had come before. He didn't remember the city of angels before sin much, as one of the first things he had ever done was sin. 'I still remember him. Golden-haired and bright eyed, the devil cooing in my ear to take the pretty rings I liked.' But the rest of life before the war, he didn't remember well. He should have been like Uriel, should have kept his own library of the world he needed to remember.

It was one final hesitation before Uriel surrendered. "You can go to where my oldest scrolls are and read the truth for yourself. If our world will end soon, alongside that of man, then I won't feel shame for much longer." Dina realized he still held his book, his human likings. "So go and read, if you like, but it's in an old script. You'll have to learn it."

"I'm not very good at reading," Dina lamented because he was not good at quite anything at all. "Can't you read it to me?"

"I can't." However brisk his response, Uriel didn't sound so cold for once; he was like the fire still before the both of them, crackling and warm and dying. "You should learn, then you should read the histories as I've written them. Then, afterward, you should..." His voice — uncharacteristically uncertain. "You should climb up into the cosmos and see the stars for themselves." He extended both his thumb and index, curling the rest of his fingers. "Travel forward, do not veer to the left or right, until you come upon a star. The stars are always moving, so I can't tell you which one you'll meet first that way, but if you don't go straight, you won't find your way back. I want you to touch it, try speaking to it. Sometimes, they talk in their sleep."

"But I thought the laws say we mustn't leave Heaven without purpose—"

"I'm giving you purpose." Uriel turned his head to him. "Do as I say. I'm still your prince. I want you to know the entire truth, not the kinder version that Heaven has invented so they can sleep soundly. I can't go with you. The Lord has ordered me to study the Earth for some years. I'm leaving very soon." He breathed in deep, then exhaled slow. "I need someone to know before we're all gone."

"Uriel," Dina called, his eyes squinting in innocent fear. "Do you really believe that our world will end the same as the humans'? Do you believe all us angels left here will fall?"

"I heard that all of time will end soon from God's own mouth."

Threats of God collectively punishing all angels had been shouted from the rooftops when the Watchers' sins reached Heaven, when Dina was thrown out into the street. He remembered a kick against his head, hands grabbing his clothing, spit landing on his face. They said the sinners had caused this, surely Azazel, surely Armoni, or any of the others. But it had been Armoni and Azazel that so gently led Dina through life in the shadows after the war, who were so patient with him, who preached hope with kisses to his cheeks. "Will I see old friends again before the end? I want to."

Uriel whispered, like he didn't want their Father to hear: "If God is merciful, He will allow you to forget them."

CHAPTER 3

His father was dead. In a town bordering a nation like Babylon — they found the man hanging from an electrical cord, a cloth bag over his head, his wrists bound behind his back, his legs severed to end in a few ribbons of pink-red, tossed occasionally by the breeze. He wasn't alone — five other bodies hung beside him on the overpass, dangling above a road of vehicles that either passed hurriedly or skidded with a screech of tires and swerved to halt right before daring to cross beneath corpses. His aunt had tried to cover his eyes when they all found him, but the boy had already been staring for several seconds, his blood cold in the scorch of summer. Tadeo was his name — the boy of eleven or twelve years — and he had been squinting, trying to read the words on the banner that was plastered right below the dead men.

Tadeo was his name, even when he came to realize that the screams of horror came not from his aunt but from himself, and his name didn't change even when he doubled over with wet gasps scratching at his throat. Beat after beat, his heart punched the front of his chest, terror about to shatter him inside. Tadeo was the name of the body he felt himself wrenched away from when he collapsed against his family, their hands all coming over him, like thinking to bury him. Like they would lay him in the grave alongside his father.

He would never learn why they killed him — his father — not really. It may have been a confrontation, a case of mistaken identity. Tadeo's father was not a criminal, and he had been so staunchly against them. He'd told Tadeo, in their language, "When I was younger, son, the streets weren't like this. There used to be musicians downtown, and foreigners from right across the river used to visit."

There had been no musicians downtown when Tadeo's family walked past the boarded-up buildings, heading to report his father missing after service at church. During the mass, Tadeo had sat bored, praying only marginally for the father he adored because he couldn't imagine a life without him yet. Three days with an empty chair at the dining table had bothered him, as well as the unfamiliar silence at breakfast, but he couldn't believe that he'd been kidnapped, much less potentially killed. 'You're going to live,' his father always hummed beneath his dark mustache, 'you're going to suffer.' The lines to a song that Tadeo wasn't sure he'd ever heard.

In Heaven, an angel set down his collection of fairytales and old scrolls about the beginning of time, dreaming of happily ever afters, then decided to leave paradise — heading for the stars.

Now, before the death of Tadeo's father — life had not been so kind either. As stories of murders, kidnappings, and traffickers grew, turned deeper like a gash, gaping wider — foreigners came by less, the bustling economy began to trickle dry. Less food in the fridge, and then Tadeo's family moved back into the house of his maternal grandparents, and he, a toddler, shared a room with both his parents. As the situation worsened, the state proclaimed that the rampant corruption of the police force was to blame — 'criminal infiltration' — then ordered an expulsion of all officers to be replaced with a temporary military operation. For a year, then another year, then around eight, the soldiers remained. But Tadeo cared little for any of this; he was a child.

None of this could matter to a child, and I'm certain it hardly matters to you.

So if anyone had asked Tadeo what his greatest problem was during the early years of military occupation, he'd say that his mother was constantly yelling at him. She said he didn't dress right, didn't wear his hair right, and that he didn't cook right, nor did he rub a lime on his elbows and knees to fight the darkness there, as she insisted he do. Tadeo's mother was now a hairstylist, working in a small place beside an office for currency conversion, and as Tadeo aged, the fury between them grew as large. His father was the calm eye to their storm, meeting them with gestures for them to sit and to laugh their arguments off. Two years before his death, he'd been in the room when his wife suffered a stroke, and he had carried her to a hospital, then wheeled her out, newly disabled, within a week. Tadeo's father took on more hours in the restaurant he was a server in, to Tadeo's great sadness.

Angel Dina climbed toward the cosmos with Uriel's writings in his mind about what had occurred to the stars, though he remained confused about the details. Most particularly, he didn't understand God's behavior. 'I believe Uriel,' he thought wholeheartedly — but God couldn't be so cruel to disfigure angels into burning spheres of fire and leave them like corpses above. As he struck his wings, broke past the golden sky, he stumbled onto the cold abyss of the universe only to then swerve clumsily, trip and plunge toward the floor of the cold universe. He landed with an erratic flutter of his pale wings, and then lay over the wet ground, seeing all of space from its very edge. With every galaxy a speck in his silver gaze, he stood, then began walking along the void.

The story of Tadeo's life is relevant; it had thus far been a moderately unfortunate one. His mother was now in a wheelchair, struggling severely with lifting either hand, never speaking, half her face in permanent stillness, the occasional dribble of saliva slipping from a corner of her mouth. Before his murder, Tadeo's father asked his wife's coworkers to teach him how to do cosmetics, and he would paint his wife's face gently, patiently, knowing she wished she still could. Tadeo began to cry often, wishing he had loved his mother deeper when she could do more than groan at him, but how could he have known? In the same vein, he wailed in a deep, tortuous agony for the kind father after he lost him, having never thought of this, never imagined a life without parents.

Dina adjusted his hair and veil, then turned his face to a great, humming star so massive it appeared closer than it was. Blinking a few times, the angel approached, interlocking his own hands, tilting his head. Is this what Uriel had wanted him to see? The star was little more than a ball of yellow-red, but its consistency was not like fire — rather, it was thick as blood. It could have been a sphere of gore, burning and screaming in forever torment. At the same time, it was beautiful, warming Dina inside as he was heating on the outside. "You're beautiful," he told the star, each step making him smaller and smaller in its massive presence. "The most beautiful thing I've ever seen."

Tadeo grieved; he grieved so greatly that he wailed to his relatives: "The world is over. The world is ending." How can all these awful things be happening? "God, why did you do this to me?" His grandparents ran their hands along his back, even the paternal ones who'd traveled from their hometown much further south. "Please give me my father back. My mother and I need him. Please. I'll do anything. God, please don't leave me without my parents." Some relatives suggested migrating to that nation they bordered, but it was so expensive, so difficult, and they were a large family. Who should escape? Who should be left behind in this war?

Before Dina could speak another word, he bore witness to the star before him suddenly twitching, limbs curling out from its sides, the arms reaching upward in a towering stretch as its legs unfolded beneath. Its silhouette lost some of its roundness to morph into the vague shape of an angel with a face. On it, there was a pair of enormous eyes like flaming coals and several mouths that were each magma teeth and magma tongue. Its yawn was loud, harrowing, rattling nearby moons and skipping comets. Then, before the little angel, the star lowered itself to an animal pounce, bringing its face just some breaths away from Dina. "Oh," Dina breathed, wonder filling his heart. "Like this, you're even more beautiful."

The star spoke in a saccharine voice like honeyed dates: "Angel."

And Dina felt a shiver creep up his body. "What are you doing here?"

Dina stared with wide eyes, parted lips. "Me...?" His voice drifted, though naturally; he noticed that whenever the star spoke, it did so with a certain distance to each syllable, something that trailed further and further away like smoke from a cigar. "Well," he began, then echoed himself. "Well. I'm here because the archangel Uriel ordered me to come." The sun seemed to tilt its head, light flares falling onto its shoulders like waves of hair. "But he told me that all the stars were sleeping. You seem wide awake, or are you talking in your sleep?" There was warmth on the cheeks of the youngest angel, and he realized he felt embarrassment without explanation. But angels are made of shame, can hardly feel anything else.

"Sleep? Oh, I suppose I was asleep once. I dreamt for billions of years, but now I'm awake." With one appendage like a hand, the star waved dismissively. "In all the time since, no angel has come to visit me. You said Uriel sent you?"

"Yes," Dina answered, hesitant. "What do you mean no angel has come to see you? Hasn't Uriel? And—" He knew that he ought to ask now before the star might reply with another question. "You should give me your name. I'll give you mine in return. It's Dina."

Slow, languid, like a needing moan — "*Dina?*" The star grinned impossibly wide. "What a gorgeous name. It suits you, your face and your body. That's quite the body you have. It's the first angel flesh that I see so close. Is it comfortable? Are you comfortable?"

Dina placed his hands on his own chest, his ribs, then his forearms. "I think I am, or that I could be. Uriel says that body discomfort is expected for an angel. Don't you feel some discomfort as well?"

"None at all. I don't have a body." Like a predator, the star stalked closer, bringing its fiery face dangerously close before Dina's figure. "I was asleep for a long time, but last I was awake, I was watching all you angels in Heaven, and I was watching the Earth too. It's so far. I could hardly see anything of you all. I was always curious if angels were happy. Are you happy?"

Swallowing, Dina glanced behind him, saw darkness, then looked forward once more. "You've been awake before? But Uriel said that all of the stars have been asleep since before Heaven was built."

"Oh, but what does Uriel know?" Snickering, shaking shoulders. "Why would we want to talk to him?"

"He cares about you," Dina replied. "He's filled his library with stories dedicated to you."

"No more talk of Uriel," went the long, irritated sigh that responded. "I want to hear of you." Dina parted his lips, wanted to ask why. "I asked if you're happy, but you didn't answer me. That must mean you're not. If you're not, then why would that be?"

Instantly frowning, shaking his head, the youngest angel argued, "That's not true. In Heaven, all of us angels are happy." They had no choice. "But..." He tilted his head, walked his gaze toward the dark of the void embracing them, staring at a dot of pale blue in the distance; it may have been the Earth but it could have easily been anything else. There was nothing special about it from here, and from this distance, one might understand how God could live with the blood on His hands. He may not even notice it, walking along the nebulas, crushed life beneath His feet, stuck to His sandals. Surely, there were other Earths, too; did they also carry Heavens on their crowns? Dina wondered if there were other angels, somewhere far away. Another Dina, another Dina in every direction. A universe, a labyrinth of mirrors.

"What bothers you, angel?"

Dina could forget his troubles here, but he also could not, noticing now a quiet buzz from the abyss — God's chest rumbling as He slept, perhaps. "I've sinned. I can't be happy if I've sinned."

"Sin? You disobeyed your Creator?"

Shutting his eyes, lifting fingers to touch the lace of his veil, the material too soft to scrape, but Dina still felt as if his fingers bled. "It was a long time ago." He remembered the sensations of feet striking against his chest until they broke it down, like a door, and some of his ribs snapped downward, pierced straight through his heart. Agony had filled his mouth hot, wet. "Satan's angels hurt me during the war, but I deserved it. Everyone saw that I had rings that didn't belong to me." 'Even if on broken fingers, held up to the light that was returning to Heaven slow, like a drop of ink in water.' "I took something that didn't belong to me. I did it even before the war... Satan told me that I would love them, so I should slip them off this angel's hands while he rests. His name was Phanuel. It was a sin. I committed sin against him." 'I thought God's angels would save me after Satan and his followers tortured me, but then they hit me as well.' But they were right to do it, unlike Satan's angels. Suffering can be good, can be needed punishment.

'Sometimes, God needs you to suffer.' For the right reasons. 'Only God can punish me.' A body built for only God to hurt. Only God's striking hand can be righteous.

The star asked again, "Are you happy?"

"I could be," Dina whispered, eyes fluttering open, but his vision hazed, distant as he turned it back to the star. "If I could be forgiven, I'd be happy." But God had already forgiven Dina; His mighty hand had taken his bruised face, dragged along the angel's bottom lip with a thumb, threatening to press it inside, slide along his tongue like human Eucharist. "Though my Father said that He has saved me, I worry that I'm not. Maybe I'm good again but I'm not good how I once was." The angels do not have Eucharist; there has never been a Messiah for the angels, no savior to eat alive. "I wish I could be pure again." Wish he'd never committed the sin at all.

The angels had torn the rings off his broken fingers, left Dina on the road, left the canyon in his abdomen there to continue bleeding, red in rivulets falling to the once-gold street. To Phanuel, the angels had gone to return the rings. 'They left me there.' Someone had spit at Dina and said he'd asked for it, for what he'd received.

"God's forgiveness isn't enough for you."

Painfully — "Am I a bad angel?"

"You want it all to end."

"No. No, no." Dina blinked, stared up at the beautiful creature. "But I miss my friends, and I wish God's forgiveness was enough for me. I wish I didn't... want so badly." 'There's something wrong with you, Uriel always tells me. He says I act and I hope like an angel just a few days old. I don't know how to be sad, he says. An old angel knows how to be sad, doesn't cry anymore. But I cry. I cry like I was born yesterday.'

"I know," said the star, "how you can make everything right again."

"But everything is... as it should be?" He hadn't meant to sound unsure, but Dina was only a few days old. He had been a few days old for millions of years.

The human boy. His name was Tadeo. One day, he finished his school day, picked up his backpack and slung it over a shoulder with a sigh, saying nothing to no one, not even those girls he considered friends. How could he want to speak to other people? He wanted no one but his father, the man who was dead, but it had been months now since his funeral. All he could think to do was take his classroom desk and smash his head against it, but instead, he got onto his feet, brushed past a student who was hurrying forward to speak to the teacher. Heading for the open door into the hallway, Tadeo took the front of his button-up in a fist, tugging on it to have the fabric unstick from his sweaty front. He would walk home today; he would stop by the convenience store for a few things for his family and perhaps an umbrella.

Dense and wet on his skin — the humidity made him grumble. It was enough to make him miss the usual unbearable dryness of the town as he tried to survive the crowded school building and move onto the streets. From the classroom window, he'd caught the gray clouds, and now he saw them with a huff because he'd like to be thankful for the rain — the river needed it — but Tadeo didn't appreciate gray darkness in the afternoon. Grumbling, he went on his way, staring at a vehicle ahead, parked at a corner indiscreetly — something like a large pickup truck in camouflage greens, the bed armed with railings on the sides and a stand for a machine gun. Two men were there, soldiers in helmets and clothes the same pattern as their car, with bulky, dark automatic rifles in their arms.

Tadeo walked past them, didn't give them any attention.

In the sky, the star said, "Everything isn't how it should be.

Wickedness has corrupted God's creation. Angels have fallen. Angels have fallen a second time." Dina flinched, remembering his friends. "Man was banished from Eden for their wickedness. And though they were offered salvation, they've become the most evil creation of all."

"No," Dina said, though he was remembering now how Uriel had said man would destroy Heaven. "That's not true. The humans are beautiful and good and mystical." In every fairytale, they were. In all the stories, the princesses and princes. "They always choose good in the end. They love God so much."

As Tadeo left the store, he noticed the same soldiers he'd seen by his school in the parking lot. They'd brought their car as well. He only saw this because one of the men was stepping away from it, moving toward the entrance, toward Tadeo. Trying to step aside, Tadeo was intent to head home, but a gloved hand came over one of his shoulders. As the soldier spoke, Tadeo stared at the man's shoes, noticing that they were more like sneakers than combat boots. His heart was sinking, somewhere cold, like he was falling off a boat into the middle of the ocean. He'd been born on the beach, his grandparents told him, a few hours away. Firmly, the soldier said Tadeo must come with them.

Tadeo replied that he had to get home, but the soldier said they would take him home afterward.

"You don't know them," said the star.

"I do," the angel insisted. "I read their stories."

"But you see evil there too, don't you?"

"I... suppose I do."

The soldiers sat Tadeo in the back, between two men. It'd be difficult to see him from the windows — though as the truck rattled around, the boy peeked over a shoulder to notice the road becoming quieter, emptier. He asked where they were taking him, beginning to shake, his lungs closing. They didn't answer.

"The only way to destroy wickedness, Dina, is to destroy the world. If you want forgiveness from your fellow angels, you must end all things."

"No. I don't want to...."

"It will all continue how it is. Life will only grow more wicked if you do nothing."

"But not me. Find another angel, star. I love humans." He'd never known one, not well. "I couldn't."

"Don't you want to put an end to evil?"

The three soldiers brought the boy to a car lot, where they raped him.

"I... do."

Afterwards, the men stepped away, talked again.

"Then the world must end."

There were a few options for what the soldiers could do with Tadeo. They could sell him, they could kill him. But it was going to rain soon, and it was still early in the day. They could also send him to one of the extermination sites, right outside of town, lower his carcass into acid, leave a few bone shards to be found a decade from now but maybe never to be identified. A grieving boy's face on a missing poster to hang in the plaza for each of his birthdays to come. Tadeo. Tadeo Morales. His father told him that his name would've been either Angela or Tadeo, depending on what he was born as. Girl or boy.

Behind a car, Tadeo was moving, must've woken up. The men heard him, so one made the decision right then for what to do, and he told the other soldiers to stay on the road as he reached for the gun on the truck before marching across the lot to where the boy was. Without a second thought, the soldier aimed, and the crawling Tadeo turned back his head to stare at him. Briefly, the sun streamed down from between some rain clouds, already drizzling, and the light shined onto the man like Heaven peeking down. The shot was quick, direct, booming with the recoil of the machine, the fire within, and a skull opening, ending.

Lowering his weapon, the soldier turned his back on Tadeo, walking back toward the other men. He called out to them about being hungry. Should they stop by a store for something to eat? They could also go into a restaurant. So many options in life.

"The world," whispered an angel, "must end."

It was as they were preparing to leave, but not quite in their truck yet, that the men heard that car by the body jostle sharply. The three glanced back, saw nothing. One of the soldiers shrugged, then said that he was tired because they'd all woken up so early and suggested they all go nap somewhere before they eat. The hungry soldier shoved him, starting to argue, when the third man, fiddling with the car keys, suddenly, was wretched away, pulled deeper into the lot so fast that the other two almost didn't see the great, clawed hands that'd taken him by the legs. But they both saw perfectly well when those hands grappled their shouting friend's head, his knees, before pulling him apart. It was both fast and slow, the first breaking bones creaking before they snapped and blood, intestine, flooded onto the dirt. A beast, crouched right where Tadeo had been laying dead only a minute ago.

The tired soldier remained paralyzed, but the hungry one lifted his rifle again hastily, shot once, twice, again, again. With each fire, he took steps closer toward a creature his mind refused to comprehend. The monster — who was a mere haze of rippling gore and eyes and mouths — took every bullet as it dropped its victim. Then, it turned, took to matching the man's steps, creeping closer. Screaming spit in the giant's face, the soldier refused to surrender until every bullet was wasted, until he had no choice but to raise the weapon as if a bat. The beast, however, pounced forward to crush him between a thousand teeth. Biting off one limb, then another; it would have been a deliciously slow torture if there hadn't been a final man to take care of. When the beast jerked to look at the remaining soldier, it reached for a sprinting leg. The man tried to shove his gun into his own mouth, but with a violent yank, the beast pulled him into the massacre, and the missed shot flew up to the clouds.

Resurrection only comes to those who suffer for it.

CHAPTER 4

He was furious, of course — Metatron. Dina had returned but stood still before Uriel's home with his veil slipping back from his head, tangling in the onyx threads of his hair, whereas his pale robes were askew, eyes frozen wide with his irises darkened as if staring at the sun too long had burnt him; perhaps, it had. The man-turned-angel stood at the open doorway with a bewildered twist onto his elderly face in the city of youth. "Where in the name of God have you been?!" His voice was loud enough to rattle the dozen or so nearby angels that were already listening in while in the midst of heading to their duties — much of which had become constructing homes for the coming humans.

"Metatron," Dina whispered, the white of his eyes red, almost bloody, and his lips twitched upward, a smile for a fraction of a moment. "I saw a star." He lifted a hand, finger directed at the sky. "He was beautiful, and he told me... how the world must end."

"What were you doing there?" Metatron snapped, stepping out and toward the young angel. "I had no one to serve me for many meals, and now you tell me that you've disobeyed the Lord to wander the skies? God should punish you. He should have your wings torn off your back!"

A flicker of reason and fear passed over Dina's scorched eyes.

"Mm," he blurted. "But— Metatron, I went with Uriel's permission. He ordered me. He ordered me to go see the stars." His feet were weak beneath him, quite suddenly, and he wavered in place; he was still blinking the dark spots from his vision. The sight of the gorgeous star with an unfathomable shape, indeed, had begun to burn after a while, but he hadn't been able to turn away from his smile, his coos. 'Once, there was a beautiful angel who was so beautiful I couldn't linger my gaze too much. His eyes were golden, his skin was shining bronze, and his lips were soft, fluttering against my earlobe when he whispered to me.'

Dina liked beautiful things — rings, stars, and angels. Once, Azazel had told Dina that he was beautiful too, but Dina didn't think so. 'You'll grow into it,' he'd teased, but Dina had not grown. Since the war, he had been stunted, killed.

Metatron struck him, as he often did, as he had before Dina spoke to Uriel and left for the stars. Stinging, like before, the young angel's head jerked to one direction, his feet stumbling again, but this time he had no moment to recover. The man-turned-angel took Dina's veil and hair in a fist, then wrenched him forward, began walking, dragging the young angel. "You don't answer to Uriel," came the harsh scratch of Metatron's voice. "Come with me."

Looking to all the angels watching, Dina whispered, "The stars are waking. They said I must act." Many angels were grimacing and turning away now, one even outstretched a wing to cover the view of Metatron forcing the angel into Uriel's home. "Metatron, please listen to me."

"Be silent."

"What are you doing?" Dina lifted trembling fingers, touched the wrist of an old man as Metatron kicked the door shut behind them. He thought that he might be released the moment he was pulled inside, but he was yanked down the hall, toward the seating area. "Where are you taking me?" 'The books? To clean?'

"When you knocked over that book, you almost found it." Metatron brought him into the same corridor that the two had been in when Dina had dropped his collection. "I had a new room made without Uriel's knowledge. It's where the dictionaries for all the languages of humans are being stored. It's disorganized. It all needs to be copied and rewritten to the key that I've prepared to standardize it."

Dina tilted his head, blinked a few times. "But, Metatron, the star—"

"I could be taking you to God," the old man snapped just as he kicked at the carpet below them, rolling it with his foot to expose a wooden latch and door in the flooring. "I could tell Him how you've disobeyed again, how you are a sinner who should have fallen and how now you've spoken to stars without permission." After this, he lowered himself to grab the latch and pull the entry open into a dark tunnel leading downward. "Instead, I'm giving you work to do. You should be thanking me." Dina stared. "Thank me."

"Thank you," Dina breathed, feeling Metatron's hand finally release his hair and veil. "I'm sorry. Please don't tell the Lord that I've sinned again—" He was shoved — quick, unceremoniously. Wings sprung out, only to slam into the walls of the tunnel; and so despite the rather short drop, Dina scraped his feathers and his sides rough enough to draw blood, which only stung worse when he crashed onto the ground. Shouting sharply and gasping in some of the dirt that was kicked up, Dina writhed for a moment. And Metatron looked down at him, expression irritated. "No— Where's Uriel?!" Dina, lifting a throbbing head, called: "Where is he?!"

"Already gone," called Metatron. "So there is no one to argue on your behalf. Get up now. There's a desk there and some candles. I'll throw you some cushions and blankets to sleep with soon, and some food when you need it."

Feeling one pale wing twitch and bleed beneath him, Dina's face only twisted in greater confusion. "Why? Do you want me to stay here?" He tried to sit up, grunting, and looked behind himself to faintly see the shadows of a stone desk, a triple candle holder of black metal, and piles upon piles of manuscripts, scrolls, and loose leafs creating thick walls from every direction except where the desk was.

"You will be less trouble down there. You hardly leave this house as it is, so why do you cry to me now?"

"Please." Dina begged, eyes itching. "I'll be good. I want to be good. Please don't leave me here."

"Finish the standardizing within a century, and you'll be good and free," said Metatron, then he took the wood latch, pulled it closed, and drowned Dina in near complete darkness.

The angel didn't move, not for many minutes, his hands falling to the ground, curling into trembling fists over it and feeling each grain of dirt dig into his skin. 'He won't tell God what I've done if I just do as he says. Uriel will return soon. He told me when I sat with him that it would only be a few years.' 'But you don't have a few years.' 'I do, I do. I'll live forever.' 'The end has been delayed too long.' It was here that Dina paused, lifted his head. 'Delayed?' 'Hello, Dina.' The angel startled, one hand flying over his mouth but not quite clamping over it. Instead, his fingers touched his lips, trembling. What was that? It was entirely indistinguishable from his own thoughts, except that Dina was sure he hadn't thought that. Why would he greet himself without warning? 'Hello?' he tried.

What may have been a voice in his head replied, 'I can't see into Heaven. There is no starlight there. I can hardly speak to you.'

Dina asked himself, 'Is that you? The star?'

'I can see the Earth, Dina.'

'What do you see?'

'I see that the end of the world is beginning again, but it'll be stopped if you don't act.' Dina nodded to himself; he knew Uriel had been directed to Earth and that all the archangels occasionally visited humanity; perhaps, they frequently halted the end times in its tracks. 'You must leave this place. Go to Earth.'

Frowning, Dina tried to reply, 'Metatron trapped me beneath Uriel's library. He wants me to copy the human languages and standardize their tongues.' He lifted his face, as if he could speak through the floor he was locked beneath, past the house, through the bright firmament that protected Heaven from the stars. 'What should I do? I don't want to rebel against Metatron. I want to be good.'

'There's no need to rebel yet. He was right to put you where you are. Before you visit Earth, you must learn the human tongues.

Learn as many of you can. You must also learn human history if you don't know it yet.'

'I don't like their history,' Dina answered. 'It's too complicated for me. I prefer their stories for children.' But he remembered how Uriel always snapped at him for reading the wrong things, for his love of fairytales and fantasies. He liked morals, he liked happy endings. 'But I suppose I can try.' Finally, he planted a foot down and reeled up his body to stand. The room, however, seemed to stretch before him, all the writing tunneled around him becoming clearer as his blinking eyes adjusted to the darkness. 'There's so many human languages. It would take another eternity to learn them all.'

'Then you'll have to learn the most abundant ones.'

'I don't know what languages they speak on Earth today.'

'I will help you, and I will teach you how to pronounce their words.'

Dina paused, staring before himself at the desk where he would surely begin work copying everything soon. He might sleep there as well, if Metatron were ever to drop down the blankets and pillows he promised. 'Thank you.' The walls of books at either side of him curved toward each other, threatening to topple and crush him. 'I'm happy you can still speak to me. I don't like to be alone.'

'You'll never have to worry about being alone again, Dina.'

The young angel reached the desk, taking the wooden back of the chair and tugging it aside; it was rather simple, which was odd. All the handiwork in Heaven was typically more ornate, even after the war — there was nothing to do in paradise except pray and focus on the details of every piece of labor. Enoch must've had this made recently, quickly. Humans always work with such fatal urgency. Dina saw that there was an open book before him and touched too-thin papers before feeling the boards at the end, which were flimsy and nothing like the old leather that bound his fairytales. Dina didn't know yet about work meant for mass production; he was an angel. Though he was a sinner, alone in Heaven without friends, he was an angel.

For the first year in the dark, Dina mostly copied, following

Metatron's orders and listening to the star's as well. 'Good,' the star cooed when Dina parroted new phrases to him. 'You're learning well.' And he began to formulate what the largest branches of language might be, though imperfectly — focusing on surface-level similarities such as tonal use, rather than similarity in syllables. He was no angel of words; Dina didn't believe he was the angel of anything. 'Oh, do you think so?' Scratching, scratching — the angel's quill on paper filled the silences between Dina's own breaths and the star in his mind. 'I think you could be the angel of anything you like.'

'I want to be the angel of whatever my Father desires.'

'Why? Make something of yourself instead.'

'That's how the devil speaks.' And Dina bookmarked a page, thinking to return to it after he slept in the cot that Metatron had thrown down two weeks after imprisoning the angel. 'I remember it. How he speaks. It's one of the few things I remember of before the war.'

'God will never tell you what you were made for.' Before Dina could reply, the star added, 'But if you don't want to decide what you're for on your own, then I will help you.'

Dina's lips twitched at the ends, wanting to smile. 'You will?'

'All angels are tools, weapons. I'll wield you if God won't.'

'I want to be wielded.' He would like to be used.

'I'll make use of you.'

The second year passed quicker. Metatron seemed happier in an empty house, an angel in its basement to do the work he didn't want. Dina had largely accustomed to the darkness now, and to the lovely praises of his star, and a few tongues. Unfortunately, he had spent too long becoming half-conversational in ancient languages — according to both the star and Metatron — which were apparently not spoken on Earth anymore. Appropriately, Dina was told these were dead languages.

'How is it dead? Where did it go?'

'All its speakers have died or moved on.'

'We angels move on from things, but we can always return when we wish. Do you think the humans will return one day to their old ways of speaking?'

'Humans are like angels — forgetful, but they're not as skilled at recording their history. You can hardly remember your infancy, such is the case with humans. They don't remember their first tribes or cultures. They'll invent stories.'

'I invent stories too, sometimes, when I want to feel better about the past.' It feels wonderful to admit to someone. 'We're not so different from humans.' Dina missed his fairytale books, but Enoch wouldn't give them to him.

'You miss paradise.'

'I don't remember it.'

'But you long for it.'

'Terribly.'

On the third year, the star reminded Dina — though he'd done this many times before — to study human history, but the angel distracted himself with a new language. 'I will get to it soon, I promise. Star.' He didn't know his name. 'There are so many ways that the humans write. Some of it is so similar to the way we've written in the past. It's like they're repeating our history.'

'For the angels, the world ended twice. Once, when God created the stars, and a second time when Satan fell. The humans have suffered an end when it all flooded. They must all know to burn now.'

As Dina tried to sleep — at some unknown hour in maybe the fourth or fifth year — he lay sprawled on the cot, thinking of a story he'd read of a princess in a tower, trapped, waiting. 'She was beautiful with long, endless hair. One day, a prince heard her singing, and he tricked her into letting down her hair before climbing up to meet her.' 'He must've fucked her.' 'That's a sin.' 'But it's what humans do, and it's what the sinners do, and what the fallen angels do. You're a sinner. What's stopping you from doing anything?' 'God will be angry at me.' 'He will be angry at you no matter how you act, Dina.' On the sixth year, Dina recounted another children's story to the star, and the star framed it as a tale of lust once more. Dina listened longer this time, one hand over his stomach, thinking and also not thinking.

'You should know some of the evils of the word,' said the star, 'before wickedness is gone forever.'

'But won't I become wicked and God will do away with me too?'

'You will be done away with no matter what. You know that you've died already, Dina. You will die again. Eternal life is to die an infinite number of times.'

On the seventh year, the star offered his name, which was Apsinthos.

'The world should end, the world should end.'

'You will do it.'

'God will be happy?'

'I will be happy.'

'I do like you. Very much.'

The eighth year — the languages with the most numerous speakers in the world were perfectly known to Dina now. Impatient, however, Apsinthos began to urge Dina: 'That is more than enough now. You need to visit Earth. You've spent enough time here. Human life is so short. What has been mere seconds to us has been enough for millions of births and thousands of deaths on Earth. You must leave.' And so when Enoch next opened the latch and called out, the young angel hurried to look up at him, veil gone, hair frayed, unwashed for days, eyes bloodshot. Parting his lips to ask if he could be let out now, but Enoch shuddered at the sight of him, told him he'd send down a bucket of water. The next time that Dina begged, Enoch insisted the young angel was not done.

'We're losing time. Dina. Dina, the world's apocalypse will be halted by those who don't understand why it must end. You must leave this place.'

'The world must end. The world must end.'

'Attack Metatron!'

'Beneath his skin, he is like chariots, fire, and wheels. I am nothing but wings. He will make me dust.' He slept little now, a plate of food untouched and stacked with another full plate at the front of the desk, which already was buried in a disarray of paper, ink, books, scrolls. 'And I am to serve him. When he stepped into Heaven, the Lord's booming voice called out for us to serve him.'

'You must act, Dina.'

'I'm sorry. I'm sorry.'

And it was on the tenth year of the youngest angel's imprisonment that archangel Uriel finally returned. He did it with a detesting, exhausted sigh as he landed by the great fountain at the center of the eternally divine city. Then, he looked all about himself, saw some white-robed angels who'd been passing by, who all staggered to a stop to bow and intertwine their hands together in respect. If Metatron had done some good, Uriel supposed, it was that the other angels now seemed to appreciate the stern, scornful prince of wisdom some more. Their old Uriel had never struck them or snarled, at least not in excess, and he was an angel like them, not a man who argued angels were not capable of thought and were all instruments for human salvation.

An angel took Uriel's arm — tight, urgent.

Tilting his head to the side, the eldest of the heavenly host quirked a brow at a smaller angel of wavy hair, the color of almond, gathered into two braids. His face was freckled extensively — instantly, Uriel thought of Dina — even if this was clearly the archangel Gabriel. Like everyone else, he donned a colorless tunic, but a rebellious white lily was tucked by his left ear, whispering, humming. "Uriel—" the youngest prince called, his brows curved in worry, his pale pink lips opening, then closing. "You've returned from Earth."

"Yes," said Uriel briskly, looking to their surroundings again to see the same Heaven he'd left years ago. It was quite the contrast to the deplorable plane in which the living humans toiled; a part of him was still shuddering at all that he'd witnessed. "What is it?" Uriel tore his arm away, swallowing thick. 'That is why you sent me to Earth, isn't it, Father? To see and to shudder?' But Uriel had shuddered in Heaven, too, in the last many centuries. Every time he noted all the new homes that the angels had built, sitting empty and waiting for human to fill them — Uriel would feel all his blood run cold. "Do you have a message for me, messenger?" It could have been a joke, or it could have been an insult; Uriel wasn't sure.

Gabriel said, "I need to talk about the state of the Earth with you. Hardly an angel in Heaven knows how frightening humanity has become, but— There's something else that I needed to tell you about. Immediately." Uriel made a noise of affirmation just as he took the first steps, relieved to feel the road of Heaven beneath his sandaled feet again. "It's about Dina." Then, Uriel stopped once more but maintained his gaze down the road, toward a crowding of angels headed somewhere, likely to a temple to pray or feign praying as best they could. "Metatron hasn't let him out of your house in years. I saw Dina arrive from... Well, he said from the stars. Metatron wasn't pleased with him, and he dragged Dina away. When I confronted Metatron, he told me Dina was being reclusive, is all." Uriel sighed harshly, and then he murmured that he would deal with this. "Ah, good. I thought I needed to tell you immediately because I know that you care about him—"

Scoffing, Uriel unfolded his wings. "Is that so?" Then, he took off back into the air for a flight that lasted mere minutes. The door was ajar when he arrived, flaring the prince's already simmering anger, and he threw open the entrance and shouted, "Metatron!" Slamming the way in behind him, he immediately moved through the hall, face twitching at whatever that old man had done now. Uriel soon found him in the seating area before the library and didn't waste a second: "Explain to me what I've been told."

Lounging on a divan, Metatron was scribbling on his parchment — sentences on something regarding human language. He lifted his gaze, then furrowed his brow. "Welcome back."

"Gabriel tells me that no one has seen Dina for several years." When the man-angel scoffed, Uriel grit his teeth, hardly felt himself move before he found his fists around Metatron's robe, and he found himself pulling him off his seat harshly. "Don't be obtuse. He came back from the stars, and you're punishing him. I gave him the order to go, Metatron. I'm a prince. I was the first prince. I was the first angel. Tell me where Dina is."

Staggering, spitting, then laughing in utter bewilderment. "So it is true? You sent Dina to lose his mind?" Metatron shoved him back, and though Uriel stumbled, he did not let go. "Don't be an idiot, Uriel! I locked him up for his own good. He returned from the stars speaking in riddles, whispering, making no sense to anyone. He spoke of the stars telling him to act."

'The stars,' Uriel thought to himself, eyes widening, long dead hope resurrecting in his chest. 'They must've spoken to Dina. To prevent the apocalypse?' The stars must be rebelling against God's apocalypse plans; they must know that humans have no place in Heaven or in the skies. "Where is he?"

Metatron was quiet, then: "Why did you send him to the stars, Uriel?" But, in the second of silence, the prince noticed distant thumping, and he caught Metatron's scowl before he released him, taking off running in the direction of noise. Metatron shouted after him, "You're a moron! I hid him away so that he could return to normal, but he's no better than before! Leave him where he is or watch how he'll bring madness to your streets how Satan did!" Uriel wanted to shout that Enoch had no idea what he was talking about; he had not been there for when Satan was born, was not there for the war.

The wooden door in the ground was beating like a heart in between a ribcage of fallen tablets and scrolls, some muffled groans at the other side — pained or perhaps starving. Though there was a silver lock, it was open, and as Uriel dropped onto one knee, he took the latch with both hands and, grunting, lifted it.

Though angels did not rot or age, the youngest angel had come close, his hair in such tangles with his lace veil that it seemed to have interwoven with it, his once-white tunic a dirty beige, lips cracked dry. Angels cannot die, no matter how deprived they may be of anything, but they come close; they suffer to a grave, but they never lie it. At least, that is what Uriel had once thought. "Dina," he whispered, catching every detail in that confused, innocent expression. For the first time, his hands itched with the want to touch someone, his arms ached with the need to pull Dina close and squeeze him tight and apologize for not having done more. Instead, he said, "You must go."

"Uriel," Dina barely managed, legs and arms pressed hard against the narrow tunnel so that he wouldn't slide back down into dim candlelight. "You're home."

"The stars spoke to you, didn't they?" Uriel asked even though he could hear Metatron's stomps, his grunting, so close behind. "You must listen to them." 'Do what they haven't thought me worthy of.' He reached for Dina's hand and pulled him out of the hole, then squeezed his fingers. "Please. I'll hold back Enoch as you run." Without hesitating, Uriel let him go, spun around, then threw himself at the man-angel, tackling him against the wall of tablets, taking his head, slamming it down onto the stone. In a bloom, blood spread beneath the crack of a skull soon to give way to angry flames. 'Save us all, Dina.'

Hurriedly, fluttering his wings, Dina took steps backward, heart in his throat, shaking, all his vision blurred. It was so bright in the library compared to his prison that he was nearly blind, but his muscles remembered the paths he'd taken for thousands of years here. Taking off in the opposite direction of the labyrinth, he searched for another way out. 'I will end it. I will end it all, Uriel.'

The priest who led mass today was unfamiliar. Under the flickering light, his dark eyes appeared to shine golden, as if lit aflame, and his smile was wide, and when he spoke, it was slow, curling over the syllables. And he was beautiful, as well — his jaw sharp but not overly masculine, his lashes long, his figure slim but not bony. It was always wrong to stare so much at other men; nonetheless, Tadeo couldn't trail his eyes much further than him, this holy man who seemed too beautiful to be holy. Purring, serenely, he said: "Go in peace."

From one of the back pews, the young man — Tadeo — sat beside a wheelchair, pressed up to the wooden seats, with an older woman slumped in it, her eyes dazed, her tanned hands on her lap, almost in prayer. At his other side, there was a young woman, sitting with her jean-clad legs crossed. Joana, stealthily hiding earbuds in her abundance of dark, loose curls, pursed her lips and furrowed her brows as she tapped at the phone her earbuds were leashed to. Quietly, Tadeo said, "Amen," for the three of them. Then, Tadeo maintained his gaze on the ground and tried to pay no mind to the procession of the beautiful priest and the altar servers down the center, walking away from the altar. Instead, as soon as it was socially acceptable to do so, Tadeo lifted his body to stand, expelling an uneasy breath from his mouth. 'Where is Toño?' Where was the usual priest?

Over the still-singing choir, Joana said, "He should be outside." She had read his mind, had the terrible habit of doing so. Then, her gaze flickered up at Tadeo gravely, and she announced, quieter, "There was a massacre a few hours south." Before the young man could ask, she elaborated: "On a highway, probably heading up here to the border."

"How many?" Tadeo murmured, though there weren't many churchgoers here with them, unsurprising given it was a weekday. Only elderly people were around, almost two dozen, a few middle-aged folks who had something immediate to pray for, and a stray dog that nobody had the heart to kick back out into the warm winter day.

"They don't know yet but at least ten, five of them women." A gruff rasp of Joana's smoker voice — as if she were forty years old at just the first year or two of her twenties.

"Do you think *el padre*—" the father, the priest Toño "—called because of that?"

"No, unless he knew about it earlier today," Joana answered promptly, then clicked her phone to turn off right as Tadeo was going to peer over her bony shoulder and stalk whatever the source of her information was. "But he texted me during the mass. I don't think it's anything big." If it was, Joana probably would have been the one to tell Tadeo, not Father Toño. "I'll come with anyway." Tadeo was about to ask if Joana could take his mother home instead. "I'll take your mom back to your house while you deal with whatever shit he needs." Tadeo snorted a bit.

The mind-reading; sometimes he really believed Joana could hear thoughts, not just his but everyone's. Tadeo had no reason to think otherwise. He believed in the divine, and he believed in magic and miracles. He was a miracle himself.

As Tadeo shuffled out of the pew to take his mother's wheel-chair, the light of the stained glass window nearby painted him. In the last ten years, he'd aged finely from young boy to young man. His hair was now much shorter, however uneven it was, and his face had lost its roundness finally, and his hips were slimmer, his shoulders wider, his skin a touch darker. Proper men's clothes fit him now — loose jeans and a belt, a long-sleeved pale shirt. His crucifix rested against the first buttons of his top, the beads cool around his neck. Truthfully, there was nothing remarkable about his appearance; he looked like his parents, his neighbors, most of everyone he knew. He could have been anyone in a crowd were it not for the bandages covering the upper right half of his skull, lines of white barely avoiding the small piece of his ear that remained and fully covering the hole where a right eye should be. The shot that had killed him once, the mercy kill.

The churchgoers nodded politely, nervously, at him. Many of them knew who he was, though they never said it. Recently, Joana had informed Tadeo that they were all merely happy that he went to church, that he used his curse for good. 'Curse?' Tadeo had echoed, almost laughing. 'It's a blessing, isn't it?' Joana had either not heard or ignored him, but when Tadeo repeated himself, she just chuckled that it may be a blessing but an ugly one. She didn't blame anyone for seeing a monster. 'One day,' Tadeo had said, 'they'll know I was a saint.' Joana had said, 'You have to die to be a saint,' then she'd turned her phone and showed him an address, telling him where to go, where a murder of two was needed, 'so you might've missed your chance.'

Helping his mother's wheelchair over a curb and onto the plaza that the tall church was connected to, Tadeo saw, indeed, the priest he'd been looking for. Toño — a very stout man, wearing plain pants with his Roman-collar shirt — sitting at a bench, not far from a woman who was selling corn on a stick. However urgent he'd sounded in his voice message to Tadeo, the priest seemed utterly at ease, nibbling on the corn, staring off into the green where a few were enjoying the last hour of sunlight before dark, before they'd likely all shuffle along home and lock the doors and cover their windows and keep to themselves. Gripping tight the handles on the wheelchair, Tadeo reassured himself, 'Well, it's better than before,' because he was certain that was true, however much work remained to be done. Just as he reached the priest, the man looked over at him, chewing, and he waved a hand invitingly.

"Father," Tadeo called, "I'm sorry. I thought you were leading the mass, and I thought I might as well go, and that I might as well take my mother."

"No, no," he said quickly, standing up, taking a few steps to Tadeo, "I'm the one that's sorry, my son. I should have let you know." Then, the priest smiled down at Tadeo's mother and placed his hand on her shoulder, squeezed reassuringly. "Good evening, ma'am." She didn't reply, never did, but he always said it anyway. "I," the man began to Tadeo again, "told Joana that I was out here in case you wanted to step out of the service."

"I didn't bother telling him," Joana finally said, snorting, then elbowing Tadeo to the side. Firmly, her hands came over the handles to Tadeo's mother's wheelchair. "Did you hear about the massacre, Father?"

The priest's brow furrowed. "When? Today?" Joana repeated what she'd told Tadeo. "My God, that's terrible. No, I haven't heard of anything." His voice was small, and he absentmindedly twirled his corn at the ground. "May their souls find their way to our Father and find peace."

Tadeo almost echoed him, but Joana spoke once more: "What about *your* migrants? Safe and happy?"

"Safe," he said quickly, nodding. "No incidents there— What I called you about, Tadeo, is that— Do you remember that house where they were holding those five people? Last month." Three men had been there, holding five hostages and seeking ransom before finishing the promise to get them across the border. The five had been horrified when Tadeo stepped into the house and killed their captors, and every one of them was now in the shelter with the priest. However, they'd traded extortion for limbo. Many of those in the shelter had been there for months, even years for a few.

"Yes," Tadeo said. "Do you think there might be people held captive there again?"

"I don't know," said the priest, "but that woman who lives nearby told me she heard a lot of noise in it recently. I just wanted to ask if you could look in there and make sure it's nothing to worry about?" Already, Tadeo was nodding. "Good, good, thank you, *mijo*." He reached for Tadeo now and patted his shoulder the way he'd done to his mother. "Oh, and before you both go — what did you think of the priest leading the service? He's new; he got transferred in, very suddenly, actually. Father Ángel."

"Father Ángel," Tadeo murmured to himself. "He was— He was good." Turning to Joana, he hoped she'd have an opinion, but she was putting her earbuds back in, and Tadeo remembered she'd been listening to music during the entire mass. She hated mass — not because she was an atheist, as far as Tadeo was aware — but just because she found it to be a waste of an hour.

On her phone, Joana was putting on the single of her favorite pop-star — a beautiful blonde woman often called, 'The Harlot,' after the the title of her first studio album. "Let me drop off your mom, Tadeo. Tell me if you find anything in the house or if you kill anybody." She began turning the wheelchair before stopping, tilting her head over her shoulder. Whispering, she added, "But do me a favor and don't kill any soldiers, even if they're killing babies or whatever. Do you hear me?"

Tadeo blinked in confusion. "Huh? Why not?"

"I'll tell you tonight," she said, then began walking away with Tadeo's mother, humming along to the song blasting into her ears and leaving the young man there sighing and shifting, looking down at the ground.

"Your mother is looking well, *mijo*," said the priest chirpily. "Is she on new medication?"

"No," Tadeo replied quietly, and he listened to a child cry nearby as a mother wrestled with him. "No, I just hope it's been my prayers." If only she could have a miracle, the way Tadeo had.

With a polite farewell, Tadeo headed off, walking. He tended to travel on foot, just to ensure that the streets he patrolled were safe. He turned his head in every direction, catching some soldiers and their tanks, but they didn't confront him. They didn't do that very often, anymore. To himself, Tadeo often hoped that some of the soldiers thought highly of him, appreciated him culling their ranks of the corrupt, but it never felt that way. Like the locals, they knew who he was. Surely, there wasn't a soul in town that didn't know what he was, except for those who had the misfortune of stumbling onto his territory. Like Father Ángel, perhaps. 'He smiled too much,' for a priest, however beautiful that smile was.

Some teens pointed him out, murmured to one another, and one old man shuffled by quickly. A child in the back of an old car on the wide road perked up at the sight of Tadeo on the sidewalk and waved excitedly. At times, Tadeo wondered why he was a secret, but if the locals couldn't stand talking of the war, they probably couldn't stand talking of the end of the war either. And that was what Tadeo was — the end of the war. The town was cleaning up. More innocents wandered around after sunset. There would be less fear soon. Tadeo hoped the people would stop fearing him too, soon. Whispers around corners and in alleys only spoke of a terrible monster, who killed terrible people.

An hour later, the resurrected young man arrived at his destination. A one-story home with graffitied walls and overgrown trees that had invaded through the gaps of boarded-up windows; it'd belonged, surely, to a family, once. There were a few children's toys left behind in the yard that Tadeo, pushing open a fence gate, was stepping over. And there had been a mass exodus, ten years ago, maybe more than that — thousands of families hurrying to cross up north or scurrying down to a safer city. What would those who lived here think of what their home had been used for in their absence? What did all those who'd left think of this place? Tadeo hoped they'd return one day. 'And it can all be like none of the war ever happened.' Approaching a door, skewed to the left and hanging on by only the top hinge — Tadeo pushed it aside gently and strode in. Narrowly, he missed the shards of a beer bottle on the ground, and his sneakers crunched on the dirt over the tile instead. He allowed the door behind him to half-close.

One of Tadeo's hands went to his waistband, and he gripped the handle of his pistol for comfort.

Dust sprinkled the dark air, with the only light streaming down from gaps in the old ceiling. It was a living room before him — the couch from the last time he'd been here remained, and so did all the wrappers of junk food on the coffee table. A crucifix and a candle dedicated to Mary were there too, but the candle was tipped over. It hadn't been last time. Slowly, Tadeo flickered his gaze back up, and he exhaled slow through his nostrils, and he listened. One of the trees that'd invaded was shaken by the wind, banged into the window, but otherwise, there was silence. 'But something is wrong.' He could sense it nonetheless. 'Someone was in here.' Maybe it hadn't been a trafficker, maybe just a burglar; Tadeo didn't hurt burglars; he only killed killers, abusers. 'Maybe it's nothing.' Even still, Tadeo could feel monstrous limbs restlessly moving beneath his skin, his jaw aching, wanting to sprout new teeth, his joints wanting to bulk, his back aching with the want to spread wings and grow eyes.

It was always a pain to transform into a beast, though; he didn't like walking home naked.

Tugging out his pistol, Tadeo stepped toward the open kitchen area with its dead appliances and empty space where a fridge had surely been stolen. As he did, however, he noticed a feather on the litter of the floor — among soda cans, food wrappers, and roaches. Tadeo approached quickly, crouched to grab it, then lifted it. It was long, definitely too long for any local birds. Could it be exotic animal trafficking? Tadeo had never come across that, but he supposed anything was possible in this bizarre world.

As if to answer his muse, a sudden force struck him from above, at an angle, throwing him harshly over a pile of trash and making Tadeo drop his gun and snarl at the weight over him. "Get the fuck off!" Tadeo yelled, ripping an arm away from whatever, whoever, was trying to hold him down and turn him onto his back. Talons burst out through the skin of his fingers, as well as a partly winged appendage at the forearm. Eyes, too, began to tear open in a bloody spectacle all along his arm. Just as Tadeo flung the attacker away with inhuman strength, he saw them through a flaming eye at the back of his hand.

"Ah!" cried out the creature, slamming into a kitchen wall, then crashing into some wooden cabinet, taking two plates down with them in a deafening clang as the attacker flailed, white wings flapping erratically behind. "Ow, ow." Over their head, they had been wearing a fabric like lace, but it was slipping down to their neck, revealing dark hair, much of which had fallen over their speckled face. His long robes were white, or rather had been, but smudges of brown had stained the entire outfit beige. He could have been a human, but when he faced the recovering, standing Tadeo, he was suddenly, unimaginably, beautiful. And he breathed in a pretty, soft voice, "You... It's you."

One of Tadeo's arms was still a living, trembling mass of talons, eyes, bubbling skin. It burned, screaming out in agony that Tadeo clenched his teeth and bared. "What are you?" He staggered back, but he didn't humanize his arm yet. "Who are you?"

"You're... Tadeo." The creature moved onto his hands and knees, trying to set a bare foot down. "It's you. You're Tadeo." The young man in question narrowed his eyes, he saw some of this creature's wings dragging against the litter, and he cringed as if he could feel every sticky, textured trash tangling with each feather. "You're him, aren't you? You're the one who died and resurrected. All of your wounds were healed."

Hesitating, Tadeo drew in breath after breath. He wasn't stupid; it looked like an angel before him, not too dissimilar to those he saw in church, in statues, on candles. "Not all of my wounds," he corrected quietly. With his more human fingers, he touched the bandages over his right eye. "This one, this part — it's never healed." The shot that had killed him. "But who are you? How do you know?"

"I'm an angel."

"Angel." Lowering his hand, Tadeo shook his head but not in disbelief. "Did— Did God send you?" He took a step back, reaching for his beast hand with his human one, trying to soothe it now, the pain so great it made the rest of him tremble. "What are you doing here?"

Dina's eyes were silver. "I must help you," he whispered. "I know what's going to come." Slow, he rose to stand tall, his lips parted in an almost childish wonder. "The world is going to end, Tadeo."

Tadeo blinked, then flickered his gaze to his ruined arm, each eye slowly shutting, talons cruelly shredding their way back in. 'It's true then,' he thought. 'God did this to me.' Outside, he could hear the sounds of his town again, and the heavy tires of army trucks rolling by. 'It's all true. Fuck, it's all true.' His heart was heavy, and yet it rose, scratching its way up his neck and pulsing beneath his only eye. "The end of the world?"

"Yes." The angel was nodding, though Tadeo only saw it from his peripheral vision. "I've come to... help you."

The young man felt a fear creeping along his skin, so cold that he felt like a boy again. "The world already ended," he found himself whispering, taking a step back in the terror beginning to rack its claws up his body; shock and fear and confusion in one crude mixture always did remind him of that morning he'd found his father, that year of his life, those days that his town began to crumble all around him. His gaze flickered back to the angel, and Tadeo said, "The world ended ten years ago."

CHAPTER 6

'Apsinthos, tell me what you've done now.'

'What you have been too much of a coward to do, Kimah.'

'You will stop speaking to that angel.'

'I'll end this eternity of suffering at last, and I won't wait for the blessing of any of the other stars, not even you. There are trillions of me burning in the sky with you. I'm shattered across all of the darkness. Can you feel me? Some stars hold pieces of you, pieces of me. Do you ever feel me burning against you and think of the Uri you so loved?'

'The prophecy is not true, Apsinthos. There will not be an end of time or suffering. The only thing you might end is man.'

'If only man will end — then why do you stop me? Let me be so gracious by slaughtering every last one of them to end their misery.'

'Now you pretend to be noble? Now you say you are ending them to bring them salvation from suffering? Your only concern is you.'

'My only concern is me? I am hardly me. There is no star in the sky that is me alone. If it were not pain enough to burn, it is even worse to never know quiet, to have once been whole, to have split into trillions of pieces over billions of years. Time is endless, you tell me. Pain is endless, you tell me. If that's so, I'll create end. End in its entirety. It's the only manner of destroying myself.'

'I will have the other stars tear you apart with their teeth. You will be split into a trillion more pieces. We will scatter you across the emptiness, and we will never grant you a body of your own. Apsinthos, you will stop doing this.'

'Perhaps if I were just one star and not pieces of every star in the heavens — I would be content to end nothing more than myself. It is your cowardice that gifts me the joy to end you all with me. To end all things with me.'

'You will leave that angel.'

'He is my angel now. He will be my messenger. He will be my body. I've enveloped his mind so completely that you will not be able to speak to him now, Kimah. I have learned from all the times I tried to speak to man. I have learned from what we did to the angel of the stars. This one will only hear me. And I am noble to do it. I will end your suffering, too. After it is all over — you will absolve me.'

CHAPTER 7

Michael was supposed to torture Uriel today.

Instead, he was laying in bed, feeling too warm, almost like he were still burning in the heart of Heaven. There was, however, the echo of bird chirps in his ears, a remnant from his dreams of Earth. It'd been years now since he'd last been ordered down from paradise, and yet he kept seeing it every time he closed his eyes. Even with such great duties to focus on — Uriel's punishment, the chief prince's revenge for all that the wisest, oldest archangel had made him suffer — Michael still found himself thinking of Earth. Might God send him there again, after the torture? It would mean the end of the world if he descended to human land so soon, but he wanted it nonetheless. And for an angel — the apocalypse was a good thing, a blessed thing. For many men, it was a blessed thing as well.

Since the time of Christ, Michael had lived in barracks: a stone fortress on a road that ran through the center of the city and to the closed gates, shielding them from clouds and, recently, any humans that might pass by in their metallic, flying beasts. Rising, slow, to sit up and rub an eye, the chief prince was plopped over a colorless mattress in a room of stone, sparsely populated with plain furniture. The room wasn't entirely undecorated, however; the wall before him upheld a mural of Jesus and his mother. Certainly, an angel had painted the image thinking Michael would appreciate it.

He did not. Huffing, Michael kicked away the bedsheets, pivoting to set his feet against a thin, beige carpet, patterned but not excessively so. 'It's late, isn't it?' He had no clock in the room, and Heaven's light hadn't set since the angels' first war. Perhaps, he'd missed the hour chosen for Uriel's punishment; a part of him hoped that was so, though he knew it would just be rescheduled. God cared little for punctuality. Uriel's punishment would come, the end of the world would come. What mattered to Him was the promise more than the reckoning. The Lord liked to live in waiting, edging.

Additionally, Michael was hungry. He grimaced at the churn of his stomach, trying to fold into itself just to satisfy its emptiness. 'Earth food,' he longed for as he pulled himself onto his feet with a sigh. First, he went for the armor on a stand by the entrance, which was just a few steps toward the door when one is of saint Michael's stature. Then, he bound his body in the silver, reached for his reddened cloak and pulled it over his shoulders. Only his helmet did he refrain from for now, holding it in his left gauntlet while his right reached for the handle of the door. He could snap it with his fingers if he simply tensed his muscles, but for now, he pushed it forward.

Stepping into a narrow corridor with a low, curved ceiling — Michael reeled in some cold air through his nostrils with no hint of any brisk, earthy smell. But there was no time to continue with this fantasy; Michael saw his friend Phanuel with all his hair in a braid, sweeping at his back like a dark pendulum, the nature of his feathery layers curling many strands away from its form. He'd been in the midst of hurrying down the hall, toward Michael, before he saw him, stumbling over his own sandals — leather, a rarity to find in Heaven.

Almost inaudibly — "Michael." Phanuel's voice was harsh, rasped, and nothing more than a whisper. "The Lord calls for you. Gabriel is at the door." Slow, the chief prince stepped closer to his friend, and he looked at him gravely as Phanuel lowered his gaze, almost in shame. Yesterday, Phanuel had asked Michael to speak to God first; he didn't think it was right to torture an angel on behalf of a human, but Michael had reminded Phanuel that God had scorched him, that God had forgiven him but would never trust him again. And now, Phanuel didn't argue. He returned to his usual silence, the one he offered to everyone but Michael.

There came a commotion of footsteps. One, then two, then three angels turned a corner far ahead, and they called out to Michael that Gabriel had arrived; all of them — in armor.

"I see," Michael replied, then patted his friend's firm bicep. "Phanuel will command for however long I'm absent." At that, the angels' faces pulled in amusement. Phanuel never commanded; he didn't speak. "But I hope to return quickly." As Michael began to walk again, he felt Phanuel's fingers drag against his arm, as if tempted to stop him, before the touch faded. It seemed to be, could be, a warning, but for what?

Gabriel was inside the barracks by now, the only splash of color among three angels dressed in white, ankle-length robes; he was in a blue tunic, some white stars speckled on the sleeves and hem, with his white lily tucked by an ear. He could have been Mother Mary. "Oh, Michael." He smiled soft, standing at the center of the spherical room that was the entrance to the fortress. "Did they tell you already?"

"What does our Father call us for, Gabriel?" Michael was tired, though he didn't know why. "Is this about Uriel?"

"Uriel will be joining us," Gabriel replied, his eyes tinged with sadness. "All the princes must stand before God. Metatron, too, will be there."

"Will Mary be there?" Michael didn't know why he asked.

"No," Gabriel answered, voice uncertain, "I don't believe so." Mary's name was often in Gabriel's mouth. He had once said she was like his mother, but Michael had made a face at that. What did they need a mother for? They had God, and He was surely a mother as well as a father. But, Gabriel loved her, said she had given him a reason to speak for God after the flood. 'The flood.' Michael had almost forgotten of Gabriel's small rebellion following the great flooding.

With this, Gabriel led the way out, Michael in tow. The instant that they'd stepped into the city, the messenger unfurled his wings from his back, then beat them strongly against the air, flinging himself up high. Pausing, Michael felt the usual anxious flame in his chest at the thought of confronting his Father and let it simmer before he beckoned out his own wings and rose to the sky. He glanced below to see the angels walking between the stone commandments rising as high as towers. Soon, all that the prince saw was traded for the oppressively golden firmament, then the cold embrace of the abyss. One ought to mention what angels made of man-made objects reaching Heaven, but not yet — because Michael encountered none of it today.

The road to God is very simple for an angel; in a sense, all their roads led to God. Michael could have flown anywhere, in any direction, and he would have found himself approaching his Father. For a human, this would be beautiful; for an angel, it could be horrific; Michael chose for it to be affirming — of his purpose, of who he was. Michael could never be lost, would always find his way back to the Lord's loving hands. Michael saw those hands as he broke through the cosmic ceiling.

God, shining down not as a light but as a canyon of darkness. Pulling, pulling — at Michael's side, Gabriel allowed himself to be pulled closer by the Lord's weight. And he did not resist when his fall toward God stripped him of flesh to reveal fire. Michael shut his eyes as this happened to him too — uncertain whether he was allowing it, even accepting it. Nonetheless, there was nothing he could do when his other pairs of wings broke free from his body. To many angels, this spirit self was their truest self, but to Michael, it was no better than skin.

He appeared before God; he appeared beside angel Gabriel.

Near to Him hovered Metatron, Raphael, and a mostly-incarnate Uriel whose arms were still bound behind his back. The marks of torture were already on him: a burn seared across his face, craters of red dug over skin, one of his eyes swollen shut. Yet, his mouth was pressed into a fine, elegant line. He didn't turn as Gabriel and Michael approached, nor did he move as Metatron's booming voice rose to God: "My Lord, I see now that the end will truly come, as you have told us." The man-angel was a whirl of wheels and fires, whereas Raphael was a cluster of cherubic faces, and Gabriel was a plume of seraphic flames. "I believe the angel Dina escaped to Earth to end it himself."

"No," replied Uriel in a low, scratching voice, head dipped in what could have passed for shame. "You know nothing, Enoch."

Gabriel quickly interjected: "Father, I've brought Michael." He fluttered closer, then folded a pair of wings before his face in reverence. "Whatever may occur, may you be merciful — as always."

God the Father was on His Throne, appearing that day as jasper and river. An emerald rainbow haloed not above Him — for there could be nothing above Him — but at His back, His shadow of light. Only then did Michael notice that there were others by the Throne with them — dozens of angels holding instruments, their faces beautifully enfleshed while the majority of the archangels were in the dress of abomination; the Lord's choir. Michael couldn't remember the last time he'd seen them, had even wondered if they mattered to his Father at all after Lucifer's fall. 'It doesn't,' an angel had murmured in the first century after the war, 'sound the same without him.' Lucifer.

"God," Uriel spoke, "you cannot end the world."

The Lord answered, calm as judgment: "You do not care for man. Why not let them all be destroyed?"

Uriel's voice sharpened. "I know that you sent me to the Earth for ten years to see what filth they are, and I did. I saw how they dirty all that they touch, how they cannot tend to their own lands or their own souls. But if their world is ended, then they will only carry that sin here. They will not come sinless. There are no sinless humans."

Michael set his jaw, but he remained silent, unwilling to place himself on the path of God's condemnation again. Instead, he listened to Gabriel's quiet, trembling words: "Father, you can't have extended humans' time on Earth for so long without reason. Why grant them millenniums after Christ's death only to destroy them now?"

"Gabriel," Raphael called, hushed, "you shouldn't question our

Father." It was an odd phrase to hear from him, one Uriel normally would have been the one to hiss. Raphael was always very quiet before God, the anchor between Uriel's cutting strictness, Gabriel's bright curiosity, and Michael's steady obedience. Perhaps, Raphael wanted to fill the silence that Uriel had left behind by rebelling. Michael wondered whether Raphael would ever speak for all of them, if he were the last one left.

But Gabriel shook his head. "My Lord, the apocalypse would bring about too much suffering."

Metatron's voice rang out instead of God's. "The Lord offered His only Son to save mankind from suffering. It is only through the apocalypse that they may rise to paradise."

And Michael thought, distantly, that Metatron — standing now at God's left hand, watched curiously by the quiet choir — was so much like the Uriel he once knew, the Uriel who had shoved and snapped at the chief prince to remove his gaze from beautiful Lucifer.

"Only through the apocalypse," Uriel said, low and bitter, "can the soul of man rise to replace us."

"Silence," Metatron snarled. "You have no right to speak after sending one of our own to the stars and now to Earth."

"Dina is not one of your own," Uriel replied. "He's an angel."

Raphael tried to cut in — "Metatron, please," — and darted forward to stand between the wheels and Uriel's battered form. "This isn't about the angel Dina. We'll send someone after him soon. This is about the end of the Earth, if it's truly to come this time."

"Why?" Gabriel whispered, almost to himself. "Why, why, why now?" His deep frown, the quiver of his lips, and even the tilt of his eyebrows were nearly visible through the feathers veiling his face, but what couldn't be seen could be felt. All around them, there was only feeling, the sensation of soft wings, scorching fire, the tremble of the harp strings from God's choir.

Michael faced them again — plain, beautiful angels with their heads bowed, fear and confusion etching onto faces meant for praise. 'What are you doing here?' They looked lost, almost humanly so. And Michael began to wish he'd brought his sword, something solid to hold — the weapon's hilt like the hand of a friend. A blink, then all the light around them fractured like stained glass. Mirages emerged in every direction around them in the shapes of chairs, thrones — stacked as an endless tunnel — all empty and eager.

Then, the Lord's voice, vast, tender, unendurable: "Why now? Because I know their deeds. It is written that some have persevered and endured but have forsaken my love. But to whoever is victorious in hearing of my spirit, I offer the right to eat from the Tree of Life and join me in paradise. And I know of affliction and poverty. I know, too, of the church where Satan has his throne. I know of the prophet adulators whose children I will strike dead. Those dressed in white are to walk with me; their names are already written in the book of life. Listen to my words, for they are holy and true. The new Jerusalem will descend from Heaven. I know each deed of the churches on Earth. The rich who say they need not a thing, but I know they are wretched, pitiful, poor, blind, and naked. It is only those whom I love that I rebuke and discipline. I stand at the door and wait for the knock. Those who are earnest and repent will come in to eat with me. They will be with me."

At His word, the thrones filled, but not by angels. Figures of age — flesh stringing into the form of elders, of bodies like Enoch's before his transformation; and there were twenty four of them by the Throne. The choir didn't look to them, but they began to sing in four voices, "Holy, holy, holy is the Lord Almighty, who was, and is, and is to come." The elders chanted with them: "You are worthy, our Lord and God, to receive glory and honor and powers, for you created all things, and by your will they were created and have their being."

Yet, Michael's gaze wandered — to Metatron, the conglomerate of burned chariots, then to Uriel, who remained unyielding, and lastly to his siblings Raphael and Gabriel, who maintained trembling devotion. Wings and light crowded around them, as if the totality of all that was occurring here had to swell in size to contain itself.

More voices were joining, and the song grew until it was no longer song at all but a living creature, a beast.

In His right hand, the Lord revealed a scroll, not of parchment but of flesh and blood. And it dripped gold from its seven seals to leak into the choir's mouths. But Uriel cried out, raw and furious: "Who is worthy to break those seals and open the scroll? No one in Heaven, God. No one on Earth or under the Earth can!" A lurch of pain in Michael's throat tore up pearls from his eyes, almost blood, nearly tears.

"Do not dare weep!" thundered Metatron. "See the Lion has triumphed. He will come to us now. He will open the scroll and every seal." Michael's heart was not within him; there were no beats to stagger or stop; he was nothing; he didn't like to be nothing, he wanted flesh, needed to be gripped at his hilt and wielded. "Bow all for the savior the Lord has granted us! The Lamb!"

Then Michael saw a Lamb, appearing before them as if slipping from the fingers of a great hand between the angels — hundreds now, thousands — and God. As if slain, he lay limply, one leg swaying before it touched the center of creation's crown, then he opened one golden eye, the same shade of sunlight as his hair, streaming like burst stars. In shackles of every precious stone — jasper, sapphire, chalcedony, emerald, beryl, topaz, jacinth, and amethyst, and every other — and in a fine woven tunic and hefty robe, he stood. The Lamb, bloodied like he had withstood the rain and flood of slaughter. Or like he had just been born. Beautiful, still.

The choir angels sang for the perfect Lamb, who limped, wounded at the head and at the heart to bleed onto his own feet. Strumming their hearts, the singer urged, "You are worthy to take the scroll and to open its seals, because you were slain." When they fell before him, it was to prostrate, as if the Lamb was their idol.

'Lucifer?' Michael felt as if he'd faded into pure light. No mouth, no touch — he was reduced to a witness. 'Satan. Lucifer.' Here he was, combing his hair with fingers as the incense smoke of golden bowls reached him; here he was, his face in a drowsy, young expression with half-lidded eyes, lips slightly parted. 'Lucifer, how have you come here?' The chief prince flickered his gaze in every direction, but no one was shouting, 'Devil! Cast him down, Michael!' Why did no one see that the Lamb was the devil, the great opponent of God? 'Why are they not afraid? Why does no one see you how I do?'

"And with your blood," the choir angels praised, "you purchased for God souls from every tribe and nation. You have made them a kingdom and priests to serve our God, and they shall reign on the Earth!" The highest Heaven was now too dense in souls, in people, in all of the fears scalding and skinning Michael's very soul. Ten thousand times ten thousand angels circled the Throne, an ocean of wings, faces. Michael could no longer tell one voice from another — the hymn of the choirs and elders, of all the living creatures, became the pulse of a single divine heart. God's heart. We are all the Lord's organ, His very body. "Worthy is the Lamb, who was slain, to receive power and wealth and wisdom and strength and honor and glory and praise!"

The chief prince of Heaven strained to see Raphael, Gabriel, or Uriel in the hoard of life, crushing against one another, so close to bursting out, beginning all of time anew. But he could not. His gaze remained on Lucifer alone, the Lamb. He was taking the scroll from his Father's giving hand before turning back to face Michael. He looked curious for a flicker, then smiled wide enough to squint his golden eyes with all his familiar, ruinous grace. He was mirage, illusion — this slain Lamb. But his lips shaped around a single word, 'Michael.'

Michael remembered: he had been born to God with a lamb in his arms.

"To Him," sang all the angels, "who sits on the Throne, and to the Lamb, be praised for your glory and power! Forever and ever! Amen!"

"Come," said Lucifer, the Lamb, to Michael, the prince and saint, as creation convulsed, and they sunk into a collapsed spectacle of worship. "Come and see!"

CHAPTER 8

Dina could very well remember how Apsinthos had guided him to avoid the bird-shaped, enormous metal beasts whizzing past by having the angel fly through the clouds — in utter pale blindness, in suffocating, freezing humidity. Often, he would pop his head out from the top of the white cotton mountains, silver eyes pointed upwards. Apsinthos would hiss, 'Don't look at them.' But Dina would watch the airplanes swim by overhead, his mouth opening to make a childish noise of awe. He'd even squint to try to look through the pinhole windows, but he had yet to make any human out of it. 'I want to see one,' he'd think excitedly. 'Beautiful humans, beautiful humans.' Princesses, princes, cupids, sirens; he wanted to catch one, if even from the corner of his eye.

Apsinthos, eventually, had instructed Dina to descend where the air grew a little drier, warmer. To do so, Dina tilted his fluttering wings, plunging quickly into the night, partly longing for the star to say, 'What a good job you've done, Dina. What a perfect angel you are. Your obedience is greater than anyone's.' But Apsinthos spoke only of the end. And it'd be wrong to say that Dina hadn't asked himself, after being released from Metatron's cage for more than a few hours, if he really wanted the apocalypse, especially after remembering that Uriel had explicitly wanted the world not to end.

Apsinthos hadn't reacted to Uriel's pleading in the seconds before the young angel had escaped Heaven, and Dina kept waiting for him to do so — though it'd been days already since he'd left, surely. He wasn't certain. The sun ran from the angel, leaving him in its bright dust without a helping hand of time; was it daybreak or nightfall that Dina chased?

Finally, Dina was able to see humans. After his descent, he settled in a sort of place he'd never seen before. The stout buildings were not unfamiliar, and he had seen, in illustrations, something akin to horseless carriages — fueled by dark ink that they bled out in smoke — though the vehicles he encountered on the road were far stranger. Turning his head one way, then another, following the distant sound of voices. A lovely four-legged animal trotted ahead — a hairless dog — and insects were humming somewhere. Dina peeked around a corner to a bustling street, humans chattering beside a bright building with outside seating and a rotating, inverted triangle of blood red meat. A man was sawing at its sides, then dropping the slices to a thin circle of corn. Momentarily, it was foreign — the scents, the food — but the longer Dina stared, the more familiar it became. Uriel had once bemoaned that all that humans had created were mere imitation of angel creations, and all that they created, that weren't derivatives of angels, were pure wickedness.

Uriel, the prince whose hand felt right against Dina's face. Uriel, who didn't want the world to end. The very same archangel whom Apsinthos continued to ignore.

Ahead, a man called out to the mysterious figure at the end of the street, and Dina's heart jolted. And Apsinthos told him not to speak to them before Dina turned on his heel. Like the sun, he ran, heading nowhere. When he'd found the house that Tadeo would fight him in, Dina had hurried inside, all the dreams of meeting humanity fading for a second, replaced by a sudden horror that he couldn't place.

But here Dina was now, sitting on a flat, white wooden chair, hands on his lap, his lace veil over his waves of dark hair as stained as his tunic, his face turned toward a television.

"According to the Gospels," Tadeo was saying, voice uneven,

trembling, "Jesus said something as he was dying on the cross." His hands were over the table, over the mantle, with his fingers scratching at each other. "In Luke, Jesus said that he hands over his spirit to God. But in John, Jesus says, 'It is finished.' But, then, in the books of Matthew and Mark, Jesus says, 'My God, why have you forsaken me?' I don't understand." He lifted his gaze, tepidly. "So, if it's okay to ask, angel, I want to know... What were Jesus' final words?"

Dina blinked, but his head was still facing away, his attention on the television in the living area at the other end of the room. "Hm?" His lips had been parted, eyes wide, as he reeled in every flash and static from the talk show that was playing. "Jesus...?" Slow, he turned back to the human. His wings were folded behind him, pulled close but perfectly visible.

"Yes." Tadeo cleared his throat, nodding. "Yes. Jesus. Did you hear me?" He frowned a bit. "I asked about Jesus' final words."

Dina's gaze began wandering again back to the television. "Oh, I don't know."

Sincere and oddly childish, Tadeo called, "What?" Dina's accent was strange, every syllable inflected wrong yet somehow still understandable. There was also something very familiar about it, but not in the sense that Tadeo had ever heard it before, rather like stepping into the room you'd been born in. 'Maybe,' Tadeo had been wondering, 'the angels speak in the language that we humans long forgot.' "You don't know?"

"I wasn't there when he died," replied Dina simply, then startled when the door thudded open, the hard stomps of someone staggering inside following. "Hm?" He twisted around, one hand going over the top of the chair, whereas Tadeo instantly shot to his feet, swearing to himself.

Just as she was shutting the door behind her, Joana swung a yellow plastic bag by her head and said, "They were having a two-for-one sale at the *panadería*, so I got as much as I could." Though Tadeo was moving, attempting to get in the line of sight between her and the angel, he was too late. Dina stared, his shining eyes meeting deep brown irises embracing large pupils that reflected the angel's face in all its perfect, speckled smoothness.

"Joana," Tadeo said.

"Joana," Dina echoed softly.

"Who the fuck are you?" Joana asked calmly, a sharp wail sounding nearby, though she didn't turn her head even when Dina did; Tadeo's cousin was in the kitchen with her infant child. Taking some steps, Joana moved away from the door to set the bag of bread at a coffee table in the living room before heading straight toward the angel and Tadeo.

Tadeo answered: "He says his name is Dina. He's an angel from Heaven."

"Oh?" Joana laughed, then turned her face to the kitchen. "Hey!" she called. "Did you all hear me?! I brought some bread!"

"My granddad's out," Tadeo sighed, hearing his cousin's baby cry again. "He went on a walk with my mother." Or rather, he was walking as he pushed along her wheelchair. "My grandmother's out in the back, in the garden. Most of my cousins haven't seen him yet."

"Mm, so what were you planning?" Joana laughed again, but it seemed somewhere between sincere and bitter. "A *carne asada* to intro-duce him to everyone?" A barbecue. "Or what?" Finally, she reached them, pulling out a chair beside Dina and now speaking directly at him, "So, you. Angel. You told my friend that you're an angel."

Dina blinked, then nodded. "That is what I am. Your name... is Joana?"

"You talk weird," Joana commented, but not cruelly. "But yeah. Joana Hernandez. What's an angel doing in this shithole?" Tadeo almost sighed again.

Tilting his head, Dina answered slowly, "I'm here because the world will end soon."

Joana hesitated, but not in shock, then said, "And? Are you here to stop it?"

Tadeo huffed, then said, "Of course he is. What are you so mad about? I have an angel in this house, and you're mad?"

Ignoring him, Joana nodded her head at Dina again. "I want you to answer me. How are you going to stop the end of the world?" The angel parted his lips but hesitated. "How are you planning to do that? Is the devil here?"

"The devil—" Tadeo had repeated with the intention to scold Joana again before he realized the weight of the question; he turned back to Dina. "Is that true?"

Jolting, flushing, Dina shook his head. "No. I don't believe so— Though... he could be."

"It wouldn't surprise me," said Tadeo, leaning back against the table, reaching for a plastic cactus-shaped salt shaker and fiddling with it anxiously. "The awful things that have happened here can only be the work of the devil."

Dina said, "I don't understand what's happening here. In this place."

"Hasn't God told you?" Joana asked, and Tadeo realized how calm Joana was — she had never been one to shriek in shock, but there wasn't as many questions as he expected, not even a flicker of surprise that Tadeo had been right that the miracle of his resurrection was God-granted or that the angels were watching over them. 'Maybe that's why you're so quiet,' Tadeo wondered, 'you don't want to admit that you were wrong that God has abandoned us.' Or admit that God was real, after all. Because an angel in the room didn't only mean that an angel existed but that God did, that Jesus did. The Messiah. And Heaven. Paradise. Confirmation of your religion didn't feel as triumphant as one might've expected.

Before Dina might've answered, the front door opened again, and it was an old woman, leaning on the arm of a middle-aged man, one of Tadeo's uncles in jeans, a polo shirt, and a white *tejana* hat. "Ah, Joana, good afternoon. And you—"

"It's the angel," the grandmother answered. "Tadeo said he found him." Fondly, she laughed when the uncle let go of her and scrambled over.

"Angel—" he said in awe, putting his hands together, trying to lower himself onto one knee but taking awkwardly long to do so. "Oh, it can't be. Dear Father, how blessed we are."

Joana smiled at Tadeo's grandmother and announced that she'd brought them bread from the bakery, not paying any mind to what the uncle was doing. When the grandmother neared her, she kissed Joana's cheeks in greeting. But, after this, Joana looked gravely at Tadeo, nodded toward the kitchen — where there would be a way into the yard, where she most preferred to talk with him. Tadeo shook his head warily, murmuring that he wanted to go out and find his mother, and Joana paused, before sighing.

"We can talk tonight," Tadeo reassured before stepping away to allow his family to fawn over the angel.

Dina stared at the man kneeled before him, confused and almost frightened, and he lifted a hand, wanting to put it on the man's head to lightly push him away. 'A man shouldn't worship an angel.' But the uncle took the angel's fingers in his calloused own, clasped his hand, then brought it to his mouth and kissed once, twice. Immediately, the angel almost yanked it away and cried out, but he remembered the illustrations in the books he liked; he remembered the princesses having their fingers kissed by charming princes. And he felt warmth rise to his cheeks.

The man was saying, "My God, what an honor for you to be here. We are blessed. Despite everything, we're so blessed."

The grandmother affirmed it: "Thank you, my Lady. My Lady of Guadalupe."

Anxiously, the angel drifted his hand away, and he felt the presence of someone come up to his side, lean down and nudge at his shoulder — Joana. She said, "Hello."

Dina blinked up at her. "Hello?"

"How's Tadeo treated you?" she asked, suddenly amicable.

"Tadeo?" Dina saw that the boy in question was wrapping his arms around his grandmother and kissing her cheek before he turned down his head so she could kiss his forehead. "He... asked me about Jesus."

"Yeah, he's a real fag about Jesus."

The uncle burst out into a wheezing laugh as the grandmother hissed, "Joana!" At the same time, Tadeo let out a long sigh before saying he was going out to look for his mother and grandfather.

Dina, meanwhile, realized his language learning hadn't been as thorough as he'd thought.

But some hours passed uneventfully, the uncle ushering the angel to the couch and immediately telling him of his experiences with God, and asking quite frankly if he was going to go to Heaven, while Dina turned his face back to the television and stared at every spectacle of color and noise. He watched it so intently that the man soon surrendered and went to speak with his daughter and her baby. And, soon, Dina had moved onto the floor, closer to the enormous, bulky television — "*Angelito*, you're going to hurt your eyes!" the grandmother called — but he leaned even closer in fascination, almost pressing his face against the screen. He didn't seem to notice when Tadeo returned with his mother and grandfather, nor did he seem to care at how the family moved around him, going about their day.

That night, a dozen members of the family and an angel were gathered between the crowded dining area and living room, some having to stand by a long table at the wall. This table upheld a nativity scene currently; before that, it had been an altar of portraits and candles to remember the dead. Though the Day of the Dead was long gone — and a tradition that Tadeo's paternal side was far more attached to — they had kept most of the portraits, now on one side while baby Jesus was on the other. There was a Bible, too, in a corner that only Tadeo ever read because his grandparents were not great readers and his parents, though religious, had always found their faith more in whims and what their own parents had taught them, rather than anything in the scripture itself. But none of his family had come back from the dead as he had, so one shouldn't be surprised that Tadeo believed a little harder than anyone else.

Tadeo could see the altar and nativity from the corner of his eye from where he sat, his plate already finished before him. They'd had roasted chicken and tortillas, along with some tamales left over from Christmas. Soon, it would be the day of the 3 Kings, and the family would cut open a *rosca*, searching for an infant Jesus in the bread. Then, they would make tamales again, much like the ones that the angel beside him was shoveling into his mouth with his hands, not bothering with a fork, eating almost like the stray dogs that travel over roofs.

Tadeo's grandfather was asking, "Do they have tamales in Heaven?"

Nodding, Dina swallowed his meal down, then turned a bright smile to him. "Very similar!" he chirped, and the old man sighed in relief.

When a shoe kicked at Tadeo's ankle, he assumed it might've been a little cousin, one of which had a habit of crawling under the table and grabbing at any limb he could, but when he was struck harder, Tadeo jolted and turned to Joana. She was chewing and nodding her head, silently urging Tadeo to speak with her again. And Tadeo looked away.

"We're really grateful that you're here," said the grandmother, who was just near enough to take Dina's hand and squeeze it. "Our family has suffered so much. But with an angel in our home, it all feels much better. I've been wanting to ask about my daughter's husband." Tadeo's father; Tadeo's mother, meanwhile, was being fed by her brother, who dabbed at her mouth with a napkin. "Is he in Heaven? He was a good man. He's in Heaven, right?"

"Heaven?" Dina echoed, then turned his head when an older cousin called out:

"My best friend! Her name was Imelda de la Cruz. She was so sweet, but she died in a crash five years ago. Have you ever seen her up with the angels?"

A smaller cousin then said, "Oh, my friend's dad died two years ago! Is he in Heaven too?"

"I... don't know," distantly, quietly, Dina answered them all. "I suppose I don't... know all those in Heaven. They might all be there, but I'm the wrong angel to ask. Forgive me."

Joana's sharp grumble cut through: "Yeah, you don't know shit about anything, do you?"

"Joana," Tadeo said harshly, tired now of whatever the hell her problem was.

But Dina affirmed her kindly. "No. I don't know much... Forgive me for that too."

Silence fell, even the scrapes of cutlery on plates stopping, before Joana said: "This town was taken over by traffickers, so they could hold a route to the north. Do you understand that, angel? Do you know what drugs are?" Almost immediately, Tadeo opened his mouth to cut her off, but he stopped when the angel jumped, nothing but bewilderment on the face Dina was tilting in confusion; 'you, really, don't know anything?' "The state thought our police were too corrupt to save, so they expelled them all and put us under the military. It didn't work. The soldiers are also a lot of fucking criminals, and around ten years ago, there were massacres here, and the state didn't give a shit about any of us. They called us ungovernable and left us here to die." And now the infant in Tadeo's cousin's arms was crying again. "Ten years ago, Tadeo resurrected, too."

Dina whispered, "I do know of that."

"Ten years ago, he came back to life, and a few years ago, I convinced him to fight for us, to kill the traffickers and the soldiers that work with them. This is the most peaceful life has been since the massacres. And now you're here because you want to stop the end of the world or end it or whatever the *fuck* it is you want."

"For fuck's sake Joana," Tadeo found himself snapping, a fist curled on the table though he had begun to wince as if in pain. "What's wrong with you?"

"We have enough problems right now," Joana finished, then turned to look at Tadeo directly. "They're cutting off our gasoline."

"What?" Tadeo's grandfather said first. "The gasoline?"

"And they're sending more soldiers," Joana said, her scratchy voice breaking tensely at the end. "They want to choke us until they figure out who's been killing the criminals and who's been killing the soldiers. They haven't announced it so that it can be a surprise attack, but when they do, they'll tell everyone they're trying to kill a kingpin."

Tadeo's blood was cooling rapidly, his hand shaking now. "I'm not," he said tightly, "a fucking criminal."

"Well, what else is the world going to call someone who's killing soldiers, boy?" Joana leaned back into her chair, reached for her glass soda bottle, brought it to her mouth, gulped down the last of it.

"Tadeo," called the uncle, "relax, son. They don't know who they're looking for. You should hide. They'll leave as soon as they can't find you, and no one will betray you. The town loves you."

But Tadeo was frowning, afraid; he hadn't felt loved in church or on the street. In fact, it'd seemed like everyone would jump at the chance to betray him. 'But I only kill bad people. I'm a good person. This world is crazy, God. They think I'm a monster for trying to save my people.'

"Din-ita," the grandmother was saying, wiggling to try and stand around the crowded table. "Come, come," she urged, scooting as close to Dina as she could, then touching his shoulder gingerly with a trembling, wrinkled hand. "You need to get out of those clothes. I'll tell you where you can wash up and where you can sleep. I'll find you something clean to wear."

The angel remained seated for a moment, his eyes wide, listening to the silence, before he nodded, whispering that he would like to be clean again.

CHAPTER 9

As the beautiful priest Father Ángel flipped through a binder, he landed on a clipped magazine cover of what appeared to be a woman — blonde, blue-eyed, with long lashes that evoked the rays of a sun, full lips coated ruby red; of her figure, there was the expected fullness of a celebrity and thinness in the right places and long legs, a perfectly coy silhouette. They called her the Harlot — the words were written in lipstick across the bottom half of the page, obscuring her groin. She hadn't wanted that name, those who despised her and those who loved her both embraced it. In the photo, she was posed with hands framing her face, right hip jutted one way, and her face was sultry, knowing. Father Ángel stared at her.

'Ángel,' she said, 'the people are asking where I am.' Ángel turned the page to look at another section of his binder, the notes on some deals — though he'd written them in a sort of Vigenère cipher — he still heard her. 'You can't be here long. The stage misses me. And you look so ugly in that cassock.' The priest gathered the information he needed, then he shut the binder, and he slipped it back under the false bottom he'd created in the desk of his rectory room. A window nearby buzzed with the insects fluttering on the opposite side, and he heard distant bird songs. 'Be quick with what you're here to do. The people want another album. They miss me. Don't you miss me too?'

As the priest made his way to the wardrobe, he passed beneath a flickering bulb, and in a fraction of a second, his shadow appeared horned with a tail trailing by his feet, but with four wings hanging heavy from his back and three other faces pressed against his copper-red own — one like an ox, another like an eagle, the third like a lion. He lifted a hand to the wooden door of the wardrobe, pulled it open to reveal every clean cassock he owned before reaching to wiggle the board at the back. Another false end, another lie.

He removed the panel and set it aside to reveal his emergency outfits. A dress would do for tonight, wouldn't it? Should he wear the one that ended on his upper thighs, hardly concealing the perfect intimacies the devil could tempt even the holiest men with? Or, should he wear the tighter dress that fell to his ankles with a long slit that crept up higher on his thigh than the first outfit? Surely, he'd love to sit and ponder, but the beautiful priest had places to be and people to be. The night was young.

Somewhere else in the same town, the young angel Dina was sitting on the roof, legs hanging off the edge with a half-finished pink *pan dulce*, sugar bread, in his hands. He wore now a sweater whose hood covered the top of his head and long jean shorts that fell to his knees, as well as a pair of sandals that were too small. He watched the smoke twirl up and away from a grill — made of bricks and iron fixtures above a grave of burning coal — that Tadeo's uncles and male cousins were crowded around, with one young girl among them who kept trying to help. Large cuts of meat were roasted there, alongside some cactus pads rid of their spikes and both corn and flour tortillas, and there had been onions, tomatoes, peppers there as well, but they'd been moved to a stone mortar that an aunt beat a pestle against, crushing all the darkened vegetables. From a speaker set on a table where the younger children were chattering — upbeat, rhythm-heavy music blasted. Tadeo stood not far from it, as did Joana, as they argued in whispers, or perhaps hisses.

'I never,' Dina told Apsinthos the star, 'saw this in my books.'

The angel turned his face and sighed a little, catching some of the street from his periphery. There was a boy who passed by on a bicycle, followed by a group of laughing friends. In the distance, he heard a bang, but it was rather muffled, and another one. Two gunshots, but only two. Nothing to be afraid of. Dina knew gunshots, had heard them as he lay hiding in that house Tadeo found him in; he'd peeked between the boards of the windows and seen men with firearms in their hands. 'I don't understand,' he thought then and now. He continued to think of what Uriel had told him in Heaven, that this world shouldn't end, and what Joana had spoken of.

'There's so much of humanity that you still have to see for yourself,' said the star in his head. 'Why don't you take a walk?'

Dina hesitated. 'They'll call me down for their food soon.' His gaze flickered to his bread. 'They were excited for me to try it.'

'You won't be long.'

And so Dina finished his bread, rose slowly onto his feet and climbed down, heading for the street. If he wouldn't be long, maybe the humans wouldn't notice. Only once he was on the road did he wipe at the crumbs on his mouth.

Meanwhile, the priest opted for the shorter dress, taking and folding it elegantly into his duffel bag before heading out into the night. He had a driver waiting — a simple bribe — to the nearest airport, where the bribe had been more difficult, had involved a call to the governor from the right person. Nonetheless, the private jet arrived safe, and, if all went well, there'd be no need to do this, this trip, again. Picking at his nails, the priest wondered how he'd explain the lack of acrylics, and he ignored the buzzes of his phone in his pocket for now. It could be Toño, who might've watched the beautiful, young, new priest sneak away, or it could have been the governor. It could be anyone. Father Ángel would ignore them all the same.

Leaning his head against the car window, he watched the quiet streets, and he thought of all he'd heard about how there was nothing but war here. Shootouts, mass graves, burning cars, hanging bodies, decapitated journalists. The people, however, were largely silent of what was happening, what had already happened. A quiet war — but Father Ángel knew that quiet wars were as horrific as the rattling, screeching, booming ones — they were simply longer, happened over generations — and sometimes they exploded too, in a final act, like the universe beginning again.

Not thinking of the danger of doing so, Dina walked in the center of the street, following flickering streetlights. He wondered where the glow in them came from, if man had captured the small stars in the sky and trapped them in jars. Some wind rustled nearby leaves, and he tilted his head to look at a home on the opposite side of the road — graffitied, overgrown with ferns and a tree, all behind a simple fence. Dina approached, peeking in between two thin bars to see a shrine within arms-length. It was of a woman with her hands together in prayer, wearing a red gown and a robe of green with yellow stars speckled on it, her feet supported by a little angel.

"Mary," Dina recognized, but then frowned. "You're all alone." The paint was faded everywhere, scraped off in sections, and her shrine itself was weathered at the corners.

Slow, Dina's gaze trailed down, and he saw, right by the angels holding Mary's feet, a small, faux-leather square. It was thick, though its length wasn't much longer than that of his hand, and when he reached between the bars, grasped it, it fit perfectly in his palm. He pulled the small book out, fingers brushing scratchy, torn pages and a curved binding that was frayed at both ends. Over the front, there was the title of the book, its version, as well as an embossed golden crucifix.

On board the private jet, the priest changed into his dress, let down his naturally golden hair, and he changed the contacts in his eyes from browns to blues. He, then, began with makeup. But as he stared into his small vanity mirror, he imagined a hand over his own, and he thought — momentarily — that there was someone standing behind him with eyes a shade much brighter than the ones the beautiful priest had slipped on — something more like sapphire, more like sky. His last memory of Azazel said nothing, simply lingered, and he did so for the majority of the many-hour flight.

Angel Dina, on the other hand, flipped idly through the Bible, looked back to the Mother of God for a moment, then he turned to begin walking again with the book in hand. As he left, he listened to all the distant noise of houses full of life and those deathly silent. He passed by piles of garbage, and he passed by some bowls of water that must've been left out for strays, and he saw, in the distance, a pillar with a great, glowing sign attached to the top. He could read it to say something, but it wasn't a word he recognized. Though he was tempted to step inside, Apsinthos warned him — 'You have no manner of paying.' Dina wanted to say he did. He had a soul; he had a body, too; he had a body to pay with. Maybe Apsinthos heard him; he said, 'You have no money.' Dina had encountered that concept before in his books, but he hadn't understood it there, and he didn't understand it here, now.

Nonetheless, he turned slowly and walked away from the convenience store, though he saw some young people talking inside happily, then laughing. For a moment, he imagined being among them. He thought of how he'd once sit in between Azazel and Armoni. He thought of them, and he thought of Uriel once more, who'd wanted the world saved. 'Dina,' said Apsinthos, 'go to the river.'

Father Ángel arrived in a city of fluorescent light, skyscrapers, and fortune, and at the airport, as expected, was a chauffeur. After this, it was a half hour to the casino, each minute of which he spent with his eyes shut firmly, trying to make up for all the sleep he should've had on the jet. It wasn't enough; it was never enough. As the driver pulled up to a seven-floor, wide building, the beautiful priest opened one eye in a squint. Though the arrangement had been to close the casino for a private event, there were more people than planned moving in and out of it, many older folk. Oh well.

Long ago, the beautiful priest had learned to accept collateral damage. All humans died eventually, and almost all of them died miserable deaths. And he didn't often torture them, he was often quick, and there was something so comfortingly impersonal about a devil responsible for your death; there was nothing you could have done differently, it wasn't someone you loved, it wasn't the world that you hated. It was something so much larger than you could ever know.

Tapping, his stilettos climbed up a line of steps toward the entrance into the casino, and he licked the gloss on his lips for a taste of its cherry flavor. The double doors were guarded: security stood at either side, asking for identification from the priest, informing him that this event was closed. Without a word, Ángel retrieved a wallet from his purse, offered an I.D., and then smiled pleasantly as he was allowed in with another few taps of his heels. Soon, he was crossing them over carpet, which was colored red-orange and decorated with yellow geometric shapes in a vague floral aesthetic. Tassels of blonde hair bounced against his shoulders, curling toward the jeweled, designer necklace he wore, whose style matched his bracelets and dangling earrings. As for his dress — it was a seven thousand dollar piece of pale lace beneath crystal embroidery, with some black bows on his shoulders, though one was, tastefully, on the verge of slipping off. Coyly over his bottom, he held a clutch purse as he moved through a hundred people.

The slot machines were singing, whirring, but the priest headed toward the circular bar at the center of the enormous room first, where there was what appeared to be a young woman standing before the bartender, sipping from a tall glass with a salted rim. Her nails were acrylic and half pink, half white, and her hair was a tender, soft pink in loose curls. "Gemory," the priest called, watching the woman jolt, then turn on her heels to reveal her short white dress with a low, V-shaped collar.

"It's Sarah here," sighed the demon, but she smiled fondly, reached for the wrist of Father Ángel and leaned to kiss his cheek in greeting. "I forgot to tell you, didn't I? Forgive me, darling." Neither she nor Ángel seemed to fear anyone hearing them and piecing together their lack of humanity. "Your man has been looking everywhere for you, so don't bother trying to hunt him down. He'll come here any moment now." There was some music playing from a speaker by the rows of liquor — popular radio music but its volume was quite low.

"Good," said the priest, then turned to cross his arms over the bar, bending over it to call for a flustered man polishing a glass to make him an old fashioned. Then, Ángel tilted his face back to Gemory and asked, "Did you bring what I asked for?"

Reaching into a pocket of her dress, Gemory picked out a pack of cigarettes and said, "It's behind the counter." Then, she leaned in, whispered, "*He* knows," referring to the bartender hurrying to make the beautiful priest his cocktail. "He said he wouldn't tell a soul for the right price."

"Mm, you always think of everything," the beautiful priest teased. "You always ask why I grant you so many privileges as if you don't know how competent you are." Cheeks darkening scarlet, Gemory huffed, looking away, and pulled a cigarette out of the box for herself, then another one. "They do say that if you need something done, send a woman."

At that, Gemory giggled more timidly, then placed one cigarette between her lips and offered the other one to the priest. "Don't think I don't see how you're trying to butter me up." Just as Ángel took the offering, tucked it into his mouth, she reached for the lighter in her dress and flickered its flame. She leaned her face closer to the other. Both of their cigarettes, then, lit with a single spark, and the priest breathed in the tobacco just as the bartender returned with his drink.

"It's why you're here, Sarah," the priest said, one hand coming around his whiskey cocktail, orange as the setting sun with a cube of ice sitting in the middle. He lifted his drink and picked the cigarette out of his mouth with the same hand he was using for the old fashioned, and he sipped. "Mm, you're here to help me." He caught a flicker over her eyes, something she'd probably strangled to smother, to not betray whatever she was pretending not to feel. "You wouldn't like to be ordered to return to Hell, would you?" This time, she allowed fear to tug on her features, and the beautiful priest smiled at her. "Hopefully, you're not doing anything you shouldn't. Not... talking to anybody you shouldn't. Because if I do find out that you know his whereabouts, Sarah... Mmm, well, who is to say?" Slipping the cigarette back between his lips, the priest turned to lean against the bar again, staring at the spinning slot machines. And he waited in the tense silence.

Dina returned to fiddling with his Bible as he walked, following the direction of Apsinthos. There were distant sounds, particularly of cars passing by and of distant humans and buzzing insects, dogs, but ultimately the roads were silent. It reminded him of Heaven, and he thought of what that girl Joana had said, how such horrible things had occurred here. As he stepped out of a neighborhood and saw greenery and what appeared to be the slope to a river — the angel thought of how terrible things had occurred in Heaven, as well, and how quiet the city had become after that. He swallowed, thickly, and moved past a stout building of colorful, paper-like shapes — piñatas — hanging off the ceiling with a family still sitting around, chattering, working despite the nighttime. Dina was still accustoming to that — daily darkness.

Hesitatingly, the young angel walked toward the river and here, too, he saw life — a man and a boy at the bank, the older one fishing. The water didn't rush ferociously, nor was the surface very high, but nonetheless it was an artery of water splitting the Earth. Dina approached the fern-filled shore, far from the humans, and crouched to touch the water. "Oh." It was murky, almost thick, in a way he'd never felt before, and then he flickered his gaze upward, and at the other side of the river, he saw two figures on horseback. 'Like the princes in my stories,' Dina thought, but they weren't dressed in royal, bright garb and instead in dark green uniforms.

These horsemen — they stood still, and they might've been staring at Dina, as if waiting to see if the angel would try to illegally cross over. There was hardly anyone but these green horsemen on the other side of the river, where the homes seemed taller, less cramped. There were no fishermen on the other side, only horsemen. Fishermen versus horsemen.

Apsinthos asked, 'Do you remember the last story in the Bible?'

At the casino, the man that the priest had been waiting for finally arrived; he had been looking for Ángel, just as Sarah had said. Sarah, Gemory, who had disappeared more than a few minutes ago. She was smart; she'd pieced together what the priest was here to do.

He'd always liked her because she was intelligent; hopefully, she would continue to be and spill the secret that the priest really wouldn't want to punish her for. But he could very well understand being unable to disentangle oneself from a relationship. After all, that was why the beautiful Ángel was here now.

"I didn't think," came the husky voice of an older man, breath brushing his ear, "you'd come." A hand slipped to settle itself on the lower back of the priest.

"You said you'd pay for me to play with any slot I wanted," answered the priest, huffing out a sigh, then sipping from the third old fashioned he'd had so far. "You're not going to go back on your promise, are you?"

"Oh no," said the man with utter warmth. "Play as much as you like, sweetheart. While you've been gone, I secured that share I was telling you about oh, what was it, last January? And the great arms deal went through, too, so there's a lot of money being made, a lot of slots for you to play with."

"Arms deal..." the priest echoed, then tilted his face coyly at the man and didn't react to his fingering of the jewels on the dress. "Deal to who?" The man specified. "I don't suppose you're doing this for more diamonds, as if they're not all already yours." But the priest was playing dumb; the arms funneling to the rebel groups would ensure that the diamond trade and all the enslaved children mining them would continue to be his. Some men must keep a foot on the neck of nations to remain upright; some nations must keep a foot on the neck of nations to remain upright. But pressing too hard might tip a man over, might tip a nation over. Even a nation like Babylon.

"Not diamonds, no," he laughed. "You always make these leaps that I don't understand, doll." All roads lead the same way if you only know how to build forward. "And that isn't all, there was another deal in that country you said you've been in. With the military."

"It comes with provisions, I imagine," mumbled the priest. Almost certainly a promise to keep the migrants from reaching Babylon, almost certainly to capture some expendable criminals and scapegoat them. It's a delicate balance between pretending to help and pressing hard on the neck.

The man was laughing and ignored the beautiful one's remark. "I have a question for you. You know about who." It'd been ten years since the subject's death; they didn't say his name; it was always safer not to, even when they booked a casino, a house, a room privately. Friends, colleagues, were all talking, drinking, fiddling with slots, and the priest returned to watching the colors whirl. "I did some private investigating. All this time, I couldn't help but wonder if he was hiding out in his home country with a new collection of children." He'd been a sex trafficker. "I tried to hunt him down. He should know I'm a friend, I thought. I thought.... he was too powerful to kill, even if he had enemies in every corner. I mean, all his blackmail, doll — he seemed untouchable. But then, I spoke to some authorities." Quiet — "You were never the same after he died."

"A girl can't grieve?" Ángel chuckled, but he knew he was caught. It didn't matter. What was more concerning was the arms deal — further violence in the town he'd started the day in might only cause trouble, not to mention that the strand of survival for Babylon was thinning. This would not help. He had to send a message to Babylon; he had to do this for reasons beyond petty annoyance with the blood diamond billionaire.

He was laughing again — the man, and he ran his hand up and down the slim back of the demon. "I missed you, I really did. The other girls aren't like you. Not as charming, not as pretty." It'd been a year since they'd last slept together, and almost a decade since the apex of their relationship, and the priest distinctly remembered how the man had said, 'You must be an angel,' as they'd laid together in the aftermath. The man hadn't cared for the death of their colleague back then, too glad to be the one fucking the priest now. "But about... our friend."

"The timing of his death did seem rather convenient, didn't it?"

"I saw his body; the authorities showed me the pictures." The man finally, draggingly, removed his hand. "And they lied about his suicide."

"Can't a man kill himself with three bullets to the head without conspiracy these days?" Setting down the cocktail, the priest hoped that the doors were locked, though they didn't have to be; he would be quick. "And God forbid he burn his body to ash after his death too."

The man, again, snickered, but this time with a touch of disbelief. "I told you that I missed you. And, listen, if you're the one behind the untimely demise of our friend, you don't need to worry. Whoever you work for — because I know there must be someone — let them know I'll be their friend too. I'm a reasonable man."

Finally, the priest lost his patience, and he slapped the hand that the man had tried to set on his waist with nails that seemed just a bit too sharp. Some wrinkled skin clawed off in gashes of deep, dark red. "Stupid fucker. I don't work for anyone." And the man hissed and jerked away, stumbling backward.

At the river, Dina flipped through the Bible again, as he'd been instructed to do. The pages were riddled with holes, and more than a few times, he had to swipe away at insects squashed between pages. Though it would normally be too dark to read, proximity to the border ensured ample light from posts on both sides of the river. Regardless, he squinted, and his lips mouthed the words he read silently, fingers tracing the bottom of the letters as he moved along the scripture. Despite being locked in a room with literature for so long, Metatron had primarily given Dina dictionaries, and when the angel had read the Bible, he had studied it for language, not meaning. And Uriel, too, had always discouraged Dina from reading it and called it 'utter fantasy.' Now, he wondered what it all meant, why it mattered.

Dina whispered, "Then I saw the beast and the kings of the Earth and their armies gathered together to wage war against the rider on the horse and his army. But the beast was captured, and with it the false prophet who had performed the signs on its behalf." He turned some pages, then read some more, "The beast was given a mouth speaking arrogant and blasphemous words, and it was allowed to exercise authority for forty-two months. And the dragon gave it his power and his throne and great authority. One of its heads seemed to have received a death blow..." He thought of the hole in Tadeo's head, and then he blinked in confusion.

Just as the man in the casino snapped, "What the fuck was that? You stupid bitch. You gold-digging bitch. I know you did it." He cradled his hand to his chest, but just as he opened his mouth—

"Mm, is that...?" The priest looked at the bar, and he noticed the faint music again, the melody and its lyrics. "Oh, it's the Harlot." The gorgeous pop star, who was on hiatus to prioritize her health for some time. "I'm her biggest fan." A smile began to curl on pretty painted lips, then a grin bloomed, alongside a flirtatiously raised bare shoulder. "I've been told I look just like her. What do you think?" The man looked utterly bewildered for a moment, but then he blinked once, twice — either because the realization was sinking in or because the priest had just hopped onto the bar counter, turned over, then disappeared onto the other side. As Gemory had promised, the weapon — a long, obsidian-colored assault rifle was tucked beneath the counter.

"What are you doing?" the man called.

Humming to the melody, the priest reached for the gun, noticing from the corner of his eye as the bartender hurried away. "I suppose I could have had a worse time with you," Ángel said, gripping the handle. "But don't worry, Babylon will miss you even if I won't." Maybe Gemory had been smart enough to lock the doors on her way out, or to pay off the security guards. Even if she hadn't — the priest was guaranteed a good massacre just by virtue of how far the exit was. Casinos were labyrinths by design. Lifting the weapon, Ángel pointed it at the first casualty, and then watched the wicked man's body thrown backward at the first barrage of bullets. Those behind him burst into red similarly, bones splintering, muscles bursting. And then, all those running and shouting followed.

'The book,' said the star to Dina, 'of the end times. Of the anti-Christ.'

'Is this about... Tadeo?'

'He doesn't know what he is. You must guide him into becoming a false prophet. The way I've guided you, you must guide him.'

Dina kept, kept, thinking of Uriel, of the old archangel

desperate to stop the apocalypse from ever happening. 'Forgive me.' It seemed this truly was God's will. 'Uriel, I wasn't sent here to save them or to save us.' And neither was Tadeo.

In the midst of massacre, the beautiful Satan listened to the agony and fear, drank it all in, as he lifted his stilettos over bodies and walked. He'd have to leave now; he'd have to tell a story the people would believe. He had to avoid this much carnage again any time soon. "Oh Tadeo," sighed Satan, "what ever will I do with you?"

CHAPTER 10

On the television, there was something about a terror attack in a faraway casino. It shouldn't have warranted so many hours of news time — after all, the migrant massacre down the road had been so recent — but some important people had been killed here. A friend of the president up north, of Babylon, and a top executive of a diamond company. And there are some lives that matter more than others. Tadeo may not understand this, not yet, but Joana did, sitting beside his mother and raising the volume on the television. At her other side, the angel Dina was sitting with his arms folded over one of the armrests of the couch, his cheek resting on his inner elbow.

A commentator was insisting that this terror was a global sin and that a nation like Babylon should be wary, for it bordered a place infested with crime and terror. After all, there was a massacre of migrants, down a road, just days ago. At that, Joana snorted before a hand came around her own, reaching from behind the couch, to yank the TV remote from her hand.

"Put on a movie," Tadeo sighed, "or just anything that isn't going to depress my mother or our angel." He pressed on the channel button a few times until he settled on a film from a few decades ago, a comedy. Dina immediately perked up, only to tilt his face and wide eyes to Tadeo, as if he'd just remembered the young man lived here too. Then, Tadeo tossed the remote back onto the couch and adjusted the cloth bag over his shoulder of extra clothing.

"Are you heading out already?" Joana asked, nodding her head at the hat that Tadeo wore — a *tejana*, old and darkened brown. "The soldiers shouldn't get to town for another couple hours. But, I have a gift for you — before you go." She slapped her hands on her knees, and the angel Dina turned to look at her, too, as she stood.

He'd been strange the last few days — Dina. Tadeo had noticed; the angel was quieter, spending most of his hours beside Tadeo's mother in the living room. All the angel did was watch television, and he had yet to elaborate on the end of the world or saving it.

Setting his jaw, Tadeo looked to the wall by the nativity arrangement of biblical figurines and Day of the Dead portraits, where he saw what he'd expected. "I don't need those," he said instantly. Against the altar, there were two long automatic assault rifles. "I have what I need." A pistol and a Beast beneath his skin. "But thank you." However level his voice, he couldn't force it to sound sincere. He'd told Joana a hundred times that he didn't want more firearms, but she continued insisting that he shouldn't rely on transforming into his monstrous self, that he should use regular weapons and rely on his abilities to heal. Often, she'd remind him that there was no telling what could happen if a video of Tadeo as a beast leaked to the rest of the world.

Joana rested her hands on her lower back, looking suddenly quite old for someone not much older than a teen. Pursing her lips, quirking a brow, she said, "If you can't do the smart thing for yourself, you should do it for your family."

Tired, Tadeo let out a breath and decided to walk toward the door, saying, "I'm not going to war, Joana. I'm just going to speak with the soldiers." As he moved, he heard the couch creak — the angel slowly rising to shuffle closer. "No," he said quickly, stopping, twisting back to face Dina. "I'm sorry. I should do this alone. Is that alright? God will see, and if I can, I wouldn't want an angel to see if it all goes wrong."

Dina blinked in confusion, hesitated. "I," he paused, "suppose so. I can wait here with your family." His voice was soft, and when the wail of a baby in the kitchen — the infant of Tadeo's cousin — sounded, as always, he startled.

"After this is over," Tadeo added, "we can talk about what to do about... the end of the world you told me about when we met." Then, he tried a weak smile. "I just have to save this town before I can save the world." The angel's eyes flickered, but he didn't say another word, and his expression seemed to fall away and leave nothing in its wake. Tadeo had seen Dina do this a few times, but he'd never known what to make out of it, a part of him believed that this was Dina receiving guidance from Heaven, something he wasn't supposed to share. "I'll go now." He shifted from one foot to another. "I'll be back soon." Before heading for the door, Tadeo quickly went to press a kiss to his mother's hair to try and soothe his trembling heart. He said goodbye another time, and then he headed for the door.

Dina stared in that direction for a few seconds in silence before he heard the sound of steps coming up behind him. Joana's voice stiffly said: "I taught him how to shoot." Dina turned back, staring at the young woman, or old girl — whose eyes were dead set on him, both her hands slid into her back pockets. "Everything he knows he learned from me." Nearby, the baby was still screaming. "I've worked really hard on him."

Dina had noticed this before, but he really asked it to himself now: 'Why aren't you mystified by me?' All of Tadeo's family had been. 'You're not afraid of me?'

From the kitchen, Tadeo's grandmother shouted for Joana's help with something, and she called back, "*Voy*." I'm going. She turned on her heel, but before she walked away, she stopped and added in a murmur, "And he's done a lot of good, but he has a lot left to finish. Something to keep in mind before you do anything."

'Who is she?' Dina asked Apsinthos, but the star didn't answer.

As Tadeo walked, he felt the ghost of Dina's angelic gaze lingering on him. He'd killed before; God knows he'd killed before, but an angel's presence made him so much more aware of his sin.

'But you know,' Tadeo called out to Heaven, 'that it's self-defense. I'm not violent because I want to be. You did this to me because you know, God.' The first blood you spill never leaves you, and he could still taste the meat of the first soldiers he'd slaughtered in an empty lot ten years ago. 'Jesus, you know holy war is necessary sometimes. To defeat evil.' Jesus had tried peace first too.

Even for Tadeo, the walk in the warm winter afternoon throughout the town was strenuous, but he always avoided using a car when possible, didn't want his grandfather's car to be implicated.

Right outside of town, along the highway, there was an overpass with a wall of missing-person posters. Countless people disappeared since everything had all begun nearly two decades ago now, maybe farther back. Tadeo struggled to know when everything had turned into this — this wall of faces, smiling or serious, some cropped from what must've been family photos, friend photos. As he set down his cloth bag and leaned back against a pillar — avoiding covering the images of the people — he distantly remembered his grandfather rushing to gather all the pictures of Tadeo's dad after he'd been missing for too many hours. They'd used a photo of Tadeo, his mother, and his father at a park; a perfect day now forever associated with kidnapping, torture, and murder.

'Kidnapping, torture, and murder.'

Immediately, Tadeo shut his eyes, stopped his thoughts. His blood had begun to cool. If he continued remembering, he would lose sight of where he was and what he was supposed to do. He'd learned that you never learn to bear it — the world that you're born into. One had to forget to survive. Reaching for his hat, he removed it to begin fanning his face. He pointedly tried to think of dinner. He hated to stand under a bridge — the corner of his eye always tricking him into believing there were bodies swinging beneath like pendulums on a clock, their feet dangling how angel feet might dance while they fly. He had to think of dinner and nothing else. Nervously, he reached into his pocket, retrieved a plain black bandana and draped it over the bottom half of his face. It made him feel like a bandit from a film; it helped to pretend this was all fictional.

After a few hours, the streets had grown quiet, and there was a moment of relief from passing vehicles that'd heated the vicinity enough to make Tadeo, sitting against the pillar now, bathe and roast in his own sweat. But he knew the silence wasn't a good sign; something had blocked traffic up ahead. Grunting, then, Tadeo rose to his feet, taking his gun, and stepped onto the road, moving to the dead middle of it. He began to walk. He breathed. He was alone, marching toward the silhouettes coming into view on the horizon, moving faster toward him than he was heading toward them. Most shapes were hefty, camouflage-colored cars, with four to five soldiers on the trunks — but there were smaller, more compact vehicles following behind, certainly with more armed military. Tadeo faced them alone.

As the first truck stopped just a few yards away, one of the men shouted for Tadeo to put his weapon down on the ground, but he didn't.

"Why are you here?" Tadeo shouted back at them, lifting his pistol to hold with both hands, though he could feel something already squirming beneath his skin, eager to burst and make a massacre of this. "The person you're looking for is me." He didn't take his uncle's advice to hide; he knew if the army didn't find him then they would just find an innocent person to blame. "But I'm not a criminal. I've only hurt traffickers and soldiers who've abused their authority." All the trucks before him were coming to a stop; there was a helicopter trailing behind. "If you look into every man I've killed, you'll see that it's true. I've done nothing wrong."

"Lower your weapon," ordered another soldier, but this time muffled through the radio of his car. "And surrender yourself peacefully."

"I've done nothing wrong!" shouted the anti-Christ. "Listen to me! I've done nothing wrong!" But then he hissed when the first shot fired, swiping past and scraping his knee, enough to burst open the joint, make his ankle twist. The shattered leg tipped his whole body forward. "Agh!" he cried but caught himself, both hands still on the pistol, injured leg bent over the ground while the other held him up firmly. "Fuck you!" His voice grew throatier, guttural. "Fuck you all you fucking bastards! You're the criminals! Corrupt mother-fuckers!" But he focused all his pain on his knee, and then he shook it and, instantly, even quicker than an angel could heal, something only like Jesus had done with a touch of his hand, the bones jerked back into place.

Some soldiers noticed the healing, but many didn't, standing and sitting too far away; for most, it was too late before they did.

The first thing to tear from Tadeo was something like a spider limb, enormous and partly feathered, out from his left rib. The appendage stretched impossibly fast toward an armored truck, then swung at it like one might swat a fly. Like the car was weightless — the limb rammed it against another car, then another, crushing them against each other with all the soldiers still inside. A choir of screams sounded in between the metallic screeching, the panicked gun shots. But talons jutted out of the limb's front end to dig into the first truck it'd grabbed.

And then, firmly, Tadeo took hold to launch it up into the air, toward the helicopter that'd been calculatingly pulling back as a sniper perched there took their shot. It hit the anti-Christ, stag-gered him back as the bullet drove through his chin and throat. But, at once, the helicopter was also struck, the crushed vehicle sending it spiraling backward, then down. As this occurred, another half-winged appendage tore out from Tadeo's opposite side, and more — then all of his body was swelling and morphing into pure limbs and mouths and eyes. A giant, a beast.

"Turn the car around, you stupid fuck!" a soldier shouted at a driver as the monster of the anti-Christ moved into a pounce, then a sprint toward the half a dozen trucks left. "Idiot!" The others began shooting, firing and firing away at the beast who took each bullet without stopping his chase.

And as the helicopter crashed nearby in a burst of fire, Tadeo reached a truck, took it with two great, god-like hands to bend into a crescent, listening to the gurgled yells and crunching bodies of those trapped inside, before other hands grabbed at a scrambling army, trying to jump off their car. He pulled them into the shredder of his sharp-toothed mouth, ground them to red dust. Once they were rubble in his mouth, Tadeo spat them at the tires of the trucks that'd turned around, that were hurrying away, whose soldiers no longer bothered with shooting. They ran; they were all running.

'I didn't do anything wrong.' He killed bad people only. Tasting blood, he reminded himself of what they'd wanted to do and what soldiers could do.

Until the pain was too much. Everything, everywhere, began to howl in such stinging pain that Tadeo let out a cry, and his monstrous body stumbled around, losing limbs with each step. Gurgles of blood gushed out from a beastly stomach, out his largest mouth. Choking up, Tadeo felt his hands, no longer carrying talons, rise to his face as if to shield his agony from God. Ripples of agony continued to course through him, like waves, like he was an ocean of misery, and after he'd reached the wall of missing posters, he was on human feet again. His face was bare, and he was mostly naked, the shreds of his clothes on the ground. Thankfully, his hat was still in one piece, tossed to the side.

It was enough for him to catch a sharp, hoarse breath, to feel his heart begin to beat once more.

"Fuck," Tadeo whined, shivers violating every part of him. "Jesus. God." Then, "Father—" Then, "Dad..." Hurriedly, he went for his abandoned pistol on the ground, then his cloth bag by the pillar to yank out his spare shirt and pants. Trembling fingers buttoned his top and pants before Tadeo took his hat, lifted it to his hair, leaving bloody fingerprints on the rim.

But then there was one last shot — Tadeo felt it sink in through his back, tear through his spine perfectly, split apart his tissues, and burst his pounding heart open to cut itself out through his sternum. His mouth filled with the bloody taste of silver again. And, like before, he didn't fall. He'd been taught never to fall, to die standing if he must. So Tadeo merely staggered, strings and clumps of red and pink falling out of him — his own heart — before he turned his head, slowly, shaking and shaking in a crescendo before its note cut off abruptly.

Half hidden behind an overturned truck, there was a soldier still standing with a small handgun, surely a backup, pointed straight at Tadeo. If he squinted, the anti-Christ might've noticed smoke still trailing from the pistol, but instead, he only noted this soldier's bared teeth, his furrowed brow, and his yell as he shot another bullet. This one hit Tadeo in the chest again and sent him crashing against the pillar of the overpass, almost into the wall of missing people.

"Get the fuck," snarled the anti-Christ, "out of here!" He lifted his pistol, firing once, missing when the soldier sidestepped and aimed again. This time, the soldier didn't get a hit; Tadeo jumped behind the column, pressing his back against it and hissing as he felt his heart stitch itself back together. "Get out of here!" he shouted again. "Tell your commanders what happened! Tell them this is what happens when you treat me like a criminal!"

"Go fuck yourself!" A throaty voice yelled back. "What are you?!" And Tadeo flinched when a piece of concrete chipped off by his head, his chest rising and falling, lungs inflating even if that only made more blood pour down from his chest. Spots of black bloomed everywhere across his vision; he was exhausted; he was healing too much at once. "Face me, son of a bitch!"

"I told you to leave and tell the others what happened here!" shouted the anti-Christ, and he managed to peer behind him, see that the stranger had stopped hiding, was approaching the overpass hesitantly, his gun's aim not wavering even a centimeter.

"Fuck off—"

Tadeo stepped out, and the stranger managed to shoot first — the bullet grazed the anti-Christ's head, tearing right through his ear — but Tadeo's shot was so immediate that they both fell back and yelled in unison. Crimson splattered against the concrete the anti-Christ landed against, his left hearing submerged instantly in blood, and his neck warming as it spilled. But the stranger was yelling in agony much louder, leaning against the toppled car he'd emerged from behind of. Redness spluttered out of a mangled hand that, seconds ago, had been holding a gun now on the ground.

'I should kill him,' Tadeo thought as he panted, desperate for the taste of air and not blood; his heart was only a quarter re-made.

"Fuck you. Fuck you and your fucking mother," the soldier was groaning as he slumped, seemingly in surrender.

"I told you," the anti-Christ murmured too quietly, "to leave." 'But now you missed your chance because maybe I can use you instead.'

CHAPTER 11

"Raphael, you must believe me."

"Michael, I don't think you're lying, but listen to yourself. It sounds like even you don't know what you saw."

"I know that it was him. I know that much."

"But that's not what I saw or what anyone else saw."

The angel Gabriel didn't look back as the voices of Raphael and Michael continued to rise in fright; the chief prince's voice tinged frantic, while Raphael's trembled in unease. Meanwhile, the messenger archangel was staring at Uriel, slumped to sit on the ground against a stone wall, his head dipped forward, his body no longer so tortured but some blood still over his dark skin, dried, appearing almost like paint. "Brother," Gabriel was calling softly, lowering onto a crouch to touch the old prince's hand, brushing the wrists that had been chained together so recently. "Are you alright, Uriel?" Metatron had been the one who'd bound his arms, who'd brought Uriel before God to be tortured.

There was an empty gloss in Uriel's eyes; staring into them meant seeing your own face reflected by the orange-fire of his irises — like seeing oneself burning in Hell.

Some time ago, Gabriel had asked Mary, 'Where are you going? Are you returning to our Father?' He'd been seated at a table,

94

fiddling with a piece of bread he'd lost appetite for. He hadn't been staring at her, but he'd felt her presence at the doorway. 'Mary?' There was no reply. 'Are you going to your Son and your Father and your husband and your God?' Silence. 'Do you ever hate me, Mary?' Even if she did, where could she run? There is God or there is fire.

"You must believe me..." the chief archangel was imploring with a choking, strangled voice. "You must believe me."

"Speak to God, Michael."

"No... No, no. I'll put a sword through my own throat so that I don't have to speak a word to Him."

"He can hear your thoughts— No. Put your hands down, please. You're going to pull all of your hair out. Don't hurt yourself."

Gabriel continued to stare at Uriel and thought of the last time he'd tried speaking to the Mother of God, had waited for her voice to respond to his questions and her maternal touch over his hair before she left the house, returned to the side of her Father, who was also the Father of her child. 'Do you ever hate me?' he wanted to say again. 'Do you ever think that I came to you when you were too young, or that I neglected to tell you just how your Savior would save you? Do you ever wonder if I took advantage of the love you had for a God you didn't know? I'm just a messenger. I hope you can forgive me.'

Uriel blinked, and then he raised his face, made eye contact with the youngest archangel; he noted Gabriel's distant expression and realized all the time he'd lost, as well, in his own head. He couldn't be another Gabriel. He could not follow the same path. Jerking his head to the side, Uriel snapped, "Be quiet, Michael. Whatever you've imagined, it doesn't matter!" He looked back at the messenger angel, then added: "And you, get your hands off of me."

Jumping, Gabriel clutched at Uriel's hands a little tighter. "Are you still in pain?"

"You're all useless." Uriel ripped away his arms, then shifted to climb onto his feet slowly, staggering. "We can't do this. None of you dare to leave this room." They were in the same barracks where Gabriel had met Michael earlier, the same ones where Michael lived, but in another room, one with no furniture beside stone benches, stone floor, and candles. "If the four of us travel to the Earth together, at once, the apocalypse will begin."

It would be another mark on the list of events that Revelation had foretold. If Revelation was prophetic, this would trigger the apocalypse; if Revelation was not prophetic, then the angels would act like it was. That was the riddle at the center of it all, to Uriel — was Revelation a prophecy or was it absolution for what lay ahead? One can clean their hands of anything if one says it was pre-ordained. 'Is the Book of Revelation prophecy or absolution?' he echoed to himself.

"None of you understand," said Uriel. "You don't know what it will do."

Michael's breaths remained unsteady, and his face was still turned to a corner of the room, but he grunted out, "*You* know nothing, Uriel. You've always thought you understand God, but you don't."

"Idiot," Uriel snapped. "All you do is follow God's orders without wondering why He hands them."

Raphael furrowed his brow, both hands on his staff, his voice taking on a sternness that it'd rarely ever taken — "Uriel, you've been the one to emphasize how important our submission to God has been for billions of years. You warned us to fear God before any of us even had a reason to. And now you're rebelling? What has become of you?"

"Once the humans rise to Heaven, the Lord will have no need for us. You have seen Metatron. Soon, God will transfigure all the humans such as He did to him, and if we angels are not sent to burn, we will be made servants to man."

Gabriel, slowly, stood, his hands before himself, fiddling. 'Mary,' he thought. 'I didn't see you at the Throne. Were you behind it?' He turned to face the other archangels, seeing Raphael's bewildered eyes and Michael's tight, frustrated expression. He parted his lips, but he didn't speak. 'Where have you gone?'

Raphael spoke again to Uriel, "What are you suggesting then? You want us to lock ourselves in here? You want us to *rebel*?"

Quiet and stiff, Michael replied, "If you rebel, the Lord will have you punished."

"Yes," Uriel laughed darkly, "and I'm sure you're very eager to tear my wings off like you did to that little devil you still fantasize about."

Instantly, Gabriel stepped before Uriel, but Michael had already swung his fist, and it struck the messenger angel across the top of his head, so hard it sent him to the ground, his skull crashing against the stone, instantly cracking open. His mouth, his senses — all overwhelmed with blood, its metallurgic heat, its rush out of him like a broken dam flooding the ground. 'I still remember,' Gabriel thought as he felt, distant like a dream, his body jerk and shake, 'when Lucifer punched me. With everyone watching. The way he curled his palm, the angle of his elbow.' Michael had taught Lucifer how to punch.

"Michael!" Raphael yelled, raising his staff and roughly shoving the chief prince aside with it, but his voice cracked, and his gasp was horrified. "Look at what you've done."

"I haven't done anything," Michael seethed, his gaze not even flickering in Gabriel's direction before he stepped forward, grabbed Uriel by the collar of his robe then slammed him against the wall enough to rattle the oldest angel's body. Uriel managed to keep his head dipped forward, avoiding his skull slamming into the stone enough to break open how Gabriel's had but nonetheless still striking it enough to make him grimace. "And you—"

"You're a killer," Uriel spat. "God has made you into a killer. You'll even break open the head of another prince of Heaven."

"You don't know how lucky you are that our Father decided I don't torture you, after all." Michael, from a rage building in the very back of his throat, growled. "But now you will leave this room. You will follow His orders. You will do as He says."

Raphael retrieved a long vial of water from a pocket in his robe and dumped it entirely over Gabriel before laying his hand on the split of the skull, where brain matter itself was cascading out. But Gabriel was still conscious, would always be, and he continued staring at Uriel and Michael, who appeared more like shadows than angels through all the fog over the young angel's eyes. 'Mary, did you know the end was coming?' He hardly felt the healing, the same way he'd hardly felt the pain. 'Did you know, the same way you knew your son was going to die?' He shut his eyes, for a moment, and he tried to listen to Raphaels' hums, tried to lose himself in the delicate work of his fingers. 'Your son, who your Father put in you.'

"You cannot make me," said Uriel. "I will not destroy the world for God. There will be *no* blood on my hands, not in His name."

Hazily, Gabriel felt himself tugged closer to Raphael, who was on the ground with him, and he rested his healing head against his friend's chest. Even with all these recent memories badgering him, he found himself reminiscing, too, on his first days as a prince, how Uriel had ignored him, how Raphael had taken his hand and put his wing over him and led him through the perils of authority. Raphael had reassured him that responsibility was nothing to be afraid or ashamed of. He'd seemed so wise, though it was Uriel who was meant to be the angel of wisdom.

"Uriel, forgive us," Raphael called, his talk making his chest rumble against Gabriel's cheek. "But we must follow God. We have no choice but to be obedient to Him. We're His chosen. If you won't follow His word out of love, then remember your fear of Him."

But now Gabriel felt older than them both. As his skull closed, and all that remained of the injury was dried blood by his ear, he pushed his body away from Raphael's, though not without dragging his hand over to his, squeezing the fingers that had healed him. Parting his lips, he heard his own voice say: "I don't want to bring apocalypse to the Earth either." He said it simply, like it wasn't the great rebellion that it was. "I will stay here with Uriel. Michael — you and Raphael may do as the Lord has ordered, but I cannot."

"What?" said the angel of healing first, his eyes wide, his mouth opening and spluttering. "Gabriel—" Except Gabriel pulled away from him entirely to climb onto his bare feet, then putting one over the other, approaching Michael, the towering chief, the angel of strength. "What are you saying?"

"I said that I won't end the world," Gabriel said, and he looked up at Michael as the prince inched his face to stare back, his eyes as wide as Raphael's but overbrimming with rage.

Michael, tense, slow, asked, "You're going to rebel?"

"I want," Gabriel answered, "to speak to Mary—"

"You don't answer to Mary," Michael snapped. "You answer to God, Gabriel. Our Father. The Lord and Creator of everything."

"I will answer to Him," said Gabriel, "after I speak with Mary."

Uriel chuckled and now he was the one stepping between Gabriel and Michael with a twist of amusement on his lips. "Well, you can take Raphael with you to destroy the world of man, but I won't leave this place, nor will Gabriel. What I saw in those ten years that the Lord had me watch them disgusted me. They starve each other, they harm their oldest and youngest, and they've created weapons so destructive that even I can't comprehend them. Will you teach God's army about firearms, Michael, or will you allow them to descend to Earth with our ancient swords and spears? Will you tell the angels that the Earth and man we knew are long gone, that the world of prophets and Eden and miracles died long ago? Will you show them how the humans have already surpassed us in their few centuries alive, or will you allow the angels to realize it the moment a nuclear light is pointed in their faces?"

Now, it was Raphael, climbing wobbly to his feet, who snapped, "Uriel, you're not making any sense." He took his staff with both hands, and he wavered in place, so much that Gabriel found himself moving toward him quickly so that he could keep the healer angel upright.

"I avoided seeing the Earth since the beginning of their last century," Uriel elaborated flatly. "Their wars filled me with such rage that I vowed to never look at the humans again, but God commanded it, and now I know that the world has only grown so much more wicked. And I'm certain the Lord knows the trip wasn't going to convince me of apocalypse but that it would only strengthen my resolve against it — despite that, He sent me. He sent me to learn that, however cleansed they are of sin, I will always remember the destruction the humans have caused, how they've created evils even greater than the devil's."

"Human weaponry is weak against the will of God," Michael said. "You're blinded by spectacle, like a child." Uriel scoffed, laughed. "And speak all you want. It doesn't change that you've been commanded to do something and you must follow orders or risk being tortured by our Father." With one step forward, the chief prince brought his face even closer to Uriel's, and he added, quietly, "And if you're too rebellious to save yourself, then what about Dina?" At this, the oldest angel tensed. "Will you allow me to find Dina on Earth and have him punished for trying to halt the apocalypse? That's what you sent him to do, isn't it, Uriel?"

Gritting his teeth, Uriel managed a strained, "*Michael.*" Behind the chief prince, a door was opening, and there was an angel there, shaped like an elderly man in a long robe. "You've seen that God lies to you, and you choose to ignore it. And you still kill for Him, believing He'll keep His promise to save you, save you from what you've done."

"All of you," Metatron barked. "What are you arguing about? The Lord has ordered you to mount the horses of the end."

Uriel continued: "But there's a part of me that pities you. I know that hopelessness. Billions of years, I lied to myself and smothered the doubt that there could ever be more than this. I still believe rebellion is death and is worse than death and is *suicide,* one of God's most detested sins. But how far can you follow your Lord before seeing He has merely destroyed you and everything you've ever loved using your own hands?"

Metatron grunted, then stormed inside, revealing Phanuel close behind, face twisted with curved brows and parted lips, sad and fearful; he must've heard Uriel's words. "I *said,*" the human-angel called, "that the horses are prepared, and there is no time for you four to argue in here. You all see why God prefers man over the bratty children you angels can be?" Though the elder wasn't armored, Phanuel was and the corridor of angels was as well.

Uriel murmured, "That's not what you said, Enoch." Then he stepped away and took some steps toward the door in capitulation while Michael swallowed thick, looking at the ground, his muscles cold, his blood missing, his body empty.

Nearby, Gabriel touched Raphael's arm and told him quietly, "I want to speak to Mary."

"Please," Raphael whispered, "don't say that to Enoch. Don't say that to God. Now is not the time to rebel. I implore you, Gabriel."

Gabriel wanted to say, 'My heart doubts the end times. Once, God said a flood would kill all of man. Then, He said all of man was saved with the sacrifice of His son, but now He will destroy them all.' His heart ached. 'Mary, can you soothe my doubt?' One day, you begin to doubt in God, and then loving Him is never really the same. Believing in Him, even surrounded by faithful angels, is never the same. The memory of doubt will follow you forever. You will pray, drowned in the memory of just not believing how you used to. And so Gabriel forced himself to stop thinking of God's Mother, but then he thought of his Father, and he couldn't help the feeling that — 'If I ever come to love you again, I will still remember the day that I stopped. I will remember what you did, and what you didn't do.'

Michael answered Enoch quietly, "There are some things I must discuss with the army first, but Raphael and Gabriel may go ahead." He didn't bother to look at the two angels in question. And when Metatron began to argue, Michael emphasized, "This is imperative, Metatron. And there is more time than you think. I already have eyes on the anti-Christ." His heart was in his ears, echoing, echoing. 'You think my pride makes me foolish, but it does not,' Satan had said to Michael once. 'Suicide,' Uriel had said.

Uriel was silent, Gabriel was silent, and Raphael was too, and Metatron smiled at this, surely feeling like a chief prince as he ordered, "Then let us go with God."

There were horses waiting for them — armored, winged. The Lord had created them for this, the first animals to appear in Heaven. Four of them for the princes, the horsemen.

CHAPTER 12

"Torture him," said Joana as she tapped her fingers against the wheel.

The gasoline had, suddenly, run dry, but only in some stations. There was no chaos yet, and after Joana had shouted at Tadeo for massacring the soldiers, she'd sighed nervously, then checked her phone, then said that it would take at least a day, maybe a few, before all the stations in town were affected, before the residents realized this was a much graver situation than they currently realized. For now, those people with empty tanks simply traveled further to where the fuel still flowed. They didn't know that Tadeo was responsible yet, or that they were being collectively punished for not condemning him. So, he had time to act, to get the gasoline back, but how?

Tensely, Tadeo swallowed, sitting in the passenger's seat, not daring to turn his head and look at Joana. Instead, he listened to the shuffling behind him, then turned his single eye up toward the rearview mirror — which a rosary was hanging from — to see the angel in the backseat. Dina, sitting near the window, watching some boys play soccer and two women selling popsicles. "Can you," Tadeo whispered to Joana, though he still looked to the angel, "take Dina with you while I do this?" The angel had remained rather quiet, and

Tadeo still had yet to know how Dina wanted him to save the world. He'd gotten distracted trying to find a place to put the soldier and ensuring he'd live.

Joana stomped on the brake, tires squealing, but the pedal was weak and needed that level of violence to stop, even slowly. "Why?" she asked as if she didn't know; she was Tadeo's mindreader, and he was certain that she asked him to explain sometimes not because she needed the answer but to shame him, to force Tadeo to listen to himself. And as the car, with a huff of its engine, crept to a halt, she visibly chewed on the inside of her cheeks and turned her head to Tadeo, brown eyes half-covered by half-fallen eyelids. On their right, there was a familiar house of boarded up windows and graffiti, some freckles on its walls of bullet holes; the same one that Tadeo had found Dina in. Past its ceiling, the sun was falling, the sky painted in a red sprawl with some hints of playful yellow and pink and pastel blue over the quiet neighborhood.

Tadeo thought again of how many people had abandoned town when the violence began. Much of them had managed to cross the border into the northern nation before it became as militarized as it was now. It was better over there, they said. It was all they said, really. It was not good, but it was better; he supposed that some people learned to be happy with better, rather than good.

"I don't want him to see," Tadeo finally said, "or you."

Joana snorted at that. "You don't know how to torture."

"I know enough."

The angel, slowly, turned toward the two humans at the front seats of the parked car. Today, he was dressed in loose shorts and a baggy t-shirt with an advertisement printed over his chest; over his head, he wore a cap with yet another company name printed across it, but the lettering was so faded by now that he couldn't read it. His hair was in two dark braids, braids which Tadeo's grandmother and cousin had happily made for him, speaking of how they missed doing the hair of a girl in the family that must've disappeared or died. Just as Dina had begun asking where the granddaughter was, Tadeo hurried him out the door to meet Joana at the car. "Is this," Dina called, "where you're keeping the boy you spoke of?"

"He's not a boy," Tadeo corrected, though gently, for he was speaking to one of God's messengers. "He could be my age." He hesitated; he felt like a boy still. "I need to get some information out of him to fix this gasoline problem. But, I want to do it alone."

Joana snorted. "You don't even know the questions to ask."

"I do," Tadeo insisted, but his brow was furrowing as he reached for the door, pulled on the handle, then pushed it open roughly. "Stay in the car with Dina."

"Order me around like that again, and I'll cut your other eye out," Joana snapped but didn't stop Tadeo as he stepped onto the sidewalk and went for the pistol and ammo he'd been holding by his feet. "But I'll take the chance to go to the gas station we passed by. I haven't checked that one." Tadeo frowned deep as the ocean. "My guess is they're probably going one-by-one, but who knows. The private companies might last longer. If you can get this mother-fucker to tell you who you can kill to get the gasoline back — that's all we need." Firmly, Tadeo nodded. "I'll be back soon." Then, before Tadeo could shut the door, Joana craned her face back and barked, "Angel, come up here! I'm not your chauffeur."

Jolting, Dina swished his head in Tadeo's direction, as if to ask for permission, but Tadeo simply stepped further into the sidewalk, leaving the door open and turning around as he walked past the broken gate, moved along the path.

"Tadeo! Tadeo!"

The man in question glanced to his right, seeing some children who'd been playing, waving their hands and cheering for him, one of them saluting if he were doing it to a flag. 'What?' Tadeo shifted uncomfortably, strangely warm over his cheeks, then raised a hand to wave. 'Do I salute back? Do they know who I am?' Of course they did, many knew, in whispers; he imagined the children listening to their parents' warnings of a beast but reacting with awe, wanting to turn into monsters as well. Impulsively, Tadeo saluted, but the children broke out into squeals of laughter, turning to one another and mimicking him immediately.

Then, he sighed. Whether Tadeo was turning into a saint in their eyes or not, he supposed one could never escape the bullying of children. Behind him, he heard the car door shut, and he looked to see Dina in the passenger's, staring at him again whereas Joana maintained her sight on the road. Before long, the car coughed some exhaust behind itself, and the two were speeding down the street, turning rather sharply onto the main road. After this, Tadeo finally headed for the door, his breath uneven, his heart beginning to knock on his chest and ask if he was here. He was, he was. 'Somehow.' He was still alive, though he had died.

Reaching into his pocket, the anti-Christ pulled out a keyring, used it on the multiple locks he'd attached to the entrance, then stepped inside, locking the way in behind him.

Stopping at a red light, abrupt and harsh, Joana remained in place while Dina swung forward then back into his chair with a little surprised, almost frightened noise. The too-long line of vehicles before them indicated what might've been a crash up ahead or some other road blockage — criminals used to leave burning cars along the streets to frighten civilians and lead them away, but it had been maybe a year or two since then.

"Dina..." Joana rolled the name over her tongue, watching Dina turn his head from her periphery as she reached to turn up the radio, wondering if there would be anything about the massacre Tadeo had committed, but her hearing was overwhelmed by static and regional music blasting from a car beside them. "I'm curious about you." The angel parted his lips. "I've been trying to figure out what you want. If you haven't killed Tadeo already, then what could you want?"

At the same time, Tadeo was turning the dial on an electric lamp on a pale plastic table he'd found the same day he brought the injured soldier here. The yellow-ish glow swelled to fill the darkness of the small, square room like an inkblot, and soon, Tadeo found himself staring at the hunched-over figure whose wrists were tied behind a plastic chair whereas his ankles were tied to the legs. He remained in the same camouflage pants as before, but his jacket had been removed to leave him in a stained, sweated, bloodied white undershirt; two metal dog tags were laid against his strong chest, rising with each unnaturally steady breath. Engravings on the silver read Dante Perez, as well as offered a number and blood type. Now that they were not shooting at one another, Tadeo could examine his features better — the black hair fading to a buzzed trim at his neck, the darker brown skin, the almost black eyes, the strong jaw, and the thicker brows, a bead of sweat dribbling down from them. One of his hands was bandaged, rather amateurishly.

"Dante," Tadeo tried for the first time, though he had read that name before. He'd noticed it as the soldier kept fighting against losing consciousness and against Tadeo's grip on his jacket as he dragged him across the mud, heading back into town.

"Get it over with," came a low, husky grunt.

Tadeo stared, feeling the dryness in his throat harden into beads he had no choice but to swallow down into his stomach, however much it weighed him down. "Get what over with?" He did what he always did when he had the urge to tremble: he clenched his teeth and lifted his other hand, the one with the firearm, setting it on the table, far from the man's reach if he miraculously managed to escape his bindings. Tadeo always had to plan for miracles; he was a miracle himself. "Do you think I'm here to kill you?"

"I'm not going to tell you anything."

Tadeo swallowed. "That would be stupid of you."

"Chop my legs off and I still wouldn't tell you shit."

"What if I chopped that head of yours off?"

"Then I wouldn't be able to tell you anything even if I wanted to, dumbass."

Quickly — Tadeo twisted, kicked back a leg, then swung it around to slam his shoe into his captive's jaw with a dull thud followed by the screech of the plastic chair and the strangled, deep cry in pain. The man lurched to the side, gasping and spitting but there was no blood yet, even though the side of his face immediately reddened. "You're the dumbass. You don't even know what I want yet." But Tadeo lifted his foot again and set it down on the chair, between Dante's legs, lowering himself to bring their faces closer and added: "You're lucky. I could have left you to die out there."

Dante, slow, tilted his head over at him, his shoulders trembling with his fluttered breaths. "Oh lucky me, I've always wanted to get disemboweled. Why are you in my face? You want a kiss, faggot?" The response this time was a punch, striking the same side; Tadeo knew the sting of it would be worse, and he was right. He remained in place with his foot on the chair as his fist whipped to have Dante jerk once more to the side, this time blood shooting from between his lips to bead the ground in red.

"I'm going to ask you a few questions. You're going to answer them," Tadeo continued.

"Fuck," said gurgled, "you."

"Why were the soldiers sent here? Violence has been at its lowest for the last few years."

"What are the hell are you? How did you kill all those men?"

"Answer me." Tadeo trembled, wishing more than anything that his body wouldn't betray him. But he hated the way soldiers spoke; he hated their humor; he hated the way they carried themselves. He hated soldiers. 'None of you are good.' He wished he could get away with slaughtering them like the traffickers. He wished he could have killed those men slower. 'All of you soldiers, scum of the earth, rapists, motherfuckers, demons.'

"You turned into a fucking monster."

Lifting his fist again, Tadeo didn't bring it to Dante's face; instead, he smashed it down on the bandaged, bound hand, over his pinkie finger. At the howl in pain of the bones cracking beneath, he replied: "I'll become a monster again if you don't tell me why you were sent here." Dante shook his head, teeth grit, and so Tadeo lifted his fist once more, this time dropping it onto the middle and ring fingers with a hard stomp that cleanly snapped each digit and brought out another angry yell. "Why are you here?" Panting hoarsely, Dante didn't respond, and Tadeo had to try not to grin, to revel in the agony of the soldier. "Why are," Tadeo repeated, taking the soldier's thumb and index between two fingers, feeling Dante frantically struggle in the binds, broken fingers flopping about as he did; Tadeo could deliciously taste his panic now — "you here?" And as he crushed the two last digits on Dante's left hand hard against each other, so tightly that with a bloody tear, the thumb and its tendon was pulled out from its socket, skin splitting open to drop far more blood onto the ground.

Screaming, as high and as desperate as he had, Dante finally spat right in Tadeo's face: "Because of *you*!" His voice broke instantly, and he doubled over, groaning and clenching his eyes shut. "Because," he echoed himself, "of you. Because of you!" Hiccups broke in between syllables; he was trying not to cry.

"Why?" Tadeo released him, staring down at the hand he'd mangled, twitching uselessly, the section at the wrist gushing blood, more than he'd intended. "Why would the state send soldiers because of me? Do they think I'm a criminal?"

"You *are* a criminal, dumbass." Weak, groaning. "You murdered the soldiers. You're fucking torturing me." Dante shook his head again, but like he was trying to wake himself. "We were sent here to capture you."

"I only killed the soldiers because you all attacked me," Tadeo spat, finally removing his foot and moving away, taking a few steps back to lift a hand and shakily run it through his hair, damp, sweatier than he'd been expecting. It was too warm in here; without thinking, he lifted an arm and wiped the drops on his brow with his sleeve. "I'm not a criminal. I don't kill innocent people." But he could reasonably assume what Dante would respond with. "The soldiers I've killed in this town for the past few years— I only did it because they were corrupt. They were no better than the criminals they were supposed to protect us from. All of you are corrupt."

"Think whatever you fucking want," Dante hissed, his face twitching in a deep grimace as his broken hand continued to bleed. "You think you're targeting bad people but all anyone sees is more bodies on the streets. Do you think you're a saint or something? Am I supposed to believe you can turn into a giant monster and that you're fighting corruption like some kind of fucking—?"

"I'm trying," Tadeo cut off, "to protect this town. That state left us all for dead. It's been ten years of this shit. We were all abandoned for the criminals to turn this place into a war zone. All I've wanted is to run them out of town because none of you ever could."

Elsewhere, Joana was climbing back into the driver's seat and groaning, taking the door then slamming it behind her. Dina was still staring at the gas pump they were parked beside and the taped paper over the dispenser that read that they had no gasoline. Minutes ago, Joana had gone into the attached convenience store, leaving the angel behind with the local radio finally working to broadcast a young woman informing listeners that there were reports of disruptions to certain oil pipelines but that authorities were looking into the issue. "Not a drop," announced Joana as if Dina could understand. "And no sign of the gas coming back anytime soon." She jerked the gear stick back, setting the vehicle into reverse and inching it back to angle it toward the road. "So, we're fucked, or at least the people are." Setting the car back into forward driving, she waved a hand at an extremely tall truck passing by with eighteen wheels. "Those are fine. They're getting their gas before passing through town, but within a day or two, there's going to be chaos."

Dina asked quietly, "Why? Can't you all... walk?" He thought to speak now just to prove that he wasn't mute; he hadn't answered Joana earlier, after all.

Harshly, Joana reeled in a breath and said, "It's too complicated to explain." She turned the car into the main street and murmured, "I'm going to head out to see my dad now. Do me a favor and don't tell Tadeo." When the angel parted his lips, Joana added, "I'll tell him myself. Later."

The star in Dina's head, Apsinthos, replied: 'Be cautious around her.'

'Why does she think we want to kill Tadeo?' Dina asked.

'She must think you're here to stop the end times, but that means she knows Tadeo is the anti-Christ and that he must die to prevent the apocalypse.'

"Right now," said Joana, "we're going to the club."

And Dante panted and panted, finally replying to the anti-Christ, "So what now? Are you going to kill me for being corrupt like all the others? If you will, just do it. Stop wasting time."

Tadeo shook his head. "I need more information. Why was the gas cut off?"

"I don't fucking know," said Dante. "Why would I? I'm just a soldier. I wasn't even going to get sent up here, but they decided last minute that they needed more men. I don't know shit. Don't believe me if you don't want but it's true. I don't know shit. You couldn't have picked a worse guy to torture for answers. I have none. We were sent to this shithole after being told that criminals have some kind of machine or person massacring the soldiers stationed here. The gas is cut off probably to keep any criminals from escaping during the confrontation today, but I don't know. That's not normal. We've never done that before."

"The only people the gas cut-off is going to hurt is innocents," Tadeo mumbled, crossing his arms and turning back at the door, thinking of the children he'd seen. "There aren't a lot of criminals left here at all."

Joana parked some streets away before stepping out of the car and shouting over at Dina to follow. As the angel crept out onto the sidewalk, he heard the hooting of some men from another vehicle, sharing beers and nodding their heads at a woman who walked past in a shimmering dress. Above, the moon was settling into its dark cradle, peeking out only a sliver of itself, whereas the clouds were oddly dim. In his head, Apsinthos reassured, 'Do as she says for now.' Dina nodded obediently, then spun around, following after Joana, who had just taken to walking toward a corner. 'Good.'

Past a few streets, they made it to a rectangular, dark building with a sign over the door with cursive lettering and neon lighting. There was a line of humans outside it — the longer-haired ones wearing dresses and the short-haired ones primarily in pants; the angel glanced down at his long shorts and sandals and began to feel extremely cold and ashamed. Before he could verbalize this to either Joana or even Apsinthos, the girl had hurried past the line, nodding at a figure in black by the doorway. He'd been in the middle of speaking into a phone, though he waved a hand, allowed Joana to breeze past him. "Who," the man said, twisting the bottom of his phone away from his mouth for a moment, "is this?"

"Just an angel," answered Joana, and the bouncer quirked a brow but seemingly decided not to waste time arguing.

Nonetheless, Dina felt suspicious eyes climb up his body as he stepped into the club, and there were some whistles behind him, which only made him feel more naked, more ashamed.

Dante was laughing: "What now?" He grinned weakly, his teeth reddened, at Tadeo. "I don't have any information to give you, and you're pretending to be a vigilante while torturing someone who came to get rid of whatever was slaughtering our soldiers. It's so stupid. This is so fucking stupid. There are criminals here. Do you think you made them all run away? They've just learned to be quieter about whatever they're trafficking through this place. If there weren't any criminals left here, then who is paying off the soldiers you're killing?"

'It's too loud in here,' Dina thought instantly. 'Too crowded.'

Bodies were pushing up against him from every side, the bass of the music thudding against his heart and head. Flashes of light, of every color, were blinding him every other second, and though he was rather tall, tall enough to see over the heads of quite a few, he was half-blindly following Joana ahead of him. She swerved in between every dancing figure, expertly avoiding their swaying arms with ducks and sidesteps, whereas Dina was just taking each hit. The stench was sweat, was horribly earthly, was salted, and horribly damp. Just as the crowding grew less and less dense — a bar with a hundred glass bottles behind a long counter came into view. Almost two dozen people were there, many coming and going between the dance floor and the bartenders, but at the center, there was an older man, dressed in a red button-up, rosary on his chest, dark *tejana* hat on his head, and there was a short, wide glass in his left hand with a square block of ice among sunny-orange liquid.

There were three other men at his sides; one nudged the central figure before he turned back and looked at Joana. With a grin, he gestured her over and said, "Joana, there you are. What fucking mess we're dealing with, no?"

"Hi," Joana greeted, "uncle," though he was nothing of the sort. And once she'd neared him, the man pulled her into a one-armed hug, patting her back, then kissing her cheek.

"Who's this you brought with you?" He stared at Dina over Joana's shoulder and smiled amicably before Joana pulled back.

"I don't have updates on the captured soldier yet," Joana said. "My guess is that the state is trying to take on Tadeo because he's been killing too many soldiers, so they think he's with the traffickers. But that doesn't make sense to me. I was wondering if all that Tadeo is doing is disrupting trade — the legal kind — and the other side of the river is getting involved. Where is my dad? Is he not here yet?"

"Don't sound so sad, *mija*," the man said. "Nothing to be worried about yet. We have gasoline, oil, and we'll be selling it at a good price to the people if they come to us. We will take good care of them." He grinned, then squeezed her arm. "And the state knows he's working for us." The traffickers. "Even if he doesn't mean to." The kingpin, of the traffickers, laughed warmly.

Joana ran her tongue over the gums at the back of her lower teeth, tasted blood. 'Keep having him kill our competition,' he might as well have said to her ears. 'Keep controlling him for us. You will be rewarded handsomely, girl. Aim him in the right direction.' And there would be peace, but only because the turf wars had ended, and now the town was in the iron grip of one group, one man, a kingpin of substances and bodies and blood.

"Have a drink," cheerfully urged the kingpin, "I won't tell your dad." Without missing a beat, he teased, "Just how I don't tell him about you and my daughter."

Tadeo, slowly, said what Joana had told him they should ask as they left the house: "What can we do to get the gasoline back? Who can I talk to? I'm not a criminal. I have no shame."

"I wouldn't know," said Dante, and an odd silence followed, broken only by the drops of his blood falling from his hand. "I'm just a soldier. How many times do I have to tell you? You're so fucking naive. You think you can just end things by killing the right people."

"I have one last question for you," Tadeo said, and when Dante didn't reply, he asked it anyway: "Do you want to live?"

"Dina," Joana said as she was handed two tall, cooled glasses.

"Come, have some of this." The angel waited, but the star in his head said nothing, so he took one glass, lifted it to his lips and felt the rim burn his mouth from how cold it was. He sipped anyway, then made a face at the taste. "Good, right?" Dina wasn't sure, but he experimentally tried to have some more, though he flinched again. "That guy wants to dance with you." She jerked her head at one of the men by the bar, beside the kingpin she's been talking to. "You should. We might be here a little while."

Dina instantly shook his head. "I can't—"

"What, you scared of God? Scared of looking gay?" she laughed. "Isn't the world going to end? Try it. See why humans love sin so much."

Again, Dina waited for guidance from his star, but there was none, and so when the man approached, he allowed his free hand to be taken, and he felt himself pulled toward the crowd.

Dante answered: "Of course I want to, idiot. Let me go."

Tadeo said, "You know too much about me for me to let you live."

"I don't know anything," Dante drawled. "I don't even know what you fucking are. I saw you turn into some giant... thing. I saw you turn into a giant. If you're going to kill me, at least explain what I saw."

Tadeo inhaled through his nose, considering ending this all, ripping out the rest of the soldier's arm then his head. Instead, he confessed quietly, "I don't know. I don't know either. Ten years ago, I died, and I came back from the dead like this. I think that God blessed me." Dante's expression flickered with something, perhaps surprise. "I could turn into that... giant. I was ashamed after I came back from the dead, though. I refused to go out. I even let my family think I was dead for some time." Cautiously, he took steps toward his captive, looking down at him much calmer than before. "After I showed them what I was, what I could do — they were scared of me."

"Why did you start killing criminals?" asked Dante with a level-headedness that surprised Tadeo as well.

"A friend." Joana. "She made me do it. I was scared of myself, but she told me I had a duty."

"Hm." Dante laughed, though it seemed humorless. "So, you resurrected. God blessed you. Of course."

Tadeo glared his single eye. "You saw it for yourself." And, without thinking, he reached for the bandages of his face, tugging them harshly aside to show the enormous gape in his head, how it passed all the way through, how all the brain matter he had remaining was visible at an angle.

Except Dante was looking at his feet again. "I did. I really fucking did."

"Then?"

"I don't believe in God," he confessed, "but I suppose I can believe in you."

CHAPTER 13

Dina lay in bed, facing a wall. There was no nausea in him as there had been last morning, but his mind still flashed with the lights, the sensations — a hand on his back, the burn in his mouth, the deep hole in his stomach, each thud of the music and the bodies dragging against him. A pair of broken lips, husky against his ear, wet tongue, teeth scraping. Black inkblots bled into his memory — a dark shadow where the man's face should be — and he found himself unable to remember chronologically. He had been drinking one moment, then the man had a leg between his own, then he was by himself, briefly, at the center of an oval of people, who clapped their hands and cheered. He'd been dancing for them. Angels love to dance, about as much as they like to sing — though this is often never written about. Dina himself had never danced much, only a few times in secret with Azazel and Armoni and a handful of other times in his short life before the war. The first time he'd danced, it had been with angel Lucifer.

Ta, ta, ta — Lucifer's feet had hit the table they were on top of.

Dina could still feel the leg of the stranger pressing up between his thighs; he could still feel his breath caught in his throat, the stutter of his heart. 'Dina,' called the star Apsinthos. The fingers squeezing his waist, the chorus again and again, the spinning of the room as he was handed drink after drink. 'Angel.' Suddenly, a certain goodness had lit aflame in his belly, nascent and novel. It had been wonderful, all the touches. 'Are you going to waste another day in bed?'

Finally, Dina lifted his body, so abrupt that he expected for a wave of nausea to hit as it had the previous morning. "Hm?" 'You're still here, still in bed?' "I'm sorry," he whispered. "I'm sorry..."

Slow, the angel readjusted, saw himself donned in shorts and a shirt too small, that showed a sliver of the brown skin of his belly. Nearby, he could hear the shuffling of feet, furniture, the murmur of talking. And he remembered he was in the home of Tadeo, the anti-Christ. The voice of Uriel, again, again, echoed in his mind, telling Dina of the apocalypse that must never occur. 'What am I doing here?' This place that was nothing like the forests and castles in his fairy books. Abruptly, he remembered the sensation of the books in his hands, and the deep reverb of Uriel's voice nearby, telling Dina to go to bed. He remembered flushing, lifting his chin, staring at the old angel nearby, standing by the dim glow of candlelight.

'Very few times,' Dina thought, 'you were warm to me, Uriel. But I cherished those moments. After losing Azazel and Armoni, I thought I'd never know kindness again from an angel. Sometimes, you handed me bread, and I thanked you with all of my heart. I thanked you for telling me to rest. Thank you for letting me live with you even if you don't want me here. Once, Uriel, you said that you didn't mind me. Once, you grabbed the collar of my tunic and told me not to touch you ever again after I tried embracing you. I never want to see you angry at me. If I ended our world, would you forgive me?'

'Don't apologize,' said the star, 'angel. Do you still feel ill?'

'What happened to me?'

'You were drunk.'

'I've been... like this before.' Once or twice in his short life before the war, and a couple more times in the dark with Azazel and Armoni. 'It was more intense this time. I wanted his touch — that man's. I think he thought I was a woman. He used terms for me that I know they reserve for women. I liked his hands, though I know it's against the laws of Heaven to think so. He pressed his body to me, and that's against the laws too. It's a sin to enjoy it.'

'You're already a sinner.'

'But I cannot ask for forgiveness again.' Dina hesitated, then — 'Is this right, Apsinthos?'

'Is being touched right?'

'No. No, I mean being here, on Earth. Uriel said that humanity shouldn't rise to Heaven. And I like Uriel. He's always been right. He's the angel of wisdom.'

'I think you confused your conflicted feelings on desire with your feelings on being here, sweet Dina,' said the star as the young angel grimaced, almost shaking his head. 'You drank too much, and you felt the affection of a man; you aren't thinking right. If you were, you'd remember that you were never doing this for that archangel Uriel. You were doing it for God. It's what He desires; you read it in His scripture for yourself. He will love you if you do it. You want to be loved by God, don't you, Dina?'

'I do,' the angel surrendered, 'more than anything.' He supposed he should crave God's love more than Uriel's; he supposed that is how a good angel should feel.

'To fulfill the prophecy of Revelation, you will have to sin. You may have to lie, to covet. How the angels have had to kill humans for God, you will have to commit some sin for the greater good.' The star paused, then it asked, 'Have you ever pleasured yourself with your hands, Dina?' The angel gripped at the bedsheets as his muscles tensed, and his cheeks warmed. 'It wasn't a sin once to do it. In the time before Satan, there was no sin, just acts of pleasure and acts of pain. When time has ended, there will be no such word for sin anymore. You may be able to feel pleasure again how that man made you feel. Do you want to?'

Dina swallowed thickly, and he remembered the stranger again, his hands on his hips, his waist, the man's huffing, and the building heat in between the angel's legs, the almost painful tightness that had nearly bent his knees unwillingly. He imagined having knelt, then, unable to hold himself up, staring up at the man as if he were God. His sighing face nearly pressed to a clothed pelvis. "I shouldn't." 'I shouldn't want it. I shouldn't have hoped he'd grab my hair and force me down onto my knees.'

'But you do want it. You want to do what you shouldn't. Bring your hand between your legs.' Dina was relieved it was a command, that he didn't have to live with the guilt of doing it on his own accord. Apsinthos was very considerate, he thought. The star was kind to him, perhaps more than Uriel. And he couldn't fall the way Azazel or Armoni had; he was already here. Trailing a hand down from waist to thigh, the young angel glanced down between his legs. 'Closer.' Biting his lip, Dina palmed properly at the place of damning and, sharp, gasped, toes curling at the new sensation, hips stuttering up. 'Run it up, down.' He did, caressing with his fingers and instantly clenching his eyes shut. Inside his abdomen, it felt as if a knot was tightening, tightening. 'Slowly.' His hands trembled, but they ran up, down — just as ordered — up, down. 'Sin feels right, doesn't it?'

Quicker, Dina's fingers worked, and he had to bite down hard on his cheeks when a sudden jolt of a sound almost spilled from his lips. His hips continued rocking forward, chasing his touch, moving together as if reeled on the same hook, and his free hand went behind him, grasping the pillow he'd slept on before he might fall over. Breaths were coming shorter, refusing to stay in his mouth, as if he were running, chasing. What could he be chasing? All he knew for sure was that his fingers were damp now, as if he were working them into his mouth. He imagined that, the weight of something in his mouth. He imagined weight, over him, his entire self.

The face of Apsinthos came to mind, his fiery features and enormous size. How warm would it feel to be held down by the bright body of a star? How warm would it feel to have a star burn his way inside and fill the angel with flames?

When Dina's thighs were spasming, the star said, 'Finish. Do it for me.'

The angel, blinded by need, felt the throb in him almost painfully now, the discomfort like a limb tied down, like an urge turned panicked need. He couldn't stop his gasps anymore, though he kept them as soft as he could, trying to ignore the noises of the house. 'Apsinthos, are you looking at me? Do you like seeing this?' His body jerked, as if revolting against the goodness twisting him up inside. One foot kicked helplessly, and he turned his face, eyelids half-closed. 'Please.' He slapped a hand over his mouth as he finished, overwhelmed by the pulsing sensation of pleasure in him, so strong that he was certain he'd died of ecstasy and risen up to the stars himself, met Apsinthos again with his great smile, his fire hair. Dina would be tiny in his palm, but if the gorgeous sun lifted him, Dina would get on the tips of his toes to brush his lips on his.

'Apsinthos,' he thought without meaning to, his pale wings partly fluttered out of him, his skin feeling too tight over every scorched thing that made an angel up. 'I want to see you again, Apsinthos.' He wanted to kiss him, wanted the world to end how all stories ended — with a true love's kiss.

'When it all ends, we will be together, angel.' And the angel smiled. He had felt good, and he was happy.

Elsewhere — a pink-haired demon woman was sitting leg-crossed at the other end of a coffee table in a crowded café. She was holding a smoking cigarette, shortened to about half its full length between her fingers, and her bright red lips were pursed in annoyance beneath hefty sunglasses. "There's not much I can do. Even if he doesn't have me dragged back to Hell, he has more than enough power to have me take the fall for all his crimes here on Earth. That's why he has me be his accomplice, I think — not because he *really* needs me to bring him weapons or anything, but to make sure that if I ever step out of line, he can have me thrown in human prison." When the demon on the other side of the table snorted, Gemory, the demon woman, sighed and insisted: "You don't know how good he is at framing people."

"I'm well-aware," said the demon duke Asmodeus, "of how *excellent* he is at blaming others for his own actions, actually." He was dressed in a gray wool coat, sleek pants, leather dress shoes, a golden ring, a silver watch, and a black face mask over the end of his nose to his chin. For the last two or three centuries, Asmodeus' onyx-colored hair had been trimmed short to create messy bangs at the front whereas the back was sweeping a few finger-widths past the nape of his neck. As for the infernal horns the great demon used to carry, they were not what they used to be — they had both been broken long ago, then sawed flat closer to his skull, almost entirely hidden in his dark hair. "But you shouldn't feel guilty, Gemory. I owe you plenty for trying to keep this... quiet."

Gemory breathed in slow, then tapped the end of her cigarette out on the ashtray on the table. Typically, she'd be more careful with how she moved, how loudly she spoke in their demonic language, but there was no better place to hide a devil than in a crowd. "I warned you," she said lowly, "that you couldn't keep this up long. Were you really only here for *fun?*"

Months ago, the demon duke of lust had rolled over in bed, settled his mouth over the half-asleep fallen angel of fruit. He'd drunk his gasp, then reached to play with Rosier's necklace as he kissed him some more. Whispering, Asmodeus had said they should go to Earth. Rosier, softly, had asked, 'Have you asked Satan? Or Baal?' But Asmodeus had said their approval didn't matter. If Satan had the audacity to care so much, then he should be here to stop them. Then, he'd kissed at Rosier's cheek, then his neck, and said, 'Let's leave, darling.' Wrapping an arm around him and squeezing firmly. 'I'll marry you again. There are some places left on Earth where we haven't wed, and I don't want to stop marrying you until every grain of dirt has known that I love you.' Rosier, such a soft demon, surrendered to this, of course.

Asmodeus said, "I told you. It was business." That wasn't a lie. "The clubs do well enough without me being here to manage them, but there are always legal issues, journalists to get rid of." There was always someone who looked too deep into the scars that certain clubbers would leave the building with; contrary to popular belief, organ harvesting didn't often kill the victim, and their victimhood itself wasn't an easy thing to argue for. They would sign papers, they would receive a decent payment, and they would leave in some pain but happy to afford another meal. Asmodeus never considered himself so evil; it was the humans who bought, and it was the humans who sold. All he got out of the exchange was a cut of money and some new body parts. He wasn't so monstrous anymore, hadn't been for many, many centuries now; on the outside, that is; he couldn't speak for what existed beneath his skin. "Hell is also miserable."

Gemory abandoned her stubbed cigarette and crossed her arms. "Worse than it was last time I was back home?" She said 'home' slow, bitterly.

"Well, right before we left, Baal whipped Moloch for trying to free some demons from the prison." Asmodeus chuckled over the other demon's sigh. "He's not very bright — that Baal. Satan would be smarter than that. He would have created division between Moloch and his friends. Divide and conquer, the humans call it. For as much of a bitch and bastard that Satan is — he was good at ruling Hell." 'And so why haven't you been in Hell anymore, Lucifer?' he wondered. 'What won't you tell us?'

"Hello, hello," came a kind voice nearby just as Asmodeus smiled and Gemory rolled her eyes. "Forgive me for the wait. The line was longer than I thought it'd be." With both hands, the demon Rosier held a pastry — a horn-shaped bread with a drizzle of choco-late — on a simple, small plate. Like Asmodeus, he had a wedding band, but he also had a deceptively simple engagement ring that must've cost the price of a city home or two. "What's happening?" He wore a sweater, a scarf, and a close-fitting knit cap. Long ago, he too had his horns sawed close to his head, and though he hadn't cut his obsidian-colored hair any shorter, he now tied back some strands of it.

"The devil isn't happy," Gemory muttered.

"He never is..." Rosier finally set the plate down on the table, between Asmodeus and him, then settled on the chair beside his husband's. "But, I suppose, we'll have to return then?" As he spoke, the duke reached and took one of his hands, running his thumb over Rosier's knuckles. When Gemory noticed it, she remembered how terribly she'd craved Asmodeus's gentle touch once, and it was both tragic and wonderful not to crave it anymore. Sometimes the birth of desire can only be bested in joy by the death of desire.

Asmodeus said, "We should go willingly."

Rosier looked over at him, blinking twice. "Are you sure?"

It had been a wonderful few months; it really had been. "I don't think it'd be a good idea to bring Satan's wrath down upon us, not right now." While Asmodeus would often go to his clubs, Rosier had never enjoyed it. He'd say, 'No, no — I'll stay home,' one of Asmodeus' many expensive condos across the globe, high on a tower with a perfect view of the skyline. Though Rosier hadn't liked Earth as much in the past century, he'd found it very nice at times to walk in the dark; many times, Asmodeus would join him. Though, there had been difficult days between them, as well. Many of them.

The duke felt Gemory's pitiful gaze; though her sunglasses hid it. Asmodeus said, "I don't want you to get hurt." He nodded forward. "And I can't ask Gemory to risk her life for us anymore." At that, she laughed.

"I did it for you, Asmodeus. You're my friend," she replied. "I would really like to think that we can be friends, anyway." Gemory paused, then looked at Rosier, who parted his lips, then disentangled his hand from Asmodeus' to reach for the croissant. "And I wouldn't wish Satan on my worst enemy." Rosier tore a third of the pastry off, then he extended it to Gemory, wordlessly, with nothing more than a nervously sweet shine in his faux hazel eyes, but she shook her head solemnly. "You have it. Who knows when you'll get to have another human pastry?"

The demon of fruit hesitated, and he wished he could have said something, but he didn't know what would suffice to convey what he wasn't sure he felt.

In Tadeo's home, the anti-Christ had just returned. He came in through the doorway, shut it with all the locks behind, then grabbed the hat off his head and set it down on the nearest table. For once, he'd traversed the town without a firearm, figured it wouldn't be necessary for the short trip he was making to the hospital, a mere ten-minute walk away. 'How,' Tadeo had asked, 'is he doing?' The doctor in his office had sighed, glanced over at his secretary-nurse past the open door into the waiting area, then told Tadeo quietly that Dante's hand was beyond repair, and that the soldier was still in an urgent care room on the first floor, not speaking to anyone. 'I'm sorry for making you do this,' Tadeo had wanted to say, unsure now if he'd even said it. With a sigh, he stepped into the living room, where Joana was watching the television with his mother beside her, as usual.

"So is he dead?" Joana asked simply, not looking at him.

Tadeo swallowed, then moved across the room, headed for a door near the bathroom, where he was sharing a room with the angel. "Are my grandparents home?"

"I asked you a question," Joana said, but her voice wasn't strict as she stood, then rolled her shoulders, stretched her arms over her head, and trailed behind Tadeo. "Is he dead? Did he die of blood loss?"

Through gritted teeth — "They have to amputate his hand." Joana whistled. "I'm not proud about it. I didn't mean to take it that far. I got mad at him. It's his fault for making jokes."

Joana finally said, "Your grandparents are at mass." They reached the door to the bedroom, and she moved to lean on the wall against it, staring at Tadeo gravely. "And so the soldier — how does he feel about the fact that you've made him lose a whole ass hand?"

Tadeo took a deep breath, wishing now that he'd just come in through a window to avoid discussing this with her. "He's not talking, but he hasn't tried to run away. I'm not worried. Who would believe him? I mean, he doesn't believe it much either. He especially doesn't think that God is the one who did this to me or that I have an angel in my house." He hesitated, then added, "But there's not a lot of cars out there except for the trucks passing through to the border, and they're getting really angry about all the people trying to hitchhike across town on them, so maybe he's going to have to stick around anyway. Has the TV said anything about the gasoline?"

"They're blaming the criminals," Joana replied with a shrug. "The story is that they fucked up a pipeline while trying to steal from it during a confrontation, and that, for now, the state is going to hand out gasoline at a few stations. Should've started today, actually."

Tadeo nodded his head again, then finally knocked a fist against the door. "Dina," he called.

"He's still in there," Joana said as if that weren't obvious. "He still hasn't left the room."

"For fuck's sake," Tadeo grumbled, "what did you do to him?"

Joana laughed and raised her hands. "I told you. I just handed him a beer or two after we came back from checking the gas stations. How was I supposed to know angels can't hold down a little alcohol?"

"Dina," Tadeo called again. "It's Joana and I. Can I talk to you? I need to know something." He took the doorknob, saying the angel's name again, began turning it before he felt the handle yanked away from him. The door swiveled open to reveal the tall angel looking flushed, hair in a tangled web around his head, his entire body wrapped in the bedsheets like he was trying to hide within it. "I'm sorry," Dina said quickly. "I was asleep. What is happening?"

Tadeo blinked, turning his head a little to see into his room — the twin beds, the Mary of Guadalupe figurine in a small wooden table between them, the peeling wallpaper; this had been his mother and her siblings' childhood bedroom once. "Nothing right now. I wanted to talk to you. Can we go to the living room or the kitchen—?"

"We can talk here," said Dina, wrapping his arms around the bedsheets tighter but scooting forward. He reached behind him, shut the door, then echoed himself. "We can talk here..."

Hesitating, Tadeo glanced back at Joana, then at the angel. "You told me the world is going to end." Dina blinked, then nodded. "Does that mean we're in the apocalypse? The biblical one?"

"Yes," said Dina, firmer. "It's the biblical apocalypse."

"Everything that that Revelation says will happen," the anti-Christ answered, "will happen? There will be plagues and rivers of blood, and a star will fall into the Earth, and Jesus will return and take a few with him, and the rest of us will burn forever?"

"Yes," the angel said again.

"How can we stop it?"

Dina stared, and he tried to remember what he'd read when he'd first realized who Tadeo was, why he mattered to the end times that he wanted to prevent. 'He really doesn't know,' Dina thought, 'what he is meant to do.' Apsinthos had already told him that, but it was difficult to stare at the genuine, wide-eyed, pleading expression of the young man before him, knowing what he was, what he was born to do — to kill the ones he loved, to destroy what he was fighting so hard to protect. 'Don't pity him,' urged the star, or perhaps it was Dina himself. 'To fulfill Revelation,' said Apsinthos now, 'we will need demons and those angels bound beneath the Earth.' Dina almost gasped. 'Those whose anger and rage has been carefully nurtured in their bindings, so that they kill a third of mankind.'

"Hello?" Joana impatiently called.

The angel, eyes hazed as if he were asleep, whispered: "The Watchers. We must release the Watchers."

CHAPTER 14

The Lord has a sense of humor. It was raining when the angels descended from Heaven on winged horses into a remote, forested area. Even for those who'd traveled to Earth recently — Michael, Uriel — it was difficult to not immediately recall the brisk, chilled air of the days that the world of early men had flooded. The waters that had buried the children of the Watchers and their mothers, the women who'd loved angels. Though there had been men, too, that loved angels. Michael knew that better than anyone. His sword was always heavy, always seemed to drip blood, as if there was still the body of a winged child skewered through it. He never forgot. He never forgot the Watchers, and the devil that he'd destroyed them with.

But, right now, Michael held the reins of a pegasus the color of blood beneath its silver armor. He stared up at a high billboard on the side of the road with a celebrity plastered over it. Lounging on her side, she wore a short, tight dress, blonde hair curled and half trailing over her body, the other half on the flooring she laid over. Bright eyes were blue, ruby-red lips parted. The chief prince couldn't read in the language, couldn't decipher 'The Harlot' printed across the bottom. Even still, he furrowed his brows at the celebrity with an inexplicable, sinking feeling in his chest, like one were looking at a butchered corpse, wondering if they were familiar to you and knowing the body was too destroyed to ever be able to tell.

All the other angels were nearby, two hundred — like the Watchers had been — with more instructed to come soon, all over the grass rather mundanely. Because of the rurality of their landing spot, heavy darkness had masked the army of the apocalypse's descent into something rather unspectacular. Such darkness had been unnecessary, however; the angels were hidden to human eyes by the Holy Spirit — a work of God after the great flood — but Michael preferred coming across the least amount humans possible for now. The angels, on their own winged horses, looked around with juvenile curiosity; very few times had the vast majority of angels seen the Earth after what occurred with the Watchers. And Michael was already dreading to tell them that they'd really ended the world then, that this was a new Earth with new people, new weapons, new trees.

"Michael," someone called.

The prince looked over his shoulder, saw the one who'd spoken — Gabriel, who looked ridiculous with his earnest, freckled face and silver armor over a black horse. At his left, over a white horse, Raphael was similar, though he wore a helmet that obscured his head, and he had his staff strapped to his back in lieu of a sword. Uriel wore the helmet as well, sitting perfectly still over a horse, similarly pale to the angel of healing's. "What," Michael began, "is it?"

"What now?" he asked as Raphael sighed, as if nervous on Gabriel's behalf. "What do we do now?"

Upon return to the town that bordered Babylon, Satan was met by a truck with tinted windows. He hadn't planned to be picked up, not here by the airport, but there was a gun in his cassock. He hadn't hid his blonde hair, nor drowned his face in cosmetics yet. On the jet, he'd begun to powder his face using his small, golden-rimmed vanity mirror before he thought he'd caught someone over his shoulder. The Watcher Azazel, again — with a bleeding hole in his chest where his heart should be. They'd spoken recently, not long before Satan had left Hell. One of the things Azazel had said was: "Your hand shakes when you line your lips."

The window of the car rolled down, and immediately, the devil scoffed. "You love to infuriate me, don't you? You want me to beat you and yell at you." Nonetheless, he strode to the truck, pulled the passenger's seat open, slid onto the chair with his duffel bag, and sighed. "So long as I touch you, you don't mind if I slap you."

The demon Baal was in the driver's seat, his horns not as large as they used to be but still thick, still undeniably of a beast. He was dressed entirely in black but in a coat too thick for the weather. His hair had been cut short, though not to the extent of most human males either; it was still long enough for the devil to braid, as they both liked. And as for Baal's eyes, they were red in both the irises and the whites, everywhere — long ago, he'd had his eyes stabbed, and they'd never fully healed. All over him — there were scars. He was like an old god, a golden calf. "The gasoline," Baal began, "you asked the spies for is all in the back. Some men tried to approach me." Reaching for the gear, Baal yanked it into place to began driving. "I didn't kill them, but I was able to scare them off. Should I apologize now for being here?"

"Tell me why you came first," said Satan, twisting to fold his arms over the center console and lean toward Baal.

"I missed you." Baal hesitated, then he added, "And Moloch is causing trouble."

"Ugh," said Satan, and then, "You missed me," to which Baal chuckled; it was warm, deep. "But what about Moloch? I've told you what to do about him and his followers. If you can't manage these things, I'll have Gemory take care of Hell for me instead. Do you want that?"

"The demons all miss you too," replied Baal, glanced at Satan, and tilted his head. "And they're asking a lot of questions." At that, the devil let out another frustrated breath. "I just wanted to come warn you and to see you." He returned his attention to the road as one of his hands reached over, claws gently tracing Satan's cheekbone, down to his chin, grazing his mouth. The same mouth he'd failed to nicely trace with a lipliner on the plane, before Azazel's voice had echoed in his head.

"You will return soon," ordered Satan but didn't fight Baal's touch. "And you'll take care of Moloch and reassure all the demons that I'll be back within a month."

"As you wish," said Baal, obedient, proper, earnest.

Michael finally answered Gabriel: "We must do what the prophecy says."

Uriel said: "That's impossible. There are names and places all over that story that aren't true of any existing things in the present we're in. Are we supposed to take it all as metaphor?" He barked out a laugh. "If it's all metaphor, then whatever fulfills each seal of the apocalypse can be utterly arbitrary. How convenient."

Before Michael could snap back, Raphael interjected, "The Earth is enormous. Maybe we should all head in different directions. We must find those who will be saved by God first, shouldn't we?" To him, that was what mattered most. "We should avoid the bloodshed for now."

Michael shook his head. "I'll head south to where the anti-Christ is, and you all should remain in Babylon. I'll ensure he doesn't interfere with the rest of you finding the good humans, and you three should take the army with you." He faced the other angels, then he said, "The Holy Spirit will cloak you from human eyes until you reveal yourself willingly," before returning his gaze to the princes. Raphael nodded, Gabriel looked away, and Uriel didn't react at all. "And," Michael added more unsurely, "there is also the devil to take care of."

"To return to God?" asked Uriel, but Michael didn't answer before he made to leave.

Far away, Baal and the devil fucked in the car. They lowered the front seats; Satan laid back; he allowed the demon duke, the regent of Hell, to kiss him all over. He wondered briefly what any passerby who managed to peer through the tint and fog of the windows would see. A beautiful priest with hair too long being devoured by a monster. Baal held the devil's thighs as he drank, as if it were wine or as if it were blood, from between the beautiful one's legs. Encouraging purrs slipped from between Satan's lips, and he brought a hand to Baal's curls to tenderly scratch at his scalp. He held him just as tenderly as Baal went to move over him, mount him. He kissed Satan, mouth still damp, and kissed deeper, and kissed softer. The demon prayed to Satan, for mercy and for love. And like God, the devil returned love as meager scraps off his dinner table.

Claws hugging Satan's upper waist, prickling at his ribs. His hold was overly delicate, like the demon was the priest and it was Eucharist in his hands. Like fucking was sacrament. Rubbing his face against the devil's neck, his face, pressing his mouth on his, parting it, asking for a tongue to snake inside. It was fucking, rough yet slow. Satan grunted, then cried out breathlessly at the burning in his core struck again and again, rocking his hips back against Baal. They kissed, once more.

"I love you," Baal whispered as he always did, "Lucifer." He still called him that, at times.

Sometimes, when Baal said that he loved him, Satan's lips parted, quite prepared to say something back. It could have been that he'd developed the urge to say 'I love you,' recently, but why would that be? It was too late for love. It may be the end of the world, and all would be destroyed soon, including love. Yet, he kissed Baal slowly, like he really did enjoy kissing him. Maybe he did. At the end of the world, maybe he did.

Satan said, "You know that Lucifer's dead, don't you?" But maybe Baal was well aware, and it was just a ghost he loved.

Michael rode away on his horse, leaving the other archangels behind, heading for the land right across Babylon. His jaw was set. He thought of God. He thought of everything that he had to do.

The two demons laid in silence for a while before Baal removed himself, cleaned the devil, then fixed both their clothes. After this, he finished driving him to town, mentioning all the gasoline tanks in the trunk again that he'd gotten from one of Satan's other few spies on Earth, of which Gemory was a part of. He mentioned, more tensely: "Asmodeus and Rosier are still missing."

"I know. Go fetch them," said Satan, quieter, curled up against the window and tired. "Have Asmodeus punished for it. And I will return to Hell, soon. Soon. Once I finish here." The devil's children missed him, needed him. He'd never been absent without so much as a visit for this long, but he could feel his phone buzzing in his pants, one of many phones. Many lives; it was difficult to remember the most important one.

Before arriving at the rectory, Satan finally hid his blonde hair, and he applied the correct brown eye contacts and adjusted his makeup to appear like an honest young man. Baal tried to help with the dozen gasoline tanks, but Satan ordered him to stay hidden in the car. And so the devil priest brought all the tanks into the rectory's garden on his own, ignoring the sounds of the migrant shelter nearby. It was already morning, after all. "I'll," the devil began once he realized he needed to hurry along this farewell, "be home, soon."

"Please," Baal replied. "Hell needs you." Satan smiled at that, blew him a kiss, then slammed the door shut so that he could head to bed.

The next morning, Satan, the beautiful priest, was awakened by the good priest, Father Toño, shaking him. "Ángel!" he shouted. "Ángel! You're okay— Oh Father in Heaven, you're alive." He was trembling, lowering himself onto the mattress, hands refusing to leave the devil's shoulders for even a second. "You don't know how afraid I was. I called you a thousand times, Ángel. Are you crazy? Don't ever do that again, brother. Please, don't ever do that to me. Where were you?" Staring with eyes slightly widened, Satan said it was just two, three days, that he'd been in the larger city down south to speak to the prior bishop he worked under. Father Toño, however, sighed, finally loosened his grip but still didn't let go. "I never told you, but the priest that was here before you — disappeared. He was kidnapped after he tried to protect some of the migrants against the criminals. They took him. I pray every night, Ángel, that he isn't really gone, but until God tells me otherwise, there is just my memory of him, a good man. A great man. And there's you. Please. Answer my calls if this happens again."

"I will," said Ángel, the devil, and smiled a little. "You don't have to worry about me, Toño. Even less with that boy, Tadeo." Father

Toño flinched, as if in shame. "Come with me. Let me show you the gasoline tanks that I brought from the city."

"Oh? So you know about the gas?" Father Toño pulled back as Satan slid away from him. "That's good. There are some migrants that need to be driven to the border today. I wanted to do it myself, and there were some soldiers I was speaking to for gasoline, but this works out better. Thank you, Ángel."

Ángel rose from the bed, heading for his window, peeling back the curtain, staring at the sky. "Mm, God whispered to me about the gas. I'm glad He did." He felt Father Toño tense again and smirked. "I'll join you on the drive." Satan always enjoyed the role of priest; a few centuries ago, he'd managed to reach the papal bed and gotten fucked on it. Priests and pastors and religious men hadn't changed at all since then, no matter how much the world beneath their feet did.

After this, they both went about the morning, had service, ate, then went to the shelter, the larger hall next door, where families and some lone individuals, totaling two hundred, ate the meals that the few nuns and some volunteers had prepared. Walking between all the plastic tables and chairs, the two priests began gathering those due for the immigration office. It was half a dozen people only, four adults, two children. Gently, the priests urged them to follow to a large van.

Michael the angel arrived over the border and hesitated. He guided his blood-colored horse toward the bridge out of Babylon and gripped the reins tightly, listening to the excessive honking of the cars heading up north and those heading south. In between the vehicles, he landed, then rode steadily, careful to avoid touching anyone. A few humans were selling across the southern part of the bridge — particularly women in long skirts, as well as children. They offered artisanal trinkets, some beaded earrings, and candies. A man nearby cleaned a car's windows, then knocked on the driver's door to ask for coins.

It was not the first time that Michael had seen this, and it was quite the familiar scene in general — humans traveling, humans and their commerce. But it'd been an eternity since he'd been tasked to destroy this, to harm them. Stopping, he decided to climb off his horse, setting it at the center of the bridge, before he flapped his wings. Michael rose into the air and breathed out nervously.

In the migrant car — a little girl was chattering with her father in the creole language of the island they originated from, a young indigenous boy who'd left his home alone sat with a middle-aged woman he'd met in a caravan, who was talking to another woman, who held a crying infant, and there was a quiet older man. On the radio, there was news. Before them, there was a nearly desolate road. The beautiful priest stared at each of the pedestrians they passed, many whose gazes lingered. "Hm," the good priest was sighing, "maybe this wasn't a good idea."

"You're right," said the beautiful devil. "One of us should have stayed behind in the shelter. There could be a massacre happening right now, and we're letting it happen."

"There's no massacre happening right now," the good priest grumbled. "What I mean is that we might get attacked. I was just hearing about some cars that were stopped by criminals and got their gasoline stolen."

"Oh dear," said the beautiful one. "I'll pray a Hail Mary, in case." Again, the good priest sighed. "But don't worry so much, brother. We're almost there." He nodded his head at the bridge coming into view, though they were headed for a large building across the street from it. "Look, there's so many soldiers." Dozens of men were stationed both at the immigration building that the migrants had to be processed through and by the bridge entryway, brandishing their hefty firearms and camouflage.

"A lot of them," Toño replied, less cheerily, then jostled in his seat when one of those soldiers was stepping up to the road before them, lifting a weaponless, gloved hand, palm facing them in a halting gesture. "Oh, what do they *want?*"

"For fuck's sake," added the older man in the back, to which the beautiful one chuckled.

"Hey now," Toño tried to coax them, shifting the van into parking. "Don't stress." Other soldiers were approaching now, perhaps eight or nine. "I'll talk to them," said the good priest, almost insisting. "I'll talk to them—" As he rolled the left window down, the first soldier was already commanding:

"Out of the vehicle. All of you."

"We're from the shelter on Private Street, and we have," Toño tried to interject, "an appointment with the migration office. Look, I have documentation for everyone here. Ángel, can you pass me the folder I have on the side there—"

"Out of the vehicle, now," repeated the soldier, firmer, then banged his hand on the side of the car with a metallic thud. "Hurry your asses up." His sharpness chilled the blood of every human in the van, including the good priest, whose eyes widened in confusion, but when he opened his mouth, the soldier lifted his long firearm, pointed the barrel between Toño eyes. Instantly, those in the back drew a breath, and the infant hiccuped with the first bubbling of a wail. Again: "Get out of the fucking car."

Swiftly, calmly, the priest Ángel clicked to unlock the van and urged with a quiet voice: "Everyone, step out of the car. To the right." The left had the most crowding of soldiers, and Satan was certain the migrants realized this too, as they didn't hesitate to hurry in the direction he indicated, almost stampeding over one another. Meanwhile, he remained in place, waiting for the soldier to lower his gun away from Toño, and he listened to the radio.

"The president has reportedly retracted his statement—" Static was seeping out like blood from a wound. "He trusts that—" It was a nation like Babylon, up ahead. To those headed there, Heaven and Hell, at once. "It was—" Slowly, the man began to trail the end of his gun lower, lower, before he grabbed the handle of the door, wretched it open abruptly. "It was a misunderstanding, according to the Speaker of the House, but there is something to be said about the complete lack of government control at the border. A recent massacre of soldiers outside the border town of—"

"Wait—" the priest Toño tried to say again, but he was grappled at the collar of his button-up, then yanked out.

"You get out too," the soldier snarled at the devil. "Get out and put your hands up."

The beautiful one didn't hesitate, reaching for the handle,

turning it, pushing open the door, and stepping out elegantly. He raised his hands to the back of his head, stepping away from the vehicle, toward the migrants they'd brought with them, standing off the road, off the sidewalk, over the grass. Behind them, there was the decline of a hill that led down to the river that the border bridge loomed above. Each of the migrants was cowering, some hunching, hands over their head. The woman with the infant was low to the ground, curled over her now screeching child, while the father was holding his daughter behind himself. As Satan stepped toward them, he also saw — across the river — horses, four horsemen patrolling the border. All they did was watch.

"To the river," shouted the soldier who was shoving the good priest toward the group. "All of you." Now, there was begging, one of the women crying, pleading, shaking her head and putting her hands together, but another one of the soldiers shot at the sky with a horrible, curt boom that made nearly everyone scream, lower their bodies more, begin shuffling back and toward the bank, feet unequally sinking into the mud so that they all staggered.

Satan followed, eyes maintained on the horsemen. There was another figure, high over the bridge to Babylon, hovering over the river in a blinding shine of divine armor. Great wings were spread behind him the color of the Earth, and a bulky sword was over his back, handle by his helmet. And as the devil priest followed the people into the cold rush of the river, first dampening his socks, then his exposed ankles, then seeping through his pants — he saw that this figure was dressed in a reddened cloak. It was quite ridiculous, almost anachronistic — but as was the glow over his head, as were the wings spreading out from his back. Yet, no one was reacting. Couldn't they see him?

"What do we do, Father?" whispered a young woman, one of the migrants, who was cowering against the beautiful priest's side. Behind them, the soldiers were still barking orders, telling them to sink deeper into the river, lifting and pointing their guns again. Satan didn't look at them, instead touching the woman gently at her upper arms, whispering for her to be careful as they trudged through the river water.

Then, he murmured: "Do as the soldiers say. Do not be afraid." The angel in the sky fluttered his wings, approached, watching, but his gaze seemed fixated on the beautiful priest. Suspicious, curious. They could never quite hide from each other — Michael and Satan — whether behind a helmet or behind a painted face. They would always feel one another — nearby.

"What's going to happen?"

Releasing her, Satan moved past the migrants, who called after him, heading toward the bank again, where the good priest was holding up his hands, still demanding answers. "You!" called one of the armed men. "Get back in the river!"

"The rivers will run red with blood," the beautiful devil mused; it was a line in the Book of Revelation; he would know; he'd known it in every language, in every time, since John first wrote it. He watched the soldier who'd spoken twitch, finger shuddering against the trigger, barrel pointed at the devil. Other soldiers shouted, turning their weapons to Satan, as well, and just as Father Toño started stammering, demanding the other priest step back — the devil spoke once more. With both hands raised by his head, palms facing the soldiers, he stepped before Toño, though not without brushing past him, whispering the word, "Left."

"Ángel?" the good priest helplessly called.

"Ángel," echoed the devil, feeling a looming presence, a shadow trailing closer until it sprawled by his feet. "There is one with us now." Slow, a smile began to bloom across his lips, curling them back, exposing perfect teeth. He reached into the pocket of his cassock, gripped the stout revolver hidden there, then twisted. Right above, there he was: the cloaked figure with a silver helmet obscuring all of his face and chains dangling from one hand. However bulky the angel's armor was, Satan caught a sliver of exposed skin between chest plate and head, aimed, shot.

The harsh bang was followed by the hiss of the bullet, then the splatter as it cut right through the angel's throat. Blood, strings of meat, flesh, from Michael the archangel, dribbled onto the river, staining it like oil in sea. Though the humans couldn't seen him, they saw the red of his blood and the ghost-silhouette of a body.

But, as shouts rang all around, Satan didn't linger, didn't even stay to watch the saint flutter erratically in the air, plunge down what amounted to two stories. He did, however, catch Michael's helmet jerk in his direction, so sharp his neck might've snapped had it not already burst.

The devil took off, sprinting to the right in the few seconds that he had before any of the armed officers, at either side of the bridge, could recover from the shock of a killed ghost. The bangs of more shots were quick to follow him, as well as the burn of grazing bullets. Shrill screams surrounded him, all of them. Michael yelled out, choking on the blood in his mouth.

But the devil ran like it was God after him.

CHAPTER 15

"Don't be difficult," Joana's father had told her the night before. "Get your boy to deal with this shit or else you'll see what I do to you. You don't know how good you have it. Your mother and I would have killed for all the things you have — that nice phone, those new shoes. Don't let that boy kill more soldiers but have him find out why they tried to kill those people. Do you hear me?"

"Yes, dad," she'd said. "I'm sorry, dad."

The words had echoed in her skull that early morning from the backyard of Tadeo's home, where she often slept in a hammock beside where they had their *lavadero*, a washboard utility sink; many times, Joana would help Tadeo's family with running the soap over the ridges of the board side before laying clothes there to begin scrubbing. Joana had more than enough laundry to painstakingly do in her own house, but sometimes she'd snicker at the thought of her mother forcing her eldest brother to help instead. If nothing else, bringing the money to the family meant she didn't have to do the dishes so much anymore, didn't have to worry about mopping after her youngest siblings. She could be a person, not just a daughter. But selling her soul really hadn't been what she wanted once.

The last few days she'd been holed up in Tadeo's family's house more than ever, wondering, 'What the fuck is going on? What the fuck am I going to do?' The soldiers had attacked two priests and several migrants, killing three of them, in the face of a thousand witnesses, including the patrol at the other side of the border. Up north, the story was that the traffickers had infiltrated the state forces across the river, that it was the criminals that had ordered it. But Joana knew that wasn't the case — even without calling the kingpin, she knew that he wouldn't have ordered something like this. What for? Criminals are quite deliberate with violence, but if Joana had gathered anything from the televisions, it was much easier to believe that they were irrational, indiscriminate, violent monsters. Demons, they called them.

But even demons are deliberate; they are purposeful.

'I'll have to,' she thought, 'keep Tadeo down.' She would tell Tadeo to lay low for a few weeks, that the massacre was a punishment from the state for what Tadeo had done to the soldier; after all, maybe it was.

Then, there was a sudden, sharp whine nearby, then a snort. "Oh for fuck's sake," she said out loud, wheezing out a cough like she were in the midst of smoking as she fought against her hammock to get back on the ground of the yard. "God fucking dammit, Tadeo."

At the other side of the house, past the front yard, nearly on the road but with one foot still over a cracked sidewalk, Tadeo was breathing in nervously. The sky clung to darkness and warded off dawn, the rays of the sun at the horizon exceptionally dim; it might be a cloudy day for once. Beside him, an Azteca mare stood tall with dark brown skin and an even darker mane, as opposed to the much lighter, milky-coffee color of the saddle that the young man was adjusting. The angel Dina was standing right in front of the horse, eyes wondrous as he tapped her snout. When the door slammed open, crashing against the edge of the adjoining wall — Tadeo didn't dare turn, though Dina did immediately.

"Stupid fuck!" Joana yelled even though one of Tadeo's uncles and his grandfather were hurrying behind her, telling her to lower her voice or she'd wake everyone in the neighborhood. "Do they know, Tadeo? Do they know you're trying to take your ass to *Hell*?"

"They already know everything," Tadeo replied stiffly, tugging on the saddle a few times just to check its firmness before setting a foot into one of the stirrups. Grunting, he lifted himself, throwing his other leg over the mare's back to mount her.

Dina stared at Joana tensely. He hadn't forgotten what he saw at the club, and he'd begun to bite his tongue in recent days after she'd snapped at Tadeo to not even consider leaving the town for the sake of the Watchers. Even that soldier Tadeo had tortured had been sent on his way already; Dina had awkwardly stood nearby as Tadeo spoke with the other young man outside the hospital, urging him to return to his family, to get himself uninvolved for his own good. There had been no progress in Apsinthos' apocalyptic plans thanks to Joana's manipulation. And, now, the angel fluttered his wings, partly hoping the star in his head would make the snide comment he had the urge to grumble.

When Apsinthos was silent, however, Dina spoke: "Joana." He tried to speak calmly, authoritatively — the way Uriel always did. "The end of the world is at stake. Tadeo must do this."

"Bullshit," Joana snarled at the angel, stepping up to him, tilting her head up without cowardice to Dina's divine presence. "If Tadeo leaves this place, everyone's lives will be in danger. Haven't you seen how the soldiers don't give a shit about us? If Tadeo leaves, and the criminals notice he's gone, they might take the chance to worsen the violence again."

"I won't be gone that long," Tadeo grumbled. "It's just three or four days on horse, and freeing the angels trapped beneath the Earth should be simple enough. We're not going to Hell, just halfway there." Joana laughed meanly, but Tadeo adjusted himself, looking down the road, not letting her interfere.

Dina, meanwhile, turned his head back to Tadeo's family as they moved to tell Joana that Tadeo could make his own decisions. His grandmother and one of his aunts were appearing at the doorway as well, and Dina was sure Tadeo's mother was probably in the living room, listening as much as she could. Distantly, the angel could hear a dog barking, and he tilted his head to see one such creature — slim and hairless — on the roofing of a home nearby.

"*Tío*," Tadeo called to his uncle. "I'll bring her back to you as healthy and happy as you lended her to me."

"It's no problem, *mijo*," his uncle said quickly, stepping toward him, patting the mare's behind. "Just stay safe." Most of Tadeo's family didn't really understand where he was headed, but with an angel by his side, they assumed they had no choice but to support him. And as Dina heard the other members of his family wishing him luck and waving, asking if he was sure he'd packed everything, Dina adjusted the hoodie he wore, as well as the jeans. He'd been offered a hat like the one Tadeo often wore, but he preferred the hood.

"I'll be back soon," Tadeo reassured his family. He had a backpack, which the angel had watched him fill with water, food, and ammunition the night before.

"You're going to fuck everything up," Joana said sharply, and though Tadeo visibly swallowed, he took the reins and wished her farewell.

With a tug, the anti-Christ guided the horse into a steady walk forward, and Dina followed on sandaled feet, glancing back over his shoulder at the waving family. They said, "Goodbye, Dina!" as well, making him startle at first, then jerk his hand up to wave it back. The grandmother shouted, "Take care of our Tadeo! May God bless you!" The angel realized he no longer knew if he was blessed, and as he went after the young man down the road, turning a corner into another neighborhood, he fiddled with his fingers nervously.

"Are you sure this is the right way, Dina?" Tadeo's voice leaked into the angel's thoughts as they traveled together, a few neighbors peeking out of their windows, looking up as they ran a broom over the sidewalk. There weren't many soldiers, but they stared at him, too, from corners. Few cars populated the streets, as well, as the gas shortage grew tighter and tighter. Cargo trucks continued to pass, through, headed to Babylon.

'It's not far from where the anti-Christ was born,' Apsinthos had said, 'at the coast. Many years ago, a drill cracked the Earth there, and it gushed black blood into the ocean. The crack was so deep that it opened a wound into Hell. The Beast must've climbed out from there before it entered the boy.'

Yesterday, Dina had heard this in the bathroom with a bucket of water, a cup, and soap, naked and crouched on the flooring, wet hair over his face as he listened to his love. 'Isn't Tadeo the Beast?' Each droplet that rolled from his body and landed on the tile was loud as a gunshot, and he shivered. He didn't like the water here — too rough, all the Heaven crystalline smoothness missing.

'The Beast is inside him, but Tadeo is not the Beast; he is the tool of the Beast, an anti-Christ.'

Once they'd left the town behind, they turned off the road and onto grass, and the angel spread his wings and began to fly overhead. Only then did Dina realize how long it'd been since he'd flown — stuttering from left to right, focusing too much on the balance of his wings when he'd once flown like instinct. Nearly, he missed the start of Tadeo's questions.

"So what is Heaven really like? Is Jesus there? Is St. Peter at the gate? Is our Mary of Guadalupe there? How is God? How does He feel about all of this?" For hours, Dina deflected questions or offered half-answers or admitted he knew nothing. He tried to emphasize that he wasn't a great angel, just one that cleaned the house of a prince. "But that's a great thing, isn't it? To look after the house of an archangel? And God has sent you here, which means He has great plans for you, Dina."

"You believe so strongly," Dina murmured as he flapped his wings, slowing his glide but looking ahead at the brown dust of the Earth, the shrubs, and the cacti with pickled pears gleaming, "in God's love." He didn't know why he said it like he didn't understand. Dina was an angel, and yet faith felt so foreign to him. He supposed there wasn't much to have faith in if you'd seen the Lord's face. Angels didn't need to believe in God; they needed to fear him.

"Thank you. I do. It's what helps me find peace. Life hasn't been easy for me, and— Uh. Well, when I— When I returned from the dead, I wasn't like this. I spent an entire year here, in this place. I ate the cactus, and I ate snakes, and I ate soldiers. I was so angry that I thought I'd die. But then I returned home, and I stole from every place I went to. I didn't care who I hurt. Joana found me. After that, I also started going to mass again. It was the only thing that would make me feel better. I told myself that at least God loves me. At least God will accept me. He made this beautiful world, and we must keep it beautiful. And He put us here to fight. My father used to say we're here to work, and that's true. He also said we're here to take care of our home and each other; that is what He made us for."

"I... hope you are right. I hope that is what the Lord has always wanted." What else could Dina say? "I would like to think so."

They didn't encounter anyone, though they did hear a faraway buzzing that they assumed was from the faraway road. Many times, the angel turned back, and he'd catch some grass rustling, and a few instances, he considered flying closer, but the boy would kick his horse into a gallop and Dina would choose to follow. It was surely just an animal — a javelina or a deer or a snake. He didn't mind that. Thus far, he'd found animals to be wondrous and kind. If Heaven were full of animals, it would indeed be Heaven.

At sunset, the boy, horse, and angel settled by a sprawl of prickly pear cactus and agaves. Tadeo reached into his backpack, retrieved a foldable silicone bowl, then set it over the ground. Then, he reached for one of the jugs of water attached to the horse and uncapped it to pour into the bowl. "Drink," he urged the mare, who whined at him, stomped her foot. "Please."

Above, the sun was creeping toward the horizon with a crowd of yellowing, pinkening, and every shadow was leaking out further from its source, as a stroll of wind ruffled the feathers of Dina's wings. He hadn't tucked them in yet and they cast a dark silhouette on the ground that distorted the shape of his body into something larger than it was. Beside him, Tadeo opened the pack with the food he'd rolled up in aluminum. He'd brought a portable stove, but the boy didn't bother using it today. Instead, he began setting up the tent, at the same time he took bites from a cold, bean and cheese taco, asking Dina if angels slept in beds up in Heaven.

"We invented beds," Dina answered softly. 'We invented most things... first.'

Apsinthos finally spoke: 'All that humans have done are derivatives of what angels have done.'

'You sound like Uriel,' Dina replied, setting down into a crouch, watching the Azteca nuzzle her nose against the water. 'But maybe he was right that the humans were created to replace us.'

With a huff of exhaustion, Tadeo moved between his tent and outside, removing his hat and fanning his face for a moment just as he was turning to Dina, opening his mouth and waving the last of his taco, before he faltered. He blinked, eyes widened, as he looked at something right beside the angel. "What—?" left Tadeo's mouth, then, "Hey! I saw you, fucker!" Dina turned back curiously, listening to the sharp noises of the mare beside him at the undeniable sound of feet padding the ground, of someone hurrying back. "Oh my fucking God, it's you?" In his dark green pants, hefty black boots, and the same open army jacket he'd donned as he shot Tadeo to pieces — the soldier was cursing, reaching down to grab the bike that he'd dropped. "Dante?"

"Fuck you," snapped back in an instant.

Stomping over the uneven, rough terrain, Tadeo left behind the curious angel and stuffed his dinner into a pocket as he said, "You followed me? All the way here? What the hell is wrong with you?"

Dante succeeded in lifting his bike off the ground and grunted, his face still pointed away from the anti-Christ, mouth settled in a pout. Now that Tadeo was closer, he saw the folded sunglasses over Dante's tank, right beside the dog tags, and the bandaged stump where his left hand should be. "I was trying to hitch a ride out of town." He paused. "But the trucker I was calling got pulled over by a bunch of criminals, and they stole his gas right in front of me. Then, I saw you. I saw you and—" He turned his head, and his gaze landed on Dina. "An angel."

"I told you," said Tadeo, "that I had an angel with me. You didn't believe me." He finally reached the soldier and stopped, unsure what to do with his hands, just how threatening he was supposed to be.

"Now, why the fuck would I?" Dante laughed, spreading both arms at his sides as if to gesture at all the absurdity of the world.

"Forget about the angel," Tadeo snapped, feeling his face twitch. "Why did you follow me? What the hell is wrong with you?"

"You can turn into a giant monster, dumbass. You think I don't worry watching you run off into the sunset? I wanted to see where you were going and what you're trying to do, but now I'm stuck in the middle of the damn desert." 'It's actually not a desert,' Tadeo resisted saying. "And I'm going to die of thirst because of you out here."

"And what?" Tadeo laughed, deciding to turn around, begin heading back toward his tent, all the while the angel continued standing there beside the horse, saying nothing. "Do you want me to give you water? Why don't you just go back into town or get back on the road and find a truck to take you somewhere else? You don't believe in God, so I don't expect you to believe in what I'm trying to do."

Dante clicked his tongue. "Wouldn't Jesus offer water to an enemy?" Tadeo stopped again, facing his angel and horse, seeing now that the sun had almost wholly fallen past the flatland horizon. If he'd gone south, he would have reached mountains many hours ago, but he was headed toward the sea, somewhere he hadn't visited since his father was alive. "So? Come on, church boy."

Tadeo clenched his teeth, then crouched for one of the plastic water bottles he'd left at the foot of the tent. "I didn't bring much, so try not to finish it." He lifted his body back up, twisted back, then extended it with a scowl.

Dante, suddenly, smiled, moved toward Tadeo, and took the water bottle. "Thank you." He unscrewed the top, looked to the angel Dina, then said, rather politely, "I'm Dante Perez." He offered his un-bandaged hand, which Dina blinked at before reaching out, touching his fingers. "Oh—" the soldier breathed just as the angel took hold of his palm and gave him a gentle shake. "You're really an angel. I already saw your wings, but... wow." He was quite stout, the angel noticed, but he was handsome with a sharp face and a large grin.

Tadeo snorted and began fiddling with the tent, trying to ensure the dual sleeping bags had been set up, before finally returning to his dinner. "Tomorrow, you're going to head back." Dante released the angel's hand and opened his mouth. "Don't ask questions. You're not going to understand, and I don't want to bother."

So, the soldier turned to the angel instead and called, "Beautiful," though he used the feminine suffix. "Can you explain what's happening for me?"

Dina felt his cheeks warm and, flustered, smiled. "We're trying to travel halfway to Hell."

"Dina," Tadeo sighed in irritation, but Dante's laugh cut him off, and the anti-Christ finally stuffed the last of his dinner into his mouth.

"Really?" the soldier said, removing his jacket, then setting to plop onto the ground so that he could sit over it. He brought the water bottle to his mouth as he settled, chugging down as much as he could.

"Yes," said the angel because the star in his head wasn't telling him to be quiet. "We plan to free the Watchers. They are angels who were bound for their actions that led to the great flood that nearly ended humanity. We're trying to stop the final apocalypse."

"Wow," commented Dante, then his stomach grumbled, and he glanced down at it like it was a beast of its own. "Well, I hope we stop for some more tacos before we go."

Tadeo jolted. "What—?" Once again, he started walking toward the soldier, who didn't lift his face to Tadeo. "*We?* Tomorrow, you're going back home. Do you fucking hear me?" It was darkening extremely quickly, far from civilization as they were, and the angel was turning his face up to the sky to see the twinkling beads of light on a black canvas — and this went on for several seconds of silence. "Hey? Answer me." Dim, difficult to make out as night took hold, the soldier's face was expressionless, his eyes distant. "I said to answer me."

"They think I'm dead," answered Dante, then finally turned to look at the anti-Christ. "I called my mother, and she cried and said that they told her I disappeared during a drug bust operation in the south. They told her there had been explosives, and that I was definitely in the rubble. They told her that they would send what was left of me as soon as they could." He stopped, then shifted to plant his remaining hand behind himself, lean back on it, and then inhale slow. The air was chilled, and yet he'd removed his jacket to show his muscled, lean arms. "It was all bullshit." His stump of a wrist was on his lap.

Tadeo swallowed, then asked, "You don't think it was a mistake?"

"They knew about you, obviously, some of the higher-ups. If they hadn't, they wouldn't have sent us to kill you, but now I think they've known exactly what you *are* for a long time, that you're a demon-thing." Tadeo's eye twitched, but he didn't bother correcting him; instead, he found himself stepping back, turning halfway. "Maybe they also know exactly who you've been killing — which soldiers and which criminals. They're keeping a lot of secrets. And don't misunderstand — I know better than anyone that the state is a lying piece of shit that covers up corruption, but lying to my own mother, covering up where I went, who I was trying to kill. Why lie about that? Why not say I died up north in a shootout? This is more than they've ever done. They don't want the people to know about you."

Tadeo wished he'd lit the electric lamp that was still attached to the horse's saddle; the darkness was tiring him. "You should go home to your mother."

"I really should. I should tell her about this stupid fuck who tore my damn hand off, that lost me my job, that is responsible for how she's going to have to get back to cleaning houses." At that, Tadeo tensed, and he wanted to say that he didn't mean to take it that far, but he knew that he had. "And well." Dante chuckled a little. "I'll stay dead for a while. I don't want them to find out I'm alive yet." Before Tadeo could ask — "I only joined the army because I didn't want to get dragged into trafficking." He named the town he'd come from. "I was like you back then. I thought we could all just kill the right people to make things better and that if I traded the criminal gun in my hands for a soldier one, then I'd do good, but in the end, I was still holding a gun." He faced Tadeo more gravely, then said, "So you and the angel are trying to stop the world from ending, right? Is that even still possible? Everything is so fucked."

The two humans turned to the angel, who stared at them, his eyes as silver as the full moon over his head. 'Oh,' Dina thought, 'I suppose they want my reassurance.' A churn of guilt turned his stomach, but he tried to smile, to nod, to angelically hold his own hands. "Yes, there is hope. The world can still be saved, but we must act. This is God's will." 'Oh, I really don't like that, telling lies.'

"Hm," said Dante, "I don't want the world to end."

Tadeo quirked a brow. "You're going to help me?"

"No. Don't get ahead of yourself," Dante laughed. "But I want to see more of what's going on, whether you want me to go or not." Then, the soldier yawned and rolled his shoulders, murmuring, "Let me sleep an hour, then I can keep watch all night."

Tadeo scoffed, then stepped toward the tent. "Keep watch of what? The cactus? Get some sleep instead. We should all fit in the tent, but leave the middle section to the angel because that's the most cushioned part. Are you hungry? I have another taco in my bag and a stove if you want to heat it."

The soldier waved a hand. "I'm just tired. How early are we waking?"

"Dawn."

Dina dipped his head and crawled into the tent, the rocky ground barely cushioned by the thin lower fabric, even though Tadeo had thrown some blankets inside. Without another word, the angel laid down, pulling his knees a little closer to himself because he was too tall for the flimsy little home he'd have for a few hours. There were times all he could do was breathe out nervously, realize how far from Heaven he truly was and how much his life had changed after a hundred million years of stagnation. His star was quiet today, but he sent him a loving prayer, then allowed his eyes to flutter shut. His wings ached beneath his skin.

Outside, Dina heard:

"No, dawn is fine. We're really going to Hell? Really, really?"

"Yes."

"Pfft. To be honest, I still don't believe in Heaven or Hell or God even if angels are real — but I'm willing to look. Hey, don't make that face at me. You should be excited, *güey*. You're going to be the first saint that goes to Hell."

CHAPTER 16

The anti-Christ, the soldier, and the angel arrived at the coast within a day and a half, a few hours before sunset. Sparse vendors were scattered along the stretch of sand and rock, but Tadeo guided his Azteca mare away from them, away from the beach. He headed toward the tiny town adjacent to it, to meet with his aunt and uncle who ran a small convenience store. Dina had been, gently, ordered to stray behind, on the sidewalk, but Dante had been unshakable. All throughout the ride, he'd been pressed awkwardly to Tadeo's back, occasionally bumping his head into the anti-Christ's hat every instance that the horse jostled about too much. When the aunt asked who the green-jacketed man at the patio was, as Tadeo set some belongings down in the living area and thanked his relatives for taking care of them — the anti-Christ sighed, then grumbled, "Some weird man who is following me." Tadeo hadn't thought that Dante would hear, but he noticed a sulk on the soldier's face that remained even after he, Tadeo, and Dina finally headed to the beach, now on foot.

Whistling low, Dante stared at the horizon, dark sunglasses over his eyes, standing between the angel and Tadeo, his combat boots some steps away from murky blue water climbing up the shore. His voice was rather tight: "What now?" However much they hadn't spoken of it, the phantom pain of bullets and an amputated hand hung between him and Tadeo like wet clothes on a wire. "We're not going to swim out there, are we?"

"I'm not sure," Tadeo admitted. "We got here later than I hoped. It might be a better idea to go back to my family and sleep, but Joana's already pissed at me." The air was cool; the waves were a lullaby.

"Who's that? Girlfriend?"

"She's a lesbian," Tadeo answered, "and she's more of my boss." Without elaborating, he turned to the angel nearby. Dina's dark hair was tangling with the wind, and his eyes were distant. Time after time, Tadeo would catch the angel's lips shaping into words never uttered, like he were speaking silently to something, maybe himself, maybe God. "Dina?" Tadeo called. "Do you know what we should do from here?" The angel's gaze remained empty, his lips parted — an expression unchanging as if he hadn't heard. At that, the anti-Christ furrowed his brow.

"Alright," said Dante, then adjusted his jacket and trekked down the slope toward the tide lapping at the sand.

"What are you doing?" Tadeo walked after him without thinking, dry sand crunching beneath his boots before sharp splashes sounded below. Instantly, the sea began to claw up his ankle, and once it reached his jeans, it seeped through in such cold that he instantly shivered. "Shit—" Dante trudged through the water quicker, even as it began to rise to his knees, his thighs. "Hey! What's the matter with you?"

"I'm just walking." Dante reached for his sunglasses, tugged them off, then folded them at the collar of his shirt. "It's cold as fuck."

"Yeah," Tadeo sighed harshly. "It is." Just as the soldier slowed his movements, water having reached his waist, the anti-Christ halted his steps, feeling the tide rock against his thighs. Around them, it was quiet — just the hissing of the wind and some distant seagulls. Turning back, Tadeo stared at the desolate beach and the angel still standing at the shore, looking ahead, toward the setting sun. The haze in his eyes remained, as did the slight moving of his lips, almost as if he were lowly singing now in between the whirls of the ocean. Saliva balled in his throat — Tadeo remembered how his father used to sing beneath his breath, the words less like lyrics and more like a comforting chant.

Rolling the tension from his shoulders, Tadeo turned back to the soldier and called: "Dante! Come back here! We should wait." Shockingly, Dante did stop, though with a stumble; then, he tilted his head back at Tadeo, though his face was twisted in confusion. "What's wrong?" Dark brows tugged together in response. "What is it?" The soldier's mouth parted, but it wasn't Dante that answered.

Behind him, Tadeo heard Dina say, voice soft: "It's in the water."

Tadeo's face was turning to see the angel, halfway there, when there was a sudden thump against the ground beneath his feet, then a ripple of the murky blue surface, like they were all standing on a dead heart that suddenly beat again. A gasp skittered from between his lips. Then, Dante was looking perplexed once more; then, his body jerked, in place, then to the left, then diagonally downward, making him stagger. A flicker of panic passed over his features before Dante, abruptly, flailed and was yanked down with such force that all the water around him shot up high and sharp. In an instant, the soldier's body disappeared beneath the surface, and it didn't come back up, not a second later, nor three seconds later, not a hint of him.

"Dante!" Tadeo managed to yell now, throwing one foot before the other, trudging through the sea with all his strength to move quicker than any real human could. Not even bubbles of air dribbled up the ocean that Dante had been pulled under. With no other recourse, the anti-Christ tried to look back again: "Dina, something took—" The angel was staring at him with wide, silver eyes. Then — "Agh!" — a thousand hands came over Tadeo's legs, fingers gripping the fabric of his pants before tearing through to tangle with his skin. A mouth opened to scream, but he didn't have the chance — as he was wrenched down into heavy, crushing icy water that soon rushed past his lips as his body was dragged deeper into the open sea. He threw out an arm, then another, willing bone and feather to jut out from his body in a burst of pain, blood. A redness, sprawling out like ink on parchment. His eyes blinked, blinked, bleeding out all the salt water until Tadeo could see clearer. As if in response, the monstrous hands on his legs were becoming one, becoming a single limb attempting to crush his lower half. It was a slimy limb, scaled — it was like the body of a fish or a serpent, and the anti-Christ finally saw exactly what he felt.

A sea serpent of blue-green scales and a head the size of three men standing on each other's shoulders. On a long-snouted face, bulging eyes were darker than the ocean floor, a mouth was wide enough for several thin tongues to hang out, fluttering like streamers in the wind. Spirals of its body crowded all of the constrained Tadeo's surroundings, and he was held in place by one such spiral.

Lungs fully filling now of scorching water — he saw another coil, this one around the body of Dante, who was slumped in its hold. A third coil was still broken up into several appendages — not unlike the multitude of limbs, or what had felt to be so, that initially seized Tadeo; they grappled a struggling Dina, one wing fluttering uselessly, the other one crushed in the hold. The angel's panic was less than the soldier's — his face more confused, almost hurt, as if he'd been betrayed. 'What is this?' thought the anti-Christ. Except he already knew. It was a sea monster.

In the Book of Job — Tadeo remembered clearer than anything — a line read, 'Can you pull in the Leviathan with a fishhook?' Skull full of water, choking on every drop of it, he saw how flames still managed to trickle from the monster's nostrils in dark red. 'Will it keep begging you for mercy? Will it speak to you with gentle words?' The coils of the Leviathan's body moved like gears, and if it weren't for the rocks at the sea floor beneath them inching and inching past them — Tadeo wouldn't realize the monster was moving, bringing the three of them somewhere, in a direction almost certainly opposite the shore. But how to be sure? 'Any hope of subduing it is false; the mere sight of it is overpowering.'

The sea was too empty, no fish, no great mammals. The ground spared a few specs of sand to blow past, as if dust in breeze, but Tadeo couldn't catch a glimpse of even crabs or critters. Each breath

brought a barrage of salt into his mouth, but he could not die —
'I've already died,' — and neither could an angel, Tadeo was sure,
but the soldier in the hold of the Leviathan was scarily still, head
dipped forward. Gritting his teeth — Tadeo didn't want him dead,
no matter how much Dante had shot at him before. He'd already
had his revenge, and he didn't allow for collateral damage. Tadeo
hacked on the water some more then twisted one way, the left,
trying to shout in exertion, in pain as limbs sprouted, then
retracted, from his joints erratically. But it was to no avail, and the
water was growing heavier on their bodies, and all their world was
growing darker.

'Nothing on earth is its equal—' Tadeo's heart was as frantic as
his body, tearing through his skin and clothing, gushing crimson out
of him, but he was reduced to feeble kicks. 'A creature without fear.'
It had been many years since Tadeo had felt terror like this. So
recently, the anti-Christ had decimated dozens of soldiers and their
tanks. 'I've never had an equal to fight,' he realized. 'Not since I
turned into this.'

The Leviathan, abruptly, dipped its head, plummeted with all of
its body, taking the angel, the anti-Christ, and the human with it.
Hard, they rammed into the ground, and Tadeo shouted out when
he slammed into the seafloor. Thrashing, he tried to lift his head,
but he was being wholly dragged against the rocks, each one digging
into his side, his head. Once again, he was choking up on water, and
his head felt light in between all the thumps of pain. Dina's voice
sounded — yells and shouts for Tadeo, but they were muffled. He
could hardly see now — the surface a dim glow far above. 'Like
Heaven.' He could remember the light he saw when he'd died, the
flicker at the end of the tunnel.

Weak, Tadeo almost didn't notice when the ground took on a
decline, and he felt as if he were traveling down a slide. Squinting,
Tadeo could only feel the now many rocks that were striking against
him and make out the shape of what might've been a giant dark
maw of stone. Like a cave mouth. The Leviathan slithered inside,
turned like a shadow, and the soldier — surely dead by now — was
pulled in first, then the angel who was looking at Tadeo in despera-

tion. Then, finally, Tadeo felt himself reeled into pitch darkness. Shaking, shuddering — the water instantly became cooler, and almost denser, and though he struggled to see, he noticed a ceiling coming over him, hanging down rock icicles like teeth. The ceiling, in fact, was approaching rapidly, and the floor kept trailing downward. Uselessly, Tadeo jerked a little, but as the cave closed in around him, more and more until he could feel it crushing the Leviathan's body and his own together. He turned his head, shut his eyes, gasped and gagged on water.

'I can't move,' he wanted to scream, limbs crushing against his sides. 'I can't breathe.' His organs felt squeezed too, and the cave was tightening so much around him that he was even losing his ability to struggle. 'I can't move.' It was so dark. 'I can't move.' Was he still going deeper? His legs were uncomfortably pressed together. He couldn't even turn his head anymore. Black, in every direction. Some muffled sounds. Dina was gone, was quiet. Dante was dead. 'I can't move.' Not even the room to shiver. 'It's so dark.' He couldn't move. 'My ribs—' When he tried to breathe, his shoulders, his chest, scraped the walls.

Then, the water ended, and there was — his hair wet, his clothes drenched — dryness, air. Tadeo spewed out the ocean, felt it like vomit, but his body was still crushed, and he couldn't see. Where was he? Distantly, he heard screams again. 'Like howls of animals.' But there were inflections in between, languages like no animal Tadeo had ever met used. Those were people — screaming. It wasn't Dina, nor Dante. 'Hundreds of people screaming.' Some more rivulets of saltwater dripped from his gasping mouth. 'People. Where are they coming from?'

His foot jerked, his leg shifted. Then, he could turn his head. The cave was easing up on him, as was the Leviathan's hold. Tadeo looked toward his feet, wanting to see if the angel or the soldier were up ahead, but there was only darkness. And there was only darkness as the space he was pulled into grew wider, wider. Instantly, he sighed in relief, but it was only temporary. He soon wiggled his fingers, dismayed to not feel anything against him. When he lifted his head, there was new freedom, too much freedom. Then, the sea serpent released his body, and the rock ground scraped his front one final time.

The anti-Christ fell into pitch darkness and the symphony of agony. He scratched at the emptiness he fell into, twisting, searching. He shouted — "Angel!" — but the screams were rising in volume around him and muffled his yells. "Angel! Dina!" Heat grew all about him too, like he were falling into a furnace. "Dante!" Kicking and kicking, realizing the fall would never end, he groaned and tried to curl his body forward. He ground his teeth; and stinging, twin mouths opened at his back, whipping out feathered tongues, too wet to fly. "Fuck." Another pair of mouth-wings tore through his arms, and his legs shook, bled, as Tadeo twisted and screamed out in pain to join all the other howls of agony in the air.

Who were they? The damned, surely. 'We were looking for Hell.' They hadn't planned to go there, just to meet the captured angels halfway. Was this halfway? The shouts were so loud now that he could make out certain voices. A higher-one, feminine. A lower one, masculine. Were those children? No. That couldn't be. 'Hiccups. Crying. Gurgling.' Tadeo took his own top, dug his claws into it until the fabric tore. He was sweating, coughing out the heat, the sudden sizzling on his skin. 'I can hear—' Once again, he panted, but it was a different terror now that seized him. 'I can hear them choking on their blood as they scream.' Those couldn't be children, those couldn't be scratchy elderly voices, those couldn't be, could they? And were those animals? Those howls? 'No.'

Roughly, the sprouted wings at his back, his arms, his legs struck the air, jumped him a little in the darkness up or whatever way it was that Tadeo's head was pointed. He couldn't even decipher if the screams came from below, from above, or from all around him. The thudding pain of his head, the many eyes rippling open down his face, did nothing to help him see. He could feel his own skin swelling to triple and distort his shape. Though he shouted one more time — "Dina! Dante!" — his boyish voice was gone, replaced with a guttural monster groan.

Then, a light — a dim glow in the direction of the anti-Christ's feet that was bursting like a dying star.

Dina saw it too as he fluttered his eyes open with a dull throb at the back of his head, feeling too warm, too empty of air in his lungs. 'What is this?' He was falling. 'I hit my head when I was in the cave.' And now he was plunging in an endless dark, hearing distant screams. When yellow-orange flickered in the air above, it took some blinks before the angels realized heat followed with it — fire, so great that it illuminated the face of the Leviathan that breathed it. Like a comet, the flames streaked across the pitch black, toward a many-winged giant. "Tadeo?" Dina whispered groggily, but all the bleariness was shocked away as the light engulfed the anti-Christ's beastly body. "Tadeo!" Tadeo screamed as he was scorched. "Tadeo!"

Before Dina could pull out his own wings, he felt something take him by the torso, wrapping around tight in the sudden shape of links. 'Chain?' It tightened onto his lower ribs enough to bruise, to cut — with one end trailing off into the unknown whereas the other end, approaching rapidly, was a metallic sphere, spiked to appear like a star, a morning star. The teeth bit deep into Dina's chest, and the angel screamed. So roughly the star dug itself in further, the angel was pulled in a direction he couldn't make out. Like the cave at the bottom of the sea, wet rock soon scraped against him, but he could do no more than jerk and twitch over the red, slick ground of a tunnel. His wings were trapped beneath the chains, his body pulsed in pain — but he saw as, yet again, a light bloomed before him.

A figure with a long torch was laughing, saying, "It's an angel!" The figure at his left was tall, almost all of his body obscured by a dark cloak that hooded his head.

Holding the other end of the flail that was torturing the hiccuping, wheezing Dina was a great, burly demon with bull-ish horns. With a hardened, scarred face, he carried also eyes reddened in the whites, as if his arteries had burst open long ago and refused to stop bleeding. For clothing, he wore a heavy tunic, excessive robing, a red sash, and sandals. A golden laurel wreath crowned his head.

"Who," asked Baal, "the fuck are you?"

CHAPTER 17

After some time had passed — Satan, of course, returned to the church. The devil traded his torn clothing for a new dark cassock and had to hunt for a scalp, peeling it off a poor man's head in the dead of night. To sate his hunger, he had found the rotting pieces of a goat discarded outside a butcher's shop, crouched over the ground, ate it. Many have depicted him with goat eyes throughout history. He had seen just about every statue of himself, painting, sketch, from the greats and those who will be forgotten after death alike. Few times had he been beautiful. Some of this is by his own design; his perfect lips had shaped lies by the ears of emperors, kings, chiefs, and popes, whispers that he had burnt up in the fall, lost all the beauty of an angel. It was true to an extent. His face was a disguise. He was a lie. Beside every translator, every scribe, he had been a lie, every life. A million lives Satan had led all throughout history, in every place, in every kind of body. From one end of the world to another, he had been running. Chasing a thread until it brought him here.

He returned to the church, of course he did. He had no other life ready for him to take, and he had unfinished business here, a killing to do. And Tadeo was nowhere to be found.

Satan arrived at the rectory at in dead of night with hair in a different style than before, glow beginning to seep through his false-brown contacts. His exhausted gaze bled down onto his body, wavering in place, wrestling to stay up. But this could have been an act, one of a tired priest. The devil is a liar; he may lie so much that he no longer knows the truth.

"Ángel," someone called, many called. Standing in the room were several nuns, two other women, a tall man, one of the migrants that'd been in the vehicle when the soldiers attacked, with his daughter on his hip. "Ángel!" Unlike all those who stood, the other priest, Toño, was slumped in a chair, looking nothing like a middle-aged man and more like a terrified little boy, his face crinkled as aluminum foil in deep worry.

"Where have you been?" asked one of the nuns. "What happened? Have you heard all that—?"

"Was it God," said the priest Toño quietly, "that guided you this time, as well?" His face had paled a shade, and now Satan noticed that there was a blanket draped over his lap, failing to conceal a white cast on his left foot, propped up over a short stool. But his eyes gleamed with a sadness and a hope, a dual grief and joy. "Ángel," he called, "you saved the lives of these two." The migrant man, stepping toward Satan with his sniffling daughter. "You might have saved mine too. Thank you." 'Whatever it is you are,' the good priest thought, 'thank you.'

"Thank you," said the migrant man in question, taking the hand of the devil, squeezing, and then bringing it to press to his own forehead. "I haven't been able to sleep since. I owe you my life. Whatever you shot at, it distracted the soldiers" — Satan had intended that, yes — "and you saved me and my daughter." When was the last time Satan had saved a life? He was a monster of collateral damage.

"Whatever it was you shot at," the good priest said now, "when it fell into the river, I thought I saw the shape of wings in the water ripples. What could it have been? I heard the name 'Michael' in my mind."

"Michael," Satan echoed, "would not do something so terrible, would he? If it were the saint Michael in the sky that I shot at, he would have been watching innocent people die without acting. Our saint wouldn't be so cowardly... would he?"

A silence hung over all those in the room, for some seconds, before the good priest, quietly, said, "There's going to be a Mass early tomorrow. I would like to lead it. Please, Ángel, be there with me." When his voice shook, he added, "I need to sleep. You should sleep too. You're right— You're right that it couldn't have been Michael."

They regarded him with suspicion — the nuns — but Satan went to bed, wondering how long he'd have here. He'd exposed himself to the angels; he should leave this place for good. But he'd watched Michael's blood dribble onto the river. The rivers would turn red with blood, Revelation warned. The water had remained blue, green, and yet it was difficult not to fear that it was all darkening into a crimson shade now, every second he faced away from it.

The next day, he decided to take confession in the church. So much of priesthood was boring — multiple long services a day, paperwork, planning the masses for the holidays and weddings and fifteenth birthdays, and then the added labor of processing migrants in the shelter, transporting, organizing identification, calling authorities, receiving the occasional threatening call — but the confessions were quite fun. As he readied himself for it, he gelled his stolen hair and spent a few minutes applying several layers of sparkling pink lip gloss over his plump mouth. Satan, after this, finally went into the small church building, planning not to bother pretending to bow for the altar today as he crossed past the pews.

Then, Satan stopped, the echo of his steps on the tile too loud. He'd just reached the center of the church and was facing the altar, the hanging Jesus Christ, the sunny monstrance holding the Eucharist. No one sat at the frontmost seats, and as he turned, the devil saw that all the other pews were empty as well. He couldn't recall a time the church had been this desolate.

The tall double doors of the entrance were shut, a wooden panel barring the interior side. Only then did Satan's breath tangle with his tongue. He had never seen the doors locked, and the other priest, the good priest, was in no shape to do it himself, and he never would — always insisting the church should be open to anyone — the locals, the migrants, even the criminals. He still believed in the criminals. Anyone can be forgiven, according to him, according to God. For centuries, Satan had heard this sentiment and asked: why should anyone want God's forgiveness? What made His forgiveness so special? The Lord is but a narcissist — because what good does it do to apologize to a distant God instead of those you've harmed? Why move to absolve yourself instead of making amends? This is pure narcissism, too, on the part of the sinner. The devil would know; he is the mother of vanity.

A sprinkle of dust fell before Satan, onto his mop of dark hair, and a creak sounded on the ceiling. He tilted his face upward, and his lips parted, but he had less than a second to react, to reach into the pocket of his cassock and grip his revolver. As fast as sunlight, a silver gauntlet of a hand grappled his throat, then great wings the color of the Earth stuck to propel both Satan and his captor toward the altar. The edge of it crashed against the devil's spine before the angel pinned his head down against the marble, fingers digging into his neck, shy of crushing it by just a pinch. Teeth clenching and baring themselves like he were an animal — the devil found a bulk of armor holding him down, a helmet with slits over where the eyes should be perfectly obscuring a face. "Angel," the devil gritted out.

"Where is the anti-Christ?" demanded the angel, and Satan could not laugh, so he wheezed. "Where," said the chief prince again, sternly, angrier, "have you hidden him?"

"I can't remember the last time I saw you. Was it when the Son of God bled to death?"

"I'm not here to talk with you."

"You never talk to me anymore."

"Tell me where he is."

"Do you talk to anyone? I hear that you don't. You speak in God's voice. You are the angel of God. Do you remember what it feels like to speak for yourself?" Then, Satan grinned wildly. "Why were you over the bridge?"

"If you don't answer me with your next words, I'll set your head atop a spear. The rest of your damned body will fall into the lake of fire. You will be tormented for the rest of eternity in the flames, devil."

"Hell is my home," said Satan, snickering, serpentine. "The fires can't hurt me anymore, Michael." His hand trailed, slowly. "And when Heaven falls, maybe you'll all learn how much better it feels to burn." The monstrance's base was cold around his fingers as he took it, and it was heavy as Satan lifted it over his head, brought it down onto Michael's helmet. No piercing of the silver armor — but the gold shattered, the glass-embraced Eucharist, round and the size of a palm, cracking in half and falling, made the saint shift backward. However, Michael didn't let go, his grip deadly, unrelenting. "Fucker," the devil hissed, smashing at Michael's helmet a second time, each piece of the gorgeous ornament that had so tenderly cradled God's body clanking to the floor.

"Tell me," grunted Michael, "where he is."

"You're a faggot. You're a sinner. You'll go to Hell to be tortured no matter how much you kneel for your precious little God. You remember, don't you? I was granted Hell because of you." Another wheezing laugh. "Because you failed your Father. Because you could not resist me. God's chief prince couldn't keep his hands to himself. He couldn't help but touch the devil and rut on him like a bitch in heat."

"Don't try to provoke me," said Michael; he must've prepared for Satan to jab at his wounds. "Tell me where the anti-Christ is."

"You will never find him."

"I will destroy him as I will you. God will be victorious over evil."

Satan huffed, bored now. "You were watching men massacre innocent people before I shot you. Is that victory over evil to you?" Though the saint's face was hidden, the devil felt the tensing of his muscles like they were attached to his own bones. "The Lord has always been behind the worst of mankind. He has been in their mouths as they slaughter non-believers, but I have hardly ever seen it so clear—" He breathed in, shakily, body beginning to ache and burn inside beneath the prince. "How far gone you must be to not recognize it even now, even after all of humanity has shown you the depths of God's cruelty."

"I told you to answer me."

"Maybe I am like you — too dense, too stupid, to answer." Satan shut his eyes for a moment, listened to the noise outside the church, every distant man and woman, child and elder, as well as the birds, the sound of cars. "You will never find him," he echoed. "You will succumb to me like you did when your lovely Father flooded the world. You will burn up in the hellfire that you are responsible for." Finally, he reached into his pocket.

"You will not lead me astray."

"How can I lead astray someone so far gone?" Satan yanked out his revolver, pressed the barrel against Michael's helmet, held it there. "Release me."

Michael, still, did not. "Is the anti-Christ in this church?"

"Maybe he's buried beneath it."

"Why do you disguise yourself as a man of God?"

"A woman of God was more difficult to be. Why have you come to the Earth?" Satan felt the cold around his neck ease up, and he heard the drag of Michael's foot shifting backwards, surrendering. "Why were you over the river? Don't tell me the world is ending. Is it real this time? You should have warned me. I would have dressed for the occasion."

"The other archangels have come to the Earth," he replied, steady, "and they are stationed in the Babylon you so love. At my word, they'll have it destroyed." After Satan had shot him, Michael returned to the archangels — the other princes. 'They were doing nothing, standing together over what they, the three archangels, had come to the reasonable assumption was Babylon. On the top of a skyscraper, on horseback, staring down at opulence and modernity.' They looked at Michael, and Uriel had said that he and Gabriel were not going to remain here.

'I'm sorry,' Raphael had said instantly, his eyes pained and lowered. There was a scattering of other angels far behind him, peppered on other high buildings, staring down in wonder, fascina-tion, at the world they had been sent here to destroy. 'I tried to convince them to stay, Michael—'

'I'm going to find Dina,' Uriel had interjected coldly. 'And Gabriel will return to Heaven.' The messenger angel had turned his shameful gaze away. 'We will not partake in this, Michael.'

'The devil has found the anti-Christ,' Michael had said, though he wasn't certain, and he saw Gabriel and Raphael lift their heads swiftly while Uriel remained expressionless, stone. 'He works as a false holy man among the anti-Christ's people. If you want to stop the apocalypse, it is too late. The devil already wields the Beast.' In the present, the prince was removing himself from Satan, looking down at him, and he said: "The angel Dina is here, too, isn't he? Are you working with him?"

"Dina," Satan echoed, as if he'd never heard the name.

"Uriel looks for him."

"I see," the devil chuckled. "What should I answer? You won't believe my words, no matter what I say." He tilted his face up, almost coyly. "But why would an angel work with me? Is there havoc in Heaven?"

'You will,' Michael had snapped at the other princes, 'come to the anti-Christ's stronghold when the sun grows dark. We will capture the devil and the anti-Christ, and then we will move forward with the saving of the pure.'

'Who are the pure?' Uriel had asked. 'Who are the pure, Michael? Do you know?'

Now, Michael dismissed, "He's nothing more than an interfer-ence, trying to do good for Uriel and for God, but he is easily manipulated. And because Babylon is the nation of sin, and you are its whore — you might have tempted him, as you tempt everyone."

Giggling — "The *whore* of Babylon?" He reeled his body off the altar, stood over the remains of Eucharist, and drew in breath after breath. "But we aren't in Babylon, Michael. Look behind you. There's a pretty statue of you there. This is a place of faith, the *right* faith." Careful, the chief prince turned his head, to the right, as if he knew instinctively. And, yes, there was a figure on a podium there, named San Miguel, beautiful and blonde and pale-skinned, one hand lifting a sword and one foot over the coiling of a dragon. "But I'm sure you already know this nation, this town, is not Babylon, and so then I wonder what you're doing standing here? Why are you looking for the anti-Christ? If you want to fulfill the prophecy, then Babylon must fall before the anti-Christ is killed."

"Don't quote the scripture at me," Michael snapped, turning back to face him, and the devil could sense he was clenching his teeth. "I won't kill him—"

"Only capture him?"

"And I will capture you too, Satan," the prince added, lower. "You will be brought before God." Lowering his gun, the devil shook with laughter. "In exchange for Hell, you swore that you'd return to the Lord, and you would accept His resurrection of the angel of worship that you destroyed. But, instead, you've schemed, time and time again positioned yourself like a god of this Earth. Christ, the Son, was crucified because of you. And you committed an abomination because of your recklessness, your *pride*. And I will bring you before the Lord so that you repent before He tears you apart and creates a reborn Lucifer from your corpse."

Satan was quiet, smile falling slow — all the humor gone. Silence. It was enough to seemingly unsettle Michael, who shifted, waited. Over a shoulder, the handle of his sword loomed in threat. But the prince, in all his pale armor, gleamed the church's light. He could have been a ghost, standing among artifacts of saints, angels, of a bygone time.

"The prophecy of the Revelation," said the archangel slowly, almost with a nervous shake, "will occur. It's greater than you, than me."

"Those were words written by a man."

"God inspired those words."

"Maybe God inspired a lie," replied Satan, then he watched as the chief prince turned to show him his back, wings curling in to tuck into them, perhaps slip back into his body. "And where are you going now?"

"The anti-Christ will have no choice but to reveal himself soon, and I'll wait until then. Consider this my covenant with you."

Satan, then, snorted. "Didn't you say you'd torture me for refusing to tell you where he is? You haven't changed since we last spoke, too cowardly to hurt me, too cowardly to save me."

"I have seen your face everywhere on this Earth," said Michael, marching toward the door. "You are their performer and their priest, their god. This is a wicked place, and all there is to do is destroy it, as God has promised to do. The evil will suffer and the good will rise to Heaven."

"And replace the angels?"

"The time of angels has passed. We are all corrupt. It is because of you that we are not worthy to care for God's eternal city any longer." Michael paused, then he turned back one last time, helmet still shielding however much he might be frowning or hurting. "You will not be victorious against God, Satan. You did not win the war for Heaven, and you will not best our Father this time. I will follow the prophecy. It has been written. God will be victorious. He is good."

The devil slipped his weapon back into his cassock, bit the inside of his cheeks, and waited before it was obvious that Michael was the one who wanted to hear some final words, perhaps a good-bye. "But are *you* good?"

"I will do as He says." How dearly Michael must've missed talking to Satan. "Because we angels are all sinners now, I will not bother with sanctity when I hurt you." If Satan could pity, he might've pitied him. "I will treat your body with no grace, no holiness. I will desecrate every inch of you. When I capture you, if the Lord allows me to be the one to kill you."

"You love it when we argue. I give voice to your doubts."

"Farewell, Satan. I will burn you when we meet again."

"You will miss me."

"Perhaps, I will burn us both." Then, the angel lifted the board he'd placed over the doors, set it aside haphazardly. Michael tried to expel all the fury in his heart that should be fiery anger but was weighing into dense misery he could not do away with. God, help him, God, help him. Every step forward in the dark evening was an inch toward apocalypse, the few stars above twinkling in the dark abyss. 'It will not be like before.' He would do it right this time. But, his heart ached as he admitted who he must speak to, who he should have come to first, no matter how furious it may make her. 'Joana,' he thought. Joana.

CHAPTER 18

There is no center to Hell. Wherever it was that they took Dina was unknown to him, but he felt that it was not the center, in the same way that if he were to slip his hands inside himself, however unfamiliar his gore might be to his fingers — he would know where the heart is. His hand could take it, feel the thumps of his life. But there was no such heart here, no pulses. If Hell had a center, it wasn't here, but if it wasn't here, then it was nowhere. He found himself kneeled over smoothed rock, terribly warm, in a rare space between all the extravagant carpets, nearly as red as the walls — of stone, as well. Much of it was obscured by plain banners; if this were Earth, they might've carried an emblem of a king or nation but they had little more than simple embroidery at the corners. There were many fires, joining the sea of red all around, but they were concentrated on the tops of tall torches lining the hall.

Satan's throne, at the peak of a steep stairway much like that of the devil's old home among the caves of the Earth, was ornate, golden, and there were great bones at its head, curling up so that anyone who sat on it might appear to have horns — but it was empty. Lonesome, the other bone accents on the massive seat remained still, as did a cloth strung upon it like a diagonal sash on a torso. Baal did move to stand before it, however — the throne of his king. His shoulders were tensed, his hands were fists, and though his back was facing the captured angel, he soon turned his face to reveal a clenched jaw, glared red eyes, an angry curl to his upper lip.

"Who are you?" grunted the chief duke of Hell.

Dina stared up at him, instinctively wanted to place his hands before himself and fiddle his fingers but his wrists were locked together with bulky, rusted cuffs, listening to the shuffling of a demon behind him. Earlier, the one in the hood had slipped away, murmuring something to Baal that the angel hadn't heard. This had occurred as Dina was dragged through a narrow passage in the cave he'd been pulled into, as they had stepped out into a great hollowing in the red rock that encased Hell. Here, there had been a tower, though its likeness was not like most tall edifices of Heaven, nor any of the multi-story buildings of Earth. Instead, it resembled an amphitheater, the walls composed of archway after archway, so reminiscent of the great arena where innocent angels brawled before Satan's corruption, except far too tall and thin. When Dina had come upon it, his face had tilted up and up and up, trying to take in the impossibly towering structure of Hell at its faux center.

"Answer me," Baal grunted, twisting his body, stepping toward the angel. In one hand, he still held the mace with its starred sphere on a chain, still dripping heavenly blood.

Dina was still wounded, of course, red soaked down the torn front of his hoodie, soaking the company name printed there. He couldn't help but oddly pity it, the company name, though it was his own chest torn open and pulsing in pain. Like a heart — the pulsing. "Dina…" he answered slowly, warily, tongue still tasting the metallic tang of his bleeding. "That is… who I am." As they'd walked Dina down the steps toward the devil's tower, he'd realized there were other buildings in the vicinity — stouter and some of wood, some of rock, some of mud. The demons he saw — a few with animal heads, many with animal limbs, most with horns and tails, nearly all angelic beauty lost — were cleaning stone pathways and scraping off their walls clumps of red-pink like flesh. 'It even breathed, like flesh.'

"Dina," echoed Baal, took a second to glance at the demon behind the angel, then returned his attention to Dina. "What are you doing here?" His tone was stiff, even irritated, but he didn't raise it. "Did your God send you here? Or was it your chief prince?" Slowly, his hands began to work coiling the chain around his palm, the sphere coming to be held carefully by his claws. "I know that you little angels can't lie, but if you spare any details it'll be your head you lose next."

Imagining the sight of his body, twitching and decapitated, Dina swallowed and felt his body shudder. "I—" 'Where is my star?' What should he say? "I'm not here on Michael's orders, and I'm not here on the Lord's either." Baal, slowly, growled. "It's true!" Dina added hastily, turning back up, struggling against the cuffs of his hands because he so terribly wanted to interlock his fingers before his face and beg. "I'm not here for anyone except myself."

"Then what the fuck do you want?"

Dina, frantic, tried to think of something, some half-truth, something his star would guide him to say. Instead, he blurted the truth: "Where are the Watchers?" Baal's eyes, instantly, widened. "I'm looking for my friends— Azazel. Armoni. They left Heaven to help the humans. Many things happened. I cannot tell you what — but I know that there was a Flood. The Father commanded me to see the Earth and tell the man Noah that the end would come and that he should build an ark, but I never understood what happened. I was told the Watchers corrupted themselves with women and there were giants, but I never understood. I never—" He was not only being honest to the demon now; Dina was confessing a secret to himself. "I never believed it because I didn't understand. It didn't sound like something my friends would do. Believe me that this is why I am here in Hell. I didn't mean to come to Hell. I was only searching for my friends—"

"Okay, shut your mouth," Baal interjected, brow twitching. "I don't give a shit about what you think about your stupid friends." But then, he inched away and laughed, bitterly, meanly. "But the Watchers? The whore angels? It's been thousands of years, and you've come down looking for them now? Who are you?"

"I told you," Dina whispered, his chest stinging, his face grimacing. "My name is Dina."

"I heard you the first time, idiot," Baal snapped. "But who *are* you? I don't remember you from Heaven." He snorted. "Are you an angel of stupidity? Are you an angel of any importance? I doubt that your God has appointed a new archangel."

"No, no, I'm not an archangel," Dina answered softly. "And I'm an angel of... nothing." Angel of nothing at all. "Angels do not need purposes anymore." Uriel had once told him that. 'I miss Uriel. Without him or my star, I have no one to tell me what to say or what to feel.' When Baal raised an eyebrow, Dina tilted his head and explained, "Because us angels have no other purpose than to prepare Heaven for humans. This is how it has been for many centuries now."

The demon behind Dina laughed, almost like a bark. "What? Prepare Heaven for humanity? What does He intend for you angels? Is He going to cast you down or are you all to be slaves?" Dina struggled with that word but understood it well enough to frown.

Baal answered: "Satan told me of this." He lifted his arms and crossed them over his chest. "He told me that God has abandoned His host, that the angels are like shit to Him. God only cares about humans now. It has been this way since Christ." At that, Dina nearly tilted his head. Was that true? He knew little of Christ but he could remember that this had all begun following the Flood. 'Michael tied at the center of Heaven, burning.' "But it doesn't matter. What God thinks of His angels is no problem of our own. If He wants to burn them, then we should let them burn for their cowardice at the beginning of time." The Fall. Had that been the beginning of time? Dina wanted to swallow and say there had been a time before then. There had been angels before Satan, and there had been angels before man.

And, surely, there would be angels after man, wouldn't there?

Suddenly, Baal's foot drew back, swung, and struck the kneeled angel hard against the jaw, sending him thudding against the ground with a sharp cry. "The affairs of angels," he began before setting his sandal down over the side of Dina's head, pressing down uncomfortably, enough to ache the area by Dina's eyes, "is of no importance to us." Gritting his teeth, Dina shut his eyes but they nearly opened them again instantly when he impulsively tried to move his hands again and, oddly, he felt them inch apart. "If you want to see the Watchers, then you can see them from where you'll be chained up with them."

Dina's fingers wandered, touched a finger tip against the bolt that was supposed to be screwed into place only to feel it wobble and slightly twist. Heart quickening, breath catching — he could give it a few more twists and pull the cuffs apart. But no, he shouldn't. 'He will notice. He will hurt me.' And would it be so bad to be imprisoned beside old friends?

"Are you sure?" called the demon behind, stepping over the angel's sprawled legs and chuckling. "Shouldn't you wait for Satan to call that order?"

Dina felt Baal's foot tense before he heard the duke grumble, "Are you questioning the regent of Hell?"

"I am," replied the demon slyly. "I can do that, can't I? You're no devil."

"How many times must I fucking say it?" Immediately, Baal removed himself from over Dina, turned around, grappled the demon by the throat and snarled. "He has given me the authority to command and rule Hell while he is absent."

A clawed hand took and dug into Baal's wrist, but however roughly the duke was choking him, the demon still managed to spit — "So you say, so you say. We can't be certain if Satan isn't here, can we? Why won't you tell us where he is? How can we be certain you're not hiding him away?"

"You have no faith in your god?" Baal hissed.

"It's *you* we have no faith in."

'I can only do this now,' Dina realized, his heart thudding, up in his ears, in his mouth. 'No, no, I shouldn't. I'm good. I will do as told. And I will see my friends.' But he had left the anti-Christ behind. 'Tadeo.' And that soldier boy. 'What is the right thing to do?' He shouldn't listen to a demon. 'My star told me to guide Tadeo.' Before him, Baal had just sunk in his talons, a burst of blood gushing out from the mouth of the demon in his hold, but he snarled at him once more, demanded respect as the regent of Hell. 'I have to do this.' But where to find the bravery? He wanted to look inside himself, find it, but there was no time. 'I have to act.' He would find the bravery to act another time. 'I will be back for you, Azazel, Armoni.' Quick, he twisted the screw in his cuffs.

Meanwhile, Dante was tasting salt. It dribbled wet from his bottom lip, rolling down to his chin, then falling in rivulets along his throat, almost following the arteries. Weak, he blinked, fluttered his eyes, then felt a cough wretch itself out of his mouth, expelling more of the sea water with such force that it startled him back to full consciousness. "Fuck," he said automatically. His arms were above him, though he could barely see them in the dark, and his legs were in line of sight too. Air was rushing past; he was falling. Seemingly, it was endless, in every direction; there were no walls to his left, nor to his right, and glancing down, there was mere abyss. Above, the emptiness would have continued, but there was a long, coiling creature, larger than anything Dante had ever seen, and there was another figure, a many-winged thing of several mouths and eyes, though it was blackened and crisped, burnt. In between the two, there were bright flames. A few seconds passed, then Dante realized the fire was coming from the great serpent's open mouth.

Without thinking, the soldier padded all over himself, his damp clothing, until feeling the familiar shape of a dark pistol tucked into his waistband. Unloaded; he had kept the magazine in his pocket in case, always holding the anxiety that the gun would go off in his pants and castrate him. Now, he yanked the weapon out, held it against his chest with his handless arm before shoving his fingers into his cargo pants to free the magazine and click it into place on his pistol. The smaller creature above him bore great resemblance to the one Tadeo was, though it looked like he'd been charred on a grill as he was taken by the tail of the Leviathan, then whipped from one side to another. Against the enormous snake, Tadeo was horrifically losing what might've been a fight but seemed more of a homicide. It almost made Dante laugh. 'That's for fucking up my hand,' he thought.

But then, he watched carefully, saw how Tadeo roared out in pain in a way Dante had never heard. It was a horrific, shrill sound, and it scorched at his ears. 'Fire.' He saw how one of Tadeo's hands was barely out of the flames, grasping helplessly. Bubbling, the beastly skin there was the only part of Tadeo not scorched into a crisp, and to heal, a trail of new skin stitching itself back together over and over climbed down Tadeo's body from that hand.

'Would you be able to heal,' Dante wondered, 'if your hand wasn't safe?' If all of him burned?

Swallowing, Dante raised the stump of his left wrist to help him better support the pistol as he aimed. "Fucker!" he shouted. "Motherfucker!" Whether he was calling to Tadeo or the Leviathan, he didn't know, but it didn't matter; they didn't turn, probably couldn't hear him. But Dante was willing to trust in the half-human above and shoot the snake if it meant stopping this eternal fall.

So, Dante pulled the trigger. The recoil was nothing new, his shoulders quite accustomed to taking the blow, but the bang was oddly muffled to him, as if the sound was soaked by the darkness around him. Squinting, he followed the trail where the bullet should've gone, and when he saw nothing hit the bigger monster above, he was sure he'd missed. Except there was a sudden spray of blood that poked a minuscule hole through the Leviathan that made its whole body twitch. The pain must've been even less than a paper cut, however, as the Leviathan didn't turn its head, made no indication that it even noticed. Biting the inside of his cheeks, Dante aimed and shot once more. Another bleeding hole. Then, he shot a third time, fourth time. On the fifth, the Leviathan finally shuddered, its entire body rippling, before its mammoth face whipped down to Dante, eyes and mouth opening wide, a million teeth illuminated by fire-saliva.

Dante's heart stopped; the beads of sweat on his forehead ran cold. His finger twitched anxiously over the trigger, but he bit down a swear for now. 'Fucked myself over,' he thought gruffly. 'Ah well.' There had been nothing else to do, anyway. The Leviathan roared in his direction, rattling Dante's eardrums but if he was good at anything, it was taking the pain, gritting his teeth. "Motherfucker," he finally said. Above, the snake barreled toward him, loosening its hold on Tadeo. Dante fired another shot, pierced an eye; it cut right through with hardly a reaction from the beast. Instead, fire was building in its mouth, beginning to fall like drool, beginning to lap like its tongue. By one of its coils, Dante saw the beast Tadeo strike the air with wings, and though he wasn't sure, it seemed like the charring and ash were flaking away from him, revealing a bloody but thrashing Tadeo.

Tadeo reached the Leviathan's head in time, grappled it, then yelled with exertion as he pulled up the monster's face, diverting the fire to a wall. Again, the flames engulfed the anti-Christ, who let out an agonized scream, but it struck, too, at the Leviathan, whose cries in pain only flooded them with greater fires. Far below, Dante was hot as Hell and shaking, but breathing, still breathing. Alive for now.

At the same time, Dina was flying. He had heard Baal yell after him the second he pulled his arms apart, still cuffed, and sprinted toward the door, but he hadn't stopped, no matter how terribly he wanted to. His heart was screaming at him to run, to return to the surface, which had seemed so simple compared to Hell, this Hell. His heart, too, told him to duck, to slip between the open doors and lower his head to avoid the whip of Baal's mace. He felt it tug at his hair but not tangle. The relief almost killed him, as did the fear. Hurriedly, he'd torn his wings out of his back, then struck them against the warmth around him to fling himself high, far above the stout, square buildings dribbling flesh like water from rain. As he did, Dina saw demons of all kinds turn their heads up, most smacking a hand against the shoulder of whoever stood beside them, pointing, shouting. Then, he noticed some of them hurrying for javelins, spears, a few slingshots.

"Stupid fucking angel!" Baal was snarling. "We'll throw you into the pit of fire with your whore friends! I'll rip you apart! We'll grind you to pieces for the sinners to shit on!"

Dina tried to ignore his wobbling lip, swerving in every frantic direction, trying to avoid every swing of Baal's mace, and when he heard a bang, like a gunshot, he allowed himself to fall quickly, sleepily. The first two, three, times, it worked, though his foot was pelted by a rock so hard that he felt his knee twist far too much, almost snap. The hit made Dina stagger, but he recovered just in time to see the cave that Baal had led him and two demons out of earlier. Again, Baal yelled, but the angel maintained his focus on the approaching crevice, even as some demons sprinted up the rocky steps to try to reach them. But then, Dina felt a thud through his hip, a thrown stone bursting open with an implosion of pain that blinded him, made him scream, swerve, crash into the side of the cave entrance.

He skidded against the ground, once again crying out in pain through the sudden blots of darkness in his vision. Yet, he could see the end of the channel, the darkness that he'd been falling through before Baal appeared. Behind him, he could hear him yelling out orders to seize Dina and dismember him slowly, to feed him to the sinners. Dina could hardly move his twitching legs, but he still reeled up his wings, beat them, dragged his injured body against the ground with each flap. He used his hands, as well, placing one before the other, almost as if he were crawling. His wings continued pushing him forward, fingers continued scratching at the ground.

"Angel! Stupid fucking *angel!*" bellowed Baal from behind.

Dina, finally, set a foot down, then kicked off of it, falling into the abyss he'd been in before. Folding his wings close, the plunge was fast, terrifying. But freeing. As the air rushed past, into his mouth, his hair fluttering behind him, his blood trickling in beads upward — he almost felt good. Free falling felt good. He could see light below him, violent and warm. The sea serpent that had pulled him to Hell with a smaller monster strangling it, trying to hold its fire away from whatever was below even if it meant burning them both. "Tadeo!" Dina screamed. "Tadeo!"

The anti-Christ twisted his horrible face up, and he shouted back, "Dina! Help me!" His grip on the Leviathan was slipping, and soon it was thrashing again, no longer breathing fire, trying to shake off Tadeo with harsh whips of its body.

"We must go!" Dina stretched out his wings and fluttered them, feeling each feather shift. "Fly up with me! We must go!"

"*Angel!*"

Dina turned back, saw Baal, breath reeling in. He put up his hands and swerved, trying to dodge the mace, succeeding again only enough that the spike of the starry sphere dragged at his forearm, yanked back to pull out a chunk of skin. Blood, again. Pain, again. By now, the angel could only whimper in the pain, realizing how hoarse his throat was from screaming. He kicked, trying to jerk his body away as the Regent of Hell reeled back the sphere, swung the chain around behind him. Dina squinted frightfully, realizing he was trapped between a sea serpent beast below and the horned one above. He had been wrong to run away. He should have listened to Baal when he could. He shouldn't have come here. Baal threw the star of the mace out at him again.

Then — Dina was tugged backward, behind something, and a clawed, charred hand went where his face had been. The claws caught the sphere, each of its spikes poking through the fingers, the palm, even an eye at the back of the wrist. Almost consumed by the feathers of too many wings, Tadeo tightened his grip on it, then yanked down, pulling the suddenly-pale Baal down before he could let go of the handle of the mace. The demon did release it, then tried to beat his ancient, featherless wings. Mercifully, Tadeo didn't pursue Baal before the Leviathan began screeching again, and heat began rapidly approaching from below. "Fly," the angel whispered, feeling one of Tadeo's other hands gripping the back of his shirt. "Fly, Tadeo!"

Baal retreated, swerving into a crevice in the dark walls of the abyss, and the anti-Christ dropped the mace, hand bleeding until the blood dried, and instantly, the cuts sewed closed, and he breathed out to feel the burnt of him began to chip away into the darkness. Tadeo, obediently, beat all his wings, pulling Dina up with him, who was fluttering his own wings and trying to keep up. How far above was the place they'd fallen from? Tadeo couldn't think, couldn't even guess. Panting, panting, all the pain of what he'd suffered in the last hours was fogging his head. Groaning, grunting, all he could do was bear it. He would have to cry it out, like a child, but not yet, not now. He listened to instinct, to flap all his wings faster, faster, until he was nearly dragging Dina. Maybe the abyss would go on forever, but he would have to keep flying up to escape the flames for his own dignity if nothing else.

He was in pain. So much pain. The world was spinning. The pain. Beat after beat of wings. He must listen to his instincts, the beast inside him that could have had a mind of its own. It was bleeding with him. 'Tadeo, keep flying. Up, up.' May they arrive in Heaven. The pain. In Heaven, there must be no pain.

"There, Tadeo!"

In the darkness, he had the angel guide him, through what must've been a gap in the rock ceiling, then through a narrowing channel that Dina climbed in through first. Tadeo followed, folding all his wings inside his body with a groan of pain that he couldn't fight tears over now. Each new mouth and eye on him shut, then began to heal over, pale like scars. As the rock around him crushed him, he tried and tried to grow smaller. He crawled, crawled. Without even realizing it, he was beginning to choke on water, but his lungs were already full of blood. Just as the ocean cave eased up on him, the anti-Christ began to limp, no longer able to trudge along even when the angel called his name. Celestial arms came over a humanizing, naked body, then Tadeo shut his eyes, feeling the angel use his wings to toughly push themselves up faster through the water.

When they finally arrived to the surface and night sky, Dina embraced Tadeo tightly, choking up on either the sea or tears — regardless, it was salty — and he rubbed his face against the boy's drenched hair. He kicked weakly, trying to bring the anti-Christ to the distant shore. Calm, the tide pushed them gently, encouragingly. Half an hour it took, so long that Tadeo was gurgling and stirring by the time Dina was finally able to pull them out of freezing water onto cold sand. "Tadeo, Tadeo," he was crying, "Tadeo."

The anti-Christ could feel nothing but the angel collapsing on top of him, weeping for his dear angel friends that he'd somehow abandoned by doing this. Not understanding, Tadeo simply laid there, his body healed but aching everywhere. It was such pain that he almost wanted to hurt himself just to feel in control of the agony for a mere second. "Angel," he croaked, and Dina hugged him tighter, before Tadeo blinked, began to see the crescent moon over them. "That was... We were..." His voice was throaty, still burned. "The Leviathan.... And..." His heart petrified, fell. "Dante."

Dina tensed over him, then lifted his body slowly, faced him with all the fright of Heaven and Earth.

"We left Dante," Tadeo breathed, "in Hell."

CHAPTER 19

It was revenge what Asmodeus had done. Petty, perhaps, but it was always the little things that infuriated Baal the most, and if Asmodeus couldn't kill him, then the least he could do was send the regent of Hell into a rage. Obediently, Asmodeus had said, "I'll bind his hands," about that angel Dina, gesturing for Baal to lead the way to Satan's tower, and that stupid, stupid Baal had nodded and hastily moved on ahead. 'Dumb fucking dog.' A single twist of the screw, just loose enough that the weepy, bleeding angel should realize that he wasn't really restrained if he tugged at the cuffs once or twice. Maybe Baal would catch the angel instantly, but he'd at least be annoyed. If Asmodeus couldn't kill him, he could irritate him. If he couldn't send Baal to Hell, then he could make his life one.

Currently, the demon was moving in between a crowd, in some other part of the underworld, one foot beginning to drag no matter how many iron bars he'd attached to the calf bones to try to force his body to accept it. One of his hands kept twitching, looking for his typical cane. All about him, there was pale fog, and the rock ground was warm with blood. Demons were all rushing in opposite directions, but that didn't stop claws from grazing his arms, then a voice saying, "Duke, do you know what's happening by the tower?"

"No," replied Asmodeus. "Baal must've fucked something up."

Then, he continued on his way in the all-encompassing, blinding paleness, ignoring the stench carried on its back. Behind, he heard the demon call for him again, curiously, but Asmodeus ignored it. He ignored all the chatter of demons around him, as well, and he ignored the distant howls and groans of the tortured dead. However, at one particular gurgling noise, the duke couldn't stop himself from turning his face upward to examine a bubbling, pulsing mass of wet redness. Whatever it hung from — the ceiling — was lost in darkness and the fog, but Asmodeus knew it had a wide base and a sharp peak, almost like a limb reaching down. A pyramid of flesh. Yet — any squinting demon would notice faces, mouths wretched open as if in screams peppered upon its body. Some loose limbs dangled from the pyramid of flesh, but from the neck downward, the individuality of bodies, of the victims, melted into one blended mass.

How terrible. Asmodeus had really not wanted to return here so soon. He missed the city he'd been living with Rosier, and he missed the sunsets, and he missed the technology, and the convenience of food, labor, and other kinds of service work. In Hell, one can't order a meal on command as easily, even a duke. Of course, Asmodeus was not always fond of the socio-economic situation for contemporary humanity — even as an outsider who could reap the benefits and none of the consequences — but he was not an angel, he didn't bother to cast a judgement on them. He never missed Rosier's downtrodden expression reflected off a passenger's seat window, however, when the younger demon looked at the state of the Earth.

In the present, Asmodeus found himself alone, all the demons disappeared into the dense fog. He could hear the shuffling of their feet and the pain of the flesh pyramid above, but now it was silence also echoing in his skull. If there was anything worse than the loudness of Hell, it was when it grew quiet. Slow, he turned his head, wondering of the abyss angel Dina had fallen through. He listened for it, heard the usual tumbling of rock and dust, but also the whip of a falling thing. The angel again? He turned his head up, saw the flesh mound. A corpse hand was reaching down for him and, without thinking, he took it.

The pyramid of flesh pulled Asmodeus up, and he set his good foot upon it — clawed— and then the flimsy human one. He breathed, rolling one shoulder, as the direction of gravity turned upside down. Letting go of the corpse hand, he trekked cautiously, hearing the squelches and agony wails beneath his feet. They faded into the usual noise of Hell as he continued onward— the dark fall where the angel might be. To pass the time, he kept thinking of his beloved husband.

Marriage always helped to lift the fallen angel of fruit's spirits, and Asmodeus was already itching to host another quiet wedding somewhere, to fall into a fantasy where the two of them were humans and wishing love until death meant something. During their most recent honeymoon, Rosier had laid over Asmodeus' chest and confessed that he occasionally dreamed that they had never been angels, that they might've been childhood friends turned adult lovers, that they had families and heritage and graves waiting for their rot. The duke had never understood the craving, especially from someone so oriented toward fruits, trees, nature.

'Do you ever hate the humans?' Asmodeus had asked.

'I wish I could,' Rosier had confessed softly.

'You should hate them. If they weren't hopeless, they wouldn't all be in Hell.'

'Not all of them are there. And there's this old woman who runs a shop with her granddaughter next door... I think they're good people, Asmodeus. I really hope so.'

One night, Asmodeus had caught the smaller demon sitting on the sidewalk, sniffling between hushed, raw cries, cigarette in one hand, saying he wished they'd never met. 'I love you,' Asmodeus had said, 'if we hadn't met, I don't know what I'd be doing. We've always been beside each other, Rosier. It's always been you and me. I don't even know who I *am* outside of you. But—'

'If you ever leave me, I'll die,' Rosier had wept. 'You put your roots in me, and now I depend on them to breathe. If only we had never met— If only I didn't need you more than I need my own heart.'

Creeping behind him, a few limbs of the pyramid were brushing past Asmodeus, reaching out into the dark canyon. He, simply, watched as the flesh-hands reached out to push a falling person, then grab at him, reel him into the gap in the wall where Asmodeus stood. To the duke's feet, the thing, this *person*, was dragged to, then left for him as the peak of the pyramid itself retreated. "Hm," the duke said at what he was sure was dead.

But there were many good days for Asmodeus and Rosier — many, many of them. Rosier detested television and still struggled with anything electric, but he'd enjoyed a bulky tablet with simple games on it and often laid his head on Asmodeus' lap as he played. They'd somehow never run out of topics to discuss, to laugh about — not as angels, as demons, in Heaven, in Hell, nor in all the earthy cities. Most mornings, they dressed each other, and they kissed constantly, as much as Rosier would allow. They fucked less often, as much as Rosier would allow.

The young man at Asmodeus' feet grunted, shifted, tried to lift his body, then slumped back down onto the flesh. "Fuck." An arm slithered across his torso, clutched at the white tank beneath his open green jacket. "Ah—" He twitched at his own breath, and if the duke could recognize anything, it was the sound of pain. Trembling, the man tilted his head up. "Who are you?" The duke hesitated, then pulled back the hood over his head. "What are you?"

"An angel," chuckled Asmodeus, his accent minuscule, tongue particularly good with romance languages, "like the one you were with." He leaned down and offered a hand. "You were with that angel, weren't you? Did he abandon you?"

Brows furrowing, the soldier breathed, lifted his body to sit, and groaned in pain once more — but he didn't take the demon's hand. "No. The angel was with... this other guy. Tadeo. That's his name." Asmodeus quirked a brow, lowering his offer, watching as the man wobbled to his feet, doubling over, clutching his stomach, knees knocking together; any minute now, he'd fall back over. "I don't know him so don't bother asking me shit." He looked up at

Asmodeus through a dark fringe. "You're not an angel. This is Hell, isn't it?"

"Hm, well I *was* an angel once." There was some demonic shouting nearby, maybe Baal.

"Whatever you say," Dante droned, turning back to the gape from which he'd been rescued. "The motherfucker left me, didn't he? I saw the angel go in after him. Then— Then, they flew. They fucking flew and left me falling." Asmodeus' eyes flickered behind him, but there was only fog; Baal was almost definitely furious right now, probably hunting him down. "Look at this—" Dante waved the bandaged stump where his left hand was supposed to be. "That fucker did this. He did this, and then he abandoned me down here in goddamn Hell. He thinks he's a fucking saint, but he left me here—"

'It's a good thing,' Dante almost confessed, 'that I'm going to betray him.'

Slowly, however, the duke began to shrug off his cloak, revealing the dark robe he wore beneath, and the soldier jumped. "What are you doing? Get back. I have a gun."

Just as the soldier started reaching into his pants, Asmodeus threw his cloak over Dante's body and said, "Be quiet." He turned back, then jerked his head. "You can stay here and get tortured by Baal or you can follow me down."

"Down—?"

Asmodeus chuckled at the soldier's yelp, knowing he'd just noticed the pyramid of flesh. "Don't mind that. It's just bodies. If it hurts them, they're all used to it. Hurry." He began to step along carefully, not bothering to avoid the human faces or their desperate, grasping hands. "Don't lose sight of me or you'll get lost forever."

"Wait," called Dante. "Wait!" He panted as he limped over the mangled spew of people, his face twitching, nerves tightening at his throat. "Motherfucker, I said wait." He nonetheless pulled the demon's hood over his head, then tightened it at his waist, tried to tie some of it at his side so that it wouldn't drag on the floor. "Who are you? Where are you taking me? If I'm in Hell, how do I know you're not taking me to get boiled alive?"

"Maybe I am, but what choice do you have?" Asmodeus hopped over a limb, stumbled, felt a whip of pain climb up his spine, then winced. "If the other demons find you, they'll bring you to Baal. You don't want that." He raised his head, saw that the ground was faraway, pale. "Come. There might be a way across from here." Clenching his jaw, Asmodeus walked again, but his foot was now trapped in a churning cycle of pain.

Dante breathed, then followed, obediently bowing his head. And with an apparent good intuition, said, "Your foot fucked up?"

Asmodeus didn't reply, shuffling along, squinting his eyes, searching for a tunnel in a wall that he might never find. He had no patience for this. He had no patience for Hell and its eternally twisted ways, its ticking body, its constant rearrangement. Some of Heaven had been like this, though it was difficult to remember now. 'There's a saying that the humans have, something like: There are years where nothing happens, and there are days where decades do.' Asmodeus felt that he'd lived mere days as an angel, but he'd lived a billion years since the fall. And in this life he had now, he didn't like the meandering about that the inferno demanded, even when he finally came upon a dim blotch that seemed indicative of rock channels between the walls of Hell. But only the walls here — it was different above, and it was different below. It was cold somewhere, it was wet elsewhere.

The place of damnation was quite accommodating, in a sense.

As the demon and the human stepped into a narrow corridor, the soldier whispered, "So, do you have a name?" He immediately hacked hoarsely, stumbled on the ground, which was rapidly turning to stone beneath them, as it took on an incline to the left.

Asmodeus stepped onto the incline, followed it to the left, until he'd stepped on the wall, moved along it, then he was walking on the ceiling on the cave, or rather the ground of it. Assuming the young man would follow in his steps, he answered, "Asmodeus." Up ahead, there was light. "I'm a duke of the demons." If all went well, the inferno would be leading Asmodeus home; if it chose to be kind to him, at least.

"Asmo...de...us," the man sounded out. "Huh. Alright."

Asmodeus glanced backward. "Never heard of me?" He snick-ered; this wasn't out of the ordinary, but he would have assumed someone who came to Hell with an angel at their side was likely the religious sort. "I'm in the Testament of Solomon. The Book of Tobit. I'm in plenty of books, films."

"Whatever you say."

Asmodeus couldn't help a laugh. "And what's *your* name?"

"Dante."

"Ah. Of course it is."

The soldier cursed, again, as he stumbled up against the wall, put a knee on it, as his sense of gravity tilted slowly "Slow down. You didn't tell me where we're going, *Asmodeus.*"

The way he rolled his tongue on the infernal name was taunting, but the demon took no offense, setting a hand on the edge of the rock, peering out and sighing at the sight of more fog. This could mean he was headed the right way, but it was impossible to know. Low, hollow moans sounded — non-sexual, something more like groans but too airy and tormented. "I would answer if I could," Asmodeus said with a grumble. "Hell takes you where it thinks you deserve." With that, he planted his clawed foot forward, breathing shakily, limping forward, feeling something crunch beneath him. Asmodeus opened his mouth, about to warn the human that this was almost certainly bone and excrement before deciding he didn't need to know.

Nonetheless, Dante scrunched his nose and lifted some of his shirt over his nostrils to ignore whatever the pungent scent might be. He blinked a thousand times, annoyed at how much fog there apparently was in Hell, how that didn't even make scientific sense. Dante was not a stubborn man, though, and he'd already witnessed shape-shifting and angels and, apparently, a 'very famous' demon. He was going to shut his mouth now, then. Carefully, he crept into blindness, focusing on the shape of Asmodeus ahead, listening to each sting and throb of his body, particularly when he filled his lungs. In fact, the pain was so bad that he was forced to take small, short breaths.

'Bruised rib,' Dante diagnosed himself. He'd had a friend in the military college, one of the few that spoke the same local language as Dante and who'd insist on speaking in it even when Dante would reply in the national language. His friend had suffered a broken rib after training once, and Dante had sat beside him that night, listening to his rasps. Two sergeants had kicked his friend's chest in, and they looked away when he tried to kill himself four weeks later. Nothing unusual for the place.

At his peripheral, Dante noticed a shadow, which he would have normally ignored, but then it slumped to the ground with an odd *clink*. It was a figure, doubling over, taking clumps of what appeared to be white shards and sand into its hands, then shoving it into its face, presumably a mouth. It was not a demon, or a human, or even an animal — in every sense, it was a *figure*. Gray specks composed its body, which was in the rough shape of a person, though it had no other features anywhere, no face, no clothing, no genitals. With every movement, trickles of its composition climbed up and away from it, like smoke from a burn. Perhaps, ash.

Dante, heart stuttering, twisted his face forward again, hurried with a shuffle, but only now did he hear all the groans around him in, what he believed to be, hunger. From every direction — it was coming from. Sharply, he breathed, then flinched when it stung in his chest, but a hundred figures were appearing, walking without direction. One figure of ash ran into another, and then fell and, before they'd hit the ground, they both withered away, disappeared into the fog. The other figures, though, paid no mind, most doubling over to feast on the bone-earth.

"Don't stare too much," Asmodeus warned. "They eat and they vomit and shit all that out, then they eat it again." Dante sighed. "I know you've heard all the screams everywhere. But if you're scared, it might comfort you to know the humans who burn are less than the humans who wander like this. There are more souls trapped in endless chases than in the inferno." Before Dante could ask, Asmodeus explained, "Humans are weighed down by their sins. Most of them land in Hell and those who don't are on Earth, in the leaves and such."

"What about," Dante asked carefully, "Heaven? The humans in Heaven?"

"I'm a demon. I can't answer that."

As a person of ash walked past, and Dante accidentally brushed against them — he jolted back, tried to apologize on instinct, but he watched it stagger back, its arm unspooling between them, then the rest of its body with a soft, barely audible cry. 'Fuck.' However hardened he thought he was, Dante clutched at the cloak with his only hand trembling. 'I didn't mean to,' he wanted to say, but the figure was gone. "You're saying you don't know if humans... go to Heaven?"

"I suppose so."

"God isn't real," Dante said; he was thinking of the disgusting pyramid of flesh, the screams he'd heard as he fell eternally, feeling himself roast, never dying. "God can't be real if this place is." He'd half-expected for the demon to argue, but he'd heard a laugh, then:

"You might be right."

They strolled further through the field of bone and feces, until all the people of ash began to disappear into the fog, their miserable moans fading with them. A few times, Dante witnessed what Asmodeus warned him of — the vomiting, the defecating — but the horror was quickly replacing itself with pity. There was an existentialism sinking in, of course — a 'What will happen to me?' — but Dante knew to wait for when it was a better, safer time to ponder.

The demon, however, in what was becoming eerie silence, said that no matter where humans land in Hell, they are not individuals anymore. The living dream of their sins resulting in specific torments; they dream of all those in the inferno to see them and know who they are, what they did, what they believed was worth risking this suffering. But no — they are all the same now. Death is the great equalizer. There are no rich and poor in Hell, nor are there beautiful and ugly. To ash they all return, and all ash looks quite the same.

Dante's shoes tapped on more solid rock, suddenly, and he startled. Looking down, he saw now a trail of cobblestone, though reddened in rust. The path scaled up — a hill, which Asmodeus panted as he climbed. Dante, as he'd been doing, followed. For a few entire minutes, there was nothing, but just as he was beginning to tire, even opened his mouth to ask the demon if they could consider resting, he saw a stout, circular stone building come into view, something like a cottage with sparse windows and an overgrown garden. But there was crowding outside of it, a large demon with a laurel crown and horns — Baal — and other demons. On the ground, there were two figures kneeling, held in place by grips at their hair.

One of them — Dante saw as he inched behind Asmodeus, trying to hide and have a shield at once — had shoulder-length hair with two small braids framing his face and warm brown skin and a loose, but rather modest, tunic. Beside him, there was a pale person with curled golden hair in a single, thick braid; on his body, there was a scandalously sheer, red robe beneath golden chains and colorful jewels.

"Asmodeus," Baal grunted in greeting, red eyes narrowed, mouth twitching; this was the last Dante understood of the conversation before the demonic language overrode any human understanding. "I tried to be kind to you because you returned to Hell willingly. And now what the fuck is this? Don't try to tell me it was an accident."

Dante couldn't see Asmodeus' face, but he spoke with a tightness that tensed the soldier's muscles. To demon ears, the duke of lust was saying: "It's me you want. Rosier did nothing wrong. Let him go." Rosier jolted a little. "And Armoni has nothing to do with this." Armoni was the pale one, who grimaced in what seemed shame. "I hadn't even come home to them yet."

"Well, you won't be coming home for a long time, fucker," Baal said. "You have no idea what you've done." He waved for the other demons to release their hold on Rosier and Armoni, but then added, "I hope you enjoy prison before we put you on trial for treason to Hell." Asmodeus laughed. "And who's that behind you?"

When all the demons' gazes suddenly swiveled toward the soldier, Dante's blood ran cold.

"I found him," Asmodeus said casually. "He's a human. He must've come down with that angel." He stepped aside, revealing Dante, who tensed but knew better than to raise his gun. If anything, he should prepare to aim it right into his mouth. But Baal did little more than stare, jaw set, eyes calculating, before he turned to say a few words to a demon standing beside him.

Hushed, Dante asked, "What's happening?"

"We're about to be imprisoned," Asmodeus explained without fuss, then nodded his head. "Don't struggle."

"Wait," Rosier was saying to Baal, about to rise to his feet only to be stopped by Armoni's hand grappling his forearm. "We won't leave Hell again. You don't have to bind him or that human. I swear to you that I'll keep them both here."

Armoni said, "Rosier," low, in warning. But then he addressed Baal with a determined, yet frantic gleam in his eyes, "I know this angel Dina you're talking about, Baal. Imprison me too."

Baal snorted. "Prison won't save you from Moloch, Armoni, but come along then."

As the demons went to cuff everyone but Rosier, Asmodeus told Dante again, "Don't struggle."

CHAPTER 20

"You're a real," Joana began, cellphone pressed to an ear as she swallowed down a forkful of tortilla slices fried in salsa, "fucking idiot." She was sitting cross-legged in a chair, the restaurant of a hotel, one of the only ones still open. Half the restaurants, or related food places, were temporarily closed due to the gas shortage, and most food carts had relocated to outside of major supermarkets, whereas the smaller and informal markets suffered severely.

Tadeo was sighing. "You told me that everything's been fine. No one has noticed I'm gone."

"Did you forget about the massacre at the river, dumbass?"

"But you said that there hasn't been anything that's gone wrong since. You told me that everyone thinks I'm still there. And there's — Oh for God's sake, Joana, I can't leave him there! I left him in *Hell*! That's the part you're missing. I didn't leave him on the side of the road or something. I left him in a nightmare, and it's my fault. I have to make it right."

"If it's such a nightmare," Joana replied, "then he's probably already dead." She turned away from the televisions, heading toward the entrance. "Come back soon or other people you care about are next."

"I don't *care* about him."

Joana hung up, shut her eyes in frustration, then heard a low chuckle from the other end of the table, followed by the deep voice of a man. He said, "In Hell, eh?" She refused to face him, the kingpin. "Well, we're going to need him back soon, *mija*." Scraps against the plate indicated that he was still picking at his food, a simple meal of beans and eggs with tomato, onion, and serrano pepper. "Have you seen the news? They're saying the bad men," meaning them, of course, "ordered those migrants to die." He hummed. "I didn't know that." Joana bit her tongue, then finally fluttered open her eyes again, but hazily, tiredly. "It's a good story, though. The people like a good story. The state is very mad at us, and the north isn't happy either. There was a deal, did you know? There was a deal." A grin formed between a scratching laugh. "They say that us bad men infiltrated the soldiers, corrupted them, *mija*, but no, no, they infiltrated us. For too long, me and my men, we had to listen to the governor, the businesses. There was no freedom."

Something deep, deeper than the heart, unsettled in Joana's chest, and her blood felt heavier in her veins as she whispered, "Who are we really fighting?"

Another laugh, then a disbelieving shake of his head. "This is about freedom. All of this with that boy and who you've aimed him at for us — it was about freedom for us. You can understand that, can't you? We never wanted to be part of anything bigger."

They didn't talk about much else before Joana thanked him for the breakfast, wiped her mouth, nodded at the poor waiter who'd likely walked hours to work — the state buses were too cramped — then headed out into the warm winter day. Up ahead, there were few civilian cars but what seemed a hundred cargo trucks and a handful of soldier vehicles passing through. Not far from the door, there was an old man with a bad hunch leaning against a cart of various trinkets, including a pole where various cloth masks hung from. Wrestler masks, *luchador* masks.

Briefly, Joana recalled a time, years ago, when the kingpin, before his men, before Joana's father, questioned if Tadeo was truly so obedient to her, if he didn't suspect her intentions. 'We'll have to hurt you,' the kingpin had said, 'if we find out that you're not being honest with us.' She can't remember what she'd said, but, now, she wished she'd replied: 'He believes too much in God. It makes him naive. He thinks we're all good people at heart. He believes in me. It's going to kill him, and he's going to die believing in me.'

Joana stepped toward the man and his cart of a million trinkets. And, instantly, he smiled, eyes crinkling, lips pulling back to reveal a silver tooth or two. Despite the hunchback, he moved swiftly, almost elegantly. "Oh, young lady! Good morning. Look, I have some jewelry here and toys here for a baby or a nephew or niece."

"Good morning. How much are the *luchador* masks?" Joana reached into her baggy jeans, tugging out a tiny cloth purse — with sarape stripes — unzipping it, pulling out just a few coins as the man named the price. "Thank you, sir." She handed the money to his shaking, open palm, and he clasped her hand in his own in an affirming, kind shake before he retreated. After this, he asked her who the mask was for — a boyfriend, brother — or if it was for herself, in which case he had a pink one with white flames at the top but he might need help to reach it. "The black one, please," she said simply; it had white accents as well. "It's for my friend."

The man and Joana argued for a few minutes; her begging him to keep the change and him refusing before she slapped the extra money on his cart then took off running across the parking lot, leaving him there to call after her then surrender with a loud: "God bless you! Take care of yourself, miss! Thank you!"

With nothing else to do, given Tadeo's absence, she went home, talked with her oldest brother, mumbled to her mother, helped with her youngest brother, then took off again in the later afternoon with the mask in her back pocket.

Heading to the border bridge on foot, she followed a line of teen students walking together, looking down at the increased number of tents creating colorful hills along the river. There were quite a few foreigners here now, migrants from southern states or island states or the other side of the Earth, distinct in appearance enough to be noticed but quick to disappear into the backgrounds of wherever they were working. Joana caught a foreigner helping change the tires of a truck, and she wondered if any of them would stay if all the wars in the world ever ended, wondered if the town was irrevocably changed in ways beyond the abandoned homes. Once she reached the bridge, ignoring the mass of soldiers stationed in its vicinity, she reached for her passport and visa.

Tadeo had always thought they were counterfeit, but it'd been easy for her to arrange getting them with the right money. And so crossing the border was simple, requiring just a few coins into the turnstile before pushing through. Again, she followed the students headed to study in Babylon — a rather diverse group of those with private education money and those with public education citizenship. Joana had never finished her secondary education on this side of the river, but sometimes she fantasized about college, about leaving town and saving nothing but herself.

"Hello," she greeted in a foreign language to the green-clad officers at the center of the bridge, showing identification before they allowed her to walk on ahead, right into the line of students, maids, gardeners, visiting family, and the like. 'If I'm too late,' she thought of her destination, 'then maybe I'll leave it, leave her.' Joana reached for her headphones, plugged her ears, then put on some regional music, then her guilty pleasure — the blonde superstar, the Harlot.

Forty minutes later, she finally arrived at the interior immigration office, had her papers checked again. The state official nodded at her, and he asked if she'd heard about the executive orders and the increase in troops that'll happen by the end of the month, and she lied, said she never heard much about anything.

After this, Joana allowed herself the sweet luxury of a taxi. She slipped into the first car she could find, made some awkward small talk with the driver. Many of those on the side of Babylon spoke the same language as those trapped outside of it. "I'm afraid," he said, "that they'll send me back even though I am a good man. I've come here only to work and for a better life for my kids." Joana apologized to him as if she were responsible. "We are good people. You too, miss. We are good people, right? Hardworking people. Not all of us are bad. Those that are bad — yes, send them back. But not me, not you."

Joana whispered, "I wish this country would sink underwater."

Finally, the pilgrimage ended, and it was dark now. With her head of curly dark hair pressed against the window, Joana hadn't noticed, staring at her own reflection in the window, in the silence following her exchange with the undocumented man driving. 'Does God ask for papers to get into Heaven?' What was the border between Heaven and Hell like? Was it like this? She had family on this side of the border too; they lived only twenty minutes from her home hypothetically, but the border more than doubled the time it took to get to them. If it weren't there, then maybe she would have been closer to them, maybe everything would have been different.

Softly, the man asked Joana if she was well, and she said that she was, and then she reached to pay him too. There wasn't much she was carrying — her father had taken much of her money. Her mother had insisted Joana be no trouble, to just hand it over because that was her *father* asking for it, and she was his daughter. She was. She knew that. And she did love him. 'I love you,' she'd told her mom too before heading out.

Suddenly, Joana was ringing the doorbell outside a three-story, wide mansion, having stepped out of the taxi and walked past three luxury cars at some point. She didn't get the chance to check if the man had already driven away before the door swung open, a distant dog barking somewhere deeper in the house, to reveal a young woman with wide green eyes framed by mascara. Her hair was faux blonde — dark roots betrayed her — and her lips were painted bright red, whereas her cheeks were dusted in pink and her jaw was bronzed. Her outfit consisted of tight black pants, heels, and a silk top with luxury printing, the first buttons almost-scandalously undone to display the upper curves of her chest. Hanging from an elbow, a luxury purse.

"Oh my God," she said in the foreign language, then laughed, clapped her manicured hands together. She continued in Joana's language: "I was just about to leave—"

"I wanted to drive us."

"You wanted to trap me in the car with you," snapped the young woman, though she immediately stepped out, pulled the door shut behind her. "You're crazy. This is why I can't stand you." Even still, she retrieved the car keys from her bag, placed them in Joana's outstretching hand. "We said to meet at the club. So, where are you taking me? Are you kidnapping me?"

"Yes," said Joana as she headed for the right car, opening the passenger door, then waiting until the woman climbed in before she shut it. After walking around the front, sliding into the driver's, Joana added, "You still have time to run."

"You're crazy," said the woman again, shaking her head but putting on the seatbelt. "Don't think I'm not mad anymore. If you don't stop acting so scary all the time, then I'm going to file a restraining order, you know."

Joana hesitated, then turned on the ignition and teased, "How many years?" Tilting a long smile over at the woman, she reached to grasp her hand. "Two or five?" The daughter of the kingpin, a girl who hated her name Guadalupe, thought it was too old-fashioned. Years ago, her father had introduced her as 'La Lupina' to a warm-faced Joana.

Lupina huffed, then crossed her legs, looked away, and squeezed Joana's hand. She confessed with the sound of a smile in her voice, "Two." Then, Joana drove off.

This nightclub was rather different than the one where Joana had met with Lupina's father — its theme neon with skulls and sombreros and cacti. EDM shook the walls and thumped against Joana's chest even from a street away after they'd parked and begun walking over. She wasn't well-dressed, and looked even less so beside Lupina — in her usual sneakers, jeans, and an oversized, plaid shirt she wore and that her mother often hissed made her look like a boy. If it weren't for Lupina's status, then Joana was certain she'd have been turned away. Instead, Lupina led her inside, down the steps leading toward the basement, dark in between glowing necklaces and the dim bulbs over the long parallel bars at the walls. A DJ was up on a podium at the furthest wall, a dance floor right before it with all the bodies that weren't standing by the small couches peppered around, each with a table holding a bucket of ice and liquor.

There was some kind of masked event today — most of the people in the building were covering their face with all kinds of coverings — which Lupina had messaged she didn't really care for, but Joana reached into her pocket, retrieved the wrestler mask. She yanked it over her face, turned to a laughing Lupina, then pulled her to the bar. Joana ordered them several shots, and then downed them quickly with her, telling her about breakfast with her father while Lupina gagged. When they finally made it to the dance floor, they were adequately drunk, but Joana took a tall beer with her anyway, for the emotional support.

'I'm not going to bring it up,' she pointedly thought. 'I'm not going to talk about it.' Joana curled one foot over another and spun on her heel to remember how to feel the rhythm of the music, almost drowned out by a singing, feminine voice. The Harlot. Then, she took Lupina's hand, pulled her close, then grasped her waist. 'It's not going to happen.' Routinely, Joana took sips from her bottle, and then went for another one, and then returned to dancing with her girl, her woman. It made her sound like her dad to think so possessively, but Joana really understood him in that moment. 'My woman, my girl.' The shapes of the room were beginning to melt, as were the sensations of Lupina's body pressed snug to hers. Another spin. Lupina ground down on Joana's leg between her own, as if they were dancing regional music out on a ranch. Once, Lupina had taken Joana to her ranch, and they had curled up on a bench swing together, listening to the birds.

They couldn't be at the club long, Lupina had warned the day before; her friends — a mixture of the wealthy from both sides of the river — had begun showing up here so often, but she was desperate to dance, to dance with Joana. 'You love to dance, but they don't know, do they?' Joana breathed against her girlfriend's neck, and Lupina shivered. 'Your friends don't know me.' Lupina pulled back, locked a hazy gaze with her. 'Your friends don't know you either. Not like I do.' Then, Lupina stepped away, turned on her heel, began walking toward the bathrooms.

Slow, Joana lowered her hands, breathing in, out, in, out before lifting her beer bottle to her mouth and taking the last sips. Half-awake, half-lucid, she felt a man try to touch her, but Joana shoved him back without thinking, then headed after Lupina. Her feet stumbled as she moved, and every kind of person bumped into either side of her, but Joana could barely hear their snaps or insults or apologies. Only the sweep of Lupina's hair held her attention. Hurrying past the entrance to the bathroom, Joana noted the beautiful women by the sinks, reapplying makeup, talking, before Joana managed to catch Lupina slip into the furthest stall from the door.

'That man your father wants for you will never know you either. Not like me.' Joana couldn't help remembering her argument with Lupina now, but she approached anyway. 'I know his ugly fucking face. The stupid cut of his hair.' The stall door was ajar, unlocked for her. 'What is his name? I can't remember. Your father invited me to the wedding already. Do you want me there? Do you think you could bear seeing me? Would you say I'm a friend or that you don't know me well, that I'm just some girl your father introduced to you some night by the grill? Can you make yourself believe it?'

When Joana stepped into the stall, shut it behind her, Lupina took her face and pulled her close. Quickly, the bottom half of the wrestling mask was folded up enough for a cherry-glossed mouth to slide against Joana's. But Joana soon tilted her face — the movement slow but feeling too quick, fast enough to jostle the burning liquor in her belly — then brought her lips to the warm pulse of her girl's neck. 'My girl. Maybe I should stop thinking like that, after all.' She shut her eyes, didn't realize it; the image of Lupina was imprinted in her mind in perfect accuracy, every detail memorized, traced by Joana's tongue in the past. A past life, it felt like. 'I want to be with you every morning. Should I tell you? My phone is ringing all the time. It's my father. It's your father. It'll be God one day, telling me it's time to march right to Hell and leave you here. Because you're His good Christian girl, and I'm a valley of death.'

Lupina slapped a hand over her mouth, like she always did, but her hips began to grind against the other's knee again as Joana set her foot on the toilet seat, too firm for how weak she felt.

'If I could talk without slurring, I'd say goodbye. This has to be goodbye, doesn't it?' Her stomach turned, but Joana bit down, listening to a soft, shaking breath slip past Lupina's fingers. 'Goodbye. When I arrived at your father's house years ago, and you came down from your room to ask him something, saw me among all the men, and I saw you, I remember thinking: What a beautiful girl.' Joana had no patience, grappling Lupina's waist, trying to guide her to put one foot on the toilet as she set her own back on the ground. Then, Joana dragged both her hands up Lupina's tall body, feeling it tremble, before she began to pepper kisses down her front. Through the top, she squeezed at one of Lupina's breasts, nuzzled it with her nose, kissed it, then continued downward until she was crouching over the tile. Lupina pulled her own pants down, and Joana yanked them lower to rub her jaw against the lace of Lupina's underwear, breathing in.

'I was half-drunk when we met. I slurred my hello. I think you didn't like me.' Joana tugged the fabric aside, then dipped in her tongue, ignoring the tight throb between her own legs — partly hoping it'd start to hurt. Her heart craved a whip of punishment; she didn't know why, she never knew why. 'But every time afterwards that I was in the house, you'd come offer me something to drink, some food. Once, you offered me some of your own cooking. You said you felt bad for me because I was just a girl surrounded by horrible men. I told you I'm not much of a girl, and your father and his friends don't see a girl in me either. What was I then, you asked. I said, I'm a weapon. I'm no girl; I'm a gun.'

Nearby, there were the sudden calls of Lupina's name, the sound of her friends. And the girl that Joana was drowning in tensed. "Stop," Lupina whispered, hands going to the top of Joana's head, clutching the mask.

'How did you get here? You asked me that constantly, how does a young girl end up at the table of traffickers and killers. Where do I begin? Would you believe me if I said I know how the world ends?' Joana was in such a daze that all she could focus on was the wetness of her lips as hands came over her shoulders, pushed her away. Lupina's face, crushed in worry, was above, and Joana felt herself tremble. Then, Lupina pulled Joana's mask down over her mouth as she shouted to answer her friends by the sinks.

'How do I explain that I thought I was divine once and that I could save my father and save all of us? I was a child. I was naive. I never wanted this. I wanted to help. I really thought, I really believed, I could be good once.' Joana was grabbed, shoved to sit on the toilet seat, and Lupina stared at her for a moment, her face flushed, eyes wide. 'You're always going to be beautiful, aren't you? How am I going to live with that?'

Lupina kissed the top of her head. "I love you," she said. "I'll call you later, *mi vida*." Hastily, she adjusted her clothing, promising a second time to call, before she slipped out of the stall, shutting it behind her, scurrying — from the sound of it — to her friends and telling them she was feeling ill. And that she'd come alone, hadn't known her friends would drop by.

And Joana listened to them all talk for a minute, as well as all the other women in the bathroom. Alone, in her jeans, her massive shirt, her mask, without anyone to hold her hair back if she were to turn around and empty her stomach into the toilet bowl. Lupina's voice was fading; the door out of the bathroom creaked. Raw, Joana's throat was beginning to burn, her eyes itched. Even once Joana was finally able to wobble onto her feet, stagger out to see all the women, some smiled, others looked away instantly.

Whatever it was like to stand among them, to be a normal girl — she didn't know. What hurt more was that Joana didn't want to be like them. She wished she did. She wanted to want.

Once Joana finally left the bathroom, escaped the club, she lifted a hand to slither beneath the mask and wipe excessively at her mouth. Her chest hiccuped, and maybe her mouth did, but she couldn't tell. She knew that she was walking. Every step was both too fast and too slow; grass crunched beneath her sneakers, and the crowd to enter the club had thinned. There was only a moon above now and a streetlamp, illuminating a quiet sidewalk that she moved along. Bushes, flowers, were coming into view, as well as a fountain — a quaint park — and without thinking, she made her way closer. Then, she found herself on the grass, not remembering how she'd lowered herself onto it. The sky above was dark, some specs of light but not many, like she'd fallen into a dreamless sleep.

She blinked once, twice.

A figure was above her. When did they get there? Unable to recall them moving, stepping onto the grass over her head like their armored feet were her halo and she was an angel fallen from Heaven. 'I used to think I was divine too,' she always wanted to tell Tadeo. 'When he saved me, I thought God sent him to me, and I was going to be a saint who led her people to freedom with St. Michael in my ear, whispering.' She stared at Michael now, in all his silver, reflecting the moonlight so that he was like a ghost. His face hidden by his helmet, his shoulder shrouded by a red cape.

"It's been a while," drunken Joana said, "since I've hallucinated you, Miguelito."

Slow, the angel's hands lifted to his head, and he removed his helmet carefully like it were his skin he was peeling off to reveal whatever horror might lay beneath the flesh of an angel. "Joana." Only a few curls not tucked into the collar of his chest plate fell over his face, one of earthly eyes and a strong, hilled nose. "You're drunk." He, tepid, lowered himself onto a knee, clanking like he were a machine; Joana now perfectly imagined opening the prince to find wires where arteries were meant to be, a time bomb in the cardiac notch. "Sit up." The archangel's holy hands touched her arms, gently tugged her body until the top half of it was off the damp green.

"Ugh," fell from her mouth, and the world twirled around her, around Michael. "Are you real?"

"I'm real, Joana. Believe that I'm here."

"You're asking me to have faith?" Something, thick and like blood, climbed up Joana's stomach, to her throat, rattled her body forward, but she didn't vomit it out, refused to. "I used to have faith in you. And in God. But here we are, and the world is ending."

"I've told you, Joana." He always said her name so softly, the same as he rubbed at her shoulder blades now. "You'll rise to Heaven, and paradise is there for you. No matter how difficult the revelation has been and will continue to be, there's a life waiting for you already in the skies. Earth has become so wicked that all there is left to do is destroy it—"

"She's my home, and my mother," said Joana, voice still slurred, though her body was beginning to slump against the prince. "Earth is beautiful. You may not think so, but I do. I do, I do." Hiccup. "There are still birds left in the sky, and there is still green. It still rains. And those I love are here. And—" Heavy, her eyelids drooped then fell. "And I love a lot of bad people, Miguelito. I've done a lot of bad. I've lied, and I've stolen. I've shot a gun. Jesus won't come down to take me. Don't tell me to confess. I want mercy, not forgiveness."

"Believe me, please, that you will be saved."

"Saved from who? Can God save me from God?" Joana touched him, feeling warmth through the cold armor, and finally, she realized that her archangel really was here, that he was not a dream. "To go to Heaven isn't to be saved. Not to me. I want my town saved. I want to return to how it was before the war."

"We can't return," said the saint, "to the time before the war."

"We can try," Joana pleaded. "Miguel, let me try."

"Heaven can— will take you."

"I don't want to go to Heaven; I want to go home. I want my mom. I want my dad." Tears burned at her eyes and in her throat, in her chest, like her very soul cried with her. "Don't make me leave. This is my river and my people. This is my soil. I'm not me without this place. This is my land. Leave me here to burn. Leave me here, Miguel. I'll burn with her."

"Joana," pained, whispered.

"I told you to leave me here, didn't I? And I told you never to come back for me. I'd rather be evil. I'd rather suffer with her than live a life, eternal or not, without her. She's my land. And these are my people. You don't understand. I can't make you understand." Her eyes opened and no longer did she find comfort in the prince. "Heaven is my grandmother's house, my mother's kitchen. The park I played in when I was little that they ruined. And you said it — we can't return to the time before the war. So there is no Heaven for me."

Michael hugged her tight, wanting to say he'd take her to paradise and show her that there was, indeed, something better than this. But she didn't want something better and, a minute later, she jerked forward in a wet, guttural cough. He took her hair and waited patiently as she expelled every last drop of liquor.

CHAPTER 21

'Iwas ten-years-old when my father left me at an unfamiliar house. An older woman led me inside, and she had me undress, then she took some photos of my body at every angle. After that, she left me alone for a while, and with nothing to do, I put my clothes back on. When a man came, and the woman let me out of the room, they talked about me like I wasn't there, said they might take me to meet another man across the river. I was a little too brown-skinned for a good price, but I would do. And I turned my head, saw the open door to the yard in the back. The man had a gun. If I ran now, he would shoot me, wouldn't he? Right in the head, or right in the back? Even thinking this, my legs started moving beneath me, and I broke out into a sprint, heading out of the house. The man, and the woman, didn't run after me; there was no way out of the yard, nowhere for me to run. But I didn't want to stop running, even if there was nowhere to go. I reached the dirt outside, and I saw tall cement walls, barbed wire over the top of them.'

'When the man called after me, calmly, I twisted back, heart beating my ribs until they cracked. Then, right before me, his skin pulled apart, then the bone, and blood spilled in between. An invisible sword, by an invisible hand, had just ripped him to pieces like bread pulled apart by your fingers. And before the woman could hurry into the house, her head tensed, like someone grabbed it, then crushed into nothing but redness, no hint of bones, of brain, or eyes. I thought I was next. I went to cover my head with my arms, and I screamed. But then, Michael, you revealed yourself to me. You told me, do not be afraid, but I continued to cry. You begged me, do not be afraid. I couldn't stop screaming.'

'Days later, my father told my mother that his boss had instructed him to bathe me before I was trafficked. I wasn't supposed to be listening to him or my mother's sobs, but I remember thinking: he didn't bathe me. He should have bathed me. If he was going to send me away, couldn't I get a bath first?'

Joana blinked, could hardly tell apart the shapes of the world before her, but she could still feel Michael's arms, and she could smell the distinctly brisk, petrichor scent of the chief prince, and there are some places that you can sense you're in even with your eyes closed. The way that the wind blew, here — she could recognize it alive or dead. A park, a plaza; it was large with pathways intersecting it like veins, and there were countless benches, some tall trees at the northern side, opposite the church at the southern end; and at the center, there was a circular gazebo, some five steps off the ground with curled railings caging the interior platform. 'It was here that we always used to talk, Miguelito.'

Hazily, she lifted her gaze and saw the chief prince, and she realized that her body was draped over his lap, wrapped in his reddened cloak. On the same bench they always used to sit on. Her head was pounding, her throat was raw, her nostrils burned.

"Something in your pocket," said the prince, slow, his grasp of the language as fragile as she remembered it to be, "keeps shaking." His helmet was missing, perhaps on the ground by some flowers.

Elsewhere, Tadeo had ridden throughout the night, unable to sleep, his mare oddly awake with him as they traveled in the darkness. The same couldn't be said for Dina; the angel was behind the young man on the saddle, hugging Tadeo's ribs and pressing his face to his warm, human neck while Tadeo held the romal reins of the horse with his free hand. His other grip was preoccupied with the phone he was using to call Joana. It was a phone he'd borrowed from his aunt, the one who lived on the coast, since Tadeo's had been destroyed from the water and, likely, from burning to a crisp by the Leviathan. His aunt's husband, too, had lent him a hat, another *tejana*, saying he should protect his scalp from the sun.

It was dark now, too late for the hat on his head to be of any use. Tadeo shouldn't worry that she wasn't answering his constant calls, should he? But he'd felt compelled to ruin her night anyway, to bother her, to want to talk to her. 'I'm scared,' he knew. He kept thinking of the Leviathan, how enormous it was, how it'd almost burnt him alive. If he'd stopped healing, if he hadn't been able to force it fast enough, would he have died? Died again? Swallowing thickly, Tadeo glanced at Dina, then he sighed. 'I didn't tell you about Hell, Joana. I want to tell you.' She was the only person that he felt he could talk to, at times. She was his only friend.

Putting his phone away, he remembered a young Joana from several years ago, shoving a radio phone into his teen hands. 'Take it,' she'd insisted. 'Contact me through this. Only this. Do you hear me?' Her hair had been braided back, though a rebellious dark curl fell to hook right between her brows, and her face had been a little too rounded still. Though they were both young, Tadeo had always been bewildered by her, how old she tried to act, how stone cold. He saw perfectly well the flash of insecurity in her eyes. She wasn't perfect; she was a child; but it was the desperate trying that fascinated him.

In the park, Joana croaked, head pulsing in pain. "How long have I been passed out?"

"Some hours. The sun will rise soon." Michael adjusted her in his lap, but he kept his cloak around her tightly. Like his body, the angel's clothes could remain hidden from any human onlookers until he decided to reveal himself, and so the two were perfectly invisible in the corner of the park for now. "How do you feel, Joana?" One of his gauntlets went to her hair, smoothed down the curls tenderly, and his empty face betrayed a touch of emotion in his eyes, something tender like an open wound.

"Like shit," Joana said honestly, then shut her eyes again. "Are you looking for Tadeo? Why should I tell you? Maybe he's gone to Hell, Miguelito. And you can't go there or you'll run into your girl."

"The devil is here," said Michael, which made Joana snort.

Tadeo held onto the reins tighter, shakily, remembering even though he never, ever, should. But he was alone, apart from a dozing angel. Maybe it was safe to remember, to not fear inconveniencing anyone with his suffering:

'When I woke up, I was naked, drenched in blood — some my own, some not. All the breath in my lung felt foreign to me beneath a foreign chest like I'd just been born. Perhaps I had. I had died, felt the bullet pierce my eyeball to have it burst, shatter the bone, burrow through my brain, do away with my consciousness in an instant. But I was awake again, and my body was different. It was like a human's once more, but the flesh was so novel against my fingertips that I could have believed I was never a person before they'd killed me. Back from the dead. I had returned from a grave, and I had killed. For this body, I had killed. I was back from the dead. Maybe I'd always been dead. It had all been wrong. Since I was born, it had all been wrong, like I sagged with rot alive and, now, dead, I had remade myself how I always should have been. But my stomach was heavy with meat. I had eaten them. I had made a backward Eucharist out of them, turned their bodies into bread on my tongue. My first miracle.'

Joana said, "Oh?" then laughed weakly. "Is the world really ending, then? Is this the end?"

Michael hesitated, then replied, "Only God can answer that." He put his hand over her forehead, as if to feel for fever, but his gauntlet was in the way.

'But the victory in me,' thought Tadeo, 'was soon replaced by terror. I realized I had killed and the weight of what had killed me crushed my newborn heart. My nails scratched at my skin until talons tore out from my fingers, and I felt my body curl forward, and I saw behind me without turning — an eye had just opened in the back of my neck. I saw the end of the road. Another eyeball must have torn open inside of me and made me see my own wounds. When a cry fell out of my mouth, it wrenched me forward, and I curled into the limbs sprouting out of me like new bones. I screamed out again, then I began to run, and I headed for the drylands out of town. None of it was freeing. It wasn't liberating. A part of me was still being killed, I realized. Perhaps I hadn't come back from the dead at all. I was on the ground, and I was with those soldiers. And it was happening now. I could feel it. Like a power drill, whirring my insides until the tissue had been made wine. But there is nothing poetic of it — the burn. It hurts. They are killing you now. Run, Tadeo. That is your name. Tadeo.'

Grunting, Joana tried to sit up, and Michael let her, but as she tried to free herself from beneath the cloak, a spell of dizziness and nausea sent her back down. "Ugh."

"Rest," Michael told her.

"I can't," Joana said. "I need to find Tadeo too."

'I spent a few years dying. It was constant. Every second, I was back on the ground, the world collapsed over me. My ribs were broken into. I was not a man. I was a tearing thing. There is nothing poetic about it, dad. Rape. There's really nothing that I can say to make it easier for you to hear. It *is* nothing, for periods of time. It all goes dark, you die, for a minute or two. Emptiness, and then you've been turned over. It's nothing really. I'm sorry. You probably don't want to know this. The details. I'm not supposed to talk about those. Not supposed to explain it. Please don't be mad at me. For telling you and for living it. I was just going home.'

'Maybe I didn't want to come back. If the pain would end, then I'd be happy to die. I'm sorry, dad. You wouldn't want me to die like that. I'm sorry for telling you. I'll stop soon. Soon, I won't bring it up again. It hurts. It's embarrassing to say where it hurts. I won't. I don't want to make anyone uncomfortable. We don't talk about that. The burn. It's a burning sort of feeling. A lot of what isn't fire burns. There are burns worse than what fire can do to you. At times, I think there is somewhere worse than Hell. There are people worse than the devil. And they are here, dad. They are here with us.'

Michael said, "It's not time for him to die. I won't hurt him."

"Shut up," said Joana. "If you're here, the end is coming." But she really couldn't bring herself to get up, to move away from the prince she'd spent so long dreaming would come back to save her like he had on that night. 'After I stopped screaming, my gaze flashed back to the piles of limbs and bones and blood— then I jerked forward with a retching. I vomited between us, but you took my shoulders, held me back, held me.' Michael didn't tell her, then, why he had been there. It was only some other night that he said he'd come to find the anti-Christ on God's orders, a Beast that had been born from a resurrected body the year prior. 'God sent you, a year too late for Tadeo. God is always sending you to find what can't be found.'

Tadeo thought: 'One day, I returned to town. I don't know why. I spent a year and forty days, forty nights, waiting, but the devil never appeared for me as he had for Jesus. And so I returned, and when I did, I told them that the child they loved had died. I was someone new. That would be easier to explain. I didn't want to tell them what I'd done to my body, so I would say God did it to me.'

Michael said: "The prophecy must happen in order. I can't kill him yet—" He paused, then teased rather nervously: "I thought I told you this."

Joana scoffed at that. "I was, what, a kid? Sorry for not remembering how your apocalypse works."

"I forgive you," Michael teased again, and Joana huffed and finally began wrestling out of his touch to sit down.

Unbelieving, Tadeo's family had first ordered him to leave their house. They called him a demon, dressed in the pulled skin of their missing child. *Nahual*, his grandfather called him. And even after they'd accepted Tadeo, he remained in hiding, in the shadows, refusing to leave. He feared his body. He feared everything. 'They asked me: Did you see Heaven as you lay dead? I told them that I couldn't remember because I was too scared to say that all I ever saw was blood.'

Joana crossed her arms and leaned back on the bench, shutting her eyes, as if that would be enough to will away the pounds in her head and the spinning of the park around her. "Why did you bring me here? You should have brought me home." After they'd met, Michael had asked where her parents were, and he had flown her there. 'When my mother saw me, she screamed at my father. My father said they'd threatened to hurt the entire family if he didn't hand over a daughter. He cried to my mother, apologizing. He cried to me, too.'

"I don't know," Michael said. "You never liked it when I took you home when you were younger."

Chuckling, Joana decided to ask, "You know, I always wondered why you came back for me." 'Why you listened to my prayers.'

Michael readjusting, appearing almost sheepish. "I hadn't meant to," he answered honestly. "I'm not supposed to step in to save humans, especially not from each other, not often. But when I can, when only the victim will know, I try to save. On another day that I was looking for Tadeo — I saw you crying in this park."

"I wasn't crying," Joana grumbled.

"You were." Michael hesitated again, then he said, "You told me that your father had become involved with bad men and that was why he tried to sell you." Furrowing her brow, Joana tried not to feel any shame for having spilled her misery to the ghost that'd reappeared to her that day; she'd been so young, after all. "You said it wasn't his fault."

Joana sighed. "I had no one else to talk to."

Michael could relate to that, couldn't he? Swallowing, the prince replied, "I regret it often, having told you so much. Forgive me."

For some time, she hadn't even known he was an angel. She sought him out some nights, always found Michael in the parks, sometimes ran to him with two corns on sticks, and they'd eat together before Joana spoke to the chief prince rather casually. 'You must've loved it. To me, you weren't some divine creature that was supposed to hold up the sky. I wasn't scared of you anymore, and I didn't pray to you. Why would I be scared of you? Any man on the street was much scarier than a ghost. That's what I was sure you were — a ghost.'

Joana said, "I don't know if I can."

She could still remember that day they'd been sitting on a bench and the prince began to tell her of the end times. 'I stared at you with big eyes, I asked what you meant, and you told me about an anti-Christ and a Beast. You would kill them one day, but until then, the false messiah will create suffering for all of the Earth. You spoke to me of God's promise to rise us good people to Heaven. Whenever I complained about the horrible things that happened in my home, in my town, in my own heart, you reassured me that all would be better in Heaven. I used to want that.'

Tadeo, eventually, decided to rest, carrying the angel Dina down with him and setting up the tent, and leaving water for the mare. Once he settled down, he realized how raw his face felt with all the crying he'd done as he rode along. The misery, now, was putting him to sleep. And, in his dreams, Tadeo remembered the days he'd started petty theft for food, for drinks. No one was capable of stopping him, and he almost prayed that they'd try it. He would chuckle to himself, imagining soldiers being directed toward him and how they'd be torn apart in his claws.

"Every time," Joana began, "that you left me, I went back home and the apocalypse shit just didn't matter anymore." Though she swore, it was detached, not angry or even upset. "I went back to a family that needed money with a father who'd traded all his freedom for a gun and the salary of a criminal. I realized that you were asking me to let all of the world collapse for Heaven. How could you ask that of me? Fuck you. Fuck you." Again, it was distant, like she was reciting a script with no emotion, like she'd planned to say this once but had forgotten why. "I wanted to save my family. I wanted to save my town." 'But I was only thirteen or so when I decided.' Three years of Michael in her life. 'I didn't understand how the world worked.'

"I never should have told you."

"I would have found Tadeo, even if you hadn't told me about him or what he was capable of." Joana answered; she doubted that, but the thought might make the both of them feel better. "When I told you I never wanted to see you again, if you were going to let the world end, I meant it." She chuckled. "But, hey, maybe you were right in the end. Look at how bad everything's gotten. It's all so fucked. I fucked up. I failed. Are you happy?" The sun was beginning to rise, to drown them in light.

"No, Joana. I don't— I don't understand what you've done."

Just some hours of sleep, then Tadeo was finally riding back to town at dawn. He was careful to keep off the main roads, passing through the quiet streets, even quieter recently due to the gasoline shortage. It was good since the exhaustion was wearing on Tadeo and his horse, though not enough to prevent Tadeo from perking up when Dina shifted and said, "Oh, Tadeo, there's a crying woman over there." So lost in his fatigue, the anti-Christ hadn't noticed, but he yanked on his mare to encourage her to stop, then he turned his head. As the angel had said, there was a woman sobbing, but she was by a man slumped over the ground. "He's bleeding." From both legs, gashes so deep that there were glimmers of white bone in between the flooding red at his thighs.

Joana's fingers twitched, craving a cigarette, as she thought, 'I asked my dad to teach me how to use a gun. He didn't want to at first — I was a girl, he said — but he gave in, one day. He brought me to the outskirts, he handed me a pistol. We shot at bottles. In the distance, I saw a bird plunge, and I wondered if I'd just killed for the first time or if that was my angel sending me a message. I didn't care. If Michael wouldn't save me again, then I'd have to do it myself.' "I thought I could just kill the right people."

Tadeo crouched by the strangers, realizing the injured man was only quiet because the light was fading from his eyes. Quick, he told Dina to get some of their water and asked if the angel could heal the man, but the angel frowned and said, "We finished the last of the water earlier, Tadeo."

"There should be some up ahead at a store," Tadeo tried to say, putting his palm over the gashes, then turning to see the woman who was eyeing the angel with wide, frozen eyes. "Please don't worry. With God's blessing, he will be okay."

"It was the criminals," she was stammering. "He was trying to post online about what's happening here? I don't know. I don't know."

Joana was quiet for a moment. "My plan was to use him like a weapon. I would get Tadeo to kill the criminals, the ones at the top. I thought we could all free the town that way. We. I thought the soldiers wanted us safe from crime and so did the politicians. I believed what they said. I used to think it was simple. Good people versus bad people."

'I went out hunting for Tadeo. It's not difficult to find him if you know what you're looking for — a teen boy without an eye. In an alleyway, I found him. Like how I'd seen my dad do, I covered my face — though all I had was an old *luchador* mask — and crept in behind a boy hurrying through with bandages over half his face, and I called out, "Tadeo!" He stopped immediately, tensed, didn't turn. Quietly, I approached, pulling a pistol out of my jacket, and I said, "Your hands are already bloody. You think that no one can see it, but I can. You killed soldiers in cold blood. You died, and you came back from the dead." He demanded my name. I didn't answer. Finally, he growled, and he turned around, and I watched as his body morphed into something enormous, something horrible.' Intangibly many-eyed, many-winged. 'But I kept my gun pointed at you, Tadeo. I will not be afraid, I told myself. Michael told me not to be afraid, even if he chose to be.'

Just as Dina was about to fly off for water, Tadeo drew in a breath harshly. "Wait," he told the angel, and he heard the woman before him gasp louder than he had. With a swipe of his thumb over the wound, the blood smeared along what was, suddenly, perfectly healed skin. "Lord," Tadeo whispered. "Lord, my God."

"Tadeo," Dina breathed, fingers rising to go over his mouth. He'd never seen this, not even from angels, not even Raphael.

"You healed him," said the woman. "Like Christ— Like Christ!"

Joana thought about smoking again. 'Tadeo and I — in a stand-off. He asked how I knew all of this. I said an angel sent me. Then, I told him that he had a duty. Duty? Yes, duty. You can kill like no one else. You can turn into a beast, but you can do good. Don't let the power blind you, stupid. What killed you was the evil that's destroying us all. Stupid, you can save this place. You can save us. You have a responsibility. A loyalty to your own people.'

Tadeo grappled his healing hand with the other, and he saw as the man twitched, blinking his eyes, returning from half-dead. Immediately after, he shot up, and he clutched the woman's shirt and wrist, shaking, as she embraced him. The woman called, "Thank you, thank you, boy. You're a saint! You're a saint!" He stood, stepped back, and whispered some words in thanks, but his heart was beginning to pound against his ribs and lungs.

One of Dina's hands came over Tadeo's arm, squeezing in perhaps the same amount of confusion as the anti-Christ. "Tadeo," the angel whispered, "how have you done this?"

"I don't know," Tadeo replied, hushed and hasty. "I didn't even *try*." He felt his cellphone vibrate in his pocket, and he wanted to reach into it, hoping it was Joana. His friend. Joana. "Come, come. Let's go."

The angel frowned at the young man's twitching, fearful face. "What's wrong, Tadeo?"

Joana told Michael quietly, "I needed help figuring out where to find the bad guys to kill, and I asked my dad. He told me, but he only told me some of them, the traffickers he and his boss were competing with. I was stupid. My dad manipulated me. I wanted to save the town, but maybe it can't be saved. There are no good guys." She wished she was still laying on Michael, that he was still holding her. 'Most saints are martyrs; God wants you to die for Him, for His love. He wants you to fail.' "All I wanted was to use Tadeo to free us, then you could come and kill him. I didn't care if you did if I just got to use him first. I would even kill him myself if I could. But I've fucked it all up."

Michael leaned back into his seat.

And Joana stared at him gravely. "I set it into motion, didn't I? I set him on the path to become the false messiah." The prince didn't reply. "Have I doomed it all?" She laughed, though it devolved soon into a wheeze that rattled her shoulders. "But I'm not evil, Miguelito. I wish I were." 'Is it the devil that makes us evil or is it circumstance?' "I wish there were good people, and... I wish there were evil people."

Tadeo didn't bother getting on the horse, taking her reins and leading her away quickly as the woman held her man and continued to shout adoringly after the anti-Christ and his angel. 'Joana,' he thought. 'Where are you? What's happening in this town? It's all so confusing. I have to tell you about Hell. Where are you?' He hadn't checked his phone yet. 'You told me to save the town. You're behind all of this.'

Dina, again, grabbed Tadeo, and he abruptly stopped. "Tadeo—"

Tadeo, shakily, lifted his gaze. 'You saved me, Joana.'

'I doomed you, Tadeo.'

At the end of the street, standing in the middle of it, there was a beautiful priest with a wide, monstrous smile, his hair blonde and fluttered by the wind. "*Tadeo*," he greeted. "We've met, but you didn't recognize me when we did. Allow me to introduce myself again to you. I'm the devil."

CHAPTER 22

Hell's prison was almost empty, and the more time passed, the greater the soldier's plans of betrayal weighed.

Asmodeus had told Dante that this prison wasn't used often — that it was more a place for threats than punishment. Most demons didn't come to the devil, or his regent, to address grievances; they relied on confronting their foe directly or on forming a mob against them, or on ignoring evil acts in their totality. 'Demons are rather,' Asmodeus had said, 'jaded to it — all the violence between us. We're not like you humans, always demanding justice. If we kept track of all the suffering inflicted on us, we'd run out of numbers. And if we asked for punishment each time, then punishment would stop feeling like punishment.' He'd paused, then turned over to sleep, as he finally added, 'What I'm trying to say is to not expect justice when Baal runs that trial. Hell holds trials for entertainment, never justice.'

But Dante had never believed in justice anyway, or he hadn't for a long time. He believed in survival. And, presently, survival meant escaping Hell, calling his commanders, telling them how to kill Tadeo.

His mother's survival, at least. 'Follow him,' a fellow soldier had told him over the phone the day after Tadeo released Dante from torture. Dante had recognized the soldier's voice from the college; he used to taunt Dante's height and call him 'humble-skinned' — brown, too native-looking. 'Learn about him,' the soldier had said, 'what kills him. You don't want your mother involved in this, do you?' But she was already involved; they had taken her in for interrogation after Dante had made the mistake of informing them he was alive. 'She's a kind soul, Dante. Don't make her suffer more.'

From his corner of the cell, the soldier rubbed at a tired eye after sleeping for what must've been hours and lifted his body to sit, the makeshift blanket of his jacket falling from his chest to lap. As he did this, he accidentally drifted his gaze too far to the left, where Armoni was sitting beside Asmodeus, the duke sleeping against the wall. The blonde jolted when the soldier locked eyes with him, and then Armoni swiftly twisted his face away, lips pursed. 'Still scared of me?'

Ever since the three of them had been marched to this place — a tunnel burrowed straight down with a collection of prison cells attached to a spiraling, descending staircase — the angel had maintained as much distance as possible. He'd exchanged words with Asmodeus, but they'd been in their demonic language.

In that same tongue, a voice called out from nearby, before hastily switching to the one Dante knew: "Hello, human? I brought you something to eat." As the soldier looked past the bars of the cell, he sighed in relief at the sight of Rosier with a basket of baked goods and a soft smile. Dante hurried onto his feet and made his way over as the kind demon retrieved a peach-filled roll and offered it. "I hope it's still warm."

"Thank you, thank you," Dante said, taking the pastry and bringing it to his mouth immediately. "You're the love of my life."

"Be careful," Asmodeus warned, his voice suddenly close enough behind that the soldier jumped.

Huffing at the duke, first, Rosier then said to Dante: "Ignore him. He won't hurt you or else he'll have to face my wrath." Dante shoved more of the bread into his mouth, hiding an amused smile and trying to imagine what the wrath of this sweet demon could ever look like. "Here," said Rosier, offering a pastry to the duke, who reached for it, only to take Rosier's wrist. Asmodeus lifted Rosier's hand to his mouth, then kissed his fingers with a sultry smile. Rosier sighed, then pressed the pastry he held to Asmodeus' lips. "Eat," he urged, then switched to their demon language. "Baal will send some guards soon. There's not a lot of time until the trial."

Asmodeus answered in the same language, not turning when Dante stepped away to look at the blonde angel still curled up in a corner. "How angry is Baal?" He reached to take the food that Rosier was pushing into his mouth, then lowered it to hold by his hip. His other hand lifted to hold the bars of their cell, his knees trembling beneath his own weight.

"Not as much as you think," Rosier said, "at least it didn't look that way to me." But Baal had always spoken particularly kindly to Rosier, even as the last few centuries had turned the regent more bad-tempered.

Dante, slow, moved toward Armoni, reaching him with just a few steps, and he extended his pastry-holding hand; he was half offering it, half trying to tell the angel that there was food. When the angel lifted his gray eyes to his, they were dark, however, and cold.

Nearby, Asmodeus sighed at Rosier, took a bite of bread, chewed, then swallowed. Then, he smiled, and he leaned his face between the bars, to Rosier's height. He whispered, "If they tear me to pieces, will you put me back together again?" The demon of fruit flushed, but he leaned to peck the taller demon on the lips.

"Maybe not this time," Rosier replied, then shut his eyes, breathed against Asmodeus' mouth. Like kissing him weren't enough, and he needed to live off the same breaths as his lover.

Dante watched them curiously, wished he could speak the demon language enough to at least ask Armoni if the homosexual-seeming relationship before him was normal in Hell. And maybe ask if queerness was, indeed, the absolute greatest evil against God. But the angel wouldn't look Dante's way, his face set in a permanent scowl.

Afterward, Rosier nuzzled Asmodeus' face one last time, then he turned over to the angel and called his name, said some words in their tongue. Armoni soon stood, brushed past Dante, and walked toward the demons. Rosier handed him some bread, though not without offering Dante an apologetic look. Asmodeus limped away from the bars, toward the soldier, and shoved the last of his pastry into his mouth. Through his chews, he said, "Human." The soldier nodded his head affirmatively. "Don't worry about him." Armoni. "He's just an angel, but his wings are clipped. He doesn't like humans. Scared of them." At that, Dante raised a brow, but he let Asmodeus continue. "Also — the trial is happening soon, so if you could—"

"Asmodeus!" a new visitor called, turning the heads of everyone at once. A pink-haired demon with strikingly human clothing — a coat, a long dress, and heeled shoes appeared, hurrying down the steps. She skidded to a stop, grabbed the cell bars. Instantly, she groaned and shouted in the demon language: "What did you do?! I heard that you came back willingly!"

Rosier, beside her, quietly answered, "Yes, we thought it'd be safer to return willingly — but then an angel fell into Hell. His name was Dina, and Armoni told me he's young and kind."

Gemory turned her head. "Oh, my dear Armoni..." Pity flooded her face. "You're in here too. And you look terrible."

Armoni sighed, finally spoke: "Hello to you too, dear Gemory." He smiled tiredly at her. "Yes, apparently Dina came down. I don't know why. Asmodeus told me that, well, the *human* there told him that Dina was searching for the Watchers."

"The human?" Gemory looked over again, then gasped, spurring Dante to jump again, this time with heat rushing to his cheeks. Just as she started speaking to him, Asmodeus interjected to tell her what language to use, then she began again: "Boy," she said. "Man? What are you doing here?"

Dante blinked in surprise at her perfected accent, then looked at the others — Rosier's patient face, Armoni's sullen glare, and Asmodeus' bored expression. "Uh. Well, I followed the angel Dina down and another human. His name was Tadeo."

Gemory brought a manicured hand to her mouth, then bit down on her nail in thought. "Mm. I can't remember a Tadeo." She stared at Dante for a moment, then her own cheeks began to pinken before she looked away and laughed bashfully. "Well, it's a good thing that I've come! I can translate for you."

Rosier said, "Asmodeus and I can speak for him, as well, Gemory."

"Oh you be quiet," she shushed, then turned back to Dante and waved him over. "Come, come. Tell me everything."

"Gemory," Armoni called lowly, then muttered in their language: "You know better than to get close to men."

"Not all men are evil," Gemory grumbled at the angel, "only most of them." Then, she laughed at her own joke and reached through the bars to touch the wrist of a still flustered soldier — right above where his hand had been amputated. "Ignore my friend. He hates humans." Asmodeus had already said that, but Gemory clarified further: "And he's only in here because he's trying to hide from Moloch, I imagine. He's his slave."

"Slave?" Dante scoffed without meaning to.

"Mhm," Gemory said, nodding. "Or a captive housekeeper, if you will. After the world flooded, Armoni ran away to us and this wicked demon named Moloch took him in. He tricked Armoni into thinking he was kind, but no, no—" She wagged her finger. "He tried to hurt him, and then well, he was saved by this other demon, Mammon, and by Asmodeus over there, and—" Dante's confusion must have been showing on his face, and Armoni's anger was beginning to heat the room; and so, Gemory sighed. "Well, what you need to know is that Armoni begged Satan for help, and Satan handed him back to Moloch. You're not safe here even when the devil is around to control the demons, so imagine how much more terrible it is since he's been gone."

But something else that Dante had just learned was that Armoni had been involved with the biblical flood. Dina had said the Watchers had caused the flood. He turned slowly to eye at Armoni, whose mouth was pressed tightly shut. 'Tadeo's looking to free you,' he thought. But there were others. Where were the others? 'Tadeo.' His torturer. 'You cut my hand off but protected your own when the monster tried to burn you up.'

When he could, he'd tell his commanders: 'I think some of him needs to stay unharmed for him to heal. If you blew him up, all of him, at once — you could get him. Kill him.'

Before Dante could ask, there were the thuds of multiple feet climbing down the steps, and Gemory and Rosier hurried, together, down the staircase to avoid getting in the way of five guards, three dukes, and the regent of Hell. Baal was dressed as he always was, in his heavy robes and his laurel wreath, as he let out a long breath. Running his gaze over the prisoners and their visions quietly, some seconds passed before the regent gestured for the guards to go unlock the cell door. "Asmodeus, I really didn't want to do this." But his voice was gruff, almost sneering.

"Try not to enjoy whipping me too much," Asmodeus bit back.

And Baal laughed. "Don't ask too much from me, old friend."

Just as there had been when Asmodeus, Armoni, and Dante were brought to the prison, there was a march. This time, however, Rosier was allowed to walk with them, as well as Gemory. The demon of fruit held the arm and torso of the limping duke, and Gemory kept herself close beside Dante, whereas Armoni stood in between the two pairs, quiet. The climb up the spiral staircase dragged for several minutes, and Dante remembered the jogs he'd done around the military college, counting every second. Sometimes, he'd force himself to count in his first language. A tongue he'd wanted to contribute to the killing of, once.

But now, he forced it out again: *'Jun, cheb, oxeb, chaneb, jo'eb.'*

As they moved into one of the trillion red, dusty surfaces of Hell, he saw pulsing, bright orbs hanging from the ceiling, organs akin to hearts, burning, illuminating this part of the infernal world. Dante couldn't remember seeing any of this when he was led to the prison. 'Hell takes you where it thinks you deserve,' Asmodeus had said. It had no direction, no sense. Without demons, the keepers of Hell, to be your guide — eternal wandering would be the fate of any poor human who ever fell in. Dante had been lucky. 'Or unlucky,' he thought, staring ahead.

There was an amphitheater there — made up of archways and bones of every type of animal — and a crowding of demons. Heart stuttering, Dante also caught other creatures moving along the arches, on the open ceiling's edges, and flying in the air — made of muscle, but undeniably shaped like all the beings whose skeletons made up the building. Unlike the humans he'd seen — in the pyramid of blood and as living dust — the animals were perfectly distinguishable from one another, and they made the same recognizable communicative noises that they did on Earth. The soldier noticed how there were animals all over the stout, flat-roofed homes here. They were colorful, and some demons apparently maintained gardens by their front gates. As Dante was shoved forward, he stumbled, and Gemory quickly took his arm and snapped at the demon guards leading them along.

Asmodeus leaned in and quietly told Dante, "You won't be asked anything yourself, I'm sure. Baal is likely to send you back to prison for Satan to eventually deal with, so just keep still, don't act suspicious."

Gemory jumped in, whispering: "I'll explain everything for you."

"Thank you," Dante said politely, then nodded, firm, up at the demon woman and smiled. He saw her cheeks flush again, and she smiled back as Armoni sighed.

"I'll stay with you all too," Rosier said to Asmodeus, back in the demonic tongue, and now the duke let out a defeated breath, but he didn't argue, fearing the wrath that the fruit demon had earlier warned of.

They walked along the stone path, then through the first archway into a shaded space where hundreds of demons were all gathered in their long tunics and draped robes and their great horns, their swinging tails. When they saw the prisoners marching in, they surged forward, trying to look at them. Many of them shouted a particular word when they saw Dante, and he reasoned it was how they referred to humans. But their eyes were wide, fascinated, excited. There even seemed to be some cheers. Dante glanced up at Gemory for explanation, but she was shouting at the crowd to make way for them. And so it was Armoni, who grunted, who tugged on Dante's arm, who tried to answer with gestures of his free hand.

'What?' Dante had no clue how he'd been meant to interpret the angel's pointing at the demons, then at him. 'Is he trying to say that they're excited to see me? A human?' But why? The blonde loosened his hold on Dante, and then they were all pushed unceremoniously past another archway, into a circular area beneath the open roof of the amphitheater. There was a pulsing, enormous heart far above, hanging from the ceiling, casting a deep red glow onto the soldier and all those he stepped into the arena with. He was reminded of gladiator fights he'd seen in films; the building style begged the comparison, but the seats seemed more cushioned, and there was a stone platform at the center, up some steps.

Once they'd reached it, Dante noticed the cuffs and bolts at the edges, some dried blood on the ground; this is where tortures must take place. And it was here that he realized the absurdity of his situation, as well, and it took everything in Dante not to laugh. 'I'm in Hell. I'm really in fucking Hell.' Were it not for how Baal extended dark wings before them, flapped them hard enough to ruffle everyone's clothing and hair, the soldier would have cackled. The regent rose high, then dived toward a platform on one of the hundreds of rows of seats; there was a throne there, but it was covered by a mantle. In the crowd, there were thousands of demons, shouting, pointing, saying things to one another.

Behind him, Dante listened to some dukes step away, followed by a few of the guards. And he turned to see the dukes leave while the guards remained. They lifted their spears and pointed them at Dante, Asmodeus, Armoni. Once again, the soldier had to bite down a snicker. Just days ago, he'd been hiding behind a tank and having a gunfight, and now here he was, about to be tortured medievally, anciently for these monsters from a religion he despised. Following the lead of Asmodeus and Armoni, Dante stepped onto the stone platform and expelled some of Hell's heat from his lungs. Rosier and Gemory remained on the steps behind them, nearby but not so close to be mistaken for the prisoners.

Baal, booming, shouted for all the demons to quiet. Dante gathered that from his tone, the inflection, and the wave of silence that passed over the demons. And when he began speaking again, he directed it at Asmodeus, an accusation, then a taunt, then a laugh.

"You were forgiven," Baal was saying to the demons' ears, "Asmodeus. You broke one of the few conditions that Satan gives us — to never visit Earth without his explicit blessing — over and over. These past centuries, you haven't heeded the commands of the devil. You know the consequences that Hell will inflict on us if left untended by the demons, don't you? The fires would rage out of control, and everything would be destroyed. Even *we* might be destroyed. And — you have also neglected your duties in Hell as duke. You were forgiven because you returned willingly, and then you thanked us for our grace by committing treason. Why is that, Asmodeus? Are you tired of being a duke? Too addicted to smoking and fucking all the time?"

Just as Asmodeus had begun, speaking, however, another voice sounded out nearby. Another demon, in even more of a roar than Baal, shouted: "Enough with this shit show!" On the other side of the amphitheater, Dante saw a grinning demon with trimmed, red hair and a large body rise to stand on a makeshift platform that three demons were holding in place beneath him. One of them was red-haired like him, named Ara. But the loud demon, named Moloch, continued: "Baal, I hate to interrupt, but this really can't go on any longer." Baal, immediately, growled and stepped forward. "Where is Satan? It's been long enough. Tell us where he is."

"Moloch," Baal snarled. "What is this?"

"It's a speech," Moloch teased. "The demons are tired, Baal." He lifted a clawed finger, jabbed it in Baal's direction. "They are tired of *you*. Where is Satan? Hell suffers without him. Hell needs him. Tell us where you've hidden him."

"Satan has matters beyond attending to his spoiled children!" Baal spat. "Step down. Step down or suffer in a prison cell."

"You can't imprison us all, regent." Moloch waved an arm and other demons in the crowd hollered, raising their fists, calling the name of Moloch, demanding to know where Satan was. "You — Asmodeus." The demon of lust in question stared forward, as if he hadn't even heard the insurgent's call. "Come on, you most of all know that Hell has become unlivable under the rule of Baal. That's why you keep running away, isn't it? You know this place has rotten."

As this occurred, Gemory brought her face to Dante's ear and, voice quiet, told him: "That demon you see is Moloch. He was a duke once but Satan had his title taken away because he was so violent." Dante blinked in surprise, trying to imagine how any demon could be too violent for the devil. "He's been trying to build an army for the last hundred years to overthrow Baal." Gemory's eyes lingered not on Moloch but on Ara, the supporter standing closest to him, with a pitiful gleam. "He... wants to be at Satan's side, but he's cruel. He's crueler than anything."

"You're almost there, Moloch," Asmodeus answered, then tilted his head at him and laughed. "If I swear to you, you'll have the favor of the majority of dukes, right?" At that, Moloch twitched, and some of his own followers snickered at their hero's goals being stripped bare so inelegantly before everyone. "Well, what would I get out of it?"

"Not a whipping," Moloch joked back. "And an angel for yourself. You'd like that, wouldn't you?" He nodded his head, suddenly, at Armoni, then muttered more darkly: "You keep stealing my slave away, after all. How about we all go after that angel you set free, and you can have your own slave, so that you can keep your hands off of mine?"

When Moloch looked at Armoni, the angel's eyes widened in terror, and then he lowered his face quickly, and though Dante hadn't understood, he tried to gesture subtly. He pointed at Armoni, and then he waved a hand at Moloch, before making a slicing motion at his neck. He was trying to tell Armoni to kill him, but the angel shook his head gravely.

Ignoring them, Moloch turned up to Baal again and said, "Tell us where Satan is, and maybe there will be no new war in Hell."

The duke, again, said, "Step down."

"No," replied Moloch, grinning, baiting him. And he soon retrieved a stone from his robes, and he flung it across the stadium. He didn't hit Baal — in fact, he missed extraordinarily well — but the second the rock left his fingers, others in the crowd cheered and stood. Many laughed, many threw stones — those joining Moloch's army — and others threw objects just to throw them.

Baal growled, and then shouted, "Take the prisoners back to their cell," before he flew up into the air again, rose high over the crowd, then slowly, almost impossibly so, lunged toward Moloch. But whatever fight was about to occur — Dante wouldn't be able to see it. He felt himself grabbed by a guard, thrown off the platform to clumsily fall onto the ground with a hiss of pain and a twist of his ankle. At the same time that he was shoved forward to walk along-side Asmodeus and Armoni, however, the guards also frantically pushed back the demons scaling down from their seats onto the arena. Dante hurried alongside the two other prisoners, with only two guards dragging them along now, toward the archways. Chaos was erupting loud, bloody — yelling, shoving, brawls, stones flying. Far above, animals looming at the edges of the ceiling cackled and howled.

"We have to get away from these damn guards," Asmodeus whispered in Dante's language, and then he threw himself against one of them, making him stagger into the crowd. Then, Asmodeus took Armoni by the arm and tried to sink into the sea of demons opposite the guard he'd just shoved, and Dante understood. He hurried after Asmodeus, Armoni, and soon, the three of them were pushing through everyone, running. Briefly, Dante looked back only to see Rosier and Gemory trying to follow, however thick the crowd between them grew.

Armoni spoke, quickly, urgently. A quick string of words, some-thing about an 'Azazel.'

And before Dante could ask for translation, Asmodeus said: "We're headed for the Watchers."

CHAPTER 23

The anti-Christ, Tadeo, stared. Cold, a breeze sweeping by fluttered the rim of his hat, and the wind whistled in his ears. There were other sounds, of course there were — distant music from some yard, some faraway talking, the sound of cars on another road, a few barks, some bird calls — but though nothing had gone still, Tadeo couldn't find it in himself to realize that the world was still moving, breathing. How could the Earth continue to beat its heart if Tadeo was staring into the face of the devil? He was beautiful. Oh, he was beautiful — the shine of his eyes, the wisps of his hair, the pout of perfect pink lips in a sweet smile, the bronze brown of his skin, even his lovingly shaped, alluring build. And yet the human felt a sudden sickness in his stomach.

Tensely, Tadeo took a step back, one hand reaching for the holster of his gun on instinct only to find his fingers grasping at his weaponless waistband. "Devil," left his mouth, but it sounded like a question. "Devil," he said firmer. "You were—" That brilliant smile was so terribly familiar. "I know you— You were Father Ángel?"

"I spent a long time looking for you," Satan replied, voice precious silk. "I learned of a Beast, but even once I had, I didn't know which human of all the ones here you could be." The boy's single eye twitched. "Eventually, I learned that some priests knew of you, and that some criminals knew of you, as well. I could have disguised myself as either, but I'm very good at praying. I was an angel once, didn't you know?" The devil half-turned, took some steps, as if just to remind Tadeo how narrow the road was. "The angel with you knows."

At Tadeo's side, Dina was wide-eyed. He looked at the monster who'd destroyed paradise, half-expecting a primal rage to build up within himself for all of Satan's wickedness that had bled and scarred Heaven as much as the Earth. Instead, the angel's mind and heart were hollow. All the anger that should be there was missing, like he'd forgotten it happened at all, forgotten why he was here. Only Apsinthos spoke — 'Don't listen to him, Dina. Do not trust him. Do not believe him. He will ruin it all.' 'Ruin?'

The human furrowed his brow at the silent Dina, then turned back to Satan and answered, "I don't care what you've come for. You're nothing more to me than another criminal. I'll rip you to pieces like I've done to them, like I've done to the soldiers."

Satan addressed Dina: "Uriel looks for you, Dina."

Eyes widening — "Uriel...?" 'Don't listen,' the star urged. 'He lies, Dina. He's the king of lies.'

"He arrived like a horseman from the north, and he has brought death with him from Heaven. He holds his name in your mouth, Dina. I saw him. He's looking for you. He says... you're trying to save the world. Is that true?"

'It's a lie,' said Apsinthos again as the angel felt his heart sink, and suddenly, he felt. He remembered. Uriel telling him to stop the end times from coming. 'The war, Dina,' Apsinthos urged, 'think of the war.' The Heaven after the war, nearly all of the Heaven he'd ever known, the roads for the sinners, the penance, and then the Watchers, and Satan's feet tapping against the table as he taught young Dina to dance. Then the warmth of the devil's breath by his ear, his serpentine tongue flickering at the lobe. Satan's first victim. His plaything — Dina. And Dina's jaw clenched, in a way it'd never had. An anger that felt as ancient as he was. Dina was ancient; he had never felt the expanse of time that trailed from his shadow but he did now. "Be silent," he whispered, "Satan."

"Answer me," Satan snickered. "Are you here to save the world from the apocalypse, Dina?"

Tadeo interjected with an angry shout: "Look around you, Satan! Look at all the horror you have caused! Look at me!" He met the devil's humor with some hysteric, high-pitched laugh of his own, then lifted a hand to grip the bandages over the burrow in the right side of his skull. His fingers slipped between the white, felt the wet ooze of meat. "You don't know— You don't know how much I've suffered because of the evil of man. And you are responsible. You are responsible!" Satan tilted his head, almost curiously. "You will..." Tadeo felt himself tense, a flash of the smell of blood in his nose, of sweat, of men; and his voice began to shake. "You will never know what it is like to suffer the evil that you have created."

"It is all my fault?" asked Satan, almost gently.

Tadeo despised that answer, how playful it was. His heart had risen to his throat, and his eyes were instantly burning. He spat, "God will have you burned! For what you've done! God will destroy you!" His breath was coming faster, and he wanted to reach for the crucifix beneath his shirt to ground him back to the present but it was missing, burnt to nothing in Hell. And now the sound of his own panting made him think of men, of a dirt ground, of a lot. The resurrection he'd suffered for. "For all the evil that is your creation, that we have all had to suffer and die for, you will burn!"

"Does it," answered Satan, "make you feel better to think so?"

"That you will burn eternally? It does."

"Does it make you feel better to believe I was the one had those men rape and kill you?" Tadeo's blood froze, breath stopped. "Would it comfort you to believe that I was the one who had your father kidnapped and strung up, that I was even the one who gave your mother the stroke, that I was the one who ordered every massacre, every torture? Will it absolve them all? Would you forgive them? Would you be able to sleep at night believing that it is all the devil, that none of this is purely man?"

'God.' Tadeo was trembling again, but he shook his head weakly, his mouth opening, closing.

"Satan," Dina said slowly. "You will be thrown in the lake of fire. It is too late now to save yourself." He felt his star soothing him, encouraging his rage.

"We will save the world," Tadeo added, his voice still shaking. "Dina was sent to me by God to save humanity, and we will do it. There is nothing you can do."

Humming, the devil took a step closer, then another, then another. Tadeo, tepidly, lifted his eyes and had to suppress a shudder. When Satan had disguised himself as a priest, Tadeo had caught glimpses of beauty behind a terribly mundane face of false blemishes and too-perfect imperfections, but now he saw all that hidden loveliness without anywhere to hide. And he was catching glimpses of horror now, utter ugliness, grotesque redness at the edges. "Tadeo," Satan cooed. "Tadeo, Tadeo. But don't you... want to destroy the world? Don't you see how it has hurt you?"

"What?" left Tadeo's mouth before he could stop it, inflected somewhere between humor and disbelief and 'let it not be' fear.

"I asked if it made you feel better to tell yourself that I'm responsible for what happened to your parents, your home, and you. You didn't answer." Satan stopped, now just slightly out of arms' reach. "It's because you know that it doesn't. It isn't your fault. You've been taught all your life that there must be some scapegoat behind the actions of evil throughout history. You've been made to believe there is a devil, one who exists to tempt you to evil, rather than confronting that maybe it is all human nature. Maybe it is man who hurts man, mothers who hurt daughters, neighbors who kill neighbors."

Tadeo swallowed, shook his head again. "Do you think I'll ever be stupid enough to listen to what you have to say?"

"I wasn't there, Tadeo, when you died. I tempted no one."

"Don't listen to him," Dina whispered. "Don't listen to a word he says. Do not trust him. Do not believe him..."

Satan said, "I did not destroy your life, Tadeo. It was men who killed you. It was men who killed your father. It's men who killed the world you were promised as a child. And you know it. It doesn't matter how many times you've read the Bible. In your heart, you know the truth. And look for yourself." He lifted one hand to gesture to their surroundings how Tadeo had done. "Look around you." His words echoed Tadeo's own earlier, down to the cadence; the young man shivered. "You have tried to make yourself a saint, but it has not saved anyone. You don't even realize how much worse it's going to get. And you tried to save them all, Tadeo. You tried to save them, but only God saves, and there is no hope."

"That isn't true," Tadeo tried to say. "I've done nothing wrong—I've tried to just end this war!"

"You want to be a saint, but God needs a sinner," Satan told him. "Do you know why you are the way that you are, Tadeo? Do you really believe it was God that resurrected you into a beast?" Again, Tadeo's blood was cooling, and he wanted to cover his ears now, to beg Satan to stop speaking, to let him believe what he wanted. Even if it was a lie, it was the only thing he could bear. "Hasn't Dina told you?"

"Satan," the angel said, his voice attempting to sharpen only to break.

"You're," said the devil, "the anti-Christ." Tadeo blinked. "Of your beloved Revelation." Slow, Satan's lip curled back, revealed a cruel, bright smile. "You are the destroyer of Earth. You are no more than a false prophet, so false that you've even misled yourself. Even if this angel is trying to set you on a path to help the world, you can't deny what you are."

Tadeo breathed: "You're lying." But he could hardly hear Satan, his face twitching, his entire body leaning away. He was hardly thinking, only feeling. Confusion, bewilderment. "You're wrong." There was a sudden churn in his stomach however, like it was attached to a gear.

Satan laughed in his face. "Do you think God turns anyone into a beast? Do you think God would make something as awful as what you become?" Desperately, Tadeo turned to Dina but his brown skin was a shade too pale and his eyes were wide, almost bloodshot in what might've been terror, perhaps fury at the devil; the angel, however, wasn't negating Satan's words. "You know the truth, Tadeo. You can't argue. You're the anti-Christ. You're the Beast. You are the end times."

"I'm not!" Tadeo shouted helplessly. "I'm no anti-Christ! You're a liar, Satan! I've only done good, all in the name of God—"

"What does it matter if you do it in His name? God has a plan for you; do you think you can fight it?"

"You're tempting me," Tadeo spat, but he was shaking again, wanting to run, his skin hurting like it was pulled too tight over his muscles. 'The thing in me. The beast. It wants to tear out of me.' His breath nearly hitched. 'No, it's not a beast! It's not a beast! I'm no beast!' "Like you did to Jesus in the desert!"

"The anti-Christ compares himself to Jesus," Satan teased. "That is in Revelation too, isn't it?"

"Don't quote the scripture at me!" Tadeo snarled, this time a guttural rasp slipping between the syllables of a deeper, monstrous voice that was not his own, was not Tadeo. A beast, a beast. Immediately, the human slapped a hand over his mouth, eyes almost bulging out. 'No.' His back stung, and he could feel his skin knotting up at the back of his ribs, the sensation bringing a grimace to an already pained back.

"Oh," Satan continued to giggle, "of course. The scripture is only correct when the right person says it, isn't it? Some interpretations are wrong, some are right. God never says which. God is always silent. Even when you were mutilated, murdered, He did not say a word to you. He does not care about you. He does not love you. And you know that too, you know that as well as you do that I'm not responsible for your suffering. This world is utter rot, and it is because of men, and God knows to end it as well as I do. He has chosen you to be the apocalypse."

Dina tried to speak: "Satan, leave us! Or I will call upon God and all the archangels. I will have them throw you into the lake of fire!"

"With the boy?" Satan answered, voice as serene and light as it must've sounded in Heaven. "That would be lovely, wouldn't it? *Me and my child* — burning together."

This time, the angel drew a sharp breath, one then both of his feet staggering to bring him backward some steps. "What?" he breathed. "Child?" Quick, Dina flickered his gaze to the boy standing beside his horse, his eyes wide, lips parted. "That isn't true." 'Apsinthos,' he helplessly called. 'That isn't true, is it?' But now the star was silent, and the stare of Tadeo was endless, digging into itself like nail pressing into a wound.

Satan didn't address the angel. "Tadeo, come with me." The boy could only continue to stare. "No one knows your rage like I do, and I'm the only one who can help you destroy this place for good. It's what you want. How long will you allow this angel to deceive you? How long will you be the lapdog for those who are using you for their own gain? The people here have abandoned you, tortured you, scorned you. That angel is using you to gain the favor of his Lord, not because he cares for this world or for you."

"That's not true!" Dina hissed, shock fading to anger once more. "You're the deceiver!"

"Come with me," Satan said once more, "Tadeo."

But then the anti-Christ cackled, shaking his head, throwing his hands in the air like he'd just witnessed a great performance on stage or in a circus. "Come with you!" he taunted, shoulders shaking with his laughter. "How much of what you've said are lies, devil?! Was it only the part of me being your child or was it the anti-Christ thing too?"

Satan laughed right back at him. "You know the truth. Deny me all you like but you can't deny who you are."

Tadeo grappled the front of his saddle with one hand, then shoved one boot onto a stirrup before yanking his body up, onto the horse. "Bullshit." He took the reins, nodded at the angel, and said, "Dina, let's check in on my family. If they tell me that there's nothing I need to handle, then we're going back for the soldier."

"Anti-Christ," came Satan's voice, low, bristled with irritation in a way that Tadeo wanted to laugh and say was very parental. "You know the truth. The angel is deceiving you. You're the destroyer of Earth, and you are the son of the devil. If you continue to deny your rage, your world will just grow more rotten and evil."

Jerking his chin at the angel again, Tadeo watched as Dina's wings unfolded from his back, beat once to toss him into the air enough to fall onto the saddle behind the young man elegantly. Then, Tadeo turned back to Satan, smiled mockingly. "I have my father's eyes," he replied simply. "The color and the shape of them. And I have the exact texture of his hair. And his nose." He tilted his head, flaunting the side profile of his face. "So don't you try to trick me that you could ever," he suddenly snapped, "be my father."

Satan stared, expression like stone.

And, without waiting for a proper response, Tadeo swirled saliva in his mouth, then spat it at the ground between where he'd been standing and where the devil was, the breeze still tossing his hair beautifully, his cassock ruffled by the wind. Dina's arms went around Tadeo's ribs to hold himself steady, wings still partly out. "You will burn," said the boy, "as God promised you would, and I will be His sword if I have to. I will cast you down. And I will save this world from ending. I am no anti-Christ. I am no son of yours. I'm just a man trying to be a saint. Now, go back to Hell where you belong!" He tugged on the reins harshly, encouraging the horse into a walk, then a gallop, quickly.

But both Tadeo and Dina half-expected the devil to come after them, somehow — maybe do away with his disguise, peel back his pretty flesh to reveal the grotesque Beast that he was, lower himself onto all fours, then chase after them. Satan, however, remained still, where he was, watching the angel and his anti-Christ as they sped further and further away. Tadeo couldn't help but think of how the image of the devil turning into a Beast could be so reminiscent of the current turmoil beneath his skin, and so he frowned deeply, shifting his attention back to the street before him just as a turn approached. It was all he could do to try to stop his mind from wandering, from even taking a second to seriously consider any of the devil's words. He knew better. And yet.

Dina bit down on his wobbling bottom lip, his heart erratic and twitching in his chest. 'It can't be true that Satan is his father.' Tadeo was right; he had very distinctive features of the human father he'd lost. 'But why lie about this? To convince Tadeo to join him?' The angel turned back again, but Satan was gone. 'And did he... believe I'm here to save the world, after all?'

Tadeo, meanwhile, was trembling, his breath unstable and feeling like it teetered on an edge. However horrifying it was to be told by Satan that you had his blood running through his veins and that you were a weapon to end time — Tadeo was far more distraught by the devil mentioning that day he'd died. 'You didn't send them after me.' Tadeo had never in his life thought that Satan had secretly ordered soldiers to kill him, especially not the way he had, and yet he was utterly sweating, itchy, tensed by Satan stressing that fact. 'It's not about that day. It's about how maybe Satan isn't behind any evil acts at all. He's not responsible for this war or any wars.' But if Satan wasn't responsible for this evil, then what evils was he responsible for? Was it any of them?

As they continued onward, the sun beginning to set, the sky blooming red as the fires of Hell — 'Tell me that this is the devil's work, God. Tell me that men slaughter, rape, war, genocide because of the devil. Don't tell me this evil is human. Don't tell me that this is just us.'

CHAPTER 24

The last time the devil had been in Hell, he hadn't stayed long, but he'd restored peace in the infernal kingdom — for the demons, though the same couldn't be said for the tortured souls — and invited Azazel to dinner.

'A demon had come to free me from my bindings, then helped bathe me in water and milk before I was dressed in a freshly cleaned tunic, my face newly painted, my body smelling of lavender. They brought me to beautiful Satan in his dining room, in his tower, staring out a window at the Hell that he'd always told me I was responsible for. He saw me through the glass reflection, and he asked me if I was happy. I said that I dreamt of us, in some paradise in the sky that I'm certain never existed now. I served you, devil, some wine, and you spilled it. You covered your hair, and you didn't sing yet, like a young bird fallen from the nest, too weak to fly. I dream of us often, Satan. You dream of us, too. You used to dream of being me. Your hand on my chest, on the wound where my heart should be, and on my stomach; you wanted to bear my own memories. You wanted to feel the touch of a man. You wanted to be loved and discarded. And you wanted to create, but you already had, Lucifer. Your first child was sin, and now your second is damnation.'

In the caves where the Watchers were imprisoned, the angel Azazel opened his eyes from the empty sleep he'd forced upon himself; grunts and rattling chains sounded nearby. The darkness before him, however, was so thick that it was as if he were still trying to dream. He was seated with his ankles chained to the ground, as always, but his hands were free; whenever he was taken to the devil and returned, Azazel would almost never be chained to the same spot. This time, he was right across from the one angel he cared to be closest to the most. There was a shadow of a figure, someone slumped with his hands chained high and spread. Grunting, twitching like a starved monster.

"Samyaza," Azazel soothed in a whisper, then he rose slowly, bare feet planting over the pebbled ground. "You'll wake the others." He stepped forward, the chains connected to his ankle dragging like serpents over the ground, until he reached his friend, lifted his hands to cup his face. Though he'd long adjusted to the darkness, it wasn't always easy to see the details, even those that he was sure would haunt him in death. If he were ever to die. 'It's difficult not to think we're all already dead.' At his touch, the shuddering angel at the center of all the Watchers stilled but not without a hitched whine. "Good, good." He pressed his face to Samyaza's, nuzzled their noses. "If Armoni doesn't come soon, you can have some of me." 'My blood, my saliva, my tears, my sweat, or the wet of my sin.' It was all Azazel had left to offer.

Samyaza panted and without speaking, he brushed his mouth on the other angel's, then lowered his head, trying to reach Azazel's chest. There was a gaping hole there, where a sword had pierced through long ago, where a heart had been skewered out of him and dug into the body of a child. An angel-human child. 'You think that I didn't see you, devil, the day that you helped kill my baby. Your paled face, your wide eyes, the sudden horror on you like it was your own beating heart cut out. Does the devil regret? Do you wake from nightmares of my child that you murdered and need absolution?' Azazel raised himself on the tips of his toes and allowed Samyaza to drink from his chest, the wound.

Samyaza never spoke anymore; he could only ever groan.

'I dreamt, too, of the first day you freed me, Lucifer. Samyaza fought against his chains and demanded for the demons not to touch me, but I reassured him. I thought there was nothing worse that could ever be done to me than what had already happened. All of the Watchers were still so conscious then, not animals as they are now. And, for the first time, I was cleaned and dressed and, wonderfully, fed, before I met the devil once more. Lucifer, the one I'd last seen standing over me and the body of my massacred child even if I couldn't remember it well then. I remember it now. Or I've imagined it now and made it true. You asked me about my child. I said all of us Watchers had children. You said mine was different. You said mine was beautiful. It was not an abomination like the others. Why? Was it because I was with a man, not a woman?'

'Why was my child beautiful? Why did it have the beauty of an angel and the body of a human? Why did it have perfect wings spouting from its back? You asked me why me, why me. What was it about me and that dead man I'd loved that had beget a beautiful life? Was it love?'

Azazel pulled away, and in the dark, he caught Samyaza's mouth dripping blood.

At another end of the prison, a torch's glow swelled as a figure, ahead of many more, stepped out from a nearly infinitely long staircase. At either side of the narrow cave tunnel in the Earth, there were Watchers, their ankles and wrists cuffed and chained to the ground. Long ago, they had all stood as if crucified against the walls, but due to a cave collapse, they'd all been relocated, and this is what'd become of their bindings. All of them grimaced or hissed or covered their faces from Armoni, who looked down at them with pitying eyes and a frown. All the Watchers had matted, knotted hair, and many of them were naked to expose all their never-closing wounds, weeping blood as if newly cut. When they, one by one, seemed to realize it was Armoni, they nudged each other, grunted, gasped — but they didn't speak.

As Dante moved into the prison alongside Rosier, Asmodeus, and Gemory, panting from the climb he'd had to do for entire days, his legs burning, his head pounding — he stopped. He stared at all the naked Watchers, their quick glances and their reddened mouths. "What?" He hadn't been expecting anything in particular, and during the climb, he'd especially not cared for whatever they found, so long as it was safe from the chaos in Hell. They'd been particularly slow, given Asmodeus' weak legs and Dante's, however soldier-trained, human stamina and the bruised ribs. They'd rested, even slept, on the steps, and Dante had begun to imagine the red cave walls closing in to the sound of the distant groans of suffering souls. He'd never met his father, wondered if he was here. But — now that it was over — he remembered expecting angels. These chained creatures hardly looked like angels anymore.

Armoni spoke, softly, and Gemory translated quietly, her hand coming around Dante's arm: "The Watchers have been held here for thousands of years. The angels worked with the demons to capture them, kill their families, then imprison them under Satan's control."

"Their families?" Dante echoed.

Rosier was the one who answered this time: "They married humans and had children with them, but their offspring were horrible, monstrous giants." Dante remembered Tadeo in his monstrous body. "But much of that history, and that the angels relied on demon help, has been buried, not only for humans. For us, and for the angels — we aren't supposed to speak much of it, even if that terrible event, that flood, is why we all came to Hell. The devil tells us that God surrendered this place to us because he had the angel Michael act as his messenger to God and form a covenant with Him."

Asmodeus was leaning on the fruit demon in question and muttered, "I've never been convinced that the arrangement is as perfect as Satan says."

Armoni spoke again, this time with a glare, and Gemory giggled before she translated: "Armoni is telling us to get to walking so that we can speak with their leader Azazel. " Dante eyed all the imprisoned Watchers around him once more, and he saw that they were staring carefully at him now, one of them baring his teeth how a dog might. "Azazel is one of the only Watchers who speaks now." However tempted Dante was to ask for more, he simply followed along as Armoni began to walk in between the walls of prisoners.

On the shore, beneath nothing but stars — Tadeo had just arrived on foot after leaving his horse and belongings with his relatives, and he began walking straight into the sea. He was still shaking, despite how long it'd been since his confrontation with the devil. 'Anti-Christ. His child.' That wasn't true; it wasn't when the devil said it, and it still wasn't. 'But what's the alternative?' He swallowed thickly, then heard splashes behind him, and he stopped, turned swiftly, and said, "No. I'm sorry, Dina." The angel in question stood still, just some steps into the ocean, following behind the anti-Christ. "Stay on the shore. I think I'll go alone."

But the angel stared back with wide eyes as his hair was tussled by the breeze behind him. "Mm?" Then, he hesitated, and his gaze lost its shine like he was in deep thought or like he was listening. Apsinthos' voice said, 'He will get lost. Hell is infinite. He needs you.' "But," Dina said softer, "you don't know where he could be now. Hell is infinitely large."

Tadeo hesitated, but then he said, "I won't look long for him." 'Yes, I will.' "But even if he's dead, his family deserves to have a body to bury." 'Like my father, like maybe they should have done to me.' The memory returned to him of the beautiful devil, his smile as he spoke. 'The devil didn't kill my father.' "Dante," Tadeo added, shakily, "was a good man. Even if he was a soldier, he deserves to be put to rest respectfully." After this, Tadeo promised that he would be back soon, and then he walked into the water slow, wondering if this, his mere presence, would be enough to call the Leviathan to him. He walked on, trekking through the ice-cold waters, clenching his teeth. Once he was up to his chest, he turned back, and he saw the angel still there, the light of the stars casting an eerie pale glow on him so that Dina seemed a ghost. Trickles of hands brushed on Tadeo's legs, and he sighed shakily, prepared to be pulled under.

Dante, meanwhile, breathed out shakily, as they reached the other end of the prison. There was one olive-skinned Watcher in particular that was strung up unlike all the others, his naked body battered with swollen bruises and cuts leaking blood, eyes darkly framed by the marks of old punches, and before him, another Watcher. In stark contrast to many of the others, too, but in a different direction — this one wore clothes, a thick, pale robe with a hood over his head, where perfect braids cascaded down to his chest. When the clothed one turned to the intruders, his dark-skinned face was also painted with grieving white markings along his empty, tired eyes. Over his chest, his tunic was cut open to expose a deep, gaping wound that dug through the clavicle, through some of his spine, scratched at some exposed ribs, and the arteries still shaped around a heart that was no longer there.

"Azazel," Rosier called, but the chained Watcher behind Azazel jerked up his head, showed wide eyes, then growled, bared his teeth, wrestled against his bindings. And to the left, other Watchers startled from sleep or the comfort of their thoughts to look over, to join their leader in spitting, barking, hissing. But not all of them — to the left, the soldier noticed one red-haired angel with a dark mess of gore where his face should be sitting still, alongside an angel with patches of paler skin and dark hair trimmed close to his head, who remained silent but nonetheless kept a cold gaze on the human. On the right, there was a Watcher, perhaps the smallest in stature, barking and fighting his restraints the hardest, trying to break free to seemingly throw himself at Dante.

When Azazel spoke, voice delicate, dead — Dante couldn't understand, but Asmodeus, Rosier, Armoni, and Gemory heard: "Has the devil died?"

"Forgive me," said Armoni. "Moloch was holding me hostage or else I would have come earlier, and with food—"

"Psst," whistled a Watcher, cutting through all the barks and shushing them abruptly, and everyone turned to the quiet one sitting beside the red-haired angel without a face; Baraqiel and Kokabiel. At their attention, Baraqiel nudged his chin in the direction of Kokabiel, who had just lifted a foot, dug a toe into the dirt, then dragged it in a few different directions, scribbling, writing. Azazel stared at the sentence Kokabiel offered, and then he flickered his gaze up at the intruders.

"Someone is coming," Azazel said. "A beast."

"My child?" Armoni asked.

"Your child," Azazel answered, "is with this beast."

The Leviathan roared as it pulled Tadeo into the cave, but this time — the anti-Christ thrashed against it, yelling back as soon as he was into the air pockets. He ripped free one arm and dug claws into the body of the enormous sea serpent. Only a dent formed across its scales but the more Tadeo shouted in exertion, the more he pressed, and the greater the pain burned along his forearms — the closer he got to piercing skin. When the cave walls began to close in around him, he forced his body to grow against it and yelled out in this pain too, burgeoning wings and limbs trying to crack the stone embracing him.

Dante, frustrated, nudged Gemory, who hastily leaned down and translated, and then the soldier blinked. 'Beast?' Tadeo?

"Kokabiel says," Azazel whispered, "that this Beast is looking for us."

Distantly, there were noises, and even Dante recognized one of the voices as that of Baal.

"God fucking dammit," said Asmodeus. "We should get out of this place." He grasped Rosier's hand, and then he nodded at Dante and said in his language, "Well, here are the Watchers you were looking for. It's not safe to stay here longer. You can come with us or you could deal with whatever beast is coming."

Gemory quickly touched Dante's arm and said, "Or I can try to bring you to the surface— We're halfway there from here."

"Tadeo wanted to free the Watchers," Dante murmured to her. "But—" 'Is that a good idea?' He glanced at them, at the beautiful one standing by the most animalistic one, then at the one without a face, the quiet one, and the small one. 'No.' Hadn't Tadeo said these Watchers were going to save the world? It didn't look like it.

Again, Baal's voice sounded somewhere, closer, as well as the shouts of other demons and the clamor of their steps on the stairs. The regent of Hell must've been flying by the whipping noise of wings. "Fuck," Asmodeus said, and then tugged on Rosier.

But the demon of fruit looked back and said, "Dante, go with Gemory! If we can— If Asmodeus and I return to Earth, we'll seek you out! Good luck! You have friends in us!" The gentle, urgent kindness made Dante blink in surprise, and all he could do was watch as Asmodeus and Rosier began running opposite from Azazel and his favored Watcher.

Dante swallowed, and then he put his hand over Gemory's on his arm, leaned up to kiss her cheek, the corner of her mouth, then promised, "Thank you for the help. I'll stay here. I have to meet with Tadeo."

Face scarlet, the demon jolted, then she raised a brow. "Tadeo?"

"The beast," Dante clarified, then took a step away from her. "Good luck, miss."

Gemory's eyes were wide, but she soon nodded and smiled. "I hope to meet you again up there, boy." She started running too, in the same direction Asmodeus and Rosier had gone. And though Dante was left now with nothing but Watchers he couldn't understand, he turned to Armoni and Azazel. He saw as Armoni lifted his chin and whistled into the air briskly, and then he lowered a saddened face. Immediately, the cave around them seemed to shake, and Dante stumbled, falling nearly into a crouch.

"Kokabiel," said Azazel softly, "has told us that we'd be freed soon."

Armoni replied, "Don't do it, Azazel."

"Don't do what? Escape?"

"Don't hurt anyone that you don't have to. This is no one's fault but God's and the devil's." Even the men and women who had so terribly hurt Armoni were hardly responsible, he thought; the Lord had made them desperate and weak. Humans were pitiful creatures, and how could someone blame them? Slow, Armoni turned and saw Dante there, looking at him patiently.

Azazel said, "You'll come with us, won't you?"

"Yes. I have no choice, but—"

Tadeo heard, very distantly, a whistle, and then felt the Leviathan that he was wrestling in the cave halt, so violently that the anti-Christ was crushed against a cave wall hard enough that he felt muscles pop and bones shatter in his legs, his hips, and he screamed now, in pain. But, vaguely, he recognized that the

Leviathan had just turned directions and was now slithering rapidly through another channel in the caves between Earth and Hell. Tadeo continued to cry out in terrible pain, but he held on tighter and tried to bear it, wondering where he was going.

There was another sound out in the staircase, another voice — Moloch. Dante cursed. How many more people were they all going to have to deal with? But he relaxed when Armoni suddenly put a gentle hand over his own and stared at him. His mouth was moving, but Dante didn't understand, and just when Armoni seemed about to groan in irritation, Moloch's words became a lot clearer, his teases echoing through the Watchers' prison. Armoni's face paled, and then he shoved Dante toward the Watchers on the ground, in between two.

"Armoni!" Moloch continued to laugh. "Baal is satisfied with Asmodeus, Rosier, Gemory, and he thinks they hid the human somewhere else — but I know you're here. Come with me now or else I'll take it out on all your friends. You would think I fuck you or something with the way you act. Come home. It needs cleaning, and I would like some dinner."

Armoni swallowed visibly, then he put a hand over his mouth in Dante's direction, telling him to be quiet. "Goodbye," he whispered, then repeated himself for Azazel. "Farewell."

Dante watched over the shoulder of one of the Watchers he was hiding behind when the same demon who'd interrupted the trial stepped in, axe strapped to his back, chuckling. Behind him, there were three other demons with torches, but they stayed back and eyed the hissing Watchers cautiously. Once Moloch reached Armoni, took him by the hair, then nodded almost politely at Azazel. "Looking beautiful as always, Azazel," he teased, then yanked his angel slave away, heading back the way he came, until the cave around them rumbled again. And then, the ceiling creaked. Moloch cursed, hurried away from where dust was sprinkling down. When the wall burst open, Moloch and his demons were already running away with a struggling Armoni shouting for his child.

The Leviathan — more precisely, its massive head — broke harshly through the collapsing ceiling, and roared. And then, almost mundanely, another beast fell down into the Watchers' prison with him — a creature of four arms, four legs, and eight erratic wings attached to a shapeless form made of eyes, mouths. Tadeo, wrestling the serpent still but weakly, twitching, bleeding. He released the Leviathan, tumbled onto the ground not far from Azazel's feet and wasn't able to chase after the sea monster when it slithered back into its hole, bulleted in the direction that its parent was being taken in.

"Tadeo," Dante called, and then got to his feet, moving past the Watchers, toward the writhing beast on the ground. "We need to get fucking out of here and—" He glanced at Azazel, who was staring forward, who hadn't seemingly reacted to any of the chaos; Dante remembered he couldn't be understood. "You can't free the Watchers. You shouldn't. It's too dangerous—"

Tadeo let out a loud groan in pain, lifting himself up to face the soldier. "Dante—" Low, guttural, desperate. "You're alive— Come with me. I shouldn't have left you here—"

"What?" blurted the soldier, but then shook his head. "What the fuck do you mean? Aren't you here for the Watchers—?"

"I'm here because I left you behind," Tadeo said, but then he rolled onto his limbs properly, looking around himself at Azazel and at Samyaza, at all the Watchers, who looked at him wildly, fearfully. Familiarly.

Azazel stared back at the anti-Christ. Once, Lucifer had said, 'You are blessed to have not seen what's become of the Earth, dear Azazel. You will not recognize it. You will wish you'd finished them all off with your flood. The hole in you, where you are still bleeding, will dig itself deeper. You will see that they will all burn with us here in Hell. You will wish you killed every last man when you had the chance.'

The anti-Christ hurried over, took Azazel's chains, first, then broke them apart with his own hands. As soon as he did, he heard the distant shouts of Hell, as he had when he fell into it for the first time, but the howls were hollower, sadder. The souls of martyrs, betrayed and angry.

CHAPTER 25

The sun dimmed.

And, in Babylon, the archangels hadn't saved a single soul yet, their winged horses atop skyscrapers as they had been when Michael had, briefly, come to tell them that the devil had found the anti-Christ. In all his absence, Michael's fellow princes had been watching the nation of evil. There had been some parades — angry ones. Some were demanding the king to act, some were demanding that he shouldn't. Few angels understood what this was about, even less thought any of it to matter. There had been a massacre just outside the border of Babylon, of a few innocents, by armed men, and before that — there had been a massacre of armed men. But most of those in Babylon continued with their lives, irritated by the parades getting in the way of their walks. Prince Uriel had gathered that the Babylonian people saw the deaths as indicative of danger to their empire, feared they would somehow become the targets of the barbaric violence of those right outside their walls.

Though Uriel was tempted to speak of this to the other archangels, Gabriel was staring up at the sun — his hair was tied back, and he was the only angel who didn't wear a helmet — and he whispered, "It's begun, hasn't it?" Raphael lifted his chin and looked with him, and so did many of the angel army, but Uriel shut his eyes instead, as if that alone could make the sun's current state untrue. "The end..."

Raphael spoke with as soft of a voice as Gabriel: "Michael ordered us to find him in that place outside of Babylon when the sun dimmed." And then he tugged the reins on his horse to walk it away from the northern end of the building. "Come, you two. There is nothing we can do now. Michael was right, and I don't want either of you burned at the stake as he was. We don't only answer to God now. We answer to man, to Metatron, and this is the fate of humans that we must hand to them."

Uriel sighed loud, then opened his eyes, saw some curious humans staring up at the sun they could stare at with their naked eyes for the first time in history. "One might ask what the purpose of all this was — the fall, the flood, and now the end. If we angels and demons were going to suffer the same fates of serving — what was ever the purpose?" He guided his horse, however, to follow Raphael's, and the youngest prince, and all the army soon followed.

The human Joana, on the other hand, groaned awake. She had just peeled her body off the bed and sat up, turned over, and saw — through a crack in the curly curtain of her hair — a little boy sitting on the floor, against the mattress, her younger brother. It'd been a while since she'd been home so long, but she made a face at him like they still playfully fought, crawled off the bed that she used to share with him, and shoved him aside as he giggled. She went over to the tall drawer by a window, opened the top drawer, pulled out a soccer jersey and jeans, then went to get dressed in the bathroom. It'd been a day or two since she'd seen Michael, and she'd spent most of the time pretending to be ill. Her father hadn't been happy, had demanded to know the whereabouts of Tadeo, admitting to him that she didn't know. It'd earned her a slap, but at least only one, and she had needed a moment of peace after having to meet the chief prince again. Then again, spending a day in bed, on her cellphone, reading all about what Babylon was threatening to do hadn't made her feel any better.

In the kitchen, Joana's mother told her that it was noon; she was already making lunch — *enfrijoladas*. Joana told her that she was going out, staring at the black vest draped by a chair against the backdoor; her older brother's, the one he wore with a mask whenever he followed Joana's father to the ranches to deal with shipments. Her mother hesitated, then ordered Joana to be careful. "I know," she told her; it was always awkward between them. "Bye. I love you, *ama*."

"Come back for dinner. I love you."

Only once Joana had stepped outside did she realize that the darkness wasn't due to the clouds. She walked down the sidewalk, headed for the corner store that was one of the few places still open during this gasoline cutoff, then saw some soldiers on their truck, staring up at the sky. She followed their gaze; then, she saw it — the sun. It was dark, though some light still bled from its circumference like an eclipse did. It wasn't burning her eyes to stare at, however, nor did it seem to bother the soldiers who squinted, one of whom raised his phone to take a picture.

"Joana."

The human in question jumped, then jerked her head to the side to see Michael standing right beside her, his winged, armored horse nibbling on a patch of grass behind him. Like the last time she saw him, his helmet was off, tucked under an arm. When their eyes met, she swiftly turned back to facing forward, and she whispered, not looking at him: "What are you doing here?" Before he could answer: "Look— I told you never to talk to me again. And I have a lot to do. They're gonna tighten the border. They want to airstrike us. Just the bad guys, they say, but I know the truth. I know what they want to do. You should go." It didn't matter how nice it'd felt to sit with the prince at a table, or how safe she'd felt in his arms after the night with Lupina. He was not safe, after all. He was not going to save her. The saint Michael, chief prince of Heaven, did not save anyone.

'You're not going to help? I asked you that when I told you about all the horrible things that have happened here. You just listened, just stared. You don't want to help me? You could help my dad, at least. Get us money. You could clean these streets. You could do something. I'll never forget how you looked at me, saying nothing, then lowering your face. I wish you had done it ashamed. I wish you were ashamed to submit to God and to the world you decided it wasn't your responsibility to fix. Why ever did I look up to you? Why ever did I get so excited to see you, to talk to you, to try to make you smile? Why did I want to make you proud? You're not my father.'

Michael said, "The end times are near. I wanted to tell you again that I'll bring you to Heaven at the proper time." Not responding, Joana reached into her back pocket for her pack of cigarettes and lighter, but she had forgotten to grab it on the way out, so she frowned. "I can take you somewhere." The prince's voice was fragile, almost desperate. "When the other princes arrive, and when the first trumpets of the end sound, I'll mark you with the blood of the lamb. And you'll rise with me. You'll be safe."

Joana snorted, then turned on her heel, the conversation making her blood run hotter and hotter; she couldn't be trusted not to raise her voice, and the last thing she wanted was to attract the attention of the soldiers. She began walking, and she mumbled, "Goodbye, Michael." The prince called after her again, and she could sense him following, along with the heavenly horse. "Leave me alone. I'm not going to tell you again." 'I sound like my father.' She was headed toward a church, without meaning to, the same one that Tadeo went to often, the one with Father Toño and the new beautiful priest. 'But when I last talked to you, I made my choice too, Michael. Better a cruel father than an absent one.'

Michael continued, "You'll finally know peace, Joana."

"Maybe I don't fucking want peace," Joana snarled, stomped past a street, onto the green of the plaza before the church, then turned around and faced Michael with all the anger she'd cradled in her chest for years, for years. "I don't want to go to Heaven, and I don't want *peace* anymore." All the televisions ever spoke about was wanting peace, about how we must pray for it. But peace? Peace is a convenient thing to pray for. Peace doesn't discriminate. You can end violence by protecting the innocent or killing every last one of them. 'Peace means nothing; peace means anything.'

Michael was quiet for a moment, and he wished he wore his

helmet to hide the pain he knew was flickering over his face. When she had come to him once, complaining about her father for hurting her, her brothers, her mother, the more that he spent time with bad men — the prince had asked her to forgive him. That is how Fathers are. They are always right, in the end. It hurts to obey; it hurts more to rebel. "You'll understand once this is all over."

"No, Michael," she said lowly. "I understand it all better than you."

'I don't regret it,' Michael told himself. 'I don't regret saying what my Father would.' But he wanted Joana to talk to him now like he hadn't said it. Was that regret? "When you," he continued, "hear the first trumpet, look for me."

"I have siblings and a mother," she said. "Them too?"

He couldn't answer that. All the archangel knew was that she was kind-hearted, even if she didn't see it. Even if she had hurt people. Michael would ask forgiveness on her behalf. He would even pay the price of penance for her. "I'm sorry," he said. Joana thought Michael was a ghost, but it was her that had been a ghost of him since he met her. Her ambition, her anger. It was familiar.

"Michael," someone called, not Joana, voice too beautiful. As the prince and the girl turned around, they saw that the plaza was unnaturally desolate, no food carts in sight, no families. Only one bench, the one ahead of them, was occupied by a beautiful priest with a wide grin.

Instantly, Joana tore a pistol out of her waistband with the force of pulling a rib out from her body, lifted, then aimed it right at the face of the devil. "What—?" she barked. "Where is everyone?" She'd nearly never seen this park like this, especially not since the gasoline had been cut off, and no one in her entire life had ever acknowledged Michael in front of her.

Satan met the weapon without a flicker of emotion, and instead he turned halfway, took a few steps with his hands behind his back, fiddling with some rings, whereas Michael's own hands had turned fists. He hurried toward Joana, wanting to grab and throw her behind himself, but then the devil spoke, and Michael's muscles all shuddered and froze. "The people here," Satan was saying in Joana's language, "are hiding. I told them to. There's going to be an attack soon. Listen — there are silver birds in the sky, but they may have gone to the outskirts by now." Joana's aim followed him until he, abruptly, stopped, and she had to take a moment to inch her gun's end back to hit right at his golden head. "There are still so many... trucks passing through. They never run out of gasoline."

Michael, this time, stepped forward, moving past Joana but not before her like a shield as much as he wanted to. "The sun has darkened, Satan." He lifted a hand, set it over the girl's, gently tugging it downward, guiding it down. Joana resisted the first tug, but then she breathed out shakily, inched it lower, lower.

"And the moon," the devil mused back, "will tint red."

Joana refused to take her eyes off Satan, to shift her aim for even a fraction of a second. "You're—" He caught the outfit, the face. "You're the priest, the new one."

"I could have been," Satan continued in that distant, soft voice, "the first priest. I might have been the first to lead worship and tell others to celebrate for that great Beast above is our God, and He is Good, and He is great." A smile bloomed over his mouth, then he turned to the girl and said, "Michael. She looks just like you."

Immediately, Michael's lip curled back and he barked: "Leave us. It is too late. The end has begun, and you will burn soon. The boy will return any moment now— The anti-Christ, the Beast—" He was trying to speak in the angelic tongue, but the devil refused to respond in it.

"My child," finished Satan, but then his face twitched, a flame igniting over golden eyes, before he reached into his pocket, drew out his revolver, lifted it at Joana before she could raise her weapon again. But Michael swerved his body and moved before her in time to catch the bullet properly in his face this time, felt it spear between his eyes, shatter out through the back to splatter Joana in angelic red. Through her shout, the prince steadied his foot, cried out in pain, in fury. "Fuck you," the devil seethed, still in Joana's language, wanting her to hear. Michael couldn't see it, his vision overwhelmed with the blindness of pain, his body still recoiling, all his blood hot and thick as it began to dribble down the front of his armor.

Panting, panting, Michael had expected the gun to hit his chest, his armor. After all, Satan had aimed for the low-statured Joana, and yet, the archangel's face was burst open, his heart pounding in his ears, water out of reach, God not healing him. The bullet had been perfectly aimed for him. 'You knew,' Michael thought, 'that I'd jump in front of her.'

"Fuck you," Satan snarled, before another bang struck at Michael's knee, made it jerk even if it didn't cut through the armor. "You damn dog!" Another shot, this one hitting his chest, and Michael felt a thud so hard on his sternum that it was as if the bruise had come before the bullet. "You couldn't live knowing I had a world of my own. You couldn't imagine not listening to your Father." Shot, after shot, after shot, and Michael took each one painfully, even if he couldn't see, even if they didn't tear. "And now everyone will die because of you! A world that didn't need to end! An apocalypse that never had to come!"

'An apocalypse that never had to come?' It hadn't fully occurred to Joana that the apocalypse really could have been prevented, nor that the devil wouldn't have wanted it. Even still, she raised her gun again only for Michael to reach behind himself blindly, grab her wrist, then stumble when she accidentally shot it against his armor.

"Shit," she said. "Michael! Let go of me! What the fuck are you doing?!" Joana yanked at his hold frantic, panicking. "That's the fucking devil—" 'The devil who doesn't want the world to end.' Just like her.

"You will burn, Michael!" Satan hissed. "You will allow God to rule over my sin because you are *cow*ardly! God will not save you from Hell! You will burn—!"

"I have *already* burned!" Michael screamed back, the upper half of his face still torn apart. "Because of you! Because of what you did to me! You corrupted me in those caves!" And he swung his free hand behind himself, grappled the sword there, then flung it forward at the sound of Satan's voice. A hiss sounded, then a clang of the weapon hitting the ground. It must've scratched at Satan's skin, at least — that was all the chief prince wanted, to tear open that perfect bronze skin, to make the devil bleed. To hurt him, to make Satan hurt how he had hurt as his body burned at the Fountain of Life in Heaven.

Instead, he listened as the sword scraped against the ground, someone picking it up.

Michael, once, had taught a young Lucifer how to hold the sword. They'd been on Earth. Beautiful, smiling, the angel of worship had looked up at the chief prince with such utter sweetness that his heart had melted. He'd really loved Lucifer. He'd really liked him. He missed his mouth, his kisses, how they'd laid tangled over the grass of paradise.

Joana's scratchy, damaged voice: "Michael! Move!" At some point, the archangel had removed his grip from her wrist. And she watched as the devil reeled Michael's sword with hands on the hilt, then stepped toward, tried to raise it before the girl had realized she was free now to lift her gun and shoot it. Desperate, she stepped back, tried to move to lift it, but her back sneaker stumbled onto a pebble and, for the first time in years, her hands were nervously, suddenly unfamiliar with what part of a gun did what. She could only watch as the devil swung Michael's sword, surely to try and cut through the armor of God. Instead, the beautiful, perfect wrist of Satan was grabbed in the air, twisted enough to make him drop the blade back to the ground with a thud.

Behind the devil — a figure like a horseman in silver armor, atop a pale steed. One gauntlet had its fingers curled tight by Satan's palm, and when he spoke, it was with a deep, rumbling voice: "Satan. Stop this." Instantly, however, the damned one tore away his arm, stumbling backward, eyes wide, back hunching like an animal that knew itself prey or was feigning to be. Nearby, there was the sound of gallops — the other angels, other archangels.

"Uriel," Michael managed through the blood in mouth, feeling two hands come across his torso, like they could hold them up. Small, delicate, yet strong grip — Joana.

Far above, there were shrill cries. Stars were speckling through the sky, and the blue was bleeding dark. All the constellations were shifting as every speck of light grew wider and wider. The stars were each letting out cries, songs, of their torture. God's first victims, startling awake from nightmares. All this at the same instant that a silver eagle dropped its first strike on a road south of the town.

Far away, the Watchers had come out from the ocean and reached the shore, breathing in air that seemed too dense, listening to the same screams of the stars as all those on Earth did. Drenched in water, Azazel was the first to step onto the sand with bare feet, lifting his face to meet a night sky that was nothing how he remembered it to be. Samyaza was close behind, hunched with a collar and chain connecting him to Azazel's hand.

Tadeo was panting for breath, a half of him still a Beast, the other half of him holding Dante's arm as they stood, almost doubled-over, in the shallows. "It's—" He looked straight at the wine-red, full moon. "It's the seventh seal. It's—"

On the shore, Dina looked up at the screaming stars with wide eyes.

And Michael put a hand on Joana as well, holding her against him, trying to steady them both as the screams continued and continued. He, alone, didn't look up in horror. He couldn't see. He could only imagine. Long ago, he'd told the story of how the Lord had made his first angels into stars, and the sweet Lucifer he spoke to had smiled, had really believed in God's mercy. He'd had so much faith once. Michael had too. He did have faith still. In what? In the end. Maybe his own end now. There are those who have faith in God's love, those who have faith in God's wrath.

Lucifer and Michael on Earth. That was lovely to remember. Michael almost wanted to say, 'Do you remember when all of us were angels,' and it was only our tears that fell, some for joy and some for any crack in the stones without a flower blooming in between? Even in paradise, we found things to grieve. Maybe there was never any eternal happiness, but there was infancy. And now Heaven is a fairytale of nostalgia. It was all better before. Take me out of this world I never asked to come to. Bring me to the gentle Heaven where this all began. This became too frightening for me, too true. Let's return. Let's return to angels before man.

PART II
NEW EARTH

CHAPTER 26

'T,' thought Lucifer, 'remember.'

'The day I heard of Christ, I said that he was no son of God. I insisted it. If he performed miracles, they were not very impressive; they were mere illusions like those of water for the dying parched. The healing — I only saw it once or twice for myself. Like the humans, I simply heard of a man of Nazareth who could be the son of God, then I was asked to have faith — but there are countless sons of God. Kings, prophets, they've called sons of God. Once, they called the angels the sons of God. So who is this Nazarene man to believe himself so special? There have been many before him that have thought themselves angels and flung themselves off high mountains. A star shone over his head in Bethlehem, as his mother birthed him into a manger, but stars shine over every child every night. As a boy, he preached to his rabbis, but I met him in the desert, and I left him because if he were a son of God, if he were God — he would have taken the world back when I offered it.'

'When he was put to death, and his body was the last one of three still rotting on crossed wood — I told him, "Free yourself. Son of God. If you are the Son of God, then take out the nails from your palms and your feet. The men crucified with you are already dead, and I have led away your guards. No one will see you leave this place. Or do you want this death for yourself? Is your heart broken by the betrayal of your own people and your most beloved disciple? Let me tell you, son of man, that he never did think you could die. He lied to himself as much as he did to you. He swore he didn't believe in you, and now he will kill himself. You were always his Messiah; you were always his Son of God. He realized it when he kissed you, once it was too late." The Nazarene man answered me with a groan in agony; blood spewed from his mouth, and the birds on the arms of the cross sang. "Or will you save him? Are you the Son of God and can you remove the nails from your palms and heal yourself like you healed so many others? You say you are here to save every soul, but you cannot even save one? Are you the Son of God? Are you the Son of God?" He was silent.'

Lowering his face from the screaming stars, the devil heard the thumps of hooves stuttering to a stop all around him, then he heard the quiet voice of a messenger angel say, "Lucifer—" Satan's gaze flashed to the east, where an armored figure was perched on a midnight-dark horse. 'Gabriel.' There was another call to his attention, and the devil turned west to see a figure on a white horse with a staff on his back, the top of it visible over a shoulder — as if that were his sword. 'Raphael.' In between the princes, there were several others on horseback — faces all shielded by the same type of helmet that Michael had worn since the war for Heaven. Wings of every color were exposed but folded close to their angel backs. No man in sight, no man of Nazareth.

Revelation proclaimed that the Son of God should be among them with a sword of wrath, but if he were here — the devil couldn't find him.

"Satan," came the voice of Uriel once more. "You've done enough meddling in human affairs and in the apocalypse. You're to be brought to God, where you will be judged, then you will be cast back into the lake of fire, as was promised." He had to shout over the yells of the stars, but his words trembled.

'As was promised in what was meant to be the Last Judgment of the angels,' thought the devil. 'God will try to beckon me to Him one last time. He does not want me to burn. He would miss me.'

Satan met Uriel's scorching gaze — almost entirely hidden by the helmet where slits in the metal hung over where eyeballs should be — with an uninterested, steady expression. Without a word, he looked to Michael again, the saint with a deep, wide wound in his face, where Satan had shot him. 'All the hate that every living thing harbors for me — and yet, all of you will yearn for me forever.' What was life without a reason to live it? What was good without evil?

"My demons," said Satan finally, "will come looking for me." He didn't bother to raise his voice much, even as the sky's hum grew louder — the shrieking stars and a distant rumble above. "They have orders to."

"Your demons will not reach Heaven," Uriel said.

"None of us will reach Heaven," said Satan, staring still at Michael, at the chief prince leaning on a girl, who stared at the devil warily. 'She could be his daughter.' He inhaled through his nose, then expelled the last of his earlier panic through his mouth. It would do no good to shoot at Michael again, and his revolver was out of bullets — but it'd felt good. Michael deserved to be put down like an animal; Satan was sure that he, secretly, craved it. However, the devil was not the one who decided what souls deserved. He did not pass judgment. He did not choose which of the dead went to Hell, nor did he choose how they suffered. The devil was just a witness; that was the privileged position that the Lord offered to him. The Lord, our God, sat with the devil and showed him that He was cruel, so that one creation, above all the others, would really know Him, know God as He cruelly was.

Michael coughed out red, and Joana put an arm on his torso, before he hissed, "You made the covenant. The Lord offered you control of Hell, and in return — you would come before God so that the angel Lucifer can be resurrected."

Satan said, "You are like a child." Michael could not really conceive of death, could he? He must think all things can be brought back, that all can be put back together again.

"You will be taken to Heaven," the saint said harsher, "devil."

As he said this, the rider on the white horse, with the staff on his back, guided his steed toward Michael. With a vial that was hooked to a sash across his waist, Raphael dribbled water over the head of the prince. The angel of healing, the prince of medicine, needed no more than a few droplets to have the fragments of the chief's upper skull shift into place, for the muscles beneath the bone to bubble and grow back as skin. With a blink, his eyes, emerald and earthy brown, returned, as did his strong nose, with the hill on its bridge, and his thick brows. His dark hair streamed down in loose curls that nestled at his nape, a few strands coming to fall over his face. Joana loosened her hold on his torso, and Satan noticed again how similar they seemed at a glance. Certainly, the saint and the girl appeared more blood-related than the devil and the anti-Christ.

'Tadeo.' Satan clenched his jaw. 'I can still feel, in my arms, the weight of a baby, its shape not much different than a human infant's, except for the folded, pale wings, nuzzling dark hair tumbling down to a soft throat. Angels don't have wings at birth; they gain them, gorily, when they first fly, but the child of an angel is born with wings without having suffered their first blood like we have.' Satan could still remember beady eyes looking up at him. 'I wanted to be angry that you didn't look like me, but my first child had dark hair too. His name was Cain. One night, I sat by the fire, holding you in my lap, telling you every detail of the first human boy. I took care of him, and I will take care of you too. If he were still here, here with us, then I would tell you to call him brother. Little thing, I will not lose you too.'

'I hope that it burns,' Azazel had said during one of Satan's visits to Hell to ask, too prideful to beg, for help rearing. 'I hope it burns with you as Hell grows hotter.'

'We are all going to burn,' Satan had told him. 'At least, in the fire, I'll be holding my child. Love is all you were able to offer yours too as it lay dying; isn't that right, Azazel?'

For as cruel as his words had been, the Watcher had simply stared at Satan warily, for the devil's voice was not as angry or as taunting as it always was. It was almost soft, fragile. Oh, Azazel must've been so sure that the devil had just stumbled, allowed his cold demeanor to slip — but the angel couldn't know how great of a liar that Satan was, how he could mimic even the most instinctive wobbles of a broken voice. He was such a great liar, in fact, that Satan no longer knew when he lied. Was there any truth to him now? He didn't know. Sometimes, his reflection sang to him, like an angel or like a singer on a stage or like a choirboy of a bygone time. Lie after lie, until they made him up.

Satan stepped away as one of Michael's hands went for the chain links across his torso. 'You'll bring me to God, then try to cast me down again, chief prince?' There were times that surrender sounded so sweet. Lucifer was dead, and Satan was elderly. He was tired. 'I'll take you down with me this time, Michael; and you'd let me.' Even still, Satan tried to shift back, away, until he heard the thumps of Uriel's horse approach. All the angels had surrounded him — Satan could see it from the corners of both eyes. He could not run, and the demons could not come save him either, not yet. 'Baal, Baal, Baal,' he wanted to grunt. 'Do not fail me.' In the distance, the sound of shouts and some cars screeching, and then the padding of feet. Humans must've heard the stars too, must be looking up at them in confusion, many in terror, a horrible few with vindication.

And then, suddenly, Joana turned her face to Michael and said, "Don't do this."

"Who are you?" Gabriel called quietly; in all his time on that horse, right nearby, he hadn't said a word, but when he finally did, Joana's head jerked upward. She'd understood that. It wasn't quite in her own language, but the divine messenger's question was so comprehensible that it felt as if she, suddenly, knew a single phrase from his own tongue. Except, Gabriel directed his next words to the chief prince — "Michael. Who is this girl?" — and, to Joana, he'd become incomprehensible again. A tonal language, only capable of brokenness in its pidgin, perfect nature; a mass of consonants with the occasional high vowel.

Michael didn't reply, tearing the chain off his body, reeling them behind, twirling his wrist.

'I can remember how it hurt still.' Satan wanted to say that he remembered having his wings cut off more than he remembered what loving Michael had been like. 'I don't think we ever did love each other. If I were not the devil, I'd say God was right all along. We knew not what we did.' He turned, slowly, to face the saint, lifted his chin elegantly, silently telling him to do it, then, to bring him back to his Father, to see Him tear Satan to pieces, then set a broken, remade angel before His prince. 'To teach Michael that what is dead is dead. There is nowhere to go, no return, no Heaven, no Hell. Lucifer is dead, and he cannot be brought back, and you have killed Satan in the fix. How many times will you kill that body you'd once kissed all over? How many times will you kill him before you can make yourself stop loving him?'

The chief prince met his gaze sternly, twitchingly, saying nothing to his faux daughter or to the other archangels, before he flung out his chain, and the devil grit his teeth as it snaked around his body to make every part of it feel the hard whip, to crack each bone beneath, then scald his skin. He staggered, without meaning to, felt the top of him hunch forward blindly. 'The day we demons stepped into Hell, it met us with flames. I told them, "Do not put them out. Control them, as I have nurtured you despite how you are as destructive and wild. Do not be afraid of the lake of fire." There are worse ways to suffer, God, than a lake of fire. We have created it together, on Earth — you and I.' God's guiding hand over his, telling Satan where to cut, where to bleed.

A growl and a gasp shot out of Satan's mouth as the chain continued to burn at him, and then Uriel said, "You will come quietly."

There were many humans now — in their pants, their shirts, in uniforms for work or for school, looking utterly mundane in the face of divinity. Satan could hardly see them, but they had wormed their way through the crowding of angels and their steeds, and then many more were steps further back, trying to peer in between with their own eyes or with cameras. Man, woman, child, elder stared with hitched breaths, and a few spoke, but the screams of the stars drowned them out, and their hushed words were not ones of rejoice. Joana, like them, didn't feel like any of this was victory. Tadeo had read the Book of Revelation to her, even when she had grumbled at him to shut his delusional mouth because she had no interest in prophecies, but she'd note the hopeful note in Tadeo's voice. It was, ultimately, a story about good defeating evil, and so why didn't it feel that way? Why was Joana feeling her heart shrink in a cold terror and gripping at her shirt with a sudden childish want for someone to tell her what to do right now when all she wanted was to cry. "Michael," she tried again. 'Stop,' she wanted to snarl at him. 'You stupid idiot. You coward. This is all wrong. You know it. You can feel it too, can't you? You don't want this either. Don't do any of this.' "Michael."

The prince stepped forward, and the stars were still screaming, and when Joana glanced up to look for them, she saw silver birds, drones, parodies of angels in armor. Somewhere, Joana could hear it barely, barely — there was a *boom* like fireworks for the new year. But Michael continued, moved to loom over Satan just as he'd fallen onto his knees but continued to stare back, eyes determined, hot with anger. Slow, Michael reached for him, using the hand that didn't hold the other end of the chain, and gripped Satan's cassock by the throat to raise him slowly, back to his feet. "Joana," he addressed. "Go and hide for now. I will come back for you."

"Don't do this," Joana now freely said, though her heart hammered in her ears. "Fuck, don't *kill Tadeo*."

"I have no choice," Michael said.

"Fuck you," Joana said. "Use some goddamn free will. Don't end the world, Michael." Her heart stuttered, then her gaze flashed to Satan once more as she realized what should have been obvious from the start: "The devil was the one trying to save this world from apocalypse, wasn't he?" Neither Michael nor Satan replied to that, neither did the archangels. And so — Joana laughed, felt her shoulders rattle with the force of it, as she inched back, blood cold. 'The world is so fucked up.' She wished that Michael hadn't jumped before her, wished Satan had just ended this all right then.

Carefully, Uriel turned his horse away, and when he gave it a light kick, it began to walk. The sea of angels parted before him, and the humans hurried to follow suit, some taking this moment to begin running, to head where so many humans must be. "All of us will escort Satan," said Uriel, "then we will return to finish the job." But he stopped to look up at the stars. "The world will be no more, and the anti-Christ will be cast to the lake of fire."

'Tadeo,' Joana wanted to wail, 'where are you? Where are you? I have to tell him not to return. They'll kill him if he returns.'

"Yes, Uriel," said Michael, and Uriel, then Raphael — who looked back to the chief prince for too long before twisting his face back to follow the angel of wisdom — then Gabriel, who stared at Michael for some moments, as well, before he turned to Uriel. Only then, the chief prince faced Joana once more, reached for his helmet, lowered it over his head. He promised again, "I will return for you."

Words a tangle in her throat — Joana watched. Michael went to a winged horse, armored but not enough to hide its body the color of blood, and lifted the chained devil on a silver saddle. When an airstrike, down just a few streets, flared the sky in orange, Michael didn't react, not when the ground rattled nor when humans yelled out in terror. None of the angels said a word at all as the people took one another's hands, began hurrying away, shouts of fear trailing behind them. Joana's vision hazed, and she felt her knees knock together. Darkness bloomed over her eyes before some hands came over her, some voices asked what had just occurred; it was Tadeo's family, his aunt, one of his cousins. But Joana could only painfully choke up in response.

CHAPTER 27

Shivering, Tadeo held onto Dante as he lowered his face, furrowed together his brows. The last of his beastly features receded slow with wet squelches, then he felt himself wobble, but one of his hands clutched at Dante's jacket a tad tighter for stability. All of his body continued to ache and itch. And he might've been too hasty to transfigure back into this body — all his organs felt tilted, awkwardly shifted from their typical positions, some too heavy. In the pit of his stomach, there was a burrowing hole that some insides dribbled into. But Tadeo could only look ahead. The angel who had led him here, the beautiful Dina, who bore an empty expression as he stood on the shore; he appeared to be listening again. In the last instance of this, Tadeo had thought he was consulting God. But he felt no holiness now, nor divinity, as water lapped at his ankles. Something was wrong. The stars still screamed.

The thuds of feet running called Tadeo's attention, and he weaned himself off the soldier's support before looking to all the angels he'd freed from the sea. Many of them sprinted, stumbling, and laughing as they came up to the sand to collapse onto it, over stomach and over knees, in what the anti-Christ couldn't help but find reminiscent of soldiers arriving home victorious, yet agonized over the horrors of war they'd endured, never once worth their lives. Up ahead, the dark-skinned, braided one stood, staring forward, still holding onto the chain leash of the twitching, one-winged Watcher.

"What the fuck is going on out here?" Dante asked, his hand returning to Tadeo's arm, squeezing it. "What did you do? How long has the sky been screaming?"

Immediately, Tadeo grumbled, "It wasn't like this before I came back for you."

"For me?" Dante tilted his head toward Tadeo, then chuckled. "So, you really came back for me, *papi*?"

Tadeo scoffed — and he did not allow himself to acknowledge the burn on his cheeks, told himself it was angry irritation — "What? You really thought I'd leave you there?" Dante lifted the wrist stump where his hand used to be, and that was answer enough. "That was different. Look, I don't need you to forgive me."

"I wasn't going to, *papi*."

"Just be glad that I have some principles, and—" Tadeo shook his head, told himself to stop talking about this, then wrenched his arm away. The water swirled around his feet at the rough movement, and he expelled some of the cool air stuck to his teeth. "Tell me what you were doing with the angels before I freed them." At that, the soldier's expression flickered, and his smile fell. "What?"

"Tadeo," Dante began, voice dropping to a whisper. "I don't think the demons are the only evil ones here." When Tadeo quirked a brow, the soldier explained: "I spoke to them in Hell, and they told me that they worked together with the angels to imprison these Watchers during the great flood. After that, God gifted Hell to them, to the devil specifically."

"That doesn't make any sense," Tadeo replied bluntly. "They must've been lying to you."

"Look, I'm not stupid enough to believe demons at their word, but there was an angel down there, too, and—" Dante, sighing, nodded his head in the direction of those they'd freed. "*Güey*, just look at them." Though hesitating, allowing Dante's words to sink deep into his bones first, the anti-Christ trailed his gaze to examine the Watchers once more, their huffs, their twitching, their stumbling, their grunts. Like animals, they panted, frantic eyes following every movement, their teeth bared.

"Tadeo..." Both the young man in question and the soldier turned their heads at the speaker — the leader of the captive Watcher angels, seemingly — the least bloodied of them: Azazel. He was beautiful and wide-eyed, but the sadness that haloed his head made him ghostly, as well. When he spoke again, it was in that angelic tongue that was utterly unknowable to humans.

"I'm sorry," Tadeo told the angel. "We don't speak your language."

Though Azazel didn't reply, he parted his lips again, then he turned to Samyaza, who was looming behind him, a low reverb starting to sound in his throat. "Be calm," Azazel soothed before he felt a tug on the lower end of his robe, and he saw one of the other Watchers had come to him — Danel, on his knees over the sand. He was rasping, eyes clenched. "What's wrong, brother?" He spoke kindly, all the animosity between them faded now. Thousands of years bound beside one another had forcefully done away with hatred. It does away with most things — it breaks one down, removes them from their interests, from experiences, from who one once was. When you become nothing but suffering, then there's little left to distinguish yourself from other sufferers. "Can you speak?"

Danel's hundred wounds bled onto the ground as he used his other hand to clutch at the hair he'd cut short — as many other Watchers had done to their beautiful, angelic locks once upkeep became impossible. He rasped, "It hurts. The stars." He held on tighter to Azazel's robe, put himself against his side as a child might. Nearby, the slow Baraqiel was dragging the body of the faceless Kokabiel before dropping the angel of the stars on the shore and doubling over to pant and shiver, wings folding back inside himself.

"Dina," Tadeo finally called, forcing himself to address the one who'd caused all of this. "What's happening?"

Blinking, Dina finally seemed to fall from his trance, and he tilted his head, as if he didn't remember Tadeo for a moment. "Oh."

Then he replied, beautiful but too hollow: "We're saving your Earth, Tadeo. This must happen to save it."

Azazel watched Dina carefully, not understanding the words but not trying to. His mind was occupied; that angel there, Azazel was certain, was his close friend from Heaven, but the great reunion he would have expected, that he'd imagined would occur if he ever saw that sweet little angel again, was absent. Didn't Dina recognize him? 'Don't you care that I stand before you? You act as if I'm a stranger to you, and I feel that you're a stranger to me.' Why?

Tadeo's answer was shakier, uncertain, confused. "The sun is dark. This isn't what's supposed to happen, is it...? I know this. It's a sign of the end."

'Lie to him,' said Apsinthos.

'Lie?' Dina replied, heart stuttering. 'But how?'

'Lie to him, or it will all be over. You must lead him to destroy the world, or you will never have Heaven again, Dina.'

'But what if he doesn't want to? If I can't convince him?'

'His wrath will consume him, angel. All you have to do is keep him on this path. He will become their destroyer. Lie to him. Lie.'

It had been one thing to feign ignorance, to tell the truth misleadingly, but lying to a distressed face was another. Dina's open mouth choked up; he wanted to confess that this had to happen, that this was the only way to end evil. They had to destroy it all. They had to die to resurrect — all of them. "It must get worse before it gets better," he told the anti-Christ. "Please trust me, Tadeo. This must occur. I understand that it doesn't seem so, but —" The guilt was dirty, heavy. "You must have faith, Tadeo."

"Faith, eh?" Dante echoed.

Tadeo glanced at the soldier beside him, noticed his narrowed eyes, tense expression; and Tadeo's heart thumped hard enough in his chest to hurt, but he returned his attention to the angel soon enough. "Is it true that angels and demons worked together to imprison these Watchers? Why?"

Again, Dina required a second of silence before he spoke again. "The story of the great flood is far more complex than what your people wrote down."

"Agh," Danel groaned, hoarser this time; then, he grunted up to Azazel again. "I can hear the sun— It's saying a million words to me at once. I can't think. I can't." A whimper, high and helpless, escaped Danel's mouth. "I've never been able to hear it, not like Kokabiel does."

"What is it saying?" Azazel calmly asked.

"I don't know," gasped the fallen angel of the sun. "I can't make sense of it. If this is what Kokabiel hears, I understand why he is the way that he is."

"He," croaked the always-quiet voice of Baraqiel, "must be hearing it all too." The nearest Watchers turned to see the body of the red-haired Kokabiel, splayed out over the ground, shuddering in harsh jerks, almost as if he were convulsing, with fingers grasping at nothing. Suddenly, Baraqiel nudged him hard with his foot, almost a kick. Unlike the others, Baraqiel's body was almost entirely devoid of gory gashes, for he had gone quietly, without resisting, when Michael's angels came for him amid the flood rain.

Dante told Tadeo: "I don't think he's telling the truth."

But Dina ignored him to say: "Think of the story of Abraham and his son, Tadeo. Think of the story of Job. To do good for God, you must confront a call that first seems implausible and cruel, and you must face adversity. You will be rewarded for it. The world will be saved. You must trust in His plan."

Tadeo clenched his jaw. "I do. I do trust in Him." But this did not feel right. "If what you say is true, though, then what do we do now?" He could feel Dante's frustrated glare on his skin, searing, but he was being careful. 'What comes after the darkened sun? I can't remember. I can't remember now. Fuck, I can't remember.'

Dante watched Tadeo's face — earnest, faithful, blinded by devotion. Tadeo wouldn't listen, couldn't listen. His faith was too strong, and it was going to get people killed. 'Then maybe I'll be doing the right thing,' the soldier thought, 'if I do what they told me to do.' He recalled falling into Hell with Tadeo, how Tadeo had healed from an uninjured hand he'd protected. 'I need a phone.' It was his mother or Tadeo, after all, and Tadeo was a murderer, a torturer. He was Dante's torturer.

Azazel called out to Dina: "What is happening?" He knew not of the apocalypse. "Who are these men?" Then, he paused, sighed. "Is it... really you, Dina?"

The young angel turned toward the Watchers finally, looking into Azazel's eyes the color of the Earth's firmament, and a pang of hurt whipped him. "Yes," he said. 'Dina, don't stray your attention. You must lead the anti-Christ home.' "Yes, it's me, Azazel." He moved to the new leader of the Watchers, inching closer, until he staggered over a rock on the pale sand. "Old friend." 'Dina, stop.' 'I'm sorry, Apsinthos.'

The features on Azazel's face softened, then he closed the short distance between himself and Dina. Spreading his arms, he welcomed Dina into them, and he felt the younger angel latch onto his torso in their tight embrace. 'If nothing else,' Azazel thought, 'you still feel as I remembered. Warm. Small, even if you're about the same size as me.' "I see," he mused. "It *is* you, my Dina." 'I hope.' With a clinking of the chain, Samyaza took a step closer, yet another noise building in his throat, but Azazel didn't pay any mind to it, not now.

"I am," Dina said. "I am. It's me. Dina. I have to tell you—" 'Dina, do not.' "The boy there... He is a monster, Azazel. He is going to destroy all of this Earth and all of Hell, but I thought to use him to free you before he has done away with all the living here. But I tried to stop him, Azazel. I did." 'You're lying.' "And I've tried — I *am* trying... to lead him to good, without him knowing. It hasn't been easy, and I see that the stars are screaming. I fear that I've failed. If that's so, please know that I've done all that I could." A knot tightened in his chest, and he felt it pull so tight that every hem of his fear, his love, his self, began to tear. "I never understood what happened to you, Azazel." His eyes burned, his throat began to narrow in a hot itch. "I'm sorry."

Azazel's hand planted itself on Dina's back, rubbed and rubbed. For now, he trusted in him. "I," Azazel started, "can't begin to explain now, but I can tell you that when we Watchers made lives here on Earth, even if we were punished for it — I learned that there are some things you do not need to apologize for, Dina." Delicately, Azazel reached for the youngest angel's cheek, then guided Dina's frightened face to meet his patient gaze. "I'm here now, brother. Let me help. We can all help."

'Beautiful,' said Apsinthos. 'You are the greatest angel of them all, Dina.'

Dina sniffed, felt dampness in his eyes, as he smiled at Azazel gently and stepped back, away from him. "We must go to the place where the boy is from." 'No one ever did pay any mind to me because I was created after Lucifer, the most perfect of us. No one knew why God would ever want to create another. I was bound to be thought a derivative, a lesser one. A lesser angel of beauty. A lesser Lucifer.' Wiping at his face with a sleeve, the angel returned to facing Tadeo and told him, in his language, "We must return to your home, Tadeo." 'But maybe it was always I that was destined to be greater.'

The anti-Christ didn't reply immediately, taking a second to look back at Dante, as if the soldier whom he'd tortured, who had every reason to lie and betray him, would tell him the truth. But Dante was silent too, lips pressed tightly together. "Hm." Wind whistled past his ears, momentarily as loud as the screaming stars. "Alright." What other choice did he have? To stay here? Even if Dina had just revealed himself to be a demon in disguise, Tadeo knew that the first thing he'd do is go home. 'Probably.' He didn't know what he was supposed to make out of the fact that the angels he'd freed from Hell didn't seem much like angels. "We'll go back. But what about them all?"

"They'll come with us," Dina said. "They'll be able to help."

"Help with what?" Dante finally spoke again.

A flicker of irritation lit Dina's eyes, but none of that was evident in his smooth response: "Help with... the situation."

Kokabiel, suddenly, seizure-d against the ground more violently, and Danel drew a sharp breath, slapped both hands over his ears, and bared his teeth, a long, pitiful cry seeping through. "Something is happening," Danel gasped. "The stars are falling. They're falling." And beside him, Kokabiel jammed his index into the sand, sharply drew lines into a pair of glyphs in an archaic angelic script.

"Trumpets soon," Baraqiel read, hardly above a whisper.

The Watchers' disarray turned Tadeo back to them, and he winced anxiously for what could be coming and for what he'd done. He tried: "Angels!" The anti-Christ knew that they couldn't understand him, but some Watchers — among them, Azazel, Samyaza, Baraqiel — nonetheless looked to him. "We will go to my town, where all my people are. It may not be safe there, but I believe in my angel that it's the proper place for us both. He's asked me to have faith, and I hope that you can all have faith in me, as well." Helplessly, he tried to look at Dina, but his eyes landed on Dante's, which were oddly stern, almost disappointed. In Tadeo's chest, a rib might've unsettled, enough to jab at his heart in a way he didn't quite understand.

Without the cue, however, Dina still translated, or at least Tadeo believed so. The angel said: "The boy says that we must return to his home now. It is better to do as he says. You saw what he can turn into." Then, Dina noticed Kokabiel and the markings that warned of the rapidly approaching apocalypse. 'The revelation,' thought Dina, 'already here.'

Tadeo adjusted himself, then began climbing further onto the shore, ignoring his own nakedness, wondering where Dina had left his clothing. "Let's leave," he called to all those Watchers he walked past, hearing the splashes behind him of the others beginning to move again. There was one series of splashes much more frantic than the others, but Tadeo didn't turn before the distinctive sound of Dante's huffs sounded behind him. Heavily, the camouflage green jacket, the one the soldier had worn on the day they met, that he had continued wearing despite his half-defection from the military, fell onto Tadeo's shoulders.

Dante grumbled, "For fuck's sake, you're naked."

Azazel was staring at the two men again as he told the Watchers: "Let us do as Dina recommends. Let us go to this boy's home, and then I'll see about us all escaping to be elsewhere." But he couldn't help but feel that Dina hadn't told them everything. Memories of a naive, innocent Dina, with tears in his eyes and a veil over his hair, were engraved into the back of Azazel's eyelids, and on the surface, they mirrored the angel that he saw, but a deep, unreasonable feeling screamed at him. Azazel glanced at Samyaza, read the distrust in his eyes.

At times, Samyaza's mental destruction, that had turned him into nothing more than instinct, was helpful; Samyaza no longer thought, just felt, just knew. And he knew something now that Azazel was still turning over in his head. Gently, he tugged on Samyaza's leash, leading him to follow the two human men. The other Watchers were quick to do so, as well, though Baraqiel had to reach for Kokabiel, who was growing limper, stiller, to carry. Kokabiel could have been a dead angel, waiting to be set down in a grave.

Tadeo clutched at the jacket that really didn't do enough to cover his groin, and he felt some warmth in his chest, confusingly so, and he coughed to let out the awkward tangle in his throat. "My clothes should be nearby, maybe with my horse."

"We're going to take that horse again?" Dante asked. "Can't we just steal a motorcycle or something? A car?"

Snorting, Tadeo jabbed, "All your soldiers are a bunch of criminals."

Dante laughed a bit at that. "Well, we need clothes for all the angels with us also." Their rags were, indeed, rather revealing, but in comparison to Tadeo, they seemed modest. "We might as well rob a clothing store too." Then, he nudged him. "By the way, why did you come back for me? Genuinely, why?"

Tadeo glared, starting to annoy with this subject. "I told you that it was just the right thing to do."

"Hmm."

Tadeo felt his nose crinkle. "What is it? Why do you keep bringing this up?"

"No reason," Dante answered before he decided to ask his own question. "How... long was I there, in Hell?"

Tadeo paused, as well. "Just a few days. Why? You don't know?"

"Hm," the soldier said again. "Didn't feel that way. Do you have a phone? I need to call my mother."

"Yes, but it's my aunt's and hardly works. Don't lose it." But just before Tadeo could try to remember if he'd left it with the horse, he murmured, "And be careful. If the soldiers find out you're alive, they'll probably kill you for trying to help me, for defecting."

'I never defected.' "Thanks."

Azazel interlocked a hand with Samyaza's, and then he whispered to him, "That boy up there must be the son of Satan."

CHAPTER 28

Despite declaring he'd return to Heaven soon, Uriel chose to remain on Earth. He managed to tug the reins of his winged horse slightly, trying to ease it from trot to a slow walk. A few angels had noticed what he was doing, but they didn't dare alert Michael, Raphael, or Gabriel up ahead. All he could think of was how silent the devil had been in the end as the chief prince suddenly lifted him onto the horse, facing the rear. Then, Michael had climbed on top, taking the reins. Their backs had been pressed together — hulking armor and torn cassock separated only by the golden chains wrapped around Satan. Briefly, Uriel had locked eyes with him — the devil. 'You should be grateful that I haven't taken this chance to laugh at you.'

It was almost impossible to remember, but there was a time, long ago, when the two of them had been in Michael's home in Heaven — Satan no more than a bratty angel of beauty and Uriel trying to stop him from destroying paradise. 'I hope it was worth it, Lucifer.' Though Uriel supposed that they'd both gotten what they'd wanted in the end — the ruin of Heaven and the ruin of Lucifer. 'But neither of us are happy, are we?' Uriel refused something as asinine as solidarity, however. He let himself fall behind, unseen, as the others ascended to Heaven. Though Uriel knew he'd be able to defend himself from accusations of defection — after all, some armored angels on their horses had been told to remain in Babylon's heart to keep watch and, perhaps, peace — his heart stuttered anxiously.

Then he turned to face the world of man — the Earth he so detested. Once, Metatron had suggested stronger relations between the divine and humanity, but it had been the Lord who rejected such a thing. He must've feared another situation like the Watchers; that had been Uriel's first assumption. But maybe God simply enjoyed the distance, maybe He loved the atheists. The Lord adored the first nonbeliever of them all, after all: Satan.

But all those humans Metatron spoke so highly of were running — in a few different directions but many toward Babylon and every soldier stationed there. Far above, the stars were screaming — and, with them, came the booms of winged metal slicing through the clouds. Drones, three or four of them — silver birds. Smoke climbed in a great sprawl from further down south, though it couldn't have been more than a seven or eight buildings that were hit. The people ran on foot, many unable to climb into the vehicles that'd been without gasoline for so long now.

As Uriel walked his horse opposite the hurrying humans, several looked up at the angel wildly, desperately, begging, and the prince recalled his exchange with Raphael and Gabriel in Michael's absence. On their walk toward any urban center, ignoring the cars driving past them on the road, Raphael had suddenly whispered. 'I have the blood of the lamb here. We could begin marking those who will be saved, though I fear it's not the proper time. The prophesied time.'

'How would we know who to mark?' Uriel had replied, though disinterested in the answer.

'Perhaps,' Gabriel had whispered, 'we should mark everyone that we can.' Ultimately, however, they'd decided to wait. Mercy should come at the right time.

Children, particularly, kept eyeing Uriel. The enshrouding of the Holy Spirit, that which had made them unseen to human eyes, had evidently fallen away as they'd confronted Satan, but despite all the stares, humans weren't stampeding to him. He'd always thought they might, might beg for miracles that the prince of wisdom was incapable of offering. But in the chaos, the humans must've realized that if Uriel was going to help, he would have already. And yet — 'my heart is heavy.' With all the disdain he held for these creatures and the nightmares he had of them overrunning his Heaven — Uriel still found himself grimacing. 'Is this empathy?' Uriel knew, after all, what a sky consumed by fire was like; he could remember running from it too.

'Are you,' Raphael had prodded, 'really going to help with this apocalypse, Uriel?' A change of subject after they had reached the largest city in Babylon.

Uriel had avoided answering; 'Dina came here with the blessing of the stars.' To prevent the revelation, he thought. 'I'm here for Dina. To help him in what he does. And if Michael interferes, I'll kill him.'

'Angels cannot die.'

'After Michael burned,' Uriel had replied lowly, 'I asked our Father why He burned him, and God admitted to me that we can die. It is through fire. If we are burned to nothing, even less than ash, then all there is left for our soul to do is die. We can heal one another, but we cannot create our bodies anew.' He paused, noted Gabriel up ahead, pretending not to listen. 'The blood of the Lamb — we need to mark all the good with the blood of the Lamb, is that right? Michael said he saw the devil where the Lamb should have been.'

The bombing didn't seem to be getting any closer. In fact, it stopped. He wasn't hearing the booms of explosions, just the hisses of the silver birds. 'Dina.' He would find him. He needed to hide before the archangels — or rather, Michael — realized he'd rebelled, but he would find Dina. 'Let me help you. Where are you?' He glanced up at the stars again, and he wondered if his old love had awoken. 'Let me help, and I can introduce you to him. To Kimah.' Kimah would like Dina, wouldn't he?

The next few days of the apocalypse were slower; the screams of the stars grew softer, more like distant hums.

On the third noon, the Watchers, the anti-Christ, and others finally reached the town's outskirts, and as they did, they came across a roadside shrine made rubble — Mary of Guadalupe decapitated among it. Not far, there were the remains of a factory, scattered trucks on their side, collapsed into themselves, one still aflame. On the other side of the road, there was a concrete, one-story home with its left side made fragments of itself, whereas the other side still had an open door and painted words on the wall that read a woman's name — Maria Cantú — and that this was her restaurant. And she sold guisados, gorditas, tacos, and much more. "Oh my God," Tadeo breathed as he saw, yanking on the reins until his mare slowed into a total halt.

Behind, Dante jostled and bumped up against Tadeo, then took hold of his shoulder to steady. "What the fuck happened?" Tadeo tensed at the touch, clenched his jaw, but he resisted shoving him away. "Did a bomb drop?"

Tadeo opened his mouth, then simply rolled his shoulder, relieved that the soldier removed his grip almost immediately. "We need to— We should check if there's any survivors."

He looked up to the army of angels following them like vultures to the dying. Though they had stayed off the main roads up until now — Tadeo had no doubt that the 199 Watchers had surely already been seen by someone or something, and he'd been anticipating great trouble but nothing at all like this. The angels were quiet, had been for most of the time spent traveling, though they often landed to touch the Earth they no longer recognized, and they had taken Tadeo and Dante's hours of sleep as an opportunity to run around, to chase each other like animals, to bleed from their wounds. 'They don't act like Dina,' Tadeo had long noticed, but Dina seemed calm beside Azazel, the one Tadeo had learned was the beautiful leader of the imprisoned angels. Azazel still kept that pale-eyed, one-winged angel on a chain leash; and Tadeo never missed how this angel — Dina called him Samyaza — followed Dante and him with a twitching gaze.

Unsure what else to do, Tadeo called, "Excuse me!" He ignored Dante's chuckle. "I want to see if anyone's trapped beneath the buildings!" Before he could try to look for Dina, and to beg him for a translation, the beautiful angel swept up and away from the cloud of Watchers, swerving to circle above Tadeo — again, like a vulture. He opened his mouth, and Tadeo heard Dina speak in the ancient angel language to the curious faces of the newly-freed ones. Tadeo swallowed, and he took this second to tilt his head and whisper to the soldier, "You can take the horse, if you want. Ride into town. I'll stay here and look through everything."

Dante hesitated, then said, "I can't ride."

"It's easy."

"I'll stay here." Dante leaned closer, lowered his voice to a murmur. "I also want to talk to you without... him being here too."

Tadeo hesitated, then bit on the inside of his lips. 'Dina.' He could sense Dante's suspicion, and he'd be lying if he said he wasn't nervous too. But Dina was an angel; Dante on the road had described demons, and they were horned and monstrous, nothing like the angel who'd been guiding him until now. 'And I already met the devil,' Tadeo thought, 'so Dina can't be him.' "Alright, but it'll be a while before we get back to town."

Whistling lowly, Dante answered: "Buy me something to eat tonight and I'll forgive you."

Fiddling with the leather rein in his fingers, Tadeo shifted a little, not sure what to say, how to really talk to the man casually; he never knew how to talk to men his own age at all. "Fine," he tried. "Do you like beer?"

Dante snickered. "About as much as I like pussy."

"So no?" Tadeo blurted, trying to joke and regretting it instantly, ashamed for responding to something so crude, but the soldier behind him laughed, then called him a motherfucker.

Soon, the angel Dina fluttered his wings over to Tadeo, and he said, "We will go on ahead to the place where you found me. If we see any humans in need, we'll try to help them, but a lot of these angels need to be healed first."

"I understand," Tadeo said, nodding his head, then moving to get off the horse. "Dante will stay here with me, but hopefully, we'll meet you in town soon."

Dina stared, then pulled a smile onto his face, turned it back to the Watchers, and in their language, said: "He wants to investigate this area, but we may go on ahead. I'll bring you all to where I landed when I came to Earth. Then, I'll try to heal all of you. We'll have to land soon. We're too beautiful to be mistaken for humans, and we shouldn't draw more attention than needed."

Azazel hesitated, but not for long. He had a hand over Samyaza's head as the younger one held onto his waist to stay up in the air as he beat his only green wing left. Then, he gave the order for the Watchers to follow and called back to Dina: "What is it that happened here?"

"The world is very different than what it used to be," the young angel replied with an odd detachment before he beat his wings and propelled himself forward like a bullet.

Pausing, Azazel waved for the Watchers to go after Dina, but he eyed Tadeo as Samyaza grunted. Azazel whispered, as he often did, "Be calm." Lucifer's child seems more human than angel to me." Too human, in fact. After Samyaza made an affirming noise, the two continued onward, behind the other Watchers. They flew high enough to see dark smoke still creeping up from some buildings, all stout. This was not a place of many towers, so there hadn't been much to level, and there especially was not now. A tall hotel remained with its metal skeleton, but its inside was bare — furniture broken, made half-ash, with not many signs of people within it anymore. Instead, the humans were scattered in the streets, staring at the darkness of burnt walls and the red blood near every airstrike grave. Azazel was no stranger to dead humans, but a heaviness nonetheless sunk into his stomach. In fact, it was because he was no stranger that repulsion sprouted where his heart should be.

How many times can you see the dead until it becomes any easier? The angel could count each body he caught — two, then three, then six — and, contradictorily, relieve some of the pain. Turn the killed from lives, with faces and hands, into arithmetic, and you can endure atrocity. One, two. Dead men at the center of four bewildered adults. Three corpses laid to finish smoking beneath the sun. Five buildings still smoking, black as oil, shadowing the Watchers. The world is very different than what it used to be.

Satan had said, 'Azazel, you're wondering why I let you out of your chains while your brothers rot.'

'You want to know why my child was beautiful, why I was able to create life, not monsters like all the others.'

'That child of yours — did it speak?'

'It told me you'll lose the war against God.'

'Liar.'

'You think no one else can do what you can, Satan. You only know how to speak to your groveling demons, the frightened humans, and the angels who dare not sin. But I'm not afraid to lie, and I won't grovel for you, and there isn't much you can take from me now. You know that. You offer me food, water, sunlight because there's nothing else that you can take.'

'Me? You descended to the Earth on your own. You let an ugly man fuck you, abuse you, and it is all your fault.'

'No, *Lucifer*.' A hiss. 'You worked with God, and you became His pawn. You've already lost your war. Do you think you're still the rebel angel? Or have you realized you've just become another hand of His?'

When they landed, it was somewhere far from the most destruction, a quiet neighborhood with many abandoned homes, though there were wandering dogs with their tongues out and their fur matted. Azazel put one bare foot on cement, for the first time, then the other, and he exhaled shakily. As the animals jogged over to them, he placed a hand over one of their heads. He couldn't remember if he'd ever seen these creatures, if they existed when he'd first been on the surface, the years with his human husband, Eitan. A nice man. He really had been, once.

Samyaza crouched beside him, and Azazel touched the top of his head how one might an animal; like an animal, Samyaza leaned into it. During all the thousands of years imprisoned, it had been Samyaza that'd been treated the most brutally. He'd been whipped, burned, tortured by demons, gagged, and took the brunt of responsibility for the flood. They had killed him, slowly. One day, Samyaza had become unable to say anything beyond slurred mumbles, and one day, he'd begun to growl and bite, and they had put a muzzle on him. The demons had enjoyed torturing all the Watchers, but when they reduced them into creatures like animals, it was not how humans return to their animalistic urges in moments of great fear. Angels had been born from stars, from light — not the Earth; their growls were not instinctive, nor natural. The way that God had made humans from mutilated animals, the demons had made animals out of mutilated angels.

'Sometimes I wonder, Satan, if you want to tear me open and take my organs for yourself. Is that what you want? Do it. Give me another reason for revenge. Hurt me more, and it will absolve me for everything that I will one day do to you.' He stared fondly down at Samyaza. 'My dear healer. My dear Samyaza. Maybe we'll have our revenge. Soon.'

Dina was up ahead, and Azazel stared at his face, trying to recall his memories of him again, every instance that the young angel had held his hands, bowed his head. Constantly, he would cry. And, now, Dina was parting his lips, but the one who spoke next was someone else entirely.

Baraqiel — hair trimmed close to his head, his skin paler in certain places as if from kisses by painted lips, and his eyes tired; his build was also tall with little visible injuries. He had Kokabiel in his arms, limp like a murdered bride. "Kokabiel has had visions for all of our imprisonment; I think he should be the first to be healed." But he didn't say it softly, kindly. He wasn't particularly fond of the angel of the stars anymore — Azazel thought — though that didn't stop Baraqiel from spending all his captivity staring at Kokabiel, pressed to his side.

Once, Baraqiel had confessed to Samyaza that he had a habit of checking for darkness in Heaven, of lighting candles to fill it. 'But then I met him,' Baraqiel had said, softly. 'Kokabiel.' Samyaza had told him that he shouldn't be so close to another, his face twisting in the disgust he'd trained himself to feel over the affection of two angels. 'Now I look for him,' Baraqiel had said. 'Now I'm always looking for him. Maybe he's my light.' Samyaza had said: 'Or maybe he's your darkness.' A corner to keep lighting candles in, to keep scratching at the compulsion.

Slow, he settled Kokabiel down on the sidewalk, right as Dina stepped up to him.

Folding his wings into himself, Dina swallowed, then reached for a bottle of water that he'd been carrying for the humans, and he spared a second to glance around them, noting the lack of humans here. 'Heal him,' Apsinthos said, 'but be wary of what he speaks of. I don't know what he'll do.' That was strange; Dina wasn't sure that he'd ever heard Apsinthos confess to not knowing something. But he followed orders, poured some of the water to pool coldly onto his left palm. He was no great healer, briefly taught by Raphael one day that he'd visited Uriel's home, but Dina's hands were careful. Soon, he'd threaded Kokabiel new tissues, tendons, and teeth. Creeping along, skin pulled itself over new bone — brown, freckled. Like the space between stars, dark irises pooled at the center of eyes born blinking. It was a slow process, but not so much that the Watchers didn't all turn and lean in to watch it happen like they'd never seen a miracle. Baraqiel stood right beside Kokabiel, and he, like all the others, anticipated that crazed smile that he'd found so dually comforted and terrified by once.

Except — Kokabiel's reborn angelic face was empty, eyes hollow, lips only slightly parted.

"Kokabiel, are you with us?" Azazel spoke, and he felt Samyaza press against his back, face hovering by his left shoulder.

"Speak," Danel urged; and the angel of the stars fluttered his eyes, but the gaze in them remained unfocused. "Tell us everything that you've been hearing. All this time we were chained, you knew what was happening on Earth, right?"

Kokabiel, suddenly, almost violently, jerked his head in the direction of Baraqiel, and his first word was, "Bara." His voice was soft, and the fallen angel of light visibly tensed, eyes widening. "You kicked me. On the beach."

Before there could be any further exchange however, a certain deep, stern voice called, "*Dina?*" The sharpness of the call made the youngest angel's heart stutter then stop, but he didn't dare move even when he heard all the Watchers do so around him. "What is this?" Uriel demanded next. "What have you done?"

Instinctively, Dina's bottom lip wobbled, and he whispered, "Uriel." He turned about, slowly, slowly, all the shame that he'd only begun breaking free from flooding back into him in an instant. "You're here—" Eyes wide, frantic — he met Uriel's face hidden by a silver helmet. "Why are you here?" He must be here to end the world. "Forgive me—"

"You freed the Watchers," Uriel whispered, low, strained.

"Uriel," Azazel replied, and all the Watchers reacted as if only at Azazel's word could they understand who it was before them. They rose from their crouches, flared their wings, bared their teeth, and were it not for Azazel's grip on Samyaza's chain, the ex-leader of the Watchers would have thrown himself at the prince and clawed him apart.

"You fucker," Danel said. "You fucker— You and all the other princes are why we suffered for hundreds of thousands of years in darkness!"

"No," Uriel answered, then reached for his helmet with both gauntlets, lifted it up from his head, then brought it to hold before his torso to reveal an expression so furious that it dug like blades into all who faced it. "You carved the path to Hell yourselves for committing abominations with humans."

Azazel, more carefully, said: "Uriel, we are already free, and we will never be bound again."

But Uriel had turned his rage toward Dina, moving toward him as the young angel staggered back, heart erratic, lungs refusing to draw breath. "Was this all for them?" he snarled coldly. "Was this to free your friends?" Dina remembered how he'd told Uriel that he wished to see his friends again, not long before he met Apsinthos. 'I told you everything. I used to revolve my life around you, Uriel, and not Apsinthos.' "Do you realize that you've reared the apocalypse or is this all single-minded *vanity?*"

'Vanity?' Dina echoed in his mind. 'Is that what this is? Vanity? I'm ending it for all of us, Uriel.' And yet when he thought of the end, he thought of Apsinthos, of himself, sitting at the edge of the universe, feet dangling, watching it all burn. Maybe it was vanity, then — but was that so bad? 'Don't yell at me, Uriel. It's not fair. Maybe I wouldn't be here if you'd been kinder to me. Maybe I wouldn't have to do what the stars knew you were incapable of.'

Uriel seethed: "Dina, answer me!"

"You," said Kokabiel, "aren't wanted here, *Uri*."

The tone was unnatural on Kokabiel — still distinctly his airy voice, but the tone was ghostly, echoing. And the prince's expression suddenly froze as he felt all his blood rush through him cold. "Uri...?"

Kokabiel rose to his feet, all those near him staggering back, gazes flickering between him and the petrified archangel. "Return to your God, Uri. Isn't that where you like to be? Return to Him. You worship Him. You serve *Him*. Your place at the foot of His Throne sits empty, waiting for your knees."

"Stop," left Uriel's mouth quickly, and utter panic stressed his eyes, his mouth as the angel of the stars walked toward him. "Stop this."

"Uri," said Kokabiel again. "You serve the one who destroyed me."

"No," Uriel said again. "Enough—"

"What bothers you? Did you prefer me dead?" Kokabiel stopped, just some feet before Uriel now, his red hair tangling with the wind, his dark eyes endless and sparkling with all the stars in the sky. "Perhaps you did because you are dead too. To me, you are dead. You are a shell of a soul. You are an abhorrent weakness. You are not the one who bled fire from nothing. You are not my eyes. You are not a half of me. What you are is betrayal."

"Enough with this, Kokabiel!" Uriel yelled, but he was desperate. "End your charade. You'll suffer a fate worse than all the stars for mocking him. You will know God's wrath—"

"*Uri*." This time, the word didn't seep between Kokabiel's lips, and the prince, slowly, saw that a shadow had come over him, over all the Watchers lifting their face to stare at something above them. "How I've come to hate you." Every syllable was a hiss, every word cut into the heavy, loathsome flesh that Uriel carried. His fingers twitched; his body trembled. He had dreamt of reuniting, of resurrection, of returning to the one he lost at the beginning of time. It was never meant to be like this. He had imagined, he had been tormented with the nightmares of completeness, of holy love again — but this was no nuptial reunion. This was not love, nor retribution, nor resurrection.

Uriel turned back, half-hoping he'd turn into a pillar of salt by God for daring to look at all that he'd ever loved and lived for however much it was damned. 'Forgive me,' he was already pleading, but he didn't know to whom.

Looming above the buildings, there was a great flaming sphere perched, made of mouths, disfigured faces, shadows, and tongues — a pulsating organ-heart of itself. A great smile might have contorted its body, a wicked fury may have burned it brighter. And, all over the Earth, many other stars had fallen from the grace of the abyss.

"Uri," Kimah said again.

CHAPTER 29

To humiliate the devil, the saint Michael paraded him through the gilded streets of Heaven. The angels did not recognize their fallen brother without his angelic jewels or flowers in his golden hair, or without a timbrel and pipes at his hip. He seemed something they couldn't decipher, a thing — not a human, for he was too beautiful, nor an angel, for he was too beautiful, nor a God because there was only one God. Stoic, Satan remained in the coils of golden chains, his back so pressed to the one of a silver crusader that the devil could very well tilt his head back to lean a cheek against one armored shoulder, breeze of hair cascading onto the saint. Except Satan maintained his poise, chin high, lips pressed fine together, eyes pensive, elegant. Hearing the cavalcade, angels opened the windows in their kitchen and bedrooms, some stepped out of their doorways; and they began to rush the streets, crowding around the procession of a hundred steeds and all the angels mounted on them.

Phanuel saw the parade: his friend Michael at the front, recognizable only by his hefty sword, prince Raphael at his right but many steps behind, prince Gabriel at his left. From the top of the fountain of life with a few others, crouched, wings flared behind to maintain balance — Phanuel listened to someone call out, "Devil!

It's the devil!" And then a symphony of hate. Angel after angel shouted as loud as the day the newborn angel Lucifer had been revealed to the city he would destroy: "Serpent! Liar! Sinner! Devil!" One took the goods he'd been carrying down a path, hurried toward God's soldiers, then flung some at Satan's face. A fruit struck at his jaw, burst, stained down to his throat, then tumbled to the ground. Soon, the host of Heaven took all that they had, throwing it with each one of their insults.

"The Lord is good!" one jeered, flinging a stone that hit Satan hard enough to rattle him but to not change his expression. "The Lord is great! He has given us the Beast to burn!"

Phanuel stared at Michael for a few seconds more, then once he felt the chief prince's gaze far from him, he slipped away.

And though Michael either didn't notice or pretended not to, Satan had been staring directly at the fountain's highest peak, at Phanuel, ignoring the others standing on the lower sections, their bare feet damp on the porcelain work. 'It's not how I remember it.' In the war, they had destroyed the fountain. 'They rebuilt it.' He'd thought this of the roads too. 'They had once sprawled like the arteries of an angel, in every direction, curling and clashing with one another, leading where they wanted — some to God, some to Earth, many to nowhere. But they've straightened.' His eyes followed the angel of forgiveness, who'd flapped himself to two buildings, then pulled his wings in to fall sharply in between. 'Do you find something too perfect about your rebuilt face too, Phanuel?'

Finally, Michael guided his winged horse to halt, and Satan instantly felt claws — the nails of the angels' hands — go for his dress shoes, tear them away, go for his ankles, yank on his cassock so harsh that the buttons over his abdomen strained, then popped off. Another stone hit at his head, enough to shove him in the opposite direction, and Satan felt another barrage of rocks thrown to beat his body, followed by food to stain his ripped clothes.

"Michael," Raphael called. "Enough with this! Aren't we to take him to God?"

"Can't the angels," Michael replied, voice cold, brittle, "have Satan pay the penance that he is due?"

Gabriel answered, uncharacteristically tense: "Only God officiates penance, Michael. Let us... bring him to our Father." The chief prince hesitated. "Now, or we will go on without you. Don't you see how Uriel has already abandoned us?" Raphael breathed in sharply, but Michael didn't react.

Instead, Michael took a tighter grip of the reins, and Satan had to bite down a laugh. What was this place? Nostalgia should have torn him open, revealed a memory of walking the streets with a basket of fruit and a dear friend at his side — but this was not the paradise he'd fallen from. The city of Heaven was unrecognizable, its buildings sharper, its people colder, its eternal sun hotter. Where remembrance should lie within him, there was a gaping hollowness instead. They had done away with the Heaven he knew, done away with the place that reared Lucifer. To never rear another rebel angel, they had done it.

The parade climbed. The chief prince led his horse upwards into flight, and all those behind him followed, until they were riding into the dome of light cradling the city, tearing through it to move into darkness. Too absent, the twinkles of stars provided even less guidance than they ever had, as if they'd sensed He was preoccupied and all fled the house of God in the few seconds they had. But Satan knew very well where all the stars were; he had read the prophecies. He'd read all the apocalyptic texts, and collected them, rid of the senseless ones and organized the Bibles for the believers. He remembered that all the stars would fall, one day, just as the devil had.

He remembered, too, the feeling of the pages when he read that old apocalyptic text from John in Patmos, nothing particularly divine about it, and yet his heart had sunk deeper into Hell than the rest of him ever had; he'd whispered to himself, 'It means nothing. Like Christ, it is mere delusion,' as his hands trembled.

All the army of the Lord appeared before the Throne without flesh as He had made them, so that they, in turn, could also see Him as He was — as nothing, as jade, as power. Michael, six-winged and aflame, removed Satan from the horse by taking him by the chains, then beating his wings. The steed bowed its head and trotted back, away from God, like other horses left behind. In Michael's hold, Satan's face was lowered, but not out of submission. He was enfleshed, in the reconstructed ruins of the body that'd burnt up to near ash in the fall. There was no soul beneath his skin that he could expose now, or maybe there was but he couldn't retrieve it — his other faces hollowed out, his wings torn out. He was mere meat, stitched back together, in torn clothing, stained and bloodied; he couldn't meet the face of God without suffering agony worse than the inferno.

And the chief prince took the devil by the back of his throat and forced him to kneel before the Lord's Throne before he said, "Worship." Below, Satan's breath audibly spilled from between clenched teeth — almost a hiss. "How you promised you would," Michael spat, "when the covenant of Hell was granted to you."

"The world has not ended," Satan snarled, jerking his body, but the prince's iron grip kept him in place. "Not a human soul stands in Heaven. No one is saved. The son of God is nowhere to save them —" He cut himself off with a guttural noise like a growl, another harsh struggle. "Get your hand off of me, coward, stupid, fucking idiot."

"Worship," Michael commanded once more.

"Fuck you," Satan said. "Suck His cock if you so need Him worshiped."

At this, all the angels observing shouted out, calling him a sinner, a whore, a damned thing that they pleaded for the silent Lord to punish. "Burn him!" they said. "Kill him, God! Destroy what remains of him! Tear off the flesh that you dressed him in! Look at how he's remade it in mockery of you! Strike him! Burn him! Kill him!" It became a chant. "Father, throw him in the lake of fire! Kill the devil! Kill the devil! Punish him!"

Satan breathed out harshly, eyes screwed shut as tight as he could to not risk meeting the eyes of his Creator. 'God. Father.' But it was tempting, it was tempting, to reveal a gaze, to lift it to the Lord. When was the last time that he saw Him? Was it during the war for Heaven? In the second before the fall, settled in His hand, the size of the universe itself, cradled as a speck of light, a pretty angel, then slipping through the fingers, plunging down. 'God.' God. 'god.'

'or it was in the garden of paradise, with a man and a woman, and i standing in between them. you too, among them. we were standing over the flowers. i thought i could hear singing, somewhere. a psalm. when I was young, when i wrote them. Worship songs. I did worship you. With my heart in my mouth, I sang for you. Your hand in my mouth, when you pulled out my voice, did you strum the chords of worship in my throat. The chords you made. i wanted to know what you made me for. for they all loved me. the angels. But you? never enough. your love did not satisfy me lord so i sought another. I became a serpent in eden. i heard worship songs off the leaves, the echoes of my voice. do you sit and listen to the memory of me, lord? for how long? I listened with you my feet in the flowers, waiting for adoring angel lucifer to step out from between some trees, hurry to you, rise to the tips of his toes, to kiss his father on the cheek.'

Satan twitched, his jaw so clenched that it ached at its hinges.

'I told the demons that there was no Son of God. He was a demented man who thought himself greater than aging flesh. He is not the first, and he won't be the last. There is no Messiah. There is no salvation. And maybe there is no God. There is only me. I.'

God's voice said: "Once I said — that because of your detestable pride — I would bring on you blood vengeance of my wrath and anger. I said I shall deliver you to the hands of the angels, so that they strip you of your clothes, jewelry, and leave you without flesh. I said that I would command a mob against you of all your lovers so that they stone the body that I fit for you. With their swords, I said, they would hack you to pieces." And an ancient tightness built in Satan's own skull, beating down into his core, his hands. "And look how all that I promised has come to pass. The anointed cherub will ask himself why this is happening to him, I said, and it is because of his disobedience."

"You," Satan addressed, refusing Him a title, a relation, "will never cease this war. Almighty, if you're almighty and true, I would not have been given the soul of the wicked to tend, nor the Earth to roam. You have all done it for me to maintain this. For the sake of war, you will never do away with me."

"The feet of the Throne burn you. You were made for the feet of the Throne, but you made its touch burn. Your sin is the fire that destroys you. The spectacle of blood and ash is your own creation. You craved to create, but you have only destroyed. Yourself above all. A rebellion for nothing; a war only for you to begin again, groveling. You were Jerusalem once, my morning star. I adorned you in every precious stone. I covered your nakedness in the finest drapery. From the ground, I groomed a flower, and I picked you and made you sing. And you spread violence. You betrayed me. You betrayed what you were created for. And you have found your death where you began."

"You will never cease," said Satan, careful, like he didn't feel a quivering, submissive fear awaken in him like the other faces he used to carry; God resurrecting the dead.

"The devil will burn in the lakes of fire, and Lucifer will be reborn, the new Jerusalem. And the new Jerusalem will present itself as a bride to God. Are you the Lamb or the Lamb's wife? On the day you were made, you were one, and you will return to what you were created for. Jerusalem will be dressed for her husband, I once said, and God will live among His people. A marriage in a New Eden. The end will bear a new beginning."

'Bride.' Now, Satan opened his eyes, and they tore themselves open. Blood tore out from his golden gaze to flood his cheeks, and he remembered how angel Lucifer had cried flower petals once. Long ago. 'Over a bed of flowers.' It had been so long ago. 'I thought you'd already married me, God, and that I had slit my own throat on the wedding bed. You will do it all again. It will never cease.' Baring his teeth, drinking his own pain, Satan refused to look anywhere but forward. He met God, the Father, with crimson eyes, in hungry agony that broke a body he refused to bow. 'Look at me,' he wanted to snarl, 'and see how I've always looked at you.'

Michael, suddenly, grappled Satan's shoulder, and distantly, Raphael and Gabriel made noises of shushed alarm.

But the Lord spoke once more: "Yet, the apocalypse has yet to pass." Satan felt a hiccup in his throat that surged him forward, then a hilarity that struck at him like the arrow from a bow. He laughed, through the agony that was blinding him slow. "Michael," He suddenly called, "why have you brought the fallen cherub before me?"

Satan, through his hysterics, almost didn't hear Michael's hurried, tight voice: "My Lord—"

"You've brought the serpent of Hell to the Throne before the promised time."

Michael tried again: "Father, you know that he interfered with the return of your Son and the apocalypse. I only brought him here for you to meet again before I hold him for the right day. The Judgement day."

But the Lord did not reply, and Satan was still laughing and laughing, curling up no matter the raw scorch in his eyes, all the bloody tears swelling. All about, angels were speaking again, to one another, then to God. Again, they asked Him to do something, to punish the one who'd had all of them punished. 'Retribution,' they begged for. 'Revenge. Give us revenge.' But the Lord didn't heed to them.

Instead, He banged a fist on His Throne, silencing the host, and urging: "Take the Beast of Hell far from Throne! Do not bring him before me!"

His wrath settled heavy terror over all the angels, many of which instantly swerved to leave, to return to their city, their cage. The archangels remained where they were, Satan still on his knees, thinking of turning back and seeing all the six wings and the flames that made up Michael to cackle at his face. 'I told you,' he wanted to say, 'that you can't quench His bloodthirst, Michael. God will never love you enough, and if God ever loves you too much, it will only hurt too.' But he could not see; he couldn't feel the floor before him. He must be dying. Darkness seeped into him like poison.

Soon, Michael released the devil's throat, then took him by the chains again. Spinning, spiraling, like he were about to tip over, Satan could no longer fight the pull of pain leading him into the abyss at the opposite end of life. When Michael, roughly, tugged on him, and Satan moved in what saw as emptiness, he felt as if he were free falling. The sensation was enough to recall the agony of his soul and flesh burning together in the fall, only one of which was able to be repaired. His soul had turned ash and scattered itself over all the Earth. But Lucifer could still remember rearing her — the Earth. He could remember encouraging the demons to mend the soil and the sea, to allow the new creatures to flourish and roam alongside them. Perhaps his soul wasn't dead, after all. Perhaps all the Earth was the devil's wicked soul, and that was why it must be destroyed. To kill the devil, you must destroy the Earth.

As Satan was pulled back into the sea of stars, far too dark, his stomach lurched, and he realized he'd stopped laughing. Only pain composed him now. He didn't know where Heaven was. He began to wonder if it was anywhere at all or if it was in the place where nothing was, if it was separate from what is, what is real. The un-real place where the angels and God lived. The lie.

It was several turns of the Earth later that Satan awoke.

He was chained, hands bound high over his head, wrists locked together, whereas his ankles were chained but not bolted in place. A healer must've wet the devil's eyes, for now he could see enough to not recognize his surroundings. The walls were stone, which Lucifer couldn't recall to have been typical for Heaven — but his memory was faulty and he had known quite the different paradise. What he could recognize, however, were the weapons. Each wall was lined with them — swords, spears, shields, maces. All of it seemed very archaic to Satan, who'd grown quite accustomed to every firearm of the Earth, including those from the place bordering Babylon, where Tadeo was. The anti-Christ, the child of the devil. Bitterly, he laughed. Then, the devil listened to the sound of a door dragging against the ground, but he didn't turn to it. He maintained his attention on the details of where he was, the links of his chains, and the dips in the stone walls. The ground, cold as the room, burned his bare feet.

But he was not naked; he had been dressed in a white tunic, like an angel. Oils had cleansed his body, including of blood, and he smelled of lavender. Even his hair had been brushed excessively, some small braids scattered within the golden sea falling from his scalp. God had declared that Satan would live another day without Lucifer being resurrected out of his body, but it seemed Heaven was not going to wait to begin the conversion back to his dead faith.

Clink, clink — an armored person was approaching, an angel. 'How long was I asleep?' Time had always been difficult in Heaven. He remembered being an angel and never quite caring for it except on rare occasions, and living on Earth had made him submit to the sun's orders on the hours. Slow, the devil lifted his face to see the chief prince before him. His helmet was missing, but Michael remained in his silver armor and reddened cape as always. His lips were pressed tight, his jaw was set, his eyes bore holes into Satan. And he had, in a gauntlet, a fruit — red, gleaming. An apple.

"Satan," Michael said.

The devil replied: "How long have I been asleep? Where am I?" His head throbbed like a pulse, and he rocked a heel, realizing he couldn't steady it well. "Didn't your God tell you that it's not the proper time for the convent to be fulfilled? You may have broken the Revelation's prophecy by bringing me here, Michael and now the world will continue. My demons will roam the Earth and rule Hell and tempt every human to turn away from God, every last one, until there are none who can be saved."

"Many times," said the prince, "I asked myself why the apocalypse never came. I suspected it, that you were involving yourself and killing the anti-Christ each time it was reborn before the other prophecies of Revelation could be fulfilled. You've delayed the destruction of the Earth for thousands of years, killing and killing — but see how rotten it has become? See what you have created?"

Satan, weakly, snorted. "Did it take that human girl saying it for you to connect everything, Michael?" He grinned, then chuckled. "Who is she? Were you so jealous of me having a child that you couldn't stop yourself from looking for one of your own?"

Tightly — "She is not my child."

"She looks at you like a father."

"Be *silent,*" Michael snarled. "You are the jealous one. You saw that God had a son, and you could not live knowing He is great and you are not. You bore a monster, devil. Even after seeing what the Watchers had done, you thought yourself different. You thought yourself not an angel." 'I remember grabbing Azazel, demanding to know what made him different, why his child was beautiful and why mine would not take.' "Is this what you wanted? You have your child now, and see how you must kill it to maintain your wicked world? It is because of your vanity, your foolishness."

"I asked you," Satan said, humor falling away, tone turning harsh, "where I am." His eyes had narrowed; his lips had pressed finer.

And the chief prince hesitated, careful, staring. "You're in barracks." Nodding his head at the walls, he added, "Where all the angels' weaponry is, where the army rests. It was built for the flood. Do you remember the flood, Satan? If you do, then why did you do what you did? Don't you remember the destruction of the Earth, all the blood on your hands—"

"Our hands," Satan, sharply, interjected. "Do you remember Azazel and his child, Michael? Do you remember how you skewered it, Michael? It wasn't me who did. It was you. It was your sword. He was never right after that happened, Michael. You broke him. You break so many angels."

Michael breathed out slow. "I gave you what you wanted after that, devil. I stood before God and negotiated your Hell, and I showed you mercy. I have shown you mercy since before you became the devil, but you reject salvation, time and time again. And you speak of the death of Azazel's child to mock me, but I saw the horror in your eyes, Satan. I know that you are not the stone that you pretend to be. Every word you say, every face you make, is pure lie." He leaned himself closer, and his breath was hot. "You are not the God that you act like you are. You were an angel, and you are the husk of one now. But the Lord has told me that the apocalypse will bring us restoration, and that to end all wars, we must return to the time before the very first. You will be done away with forever, Satan, as if you never existed. It will all be like before." Michael thought of Joana, of telling her that they could never return to the time before the war.

Satan was quiet for a second, then he tilted his head, how a predator might examine a frightened rabbit in a trap. "And Lucifer will return, beautiful and worshiping, to be God's bride." Michael tensed. "You will watch it happen? You'll listen to Him fuck me how you listen to Baal do it, too?"

"It is a union," said Michael, "of the perfect angel to God. Only you would read His prophecies to mean sins of flesh."

"Tell me then," answered Satan, "if not listen to your Father fuck him, then what will you do with Lucifer once he's been resurrected, Michael?" The devil set his feet more firmly over the ground, tried to push himself forward so that he could spit onto Michael's face with every word. "Will you tell him that his beauty is a curse to be ashamed of? Will you never teach him to fight? Will you watch Lucifer remain in Eden with God forever?" Digging his nails into the chains that upheld him, Satan heard the voice of the Lord still echoing in his skull, his taunting that the devil's rebellion had amounted to nothing. And he thought of the past thousands of years, all his lives, all his identities, all the worlds he'd ruled in this endless war. "Bring Lucifer back. Do it a thousand times." 'The Lord told me that He made me a hundred million times before my feet touched Heaven. He's going to do it again. Was God telling me, in that moment, that He will destroy me and begin again? Did it all already end? How many times has it all ended?' Satan, more hushed now, said: "You can never keep Lucifer from falling." 'It will happen, over and over. God and His devil, chasing each other in a tempest.'

Michael, just as quietly, whispered, "I know how to stop him from ever falling again."

Impatient now, Satan said: "It was your fault."

"It was my fault." Michael's affirmation made the devil freeze, note the archangel's wide, empty eyes and his own pretty reflection in them. "Once Lucifer is resurrected, he will never meet me."

"Never," Satan echoed, thinking of how much of eternity as an angel he'd had without the chief prince in his life, how routine, how mundane all of existence had been. And how it'd felt like fate, like the very first prophecy, for them to meet, in a garden, how Lucifer always met God in a garden. There is no eternity where they don't meet — Michael and Lucifer. "You," the devil said more carefully. "You cannot kill yourself, Michael."

"After the flood, after the covenant of Hell that I made with God for you — He burned me for seven days, Satan." Michael's gaze flared, as if the fires would burst out from his memory. "And the Lord and I made the promise. He would do it Himself — kill me after Lucifer is returned." In Satan's heart, something shifted out of place, and a breath fell out of his mouth, heavy. A sudden coldness trickled along his stomach, his limbs, and a tightness. Instinctive — the shock of confusion, of anger. "We will both be dead, Satan."

'It's you who is arrogant, who is so self-obsessed.' Satan dug his nails into the chains again. 'You think it's all because of you. You think everything is about you. You think you caused Lucifer to fall. He fell because he wanted to. He fell because of who he was and who God was. It had nothing to do with a weak archangel.'

"You slept for days," Michael finally answered the original question, voice unsteady, almost trembling. "Gabriel and Raphael said not to bind you, but they answer to me. And the two of them have already returned to the Earth with the rest of God's army, to anoint all the ones that will be saved. I will join them, soon, to end all things." He, suddenly, took the devil's chin with one hand. "Does the devil still eat?" Satan let out a baffled, mocking laugh. "Can he eat something that isn't the beating heart of a man?" His other hand lifted the apple that Satan had forgotten Michael held and, seconds later, the skin of it was pressing to his soft, pink lips. "Eat this."

Satan stared at Michael, his eyelids half-fallen. "No."

"You won't have anything else to eat. You'll grow weaker."

But the devil was still mulling over the revelation — Michael's final deed, his sacrifice. 'You can't imagine a life in which you resist me, resist having me bear sin for you. You think the only way to save Lucifer is to die. You think this can only end if you kill us both.'

The chains rattled as Satan dragged his tongue along the skin, then he sunk in his teeth.

'You know you have lost. You have failed your Father. You couldn't live for Him, so now you will die for Him. But, even now, you can't kill the desire in you for me eating out of your hand.' Satan chewed, smacking his lips as he did, staring up at the prince's darkened eyes. 'I used to dream of this too, Michael.' He took another bite, crunched the fruit to squelch between his teeth, and swallowed, as dribbles of juice spilled down Michael's armored fingers. Tilting closer, Satan brought his tongue there, tapped the angel's cold gauntlet, then traced up to the tip. 'When I was young, I'd dream of kneeling in the flowers and sucking the nectar out of a flower you'd hold to my lips.'

"It must hurt," Satan said, "for the Beast to carry your Lucifer's face." Michael's brow twitched, and his hand beneath Satan's chin went to grip at his blonde locks. "You have such a hurt look in your eyes, angel."

"He can be saved."

"What if I told you I can feel him, Michael? I can feel what's left of Lucifer? He told me all about you. You were so proud once, and you were so kind. You fought the other angels, and they cheered for you." Michael's cheeks warmed in a soft red; 'Oh, how easy you are.' "How couldn't I fall in love with you too?"

"Stop talking, devil," said Michael, pressing the apple deeper like he could make Satan choke on it. Indeed, a part of it forced its way into the devil's mouth, brushing against the roof of his mouth, making him gag, lurch forward. The muffled moan made the saint, again, twitch.

"He doesn't," Satan managed, hoarse through the choking, "want you dead."

"You're lying to me."

"But you like to hear it, don't you? You like to hear that he loves you, Michael. He loves you more than anything, and you're breaking his heart. He misses your kisses. He misses your touch. He misses dreaming of sinning with you—" Satan cut himself off with a hitch of his breath when Michael dropped the fruit, surged forward, took Satan's face in his cold hands, tilted his face up to his, and breathed a finger-width from the devil's mouth. His armor pressed against Satan's tunic, and his knee had come in between the devil's legs.

Forehead pressing to Satan's, Michael said, though clenched

teeth — "You're not him. You're not Lucifer." His hands dragged down Satan's front, to his hips. "But you have his face." Angrily, somberly, he dragged his mouth from the edge of Satan's lips, narrowly avoiding a kiss, then down his jaw, his neck. Here, he began to kiss, but with too much teeth, nipping him everywhere that his groping fingers, fisting and pulling at Satan's clothes, revealed skin. He breathed harshly against the devil's warming body, dampening it.

Satan bit down on his lip and, momentarily, felt a flicker of pride's flame in his chest once the prince had moved onto his knees, hands still on Satan's hips like the devil was a statue of a god and Michael was a pitiful believer. Veneration, at last. But the devil didn't feel the victorious laughter he'd expected blooming in his chest. He was chained in Heaven. He had kneeled before a God who mocked his rebellion, who was going to have the angel of beauty at his side once more. Apocalypse would strip every action, every word, against God of meaning. And, suddenly, to be a divine idol wasn't what Satan wanted from this vile chief prince. 'It must be because I know it isn't true. His belief is crazed. It's demented. He's made a cult of us.' Yet — Satan breathed out a slow, pleasured sigh as Michael mouthed at his hip, then dipped his face lower. "What is this?" he finally asked. "Why are you doing this?"

Michael panted hot against the devil's arousal, then he murmured, "No matter my actions — I know my fate."

Bitterly, Satan laughed. "You want a taste of me before we're both killed by God? You want to enjoy me?"

"I told you to stop talking."

"It's all Lucifer once wanted, too. He asked you to adore his body."

"You're not him."

"I'm not, but I have him, here, in my chest. Inside me. Don't you want to join him, Michael? If you come inside, you might find him." Satan wrestled for control of this moment again. He was the seducer; he was the tempter.

Michael gripped one of Satan's thighs, then slowly pried it away from the other, lifting, and when put his mouth on the devil's sin, the both of them breathed out painfully. *"Lucifer,"* mourned the chief prince, trying to fill his mouth, coaxing his tongue to flick amateurishly, then he brought his lips together to suckle. The apple in his other hand plopped to the ground, rolled away, and Satan shut his eyes and listened to the prince moan the name of the angel he'd once loved.

"Is it what you always imagined," Satan gritted out to stifle a cry, as he shuddered, hearing the chain above rattle, "Michael?" His hips ached, begging the devil to let him rock them forward, to chase the prince's indulging.

For some seconds, the archangel didn't answer. He continued, tilting his head one way, then the other, moving his lips like he wanted to kiss Satan here. With all his armor, it was impossible to know whether the prince was aroused or not, and so Satan tried to listen for his grunts, the kind of pleasured groans that demons always offered him. His hips twitched forward without meaning to, and Michael held him tighter, taking it. Finally, he pulled off, to speak, to brush his damp lips against him as he did — "It's better."

"You could have had it. You could have had me."

"I'm having you now."

"It's too late now."

"That's why I'm having you. Because it's too late for me. For you and I."

Satan shut his eyes and the heat of pleasure bloomed in his gut, leaning further against, into, the mouth that he refused to admit he'd been made for. He'd molded himself for other mouths. His body was no longer one of prophecy or fate. It was liberation, freedom. He was pride and death and uprooted love. But he couldn't resist the draw of the other's imperfect suckles, his desperate, frantic drinking.

Pressing forward as much as he could, bridge of his nose pressing to Satan's pelvis, Michael fluttered his eyes shut, clutched Satan's waist tight, almost enough to crush. He ground the devil against him harshly, as if forcing him, as if this wasn't a willing offering that Satan would never confess to. 'It's too late for us. You're right of that.' He dipped his head, wrestled against the bindings, wished he could do more than arch his back and feel it torn out from him. Biting down hard on his lip, the devil tried still to crush the pretty moans that had granted him nations, that had ruled Hell.

Gasping, shudders of pleasure rattling the chains, Satan felt the archangel grapple him closer, as close, as deep, as he could. Trying, hopelessly, to pull the devil's entire body into his mouth, to savor, to eat. To be eaten like Christ at his supper, feeling death on his shoulders. And Michael choked, either on tears or the devil's dribbling end. He drank like it was only the devil that could save him.

Satan could only remain there, supported by Michael's hand and Michael's chains. Panting, legs shivering, the heat in his stomach aching. "Michael," he whispered. "Michael." Broken, soft, no war left in it. Lucifer's voice.

As if man hearing God, Michael lifted his face with desperate, adoring eyes, mouth leaking sin. He rose weak, trailed his hands upward on Satan's body. When he kissed Lucifer, it was hungry, grieving. Their lips molded perfect, then broke — pressing hard enough to shatter where they locked to ensure their mouth would never fit against each other again. 'It's better to be broken than to be made for you.' It was better to be dead than to live without loving, without hating, without the other.

CHAPTER 30

Hours after texting his commanders that he was still alive, Dante received a response. From the coast, after taking the phone Tadeo had handed to him, Dante had messaged that he was still with the suspect, and that if his mother was still alive, he would tell them how to kill Tadeo. Part of it had ultimately been impulse and fear, imagining his mother killed while Dante was missing in Hell. Now, however, grunting as he kicked through the rubble with the anti-Christ, he hesitated before reading the messages on his phone. 'She's alive,' with an image attached, and 'What did you find out about him?' His gaze flickered over to Tadeo.

Among the mountains of rubble they stood over, the anti-Christ was rummaging through the blocks of cement — pieces of wall, pieces of ceiling — with clawed hands. Bone and blood were piled neatly nearby, the jigsaw remnants of someone who'd died wearing jeans and a t-shirt. His brows were furrowed, sweat dribbling down. The stars above had long quieted their screams, but the young man's face cringed in pain as if they still wailed. 'He's a monster,' thought the soldier, trying to tell himself he'd done the right thing, 'but a human one.' Then, Dante glanced at his amputation. 'But maybe a human is worse.' He couldn't return to soldier duties one-handed, and maybe his superiors would go back on every promise and kill both him and his mother. But what one thing was certain — the state was holding his mother — and one was not — that maybe all of this, that betraying the stupid, idiot Tadeo, who had saved Dante from Hell, was for nothing.

Turning away, retrieving the phone of Tadeo's aunt out of his pocket, he texted: 'Destroy him all at once, and he won't be able to heal. Get him with an airstrike. Or maybe a good grenade. It has to be all at once.' In the end, he had no choice. He'd never had a choice in his entire life. But Tadeo had. He could have refused to release the Watchers. He could have never killed soldiers. He should have never been a Beast.

"What..." Tadeo began, voice gruff, exhausted, as if he'd read the mind of Dante, who hurried to slip the phone back into the back of his pants. "What the fuck happened?" He looked around them warily, then seemingly cursed, shook his head, took some steps toward the road. "Come on. We've been here for hours and nothing." Dante moved with him, and when the soldier reached, touched Tadeo's arm, the anti-Christ tensed and jerked away. "Don't touch me."

Ignoring that, Dante simply lifted his hand, held it in the air almost as if he were presenting a calming palm to a rabid animal. "My guess is that it came from the other side." Babylon. "They were always talking about striking the criminal bases here. Maybe they finally got our permission."

"Did that restaurant look like a criminal base to you?!" Tadeo, suddenly, almost shrilly, replied, but then his cheeks flushed at the sight of the soldier's frigid, unemotional expression. "We don't have the time to deal with this— These states and their *politics*— The end of the world is at stake, and all the powerful men only think of their war and their wallets." Dante snorted, and instead of answering to that, Tadeo turned on his heel, hurrying toward the Azteca mare nibbling on grass beside the road.

Dante, again, followed but maintained greater distance this time — betrayal weighing his feet for reasons he couldn't fathom. He supposed he hated Tadeo, hated being here, wanted his damn hand back. Reaching the mare, he saw the anti-Christ climb onto the horse, scoot forward, wordlessly offering the soldier the room to sit. And Dante had to bite down another noise of amusement. With his only hand, he gripped the saddle, then hoisted himself up onto it. As he did, he looked forward, and his breath caught. "God. What the fuck is all that?"

There were spheres looming at the height of skyscrapers, low enough to shadow the town — like molten rock, their bodies coursed with reds, yellows, and oranges; there were dozens, each the size of a plane's wingspan.

"They're," Tadeo whispered, "on the other side too." In Babylon — seemingly concentrated over the city center of sparse towers among stout buildings. "But look, they—" Now, without thinking, he reached and gripped Dante's forearm with tense urgency, using his other hand to point. "They have faces." The soldier could only squint — wondering now if Tadeo might have superhuman eyesight in his body's repository of divinity — to see the detailed fiery pulses on the looming creatures, and he saw some blinking, some tearing open mouths. "And that— Is that a tongue?" Like a solar flare, a stream of light twirled to flick at the air, almost hungrily at all the people below.

"If that's a tongue," Dante said levelly, "then that one has three, four tongues. I don't like that."

"I don't think anyone would," Tadeo said.

"Really? Not even you? It could be your twin," Dante joked, then shoved the other's hand off him, which made Tadeo jump, likely realizing what he'd been doing — touching Dante, after telling Dante not to touch him. "Are we riding back now?"

Tadeo was quiet for a moment, then he murmured, "I know that you're still hiding from the other soldiers, but we can try to find you a car or a bus heading south. I know that you want to see your mother." Tapping the mare delicately with his foot, the anti-Christ began the trip forward.

Dante hesitated. "Are you telling me to go see my mother before the world ends?" Then, he murmured, "If you didn't release the Watchers, maybe it wouldn't."

"I don't know," Tadeo sighed harshly to both statements. "The Watchers aren't mentioned in Revelation. This shouldn't be part of the end." But Tadeo wasn't mentioned in Revelation either, and he'd begun to worry about the degree of metaphor they were working with. If anything could mean anything, then what did apocalypse actually entail? "But I'm not stupid either."

"Are you sure?"

Tadeo scoffed. "Dina told me to have faith, but— Look, I'll admit that it's not easy to, right now."

"All I know is that these Watchers aren't all there in the head, *güey*; they don't look like they care about helping people. And I don't think Dina has been very clear about what they're supposed to do." Dante, as soon as Tadeo made a shameful noise in agreement, added: "I told you: I met demons down there in Hell, and they were all crazy, but none of them were like Dina. I don't think you can blame his weird behavior on being an angel or even a demon in disguise. I think he's being secretive."

Tadeo remembered the devil, at the end of the road, smiling wide, his eyes shining gold. 'Except the devil wasn't on Dina's side. So whose side could Dina be on? Good or evil?' "If not to save the world, though, why would Dina do all this? I don't think he's working for evil. I really don't—"

"When I was in Hell," Dante continued, "the demons told me that the Watchers were chained for marrying humans and having kids with them. The angels captured them, but the demons helped. Satan and God worked together." At that, Tadeo furrowed his brow, even more so when Dante pressed up against Tadeo, a pistol in the soldier's waistband digging into the anti-Christ's lower back. Tadeo had handed the gun to him when they retrieved his clothes; he'd done it fearlessly, knowing he was immune to bullets, but he began to rethink the decision. "And why would an angel want the world to be saved? Don't you think that, if anyone wants the world to be saved, it would be the devil?"

Tadeo swallowed, then he whispered, "Stop touching me. Stop pressing your body against me." The devil had told Tadeo to end the world with him; Dina had told Tadeo to save the world with him. Who was lying? Could it be both of them?

Grunting, Dante leaned away but kept talking: "Tell me how the story ends, how the world ends. I don't know it that well."

"Jesus comes down. He marries the Church. There's a new Heaven, new Earth."

"Okay, so Jesus comes down and fucks our ass?"

"Can you try having some respect?" Tadeo sighed harshly, cold rosary like a noose under his shirt.

"Fuck your religion," Dante said. "But it doesn't matter what I think, does it? If that's how the book ends, I just don't think that's what the devil wants."

Curling some of the rein around a finger, Tadeo decided to leave the conversation there. He'd thought — or had he? — Dina wanted to save humanity to keep evil subdued longer, but that would just be delaying God's apocalypse. Why delay the end? Prophecies were cruel; they were an impatient hint of the end, one that made you helpless. Why fight? Why try to save anyone? Why not just kill everyone to spare them the pain of life and allow them to enter Heaven as children? It was these kinds of questions that Tadeo remembered asking as a child in church. He'd tried to be an atheist as a child; he really had.

Ahead, there were a few smoking buildings but otherwise, the town was perfectly standing still, and the chaos was less from the airstrikes and more from the hungry stars above. As Tadeo rode onto the main street, though far from the couple cars speeding in any direction out of town — the people began to notice him. Masses of them, first a handful but rapidly swelling into dozens of humans, hurried to him and called his name. It was the first time Tadeo had ever heard it from strangers. All this time, he'd been their secret, the Beast of whispers, and now — with their hands all reaching out to him, some of their faces grayed from ash — they shouted, "Tadeo!" Help us. Save us.

"Wait." Heart building to hammer against his chest. Tadeo stammered. "Let me— Let me find my family—" he tried, even when hands, frantically, clawed at his horse. "I'm sorry," he said when a young man tried to shuffle an injured teenager toward him — blood trickling down the left side of her face, reddening the whites of an eye. "I'll try to help you all soon. I'll return." Where were the soldiers? The authorities? Often, his family, his neighbors, spoke of feeling abandoned, but it seemed more true now than it'd ever been.

'It's not true,' Tadeo was thinking warily as Dante waved the people away. 'It's not true that God wants the world to end. And it's not true that I'm the anti-Christ. Because if it's true, then what?' Pleading, the people tugged on his clothes. 'What about all these people? What about me?' He knew how Revelation ended, as did God, as did Satan. 'What now?'

His home; they reached it half an hour later. Tadeo, however, didn't recognize it immediately. His family's house had never been slanted to the left, and a collapsed roof was nothing unusual in this neighborhood but one hadn't belonged to them. The windows were shattered, the uneven remnants shining like crystals over the ground, in between the slabs of wall that'd been blown off. Miraculously, amid the rubble, their pepper plant still stood with Tadeo's family huddled beside it. Enough time had passed now that they'd cleaned themselves of ash. Streaks of the gray remained, however, gathered beneath their nails, in the creases of their knuckles. The oldest woman among them, Tadeo's grandmother, rose her head first, her body still shaking — like the ash, some blood lingered — and called his name. When all the other family turned, saw him, Tadeo yanked the horse to a halt, ignoring her startled neighing. He swung his body off before Dante could even taken the reins the anti-Christ shoved into his hands.

"*Wela*!" he called for his grandmother, then, "*Welo*—" He found himself coughing, suddenly, inexplicably, as if he'd made himself sick from shock. Nearby, the crowd watched as Tadeo went for the unlocked gate, pushed it open, shoved it closed behind him to dissuade his followers from harassing the family. "What," he called, stumbling into the yard, "happened to the house?"

His grandfather had a distant look in his eyes as he shuffled closer to his wife and said, "They hit our home. I don't know why. Over the last few days. They hit a few places, just a few— All over town—" On the ground between his grandparents, Tadeo's mother was sitting, her face twitching with a cognition that the anti-Christ hadn't seen in over a decade.

"Tadeo," called a cousin, hurrying over and taking his arm. "Our *tío* Joaquín—" The one who'd lent Tadeo the horse. "Ana Karen is screaming in there with her baby—" That was his daughter. "I think they're okay, but she won't leave him. The rest of us were lucky—Joana got us out of the house, into the yard right before, but our *tío* just got in— He didn't—" Here, her voice began to break and the sinking feeling in Tadeo's own chest fell into his stomach, twisted it.

"No," Tadeo whispered, shook his head, eyes already beginning to burn. "Don't tell me that. Where is he?" His jaw ached from a sudden tensing at the hinges, and Tadeo frantically grabbed his cousin, taking her sleeves. "Tell me where he is."

"Tadeo," called the hoarse, chainsmoker voice of only one person, and the anti-Christ's head jerked to the open door to a house half-collapsed. "I told you— Dammit, I told you—" Joana looked like the others, but her clothing was grayer; she hadn't cleaned it off like the others. Against the doorway, she leaned, eyes bloodshot, mouth pressed fine — her expression like she'd been the one to aim the strikes, to kill Tadeo's uncle, to cause all of this. "He's not in one piece, Tadeo. He's dead. Don't go see it. There's a reason they're all out here."

The crowd was still watching, and the anti-Christ glanced behind briefly, saw Dante on the horse still. Distantly, there were the honks of traffic, the desperate using the last of their gasoline they'd saved for emergencies. Breathing, breathing, Tadeo reached for his hat, tugged it off, revealing hair stuck to his sweated forehead. Initially, he didn't say a word to her, felt that he should be furious at her for even implying that this could be his fault, but it was. 'It's my fault in a way guiltier than you probably meant it.' He stumbled, bringing his hat now to one hand, holding it tight at the rim, whereas his other fingers began to comb back his hair anxiously.

"Don't listen to her," said the cousin. "It was— There was nothing you could have done."

Tadeo heard the words, but he could do no more than nod in acknowledgment before he took a step forward, another two, until he'd reached Joana, whose face was still set in a mutilated anger, in deep sorrow.

"Joana," he called, voice uncertain, afraid, lowering the hand in his hair. 'I need to tell you what I've done. That maybe you were right. That maybe I shouldn't have gone with Dina. That maybe I've doomed us all.' He stumbled up to her, taking his hat with both hands, then opened his mouth slowly. He wanted to say, 'I'm sorry.'

But Joana whispered —"I'm sorry." And Tadeo blinked, once, twice. "I really am." Her face suddenly grimaced deeply, eyes softening. "I didn't know what else to do."

"It's not your fault," Tadeo said softly. "You saved most of my family—"

"I'm sorry for your uncle too," she cut off, still in a whisper so that no one else could hear. "But that's not why I'm apologizing." When Tadeo waited, patient for her to explain, Joana confessed: "You're the anti-Christ." 'No,' Tadeo thought. 'No.' But the emptiness, the horror in him was so painful that all his muscles had seized up. "You're meant to kill us all — your own family, me, everyone in town, the whole world— And I knew. I've always known."

"What?" Tadeo breathed, his throat tightening, burning.

"I found you because I knew." She staggered back, gaze flashing to Tadeo's family with a strike of grief before she spoke again and looked at him. "I met the angel Michael before I met you. He told me who you were. He told me what you could do." Momentarily, Tadeo couldn't even remember when he met Joana, like she'd always been there beside him. That didn't feel so far from the truth. She'd been the one to tell Tadeo to stop hiding from the world, to free the town from all the violence. He'd resurrected, but he hadn't really stopped being dead until she stepped into his life as a little girl with a gun and a wrestler mask."He told me he'd kill you when the time was right."

Taking a step back, Tadeo felt his eyes widen and a gash in his chest cut itself deeper. 'Hurt' felt like such a juvenile word, but it was more accurate than any other; he felt small, shrinking, young, confused. He hurt like a scraped knee.

Joana's gaze was exhausted. "But I wanted to use you first before Michael killed you. I wanted to save this place. It's all I wanted— I thought it would be easy to know who's good, who's bad. I started listening to the wrong people. I didn't mean to. It's all so complicated. I'm sorry. To you, to everyone. Fuck. I thought it would be easy."

'You thought you could just kill the right people. Like all the evil of living is concentrated in some. Like there are demons and angels of humans.' Tadeo, slowly, began to turn back to the street and crowd. 'But it's the angels that want to end the world.' "I did too," he replied; it was a confession; he was a sinner, but there was no priest on the other side of the confessional. 'You groomed me into a good lamb to slaughter.' But he couldn't blame her, could he?

"Where are you going?" her voice finally rose, shaking, feeble, sounding like she never had before — but when Tadeo spoke again, it was to his grandmother.

"I'll be back in a moment, is that alright?" His skin itched, and the monster inside of him twisted and turned, despite how hollow he felt. Tadeo's grandmother looked at him, then seemed to understand. She nodded, and Tadeo instantly leaned over to kiss her cheek before stepping away, heading toward the gate once more and the people there, waiting on their savior. Their anti-Christ. Without thinking, Tadeo lifted his hat back over his hair, and he grit his teeth and told himself to stay on his feet. To not fall — onto his knees — in grief and screams and cries despite a wobble on his bottom lip. But there was no helping the bombardment of images in his mind of his uncle's face, of his voice, his touch, his laugh. He'd never hear it again. He was still waiting to hear his father's voice again. He was still waiting to hear his mother talk too.

We spend so much time waiting for the long lost.

Tadeo reached the gate, opened it to climb onto the sidewalk, and a breath fell out of his mouth. He shut the exit blindly behind him, then caught Dante finally climbing off the mare. Swallowing, Tadeo turned away, began walking away from him, from the house.

The crowd, shockingly, didn't follow — at least not closely. They shuffled their feet from a distance, like stray dogs trailing a stranger.

Among the noise of all their steps, Tadeo almost missed the sound of Dante jogging up to him, saying, "Where are you going? My God, they hit your fucking house. And I'm sure they knew where it was all this time. They were just waiting for a fucking excuse— Needed the right moment to let them get away with this—"

"My uncle is dead," interjected Tadeo softly, hollow. "And I almost lost the rest of my family. I just learned that my only friend was just using me, knowing I would die." He continued walking, but he turned his face toward his own shoulder, not looking back at the soldier either. "What do you want, Dante?" 'What did the resurrection mean if I was born again to die? What did any of this mean?'

Dante hesitated, then he said, tightly, "I'm sorry." 'The strike didn't come from me; I sent the text less than an hour ago.' But fear churned his stomach. And so when Tadeo didn't reply, the soldier cursed, took him by the arm to force him to stop.

This time, however, Tadeo felt a whip of anger and terror shock his body, and he snarled, for the third time, "*Don't fucking touch me*!" He tore his arm away, spun around, and eyes tore open across his face, mouth crowded with the jaws of a Beast. "You can leave!" But his voice cracked. "Leave and go back to your mother—"

"I *will*," Dante said, quick, a tinge of anger and terror in his words. "I will, idiot. I'm not going to stay in this shithole."

"Then why are you still following me!?"

"I wanted to apologize," Dante snapped. "Because I—" 'Do I say it? Do I tell him he made a mistake not killing me that day?' "I followed you into Hell," he said carefully, "wanting to find out how to kill you so that I could tell my commanders. But, fuck, I didn't know what to do. I can't just go back, Tadeo. If I did, they'd kill me for knowing too much. They'd kill my mother." 'They're already holding her.' "I already lost my sister. I don't know— I didn't know what else to do." Oddly, a visible tension fell from Tadeo's face, and the eyes he'd just sprouted began to shut, his sharpened teeth began to dull. Maybe he'd wanted to hear this, perhaps have his suspicions of Dante confirmed. "So, I'm asking you to forgive me." 'For what you think I wanted to do, for what I've already done.' "You can understand, can't you?"

Tadeo flinched; he could understand; he could understand Joana too.

"I," Dante continued, "understand why you did what you did to me, too. I hate you for it, but I understand. We're all just trying to survive." He laughed then, bitterly. "Maybe you don't have to forgive me—"

"But I do," said Tadeo, his lips trembling, fighting either a smile or a frown — he didn't know. "I forgive you, Dante." 'I forgive Joana too.' Maybe he shouldn't have walked away without telling her that.

The soldier was quiet for a moment, staring at him with his brows furrowed, a crease forming between them; his mouth opened, closed, then opened again. "Why?" The word had such an edge that it may as well have been a, 'What is wrong with you?'

Tadeo swallowed, then shrugged. "It's the right thing to do." The words hurt him, though he insisted to himself that he meant it, that he was good enough to believe in the right thing. If it was true that he was the anti-Christ, he began to wonder if God would forgive him for suicide, if He would allow it just this once. He'd tried to be good. He'd thought he'd been good all this time. His throat closed and itched, and his body was beginning to slump in exhaustion. Then, he lowered his gaze, down to that bandaged stump where the soldier's arm ended; Tadeo's sin. He reached, slow, to ensure that Dante had every chance to pull away, but the soldier didn't.

Brushing his fingers on the wrist, Tadeo felt Dante' muscles tense beneath his skin. He remembered healing that woman, without meaning to, with Dina. And, with no water, no more than touch, Tadeo healed Dante's hand, then squeezed it.

CHAPTER 31

In the devil's chambers, Baal had been sitting at the edge of the bed, slumped over in exhaustion, when he was told of Satan's capture.

Since the soldier and the anti-Christ escaped Hell, the civil conflict had only grown. Moloch's followers had declared themselves authorities in several clusters of demon abodes, and fighting a war in the sprawling, ever-shifting, unyielding body of Hell was no easy feat. In the aftermath of the fall, Baal had led wars on Earth, even against Moloch, over the sparse water and resources, for anything that could relieve the pain of being alive eternally — but this was far worse, far more surreal. The souls of the damned continually wailed, their mangled bodies dribbling onto their streets. Even the demons most loyal to Baal complained that Moloch's promises were seductive, the promises of better distribution of food, of water, and even of sex for all those who didn't care for the orgies. Quietly, they suggested that maybe Moloch should indeed be the regent, that he might pair better with the devil's beautiful cruelty. And Baal had whipped them for it with his morning star, bared his teeth, angrier than he'd ever been.

But now, he sat, stared with reddened eyes and stitches stinging across his body at the demon spy who'd just returned from the surface again — Gemory. He sighed at her, shut his eyes, and said, "Go out and gather the demons. Find Moloch." Once, Satan had said common enemies could unite anything; he'd whispered it while reminiscing of how demons and angels had fought together against the Watchers for the sin of loving. "We have to face Heaven."

Gemory's face flickered with a sudden terror but not shock, then she took a step back, hand coming over the front of her robe. "Is the world really ending, Baal?" Unlike the others, she had avoided punishment for running off with Asmodeus, Armoni, Rosier, and that human soldier — Baal had thought her too valuable as a scout on Earth — but she'd been visibly anxious since. Even if he wanted to punish her, though, Baal would not be as brutal as he often was. He'd come to like her; there weren't many true women in Hell. And there weren't any true men, but Baal supposed that was for the best.

"It's ended before," Baal chuckled dryly. "What's another time?" The mattresses creaked beneath the regent of Hell as he, slowly, rose to stand, his muscles stiff. Turning away from her, he headed for one of the dressers, the one for him; he had no need for many, unlike Satan's collection of clothes for every century in human history. Baal stopped, looked to a vanity mirror nearby, where there was a golden-framed photograph — ancient and torn at its edges. In it, Satan was sitting in a chair with Baal close behind him — both in their Hell drapery, their horns, and Baal's tail. One of the first pictures of the first cameras to ever appear on Earth, snapped by a terrified human man. Baal always thought they looked so serious in it, like neither had ever smiled in their endless lives. "Go, Gemory."

"Yes— Yes, Baal."

The regent of Hell, shakily, drew in a breath. He didn't usually dare sound so uncertain, *worried*, before anyone beside his beloved devil, but he knew that Gemory wouldn't think less of him for it. Thumping, her steps headed away from the bedroom, and Baal allowed silence to linger. 'Satan,' he wanted to say, 'if God has harmed you, I'll have to raze Heaven to the ground. If Michael has harmed you, I'll have to create an entire new Hell just for him.' The devil had sat with Baal a hundred times and explained that God wasn't likely to kill him, but there were much worse things than death that He was capable of. Satan's voice had been distant as he spoke, and his eyes had shut when Baal put a palm against one of his cold cheeks. 'Will Hell burn up, as you always warned, Satan?' He took the photograph, and he would look for the chest of Cain's belongings, and he would have to accept all else that he'd lose of home. 'But the world has already ended, and we survived it once. Lucifer. We can survive it again.'

Setting his jaw, the demon dressed in a new tunic, brought a Roman wreath to his head, and then draped on a cape. He took his mace, then headed for the balcony of the great tower. It was too early to expect all the demons already gathered, but he would wait there, standing over the heart of Hell, watching them, and he would tell them to put their wars aside, for the first war in history had just risen from its slumber. "And Satan," he'd say to their horrified faces, "is gone. He's been taken from us." Already, he imagined the horror of the crowd, the manner in which they'd yell, but he'd meet their anger with his own: "We will bring Heaven to its knees." Baal — slamming a fist onto the stone balustrade. "We will end the war for Heaven now — millions of years since it began." Panting, every muscle in him twisting tight enough to burn. "Heaven and Earth will be ours."

'Speak from your chest,' Satan had critiqued two hundred years ago, laying over the divan prettily, braiding his hair. 'You're my regent of Hell, Baal. They should fear the heart in your words.'

Once the demons were here to listen — "We'll bring home their apocalypse," Baal seethed. "Put aside our battles among each other, for as demons, we all serve the one who led us to freedom. Whether you follow me or your false leaders, march alongside each other to Heaven so that our true god, our king, the one who led us to freedom, can be restored!" 'And then you will rule again, Lucifer, and I will be beside you. And we can allow God to burn up the Earth, and all of man on it. Our Hell must remain.' The crowd rallied; they cheered.

But elsewhere, there was silence, broken up by wet huffs of breath. Asmodeus, kissing, sucking on Rosier's neck while the latter simply sat back against the wall, holding the duke, staring forward, eyes half-lidded. They had done little else besides this and talk after they'd been dragged to prison by Baal and his demons. Even Rosier, who could find himself entertained by even strings of thread found himself with nothing to keep him from sleep except Asmodeus' affections. The night before — though they had no way of knowing the hour in the constant dark of the cell — he had even allowed Asmodeus to fuck him, though not without keeping his tunic on, hoping Asmodeus' body over his would shield him from anyone wanting to enjoy watching. Asmodeus' rank and respect might prevent demons from joining uninvited, but Rosier still wished for private intimacy, however angelic that was for him to think.

Soon, however, rapid footsteps sounded, then a figure staggered into view at the other end of the bars.

"Rosier!" a disheveled Armoni in furs called, then grimaced when he saw what Asmodeus was doing, but he bit his tongue; he always did when it came to Asmodeus and Rosier. Not long after they'd met, Armoni had kindly suggested that maybe Rosier and Asmodeus were not right for each other, and Rosier had told Armoni that he simply didn't understand. 'I think you don't understand it either,' Armoni had replied, 'but I won't press on this, this bruise you carry named Asmodeus. And I know that he's the only thing keeping Moloch from hurting me because you ask it of him. Don't look at me like that. I know you'll say Asmodeus is genuine in his want to help me, but we can't be sure, can we? But I do know that I owe him everything, the way I owe you everything. If it weren't for you both, Satan would have allowed Moloch to tear me apart after taking the Leviathan from me to raise as his own child.' But Satan had failed, of course; even the devil couldn't raise the abominations born from women and their Watchers.

"Armoni?" Rosier whispered at the same time Asmodeus pulled away and turned to see the angel.

Before Armoni could say much else, however, a large, armored figure stepped up behind him — Moloch. He was dressed in red as dark as his trimmed hair, and he snorted at the sight of the duke of lust pressed so close to Rosier. "Asmodeus," Moloch chuckled. "You could have joined me, my side of the war, and not have to waste away in here." He retrieved a key — stolen, surely — and jammed it into the lock at the door, twisting it, then going to grip the handle. Neither Asmodeus nor Rosier moved when he pulled the exit open for them, and he seemed as equally amused by that as catching them acting so affectionate. "But you can pick your side once we all return from Heaven."

"Heaven?" Asmodeus scoffed. "What are you saying?"

"The angels stole our beloved Satan," Moloch answered briskly, then reached for a sullen Armoni, twirled a strand of his pale blonde curls idly. "So our little wars here are on hold. I'll agree with Baal that we need the devil back before Hell drowns all of us in fire." At that, Rosier swallowed nervously. "But after that, let's talk, Asmodeus."

"It's suicide to attack Heaven," Asmodeus grunted.

"Maybe Hell needed a culling anyway," Moloch laughed as Armoni let out a breath suddenly, pushed past him to hurry into the cell, toward Rosier.

"I'm sorry," Armoni whispered to the fruit demon as Moloch went for Asmodeus, grabbing his arm, forcing him up to his feet even while Asmodeus groaned sharply in pain, knees bending weakly. "Moloch and his friends held me, wouldn't let me leave to come help you two."

But Rosier kissed his cheek quickly, quieted him. "Don't apologize. I'm happy you're safe."

"I worry about what the Watchers are going to do— Rosier, Azazel told me a hundred times that he wanted Satan to suffer, that he wanted revenge. He said he'd love to end Satan's entire world the way that Satan ended his."

"Armoni!" Moloch barked as he dragged a limping Asmodeus. "Come follow, or I'll leave you to the fires." And so Armoni took Rosier's hand and followed, tugging along the demon of fruit with him.

At Satan's tower, Baal loomed over the balcony, shouting out commands at the crowds of thousands upon thousands below — demons and the souls of animals in between. The latter howled and screeched, filling all the gaps between the endless chatter and yelling of the devil's infernal children. Wooden crates were stacked, tipped over — mountains of armor that demon talons rummaged through, all from Satan's prepared stock and Moloch's gathered one. And Moloch put Armoni to work helping to hand it all out to the crowd, trying to gauge their approximate size hastily. There were, however, weapons too. Swords, spears, but firearms, as well, those mass produced for the brutal wars of humanity. The armor, on the other hand, was earthly, but not human. Satan had ordered it all to be fashioned in a dark hue to contrast poetically with the angels', but it'd been constructed from Earth and Hell materials. None of it was particularly strong — the armor could withstand hellfire but not angel swords; if this battle were to have happened centuries earlier, the demons would have been slaughtered.

But now it would be different. The humans had created just what the demons needed to take on Heaven. Asmodeus couldn't help but find it terribly appropriate.

When Armoni handed a rifle to Asmodeus, the duke set it on the ground like a walking stick, and Rosier watched Armoni fit gauntlets over his trembling hands. Both of them were armored now, though Asmodeus' fit him too tight and Rosier's fit him too large. The demons around were raising their voices in chants, and all the animals howled in solidarity, "Heaven will return Satan to us!" they declared. "Heaven will return our king! Raze Heaven to the ground!"

Asmodeus remembered his words of suicide earlier as he kissed Rosier's helmet. 'Suicide, hm.' He was quite familiar with that, but this didn't feel like suicide; he could hardly breathe in the chest plate locked around him like a pair of jaws. There was no autonomy here. 'This is murder.' Satan's sacrifice.

"I don't want," Rosier whispered, "to burn." In the seas of fire that Revelation promised for the demons.

"The world didn't end when Christ walked the Earth. It won't end now," Asmodeus reassured him. 'I didn't even end when we left it.' Centuries ago, the never-healing demons had crawled back into Hell and stayed there partly out of Satan's orders and partly because of humanity's rapidly advancing weaponry. Once demonic intimidation and strength could no longer protect them, Earth became too much of a risk for most. He and Rosier had never stopped visiting, of course, despite Satan's laws. They'd watched how, several times, the apocalypse had almost come, then quietly receded; Rosier believed it each time.

Sitting with Asmodeus once, staring at the ruins of an empire, at the dead devastated by the disease of conquest, Rosier had whispered, 'Sometimes I wonder if the apocalypse is not one moment, one day, but it's all of them put together. The world ending, over and over.'

Baal finally led a third of Hell out into the Earth. Though he could fly, the others were made to scale up one of the endless canyons into the place of damnation that'd eventually give way into the underwater caves. As they did, the flesh of sinners followed, howling after them in their agony and blooming like flesh-flowers at their feet. Hurriedly, then, the demons climbed and when they began to reach the waters of a sea, they held their breaths and continued onward, swimming despite the weight of their new armor. Light streamed in through the murky blue, shimmering onto the faraway surface. Demons swam in its direction, toward the sharp and round bottoms of docked ships, as well as toward the limbs of humans standing in the water. There wasn't much animal life in the sea that they passed; the fish had rushed to hide from the invasion.

Rosier was slow to reach the ocean. Another duke had taken Asmodeus and insisted on helping him stay closer to the head of the march, and Rosier had quickly lost sight of Armoni, Moloch, even Baal. But he didn't mind straying behind, to see the demons eclipse him and rise hastily to pull themselves out of the water. From here, Rosier could hear the muffle of screams, then of banging — and the bottoms of boats rocking from one side to another. Sudden splashes of red smoked the water above, trailing toward Rosier, who floated in the sea like litter. It wasn't long before his lungs began to burn, but he'd been burning for a long time, and he was used to pain; he could drown forever. Nonetheless, Rosier began to kick his armored feet, feeling the pull of his sword against his back, trying to weigh him back down. But he continued, and he began to wrestle his arms against the water until the blood and the light at the surface reached him, until he felt it all bubble in his mouth. When Rosier broke through, it was like an embryo from an egg. "Hah," he breathed, but didn't hear himself over the sound of slaughter.

Demons, killing first the humans whose attention had been on the hovering stars overhead, then lunging at those who tried to intervene.

Clumsily, Baal took out some innocents with the mace — some men, some women, a child maybe — intent to keep his hands away from his guns until they'd reached Heaven. But he grinned when the beating of hooves sounded among all the screams. Angels. Panting out saltwater, he turned up at a blood-crimson moon and the burning spheres of stars above the city they'd arrived in. Babylon. There had been no more than a hundred or so humans in the water, but thousands were retreating from the shore, many falling, many sure to be dead not by the demons' weapons but by stampede, caught beneath shoes or suffocated against locked doors. When the angels descended on their winged horses, Baal saw that they carried swords and spears, and he had to bite down a laugh. There were only some dozens of angels, many of them immediately yanking on the reins of their steeds, as if at the first realization that they were horrifically outnumbered. Baal couldn't help a chuckle this time, as he ordered: "Take their horses! And we will ride into Heaven!"

"Traitors!" shouted a demon. "Cowardly shits!"

At the shore, Asmodeus barely managed to wrestle away from the demon that held him before an angel galloped by, swung a sword that cut apart the back of the other duke's throat and narrowly missed Asmodeus' unarmored head. Staggering away, splattered in blood, Asmodeus sourly thought, 'I don't want to die for Satan.' He considered running, finding Rosier and taking off somehow, but his legs were still so weak. Another angel swung a sword, and he ducked just in time to see a demon fling a dagger in the direction of the attacker, hit right at one of his wings, before five, six demons swarmed him. Like insects devouring a speck of food, the demons drowned the angel in their crowding, pulling the screeching horse down alongside the angel. All around Asmodeus, the same happened to each of the angels; one attempted to retreat only for a demon, taking the chain of a captured angel, to fling it out at them like a whip and bring him down.

"Asmodeus!"

The duke of lust twisted his head and sighed in relief at Rosier, who was running to him, trying to keep his head down. Swallowing, Asmodeus blurted, "Rosier, you were right," just as the younger demon reached him, touched him, gripped his robes tight in a modern world they had no right to be in. "It's all already ended. It's all ended a hundred thousand times." He squeezed Rosier's hand, and fought the urge to kiss him, before he saw another angel being pulled down and beat, and stripped, and Asmodeus hurried for the horse even when Rosier tried to stop him. "No— Come with me! Hurry!" 'Darling. Let's see Heaven again. You and me. Isn't that what you always wanted? To go home?'

Baal took the sword of the first angel that the demons had swarmed, and he climbed onto a panicking horse before he took the reins tight with one hand. Pressing the sword against the heavenly animals' throat, he ordered, "To Heaven." It thrashed, kicked up its hind legs, for just a second, then screeched when the blade dipped in enough to stream blood. "To Heaven!" It was more than an order that time — a rallying war cry for the demons that began to hurry onto the other horses and lift their weapons. There were not enough horses for all the demons, even if three, four, five shared one, but the rest pillaged the angels, taking their armor, weapons, and already running back to Hell. Hundreds would still be able to reach Heaven, and it would be enough to raid the heavenly city without its army. For the third time, he rallied: "All you demons — to Heaven!" Sword pointed to the skies, Baal felt the horse kick once last time.

The damned cheered, and those on the steeds of angels followed the regent of Hell as he rose up into the sky, avoiding the dark clouds and fallen stars.

In Heaven, Phanuel was in the barracks, seated, gnawing on the inside of his cheeks, eye following the figure of Michael as he approached the exit at the other end of the hall. He'd been listening to the chief prince and the devil, but he hadn't caught any of the noises that he did that first time his friend had entered with nothing more than a fruit. In other words, he hadn't heard them fuck again, but perhaps they had chosen to sin more quietly today. The events from before the war for Heaven were so distant that he could hardly remember them, but while listening, he'd suddenly thought of the parties that Lucifer would host in Michael's home, and how the two had been so inseparable, how they would sit with their legs tangled without shame in front of all the angels. Nostalgia should have struck at him, and yet it didn't. He found himself unable to enjoy any of those memories, as if he'd been silently miserable. Michael may be a prisoner of nostalgia, but Phanuel wasn't.

Michael stopped with one foot already outside, the brilliance of Heaven pouring in. He, softly, said: "I will be with God."

Phanuel whispered, "You always are."

The chief prince said nothing in return, but his shame may as well have crept out from his back like a pair of wings, one of his seraphic six. Breathing in slow, Phanuel watched the door shut. He moved to lock it, afterwards, as he'd always been instructed to do.

At the open gates of Heaven, Rosier stared up at the eternally tall pillars of pearl, then at each of the twelve precious stones that adorned the walls. Like fog, clouds were at the feet of all the horses, and as Baal rode in quickly, swinging his mace at the nearest angel, one only adjusting a pebble, to have his morning star bash at his head. Its teeth jabbed into the side of his jaw, then pulled back enough to rip out some skin, some bone — throwing the stranger to the ground with a gurgled yell. Rosier, holding the reins with Asmodeus behind him, avoided the sight even when the horse beneath trotted forward, not allowing Rosier the chance to lag behind as he'd done in the water. Unwillingly, he saw Heaven. 'Home.' But, unwillingly, he saw no such home.

Rifle cocked in his hands, Asmodeus lifted his chin, craned his neck, counting each simple house they passed and every new cathedral that hadn't been there when they lived here. No angel can memorize Heaven — it resists — but the oldest had come very close. As an angel, Asmodeus had familiarized with all the most important faces of it, and its whims, and he'd had a rough count of the amount of things relative to other things, however much that changed each second. There had been more homes, more bathhouses, more galleries, more observatories, than there'd ever been places to worship. Angels had almost never worshiped before Lucifer, who taught them to adore it, to adore God. How to be thankful when you'd never known life without pleasure? 'What have they done with you, Heaven?' he thought as he aimed the rifle at some angels trying to hurry into their homes in confusion. Before Rosier could stop him, he pulled the trigger, grunted at the recoil against his fragile shoulders. Angels couldn't drop dead, but a bullet could still pierce, could still throw them back to splatter red from the back of their bodies against a wall. Angels could still scream and run.

For Baal, there was something so amusing about this — firearms in Heaven. They did little more than brandish them, and swords and maces were far more enjoyable to torture with, but he liked how the poor heavenly host seemed so distraught. How little they must've known of humanity far advancing them. Taking a torch from the top of a stand on the street, Baal flung it at the first wooden house that he passed, angels scattering away like insects, like humans. 'Poor things,' Baal thought in the same voice that Satan always said it in. 'Sheltered little children.' Michael and his soldiers already saw what the world had become — but all these angels who never left their Father's dollhouse? They must've thought Earth was as it'd always been because Heaven was as it'd always been.

Behind the regent of Hell, the demons were all starting their own fires, galloping past to swing axes and send any nearby angels to the ground, and when an angel dared to raise a sword, they lifted rifles. There was no time for the tortures they'd invented during Satan's first rebellion, but demons still looked for eyes to pierce with the ends of their blades and they grappled hair and dragged angels on the back of their horse, then trampled them into a grotesque sludge of bone and crushed meat — still screaming, unable to die no matter what broke.

But as the demons reached the very heart of Heaven — a shadow loomed above, the only armored angel that had remained in paradise as Earth's apocalypse took place. Great wings spread out behind him — Michael, sword and chain in hand. At the sight, Baal unfolded his own wings, struck them hard enough to raise his body off his horse, to bring him halfway toward the chief prince. The silence between them was brief, and faint; *clink, clink* — they both twirled their wrists to lasso their chains. And the regent said, "Your city burns, prince."

"It is Hell that burns," hissed the archangel, who didn't waste another second before whipping out the golden links that snapped against nothing when Baal instantly swerved to the left, "and you will *burn* with it!" Baring his teeth beneath the helmet, snarling, Michael swung once more, but again, the demon flew out of the chain's way. "Abomination! Beast! Demon!" Baal laughed, so quick in the air that his voice seemed to trail behind him with the breeze that circled around the prince who, grunting, then flew after him. He continued to throw out his chain, heart thudding harder and harder, but when Baal sharply turned, Michael stuttered and twisted inelegantly, frantically swinging blindly in the direction Baal had gone. 'God rebuke you,' Michael thought, so angry that he shook, 'damned angel of *flight*.'

"No," Rosier was whispering, watching the battle from a street away, the street where he'd once lived. "Michael is going to rip him to pieces." He was panting, trembling, as the fires in the city swelled and multiplied. Their horse was walking slow beneath them, passing by homes that should have felt familiar but didn't. 'Home hasn't been home for a long time, has it?' There was a hole in his heart, and it was dually tragic and comforting to know that there was nothing to fill it now, nothing to look for, nothing to hope for.

Asmodeus lifted his head, and then he chuckled — "He'll never catch Baal."

Indeed, the regent flew upward steeply, watching again with a victorious grin as the prince fluttered his wings to stop, his chain extending to grapple at empty space as it kept, kept, doing. Baal could still hear the devil in his head: Satan, Lucifer, taking his hand, curling it into a fist, telling him, 'Fight with your strengths. You have some, don't you? If you ever wrestle with Michael, he'll win with brute force.'

'I have a strength,' Baal had said quietly. 'I can fly. I taught you— I taught you to fly.'

Satan had stared, then squeezed Baal's fingers and replied, 'Then fly.' And then he'd kissed him slow.

A whistle. Baal shouldn't have looked, but he did, gaze flickering in its direction, and he saw Phanuel, on top the rounded ceiling of a temple, looking perplexed, frightened, even when he lifted a hand to point at a stone, long building some roads away. He mouthed something, a name. It might've been Lucifer, or Satan, or maybe Baal's own, but he heard the *clink* of the chain, threw out the one of his mace in panic. Just in time — his chain tangled with Michael's, twisted then knot tight between them, but as it did, the morning star at the end of Baal's weapon swung about, then struck hard at Michael's wing, sending him back as the feathered appendage folded backward with a bloody crack.

Gasping in the pain, Michael plunged, and as he did, he grasped at the air like he'd find the hand of God to take, to keep him from falling — but the Lord hadn't done that even for His favorite angel. And so Michael hit the ground. Heavily, hard, it was enough for a sea of blackness and pain to flood him instantly, to hear the thuds of his armor banging against his strained muscles. Twitching, he tried to twist around, to stagger onto his feet but the throb in his wing jerked all of him, and he let out a noise of agony like a groan. He stumbled, he kept moving, he tried not to look at all the angels, those who stared at their prince, just defeated. Chimes rattled in his ears, and Michael tried to reach for his sword once he realized he'd dropped his chain. Looking up — 'Baal.' He saw a blurry, golden sky without him, the regent of Hell.

"Michael!" shouted an angel. "They're heading for the barracks!"

The spinning world around Michael stopped, and he reeled in a cold breath, and he looked in the direction of the barracks. "No—" he rasped. "Stop them—" He instinctively stretched his wings only to hiss, flap the one that worked behind him without meaning to, pushing him onto the fountain that, just some days ago, he'd brought Satan to. 'Satan.' "No," he seethed. "Don't let them into the barracks. Don't let them take the devil!" 'His mouth had tasted perfectly like Lucifer's, as soft and plump and sweet and maddening. Venom. Liquor. Eucharist. Wine. Lucifer's mouth like liquor. He was with me again, for a second. Lucifer. His sin, his arousal. Tempt me again, please. Tempt me again. Lead me down to Hell, and let me burn for you.' "Don't let them in!" he panicked as he dragged himself closer and closer. 'I kissed you, and I regretted it all. For a moment, I did. I should have fallen with you. Cast me down with a kiss. The kiss of death. Sin. I regret it all.'

Two angels, those not too ashamed of their desecrated prince, went to help him, grabbing his body, keeping him upright, as he looked at the sight of the barracks — the door perfectly unlocked, wide open. Phanuel, standing calmly beside it. The prince couldn't look all the way inside, but he knew that Satan was gone.

CHAPTER 32

The Watchers waited for Dina to leave, as well. When Kimah revealed himself, Uriel had stumbled back, then turned and fled like a human with wide-eyed terror over his face; he left his ancient lover in the sky, furious, flaring. And then Dina had hastily healed many of the Watchers, promising to return soon, saying he had to see someone but flying up toward the other stars. Azazel, who refused to have his heart wound closed, had watched him warily, carefully. 'You're not how I remember,' he'd thought for what seemed the hundredth time. 'We don't age, but you feel larger in my arms, like you've grown larger than yourself.'

When a garbage bin nearby fell on its side, he and the other Watchers jerked their heads in the direction. Quick, Azazel gripped the chain that held Samyaza's collar, just managing to keep him from violently lunging at a group of watching teenagers. They screamed at this and at all the other Watchers who growled and flared their wings, before twisting to scurry away. After this, Azazel raised his hand, and the Watchers slowly settled, wings folding back, snarls fading, but their eyes still wild, and he realized that they'd have to move somewhere more private before he could deal with the matter at hand.

With Kimah no longer twisting his tongue, Kokabiel giggled,

grinning sleazily at the humans, then at the Watchers, then lingering his gleeful gaze on Baraqiel.

Not much of the town had been targeted by strikes, but this hadn't stopped hundreds, thousands, of people from scrambling out of the area with nothing but what they could carry or fit in their cars. The neighborhood that Azazel walked them towards seemed particularly empty, and so he saw one larger home, gestured for his followers to come in with him, and brought them into its yard. Azazel wasn't able to keep his curiosity at bay, however; he reached to touch every wall, every column, every gate. When he was on Earth, the humans had primarily lived in huts; he'd quite liked them. They were warm, simple. His human husband, Eitan, had fucked him on the floor of his hut, and Azazel had enjoyed it until he hadn't. Mindlessly, Azazel twirled Samyaza's chain and stepped into where there was dirt, pepper plants, an orange tree, and stray tile leading into a two-story home with a flat roof.

"Kokabiel," Azazel called as the others did as he had done — touch everything, tilting their heads at every sound — and filled the yard. "Explain."

"Ah?" Kokabiel walked with a bit of a sway, like he were moving to a rhythm solely in his head, but went to grab Baraqiel's arm, "Bara, you're ignoring me. Why is that?" The fallen angel of light in question tensed and looked away, his jaw set.

"Kokabiel," Azazel called again, firmer, and the other Watchers inched away to provide Kokabiel some distance from everyone except the Baraqiel he refused to let go of. "Tell us what that was. What have you been hiding?" When the fallen angel of the stars continued staring at Baraqiel, Azazel furrowed his brow, then said, "Baraqiel, tell him to answer."

"I thought," Baraqiel whispered instead, "I could forgive you for what you did." Like a kitten, Kokabiel tilted his head, blinked wide, innocent eyes. "But you haven't changed." He tore his arm away, breathed unsteady, and then he grunted, "Answer him, Kokabiel." When Kokabiel began to speak, Baraqiel snapped, "*Answer* the questions, Kokabiel!"

Staring, then huffing, Kokabiel pursed his lips before turning to

Azazel. "The star Kimah," he answered, utterly disinterested. "Kimah! That's who that was. I speak to stars, Azazel. Didn't you know? I'm the angel of the stars. I'm their angel, and I speak for them. But they all come to me at once. They all pull my tongue in every direction. Today, today, all the others let Kimah alone use my mouth. And that is all. What else do I say? I just do as they tell me." He looked at Baraqiel again, then he giggled, "Bara, do you hear that?" The angel of light twitched angrily. "I'm answering. Like you told me."

Azazel continued: "There's more." And he felt Samyaza press up behind him, face coming over Azazel's shoulder, chin coming to rest there. "All the time we were chained, you wrote riddles on the ground."

"Riddles!" Kokabiel wheezed at that. "I don't write riddles! I just speak! Not all that you don't understand is a riddle! I've told you of boxes that sing, that speak, and I told you of great silver birds that spit fire. I told you of history. Man, woman, royalties, killings. You didn't understand, but I saw it all. The stars showed it to me. While all of you rot, I watched how men destroy themselves and each other. I watched prophecies of the end seep from the lips of ancients. I watched a Nazarene man who said he was the Son of God gurgle on his own blood to death."

"Son... of God?" Azazel whispered.

"What do you mean by that?" Danel demanded. He stood onto his feet, moved toward Azazel's side, the one not populated by Samyaza, like a guard. "What do you mean *son*?"

But Kokabiel was nudging Baraqiel again, saying, "Bara, Bara, are you listening? You won't even look at me. Should I grovel? I can get on my knees, Bara. Is that what you want?"

Danel barked: "Kokabiel, for fuck's sake! Answer the damn questions!"

At that, Kokabiel sighed dramatically, kicked the ground childishly, and said: "God put His seed in a girl! Hypocrite God! Who told us not to ever have children. But He had His own, His very own. And so that girl bore Him a man! And then he died strung up on slabs of wood! What else is there to say? The devil was there. He met the Son of God. What else is there to say?" The Watchers, however, stared with such shock that they were silent, paralyzed down to their very blood; their sin, that they had suffered more than anything for, had been committed by the God that'd ordered their imprisonment.

And, Azazel knew, the devil had committed it as well — God and Lucifer, the torturers of the Watchers, the greatest hypocrites of all. "It was... not only the Lord who had a child." He'd always wondered why Satan had grown desperate one day, grabbing Azazel, commanding him in a frantic whisper to tell him how to do it, how to have a winged child, how to not bear an abomination. "The devil." Pleading, panicking, all of Satan's perfect poise falling apart between Azazel's fingertips — all for a child, any child. 'I'll do whatever I must do,' Satan had whispered hoarsely. 'I'll have Samyaza whipped again if you don't tell me. If I don't succeed, you and your Watchers will suffer.' Azazel's voice came hollow: "And I told him. I told Satan how to have a child, a beautiful one, a winged one like an angel." Samyaza touched Azazel's hand, a moment of lucidity. "I told him because it happened to me. I had a child that wasn't monstrous like all of yours."

Elsewhere, Dina landed. His feet fell into a river that seemed a touch too red, and he walked beneath a bridge. At one side of him, there wasn't a soul except for a few stray pieces of garbage; on his other side, there were troops, tanks, smaller armored vehicles. He ignored it all, walking slow toward a sphere that was much lower than the rest of the stars, but it was dribbling its blood of fire, boiling the river water below. "Apsinthos," the angel whispered in wonder. A smile trickled along his mouth, and his eyes squinted in joy, and his body seized with love and warmth.

The golden sphere before him wasn't perfect, hardly heavenly, gurgling and churning its own body. 'Dina.' He dwarfed the little angel, about half the length of the bridge but with tendrils of fire curling out from him like wind-blown hair.

Stopping, the angel looked up at Apsinthos with wide eyes that reflected all the light before him. 'You've come to Earth.' But then he remembered Uriel, of course, and grimaced. 'Apsinthos, Kokabiel began speaking in the voice of a star, and then the star revealed itself. His name, I think, was Kimah. Who was that?' The name had been in Uriel's writings, but sparsely; Dina remembered that he'd been blind, that he had spoke to God on behalf of all the other angels. Somewhere, he had read the name 'Uri-Kimah.'

'It's good to see you close to me once more, Dina,' replied Apsinthos, 'but you shouldn't have left the Watchers. You're meant to encourage them to destroy the world. They already hold the desire, my angel. You must only guide them to Babylon, Satan's beloved empire of transgressions and sickness.' When the young angel frowned, the star finally said, 'As for Uri, I cannot tell you, but you know of his obsession with us stars. He may be able to tell you if you ask, but it's not of great importance. Uriel knows little. Angel of wisdom without wisdom. Return to Azazel, my dear Dina.'

Dina couldn't quell the cold flames in his heart. 'I think that— I think that I'll look for Uri after I speak to the Watchers.'

Firmer — 'You must know your duty, Dina.'

And the angel swallowed thickly, flinching, before he said, 'I will end the world, Apsinthos. I promised it, and I know that I want it. But I will look for Uri. And he will understand once I tell him. He is wise. He is.'

'Remember why we're doing this. For the good of God and for love. I've come to this wretched Earth to be with you before and after the end.'

Dina hesitated, then, before he nodded. 'I remember, Apsinthos. Beloved Apsinthos.' When the soldiers on Babylon's side of the river began pointing, shouting, Dina unfolded his wings and lifted himself into the sky to find the Watchers he'd left behind.

But after the Watchers had the discussion in the yard, many of them had gone off to rest, though all in the same house. One might've thought they'd run away from one another, tired of the presence of these same 199 Watchers for thousands of years — but quite the opposite occurred. Azazel was sure that many of them didn't know how to breathe without counting the sighs of their brothers in between, and so they huddled close, for the most part. They slept, against one another, within the walls of a home riddled with objects they couldn't make any sense of. Baraqiel, oddly, had chased after a skipping Kokabiel, and from the yard — where Azazel remained, now sitting with his hands on his lap — he listened to them argue.

Baraqiel was saying: "For you, I descended to the Earth. For you, I took a wife. I had children, for you." Kokabiel was giggling in response. "But all this time imprisoned, I lost all the love I carried for you."

"I don't need love from you," Kokabiel laughed, "I just need you with me, Bara."

Letting out a tired sigh, Azazel had been about to close his eyes, to think, to pretend revealing his greatest secret, something both blessing and sin, hadn't ached the way it did. 'My winged infant.' With a face like his man's, with a gaze like an angel's. 'The world that I descended to with the Watchers is long gone. Lucifer said it to me, and it was the truth.' Even the air seemed different, thicker, hotter. 'But all that happened here, all the blood we Watchers spilled — I feel like it occurred yesterday.' The years that they had spent on this Earth, with all the great animals, the humans, the marriages, the families. How far the world had moved away from it, from all of their lives — but Azazel had spent every waking moment in prison and in Satan's tower telling himself that the humans he'd loved were still out there, waiting for him on a coast that survived the flood. 'Naamah.' A child who hated angels, who hated God. 'Eitan.' My man.

At the sound of a grunt, Azazel glanced down, then smiled fondly, sadly. "Samyaza." He was on his knees before Azazel, wrapping his arms around his waist, pressing his face into his stomach. 'Dear Samyaza.' The angel who'd led them in wedding humans, who'd loved a woman named Idith, who'd loved him as well. Azazel reached to run his fingers through the dark hair of the old leader, and he heard some distant chirps, some faint birds in the middle of apocalypse. "Beautiful Samyaza," he teased, and the angel lifted a gaze to him, wide and sweet. "Pretty Samyaza," he said next, taking cheeks that flushed under his fingertips. Tilting Samyaza's face up, lowering his own face — their lips pressed together, soft, molding.

Azazel had been so eager to be alone with Samyaza again.

Deepening the kiss into each other's mouths, Samyaza grunted, then moaned highly, beastly, but with a sweet undercurrent, and his body rose higher, higher. His hands landed on Azazel's legs, and Azazel wondered if he ever thought of his human wife when he had him. The ghost of their old humans remained on their skin, between them. But they gasped against each other anyway. Samyaza's hand found the wound in Azazel's chest and pressed his fingers in gently, as if trying to fill it with himself, to be his new heart. Like they could be one, this way. The first angel to sire, the first angel to bear.

But the noise of wings soon reached them, then the thump of someone landing nearby, before Dina's voice came — "Azazel...?"

Samyaza jerked away, looked wildly at Dina, but he didn't attack, hovering over Azazel protectively.

"Dina," Azazel called softly in response, noting the disheveled hair on his old friend, his human clothes, the fire in his gaze that had burned away all the innocence that Azazel remembered being there. "You're back." He swallowed, and then he said, "I have a lot of questions for you."

Flush over his brown-skinned face, Dina panted slow, trying to catch his breath; certainly, he'd been flying above in endless circling, looking for the Watchers he'd just freed. "Forgive me— I went to pray. The anti-Christ has begun to heal all those who haven't left this place, and I believe this to be a part of the apocalyptic prophecy — for the one destined to destroy this Earth to act as a Messiah. And you must forgive me for not being able to stop him. I fear the end is soon. I'm certain of it."

As Azazel mulled over a response, he heard the familiar hacking of Kokabiel nearby, and he sensed as many of the Watchers followed the fallen angel of the stars out into the yard they'd all earlier been in. "Dina!" Kokabiel called, almost like a friend might. "Dina! Dina? You're lying. You didn't go to pray!" Dina, instantly, tensed, as he stared past Azazel to Kokabiel, who strolled along, but before he could reply — "You were talking to a star."

"No, I—" Dina's face paled a shade, then he shook his head. "I… Well, I approached a star, Kokabiel."

"Liar! You're a liar!" Kokabiel sang right back at him.

But Azazel tried to keep the conversation steady; he said. "You said that the boy who broke our chains is healing those in this… tribe of people? Why is that?" He couldn't resist the tilt of his head. "We don't know the prophecies of the end that you speak of, Dina."

"They're in a holy book," Dina answered quickly, "one of many— But this is the right one, according to God. All of the wickedness of the world will culminate in a Final Judgment. Satan will be defeated and cast into a lake of fire. Goodness will prevail, but only through the destruction of everything that is, that has ever been." His eyes ignited with the flame that Azazel had earlier noted, and his body straightened, like new life had been breathed into him by his words. Religious fervor. "The Lord will be pleased when there is a new Heaven, new Hell."

Careful, Azazel replied, "If this end of all things is so great, then why did you tell us, at the sea, that you were trying to prevent it?" This time, caught in his lie, Dina simply froze. "Did you think we didn't hear Uriel's words?" Azazel remembered them, carefully: 'Do you realize that you've reared the apocalypse?' "We rose from our bindings to chaos, and you left Uriel believing you did all of this unintentionally." Delicately, Azazel rose from his chair, and he said, "But you're not the Dina that I remember."

And, abruptly, this made the young angel's gaze darken. Dina thought, 'You too. Like Uriel, calling me vain — thinking me so single-minded, so innocent. So pitiful. Do you miss the Dina that cried over penances? The one who allowed himself to be beaten in the streets, time and time again?' "What does it matter what I want?" His tongue twisted in his mouth; he remembered Apsinthos' guidance, and he remembered how he'd stood on the coast with the Watchers and thought that he could be greater than any of the others. 'Tell me what it is you want, Azazel. Is it apocalypse? Is it revenge?'

Kokabiel's hums interjected: "Liar, liar. You lie to us. You lied to the anti-Christ!" He stepped and leaned down, as if he were standing right before Dina but remained still too many steps away. "You say you do this for God! For Heaven—"

"I do this for love," Dina interrupted, then tilted his head at Azazel. "Babylon must fall. The nation past the bridge — Satan's empire. Its roads are made of blood, its buildings of evil. Destroy it, and you will destroy everything that Satan has ever wanted to protect." It was a lie, something Dina was making up now — but Kokabiel didn't correct him, and Dina wondered if he'd arrived at the edges of truth through pure faith. "And wouldn't you like the end of times to come, Azazel? You will never be pure again. You're a sinner. I know how you feel because I'm a sinner too. We were sinners together." 'But I will make everything right again. When it is all over, you will absolve me.'

Azazel visibly bit the inside of his cheeks, and he said nothing as Dina turned around, walked away slow. 'You were crying when I met you for the first time. Armoni and I discovered you, curled into yourself at the sidewalk, carrying the bruises of a forced penance. We took your hand, pulled you up.' Azazel had held Dina to him, expecting to see him weeping or protesting, but his face was empty, accepting. Many times, Azazel and Armoni had tried to convince Dina that he didn't deserve to be hurt because he was a sinner. Over time, they'd come to know that Dina would accept any hit so long as someone touched him.

"The devil has nothing but his Babylon," Dina said tensely, stopping, his wings unfolding again from his back, but he didn't look at Azazel. "If you ever loved what the flood took from you — then end the devil's world how he ended yours."

Dina left them, and the Watchers were all silent again, even Kokabiel.

CHAPTER 33

"Forgive me," Michael breathed, "Father." If a soul could kneel, he did it at the base of the Lord's Throne, at His feet; and his six flaming wings consumed his form to make him nothing but a speck of bright. "For my weakness. Heaven burned again, as it did during the first war, because I could not contain the devil." The sensation of sinking gnawed at him, and he wished he could shut his eyes and look away from God.

"I said," boomed the Lord's voice, "that Satan would be done away with, and Lucifer would be born again from his body. A new Jerusalem will present itself as a bride — the marriage of Heaven and worship, which has already happened and will happen again. You ask for my mercy, and you continue to sin." Pain, now, consuming Michael. "Even with the body that will bear the resurrected Lucifer — you sin. Even after you were punished before all of Heaven for sullying your body, for your sins of flesh, you sin."

"He," Michael rasped quickly, "*tempted* me, my Lord."

"You already know how this will end."

Throat narrowing and warming enough to burn. 'He tempted me. He deluded me. Only because you should not be given something broken, I will refrain from ripping him in half when I see him again. But when you kill Satan, bring him such pain that the Beast will never make a home in Lucifer's body again. Please, Father. I will do anything for you to hurt him.'

God said: "The end is written."

Michael's gauntlet held the handle of his sword so tight that he could feel even the divine metal of it strain to not snap beneath the prince's strength. "Why—" he began, but then the rest of his voice fractured, and there was a sudden labyrinth of paths before him of words to say, questions to ask. "Why—" he said again, but he couldn't remember what he'd originally meant to say. 'Why does God divine punish? Divine hurt, divine ache? Why must Satan die for Lucifer to resurrect? Why must the world end for good to triumph? Why did I save a girl only to tell her that I must kill everything that she loves? Why am I here?' ' "I'll bring him back." 'Why?' "And you will kill me, too, Father." 'Why? For all that I've done.' He wished he hadn't heard his own voice in his head, his own thoughts of Joana. Her face, the flickers of pain in her eyes.

'She looks just like you,' Satan had teased.

Within all the flames that made up the angel, there was a chest that ached, and Michael promised, "I will bring Satan back to you."

"Why," God echoed.

In the town bordering Babylon — Tadeo healed. He was in the plaza where Michael had captured Satan and standing where the devil had been, propped up by a crate. There were hundreds around him, the boy's family lost among all the heads and the infants being lifted toward him. All of Tadeo's, rather gentle and anxious, calls for them to form an orderly line drowned beneath all the shouting. Some were pleading for his healing hands, others just trying to watch — each time not believing it, each time wanting to see it happen again just to be amazed a second time. Those harmed from the strikes were supposed to take priority, but all those who'd been sick, injured, and neglected years or their entire lives rushed to Tadeo in desperation.

Nearby, Dante watched; he was standing on top of a building, no longer bothering with the phone he'd been fiddling with for the hours Tadeo had spent there. The sky had grown dark, an endless void absent the stars, while the moon flooded an ominous red glow over them all, as if to prepare them for the light of hell-fire. Arms crossed over the ledge, he also saw some cars whizzing down the roads, toward Babylon, but the border was closed even for the regular trade that'd passed through when the gasoline was cut. He flexed the hand that Tadeo had returned to him, again and again.

"Here," came a grumble from behind him, and he looked to see a water bottle and two quesadillas rolled up in aluminum being extended to him from a curly-haired young woman — Joana, the one who'd gotten him into this house, one that belonged to a 'bad man' according to her. As the soldier mumbled a thanks, taking the offering, Joana explained: "Electricity is out everywhere, so every-one's out there cooking their last meals." But it didn't seem like she wanted to say much more — using her newly freed hands to reach into her pants and retrieve a light at the same time she shoved a cigarette between her lips. Pointedly, she didn't look at Dante, as if doing so would drop another weight on her shoulders, another boy to look after and betray.

The soldier hesitated, then mumbled, "Cell service is mostly dead too." She made a noise of affirmation, flickering the flame that ignited her cigarette. Though she hadn't asked, he said, "I'm worried about my mother. I was hoping to reach her." He couldn't resist the allure of honesty: "Soldiers were with her."

Below, Tadeo cured the one-eye blindness of a man, and the people cheered.

Joana blew out some smoke, then leaned over the ledge with Dante. "Is she anywhere nearby?"

"I don't know," he confessed. "I don't know if she's still home." Joana asked where home was. "I was born in Mesbilja." He specified the state. "We're from there, originally, and I think she was there now."

"Maya?" Joana asked.

"Winik atel," Dante clarified. "But I don't visit the *pueblo* much anymore." And then he mentioned the southern city where his mother worked as a maid.

"Sorry."

Dante chuckled at that. "And what about you?" He nodded his head at her. "Any family?"

"Mine is safe," Joana said. "If the strikes were really trying to hit criminals, then they wouldn't be, though."

"You're from a criminal family." He didn't phrase it like a question.

Joana picked the cigarette out of her mouth with two fingers, exhaled some smoke again. "Not in the rich way." Then, she rummaged through her pockets again. "My dad got involved with some bad people, dragged my brothers in. Dragged me in too. He was trying to claw his way up." Like the food, she offered her lighter and cigarettes to him.

Dante, immediately, set his food down on the ledge, then reached for them. "Does Tadeo know?"

"Nah."

"Yeah, I wouldn't tell him." Laughing, Dante slipped the cigarette in his mouth, flickered the lighter, then brought the flame to light the end. And since they were talking, he decided to ask, "Tadeo told me about you. All nice things. Are you really a lesbian?"

Some smoke huffed out of Joana's nose. "Yup."

"Hm." Dante shifted. "You know, I've sucked some dick before. In the military college."

"Ok. Didn't ask if *you* were a lesbian, did I?"

Again, Dante cackled, almost choking up on his cigarette. "Just trying to make a friend."

"I'm going to go." Joana swiped the cigarette and lighter from the soldier's hands, shoved them into her pockets for the last time. "Good luck with your family. I hope they're alright. Are you—" She stopped. "Are you going to leave this place too?"

"I want to," Dante admitted. "Should I?"

"You can try. If you want to see your family again before the world ends, you should probably try."

Smoke burning his throat, Dante returned his eyes to Tadeo. Placing a hand on a woman's hair, the terrible gash over her face began to close, and he seemed like a proper Messiah, like Jesus with all the worshipers. Dante's mother would kill to be here, wouldn't she? 'She would push through the crowd, ask him for help. She would tell me that Tadeo is here to answer our prayers after so long begging for God to send us help.' But she would come away disappointed. 'I tried to tell you, *me*.' Mother, in his indigenous language. 'You don't want a Messiah. You want her back.' Dante's older sister. 'Fuck.' He wanted her back too. 'How the fuck is praying going to help us?' he used to snap at his mother. 'How is it going to help *her*?'

Joana had just walked away from him, and Dante hadn't even realized until he was alone for several minutes, thinking of his mother and his missing sister. He counted all the fallen stars to try to soothe his fears, but Dante had seen so much death throughout his life, and he could perfectly imagine the empty look in his mother's brown eyes, the trail of dried blood falling past the edge of her lips, her limbs tense and sprawled. When someone's shot, their arms go stiff for a moment, and their body jerks like they're going to seizure. People defecate after they die, they urinate. Dante had seen it, had found it so frustratingly gross. It was like nature had wanted to mock humans in the end, remind them that they're just animals, foul and dirty as they are. He'd seen decay, seen the roaches and the bone fragments. If it weren't for his disappeared sibling, he might've become a trafficker and led the sort of life that worshiped death.

He couldn't blame Joana, couldn't blame Tadeo.

The world was cruel, and there was no God to blame, and they were all just insects trying to make something out of their puny lives. And yet his older sibling had loved insects, had loved those as beautiful as monarchs and as dirty as roaches. She'd fed Dante grasshoppers once by hand, and she had told him that this was a beautiful place, this planet. Dante had always troubled with romanticizing 'the land' and tradition. Hell, he liked modernity, he liked cars, he liked eating foreign foods, he liked modern medicines. But there was a gaping hole in his chest, the same as there was an empty chair at the family kitchen table. Maybe it wasn't so terrible to be an insect, to live simply and be small and meaningless.

Dante finished his cigarette, left the house, and then he wiped his eyes of the tears that'd escaped.

Tadeo, on the other hand, stayed in the square for hours, until it was past midnight. He hadn't meant to, or wanted to, but the crowd had grown wider and wider around him even as the red moon continued to rise. It was only thanks to one of his cousins, who noticed the anti-Christ slumping, that he was allowed rest. She shouted out that Tadeo was exhausted and then, afterward, she'd hurried to grab him as he stumbled off the crate. Gasping, then coughing, feeling his body tremor like the Earth with every expel of hoarse air, Tadeo almost succumbed to the dark spots in his vision.

"Let him rest! Let him rest!" His grandfather's voice.

In the fog of shapes that constituted the crowd in Tadeo's exhausted gaze, he tried to find some grounding. Briefly, he thought he saw a face like that of the Jesus he'd always seen in paintings, in books, but then he blinked, and he saw his father. Then, he blinked, and he saw a man again — this one unfamiliar but dark-haired, dark-skinned. And the passages in the Bible of Jesus duplicating food for a crowd flashed in his mind, suddenly, without explanation. 'Did they crowd around you too, Christ? Did all the people beg for miracles until you dropped in exhaustion?' No, no, the son of God shouldn't feel exhausted, and Tadeo ought not to compare himself. He was his opposite, after all. Anti-Christ.

Tadeo felt hands guide him down onto a bench, and he breathed out shakily. His head pulsed in pain. His body was heavier than he'd ever felt it. All he could do was shut his only eye for a moment, even when he heard the sound of the soldier — Dante — nearby, his voice, asking if Tadeo was alright. The anti-Christ wanted to ask him what he was still doing here, but instead, he kept feeling his thoughts on Jesus, on the Bible. He thought of walking on water, he thought of Christ in Gethsemane, begging his Father for the strength to die, to be sacrificed. He could almost see it — the olive trees, the grass. The shadow of a man, and then the armor of soldiers. The lips of a disciple, cold, angry.

He felt himself wanting to beg for God's mercy like Jesus in the hour before crucifixion.

"Tadeo," came Dante's incessant calls. "Tadeo."

Groaning, Tadeo fluttered open his eye to see his family still trying to lead the people away — easier now, due to the hour — and the soldier leaning to his height. "Fuck," the anti-Christ grunted, then rubbed at his face tiredly. "What do you want?"

"Did you hear that the electricity is dead?" Dante hesitated, then asked, "How long do you think it'll be before we all start starving?"

"Don't say that." Tadeo sighed, before lifting his gaze to the red moon. If nothing else, the fallen stars were illuminating the town nicely, almost beautiful in its haunting. Each of them breathed, and huffed, and sometimes one of their tongues would flick at the air. "No one is... going to starve." He hesitated before tilting his head up at Dante. "I thought you were going to leave."

"Kind of hard to do that, and uh, if the world is ending, I want to be with the guy who thinks he can stop it."

Tadeo winced. "I'm not sure if I can stop anything anymore, Dante."

"Me neither," Dante laughed bitterly, which oddly made Tadeo's lips twitch in a terribly sad smile.

Tadeo, then, looked to his family nearby, sharing bags of chips now and talking. Curious at that, he walked his gaze further, then pursed his lip at a convenience store nearby with its doors wide open, shelves presently being emptied by dozens of people. "I'm sorry," he said, to Dante and in general, though he felt his stomach begin to gurgle. Weirdly, he had no want to fill it. Like starvation would be enough to clear his head. Sometimes he desperately wanted pain as its own painkiller.

"Why are you apologizing?" Dante snickered. 'I'm the one who's fucked up.' "You healed my hand." He showed it off, wiggled his fingers.

"I'm also the guy who broke it."

"So what?" Dante tried to drop the tension from his own shoulders. "I shot you in the head, and you don't hear me apologizing, do you?"

"You're free to apologize."

"I'm good," replied the soldier, then both of them laughed. "Anyway, I heard they're gonna set up a carne asada nearby. You know, for the end of the world. You should eat."

Tadeo blinked. "How did you know I'm hungry?"

Before he could reply, a sharp hiss sounded above, and Tadeo jumped to his feet. Far above, there was a figure, dark face painted with white, wings spread behind him in what might've normally been a blue shade but seemed black beneath the darkness of a red moon. Even from here, Tadeo could tell who it was — Azazel, the leader of the Watchers, holding the end of a chain that connected to a collar on another angel, Samyaza. Dozens of the other Watchers rose behind him slowly; and remembering what the armored angels from God had done, all the humans who saw them cried out in fear or simply hurried away in strategic silence. Tadeo tried to raise his hand, to tell Dante, or any of the others standing behind him, that these were the Watchers. He had freed them. Under Dina's guidance, he had broken the chains that were dangling from their wrists now. But Tadeo's words died in his throat when the angels flew, headed for one of the low-hanging stars.

Hours ago, Azazel had whispered, "The Lord doesn't offer justice." Samyaza had been tugging on his tunic, grip tight, desperate — but he ignored it. "We must build it with our own hands." 'But how?'

As if hearing his thoughts, Kokabiel had giggled, catching the attention of Azazel and all the other Watchers who were still in the yard after Dina left; they saw the angel of the stars grin greatly as he lifted a finger, pointing it up.

And Tadeo watched as one Watcher threw his chain at one of the many stars, narrowly avoided its bulging eyes and mouths, whipping off a squelching piece of itself. Like an organ set aflame, the piece catapulted only to splatter against a building and engulf it in rage of fire. And then there were screams again like the town had just suffered another strike. Even the ground shook beneath, and Tadeo's breath caught as he distantly heard Dante curse. Then, another Watcher did the same as the first, sending another piece of molten sun down onto a car to explode it and send humans running in the opposite direction.

"Hide—" Tadeo gasped, looked at the soldier, then his family, before hurrying toward his mother's wheelchair, where an aunt was paralyzed. "Get out of here! Get out of the streets. Get everyone out of the streets!" Heart a battering ram on his ribs, Tadeo felt his skin prickle and begin to pull taut over growing, beastly muscle. Overhead, more and more Watchers were swarming the sky above, and the anti-Christ morphed further, lowering to pounce and run after them.

"Tadeo!" Joana's voice called, and instinctively, he froze, looked to his side. "They're all heading north! Don't chase them!" A rumble built in his throat, and his lips curled back to reveal infinite teeth — but Joana stared back, panting, hair stuck to her face in sweat. Behind her, there was another woman, one Tadeo didn't recognize, with faux blonde hair and a luxury top. "Look!" And where she pointed at the Watchers flying away from them — crossing over the reddened river — and there was a distant boom. "Don't call them back here!"

But so much rage shook Tadeo that a snarl slipped out of him, his entire body trembling, and feathers began to tear out of his body like daggers. Except, he heard screams again, and he saw, from his periphery, humans crying out in terror at him. 'Beast.' Tadeo remembered what Satan had said. 'Anti-Christ.' He remembered the devil's laugh. 'My child.' "No," he rasped, but his own voice scared him, and his heart burst, filled his lungs, his mouth, his eyes with blood. He remembered, suddenly, the copper taste of death, of darkness, of pain. The burn in him. Hell, scorching his insides. 'I'm sorry,' he'd thought in the desert. 'Mom and dad. For dying. For what they did to me. For all that I'm going to do.' He'd done it for them. He'd done everything for everyone but himself. He'd needed to be their saint, their savior, because it was the only thing that could make anyone love this mutilated boy that he was.

And then Tadeo ran — not toward the Watchers, not toward Babylon. Praying he could arrive at death again and, this time, not be turned away at the door.

CHAPTER 34

Baal said: "Michael will return for you. For all of us."

At this, Satan laughed.

Finally, the devil had returned to Hell, and he sat on his throne, curved forward, as if tired, with the screeches of animal spirits and roars of flames in his ears — all from outside his shivering tower. Like a starved stomach, Hell rattled and gurgled wetly, masses of flesh dripping down the walls and the ceilings that the Leviathan crept through. And dozens of demons were gathered, peppered along the steps that led up to the devil's chair, the few of the thousands that'd tried to rush in to see the rescued Satan. Some of them were dukes, including Asmodeus, who'd finally gotten hold of his golden walking stick again. He was out of the demons' armor already, had left with his horse, whereas Rosier remained in the dark suit. And all of them watched when Satan, dressed in sheer tunic, in jewels, in a four-horned crown, lifted his golden head, then finally replied, bitterly, "Is that any different than how it always is?" A chuckle trickled along some demons. "He has hunted me, hunted all of you, since we escaped Heaven."

The regent of Hell clenched his jaw, but a touch of fond amusement fell over his eyes.

"Don't take it as surrender, then," the devil said, "that we must leave this place. We marched from Heaven, and we marched from the Earth, and we'll continue to march for our freedom from God." 'From a wedding between Jerusalem and her Creator.' "Do not despair. Remember this not as the day that we abandoned Hell but the day Michael was defeated and the city of angels was sieged." He set his hands on the armrests, then pushed himself up to stand, all of the devils he'd reared staring up at him — all the devotion that had certainly waned in his absence growing alight again. "Now, gather the belongings you cherish most and prepare to abandon Hell." Elegantly dragging a hand through the air, Satan gestured at the trembling underworld around them. "The fires may rage, but we've ruled them for centuries. Don't be afraid — act."

At the word, the demons made noises of affirmation, some asking Satan what had happened for him to be caught in Heaven, a few still wanting to know why he'd avoided Hell for so many years, but Baal shouted out, "Didn't you all hear him? All questions will be answered later. We need to leave this place. Get to it! Hurry!" Other dukes soon followed suit, shoving some of the crowd back, toward the exit from the throne room.

Asmodeus sighed gently, gaze flickering to Rosier at the same time the fruit demon looked up at him — their mutual expressions anxious. Without a second thought, then, the duke of lust took Rosier's hand firmly, using the other to grip his walking stick and join the other infernal princes in demanding everyone ready for fleeing Hell without panic. 'Unlike the last two times we had to migrate.' He lowered his face, brought it to Rosier's ear, and whispered, "He didn't explain where we're going once we leave Hell, did he?"

Rosier shivered, then whispered back, "I don't think that he knows." He squeezed the duke's talons, and the two joined the crowd hurrying out of the tower, flooding into the largest settlement of demons in the endless sprawl of Hell.

Meanwhile, Baal pushed and snapped at the demons at the end of the lines, trying to usher them all out of the throne room as fast as possible. And once he'd managed, the regent took the enormous doors with both hands, grunted in exertion pushing them closed —

the metallic hinges screamed — before an iron bolt fell into place. The sounds echoed off the stone walls, filling the room with a reverberating boom that rang quieter and quieter until silence conquered. Loud, insistent silence, hanging over Baal as he turned his head slowly to face Satan, who was lowering onto his seat again almost weakly. He slumped, as he'd been earlier, and though Baal had to cross the room, right through the center of it, like a proud beggar approaching a king, he noted a pained twitch on Satan's mouth and empty, wide eyes. Then, suddenly, an angry grimace.

"He wants to kill himself," Satan snorted cruelly. "He wants to kill me, then himself. He wants the Lord to remake Lucifer for the new Eden. Like a new Jerusalem to wed." His voice took on a hiss, the walls of poise coming down in a way Baal hadn't heard in centuries, since the days of emperors. "I'll kill him first. I'll harness the fires of Hell to do it. I'll cook him and eat him. And I'll spit him out like he's shit in my mouth." He remembered the massacre at the casino. He remembered singing for human masses. Sometimes Satan looked in mirrors and saw her. Sometimes, he saw every harlot he'd been throughout history, every man, every woman. Words in their voices were all rushing to him now — praises, teases, songs.

Baal quietly asked, "Is it over? Tell me the truth. Are we all going to burn in a lake of fire?"

Satan shut his eyes.

Outside the tower, chaos reigned. Demons scattered in every direction, some hauling dearest possessions and others running empty-handed, a few heading right for the stolen winged horses, a couple others fighting over them. Asmodeus trekked along, grunting, his walking stick clicking against the stone, occasionally squelching when it landed over patches of Hell's flowering flesh. It was everywhere — handfuls of meat on walls, on the distant ceiling. The pyramid of mangled bodies that Asmodeus had stood on as he met Dante had crept here, now hovering over the devil's tower. And the duke furrowed his brow as he said, "We should get home quickly — get what we can." But whether they arrived promptly or whether they arrived at all depended on Hell's body leading them there.

Rosier still held Asmodeus' hand, and he shakily said, "The chest of rings is heavy." All of their wedding bands that the younger demon had painstakingly maintained and polished, particularly fond of those that had a motif, however small, of fruits. But wherever it was that they were going — could they carry the chest so far? 'What we leave behind might be gone forever. Like the tiles of our kitchen in Heaven, like the mosaics of the bathhouses. Like the ceramic pots in our old house, Asmodeus. Our trees, our beds.' As they hurried down the path, he briefly remembered the first time he'd fallen asleep with Asmodeus pressed to him, the first time they shared a bed. 'I hoped we could have stayed like that forever. I hoped that we could be friends for the rest of eternity.' But now that house was gone; they'd seen a stranger of a building in its place. Over the grave of their love, the angels had made a temple for worship.

Abruptly, Asmodeus stopped, and Rosier stumbled but saw, up ahead, what'd made his husband freeze. Moloch with a few others behind him, many of his followers, the demon Ara, and the Watcher Armoni, holding the chain leash of a winged horse. "Asmodeus," Moloch called, now in full armor, stepping up, closer to the duke with a charming smile. "I'd be careful heading that way. There's a lot of fire."

Asmodeus grunted. "What do you want now, Moloch? Satan is back, and he doesn't care about your war for his hand."

Moloch laughed simply and said, "Now, now, Asmodeus. Don't be difficult. I just wanted to ask again whose side you're on. Mine or Baal's. After we leave this place, start anew in whatever new home we make for the demons — I'm going to approach the devil and offer to be his new regent. I want your support when I do it." When Asmodeus, again, glowered, Moloch's expression began to darken. "Baal hasn't been your friend for a long time, has he? Why do you hesitate to support me, then?"

"Fuck the both of you," Asmodeus snapped, twisting around, determined to see if Hell would bring him and Rosier home if they just went in any other direction, but when he turned, he saw Moloch there, and again, Ara, Armoni, others. 'This is where you're meant to be,' Hell was saying. 'Do not run.'

"What happened between the two of you?" Moloch asked, faux sympathetically.

Asmodeus thought the better question was, 'What happened to Baal?' In the past two or so thousand years. What had happened to the amusing, simple-minded demon who'd once hung on Asmodeus' words? Who was this stranger?

In the tower, the regent in question had just kneeled before Satan, staring up at him with a set jaw as the devil said: "And what if this was goodbye, Baal? Goodbye to life as much as Hell."

Baal took Satan's hand, tenderly. "It had to end sometime. You always told me that. You told me that all the centuries of work would mean nothing one day, that God will be victorious, and that we will burn." Satan scowled, deeply, like he'd been slashed. "I suppose the apocalypse is here now, but I don't believe it all meant nothing." The burly demon, tilted his head, then quietly added, "I wish I could make you believe that. But no, I know you're too logical, too strategic. A king can't feel, you told me. He must not have mercy. He must scheme and assassinate."

Satan thought, 'I often wonder if, all these years, I was building the apocalypse myself; if, through trying to stop the end times, I was nudging the Earth closer to it. I met the most terrible men, the wealthy, the cruel. I sat with those who manufactured greater horrors than even God and Satan could individually create. I sat at their table. I did it to know all the most wicked who walk the Earth, so that I might find the anti-Christ. Every Babylon that ever rose carried my footprints. And for two thousand years, I let the evil of the Earth maintain themselves, to build their riches and power. I did it strategically. I ordered the demons to remain in Hell, to never intervene in humanity's evil. I thought only of killing the anti-Christ. I thought I could just kill the right person. I didn't think of the world that reared my child — deteriorating.'

'Each time that I killed my child, each time the anti-Christ was born again, I hunted them down, but I never looked to the world, my world, the one I bled out from my wounds to see how its rot would end us before the anti-Christ could.'

Anger building in his chest, Satan replied, "I told you mercy was useless, was weakness." God did not allow for justice. He would not have Satan eventually win the endless cycle of this game. He would have the stars align one day — the fall of Babylon, the false Christ, the rivers of blood — all at once. Satan would make a mistake one day, and the Lord had always known it'd happen like this — the mistakes would come from too many faces, too many lives. How to tend to an Earth so much larger than oneself? How to be everywhere at once? 'You cannot, Lucifer,' came a mischievous whisper in his head. 'You can never be in every place, at every time, because you are not God.' Almost hissing, Satan grunted, "This is my world, and I'm the lord of it." He had ruled every Babylon behind its kings. "All of this is mine."

Baal's gaze flickered — curious, conflicted.

"I will not surrender," Satan rasped but still squeezed Baal's hand. "I will never return to Heaven. The end of days will never come. There will be no lake of fire." He could still try to kill the anti-Christ. It hadn't worked to try to appeal to the evil nature that all the other reborn anti-Christs before Tadeo had held. There was something particularly twisted about Tadeo — he did evil sincerely trying to do good, to be righteous. And Dina, Heaven itself, had harnessed him. If Satan had been like Dina, had whispered that he held the key to saving his world, then the devil could have built his trust, could have slaughtered him. None of this, this final apocalypse, would be happening.

"There must be," Baal began, "a way to kill your child forever. Not have it be born again." Tightly, he said that phrase — *'your child'* — like it was a knife he twisted in his mouth.

'My child.' In the days after Christ's alleged ascension, Satan had been standing in the garden where the Nazarene man had prayed for his Father to give him the strength to be killed, to be tortured. And Satan had whispered that God killed, God tortured, God fucked a young girl just to know what it was like to do it, then just to have a child that He didn't have to birth. And He wanted to know now what it felt like to slaughter it afterward.

'You were,' thought Baal, 'shaking in anger, as if it was your own child who'd been crucified. I laughed then, and I asked why this mattered to you. If he were really the Son of God, then he was dead. If the Son of God was God, then God was dead.'

Satan thought: 'But Judas Iscariot was also dead by then. When I found him, Judas, he told me he followed a Nazarene man who believed in his own miracles, who said he was the Son of God. I said to him, you are young but you are wise, Judas. Who am I? I suppose I'm an angel, who was once too wise, too young. I know that a soul that believes itself to be like God will, one day, demand violence. He will take your flesh and your blood. You looked at me, Judas. You said, but it is the Nazarene man who offers his body to you. I told you, he offers his body to you because you can't offer your own; he already has it.'

Another time, Iscariot had said: 'Sometimes, I find myself believing in him. When he came to me in private, I spat at him, and I laughed in his face. Angel, I told him, "Son of God? You are no Son of God!" I took him by his clothes, pinned him against the wall, and I shouted, "You are no Son of God!" He called my name — Judas. Then, I said to him: "God would not become a man. Even if He wanted to, He could not." And Christ stared at me and let me keep speaking: "God could never be a man. You will never be a man. You will *never* be a man." I don't know why I said it.'

Satan felt Baal stroke his hand, as if to calm, and they stared at one another. "I have," said the regent to the king, "nothing that I can hold except faith in you." Ever since what'd occurred with Nero, Baal had dressed like a Roman of old, part of him lost forever to that time. "Nothing. You will overcome the apocalypse, and you will help us overcome it too."

'I ordered Judas to trade his Nazarene man for some gold, and Judas said he'd already made the decision. He'd watched the man of Nazareth walk on water. One by one, the Son of God had shown his followers not to doubt, but Judas doubted. The miracles of God's son irritated him, and no longer did he bother to sit and explain them away. He hated Christ because he loved to hate him. One day, he'd stopped saying, "He is not God," and he'd begun to say, "Look at how God mocks man. He does not know what a man really is. I can see it in the way that he moves, in the shape of his face. The more I stare at him, the more I see that God has mutilated himself to become not a man but a mutilated thing, a myth, a myth of a man." And I listened to him. He must've known I was a devil, but who else lends a listening ear to the sinners?'

Baal thought: 'When I asked you again why the death of a carpenter concerned you, you were quiet. I said that he hadn't returned from the dead. His followers burned his body in the tomb, refused to face the false godhood of their prophet.'

Satan thought: 'Judas whispered that he'd trade him for thirty pieces of silver after the Passover. I told him to kiss his rabbi one last time.'

Baal thought: 'You said God had broken a covenant. He had put a child of human blood and His own blood on Earth after punishing the angels for the same vice. I asked you: "Do you really believe he was the Son of God?" You said that the question of divinity in the Nazarene man's body mattered little. Whether he lived as the Son of God — whether or not he rose from his grave — he died, to his worshipers, as the Son of God.

Satan thought: 'I watched Judas turn Christ over, and that was the last I saw of him, of Judas. His suddenly-paled face, his wide eyes. It's written that Judas regretted what he'd done. It's also written that he never knew remorse. It's written that Judas killed himself, hanging from a tree. It's also written that he fell into a field and burst open to paint the ground like the blood of Abel, the first dead man, had. Contradictions. What ever happened to Judas? How did Judas Iscariot die? The devil doesn't know. What were the last words of Christ as he hung from the cross? Even the Lord must not know. Christ and Judas, both unknown to us in their final moments.'

There were times that Satan had looked into the eyes of the Nazarene man, seen a kind boy. His smile had been bright, and he had counted sprouts outside his humble house. If God was in a carpenter boy, He couldn't remember. God was learning to be human, to be small and frail and wretched.

Slow, Baal leaned forward, kissed Satan's parting mouth. 'I asked you what to do now, and you said to lay quiet for some time. To see what becomes of Rome and to speak to an angel. To speak to Azazel.'

Sighing against the regent's lips, the devil shut his eyes. 'Azazel's murdered child haunted my dreams and my every waking moment. I had a child too, Azazel. His name was Cain. I loved him after spending so long believing that love was a dead creature in me.' When he'd had Azazel set free from his chains, Satan offered him a degree of freedom, food, cleanliness — in return for Azazel's guidance. 'How to have a child. What did you do that made you unlike the other Watchers? Why you?' Azazel had said that maybe it was love; he had loved his man more than anything. 'My love had died again with Cain.' But he'd still find use for Azazel. 'You think I'll let you be worthless to me? Oh no. Paint over my mouth and make it new, reshape my eyes, change the tone of my skin. I'll be somebody else, and you'll teach me how to do it, Azazel. Poor Azazel. I mocked him. Sad little Azazel with his little child, who can't help me get one for myself.'

Baal inched back, and he said, "I always wonder if this is how you prefer me — worn-down, tired, broken." But both their eyes remained closed. "When the anti-Christ was born, I felt as if I'd died." 'Not only me, the demon, but Baal the angel of flight.'

Slowly, Satan lifted a hand, brushed Baal's mouth with a finger. "Alive or dead, you're wanted by me." Decades after Christ's death, his followers now numbering in the thousands — 'I went to make myself like God. I visited a young man named Nero, an emperor for three or four years already. Incompetent. If anything good came of his early reign, it was due to his advisors' orders. I met the emperor for the first time in the garden, and he thought me a god. I told him I was the goddess of beauty.'

'We became lovers, and when his mother disapproved, I told him to kill her. And with my guidance, he had her to be ship-wrecked. In lapses of his guilt, I whispered he'd done the right thing. And, in a secret garden of one of his villas, I lent the emper-or's mournful soul my body. I watched him fall after that. Like the women after the Watchers, like the boy Cain after he loved a demon. Mere man — you should have known not to desire a god.

You foolish men, drowned in tales of tragedies and hubris — still so eager for a kiss from the divine.'

Baal hadn't thought much of it when Satan returned and told him that he was fucking Nero, the emperor of Rome; after all, the devil was the tempter, the tempest, of Hell. Even when Satan said that Nero was trying to hide him from the world in a hidden villa, like a captured nymph, Baal the regent didn't ask much. But when Satan, in a sudden agony, collapsed onto the mosaic floor before him — a spill of darkness broke out of his body. Half-flesh, half-blood, miscarried — 'something in me creaked, then gave, sinking, sinking.' Baal had fallen to his knees, tried to help the twitching, stone-faced Satan as it occurred. Beneath the flame of torches, Satan had looked like Lucifer again, gaze frightened and unknowing and young. Hurt.

Satan thought: 'Briefly, I was over a bed of flowers again, staring up at my Father. The petals had reddened beneath me. Time had stopped as all the pain in me had long stopped. There had been something inside me — too heavy to bear, but you had torn it out like weeds from soil. I couldn't carry it. Lord. It's fallen out of my hands. My legs. Miscarried. The weight of paradise. Satan and God in the garden. I used to ask: Beauty for what? I know now. Beauty to miscarry. The flowers in Eden must still drip my blood. But God loves me. I prayed for His love when I was a few years old. He loves me more than you. I'm his favorite. He watches me sleep. He touches my hair and traces the lips He molded. And He made Eden for us, Him and I.'

'Whatever you have done,' Baal had pleaded, 'do not do it again. Please, Lucifer.'

'That's not my name,' Satan had whispered, laying in Baal's arms, tunic soaked in blood. 'Not here. That's not my name.' 'light bearer? but i was never made to carry so much. the morning would break itself out of this body and the star burns a hole into me for you. did you create me to burn so that you might warm your hands? to bear the fire. over the bed of flowers. from my blood, over the petals, set the flames. sacrifice me, god, to your own god. tell me that one day i will leave eden. tell me one day that you will stop loving me. oh i would do anything to make god stop loving me.'

Baal, in the present, whispered, "Wanted by you but never enough for you. When you returned to Nero, again and again, I realized I can't give you what you want most." 'Another lost child, then another, before I couldn't take it any longer, and I grabbed you, and I shook you, and I demanded you to stop this, Satan, my love. God could have a son because He is God! And you screamed in my face that you were God, only you were God. You told me that I must've never believed it. I was no better than an angel, no better than Michael. I shoved you away from me, such a tightness in my throat that I thought your hands were tearing into my neck.'

"Why do you speak of this?" said Satan. "I don't want to remember that time." 'You fought with me so terribly. I didn't say it then, but you terrified me. I never thought you would turn away from me. I barely managed to resist wailing for you not to leave me here. My voice hoarse, my eyes drowned by childish tears. I'm so alone, I'm so cold, please, Baal.'

Baal sighed. "Two thousand years, you've told me that we shouldn't speak of this." 'I almost stopped loving you. The beautiful, wise Satan I'd always loved had revealed himself to be a stubborn, arrogant fool. And yet, here I am. Maybe I would have left if there was another life for me out in the world, but I handed my soul to you in Heaven, and you hold it, and my feet will keep bringing me back to you for the rest of our time before the end. I love you. When all of Heaven loved you, I loved you. When it was easy to love you, I loved you. When it was difficult to love you, I still loved you.'

Satan nuzzled him. "After we leave this place, I promise you — we'll speak of it. We need to gather our things. Cain's belongings are under our bed." 'Because of our sinning, Nero grew too crazed to rule, had just raped and married a little boy. I faked his death, then fled with Nero, but some peasants saw us. For hundreds of years, they'd claim the emperor was in a secret villa of his, waiting to return. But he died. By suicide — only many decades later than they imagined it. He grew so gravely ill in the mind that he was bedridden, hand fed. Even still, he desperately pawed at me like an animal. I should have felt wanted, but I felt like a rag. Azazel had warned me that his husband became cruel from the divinity of their love, but I had been arrogant. It's always my arrogance in the end. One morning, after I slept with him, he hung himself using his own robes.'

Kissing him one last time, Baal whispered, "As you wish." 'Months after the death of Nero, I was breathing easier, waiting for it all to be over. But—'

'My child,' thought Satan, unable to hide the pain in his eyes. 'Winged and curly-haired and soft in my arms. I had expected gore spewing itself out of me like I'd been wounded — I had been, I had been wounded, hadn't I? — but then I heard soft breathing that wasn't my own, right on the bed with me. Azazel had once whispered, facing a window, refusing to meet my eyes: "My child didn't scream. And there wasn't any pain. God never punished us with the pain of creation that humans must suffer." And I pulled it to me — the half-angel, half-emperor. My face burned, my heart swelled with pain. Curling myself around the infant, choking on what I'd expected to be victory or joy — there was only crushing sadness. I remembered holding Eve in her labor, and I remember the aftermath, how empty and miserable she'd been, and I'd pitied her, but now I understood. And the sight of Azazel's own child flared in my mind, skewered by Michael's sword. My stomach turned, over and over, grinding me up inside. My cries threw me forward as if to retch. I saw myself as a child too. I remembered Heaven, I remembered my wings, how it'd felt to fly. All of eternity in my hands, bundled. An infant. I'd wanted to create so terribly once. Azazel used to weep, thinking I couldn't hear him: My baby, my baby. The baby.'

In the following months, Baal had watched, his chest tight, as Satan carefully climbed out of the abyss of misery, holding his child so close that it was as if he wanted the infant back inside him. They were as brown-skinned as Satan, their hair dark but curled, the wings at their back a muddled white. Babbling, gnawing at Lucifer's hand — Baal prayed to feel some relief, even joy. Yet —'we were eating at the dining table once, tended to by humans you said we'd kill before we left, when I couldn't smother my anger anymore. I saw your child, felt rage rising to my face like fever. I told you, "What about Cain?" You were holding the child to your front, rubbing their back, using your other hand to feed yourself. You told me that he's gone. I raised my voice: "You've forgotten him." Your hands trembled. "You decided you'd rather fuck an animal for a new child." You stood up, the infant hiccuping, then crying out, and you told me to leave with a sudden rawness, your face flashing between hot anger and cool terror. Over and over, you told me to leave the villa. How dare I say that? How dare I? But I don't regret it. I laid awake every night, thinking of Cain, as you played with the child at the other end of the bed. You kissed their hair, preened their wings, hummed for them. I thought of Cain, I thought of Cain, I thought of Cain. Drowned in our arms.' Baal had been sure he'd never forgive Lucifer for this.

Quiet, Satan whispered, "Is a god allowed to ask for forgiveness?" 'A few years, I struggled raising the child. You came back, only a few times. I bit down my pleas for you to stay. With Cain, I'd had you beside me as I held his little body by the hearth, humming like the angel I used to be. And now alone, I sang for my new child, but it didn't come as easy as before. And this one nipped at my fingers, hungrily, constantly. They dug claws into the ground and the walls. I watched them tear into one of the humans, a woman who'd come to bring me dinner as I rested. Before my eyes, my child morphed into a beast. Wings would sprout from wherever it wished, then other groaning mouths. But I shut my eyes, curled up around my creation like that would be enough to save them.'

Baal grimaced, then he said, "I don't want apologies, not from God, not from you."

'You came back to me again, one day, Baal. A letter was in your hand, addressed to some churches by someone named John of Patmos. Revelation. An anti-Christ who will destroy the Earth and bring about the rule of God. The devil will be thrown into the fire, then destroyed forever. I read this prophecy, and I waved my hand dismissively. At the same time, I watched my child grow from a pretty cherub to a thing of boiled flesh that I realized was much like what I looked like beneath my own beauty. Had Azazel's been like this? I needed to ask him, but I refused to leave the villa. I held the baby tighter, the words of Revelation echoing in my mind. My heart still beat, I realized; it pulsed right in my ears. One day, I found that the baby had killed another human, then another, and then four more, tearing into its final victim with its mouth. I could only laugh to not weep. It was as I'd been told in Heaven; the Beast had been inside of me all this time.'

"I promise to you," Satan said, "that I'll make everything right again, Baal. I will." Rising slowly to his feet, listening to the rumble of their collapsing Hell, he gazed gently at Baal, who touched the devil's hip, then gripped it. "Amends are greater than apologies."

Baal kissed the devil's waist, and he murmured, "Is worship greater than love?" Satan stared, and then Baal confessed. He said: "I know what God did to you. I've known for a long time." And the devil breathed out heavy, shutting his eyes. "You can't make things right again, Lucifer; nothing was ever right."

'The child fought me as I drove a dagger into its body over and over, and I sobbed so loud, so violent, that any listener would have believed it was me being butchered. I threw my baby into the fire, and I covered my ears with bloodied hands to scream out in agony. My face reddened, my tears dampening my tunic, as I grieved over the floor. My baby, I wailed like I'd heard Azazel do. Forgive me. It was the first time I'd asked for forgiveness since I'd been an angel. Forgive me. Gods cannot have children. We must crucify them. I'm sorry. Forgive me for ever giving you life.'

Some decades after the murder, however, Satan heard of a monster in some other land, and of evil, and he'd realized the flesh of his child had burned, but not the soul of the Beast. The end of the world hadn't been prevented. It would keep returning, like a tide that draws away only to build itself up again. The Beast would forever find new hosts, false prophets, and the devil would have to hunt his child down each time. The Lord's final punishment — to allow Satan creation, only for that life to destroy all life. The devil had allowed himself to be tempted. And he had lost the war of good and evil, caught somewhere in between.

CHAPTER 35

Six trumpets played high from the clouds, but Gabriel didn't touch his own. Immediately after Satan had been imprisoned by Michael, he and Raphael received the order from Metatron to descend to the Earth again, continue with the apocalypse. The man-angel, too, had shoved a trumpet into Gabriel's hands and told him to breathe into it when only a seventh song was left. But he didn't, riding alongside Raphael, ignoring the music that streamed from Heaven onto scrambling, terrified humanity. All the angels were on rooftops, moving from ceiling to ceiling, watching the humans that pointed at them, recorded them. Angels have always been recorded by man, their every appearance written hastily. When Gabriel had visited Mary, she'd told him that she would remember this, tell her cousins, her husband, and her mother, and he'd smiled. He missed her, wherever it was that she'd gone since the beginning of this apocalypse.

Raphael's hands, free of the proper gauntlets, were bloody. "We should," he stammered, then sighed softly. "We should leave Babylon—" They were in the empire of evil, unknowing still of the Watchers climbing up its body. "I think we should try to smear the blood of the Lamb elsewhere, on other people. We still have so much of it, and I don't believe the demons stole any when they attacked our angels." He reached for one of the flasks on his armored waist, filled to the brim with crimson of the drained Lamb's corpse. He tilted it, flooding his palm with blood once more. "When the final trumpet sounds, the marked will rise to Heaven, saved from what continues after."

Gabriel swallowed. 'But what of all those not marked by us? The blood is endless, but our time is not. Our touch is not. The lake of fire will swallow all those we didn't reach.' But if he didn't play the last trumpet, the Lamb's blood would mean nothing, a prophecy left half-fulfilled. Everyone would burn. What was kinder — saving some or saving no one? Uriel would know — but he had rebelled and run away like the Lucifer he'd hated so terribly once.

Hesitating, then Raphael finally looked at his friend, then at the crowd of other angels on horseback behind them. The dim sun beamed down at them, and the blaze of the several low-hanging stars chased away any shadows that might have hung over them. "Gabriel. After we mark a few more, outside of Babylon, you must—"

"I know," Gabriel interjected, his heart dull, quickening. It was difficult to know which humans below were marked in the Lamb's blood or in their own — which were touched by angels and which were clawed at by their fellow humans as they tried to approach the angels. That was why they were all on high ground now — the rioting at the angels' feet had turned into shoves and kicks, and then turned bloody.

"Are you," Raphael suddenly asked, careful, "going to play it?" The trumpets above still rang.

Gripping the reins on his horse tightly, the messenger angel whispered, "When the great flood happened, we saved a few, just a family. Do you remember, Raphael? Noah, his wife, and his children, and now we must cull all of their descendants except for a chosen few. Will this continue forever, Raphael? Save a few, over and over." Then, he said, lower, "The Lord said I was responsible, for believing in the Watchers, for believing in saving what couldn't be. He does not make us all to be saved. But it was... your Samyaza who led those angels to Earth, who did it all for love. Your Samyaza—"

"*Gabriel*," Raphael, suddenly, sharply, replied. "What are you saying? The Watchers aren't... relevant to this." As they spoke, one by one, towns and cities burned under Azazel's direction — pieces of stars falling to the Earth, boiling the humans caught beneath. "Don't speak of then." For the first time, Gabriel saw a flare of anger in Raphael's eyes, the color of the sea. "Once we leave," he said, firmer, "and mark a few more humans — play the trumpet, Gabriel. You don't want to be blamed for destruction again, do you?"

But before Gabriel could speak a word of the trickle in his heart — a dust of fright, sadness, and an indignation that matched the healer's — a swiveling, metallic sound interjected, then the bang of a door hitting the wall adjacent to it. Immediately, all the angels turned to see a woman. She looked back — hunched, eyes wide, a trickle of flaking, dried red streaming from a nostril to her top lip. Abruptly, she set a foot before her, then another. She panted, "Help me—"

Raphael hastily took the reins of his horse and guided himself closer, saying, "Human, you shouldn't be here." But he spoke in his angel language, and Gabriel didn't open his mouth to translate. "You're hurt?" Fear wobbled her bottom lip, but she shuffled closer to the angel of healing and his bloodied hand. "Here, let me mark you. Then, I will heal you if there is anything wrong." She reached him, and he reached her. Bloodied hand fell over her head.

A scream followed, not long after. And Raphael jerked away, staggering his horse back. Before him, bubbles of paleness bloated out of her face, then scabs of red on her arms, her neck. Boils, rash. As a sudden coolness crushed at his chest, Raphael saw sickness. At his own hand. Pestilence. His mouth opened, as if to scream too, but the stranger stumbled away, hands rising to her face in horror. 'No,' he thought, and he heard Gabriel call his name again, watched the woman begin to run, but half his mind was recalling the flood now in regret and guilt. And the other part of him was tearing out of his body, broken by the sight. Pain. Disease. From his own hand.

Meanwhile, Dina was above the town by Babylon, wings beating slow, maintaining his place over the smoke and amid several stars, each pulsing like they were giant, grotesque hearts. 'Dina.' Several buildings below smoked — but which were a result of Babylon and which were a result of the Watchers? It didn't matter now. 'Pestilence,' said Apsinthos, 'and the trumpets. Do you hear them?' He did — six songs from above, echoing in his ears. 'It's almost over.' The Watchers had long disappeared into the horizon. 'You've done well. My dear Dina, you've done well.' The last of remorse, fading into the setting red sun. 'My sweet angel. It's almost over, and it'll all begin again.' The wind tossed Dina's braids.

'You want to feel guilty still, but paradise's reach grows nearer. You can see the horizon of beauty. We've spent long enough dreaming of the past, dreaming of love,' Apsinthos said, or perhaps it was Dina, perhaps it was Dina. 'If I must kill us all to be loved by you, then watch me bloody my mouth. I'd end the world a thousand times to be loved by you. My star. If you can be a sun, I'll be an earth of life. Let's begin again. You and me.'

From where Dina was, he could see a plaza overbrimming with humans, and he saw the anti-Christ just recently gone to walk some streets alone, in the vague direction of his ruined home. And so the greater angel of beauty descended slow, toward his victim. Pulling his wings into himself, he allowed himself to fall. Some bulging eyes of a looming star followed Dina as air rushed past him. The trumpets still sounded as he beat his wings a handful of times, tilted himself into a glide between homes. 'The homes of this town. This town that welcomed me.' Careful, he dragged a foot against the ground he flew over, then he landed in a crouch. When Dina lifted his body up again, he stood before a young man with a hole through his head, an eternal wound over his right eye.

Dina, eyes in a happy daze, smiled widely. "Tadeo."

The boy stared at him, face streaked in some ash like his family had been when he returned from Hell. No hat shielded his head, his hair ruffled by a hot breeze. Brown eyes — bloodshot. His lips were pressed fine together. His hands were open at his sides, but they trembled so terribly that they could have been furious fists. But he didn't seem angry, not really. There was a hollowness to him. As if the Beast and the Anti-Christ had been emptied out of that body and all that remained was a boy, a boy who'd tried to be good.

"You know now," Dina whispered, and though he'd intended to grin, to once again tell the star in his head that they, together, had handed God the death, the war, the pestilence, the famine that He wanted, He *needed* — he saw his own face in Tadeo's eyes for a moment, reflected. And he heard the yells nearby of women, and the cries of some young. Dina remembered the home he'd been allowed into, the one of Tadeo's excited family. He remembered being thrown out from his house when Heaven heard of what the Watchers had done. He'd wondered, laying on the ground, clutching at the abdomen that angels had just kicked, why it all had to be like this. Why does God demand pain? Why does God end the world? Why doesn't He recreate, why doesn't He tenderly, gently, forgive? Why did any of this have to happen?

Quietly, the angel turned on his heel, and the boy watched him walk away.

In Hell, a kneeling Rosier had just finished tying the strings of his sack, and he looked up to see Asmodeus, who had just stepped out of another room into the living area. Their gazes locked on one another, and then Rosier smiled gently, nervously. Right before him, on the carpet, there was an open chest; hundreds of engagement rings and wedding bands, and other forms of marriage items — nose rings, ribbons. Slow, Asmodeus adjusted the bag he had slung over a shoulder, then he thumped his walking stick against the ground as he approached, then lowered himself. He kissed Rosier's hair, slow, loving. "I'm sorry," he said, "that we can't take everything."

Rosier stared at all the artifacts of their relationship, then he touched Asmodeus' arm with a tenderness like an open wound. "It hurts," he confessed. "But I try to remind myself that this is the fate of every demon and human alike, in every war. We left so much behind in Heaven, Asmodeus, and we know now that it's gone forever. We've seen women, children, men abandon their homes, in apocalypses like our own. And you and I — we've found all their cherished things in the rubble. I know the emptiness they must feel, how many nights they'll lie awake dreaming of finding the lost, the dead. For so many, divine or earthly, there is loss, loss and loss again. It comforts me, sometimes, that we are all united by loss, by the homes we abandon." Suddenly, he sniffled, reached to find his eyes watering. "Forgive me— We should go—"

Asmodeus' gaze softened sadly, and he took Rosier's arm, tried to gently lift him up. "Before anyone sees." To Earth, before anyone sees that they ran off together again. There would be no need to choose between Moloch's cruelty or Baal's empty rule if they simply left them all behind. "But we won't have to leave the next place we get to, Rosier. I promise. I don't want to run anymore." He cupped Rosier's face, pressing his walking stick to his side with his elbow; his legs trembled. Deep, slow, the demon duke kissed Rosier, then he breathed, "I love you. I was created by God to love you."

'To love me, to hurt me.' Rosier thought of their belongings again, all that'd be left behind — their jewelry and pottery, many tunics, robes, the toys of old pets, the paint on their walls, everything collected from all of history. "I love you too, Asmodeus." He supposed he'd been made for this too, however much loving Asmodeus felt like captivity at times. He kissed back softly, gentler.

Asmodeus thought: 'I spent all of my eternal life before you begging for love. The gentle angels, the healers — I was always drawn to them. God was guiding me to angels I could break.' He pressed his forehead to Rosier's. 'I'm sorry it had to be you.' "Rosier... put on the armor that we wore to reach Heaven. You can have my helmet again." Blinking, tilting his head, Rosier tried to speak, but Asmodeus said it again, "Please." Rosier hesitated, but then he nodded, and he whispered he'd try to be quick. Asmodeus offered to help.

The process was quick with both their hands working to fasten the straps of the armor, and then they grabbed their things again. At some point, Rosier asked, "What about you, Asmodeus?" The duke said that he'd left his armor with the horse. Beneath them, the ground rumbled, an old human-crafted statue fell off a shelf, shattered loud enough to make Rosier jolt. And that was all they'd needed to take each other's hands and hurry back out into Hell. But it was already worse than it'd seemed a mere few hours ago.

Flesh had further sprouted from the ground and from every wall, every low-hanging ceiling, and they were catching fire. Between the flames — faces with open mouths silently wailing. The tortured dead themselves, boiling over. The sight sent thousands of demons on the crowded streets in every direction, each one trying to find Satan's tower, as if the devil's touch could individually save each one of them. A bitter part of Asmodeus almost laughed at how short-lived the sense of victory had been over their destruction of Heaven, but some hellfire flared close enough to make him startle. Then, he noticed how all the souls of the animals were missing, too, running away how they'd done alive to the first signs of storm. "The horse—" he said quickly again to Rosier. "We need to get on the horse." But it was by the tower — what if another demon had already taken it? "We need to get to the tower."

Rosier looked on in terror at the chaos, but he nodded, holding his bag tighter, heart pounding in his ears. 'Where is Armoni?' His friend. Armoni was the only person beside Asmodeus that Rosier really worried for, and he feared how Moloch might use Armoni as a shield against the fire. He clenched his jaw, and he breathed out nervously, pushing through the crowds with his husband. With flares lapping out, igniting other pieces of flesh, the hellfires were beginning to spread. All Rosier could do was hold onto Asmodeus' hand tighter, like only Asmodeus could keep him alive, how all the demons prayed Satan could do to them.

From high within the tower itself, the devil stared out a window, still in his regal wear, and he saw the same destruction as those on the ground, but he could see further. The people of ash in between the demon settlements were turning into smoke, rising up in coils and puffs of darkness. And Satan's gaze was cold but fear was beginning to bleed through. A ragged, tired breath left his mouth, and though all of the building was flooding now with nearly as many demons as it could fit, Satan still had a few footsteps of distance to himself and Baal, the regent almost pressed to his back, watching the furnace that their Hell was rapidly becoming. The prophesied sea of fire, forming. 'But the armor is strong,' Satan reassured himself. 'Even those who don't make it into the tower should still find themselves able to claw to the Earth.' Sharply, the tower rumbled, candles shaking in their holsters, dust spilling from corners.

"Baal," Satan whispered.

"Yes?" Immediate.

"Can you ensure Rosier is in the tower?"

Baal breathed in, seemingly hearing the unsaid words there: 'Hell isn't safe, only the tower is safe. Where is Rosier?' "Yes." And he unfolded his wings behind himself, reached to open the window before them.

Below, Asmodeus panted and grunted, and Rosier turned, looked up at him, eyes wide. "Hm? Are you alright?" His husband was limping, one of his knees twisting awkwardly. "You're tired?" His voice was high, frantic, but Asmodeus squeezed his hand in reassurance. "Should we rest?"

"No, there's no time," he rasped, his dark eyes landing on Rosier, holding steady. Then, he laughed softly, almost knowingly. "Look," and he nodded his head forward, at Satan's abode towering over them, "right past there, we left the horse, remember? We're almost there." And he dragged a foot forward, then another, pulling Rosier alongside him. "Tell me where you want to go. You like the warmer places. With all the tropical fruits, the rain, and the sun." Opening a trembling mouth, Rosier wanted to say that all those pretty places might be gone now, all those homes they'd stayed in, many of them destroyed even before the apocalypse, in earlier apocalypses between humans. "Let's settle there. Come, come." Eyes burning, Rosier nodded. "And we won't ever run again. No more rebuilding our homes, our lives, everything again and again." He hissed in pain, but he continued still, and Rosier took his hand with both of his own. "Rosier. "

"Asmodeus—"

A burst of fire nearby, from the ground itself, whipped at some yelling demons beside them, and Asmodeus and Rosier ducked in unison, missing its attack, but the horrible warmth still washed over their bodies. Together, they staggered some more steps forward, and they leaned against one another, and they approached the tower, and they looked forward. When another flare reached them, they lowered their heads, but it struck fierce enough that it threw down Rosier, who clenched his eyes shut. He held on only tighter to Asmodeus' hand, pulling his arm close, and he cried out when the armor around him heated against his skin. But Rosier didn't burn, and he curled around his belongings, and around Asmodeus' arm. He heard screams, wails, of burns, but not from Asmodeus. He almost dug his nails into his friend's, his husband's touch. Asmodeus' arm.

When Rosier opened his eyes, he gasped, almost retched, and it was all he saw — Asmodeus' arm. It ended at the elbow, where Rosier hadn't been able to cover him with his body, and there was nothing that remained beyond. No ash, no corpse, no dust. All of his body had been torn apart by the fire into nothing. Except this arm, this hand, that Rosier still held even when everything else was missing. The ghost of Asmodeus' voice still in his ear, an echo fading with each reverb. Heart stopped, not understanding. An emptiness, before him, in Hell, inside of him. He could not scream.

"Rosier!" Baal's voice. "Rosier—" Terror cutting his words.

Just an arm, a hand, that had held the young demon's face every day for an eternity. Incompatible, inseparable. The fruits of friendship. Demon of lust, demon of love; they should have abandoned their hope long ago. But they had adored one another despite, and it hadn't been enough. Sometimes, love is not enough.

CHAPTER 36

Joana was ignoring Lupina, the kingpin's daughter who she so terribly loved. They walked alongside each other on the uneven street, some gravel scratching beneath their shoes. Though she lived across the river now, Lupina frequently visited to enjoy the few pleasantries of her hometown and wealthy friends who still lived there. Once, Joana had resented that — being just connected enough to this place to dabble in the good but capable of turning away from all the bad, and that frustration tripled with Lupina. She may not have been responsible for the state of town, but her father was. Or so Joana had thought; it wasn't as clear to her as it'd been before. 'Her dad told me that it was the soldiers who infiltrated the criminals, not the criminals who corrupted the soldiers, not really.' And so Lupina's father had, perhaps, simply been carved out of something much larger; Joana could kill him and see that nothing would change. Removing the dark spot on a fruit's skin didn't do away with the rot.

"Joana," Lupina called again, sighing. "Please. Talk to me." Her manicured hand came over Joana's wrist, halting her steps. "I came all the way here for you. I crossed the bridge this way even though everyone is running the other way. For *you*."

"I didn't ask you to," Joana sighed harshly, then she yanked her arm free. Facing ahead, down the road, she saw the reddened sky of morning, and she felt a sinking weight in her chest. How was one supposed to live during apocalypse? How was one meant to continue taking steps, continue all the threads of loyalties and love? It all seemed worthless now. Slow, she turned to look at Lupina, saw the beads of tears tangled in her long lashes. 'Maybe I'm lucky.' Joana had lived all her life knowing there would be no growing up, no elder years; she hadn't let herself dream. 'But I know,' she thought, gazing at the girl she loved, 'you wanted to go to college, again. You wanted to give it one more try. I told you that you could do it.' Swallowing toughly, Joana spoke more stiffly: "I'm looking for Tadeo right now. Can you go?" Lupina opened her mouth. "I'm happy that you're alive, but you should go with your father." Then, before she could stop herself: "I hope that guy you're going to marry is alive too."

Lupina froze, lips still parted, before her brows furrowed and face twisted. "You can't be serious." A scoff rattled her before she shook her head. "Joana— I never—"

"You never what?" Joana didn't want to waste time over this, over their relationship, at the end of the world, but her face burned, and the hinges in her jaw ached. "You never wanted anything serious with me, I know." And she turned around, began walking again, though Lupina's rapid footsteps followed. "You used to tell me you don't want to be with me; you want to be a *girl*. Well, go be a girl. With your man, with your family."

"You're awful," Lupina snapped, though her voice cracked, enough to make Joana flinch. "God, you're so awful. Do you even know how *mean* you are?"

"The world is awful," Joana said.

"You don't even try to understand. If it's something *you* wouldn't do, then you think I'm stupid for trying it. If it's something *you* don't feel, you don't even try to understand my feelings. Everything is all about you." But Lupina's voice raised higher, and higher, and she snarled: "And you think *I'm* such a coward, just wanting to make my family happy, when you shoot anyone your dad tells you to without asking questions!"

Again, Joana stopped, but this time she twisted entirely around, stepped forward so that she almost bumped into a startled Lupina — "Leave me the fuck alone then!" she yelled now. "Leave me alone!" Her throat was hoarse, betraying all the rawness Joana didn't want to feel. "Please. For fuck's sake, Guadalupe, I can't do this between us anymore. Everything is over. This town, this world, and this — you and me." Chest rising and falling with almost frantic breaths, Joana stared at her sweetheart, at her sniffling and shaking face. "We're both going to die, and we're headed to different places. Goodbye, how many times do I have to tell it to you? Goodbye." If Joana had the strength, she would have shoved Lupina away, then ran away.

Lupina, however, took a step back, then a sob shook her, erupted from her lips. Lowering her head, refusing to look, Joana resisted every urge to run after her, to embrace her, to apologize. But a knife was twisting in her stomach, digging deeper as Lupina's steps grew quieter, more distant. 'My Heaven-bound girl,' she thought bitterly until her love was gone.

"Joana." Tadeo's voice, and Joana sharply jerked her face back up, and there the anti-Christ was — one-eyed, ash-stricken, standing a few steps away. Almost definitely, he'd heard the argument, maybe even silently approached to watch it happen. "I'm sorry." His face seemed tender, pitying, and it almost made Joana grit her teeth.

"Don't say that," she replied. "I'm the one who used you, remember?" Then she looked around at the shabby neighborhood. "What is this place? Why did you come here?"

"No reason," he answered softly, then cut the distance between them. "I just wanted to clear my head." Tadeo paused before nudging her lightly. "By the way, I already forgave you. I don't hate you. Maybe you were using me, but— Well, I know that you were just trying to do good."

Sometimes, his kindness annoyed her, but Joana often also wondered where it'd come from. When she'd found Tadeo, he had been like a feral animal, growling and biting at the air, hungry and horrible. Joana didn't think she'd done much, nothing more than offer a monster purpose, but maybe that was all it took for a beast not to be a beast. "Whatever you say," she dismissed, and he smiled, weakly. "Come. Everyone is looking for you. They don't even know you're responsible for those angels that just attacked, so they're not as angry at you as I am."

"I... just saw Dina. You were right."

"I always am."

Tadeo frowned. "Well, where are we going?"

"Plaza. I have bad news about Father Toño."

Dead, apparently. After making their way to the rotunda in the park where Tadeo had earlier done his healing, he saw five bodies laid respectfully beneath pale sheets. Because the Watchers' strikes had been few, and so targeted, retrieving the victims had been easy. But Tadeo, soon, learned that he couldn't bring the dead back to life. This didn't shock him, as his miracles certainly should have limits, but it didn't make the discovery any less painful. Father Toño had been a good priest, one of those who read scripture and called inequality a sin, oppression a sin. Tadeo wasn't certain of God's goodness anymore, but he'd believed it more than anything just days ago. And it had been Father Toño who'd spoken to him privately about this when Tadeo first confessed that there was a monster in him. 'Do good,' he'd encouraged shakily. 'Do good, *mi mijo*. We're with you. But remember that — we're with you, not behind you. If you want to help this place, if you want to save us, then we need to save you.' We all need to save one another.

Tadeo sat before the corpses, and he said nothing for entire minutes after he'd failed to return life to their bodies, soaking the white sheets in blood. When the crowd couldn't stand his silence much longer, each began to fidget, exchange glances, then begin to speak to him of their woes. They were hungry. A supermarket had been hit, and the power was still gone, just as the plumbing was gone. If the frequent outages of town before this, due to simple mismanagement, were any consolation now: they had trained the residents a good deal to learn to survive a while without electricity. There were many coolers stocked with ice still, which should last another few days. There were batteries ransacked to power ice machines, and boiled river water would sustain them, though maybe not for years. Worn, Tadeo looked to the hundreds nearby, some children at the railings of the rotunda; behind him, his mother in her wheelchair, his uncles, aunts, cousins, and grandparents stood.

Then, an older woman stepped forward, reached over the bodies, to offer a basket of cactus pads, cut from her own garden, some dry beans, and tortillas.

"No," he'd said, automatically, trying to gently push her wrinkled hand away. "I can't take this, and you're hungry. There won't be enough food for everyone left soon."

"But you've healed us," said the woman before him, a flood of people pressed up behind her, peering up at their Messiah. "Let us offer you something in return besides our prayers."

"Prayers?" Tadeo echoed softly, seeing Dina's face again in his mind, the serene, cool smile he'd had. "Who do you pray... to?" Some of Tadeo's family tried to interject, as if trying to explain what he'd meant for the women, but her face brightened some.

She said, "Well, to you."

"No," Tadeo whispered again, though he wanted to snap it. "Don't worship me. I'm just a man. I'm not God or Jesus or..." He stared at the bowls of food again. "Please don't worship me." 'I'm a false prophet. Don't do it.'

Tadeo's grandfather stepped up behind him, set his hand on Tadeo's shoulder, squeezed, and told the boy, "Just accept the food, Tadeo. We haven't eaten much either."

"But people will starve soon," Tadeo whispered. "*Welo*, we can't hoard the food. We shouldn't..." He stared at the bowls, and then he shut his eyes, breathed.

Dante was at the outer side of the rotunda railing, crammed between two kids peeking in to watch Tadeo perform his miracles. With his arms crossed, the soldier was keeping watch of the streets, finding them too quiet. 'Maybe my betrayal won't ever come. Maybe the army doesn't care about this anymore. Maybe Tadeo will be safe from what I've done.' Then, Dante heard the crowd's awed gasps and shouts, and he felt the children beside him jump in excitement. And so Dante turned, already expecting a miracle; even still, he felt his breath hitch. In Tadeo's hands, where he'd taken two bowls of food, there were suddenly dozens, stacked over each other, wobbling, beginning to tip.

"Take it," Tadeo was whispering harshly, weakly. "Please." But Dante's face cringed in sadness at the misery in the anti-Christ's voice.

For hours after this, the stars above town watched the anti-Christ and gurgled; the dim sun had set again, and the blood moon had risen. Tadeo remained in the plaza after his miracles this time, sitting on the grass beside his mother's wheelchair. He rested his head on her lap, listening faintly to the chatter of humans nearby. 'I'm scared for all the places on the Earth without me. Who will starve off their famines?' He'd heard trumpets when he'd stared at Dina, his destroyer. 'How long do we really have?' How long could he protect his people?

Tadeo's gaze flickered up to his mother's peaceful face. "Survive," he whispered. "You told me that's all I had to do, *ama, pero para que?*" What for?

His rest of his family was off with crowds around smoking grills, searing the meats at highest risk of not surviving another day. A final *carne asada* before the apocalypse. Some *bandas*, musical groups of regional music, had appeared, had all joined together. Some of those who'd been *mariachis* wore the traditional uniforms, others were in *tejanas* and jeans, others in sports jerseys. Lifting trumpets to their mouths, strumming guitars, and beating drums — the bands played for their families who'd come to listen and for all the other survivors.

"It's all my fault," Tadeo whispered to her. "I love you." There was a stray dog, wandering nearby, and one of the grillers tossed her a piece of fajita. "I love you and dad." He nuzzled her lap. "Everyone else too. *Wela. Welo. Tío.* Everyone. I know how this ends. I know I'm going to burn. But you're going to go to Heaven." Closer to the food, some people were starting to dance. "Don't miss me, please. Just... tell dad that I loved and missed him. And I never wanted to do this, any of this. I really love you both—" Coughing up his tears, he watched his mother's pants dampen. "Neither of you deserved this. God doesn't give us what we deserve. God doesn't give us anything at all. Don't forgive him in Heaven. *Ama*, don't forgive God for what He's done."

The crunching of grass, over and over, approaching. Sniffing, Tadeo wiped at his eyes, squeezed his mother's knee, then turned to see a cousin walking over with curved, sad brows. Behind her, Dante was wearing his sunglasses despite the darkness. "Tadeo," his cousin called softly. "I'll stay here with your mom for a bit. Go eat." Far above, the stars still hung, glowing weak like timid lanterns.

"I'm not hungry."

"Told you his depressed ass would say that," Dante said, stepped over, grabbed the anti-Christ by the arm, then yanked him up. "Come on, you need to walk a little and stop crying."

Tadeo snapped, "I wasn't crying," then wrestled his arm free and stumbled over a rock. "Can you—" He regained his footing, glared at Dante, and stressed, "I already ate." The two stared at each other for a moment, faces tense and serious, before the soldier gave him a big smile, as if he'd realized Tadeo was admiring him. "What?"

"Nothing, nothing. How about a *cervecita* then?" A little beer.

Tadeo snorted. "I don't know."

"Well, you're gonna keep me company since I still haven't eaten." Dante took a few steps, brushing past Tadeo, as the anti-Christ debated returning to his mother. But as Dante was walking away, Tadeo looked over his shoulder, saw all the people again. It was late. His family would have to go home soon, were probably drinking and chattering with all the locals and migrants, as well, who he supposed were locals now too. 'The music is nice. I could stay here forever, listening.' Those sorts of thoughts embarrassed him, however, because it was absurd to feel his heart so warmed up by the sounds of a *mariachi*. It was stereotypical; it was silly. 'If I said it right now, to Dante, he'd probably laugh. He would ask me what next? Do I get sentimental when I listen to *Cielito Lindo* too? Well, maybe I do. It's what I'm fighting for. It's what I *thought* I was fighting for. The sound of music here in the plaza again.'

"Fine," Tadeo surrendered, then he followed, trying to ignore Dante's amused chuckle.

Once they'd approached, the cooks and their helping friends

quickly went to stack three tacos, a sliced cactus pad, and a quesadilla, with a spoonful of salsa off a *molcajete*, onto a plate for the anti-Christ, and though Tadeo raised his hand to quickly deny the offering, the soldier swept in and said, "Very kind of you, thank you." Tadeo furrowed his brow before they went to one of many coolers scattered throughout the park to take a few drinks. "Get one for me, *papi*."

"Did you just ask me to come with you for the free food?" Tadeo grumbled, but did as told, taking five beer bottles between his two arms, then shutting the cooler with his foot, almost smashing the hand of the soldier that he'd healed so recently.

"Everything is free now," Dante laughed. "You're here to help me cut the line." Dante nudged him with the arm that also cradled his plate of food, and Tadeo grumbled that he was an asshole, but the soldier smiled. "Come on," he said, "let's sit." Toward a lonesome bench, Dante walked, and when he lowered his body onto it, it was with a sigh that seemed tired, much more tired that he was letting his face show. More stiffly, he said, "Relax, will you? Things are calm for once." Readjusting the beers in his arms, Tadeo bit down on the inside of his cheeks but supposed that he was, in fact, outrageously tense — in his neck, his shoulders — despite the relative peace. So, he settled to sit beside Dante and watched as the soldier brought the quesadilla to his mouth first, took a bite, chewed. "Mm." He swallowed, then reached to take one of the beers from Tadeo's hands. To open it, Dante arched his back, brought the bottle to his groin, and snapped the cap off with his belt buckle.

Tadeo swallowed, quickly turned his gaze elsewhere; out of the blue, his lungs felt emptier and his cheeks warmer. He moved to set the four other drinks on the ground, but Dante reached for another, opened it with his belt buckle as he'd done the other. "I," the anti-Christ said, "can open it myself."

"Just take it." Dante shoved it back into the other man's hand with a sterner glint in his eyes. "Stop thinking about prophecies. Enjoy the drink. Enjoy that your family is here. We don't all have that privilege."

Grimacing, Tadeo said, "I'm sorry," without thinking, grasping the cold, wet drink and listing it to his lips. "If I can figure out a way to— To get you home to your mother. Another miracle." Tepidly, Tadeo sipped. Despite its coolness, the beer burned its way down to his stomach, and the relief was immediate, as if the mere promise of drunkenness was enough to do away with his nerves.

Not replying, Dante focused on eating, and Tadeo decided to focus on drinking.

An hour must've passed, in near silence between them. Tadeo went for more drinks, glad to see that no one seemed protective over the supply, certainly imagining that Tadeo could will more beer into existence. Maybe he could, but Tadeo didn't know. Occasionally, a person or family would come to him, ask for the anti-Christ's blessing and, without knowing what else to do, he'd touch their hand, squeeze it, and then watch them leave. Tadeo had always considered himself the sort of drunk that could fool you. He could walk in a perfect line several bottles in; he could even drive, though he knew he shouldn't; he could hold a conversation without slurring, though he'd struggle to remember a word or two. 'I wonder if Jesus ever drank to smother the terror he had for himself, of what he could do. When you're drunk, you forget who you are, how you got here, and you're just living for a second. When you're drunk, you're not divine, and you realize there's nothing worse than being like God.'

Dante suddenly chuckled. "You wanna dance?"

Tadeo, only then, realized he'd been rocking in his seat to the rhythm of the music. "Ah." He set his drink down, weirdly cognizant of how rocky the ground was below the bottom of the bottle. "No, no. I can't dance."

"What?" Dante's laugh was breathy, giddy; he must be drunk as well. "You don't know how to dance? How?"

Tadeo blurted: "No, I do know how to dance, actually— I used to dance a lot when I was younger."

"I used to sing," Dante seemingly also blurted. "I always wanted to be a singer. I'm good."

"Aah!" Tadeo scoffed. "I don't believe you."

"I am, I am," Dante insisted, his smile enormous. "Listen." He opened his mouth, held a long, high note, then did a *grito* that made Tadeo burst out laughing, so hard that he doubled over, almost kicking over the beer he'd set down. "You laugh because you're jealous." Hiccuping, the soldier curled forward, then stumbled onto his feet. "So, dance? If you want to dance, then dance."

"What? With you? Like we're gay?" Tadeo was still laughing, but he shook his head. "No. No, you didn't let me finish. I can't dance. I dance... like a girl. I dance like a girl."

Dante reached, took him by the shirt. "Well, I'll dance like a girl with you."

'I did. My dad would teach me to dance. He said he'd always wanted a daughter, so that he could dance with her on her 15th. I wasn't a daughter, but for a moment, I could make myself think so, to make my father happy. He was a good man, and I thought he deserved it. He deserved to have a child that he could love.' Trembling, Tadeo walked as Dante pulled him along, and when he breathed, he almost choked on a slight evening humidity. When the soldier brought him into the gathering of a dozen or two, mostly middle-aged, dancing, he took Tadeo's hand, and he spun around under it — like a woman would. Dante pulled himself close, afterward, and Tadeo tripped only to latch onto Dante at the same time the soldier latched onto him.

'You're sweaty,' Tadeo wanted to say, but he drew in trembling breaths instead, allowing the scent of Dante's exhaustion and the liquor on his breath to lap at his face. When they began to spin together to the music, Tadeo tried not to instinctively do what he'd learned as a child, to twirl or move his hips femininely. Except, Dante did; he rolled his body, rolled his waist, bright and giggling drunkenly, and stared up at the taller man without any shame. There might've been a hundred eyes on them; certainly, there were whispers, and some taunts and jeers. But it was the end of the world, so no one did a thing about the two boys dancing away. The band played louder.

Abruptly, Tadeo tried to dip Dante, but they both stumbled, Tadeo nearly falling over the other's frightened, cursing self before the two howled with laughter. Wheezing, grinning, their hands found each other again, tighter, returned to holding their bodies together, then spinning. Their surroundings blurred as they did, and in the haze, they could only see each other.

'I've never danced with another guy,' Dante wanted to say. 'I wanted to. In the college.' He'd laughed about it with Joana, but his heart painfully pumped with the memory of his soldier training. The hazings where they'd mocked him for his erection while they fucked his mouth. First time he'd fallen in love with a man. 'But fucking was just about power to them.' And humiliation. 'I have it tough enough.' They'd call him a faggot for enjoying it, and they'd called him every foul synonym for *indigenous* for existing. 'I was happy to forget about it, find a girl one day, and feel like a man. But here we are, here you are.'

Tadeo was drunk enough not to think of the past, to not associate the musk of another man, or his touch, with anything horrible — briefly, briefly. Briefly, he could act like being close to another man was so new to him. In a way, it was. It wasn't like before. He trembled, and he was feeling the flush of his face trickle down to his core, pulsing. For the first time maybe, arousal didn't make his blood run cold or his breath ripped out of him like an intestine. "Dante, I'm— I'm gonna fucking fall, *güey*—" Dante laughed again, and then without warning, he reached for Tadeo's dark-brown hair.

Still dancing, still spinning to the upbeat old song, the two men crashed their lips together, mouths molding imperfectly, tilting, trying again, trying again, intent to force their bodies together despite destiny, body, God, blood. Their teeth bashed, scraped on their already-cracked lips, and their eyes were half-shut, tired from all the liquor but refusing to sleep and think that, for any second, this kiss was a dream.

A sudden, high trumpet shocked them away from each other, and they both twisted their heads in the direction of the band, but it'd seemed unrelated — the musician having tripped over his feet briefly. And so Tadeo and Dante, slow, dropped the heavy fear from their shoulders, turned back to each other, both their cheeks pinked. Dante was quicker to recover; he laughed warmly, and then he took Tadeo's arm, squeezed it.

"One more drink," Dante whispered. "Just one."

Tadeo swallowed shakily, but the ends of his lips were twitching upward, unsure of smiling. "We're already drunk enough, aren't we?" But when Dante took off, Tadeo followed him. He continued following even after the soldier reached yet another cooler, took out an ice-cold glass bottle, then ran off again. "Where are you going?!" he called, but followed, followed. 'It's the least I can do after you followed me down to Hell.' As Dante swerved into a street, then hopped over a fence into an abandoned restaurant with outside seating, the soldier made his way over to a plastic table, plopped down onto it. Tadeo reached him soon enough, and before he could even speak, Dante had already grabbed him by the throat, tugged him down into another kiss.

Grunting against the soldier's mouth, Tadeo felt as Dante shoved the cold beer in between the tenting at their groins. The alcohol's wetness at the seam of his jeans sent a harsh shiver up Tadeo's spine, and he rolled his face back, biting down a noise of startled pleasure. But the snickering soldier simply took the chance to bring his mouth to the anti-Christ's bared neck. Pursing his lips, Dante suckled, then licked up Tadeo's rosary beads. Setting a fist down on the table, Tadeo felt his skin everywhere suddenly strain; the grotesque thing inside him — wrestling against his heart. "Dante, fuck, be careful—"

Dante grinned against his skin, then turned upwards to peck Tadeo's mouth. "You think I'm scared?"

Tadeo murmured, "No, I think you're stupid." His breath caught and knotted, however, when Dante started rubbing the beer in between their mutual hardness. "I could kill you," he tried to say, claws starting to dig into the table. "Fuck. Dante, for *fuck's sake*—"

Dante kissed him again. "Mwah." He removed the bottle, finally, set it on the table, and then reached for the button and zipper of Tadeo's jeans. "Relax." And the anti-Christ tried, gaze flickering down to watch the soldier slide his hand into his pants, take hold of him. He grimaced before he could stop it, and he felt an abrupt whip of presentness that told him he was sobering up.

"I can't—" Tadeo whispered, but he set his forehead against Dante's, panting and panting. His hands were trembling. "I can't relax." The soldier's touch froze, and he glanced at the anti-Christ's shutting eyes.

"Oh man," said Dante, starting to hesitate. "Are you okay?"

'Never.' Tadeo knew he must look terrified, his breath unsteady, his eyes too wide, but he insisted, "I'm okay." Blindly, he reached, took the bottle that Dante had left on the table. "I just need a little more of this." Lifting it to his mouth, he downed it, welcoming the murky taste, hardly feeling the drops that rolled cold down his chin, his neck, to his white top.

Dante's eyebrows curved. "Are you sure? I can stop. Or I can suck you off quick—"

"I've never— No one's ever sucked me off." 'I want that and this,' he wanted to say. 'I want you more than anything.'

"Yeah, doesn't seem like it," Dante joked, and Tadeo laughed so weak that the soldier undoubtedly noticed it wasn't the time for humor. "Here." He brought his other hand to his own pants, and Tadeo watched the other man pull himself out, squeezed, pumped, then let out a strangled pleasure noise.

Setting the drink back down, Tadeo tried to crush the part of his mind that feared that noise. 'Think of him,' Tadeo urged himself. 'Think of Dante.' He'd tortured him. He'd broken his hand. 'Your moans remind me of your cries in pain.' He kissed Dante now, and the soldier wrapped a hand around both their lengths. Nervously, Tadeo drifted his clawed hand, put it over Dante's just as he began stroking them both. Hips aching, Tadeo gasped, raw and hoarse, but rolled them forward slowly, and Dante matched him with his own low moan.

They thrusted together, fucking each other steady. Steady, grounding almost. And Tadeo's eyes fluttered open a pinch, examining Dante — his squarer face, his darker hair, his nose, his long lashes, how his lips parted. 'Fuck, I don't want to be in love with you. We shouldn't do this.' But his cries grew weaker, higher, and he just about whimpered at the swelling goodness, at the pulses of their cocks, the wet drag of skin. The tips that kissed when they angled them right.

But no pain, no crying. Their bodies wept white sin, in just some minutes, and Tadeo hiccuped when the rush of it broke him open. But no pain. No tears in his eyes. He wasn't afraid, and nothing hurt. Dante's hold on their most delicate organs waned. This thing really was delicate, like a flower that blooms toward the sun then wilts. 'God's imperfect design.' All men with their posturing of strength, so weak between the legs. Slumping, Tadeo dropped his own hand away from them and leaned over Dante, still on the table. He hadn't been asking for a hug, but the soldier lifted a hand, rubbed Tadeo's back. Pants for breath broke the silence, which was otherwise calm, comfortable.

"Are you," Dante asked again, whispered, "okay?"

"Not really," said Tadeo honestly, noting their stained jeans and shirts, as if stained with blood.

"I'm sorry."

"No, I should thank you. I never— I never told you how I died, Dante." Tadeo pressed to Dante's throat, warm and safe, though it shouldn't be. "It was soldiers. Like you. They raped me." Rape — unambiguous; he wasn't sure if he'd ever said it like that. "And then they shot me in the head. But there's something else— I—" He'd expected to choke up, to shatter from having kept it a secret for so long.

Dante said, "I saw a photo of your parents. Your grandfather recovered it from the rubble, and he showed it to me. Your parents and," his voice growing delicate, "a daughter."

Breath falling from his mouth, Tadeo felt a devastated smile forming slow. "It's why I've always believed in God, Dante. I couldn't understand why my body wasn't mine. I felt like there was something so wrong with me that only God could be responsible."

CHAPTER 37

The Earth cracked like an egg, and hellfire erupted from where the surface pulled apart in every nation. At the heart of Babylon, where death and disease roamed as the blood in its veins, yet another thing pierced through the ground, rising far above all the other buildings, as if trying to claw at the red-tinted sky and reach Heaven. Satan's tower, the Tower of Babel, returning to Babylon; there remains a story to tell of how the Tower of Babel landed in Satan's hands, how the demons brought it to Hell — but it's a simple one. Before Christ, but after the flood, the Lord and the devil had a mutually beneficial relationship; Satan gave God a reason to rage, and God raged. The Lord had said, 'Aid in halting the construction of Babel, and you may take the tower.'

If it weren't for God and Satan having their children, maybe their little game would have continued, but perhaps He'd grown bored as gods so often do.

And now, Satan panted as he adjusted his footing, lifted himself off the ground heavily. One hand planted on the cool glass of a window to hoist himself back up, then with heavy eyelids, he stared out into the Earth, his Earth, and his nails scratched the panes. The chaos of the human city was unlike anything he'd ever seen before

— worse than all the wars he'd witnessed. Hell had risen to the very Earth — scorching every running person, grown or young alike, to dust and shrieks of agony. Behind Satan, demons groaned and many of them hurried, toward windows as well or to other levels of Satan's home, perhaps looking for the safety of their friends. The armor would have saved many, and the impossibly tall tower could fit most if not all of the demons — but this had all happened without warning. Not everyone had made it in time. Turning slow, Satan saw Baal pressed against the wall beside the window, gasping still for breath, then he saw someone sitting on the ground, pressed to a pillar.

Rosier, silent, holding an amputated arm, eyes wide and utterly empty.

Trying to halt his trembling, Satan said, "Baal, I need you to scout the area. Keep... your armor on. It won't be perfect against bullets, but it'll be enough." He wondered if Babylon could still organize its military, but he was sure that it could. The empire dies far before the war does; a lifetime that spanned every human century had taught him this. "And tell me if you see any angels."

Baal said, "Lucifer." Hushed, weak. "I think Asmodeus is dead." The devil noticed his wide eyes and his terror. "There might be others— But— Asmodeus is dead. I saw it— the fires."

Satan swallowed, thick, his gaze flickering to Rosier before he could stop himself, but the demon of fruit wasn't responding, as if he were made of stone. And something hurt inside of Satan, like a harsh scrape. He recalled the sounds of Asmodeus' voice. 'You told me that everyone was waiting for me outside. You told me I was as beautiful as they all said.' But Satan had grown to despise him. 'I told Rosier to leave you to be eaten by animals in the woods after the fall. Because of what you did. Because of everything.'

"He," Rosier whispered hoarsely, the light in his eyes still dead, "gave me his helmet."

Trying to speak through the tightness in his chest, Satan dismissed: "He protected you. You're safe. That's what he would have wanted. We should—" voice almost cracking, but he picked at the glass of the window pane once more, ignored the burn in his mouth, ignored Baal's pained, regretful eyes, and Rosier's emptiness. "We should look for any other casualties and think of what can still be done."

Baal's voice was quiet, tense. "Is that all?" He looked at Satan darkly. "Is that all you'll say?"

A flare of anger, burning away the grief, the confusion, the denial, with irritation. "You want me to grieve?" But his voice still shook. "For someone who hated me almost as much as I hated him? I don't shed tears for anyone; I'm like God. And he chose this. " Looking away, Satan felt Baal bristle. "And unless we act now, we'll lose more of us."

But Baal didn't submit. "He fell, Lucifer, because of you."

"He fell because of what he did."

"We all fell because of you."

"Baal," Satan said, stricter. "Now isn't the time."

Hollowly, Rosier stared, peering at the devil through his dark fringe, fingers drenched in red as he continued latching onto Asmodeus' hand, but there was nothing in him except confusion, loneliness. Almost childishly, he wanted to ask where Asmodeus was, when he'd be back. 'Let him return soon. We have a home to find and live in.' Where was Asmodeus? Where was the voice Rosier heard as often as his own? Where was Asmodeus? In his grip, as just an arm.

Armoni, suddenly, broke through some of the crowding ahead, hurried toward Rosier without paying any mind to Satan or his regent in a quiet, furious standoff. He lowered himself, touched Rosier, who twitched in half-recognition; he was seeing Asmodeus' face, he was hearing his voice. 'Darling Rosier, let's marry again.' He didn't move; he dreamed awake of a demon of lust, a fallen angel, who'd dragged him down from Heaven with him. But the blonde angel whispered, "Moloch told me— He saw what happened—" A gasp shot out of his mouth at the sight of the arm in Rosier's hands. "Oh no. Oh no..." When he took Rosier gently and began tugging him upward, the demon hardly felt it. "Come, come with me."

He continued to ignore Baal and Satan, wrapping his arms

tighter around the demon of fruit; and as Armoni led Rosier away, the devil didn't stop them.

In Heaven, Michael learned of the devil's tower rising to the Earth from Enoch, who'd heard it from God. Then, he'd made his way through a destroyed, quiet Heaven to the barracks, though not without fastening flasks of the Lamb's blood to his hip. He did it to tell Phanuel that he would be in charge of the injured angels and the wreck the demons had left of the city. "You know why I'm leaving this in your hands." Just as he opened the same door that his old friend had left unlocked for Baal to barge in and kidnap Satan, Michael heard Phanuel step closer to him. Michael twitched, then turned back as if Phanuel could see him through the helmet.

"No," said Phanuel, simply, in the same hoarse whisper as always. "No, I won't do that."

"I'm," the archangel replied, "your chief prince, and you will listen. If I were crueler, I would step out and tell everyone, all the angels of God, what you've done."

"Go, Michael," urged Phanuel instead. "Go to Earth. I don't want to hear from you now, and no one outside these barracks wants to hear from you either." He stepped closer, and he leaned in with a stern, irritated face, added, "How many times should I try to reason with you? When I saw the devil, strung up inside the room next door, I didn't see Satan, Michael. I saw Lucifer."

"He deceives you," Michael hissed. "He's the devil, Phanuel!"

"You can't be reasoned with," Phanuel said, then he shook his head, a flash of pain passing over his ivy-green eyes that made something within Michael shift uncomfortably. "The devil is more honest than you. Even when my own face was torn off, Satan didn't try to make me believe that he did it righteously. But *you*, Michael? You've destroyed Heaven and Earth and dared to try and convince us that any of this could be good."

"*It is good!*" Michael insisted in a sudden, shrill panic, shoving his friend back so harsh that the forgiving angel was thrown against the stone wall, and he let out a hack of pain. "That is what you don't understand, Phanuel! I follow God, and His word is good. If you think that goodness comes from anything other than His word, then you've come to believe Satan!"

Phanuel shuddered, and his jaw tightened, before he replied: "It's my heart that I believe, and it's a heart that has ached more than loved ever since the war. It aches to see what you have done and what the Lord has allowed to happen. How much longer must I hurt for God to be pleased, brother? And how much love can the Lord ever offer for us to forgive His apocalypse? How can any promise make up for this atrocity?"

Michael clenched his teeth, frustration a furnace in him. "I must leave," he managed to grit out, "but when I return— You will pay penance for what you've said."

"There's no need. I will never speak again," Phanuel promised. "Goodbye, now, prince. I hope you finally rid yourself of guilt by killing Satan and yourself. I hope you will find peace. I wish that for the both of you." Shoving Michael aside, so hard that even the strongest angel of all stumbled, Phanuel stepped out of the barracks, into the eternal light of Heaven, the divine paradise with bullet casings littering the ground. Angels collected them curiously, asking one another what they were, what the demons had wielded. What is all this that the humans have made? What have they done?

'The humans have made weapons far more destructive than the angels,' Michael wanted to tell them, but they wouldn't dare to look at him. 'They have exterminated animals on Earth, and they have exterminated some of their own. They are closer to God now than angels ever were.' The prince stepped toward the doorway, and he could see Phanuel's back, heading for a street lined with stone monuments of laws at either side, some of the columns toppled over. 'Phanuel.' He wanted to say he was sorry. He wanted to tell him that he was wrong. He wanted to tell him he was right. In their youth, Phanuel would insist he was always right, he was wiser and older, even if by a mere year or two.

'When God punished me after the war, I used to dream of Lucifer dying. One day, I saw my bloodied hands. I killed him. My longing woke Satan, and he burned himself out of Lucifer's body.' Before the war, however, Lucifer had appeared in Michael's home, wanting to love the prince in a way that Michael didn't understand. In perfect clarity now, 'I remember your frightened eyes, your desperation. There was something terribly wrong that you wanted to tell me. But you didn't. God was in there with us. You said that you loved me. You wanted me to be your God. I didn't realize you were asking me to save you from Him.'

'Why? Why?' Michael had thought at God, and he'd merely heard an echo. 'Why?'

In the tower — the devil touched the faces of some demons, examined their wounds, and he sighed into the crowd of them. Many of them held bags of belongings, all that they'd managed to save from Hell's fires, while others clutched various kinds of weapons. In their wide eyes, Satan saw his own tired face reflected, and he noticed the frightened quivers of their lips. Very juvenile, innocent-seeming. 'Now that the eternal torture we've always spoken of is finally before us, you feel the weight of dread.' "The apocalypse hasn't finished," Satan told a demon he drifted his touch away from, as well as all the hundred gathered around him, listening. "You demons defeated Heaven, and you saved me from Michael, from the God above, and all the angels. We will never know defeat. No more lives will be lost."

The words had fallen from his mouth before he could stop them, and he saw Asmodeus' loathing face in his mind.

A boom sounded in the distance, something akin to thunder, but Satan ignored it until a pair of doors at the other end of the hall opened loud enough to silence all the demons in the room. And Baal in all his armor and horns stepped through quickly, his dark, thin wings folding closer to his back. "Angels." Immediately, Satan's hand went to his revolver. "But not God's." He hesitated. "The Watchers."

A second passed, as if Satan was trying to remember what that word meant, and then he turned on his heel, headed for the window. Swiftly, he took the iron deadbolt, pulled it back, then pushed open the pane. Satan set a foot on the sill, then the other. Standing on the window, facing the apocalypse. He saw what had made that boom sound earlier — a falling piece of a star, crashing against a smaller building and the vehicles parked next to it. 'Destroying Babylon.' How much of it had the Watchers already destroyed? Biting down a sting of anger, Satan allowed his hands to curl into fists as he faced the attackers, almost two hundred angels flying forward only to slow, then hover before him, his tower, wings flapping slow.

At the front, bathed in starlight, and with pale warpaint over his face — Azazel. One hand continued to hold a chain that attached to the collar on Samyaza behind him as Azazel met Satan's stare. The other Watchers swarmed by him were panting, baring their teeth, growling — all like the animals that centuries of torture had turned them into. This was revenge, wasn't it? The Watchers destroying the world as the demons had done to theirs.

"Azazel," Satan called, "all of you —" But then his shoulders loosened, and he smiled too wide. "How about we have dinner?"

Armoni, meanwhile, brought Rosier to a cramped chamber in the tower, one of a few reserved for dukes, where Moloch had seemingly settled with some followers. They were gathered by the burly insurgent, and the closest to him was a red-haired demon named Ara, dressed in sheer, much like Armoni — both of them trying to appeal to Moloch's tastes. Except Ara had done it willingly, though with that empty look in his eyes and bitter curl to his lips that he always carried. 'Cain's old lover, Ara.' Armoni didn't get along with him, had long stopped pitying the demon who loyally stood beside Moloch and his barbarity simply because Moloch had been there for him in the aftermath of Cain's death. But for love, pain is an easy thing to excuse. Armoni had learned that well from his closest friends since he left Heaven.

He looked at Rosier in his arms, curled into himself somewhat, unnoticed as Armoni tried to usher him into an adjacent washing room.

'I never told you, Rosier, that I was excited too when we both spoke for the first time, and we learned that we were like each other but no one else. I despised fucking, and you didn't understand it. I know that our bond is why you begged Asmodeus to intervene, to try to keep Moloch from hurting me. I know, I know. If I didn't, I would have told you to leave Asmodeus' side long ago. I watched you cling to him, and him to you. I comforted you when you wept of Asmodeus sleeping with others, and I encouraged you to mind your body more, to listen to what it wants. I wanted to tell you that he's no good for you; I think you knew that I wanted to tell you that.' Asmodeus had been selfish, possessive, and Rosier had been gentle, patient, so willing to forgive. 'You would even forgive Asmodeus hollowing you out. Maybe that's exactly what he did.'

But as the two of them settled against a grooming divan — ignoring all the toppled furniture and shattered oils and the wet floor — Armoni didn't dare to voice any of that. He hugged the still dead-eyed Rosier to his side, let the demon's head fall to press against his neck.

"Rosier," he simply said, "don't... lose your mind. Demons, angels — we don't die, do we? Even humans don't die; their souls weigh down into the fires or they remain in the leaves. I think Asmodeus is in the leaves. And I think he can be brought back. He can." But Rosier remained eerily quiet, Asmodeus' arm loose in his hold.

Moloch's voice filtered in: "It's a shame. I really did like Asmodeus. Didn't we all? Very reasonable demon. Very sharp. Great fuck." His followers laughed. "But our lives will be easier without him, and it's what he gets for not standing with me when I came up to him before Hell burnt up."

One of Moloch's friends added with a snicker: "And he left behind that Rosier that he was so obsessed with. Now that he's a widow, he might need a little comfort, right?" Rosier's grip on Asmodeus's arm tightened; his fingers dug into the dead flesh. Armoni felt him stiffen, tried to call his name, but Rosier didn't react. He stared at a wall. Toward Moloch's voice.

In the grand dining hall of the tower, the demons worked quick under Satan's commands to set up the table long enough to seat hundreds, and then they emptied out some of the stored dried meats and drinks and spices. They hadn't the time for cooking, and so the plating was shamefully simple. The guests, however, didn't seem to care. When Azazel waved a hand, allowing his Watchers to help themselves — they pounced, shoved aside the chairs to grab at the food with their hands, then shoveled it into their mouths. There were few exceptions — Kokabiel, who poked at the food curiously, and Baraqiel who stood still beside him, and Samyaza, who twitched, who stared at the food but seemed to refuse to eat it if the standing Azazel didn't.

"Sit, sit," Satan urged, going to the head of the table, settling down on his chair. Baal was beside him, too, as were other dukes and demons, curious like children, a few grimacing over how they might've contributed to the state of the Watchers now. "How long has it been since we've spoken, dear friend?"

"Before you left," Azazel reminded him. "But you don't speak to me as often as you used to." He then reached for a cup of wine just poured for him, then swirled it in interest. He heard a grunt by his ear, looked at Samyaza, read the gaze in his eyes. 'You don't seem happy,' Azazel thought, then brought the wine to his old lover's lips, tilted the glass. Samyaza, dutifully, sipped, painting his lips.

Twirling a fork, Satan leaned back into his chair. "And why have you come? I never would have thought that once you Watchers gained your freedom that you'd come right back to me."

Azazel hummed, then he lowered himself onto a chair finally, setting his wine glass on the table. "We've been looking for you."

"For revenge?" Satan's tone was still light, but Baal shifted behind him. "You," he decided to remind him, "and all the Watchers will surely burn as I will." Satan's gaze rose to the window behind Azazel to see Babylon still burning. From this room, he could more clearly see how the Watchers had torn through buildings on their way to the tower, leaving a trail of rubble and bodies in their wake. 'My empire.' If Babylon fell, that would be another prophecy fulfilled. 'I need them away from here.'

"Does it ever frighten you, Lucifer?" Azazel asked, his voice soft but sharp; he wasn't going to play the devil's games anymore, much like God. "Knowing you've failed spectacularly?"

Satan's jaw tightened. "Tell me why you sought me out with all your Watchers. You didn't answer me. Are you here to try to inflict revenge on me?"

"Revenge," Azazel said again, as if tasting the word. "Revenge would be nice. But I know, perhaps better than you, that you've already destroyed yourself. You always wanted to be like God, Lucifer, haven't you? Well, you've become perfectly like him — a tyrant, a selfish, jealous, vain parent. And I'm the one leading an army now, against you. You've become the greatest evil that you always wanted to be." Satan went still, but otherwise smothered any further reaction. "I don't need to enact revenge on you. Your world is ending, and you will be tormented forever." Then, Azazel paused, the sounds of violent eating like a choir around him. "But there is someone other than you that has to suffer. Michael. Won't you tell me how to harm him, Lucifer?"

Satan thought of Michael's face as he'd held him captive in Heaven. The trembling. The kiss. The desperate, aching need masked as hatred. 'The taste of his mouth still lingers on mine, Azazel. In Heaven, he tempted himself to touch me because he held me captive. He needed me at his mercy. He still loves me. But he can only bring himself to love me if we're hurling toward death. He can only love me with a sword pressed to my throat.' Satan saw his own child in his mind, for a moment. A round face, flushed cheeks, dark hair, a grasping hand. The redness so dark that it was nearly black, the blood leaking into the flames, the smell of burning. The last few wails as Satan hacked out his own cries, begging for this all to end and for forgiveness.

In Moloch's chamber, Rosier listened to the rebel dismiss his followers, then kiss Ara noisily, hungrily, before leading Ara out as well, likely thinking that it would be too dangerous to waste time fucking. After the door thumped shut, Rosier rose to his feet, unsteady, slow, and pulled away from Armoni. He put one foot before the other, distantly heard Armoni's confused calls. Stepping into the main room, Rosier noticed all the weaponry that Moloch had lying around, including a long, sharp sword resting on the arm of a couch, the same one that Moloch was presently settling over and finishing a drink on. "Mm." He looked up at the sound of shuffling, then he quirked a brow.

'I did it accidentally once,' Rosier thought numbly, then he placed Asmodeus' arm on a counter to his left. 'All of this was an accident.'

"Rosier," Moloch began, cheery. "You were—"

The fruit demon lunged forward, reached the sword in time, and just as Moloch's eyes went wide, Rosier wedged the blade into the muscles of his throat. Hands flying to his neck, the larger demon tried to yell but managed only a wet, gurgling sound as blood splattered out onto Rosier's face. Moloch lifted a hand to Rosier's head, prepared to shove him off, as he growled and thrashed. But then Armoni was running over from the adjacent room, and he threw himself on top of Moloch, grappling his hair, holding him in place. Rosier and Armoni, both on top of Moloch. Rosier, sawing the sword until it chipped at the bone.

Moloch screamed in wrath, but when his body finally gave, his head came free. The sword clattered, and then the headless body slumped in agonized twitches while the face of Armoni's captor fell to the leg of an overturned chair beside the couch.

Rosier stared at the severed head — Moloch's mouth open, groaning, unable to piece together a single word. 'I rebuilt Asmodeus. I loved him for an eternity after what he did to me. I devoted myself to caring for him.' He felt Moloch's body jerk beneath him. 'I'll never care for anyone again.' He would never choose kindness again.

"Rosier—" Armoni's raw, trembling whisper.

And Rosier crawled off Moloch, off the couch, to Asmodeus' arm he'd left on the counter. Then, he made his way back to Armoni to grab him and take off running. The door slammed open as Rosier ran into it, and once they made it into the hallway, he yanked Armoni toward the endless spiral staircase at the center of the tower. "We need to leave." He'd planned to run away with Asmodeus, again, again. He'd wanted to run away with him forever.

Panting, Armoni looked at Rosier's desperate, bloodied face, and he wanted to scream that they couldn't go anywhere in this true world. But then he remembered the last time he'd tried to run with Rosier, when they'd visited the still captive Watchers. Armoni had called his child.

Had it followed? Sighing, broken, terrified, Armoni willed himself to purse his lips, whistle low. A screech — in the distance. Of course his child had followed; this tower belonged to Hell; and the Leviathan guarded everything of Hell. "Let's get on the Leviathan away from here," Armoni suggested softly, "and leave." Rosier squeezed his hand.

"Michael has," Satan whispered, "a daughter. If you want revenge, then do what he did to you. Kill her."

CHAPTER 38

Two young men were in bed, in a house, breathing easy — as if the apocalypse weren't raging, slaughtering the good and evil alike. Falling in love often feels like the end of the world, after all. Biblical revelation even felt less frightening in comparison. If Tadeo were brave, he'd say something like, 'I think that I love you biblically — with blood on my hands, lies in this body, and the need for you to give it all meaning.'

Dante was lying on his side, settled on the mattress before him and scrambling dominos over the bedsheets. Earlier, before moving into this lonely place to sleep alongside Tadeo's family, they'd found the dominos in some rubble and had spent the morning playing. They were only in their briefs — Tadeo sitting cross-legged, without his facial bandages, and Dante, still pouting after he'd lost rather spectacularly. "*Ya,*" he was saying, shoving the dominos away now. "No more. Fuck you." When the anti-Christ laughed, Dante said, "I'm never doing this with you again." He lifted a foot, used it to shove at Tadeo, who just grinned more. "Since you're cheating and all."

"I'm not cheating." Tadeo took Dante's ankle, pulled, and heard the soldier's yelp as he was dragged along the mattress. "I told you that my miracles don't work like that." He climbed on top of Dante, then smiled down at the soldier's huffing.

Dante stared back, and some seconds ticked by, before he nodded his chin. "Why are you looking at me like that?" A grin was beginning to bloom over his own mouth too.

"No reason." Tadeo lowered himself to peck Dante's lips, then he sighed against him. Pointedly, he ignored the fact that their groins were pressing together, already both firm from the sensation of their bare skin over each other — their legs, chests, bellies. "Hm." He eyed up Dante's body — stout but strong, his stomach lean but not too defined. He wore his dog tags, still, though he'd defected from the army, and Tadeo wore his rosary, still, though God had abandoned him. Humans are creatures of tradition, unfortunately. 'I'm going to keep praying every night, aren't I? If not for me, then for you.' Slow, Dante's hand crept over the back of Tadeo's neck, and he tugged him forward to deepen the kiss.

The soldier grunted in encouragement after that. Shuddering, Tadeo felt himself twitch between his legs. It wasn't entirely pleasant; his heart stuttered and stung. But he wasn't scared. Dante was patient, understanding. 'A bit different,' he'd said in the middle of the night, 'but in the military college, one of my superiors fucked me. I didn't want it, I think, but they do it to new guys all the time and— I'm sorry. I'm trying to say that— I don't want to hurt you. I don't want to be hurt either.'

'I'm sorry for hurting you,' Tadeo had whispered. 'God, I'm sorry.'

'I'm sorry too.' Neither really forgave the other, but neither of them needed that.

They were friends now, Tadeo supposed — romantically friends, if that made sense. He wanted to go out with Dante to get drunk and do something stupid, wanted to play games with him, wanted to wheeze in laughter with him, wanted to call him his friend as much as he wanted to call him my love, my life. Never would he have thought that learning to love could be this easy. Tadeo had expected suffering, trial and error, hurting over and over. He hadn't known romance could feel like friendship, like there was hardly a difference between playing dominos and having sex.

"Hm?" Dante fluttered open his eyes when Tadeo breathed out shakily. "What's wrong, buddy?"

Shaking his head. "Nothing. How are you? Are you hungry?" He went to touch Dante's scalp, run his hands through the black hair. They both smelled of sweat again, and faintly of semen, but there was no running water and so the most they could do was dampen a cloth with a water bottle and scrub themselves off. For now, Tadeo just lowered himself to lay over Dante, who wrapped his arms around to squeeze him comfortingly — mutual arousal simmering down.

"Not really." Dante reached across the mattress for his phone, then checked it over Tadeo's shoulder. "But I could go for..." His voice trailed off, and Tadeo felt the arms around him go rigid.

"What is it?" Tadeo turned his head, brushing his nose against Dante's neck, and he tried to see the phone screen that his friend had been staring at, but he'd just exited an application. "Do you have signal?" He supposed he'd heard Dante mention how soldiers could connect to satellites for service earlier, but hadn't Dante defected?

"Nothing." Dante's voice was tight. "I was just checking the time." But his heart was pounding; Tadeo could feel it against his chest, like Dante's heart was his own.

Outside, Joana had just left her mother and siblings when she heard something thump behind her on the street and a flutter of feathers — an angel landing. She was crouched, fiddling with a discarded bike, trying to dislodge a twig from the front wheel. A familiar shadow shaped in front of her, someone standing close behind, but she merely said, "I didn't think you were going to come back." Then — a hand over her face, streaking across it cold and wet. Joana jerked upright, twisted around, and stumbled back, the bike clanging to the ground. "Ah! What the Hell?!"

A helmeted Michael stood there, gauntlet dripping blood; he'd smeared now, across her eyes, her nose, her jaw. Marking her.

"What—" Joana touched her own face, and her fingertips

returned crimson "—the fuck is this?" Just as she lifted her sleeve to wipe it off, Michael's hand shot out again, grappled her wrist.

"Don't," he warned quietly. "The mark of the Beast is on all of humanity. When the devil bore his child, all of the living souls were marked with the Beast, and any one of them could become the anti-Christ. It is only the blood of the Lamb that can purify you and bring you to Heaven—"

"Shut the fuck up!" interjected Joana, pulled her arm away, then lifted her shirt's collar to dab at her face. The blood smeared down her neck, then she wiped more excessively, more furiously. "And get the fuck away from me." Michael tried to speak; Joana yelled out in frustration to silence him, released her shirt, and kicked a rock in Michael's direction, only for it to bounce off his silver armor without harm. "Why won't you listen to me?!" She didn't care about raising her voice, about anyone that might hear. "For fuck's sake, Michael, what's wrong with you?! Why won't you listen to me?"

"Joana—"

"I'm going to Hell!" she screamed now, feeling the words tear open her throat from within. "I'm a *murderer*! I'm a *liar!* Fuck God!"

"Joana!" Michael yelled at her, for the first time. And when the girl before him winced, his heart crushed as if in God's fist. Terror gripping it; he couldn't explain why. Joana looked afraid of him, like he'd hit her. "Please," he whispered now, pained. "Why won't you accept Heaven? It's for you. For all of you humans— Why won't you take it? Please."

But she shook her head, took some uncertain steps back, and Michael continued to ache and ache. When Joana's face flickered again with exhaustion, betrayal, hurt — everything inside him seemed to crack open. "Go already. Finish the apocalypse, Michael." That would be killing her. "Forget about me." God was asking Michael to kill her. "And leave me alone."

'No,' he thought. 'No. I can't.'

Softly, Dante whispered to Tadeo: "I remember always being surprised as a kid at how bad things get. You think all the bad things are over, and then worse things happen. All of my life it's felt like the world ended before I was born."

Tadeo swallowed, but he said, "I feel like that too, sometimes."

"Back home," Dante continued, "we still— We still have our traditions." He said it awkwardly. "But sometimes it feels like we're honoring a time that we'll never have again. Our world ended a long, long time ago." Swallowing, Dante felt the weight of the phone he set down on his lap, and he exhaled softly. "I'm sorry, again, Tadeo. I'm sorry. For— For everything." 'That is about to happen.' He'd just wanted to protect his mother.

Michael surrendered, then asked Joana before she could run, "Tell me what it is you want."

Disbelievingly, she stopped, turned back to the archangel, and then she forced a laugh as the prince removed his helmet, stared warily. "Stop this," Joana said like it was obvious, and Michael supposed that it was. "The apocalypse."

Michael didn't reply, but he listened for now, and he saw softness pass over her eyes, and when he stepped toward her, she didn't flinch again, nor did she turn around and run. "I must— I must go." He had to find Gabriel, have the last trumpet blown; those were his orders. "Please be safe." She sighed, tired, and she didn't resist when he, with a trembling hand, reached for her shoulder, pulled her closer. In fact, she leaned her head against his chest quietly. "Please. If you won't follow me to Heaven, then—" She was trembling too, and he clenched his eyes shut painfully. "I'll still find a way to ensure you're well. Even if it's Hell that you go to," he found himself promising, "I'll make a place in it that is only comfortably warm; I'll wash all of your burns; I'll cover your ears to give you rest from the screams of all those who deserve to be there." He'd kissed her forehead, slowly, painfully. "Wherever you go, I will go, as well." Their embrace tightened.

Faraway, the Watchers left Satan's tower and headed south again but settled over the tip of a skyscraper not long after. Seeing all that the Watchers had done to the nation — Azazel was surprised to see the silver birds flying out of Babylon instead of at the Watchers. 'They're destroying one another — the humans.' It reminded Azazel of the weeks before the flood, how men and women had turned on each other. Instead of uniting against the demons and angels, their tribes had looked for differences between each other to blame for war. Instead of uniting against God, the angels and the demons had fought at God's feet during the war for Heaven. 'Is this how it will always be?'

A grunt sounded behind Azazel, and he turned to see Samyaza on the corner of the skyscraper, scratching at his face, beginning the wheeze. "Samyaza," he whispered, then walked toward him. "Breathe. I'm here." He went for him, and took the old Watcher's face gently, and when he heard the thumps of others landing on the skyscraper, he looked at them patiently. But Samyaza's brows furrowed — angry.

"Azazel," said Kokabiel, his voice worryingly calm, and Azazel turned to see him; the star angel's red hair remained free from its old braids, fluttering behind him. "Revenge? Why revenge? The stars tell me..." And then he wheezed out a giggle. "That this dear Earth is already a lost cause."

"All the more reason," Azazel replied, "to have our revenge."

Kokabiel hesitated, looked at his beloved, glowering Baraqiel, then at a similarly angry Samyaza. Then he whispered, "The stars have made room for us above."

For now, Azazel didn't decipher that; instead, he began ordering the Watchers to create spears.

Soon after Tadeo and Dante's conversation, there was a series of aggressive knocks, and just as the men were jumping away from each other, Joana opened the door. "Tadeo. If you're done sucking dick, you need to get up." The anti-Christ spluttered at the same time he was scrambling off the bed, tripping over his discarded jeans on the ground, knocking down half the dominos. Over the low, weak chuckle of Dante, Joana added, "People are still starving out there, and I saw that your old house still has some of the guns I gave you in the rubble, and they should still work."

"Joana," Tadeo snapped, pulling up his pants as fast as he could and tightening his belt. "What is even the point? Look outside. You think guns can fix that?"

Grabbing his arm, Joana said, "You do what you can. Don't tell me you're going to surrender now for no damn reason."

Then, Tadeo noticed that her eyes were wet; she must've been crying recently, and he felt his gaze soften. "Okay," he said gently. "Let me just— Let me speak to my family first."

"Alright," Joana murmured as the soldier climbed out of bed.

"I have to go, also." Dante went for his pair of pants and began to step into them hastily, yanking them up his ankles, his shins, his thighs.

"What?" Tadeo turned over, having been ready to bring Dante with him. "Where?" Pulling on his white tank and his jacket, Dante headed for the door. "Where are you going?"

"Just trust me." Dante bit his lip, brushed past his new lover, then stressed, "Don't follow me. Go help people, okay?" Tadeo watched in utter confusion, and Joana was quirking a brow at him, but Dante ignored them, sighing softly. As soon as he stepped out, he deleted all the messages on the phone. 'Fuck,' he thought. 'Fuck, fuck, fuck!' He wanted to punch something, someone, as he shoved the phone into his pocket, took off running out of the house, heading for the border to Babylon as fast as he could.

Meanwhile, Joana advised Tadeo to clean up before she walked back to the streets, as well. Humans were gathered outside, probably found little to do in their homes now that all technology had died and there was little water, little food beyond what Tadeo offered to them. When he was gone, they wandered aimlessly, looking amongst each other, asking where their savior was. One old woman carried a figure of a saint that she'd modified to look more like the anti-Christ. Chewing on the inside of her cheeks, Joana moved down the road, wanting to berate everyone for this, for fulfilling the end of time by worshiping a false idol. But how was it their fault? They were just responding to a world of fallen stars and mass murdering angels.

'I like all of this better when it was just a fairytale,' she thought.

Before she could walk any further, a man suddenly grabbed her by the arm, and though she immediately cursed and tried to reach for the gun in her pants, another figure took her other arm. In a panicked blur, she barely noticed when a third figure stepped before her, brought up his knee, slamming it into her gut enough to feel like her intestines had just been crushed and forced out of her gasping mouth. 'Soldiers—' she thought, hearing some nearby cries of fright, then, 'Fuck.' She noticed their sneakers, and she recognized some faces. 'Criminals.' But what was the difference?

"I'm sorry, *mija*," a familiar voice was saying, and she rasped for breath, looked up. It was Lupina's father, the kingpin, shaking his head like this really was a shame. "Where is your boy?"

"Oh for fuck's sake," Joana grunted but her stomach pulsed in pain. "The world is ending, and you're still thinking about trafficking?"

"No," said the man, "we're thinking about surviving."

"We're all dead!" Joana bellowed. "We're all dead!" And she laughed in hysterics. "You stupid fucks think there's going to be people to sell anything to after this? We're all going to Hell!" She looked at the two men holding her up, wanting to snarl for them to snap out of whatever they'd been promised. Money? There will never be money ever again.

"It's not about trafficking," said the kingpin, and soon enough, another man stepped up beside him to finish the statement.

"It's about," said Joana's father, "the men from the other side." Babylon.

She stared at him, eyes wide. "What do you mean?" Joana's father's face was hardened, violent. "What are they... going to do?"

Unbeknownst to her, Michael the archangel was in the sky a street down. Though a few humans had noticed him, the prince had reached for the sword from his back to silence them. He watched — Joana and her father. 'I told you to listen to him once, to be obedient, that the only thing more painful than following orders was rebelling.'

Before Joana could receive her answer, the thumping sounds of what she first thought to be a horse sounded behind her, but far too fast, far too many. She turned back at the same time that the men grabbing her let go, and she breathed in seconds before she saw the beastly Tadeo barreling toward them. One of his claws reached out, grabbed her, threw her on top of his body like he were a horse. Without thinking, however, she reached into her pocket again with one hand, using the other to grip one of the wings that she was shoved in between of. She yanked out her gun, pointed it right at her father's head and, when he raised his own, she shot, shot first.

'Were you ever good? I clung to the memory of your kindness tighter than anything else in my life, but how much of it was true? Did I ever love you, or did I love the person I wished you were?'

Her father —in his second-long fright, he looked young again, looked just like the man who'd hugged her tight in the first memory she ever had. He looked like the man her mother fell in love with — soft-spoken, easily flustered, reckless, boyish — for a second only. He unfurled into his skull, red, pink, top lip pulling up, eyes pulling downward. Definitely, he'd been lifting his head, and the shot had gone through his nose, splintering it open. Numbly, Joana felt Tadeo lift up the front of his body, as if a horse on its hind legs, and her aim remained on her falling father.

Joana could hardly feel the feathers she held onto as the beastly Tadeo galloped beneath her; Joana could hardly hear the hums above of a drone. Her eyes burned, her throat dried and grew sore. Crying, she held on tighter. 'I did it.' Laughing, sobbing.

And Michael had lost all his breath, even God's breath, inside of him. It'd all happened so quickly that he'd almost not registered it, hadn't comprehended it at all. Turning his head, Michael followed Tadeo and Joana with his eyes and a shuddering crack inside of him. But it didn't ache. It should ache. He should be feeling all the dread of sin from watching Joana commit patricide. But instead, awakening from a slumber of hundreds of millions of years, of his time as an angel — pride. Pride and joy for Joana. 'You did it.' He hadn't known he wanted her to do it.

He realized what he must do, and the chief prince struck his wings against the sky and left for Babylon as fast as he could.

Meanwhile, Dante reached the border, and his heart sunk into his cold, cold body. Great tanks were crawling out from Babylon, and a dozen silver bird drones swept in between the low stars above. "Stop," he whispered in vain. Then, Dante hurried to one of the tanks breaching this side of the river, raising his hands wildly, pleading for them to stop. The military were coming from multiple bridges, impossible to stop. "Wait!" But the tank wouldn't stop. 'It's too late,' he thought desperately. 'It's too late.' They were going to bomb Tadeo to death, and they wouldn't care if their informant was having regrets. Perhaps, they had even anticipated it. What could he do, then? Dante bit his lip, and he stumbled backward, and he heard as a few civilians nearby made noises of surprise. How to make the invading army hesitate? 'Make them think I was wrong, that they're about to make a mistake.' His heart beat on his tongue, so fast and heavy that he wanted to, almost tried, to take it between his teeth and crush. Soon, he turned on his heel, then he began to run again, headed for the weapons that Joana had mentioned earlier.

At the same time, Tadeo was headed to the ruins of his home with Joana on his back as crowds swarmed to see him, not unlike when he'd arrived on horseback from Hell. Some shouted for food, for water, for more healing. If he could speak, he'd tell them to please be patient. Something was wrong. He didn't know what, but why had the criminals suddenly tried to hurt Joana? It was the end of the world. Surely they didn't believe that there was still profit to be made in extortion or trafficking or in anything at all. But then, Joana gasped and said, "Tadeo!" And the anti-Christ stumbled to a stop, trying to avoid trampling over the humans only to trip over his own tangle of legs. Tadeo crashed onto the ground but managed to turn his head toward whatever Joana must've seen. Silver birds, hissing through the air, and down the first boom of an airstrike somewhere, and then the particular creaks of a tank turning. Panicked, Tadeo's pupils thinned, serpentine.

Reaching the home of the anti-Christ first, Dante jumped past a remnant of the fencing, rushing past some of Tadeo's family lingering in the area, ignoring their questions. The high noises of the drones above answered for them, and the soldier simply shoved aside Tadeo's cousin, saying, "Run! Hide!" Staggering, he reached a wall, saw a blanket obscuring a lump on the ground that he quickly went for, panting and panting, face hot with exertion. Tugging the covering away, he saw three rifles, one revolver, and hidden beneath, a proper machine gun. Next, he searched for the ammo. Tadeo's grandfather had come up behind him, trying to demand what was happening, but Dante told him to stay back.

Coldly, Tadeo realized the army was approaching his home, and he shrugged off Joana, too quick, making her skid against the ground, scraping her arms as she yelped. But he took off, heading for where much of his family must be. He moved so fast now that the crowd couldn't follow and they, too, had just noticed the army, the silver birds. When another strike hit a building some streets away, the people screamed and began hurrying in the opposite direction that the anti-Christ headed. He sprinted, and when he saw Dante outside the home, hauling a large firearm in both hands, Tadeo initially breathed a sigh in relief. 'Dante, you're safe.' But then the soldier lifted the gun, pointed it squarely at Tadeo's many-mouthed, many-eyed head. And he pulled the trigger.

Shot after shot — *ta, ta, ta, ta, ta* — a barrage of bullets tore through Tadeo. He took them each but not without a piercing, stabbing pain for each one of them. And blindly, he stumbled, fell, growled on instinct. But — 'Dante? Dante, what are you doing?' All the inside of him burned. 'What the fuck are you doing?' A whine, like a dog, spilled out from Tadeo. But he'd never known he could even make such a pathetic noise, not in this body. 'Dante,' he thought. 'Dante?' His thousand eyes itched, and he recovered slowly, lifted his bulleted head. As the wounds throbbed and stitched together to close, he saw the soldier running at him, shouting back at a tank that'd just turned a corner, saying something had gone wrong, he was wrong. The tank obediently slowed its crawl as Dante stood before it, and he looked perfectly in place there. 'You were nothing more than a soldier all along.'

"Get out of here, Tadeo!" one of Tadeo's cousins shouted. "Run!"

"*Dante,*" Tadeo rasped out through his frontmost mouth, but it was so gurgled that he was sure the other hadn't understood. All Dante did was suddenly jog closer, lift the firearm, then whip Tadeo's monstrous head with it. It hadn't been strong enough to actually throw the anti-Christ's face to any side, but it nonetheless stunned Tadeo another few seconds, made him lower himself a little as he inched backward with such a tearing, ripping sensation of confusion and hurt inside him that he thought he was going to burst open. 'Stop,' he wanted to say, feeling Dante set a foot on him, then lift himself, as if climbing up Tadeo. 'I trusted you.' He had trusted his mouth, his hands. His smile, his words. Frantically, Tadeo began to growl, throwing his body around to knock Dante off of him. 'I loved you because I trusted you. You used me. You rotten fucking son of a bitch.'

"I'm sorry," Dante whispered; another three, four tanks were creeping closer. "I'm sorry."

Tadeo hesitated, confused, breaths erratic even as he continued to thrash how a wild horse would.

"Throw me. High. In the air," the soldier added shakily. "Please. Tadeo."

Without thinking, Tadeo grappled Dante with a hand at the end of a wing, then he tossed Dante up high between the fallen stars, and he jumped after him. Dante flailed for a few seconds up until he reached the highest point; he took his gun tight again; he pointed it at the beastly anti-Christ below. 'I still trust you.' Tadeo saw the flickers over his friend's face of terror. 'I think I still do.' Tadeo waited for the bullets to hit him once more. 'I trust you.' Dante's aim shifted, pointed at the tanks that were crammed at one end of the road, and then a little higher, right at a low-hanging star. He shot again.

A fire erupted, enormous, impossibly bright — like that in the beginning of time. Flames engulfed each of the tanks and any of the people in proximity. Half of Tadeo's family — grandfather, cousins, an aunt — standing nearby. The other half were thrown across the street, the boom louder than their second-long shrieks. And the swelling sphere of flame grew and grew. Dante fell toward it, and he looked frightened, then surprised. Lastly, he seemed relieved. The burst star took him, then spat him out, burnt up. Charred remains, then ash.

CHAPTER 39

Beautiful Dina stood on the roof of a half-collapsed hotel, realizing where the explosion had been — right by the home of the anti-Christ. In it, he had once eaten with Tadeo's family and softly admitted that he didn't know which humans went to Heaven, stifled the desire to inform them that there might be none at all. Metatron was no man and Jesus? Jesus was in an empty room, the same one where angels whispered that Mary was, or so it is said. How was Dina to know? He'd hardly ever left Uriel's library, surrounded himself in fairytales, listening to angel-tales through the open window. 'Uriel.' The last time that Dina had seen him, the archangel's eyes had been wide, horrified at the sight of a star. 'Uri,' Kokabiel had called him. 'Uri-Kimah.' And Dina remembered reading of what had happened to the stars from Uriel's old scrolls, after the prince had commanded Dina to do so.

Where had Uriel run? Dina imagined him back in Heaven, hiding from all that he had caused. 'In your libraries, scolding me for all the children's tales I liked to read. Forgive me for liking pretty things, I used to tell you. Forgive me for the delicate heart God gave me to carry. I like beauty and love. And I always liked you. I do still like you. Do you realize that I'm doing this for you? As much as me?'

The Earth seemed gutted open, revealing darkened, smoking organs that groaned out in misery, ants — humans — wandering all about it, hungry, begging, looking for their leader. Easily, the angel could see the boy Tadeo. He was half a monster, curled up on the street, and though Dina was much too far to hear it, he could feel the agonized scream ripping out of the anti-Christ's body, shaking the core of the Earth, the core of Dina.

"He has lost," the young angel whispered, "so much." In the pit of his stomach — the weight of despair, churning, revolting but not quite up his throat, to his mouth; instead, it sunk in deeper, as if it'd pull him back down into Hell. And yet, his mouth twitched with the urge to smile.

Behind Dina, Apsinthos hovered as both a divine sphere of flames and a misshapen collection of mouths, dozens of eyes, skin like pulled red linen and wet tissue. "You pity him. There is some of you that so loved him and loved humanity. You are a wonderful angel, Dina." Again, the angel's mouth twitched; his eyes squinted; his chest warmed. "But if you want to help him and his people — you must finish this. You must bring about the new Heaven and new Earth."

"I must finish it," Dina echoed, staring still at Tadeo in all his agony; he seemed so small from here. He was so small. 'I remember the sweet bread his family had given to me. How kind they had been, how kind they are. There will be sweet bread after this is all over. In the new Heaven, there will be sweet bread.' "But, Apsinthos," he called. "Tadeo is the anti-Christ." The star was silent. "Won't he be destroyed forever and not saved?" 'When Tadeo saw me for the first time, his eyes wondrous, awed, in an abandoned home in his half-abandoned town. An abandoned boy, telling me the world ended long ago.' God will only save some; God has chosen a select. The Lord has favorites; you must pray it's never you.

Apsinthos said: "It is God's will. Humanity had every chance to love Him, to be good. See how they attack one another now. This world cannot be saved." Dina knew that; he believed that. "There was no other path for humanity than the apocalypse. It all must end for good to prevail. It all must end."

Briefly, Dina wondered if any of this would have happened if he hadn't come down to bring about the revelation. "It will all end. For all this suffering that I see to be done away with forever—" Tadeo would have to be collateral damage. "It will end."

On the ground, Joana had just hurried through masses of people and stared at the destruction with fear shaking her. Tadeo's home was utterly obliterated now, whatever weapons she'd stored there gone, many of his family on the ground, groaning, many of them a splatter of red and roasted flesh now. The stench of it lurched her stomach but as she doubled over, Joana caught a tipped-over wheelchair, a woman still slumped over in it with blood splattered all over her top. However, the older woman was shivering, eyes on the mangled body of whoever had been standing before her. Joana felt a stab of pain in her gut and jogged to Tadeo's mother to take the wheelchair. "*Tía*," she said. "I have you. Let me help you up." One of the wheels was jammed into something on the ground, and as Joana wrenched it up, the wheel tore off with a shrill bang. Cursing, she still set the mother's chair right, then kneeled beside it, holding onto the armrest, panting far more than appropriate, head aching.

Looking up now, Joana saw that the crowds of people were nearly drowning Tadeo nearby, half a beast still, but he was curled up in on himself, massive eyes wide and bloodshot, all of them unseeing. "Tadeo," Joana called. "Tadeo! Your mother!" But she grimaced immediately, seeing how catatonic her friend was, his silence, his stillness. The anti-Christ could have been a statue of something, a monster, a dragon, clawed at by all the people surrounding him. They called out his name, asking for help, to save them from the soldiers further away but still here, still in the distance, the silver birds still circling. And many of the townsfolk were bleeding, some carrying the most injured, some already dead.

'They're still asking a false Messiah to save them.'

Just as some of Tadeo's relatives came to her side, looking to Tadeo's mother, Joana stood, and she marched forward, toward a scorched car that had just minutes ago lost its flame. She reached out, asking for the help of one of Tadeo's cousins to help her onto the trunk. He didn't hesitate to do it, and Joana took the final step to stand on the top of the car, over all the people. "Everyone!" Joana called. "Everyone!" In the crowd, the first to turn to her was an ashen, beautiful young woman — Lupina, again — and Joana locked eyes with her frightened own for a moment. "E-Everyone listen to me!" she tried again, cupping her hands over her mouth. "Leave Tadeo alone!" Next, Tadeo's cousins began to shout for silence too.

When even that didn't prove enough, Lupina started nudging some of the men around her, one of which had been holding Joana in place before she killed her father. He hesitated but then he raised a gun to the air, shot it twice. Two bangs rattled the air before everyone, instantly, ducked, with screams, many about to take off running. But in the opposite direction of where Lupina and her father's men had been, another two shots boomed in the air, warning the crowd to stay in place, that both directions to run were guarded. And when Joana looked in that direction, she saw her brother, pistol still pointed upward; his face was tight, his eyes were reddened. 'I'm sorry,' Joana thought, 'about dad.'

Then, she took a deep breath, began: "Our Messiah is dead! We can't rely on him. We can't sit and pray for him to save us! We can't —" The people roared out in response, arguing. "*No hay otra!*" Joana yelled back. "He can't save us! No one is coming to save us!" She almost said, 'We must save ourselves.' Instead, she said, "We all must save each other."

Faraway, Michael had just landed heavily, sword in hand, chains diagonal across his armored chest. His helmet hid a face of thinly pressed lips of resolve and tired, driven eyes. Before him — there was the greatest city in Babylon, though the sea had risen to soak the streets, water reddened by decree of Revelation. The sun above was dark, but it did enough to illuminate where the fallen, grumbling stars didn't. As he'd been told, an impossibly tall tower stood in the chaos like a gravestone, looming over blood-soaked rubble, abandoned homes and vehicles, as well as the diseased dead.

As expected, some demons scouting from balconies on the tower hurried back in, surely to warn their devil, but Michael knew Satan well. He would not hide from a challenge; he would open the doors to it. And, indeed, as the chief prince made his slow approach toward the tower, the armed demons at the double doors, triple his height and made of stone, halted their moves toward him when other demons whispered orders from their king. They, stiffly, watched Michael flare his wings and walk past them. Pointedly, he ignored the pegasi scattered throughout the lower level of Babel, who neighed in desperation at the sight of the archangel. He looked for the throne room of the beauty he'd so adored once, that he had tried to hand over to God to kill, to marry. Christ's bride, God's bride.

But Satan waited in the hall of the first floor, and he had just cleared it of all demons save a stone-faced Baal, who was stepping away from the devil, moving toward a wall to watch carefully. Dressed in the red silks of Hell, a layering robe of the same color, in jewels, Satan turned slowly to face Michael, before he smiled, cheerful. "My demons," Satan cooed, "saw you coming." Though his crown was missing, his hair fell in wisps that hallowed him.

Joana told the people: "Look for weapons and shoot back! Shoot back! If you can't find one, then grab a rock and throw it at the soldiers, the tanks, and those fucking drones! Hide the children and elderly! Protect them!" Someone shouted back that fighting was useless. "Who cares! It's not about winning! Or do you all want to roll over and fucking die like cowards?!"

Michael, to Satan, announced: "I've come to kill you." As the words fell from his mouth, the sounds of demon hissing sounded from everywhere, unseen warnings, and Baal stepped forward. But Satan lifted a hand to stop the regent of Hell from interfering. All the other infernal fallen angels, hidden in the walls, halted, as well.

"It is not the proper time," said Satan, recalling God on His Throne, scolding Michael for bringing the devil back to him too soon.

"I know," Michael replied. 'I'm here to stop the apocalypse. I will break the prophecy. I will destroy you before it was written to do so.'

Satan, his smile saccharine, thought: 'The sword of God has finally rebelled.' "Come forward and kill me then."

Elsewhere, Joana hopped off the car and yanked her gun back

out of the back of her pants, then began running toward where the invasion was happening, wondering who would follow. Not everyone did — she hadn't expected that — but as the drones' buzzing grew, as strikes burst certain buildings into flares that collapsed onto themselves soon after — more began to follow her, one after another. The young men, the boys, then the adults, the younger women, as others hurried to hide elders and children. At this, Tadeo lifted his head, but he could hardly see, still thinking of the soldier who'd burnt up into nothing, of the family he could see the remains of nearby. He whispered his friend Joana's name, and he crawled forward, wanting to help.

Satan took slow, calculated steps forward. 'Where did this come from? What has broken you?' He remembered what he'd told Azazel. 'Was it the girl?' Tilting his head, he reached into his robe, drew out a pocketknife, flipping it open, twirling it between his fingers. "Go easy on me, big brother. All I have is this."

"Liar," said the saint, sword in both hands as he began to move, and the two fell into circling each other. "Take out your firearm."

Snorting, Satan said, "You're finally learning." Regardless, he didn't reach for his gun when Michael, impatient, stepped forward and swung his sword. The devil sidestepped, lowered his head when the prince swung high, then jumped back when the sword sliced low. "You're turning on the hand that feeds you. Aren't you scared, Michael? Poor little Michael — do you know how to do anything without your Father to tell you how?"

Michael brought one hand to his chain, felt how all the demons tensed, but he gripped it anyway, pulled it off of him, smacked it against the air like a whip. "I defeated you during the war for Heaven."

"You had an army with you, then," Satan replied.

"I have something to fight for now," Michael snarled and finally threw out his chain as Satan laughed.

Elsewhere, Joana took the gun that her brother handed her and ran on ahead, ducking immediately when she heard the boom of what must've been a tank shooting. A second after, there was another harsh boom and the crackle of something exploding, followed by the sirens of a car blaring sharp again, and again. Joana turned her head back, felt herself showered by the blinking, broken lights of a destroyed van at the end of the road. She saw, then, Lupina, shoving some of the men, trying to urge them to help.

'I need you too,' Joana wanted to tell the criminals. 'You horrible, awful men.'

"Joana!" First, Lupina shouted it, then it was Joana's brother. "Joana!" Joana twisted and began running, and she heard some of the criminals' quick footsteps follow. When they came across another tank, turning its head, some of the men shot, some of them hurried for safety. Joana herself skidded to two buildings, hiding in between them and panting for breath. She grumbled, "You sons of bitches. The world is over!" Her voice raised but not much; she was too out of breath. 'Turn on the nation that you served. Turn on the ones who did this to us! All of you!" She didn't know if they could hear her. "Fight back with us!" They wouldn't, as most of the criminals wouldn't, but it wasn't about winning.

She wanted to tell the worst of the worst still in town that they were victims too, of circumstances, of powers much greater. The torturers, the traffickers, the assassins, even those who hadn't been forced into crime, those who'd fallen in to simply impress. The evil of the world is done by people, not demons, and people are made by people. Everyone in the world ought to go to Hell; we are all responsible.

Joana's brother caught up to her, and he said he would throw his grenade into the tank. If he could reach it in time, he would. "Do you think I can do it?"

"Just try it," Joana said, and he agreed. "Hit the tanks. I'll shoot at the drones." She patted his arm firmly, then took off running onto the street again, headed for the plaza. As she ran, she noticed others running with her again — mostly young boys and men, but many girls, and fathers, and eldest sisters. They carried military grade weapons — many of them. It must've been the criminals, handing them over or it must've been defectors from their military. 'I remember dreaming of this, of all of us uniting.' It was not what she'd hoped, but it would do. All her life, she'd learned to make do with the little you wrestled out of God's hands.

Turning up her head, Joana looked for the perpetrators of the horrific hissing noise with renewed vigor and a sort of sad joy. Everything was happening now, all that she'd dreamt of. At the end of time, she had done it. In the distance, however, there were winged creatures. At first, Joana felt tempted toward relief, believing it must be Michael and his army, but then she noticed they weren't armored. The Watchers.

Satan, easily, evaded the chain whip, by jumping aside and allowing it to strike at the tips of his hair. But Michael threw it out again, then again. The third time, it struck at Satan's leg, hard enough to twist it and send him down onto one knee with a hiss. Hissing, gritting his teeth. In between, Michael's heavy steps neared, and Baal shouted the devil's name. 'How terribly do you have something to fight for, Michael? How terribly do you want to save the world?'

Michael wound his chain around his hand again, and he said — "You forget. Everything you know, I taught you."

Satan knew he was powerless against a full suit of armor; Michael had learned indeed. Even still, the devil laughed, touching his pounding, bleeding leg. "I know." He had wrestled in Heaven. He had beat Michael, once. 'I remember how.' "I know better than anyone what it's like to lose and die for it, Michael." He slumped a little. "And I know exhaustion." Michael was not swayed, yet, and Lucifer looked into Michael's mask. "You said you would kill us both. Is that still true?"

Michael gripped his sword, lifted it.

"I dreamt, once," Satan said, "that God created us together at the beginning of time. Then, He killed seven of you, and he killed forty of me. This time, He wants us to kill each other." Then, Michael faltered, and he began stammering that only Satan would die now, but the devil yanked out his revolver, aimed. He shot at the sword's handle, watched as it flew out of Michael's hand before Lucifer, with his gunless hand, threw his pocket knife at Michael's knee. It was armored, of course, but Michael still jolted away to dodge, and Satan took the chance. He stepped forward, bit down a cry in pain over his leg, grabbed Michael's helmet, then ripped it off, threw it in the direction of the sword. Slow, it rolled.

Michael tackled Satan, forward, wings striking everywhere, as the devil kicked and growled.

Joana watched the winged destroyers approach, saw their scanning eyes, and she breathed out a great sigh. She thought, 'They're looking for someone. Tadeo? Dina?' It didn't matter. She saw makeshift spears in their hands, and she began marching toward them, then toward a pole, where an angel statue was perched at the top. She'd once climbed trees with her father. 'Before you worked for them.' She remembered his laugh, and his body, his hands, helping her up as a child to reach a branch, but — even in this memory — his face was blown open by the bullet she'd shot through his head. "Angels!" Of course, they wouldn't hear her. She latched onto the pole, grabbed it tight, wrapped her legs around it, then began climbing. "Angels! Angels!" Now, they were turning toward her, and she saw their leader ahead of them, the one with the white face paint.

At this same time, Tadeo finally twitched, and he tilted his massive head to the side. He almost hadn't felt it, but there was a person there, pulling at a wing of his. A woman, beautiful, coated in ash and blood, her hair falsely blonde, her roots dark, her face streaked with tears that kept pouring out from her. She panted: "Tadeo— Please help! Help Joana! She was running north!" He trembled. He could see his grandfather's face, his uncle's face. His father. 'Joana.' He had to see her too. He inched forward, but his stomach lurched, and so did his skin. He took another step, and when he heard the voices of others urging him, he forced himself to take another. 'Father.' And grandfather. Uncle. Cousins. Dante. Mother. Half a child again, dreaming of being put to sleep.

Joana climbed up to the top, grabbed onto the angel statue's neck, then she called out: "Whoever you're looking for, it's me!" All around her, the war raged, and the clash continued. Some criminals and soldiers defecting together to fight alongside the civilians. At the end of time — everything she'd ever wanted.

Azazel saw her, and he breathed out slow, thinking of his child, remembering all the fury of the infant's death that Satan and Michael were responsible. Twirling his spear, he felt anger boil over his heart, and he lifted his weapon high over his head, and he clenched his teeth. 'Revenge.' So cold that he was numbing. 'Finally.' At last. But before he could throw it, Samyaza suddenly lunged at him. "Agh—!" he cried out, twisting, looking wildly at Samyaza, grappling his arms. "What are you doing?!"

"Stop!" Samyaza rasped weakly, then hiccuped. "Stop. Please stop."

"What?" Azazel panted. Then, more frantic: "No."

"Child," Samyaza forced out, raw voice scraping up his throat. "Not children. Enough. Please." And then he whispered, "My children. Yours. Naamah."

Naamah? Who was Naamah? A child, from the flood, curly-haired, weak, starving. Azazel's eyes widened, and his breath fell from his mouth. "Don't say that name. What are you doing? I have to—"

"I saw them dead," Samyaza forced out. "Naamah. Your husband. My wife. They were all dead. Their families. Naamah with a knife in hand. Dead. All of them."

Azazel's muscles tensed. "Samyaza—" A barrage of memories struck at him — cold water, rain, warmth of falling in love, death, family. "Why this, why now?" And his face stung, and his eyes burned.

Satan shot at Michael's face, the bullet bursting through the prince's jaw, the force sending him back a step. And, just as the prince tried to steady, the devil yelled out without words like an animal in blood-red anger, and he shot once more; this time, the prince fell, onto a knee. Blood spluttered from his mouth thickly, coating his silver chest plate in red. As the devil huffed for breath, he took a few steps toward Michael, gun raised still, unflinching. He set the revolver under Michael's chin, forced up his mangled face. The prince's eyes were wide, furious, yet tired. 'I know what it's like to be tired, Michael.' Satan, quietly, said, "You can't kill me."

"End it then," gurgled Michael. "End *me*, and the end times will stop."

Lucifer was quiet, staring, listening to the wind hiss. Demons were watching — Baal and all those hidden in the walls. "It's already ended, Michael." He lowered the gun. "You've lost."

Michael said again, "Kill me."

"No," said Satan. "Neither of us will die. Even when you turn on God, you seek to sacrifice yourself. But I won't let you, you stupid God-damned martyr. You will face what you've done. You will suffer what you deserve."

"Kill me!" Michael shouted, angry, mangled face twitching in fury. "End it!"

"No," said Satan again, matching his anger with a hiss. "*We* will end it. Together." Like they had been born, together.

Though Samyaza held Azazel, and Azazel no longer found the words to order Joana's death, as if they'd traded places, as if Azazel was the one who'd been broken, who couldn't speak— the other Watchers descended like animals, aiming, hurling their spears. Kokabiel — grinning. Baraqiel — empty. Danel — determined.

The first cut through Joana's side, and just as she lost hold of the statue, crying out, another spear went through her abdomen, then another. A fourth cut through her chest. For a flicker, her eyes were wide, then calm. Joana fell slow, torn apart, thinking of a river, thinking of her family, of Tadeo, and even Lupina. The last thing she heard was the raging war, and she saw Tadeo, and Lupina, who were looking up at her. She noticed her brother, slumped; perhaps, dead too. Then, she allowed the darkness to bleed in. She fell. She was dead before she hit the ground, but there was a touch of relief on her face. Catharsis. Something like victory for once in her life.

CHAPTER 40

The statue had fallen too, shattered beside her body.

As he'd run to it, Tadeo's six legs had, with each step, weakened, then shrunk, folded. It wasn't long before there were bare, human feet beneath him, and his wings were gone, his clothes absent like he were naked Jesus choking on the crucifix, crying out to know why God would do this to His own son. And Tadeo felt nothing, initially, hollow, like that were not a person he was approaching, not a friend. A girl, Joana. Those around her didn't stop to crowd around, many hadn't even noticed; a shower of bullets speared in their direction, followed by the booms of a couple remaining tanks. The people were fighting; the people were dying. A silver bird struck nearby, collapsed a home against the person standing beside it; it must've been a warning to Tadeo, who didn't flinch, who stared at Joana. She would have wanted all the people in the world to keep fighting like this, even after she'd fallen.

'Your child hands had come over my own, not much older, and you taught me to shoot.' He'd said he was a monster of biblical proportions; he didn't need a gun. Her hardened brown eyes — an attempt at a wise, aged glare. She'd always wanted to look older. She'd insist that she looked like her father, but it was really her grandmother she looked like. She'd insist she had the aim of an assassin, and she did. Often, Tadeo and her would go out to eat. A year ago, she'd said: 'The ground grows nopal, tomato, and corn. It doesn't grow liberation. If we want to taste it, then we have to plant the seeds.' But she couldn't do it alone; no one can harvest without friends.

The resurrected Tadeo had craved violence more than anything, craved destruction. 'You told me that violence was good, even necessary.' He could be good, even as a killer. He could do good.

Coming to kneel in her blood, Tadeo touched her skewered body. Dante had said he liked her, while he and Tadeo walked and talked home, said he appreciated someone who worked hard. 'You two would have been good friends too.' He'd loved them, he realized. 'I loved you.' Tadeo had fought beside them, couldn't bring himself to be angry at them for betrayal. And yet they were dead. Empty-lidded, Joana's eyes were dark, and Tadeo gazed into them as he heard the woman who'd lead him here, Lupina, scream in agony, other shouts following after hers, from all those around him.

'What harvest?' Tadeo had told Joana. 'I only have two hands. Dante is dead, my mother can't work. We are losing everything. No, we didn't win, Joana. We've lost. We've lost.' It had all meant nothing, and the soldiers were still firing on the town. At the end of the world, they still hated him, all of them. At the end of the world, hate was all they had left. Tadeo had nothing left, too, but *hate*. Clenching his jaw, remembering, oh, remembering it all, the days of his childhood, the blooming fears, the trafficking, the fights with his mother, his father, missing for days, his body, swinging beneath an overpass, the soldiers, pulling them apart with his hands and teeth, running into the empty fields, fighting, wanting to do good. It hadn't been enough. God had cursed him. It was not enough. There would be no harvest. It hadn't been enough for Joana. It hadn't been enough for Dante. There was nothing left. He didn't hear the angel of the lace veil, Dina, approaching behind him through the boiling of his blood. Hate, at the end of the world.

He would make them all suffer.

"I," the devil was whispering somewhere far away, "feel his rage." Outside, the rotting body of Babylon, nearly dead, trying to burn out in a blaze of glory to take the rest of the world with it. "I can feel him in the greatest moments of his agony — when he died, when he resurrected. It was the same when the Beast, my child, was in other bodies. What has united them all across time has been hate." Slow, Satan turned away from the throne he'd been facing to the defeated chief prince, not many steps before the devil and far from the closed doors that Baal had dragged him through before locking them. Dim, reddened light leaked through tall window panes — the shine of the moon falling onto them like blood.

In his own golden chains, Michael's wrists were tied behind his back. He was standing, though partly slumped forward, jaw still bloodied and open. Lowly, he asked, "Why am I here? I told you to kill me; or will you force me to kill you instead?"

"Be quiet, dog," spat Baal, stepping up behind the prince. "You wouldn't be stupid enough to try again, are you?"

Michael glared forward, grunting. He couldn't afford to waste time like this. He was worried for Joana. If he failed in preventing the apocalypse, he was killing her. 'I must not surrender. I must stop this. There is still time.'

Satan said, "I've talked to the king of Babylon. I've told him to stop the attacks on that town, but—" A hesitance, then his voice returned sharper. "He's erratic. He calls on God now to save his soul." Satan laughed. "Thousands of years that I've stopped the end of the world, and now that you've allowed it to happen, you come to me with regret."

Michael felt his armored hands curl into fists. "I'm not the one who started this, Satan. *You* did this. The moment you rebelled in Heaven. The second you *had that child*! You wanted to create, Satan. Well, you have created now. Is it everything you wanted?"

"You want me to kill you," Satan said so low that it was almost a growl, "but I won't. I want you to feel every second of the apocalypse you've created. But, for now, I need to use you. You will do as I say, and you will step into the offices of the king, you will command them to stop in the voice of God."

"No," said Michael.

Satan's voice struck like a whip. "If you won't do it, the bombing will blow apart that girl you care so much for."

Michael clenched his teeth, and he spoke through them: "I'm not your weapon."

"It's all you're good for," answered the devil. "Angel of weapon. Without anyone to wield you, you're useless. You stand for nothing."

"I stand against a world that is wicked and corrupt," Michael replied. "And I know who is responsible, who I must destroy."

Baal finally spoke again: "Michael, what the fuck is it that you want?" He stepped even closer, grabbed his arm, though the chief prince almost growled in response. "Satan and I both defeated you — him on Earth and me in Heaven. Accept it. Maybe bow down to the only one who can save the world now."

"If he wanted to save the world," Michael said, "he'd kill himself."

Immediately Baal grabbed a fistful of Michael's hair, yanked hard enough to make the archangel hiss, stumble, before he was shoved down onto his knees. Michael thrashed, growling again, but God's chains at his wrists were the one thing completely unbreakable to the angel of strength. "Pray to him. Pray for forgiveness and maybe I won't rip off your scalp."

Satan hummed, then quietly said: "The world is wicked. I know that. And it is by my design." He tilted his face down at the broken chief prince. "What has bound every anti-Christ together is hate, and always, the Beast chooses the bodies of princes, princesses, of wealth and power. It's not often that the Beast chooses someone who the world has so rejected. It must've thought it would succeed in its apocalyptic plans if it hid in some dark corner that I would never look. At the same time, I know that the Beast is not a being that thinks. It is hardly rational. It is pure emotion, pure rage." His voice dropped to a murmur, "You're correct. This world is evil because of me. I rule it. It's mine. However *wicked* and *evil* it is, it's mine, *my world*." Voice rising, he looked out a window into the ruined Earth. "It will do as I say. You will do as I say."

'Michael,' Satan thought. 'I won't kill you. I won't kill you. I want to rip you apart limb from limb. I want to dig my teeth into you.' The devil thought of the damn king again; then, he thought of the emperor of Rome who'd fucked him until he lost his mind. 'I can't let you die.' His jaw was so clenched that he thought it'd begin to crack, and his blood burned until it rose up into his eyes in red flames. 'I abhor you, Michael, so much that I can *never let you die.'*

"Go for the king," Satan commanded Baal. "Order him to come here. Tell him that we have an angel of God for him to listen to."

"Yes, Satan," Baal replied slowly, and Michael coughed out some dribbles of blood as the regent of Hell removed his claws from his hair, but then he paused. "But what if he... refuses to come?"

"He will listen to me," Satan said, words paper thin. "He will *obey*."

"The world does not listen to you," Michael gurgled. "You are not God."

"*There is no God,*" the devil seethed. "There is only me. I'm the only thing left, Michael. And it's true what you say, what you've always said. I'm not God. No, no, I'm greater than God."

Carefully, Baal took a step back, but Michael glanced back at him, and he saw a flicker in his eyes of hesitation once more. And Baal looked back at him; for the first time, there was no great fury between them. "As you wish," the regent answered before turning on his heel. "I'll slaughter any of those that deny you." There was something solemn about it, like he were accepting the same fate he was threatening. At this, Michael felt a bead of cold sweat roll past his brow, toward the pulsing gore of his jaw, as the large demon left the room. He didn't know why, didn't know why he had to resist asking Baal not to dare leave him alone with the devil.

As if sensing the nerves of the chief prince, Satan reached out, suddenly, pushed a vase of wilted flowers off a nearby podium. With a sharp clatter, the porcelain shattered, water pooled, and the dried lilies lay still over the pieces and wetness like they'd been put to a lazy grave. The archangel said nothing before he felt the sole of a foot come down over his head to push down. Gritting his teeth,

Michael's face was pressed to where the broken vase was, forced up against it — the dampness and dirt and crisp petals crinkling and clinging to his exposed muscle. It stung.

"Heal," Satan ordered. "Or will you deny it to yourself just to stand against me?" A second of silence passed, a distant boom of something crashing or imploding — perhaps a star — but then the devil witnessed as trickles of water climbed up Michael's jawline and began to thread through his very skin, carefully coiling at his gums to create new teeth. "I see." Blood cleaned itself off Michael's chin and neck. "I wasn't sure if you'd still be capable." 'The demons lost their healing, as did the Watchers, not long after we turned on God. But you can still do it, of course. You're very special to God, after all.' Slowly, Michael's enormous wounds began to close.

As they did, Michael coughed out some blood, some water, and muttered his defiance again, "I won't speak to any man for you, devil."

"Killing either of us will no longer be enough to stop the apocalypse," Satan said. "Killing the anti-Christ will also no longer be enough. We've reached the point where his death would become a fulfillment of prophecy." Suddenly, the devil pressed down harder, almost stomping Michael's head into the ground, and he loomed over him with wide, endless eyes. "To break the prophecy now— We must keep him alive. The nation must stop pursuing him. The wars must end. If you want to save this place, if you want to save *her*, then you must obey me, Michael." The sight of the prince under his foot surged the devil with a contradictory glee, humor, hatred. 'I will command you now. I will wield you now, my sword, whether you want my hands or not.'

"I will never serve you, Satan," Michael grunted.

"But you will do as I wish," Satan replied with a great grin, "whether or not you want to." 'How we always do what God wants, whether or not we want to.' He removed his foot, finally, and took a step back to see Michael thrash against his bindings in fury but hardly raise his head off the ground. "What other choice do you have?" The prince curled into himself in shame, looking so delicate suddenly, so pathetic. "Poor thing." But Satan's voice was venomous, coy, laughing. "All you fought against, and here you are. How much you wrestled against me, and here you kneel. Even when you had me captured, you still failed to resist touching me. You have *failed* in everything you have ever done——"

Michael, suddenly, growled like an animal. He said: "Is this what it will be until the end? Humiliation until I accept you as my Lord?"

Satan smiled, soft, serenely. 'It's what I always wanted.' "No." 'There will be no end. This apocalypse will stop. I will save Tadeo. Maybe all of his family will be gone, but perhaps I can take their place. I'm his mother, after all, his father.' He remembered the ash he'd left of his infant. 'I can raise you.' He hadn't the chance with the Beast, nor enough with Cain. "You don't have to accept me."

Breathing out harshly, Michael tilted his face up at the devil, bloodied curl falling over his face; he saw Satan with the ruined world displayed past the cracked windows at either side of the throne. 'Lucifer.' He remembered the taste he'd had of him in Heaven, how he'd been desperate to know what it meant to fall into temptation. Michael had wanted the last thing he ever did to be succumbing, submitting. He'd wanted to know, to trade knowledge for death, how Eve had done in Eden. The forbidden fruit, Satan's perfect body; Michael had tasted it now, only to stir open a deeper hunger in him. "But it's what you want, isn't it? It's what you've always wanted. You will never stop until I do it—— Until I *worship* you." 'Angel Lucifer in the ruins of Heaven, staring at me, his eyes dead, his smile strange; he was not Lucifer any longer. He was something else. He asked me for sin, to give it to him. To create sin together, between us, between these bodies.'

Satan snorted, then stepped to him again.

And Michael's eyes were furious, brows furrowed. He remembered Satan's lips, in Heaven. When he'd strung him up with the chains, the devil had seemed so much like the angel of beauty. Phanuel had told Michael that maybe Lucifer had never died, and God had told Michael that Lucifer was devoured by a Beast that the prince's sin had formed inside of him. 'Beautiful Lucifer would peck my mouth behind trees, in empty rooms, in dark corners. I touched his body like I'd never known another angel body. I'd craved something, for the first time in my life. I had wanted him — like I could ever own an angel. Like I could be God. But I denied it to myself for Him, for my Father.' He had done it all for God, the God that was never going to forgive him, the God who was going to destroy the world of his daughter. *His* daughter, Michael's child he'd rejected. For God. It had all been for God.

Another step, and Satan leaned down, opened his lips, surely to tell the saint, again, that he had no choice, he had no will; he was a sword, he was nothing.

Michael said, "As you wish, then. I'll obey you." And before he could wait for Satan's response, he rose to his feet sharply, thrust his armored body forward to push Satan against the stairs, then pressing his weight to him. Michael's hands remained bound at his back, but he put his face before the devil's flared eyes. "I'll do what you want. I'll do what you've wanted all this time." His knee came in between Satan's legs, pressed hard enough to hurt. "Everything you begged me for."

The devil, now, laughed, and he said, "What is this, Michael? You've turned on God and decided there's nothing left but to fall into temptation?"

"I'm taking back what I surrendered to Him," said Michael sharply.

Satan stared, then his shoulders trembled with another chuckle. "You are just like your Father." But he reached behind Michael, took the chains at his wrists, pulled until they began to loosen enough that the chief prince tore one hand free, then the other. Before he could place his gauntlets on the devil, however, Satan brought the chain around the back of Michael's neck, pulled with both hands like a rider to a horse's rein. He spat onto Michael's face, then grinned wickedly up against his jaw, threatening a kiss. "Surrendered? Michael, you never had me."

"You begged for me," Michael said, feeling the fever and tightness in his body of whenever he dreamt of angel Lucifer, laying on an altar for him — a gift from God — and of when he'd spilled sick seed in the caves with the devil — learned that angels were all corrupted — and of his youth — the novel heat in the center of his body, the tempt on his hips to roll forward against the angel of worship, of beauty. To press deeper, deeper, until he broke through flesh, cut him open with a dagger if he must — anything to be inside of that body. For the first time in his eternal life, Michael allowed himself to feel all of it, the burn and the emptiness. He learned it was like hunger — wanting. It was not tender. It was not shaped of love — desire.

His hands came over the devil's upper waist in a vicious grip, struggling not to shatter the ribs all delicately arranged by his Father. "I had you," he panted. "It was only me that ever had you, no matter how much sin you made with others. It was our sin — first."

"We never sinned," Satan hissed, yanked the chain tighter around Michael's throat. Instantly, the chief prince jolted backwards, rasping with breath, and Satan stumbled onto his feet, climbing the staircase backwards slow, steady. But Michael followed, wheezing out the pain, eyes dark; and just as the devil reached the throne, Michael's hands returned to Satan's waist — 'where they belong.' He was able to lift the devil, who kicked, who glared back wildly. "You never had me."

Breath hitching, however, Satan felt himself pushed onto his grand chair, his Hell throne on Earth. "You created," said Michael, "for me. Cock and cunt and fucking." And the devil, despite himself, shivered. "You warred for love. It was all for me." 'Sin.' "You created sin to love me."

"It was never for you," Satan said before his hands went to grip Michael's chains again, tighter but not enough to suffocate Michael a second time. "But," he began to laugh, pitched and weak. "*do it. Fuck me*. It's what *you* always wanted, no matter how many times you prayed for God to make you stop *wanting*." 'Michael. You were never going to be able to live without this. Whether it be through love or hatred, you committed yourself to me. It is why we will live forever. I can never kill you; you can never kill me.' Maybe Satan did love Michael, after all; he loved hating him.

'Are you seeing this, God?' Michael thought as he grabbed at the clothing of the devil, then with a flash of anger, ripped it off. 'Once, I helped Lucifer remove his robe, and he smiled at me, eyes squinting, timid, happy.' Rabid, the prince tore at the material to expose more naked skin — a heaving chest, a pair of kicking legs, a sweet waist. The body that the devil had given the world. And Michael dipped his head, rubbed the mouth still streaked in dried blood up his torso, down again, breathing him in. For a moment, he smelled rot, then it was lavender, spring, life, honey. This was Satan, not Lucifer. He was a fallen Beast, a Beast creator. 'But if it's like this, my detested devil, then I would create sin with you a thousand times. If only to make something of this *hate* — I want to beget a new damning, a new sin, a new death.' It wasn't enough to love; it wasn't enough to hate; there must be new sin for this, for them.

The pleasure the saint had denied himself, all the need, broke free now; all the wicked, rotten will that God had called evil. He surrendered to it. Michael panted against Satan's chest, the weight of all his purity on his shoulders, rage churning his stomach. All his goodness was turning throbs of ache and sting; he was a bruise. When Satan touched the saint again, he reached for the plate over his groin, tugged it aside desperately, angrily.

'You mouth at me like an idolater to his shrine,' Satan thought, then watched as Michael brought his own hands to his pelvis, removed the armor, threw it aside. The devil ordered him, "Worship." But he said it hazily, feeling his own arousal as a scalding burn, in between his legs, where he'd been molded for love. Angel of love. "You can't help it— You were made for it. There is no will, no choice." Michael moved over him again, took hold of the devil's legs, pulling them high. Then, the saint brought his mouth to a flower, to a fruit, and he bit down, then plunged in his tongue. It was as he'd done in Heaven but not so afraid. Michael was not afraid of God anymore.

Satan released the chains around the other's neck, finally, and draped his arms over the rests of the chair, then he let out a long, wanton sound. He used to sing in Heaven. He had wanted to sing for Michael, beneath him — so loud that the Lord would be jealous. 'He was jealous, Michael. He was jealous of this.' But the chief prince soon stood and put himself over the devil. Bringing his eyes as close as possible to Satan's, Michael said, "I despise you. I hate you," at the same time he reached to align himself with the wetted entrance, teasing around it.

The devil whispered, "I abhor you and everything you ever did to me."

Michael said nothing, but when he pressed in, pressure unfolding into tight warmth — the noise he made was strangled. Hundreds of thousands of millions of years, he had denied himself paradise for a promise of paradise. The fallen angel's divinity beautifully enveloped him, opening just right. And the devil's body took it beautifully, like he were meant to be impaled to truly bloom beneath his fingertips. Like Satan was hollow, needed to be filled to be whole. "Lord," Michael said without meaning to.

"Lord," the devil echoed, breath stuttering out of him, body arching as if in pain. "Say it again. I'm your God now." But he was breathless. 'I destroyed myself, I destroyed Heaven, for this. To be yours.' But the bliss in his core felt too perfect, too right; he pulsed hot around Michael. 'For a kiss, we destroyed Heaven. And for this, we'll destroy all that remains.'

"You're nothing more than a demon," Michael said, teeth grit, and his hand fell to the armrest, hips shivering. His sin lodged inside a wound of love. He couldn't move, paralyzed. The devil had to reach for the chain around his neck, pull him down. When Michael put his forehead against Satan's, he gasped, and they shared breaths. "You're not God. You're not God." And he thrust forward, hard, and made the devil shudder, grunt out between lips pressed tight. "You were just an angel too. An angel I loved."

"Fuck him harder," Satan snarled, "and maybe you can bring him back, Michael." But he cried out again when Michael rolled forward a second time, then a third. "Can you feel it? Everything you could have had?" he taunted, then laughed when the prince moved to hold the devil's throat. "Don't be afraid, crush it. Kill me. You said you wanted to." But the chief prince, even through his anger, refrained. "You can't, can you? You want to hurt me, but you can't help but worship me." Abruptly, Satan cried out when Michael fucked into him the hardest that he'd had. "Oh," he continued through the pain, the pleasure, "you can't help yourself. Weak, weak saint. Pathetic little angel."

Gasping at each whip of pleasure that skinned up his body, Michael couldn't speak anymore, the sweet clench the further he pushed making all the apocalypse outside the windows look almost pretty with all its despair and horror. Bliss demented him. Adoring deranged him. His body seized, twisted inside. Michael's sensations, Satan's sensations melted until the prince didn't know who he was. The devil's body was his now, too; he felt every invading thrust. He was the devil. He was sin; he was death. And apocalypse was beautiful.

"Succumb," Satan whispered, "to it." His moans were rhythmic now, one after the other. "This was always meant to happen. I'm your God." He threw his head back when the prince buried in deep again, and he bit his lip not to cry out when Michael's gauntlets returned to his waist, his ribs. 'But I feel the inside of me, too. Horrible and crushing. Like I'm you. Like I'm an angel, a prince.' "Worship, and give yourself to me how you should have done in Heaven." 'Spill until I leak of you. Make me yours, how you should have done in Heaven. Make me your God, make me create for you, for us.' Create what? Satan didn't know anymore. New sins. The end of all things.

Michael grimaced, but he couldn't stop, still couldn't answer. When he kissed the devil, it was desperate, with too much teeth. There was still blood on his mouth, and Satan licked at it with delight.

For them — fucking was not enough. Nothing would ever be enough. 'Let me bleed into your wounds,' Michael thought in his madness. 'Carry me inside you forever as you burn in Hell.' His gasps had grown quicker, angrier, and the devil's entrance fluttered like a happy heartbeat around him. And Michael could fight no more when the coiling in his lower belly snapped. Collapsing over him, groaning. Distantly, the devil heard Michael whisper that he hated him again, he would always hate him. Death would not be enough to do to him, nor torture. There needed to be new sins for their hate. They must create it. From their bodies, the most forbidden love. It came in spurts, then a spill as warm as the sun, heavy as the weight of purity maintained for lifetimes — the seed of the chief prince into the bearer of the apocalypse.

At last, over a throne on Earth, at last.

CHAPTER 41

From the head of the Leviathan, Rosier and Armoni saw the state of the Earth. The sea serpent traveled Babylon — eerie, calm, crushing everything beneath its slithering body of coils and tough scales. Gripping at some of the horned skin at the top of the Leviathan's skull, the demon and the angel noticed buildings sunk into themselves, the fires of Hell breaching through cracks in the Earth to swarm at all the people, the good and wicked alike, if such a division existed. Abandoned children, elders, the weaker — and he remembered Asmodeus once saying, 'Haven't you seen enough to know that humanity is a lost cause? We demons made war, but it's men that created atrocity. The things they've done to one another, Rosier — you've seen it. How can you forgive it? How can you keep believing in their goodness?' 'I don't know,' Rosier had whispered as he leaned against him. 'But I keep believing, despite myself, despite them. Their evil wouldn't hurt so terribly, Asmodeus, unless they were kind. It's because we know they're good that their wickedness is so painful.'

In the distance, bullets battered against something, and a sharp cry was cut off, a whining animal somewhere. Dark birds flew about aimlessly, all of them like vultures, eyeing the dead.

But Rosier's own eyes were empty now, and he continued to play with the fingers of Asmodeus's corpse arm, resting in a sling across his torso. Long ago, Rosier would carry Asmodeus' head this way. After they had fallen from Heaven, after Rosier had decapitated him — he had pieced Asmodeus together again. His friend, his husband, his demon.

"Rosier," Armoni called for what must've been the hundredth time. "Rosier, please listen to me." But the demon of fruit continued his silence. "What now? Where are we going?" Armoni's voice was forcibly raised by the clamor of death that they drowned in. "Rosier." Rosier didn't turn, and yet he felt the gaze of his friend land on Asmodeus' hand, like how one might feel eyes on the back of their own neck. 'It's the same,' Rosier thought, 'because Asmodeus is my body. We were one. We were one body.' Armoni said: "I fear the Leviathan is taking us to the Beast." He remembered the soldier, Dante, who'd spoken to Asmodeus in their cage about the boy-turned-monster he'd fought before falling into Hell. "We're heading toward... a border."

Rosier almost had to ask what border, where to. He wished he could stand at the border of death and see his husband on the horizon. "There is nowhere to turn back to," he whispered.

"We shouldn't involve ourselves, Rosier, in this apocalypse."

'But we're damned,' Rosier thought, 'and fire and darkness awaits us. I would like to be dead. To be with him, I'm not afraid of death now.'

Above — the sound of feathers, and both Armoni and Rosier lifted their heads to see a couple angels, but they were fleeing upward, returning home. At the head, two horsemen led the way, one over a white horse and one over a black horse.

"They're abandoning the Earth now," Armoni whispered.

Rosier didn't reply again. He could understand them. He'd done the same — fled Satan's tower, fled the war, fled everything. He watched the angels run away quietly, almost peacefully, though he recalled how he'd pressed to Asmodeus as the demons attacked God's city.

When those fleeing ones far above reach Heaven, they'd find devastation, as there was below. But not yet. Gabriel and Raphael would, will, lead the army past the gates. Gabriel will realize he never did blow the seventh trumpet. He hadn't done it before or after the spread of sickness had finally turned Raphael against the apocalypse. The two princes will plead with God. But not yet.

Right now, the angel Dina was landing behind the slumped anti-Christ, his pale wings open but bent behind him, almost flared. He, abruptly, missed the lace he always hid his hair beneath, he missed his angel robes, he missed Uriel's library house he never stopped wandering, he missed rings on his fingers, he missed Heaven and being an angel and he missed youth. 'I'll have it back. And it will all be better.' He stared at Tadeo, crumbled on the ground, heaving, naked body trembling. 'I will sacrifice you to do it. I must. There is no other choice.' "Ta...de...o," the angel sounded out as if it was the first time he's said it. His voice was like a siren's hum, and he maintained it even through all the noise of war. "You've lost your friend."

"Don't... come near me," Tadeo whispered, shifting away from his mother and her wheelchair. "Don't... you dare come near me." Turning his head halfway, his only eye was bloodshot and wide, pupil thinned into a pinprick. "This is all because of you." He exhaled through flared nostrils. "All of this is because of you." His body was beginning to tremble, and the more he turned, the more he exposed the hole in his head, perpetually bleeding, pulsing. "I'll kill you. I'll tear you to fucking pieces for what you've done."

'Tell him that he—' Apsinthos began, but Dina knew what to say.

"I didn't kill her," the angel replied, and he recalled Satan emphasizing that he wasn't responsible for Tadeo's rape and murder. "Angels in the sky did. And it wasn't me that killed Dante, or your family. No, that was soldiers. That was Babylon."

In an angry, bewildered echo, Tadeo said, "*Babylon?*"

Dina glanced upward, and he listened to the hiss of the silver birds above, the drones, and he allowed the yells and the terror of families huddled to die together, the remnants of colorful town streamers on the ground, the blood, the tears, the begging, the useless fight back, to fill Dina with the most dread he'd ever felt. 'The world is depraved. The world is beyond saving.' "They won't stop. They won't stop killing. Since you were young, all you've known is this."

"Stop," Tadeo said, teeth visibly grit. "Stop."

"They've hated you for centuries. Your people were sacrificed to the gods of wealth and the gods of hate. Your land was gutted for a bridge into the mouth of empire. You fought to be free, and the world turned to make ruin of you instead. And they, in Babylon, are rejoicing now — can't you hear them? — and they, in all the other parts of the world who have even known of this place, rejoice. All the criminals of you, the infestation of you. They pray for all the little children here, who will grow into demons, to die a thousand deaths, mutilated for all the sins of your blood."

"Stop!" Tadeo shouted, then he twitched and twitched. But he was still covered in his family's blood, in Joana's blood, in Dante's. Joana's family must already be dead. Dante's family must be dead.

"Be angry," Dina urged him. "Be angry! The world loathes you! You tried to do good, and the world wanted you dead! Even your own family wanted to use you! They would never accept you! You resurrected, you fought for your liberation, and it meant nothing to this cruel world!" The anti-Christ let out a harsh breath of fright, of anger. "Look above you, Tadeo! Look at what this world did to those you love! It's a rotten world! It's a damned world!"

"You," Tadeo whispered. "This is all because of *you*—" It was becoming a chant. "Because of you." Beneath the skin of his knuckles, a sudden dull pain called, as if he were bruised, and this sensation balled in his chest, blooming and blooming until it began to squeeze at his lungs, force them empty of air.

Dina thought of his first memories, of dancing, of wanting to be beautiful. "This is because of them." Babylon. "And even with divinity flowing through your veins, you failed to bring down the empire of evil. All you can do now is destroy it."

When talons burst out from Tadeo's knuckles, the tips of his fingers, the sides of his palms, his wrists — sharp pain brought him a taste of relief. He couldn't resist, then, to dig his talons into his own arms, tear through his own muscle — the skin, the muscles, the pale pink layer, then the sharp red. Only hurting himself could he breathe, only hurting himself could he maintain himself here. There was so much pain inside him, and he wanted to rip it out, brandishing his own suffering like a whip. But he lifted his burning gaze, and he felt more eyeballs bubble open along his body. He saw his mother, breathing carefully in her chair, and he saw Lupina holding the skewered remains of Joana, and he saw tanks, he saw drones, saw every burning, crumbled building, every ball of light. The ground rumbled; was it the war or was it him? Was Tadeo the war? Are we the war?

"Can you feel it," Dina whispered, "now?" The angel felt it in his own heart — the rage. The rage of being born too late to know what it was all like before the war. He shouted, "End it! End it, Tadeo." 'Take me back,' Dina wanted to say. 'I want to know what it was like. I want to know what paradise was. I want to be happy. I don't want forgiveness; I want to have never done it; I want to go back. I want to be free from sin, not forgiven for it. Take me back. Please let me go back and do it all right this time. It's not fair.'

'It's not fair,' Tadeo thought, shaking in rage, feeling it in his core, in his very teeth. 'It's not fair.' Joana. Dante. Dante's family. Tadeo's father, the breeze tossing him. The smiles of his father. His mother and his father. But even if they were still here, his parents, they might not have loved him. Why had Tadeo ever wanted to save a world that didn't want him? "I feel everything," he breathed. The world had rejected him, even before he tried to save it. 'You have a responsibility,' Joana had said but to who? And would any of those who Tadeo was trying to save ever think of saving him? No; they had let him die. They had watched him step into the car with soldiers. They had let him die. The world rejected the good, long ago.

And so Tadeo screamed. He curled into himself and began to yell, every part of him ripping open with pain, with wings, with mouths, with eyes. From a narrowing throat, he wailed out, trying to sink into the pain itself, wanting to be nothing more than a bleeding wound. It burned. 'Burn.' God had made him to burn. His family had used him. Joana had used him. None of it meant anything. The crime. The soldiers. The war. What war? He would show them war. He would show them what he had died feeling. 'The pain, the humiliation, the darkness, the darkness, the misery, the violation. God in my head. In this body. This body that was never mine. That isn't mine. None of this world is worth saving. Every life, every person. It's their fault. I tried to do what no one else did.'

The ground shook, once more, and Dina stumbled back, watching all the beastly parts of Tadeo burst out of him. Every star in the air brightened to drown them in white. Heart jolting, the young angel's eyes widened, and Dina really realized then what was happening as the humans around began to scream, as silver birds were struck by sudden winds that flung them far. The few tanks remaining crushed into themselves, and hellfires flared. 'Is this it?' Dina felt no joy. 'Will it be over?' Was paradise here, right within reach? Was this how it would all end?

But it all stopped, and the yelling of the anti-Christ devolved into a spluttering cough. What followed was the lurch forward of his beastly body, shrinking back into its naked human form again, head hanging forward. Though the world around them was still loud with car alarms and screams and rumbles, the ground had halted its jerks even when Tadeo shook with a quiet, sad little sob. "Tadeo?" the angel called, bewildered. "Tadeo." But he didn't look much like Tadeo, even if that was the same face, same body that the angel had known since he climbed down to Earth. "What are you doing?" He looked like a little boy.

Tadeo sniffled, lifted a hand to rub the back of his hand against his wet eyes, rivulets of tears falling past his chin and to his neck. And he said, "Leave me alone," like a child. Like a baby, he half-crawled toward his mother. Like a young boy, he gripped one of her legs and laid his head against her lap, the eternal wound dribbling onto her pants.

"What?" Dina was the one staggering now over his feet. "What do you mean?" His voice was high, almost scared. "End the world, Tadeo. You must. Set the behemoth free from you. Kill the world that... despises you..."

Tadeo's tears streamed down the side of his face, over the bridge of his nose. And he said: "The world already ended. It ended a long time ago." 'When I died, when my dad was killed, when my mother lost half her mind, when the music stopped being played in the plaza. Before then.' Dante had been right. 'The world ended years ago, hundreds of years ago.' His father had said life was pain, but you have to live it, you have to work, you have to feel the ache in your muscles. Joana had died fighting, Dante had died fighting. It's about the struggle, in the end, the fight for the sake of the fight. 'It's not about winning. It's not about the end. There is no end.'

Dina's face paled. 'End it,' he wanted to urge. 'This can't all have been for nothing.' But every horrible miserable sound around him began to feel sharp, loud, like nails on a chalkboard. "Tadeo—Please—" His voice was breaking now, high and frightened. "Please—"

What followed was screeching, but not from Tadeo, who didn't react, nor from the machines of war. Instead, it sang from far above them all. In a sky now desolate of drones, a great head was rising from the smoke, attached to a long, coiling body. From dark scales, it dripped sea water and blood. Atop its head, there was an angel and a demon, holding on. The Leviathan. The angel Dina stumbled back, heart stopping, when the creature crept forward over all the noise of fright that surrounded it, and it lowered its head enough for the riders to crawl down.

"Dina!" shouted an angel. "Is that you?!" Armoni, climbing off hastily and running forward. His eyes were massive and round, and Rosier came up behind him just seconds afterward, reaching, taking Armoni's arm, stopping him. "What is happening? What is going on?"

Rosier, with his other hand, reached into his sling and intertwined his fingers with Asmodeus'. He swallowed, shakily, his heart heavy in his chest. He looked at a naked boy nearby, and then he looked back at the Leviathan that was staring at the same anti-Christ, curled up against an older woman on a chair, both quiet and still. 'What now?' The Leviathan offered another shriek.

At that, Tadeo looked up, ears ringing, feeling the ground beneath him rumble once more. He swallowed, and he stepped away from his mother, staggering back, staring up at the monster. As he did, he saw into its eyes. 'It's waiting on me.' He didn't know how he knew. 'It's waiting on me to end it. Like Dina, like the angels, like God.' But Tadeo took a few more steps back, and he felt an ache turn over and over in his chest. Tears, blooming at his eyes again. Shame, oddly. Where had this shame come from? "I won't do it," he told the Leviathan. "I won't end this Earth."

The Leviathan was silent, and when its tail whipped at Tadeo, the boy simply closed his eyes, grit his teeth. He remembered going to Hell. When the Beast flung him down, it was so strong that the ground cracked beneath his body, and he fell through the Earth, deeper and deeper. Tadeo felt heat, and when he opened his eyes, it was to see himself enveloped by flames as he plunged. He screamed, and he screamed. For refusing Revelation, he'd been cast into the lake of fire.

CHAPTER 42

"Babylon," Satan panted, "must not fall." Violently, he pushed Michael away from him, sharp breath reeling into his open, panting mouth. He settled a foot over the floor but wobbled and gripped at the throne behind him, the one he'd been fucked over, to keep upright. His eyes were wide; his heart was in his throat, beating a bruise. 'No,' he thought. Before him, Michael was flushed, his face a touch too pale, sweat dribbling down his body. When Michael stepped forward — the devil said, "Stay back. Stay back, you damned Son of God." 'Son of God?' In the scriptures, angels were sons, boys, for God. 'But why do I think of that now?'

"I am no," Michael replied, hushed, voice strained, "Son of God." Finally, his armored hands went to adjust his clothing, his armor, to hide himself, his nakedness, his sin. His gauntlets trembled, his face flickered with a juvenile fear. The sight twitched the ends of Satan's lips in something like humor but too angry.

"You've fallen far," Satan sneered, "Michael." He reached for his own clothes, trying to ignore the tremors in his own body, trying to remember where he was, trying to feel nothing more than delight that the chief prince had finally succumbed to him. But Satan felt torn; he felt wrong. None of it had hurt, deeply, and yet there was a churning ache in the pit of his stomach. 'I cut myself open once, looking for flowers.' He had felt something inside of him that hurt too much to bear. In between his hips, in his lower back. The pain buried inside, holding him down. 'No,' he thought. "You fought against me for millions of years only for it to mean nothing in the end. You've given yourself to me now. You're mine now." 'Why aren't I happy?' he thought. "I'm your God now." 'I told you, Michael. I knew. You would fall one day, fall for me. I know it all. I always knew how this would end.' He was like God. He was God.

Michael's brows furrowed, and his gasps finally began to wane — the heat between them simmering down into cold coal. "You're wrong."

"God is never wrong."

"You are not God!" Michael shouted. "You never have been!" But —'Satan. The inside of you.' Like a lock, like it was natural, like it was not an abomination. 'It was better than anything,' Michael thought before he could stop himself. 'Your body. Your face. Your voice.' His mind whirled. 'I'm sorry.' He didn't know why he apologized. 'There's a part of me that's still in you. I can feel the pulse of your heart. The tightening you do around me. The embrace of your warmth telling me to keep going, to press in more, to bring you closer, then away, then closer.' The greatest feeling he'd ever felt. 'Better than anything God has ever promised me.' He hated it so much that it ached his bones.

Satan answered lowly: "That you do not believe in me is your own stubbornness, nothing more." There was seminal wet in him, trickling down his legs. 'It felt right. It felt wrong.' He'd begged for it. 'Fuck me,' he'd wanted to say when he was an angel. 'Please. I'll be the first angel to die unless you fuck me. If you don't love me, if you don't hurt me, I'll die.' "But I don't need your faith." He was great with Michael or without; that was what Lucifer had learned after the fall.

Harshly, the doors opened — Baal, with a legion of demons not far behind. "Satan, they're gone. The king, his men, women."

"Check his bunker," quickly, Satan answered.

"I'm hearing that the king is dead. He was betrayed—" Baal stopped, face frozen before melting into a calculating, suspicious expression. Seconds later, he was taking another step. It didn't matter that Satan and Michael fixed their clothing; the throne room reeked of it — lust. Quietly, the regent turned his head and said over his shoulder: "All of you, prepare for an attack." They asked against who, but Baal didn't answer as he twisted to take both doors with his hands, then shut them slow, heavily, in their faces. Then, he locked them.

Satan had just settled over his throne again. 'Who is in control now?' But the truth is that the king of Babylon had never been in control; he had been one limb of empire. Power is pure arteries, a cobweb of wealth and evil, and Babylon was a headless chicken running. Its death throes, however, would bring far greater collapse than other fallen kingdoms of old. Satan had allowed slow rot to kill the previous Babylons until they fractured and another Babylon rose in the distance, but this quick, violent fall, amid all the other apocalyptic omens, was harrowing. 'This cannot be stopped easily.' What to do? What to do? A soreness in his body flared, and he grimaced, took one armrest, dug his nails into it. No, no, he had to act. He couldn't lay here in the afterglow of hate. 'It felt wrong.' He didn't have the time. There was no time.

Before him, there was the thud of Baal's fist making contact with Michael's jaw, and then the clang of the prince's armor as he stumbled back, only to then growl like an animal and throw himself at the demon. "Fucker," Baal snarled, bringing his arms up to try and protect his face at the same time that he tried to dodge the punch Michael was flinging in his direction. "Did you like it?" Baal continued to taunt. "Did my seed inside make him nice and wet for you?" Michael landed a blow right against his abdomen, so hard that it threw Baal to the ground. Yelling out in pain, he managed, "I'll fucking kill you."

"Both of you," Satan said, "we need to find my child." He lifted his face, eyes cold, and saw them grappling at each other, Michael over Baal, their faces so twisted in hate that their gazes alone could have ripped each other to pieces. "Gather the demons, Baal. And you, Michael — your sword is in the hall. If you want to end all of this, then we have to act. You can't sacrifice yourself, and you can't kill me. The apocalypse is much larger than the both of us. And the both of you."

"No," Baal and Michael said in unison, only to shove at each other again.

"Burn in Hell, then," said Satan, stepping away from the throne, striding across the room. Reaching the doors, he turned the lock, hesitated. Then, Satan looked over his shoulder and said, "Stop being so obsessed with yourselves. Vanity is a sin, didn't you know?" The ache in him continued to burn, but Satan chuckled at the demon and the archangel before walking away.

In another world, Dina was on the ground, staring at the crack in the Earth by his feet, dividing him from the Leviathan and Rosier and Armoni. He was by Tadeo's mother, and he looked to her, and — instinctively — he reached for one of her chair's wheels as it started inching toward the cracks. He turned it like a gear, trying to push her to safety, but he was watching himself move on his own. Like he was a soul trapped in the body of someone else, an innocent person. Wobbling, Dina rose to stand.

"What have we done?" Armoni breathed nearby. "What did we do?"

Rosier only thought: 'It's almost over, it's almost over.' His throat burned, his eyes itched. 'It has to be.' He wanted to tell the Leviathan to cast Satan down to Hell next. 'Find him. Kill him.' This was all Satan's fault, after all. Asmodeus would still be alive if Satan hadn't done this, all of this — God's apocalypse and the very first one in Heaven. Asmodeus would have never hurt Rosier; he would still be his friend, standing beside him.

Dina took a step back, an emptiness pooling inside of him; he was half-here, half-nowhere. Only when he felt eyes on his back, and he saw brightness bloom around him, did Dina blink. Something fiery and great loomed above — 'Apsinthos.' And Dina felt the ground he stood on and the heat of a world on fire. "Apsinthos," he whispered out loud, without looking above to the star. "Is it over?"

'He wasn't supposed to be cast down like this,' said Apsinthos. 'It wasn't supposed to happen like this.'

Together, Rosier and Armoni lifted their faces to peer at the sun looming over Dina, its flames gargling its own body, pulsing like a muscle. Armoni asked, "Dina, what is this? Apsinthos...?" Just like when Dina had seen Azazel again, he felt the weight of the past fall onto his shoulders. Armoni's fingers had once wiped at his tears, and his lips had grazed his cheeks. Dina wondered how he got here; he wondered how long he'd lived; he wondered if he was the same Dina that had stolen the rings of an angel before the war. "Dina?" He remembered Uriel. "Dina, answer me." Where was Uriel? He'd been gone a long time, hadn't he?

Though Dina didn't reply to them, someone else soon called: "Armoni! Rosier!" When the two turned their heads in another direction, whereas Dina only flickered his gaze, they saw an angel with a bleeding heart — Azazel. His face paint had smeared — as if he'd cried in white. He'd let go of the chain hanging from Samyaza's collar, and Samyaza looked the most alive he'd had since the flood. 'Forgive me,' Azazel was still thinking, as he'd gasped to Samyaza after the Watchers had surged forward, speared Joana to death. They had flown away quickly, trying to escape the murder scene only to return to it at the sound of the Earth cracking open to swallow the anti-Christ down. Now the Watchers hovered — uncertain, bloodied, waiting for Azazel to tell them what to do next.

Samyaza was still hoarse, and he continued to twitch, as he quietly told Azazel, "We should bring them with us." When Azazel glanced over at him, he noted the softness in the eyes of the Watcher who'd long ago snarled that he knew what was best for Azazel. As if recalling the same memory, Samyaza's face flashed with regret, pain. 'But it was me that became your keeper, Samyaza. I fed you my own blood, and I let you drink my tears.' Azazel walked over his gaze to Dina, and to the murdered girl and the other girl holding her body.

"Bring them with us?" Azazel echoed softly. "Where to? Where are we going?" He'd mocked Satan over dinner, told him he'd become just like God. 'But now here I am, broken over a place we helped destroy, hoping to run away and never look back. It's what the devil did, isn't it?' Perhaps, Azazel would crave godhood soon, as well. 'Will this be the beginning and the end forever?' The wound of his heart ached; the emptiness never faded. But he could feel the Watchers eyeing him. And he understood Lucifer, truly, for the first time.

It was Kokabiel who answered. He swooped down, approached Azazel, and smiled blissfully. "Above. Past Heaven. The stars have made room for us." Azazel understood now what that meant. "They're calling us home. A new paradise, one God can't reach." After this, Kokabiel smiled at Baraqiel, but Baraqiel still refused to meet his old love with anything but quiet coldness.

Armoni, below, looked at Rosier, then at Dina again, still shadowed by Apsinthos, and Azazel quickly said, "Don't bother, Armoni." Exhaling slow. "Let Dina lay in the grave he's dug for himself." Azazel didn't feel the relief he'd thought at those words, even less so when Armoni flinched, but Dina's gaze remained dark. 'I'm sorry, Dina,' Azazel also found himself thinking. 'I'm sorry I couldn't be there for you.' "Danel," Azazel then called, "can you help carry Rosier up? Samyaza can carry Armoni."

The demon of fruit clenched his teeth, hugging Asmodeus' arm tighter. 'I don't want to run.' He wanted to die. 'I want to burn in Hell.' But Armoni pressed his head to Rosier's own, and he took his free hand, squeezed it. And when Danel descended to carry the demon, Rosier felt his eyes burn and his throat close.

Michael, after retrieving his sword, dressed in silence in what might've been a broom closet. After Baal had left to follow Satan, he'd returned with a scowl and some human clothes folded over his talons — cargo pants, boots, and a tank top that'd fit horribly tight around Michael's chest. Immediately, Michael had tried to argue, but Baal had dropped it on the floor, turned on his heel, and disappeared again. The prince frowned, reached for the gift that'd surely come from Satan. And unsure what else to do, he pulled on the clothing over his enormous body, only to hide them beneath the armor he still refused to go without.

Truthfully, the chief prince should contact the other angels — Raphael, Gabriel, and Uriel at the very least, but he didn't know where they were. He had defected from God's war, without meaning to. And just as he began wondering what his fate would be now, he heard the beautiful voice he detested: "Baal says there's no sign of your angels outside; I suppose you really abandoned them, and they abandoned you." Just as Michael turned around, still missing his helmet and his chest plate, he saw the devil at the doorway changed into human clothing himself — a loose white top, frilled at the sleeves, loose pants, dress shoes — ridiculously mundane, almost soft-looking. Oddly, that made Michael's grip on his helmet tighten more than if Satan had still been dressed in his infernal, seductive sheer. "Hm." The devil looked too innocent, pretty, harmless.

Serpentine eyes narrowed, eyeing Michael's hair, still wild from sex. "Come closer," ordered Satan.

"No."

"It was an order." The devil's voice hardened, but Michael still didn't move. Swiftly, Satan crossed the space between them, grabbed the prince's hair with a painful yank. "Don't move." Michael grunted but didn't struggle, even when the devil's lavender scent washed over him wickedly. Rough but efficient, Satan's fingers worked through the prince's tangled curls, divided it into three sections, then pulled one over the other in a loose braid. Briefly, Michael remembered Lucifer's hands in his hair in Heaven — gentle, curious — but this wasn't that. And it never would be again. Hands slowing, leaning in, Satan whispered hot against Michael's ear, "You're mine now. Even your hair belongs to me."

Shivering, Michael said, "I belong to—" But he didn't belong to God anymore.

"You gave yourself to me." Satan finished the braid. Let it fall. "And you can never take it back." He stepped away. "Let's go find my child." Left Michael standing there, hair bound, body marked. Soul damned, but he had nowhere else to go.

Outside, Baal had just finished rounding up the vast majority of the demons, the others instructed to protect the tower from humans or whatever else might try to appear. It was the sort of chore that he'd typically have Asmodeus do. But Asmodeus wasn't here to help anymore, and Baal didn't know where Rosier was either. He'd heard Moloch was attacked, decapitated; he'd heard that Moloch blamed Rosier; in all the chaos, that was all he'd gathered. Really, Baal hoped it was true, hoped Rosier had given that bastard what he deserved. He set those thoughts aside for now, however, when Satan elegantly approached. Baal straightened up atop the winged horse he held captive and watched the devil climb on, settle in behind him, and whisper, "We'll kill Michael, after this. It's the most certain way to prevent the apocalypse from ever beginning again."

Baal almost breathed a sign in relief. Behind him, over the burnt ground of the great tower of Babel that dwarfed all those human skyscrapers, the demons readied on steeds, in cars, on motorbikes — whatever else they could learn to navigate fast enough. And Michael appeared at the mouth of the tower as the regent of Hell finally said, "With pleasure." When all the demons noticed the chief prince, they laughed and whistled.

Patting Baal's armored shoulder, the devil ordered, "Head for the border out of Babylon." Then, he chuckled, "You're charming when you're jealous."

"You're cruel," Baal answered, but he nonetheless leaned into the kiss Satan pressed to his cheek. After this, the devil kicked the horse on Baal's behalf, and when they went on ahead, the demons hurried to follow in a stampede.

Hours passed with Dina, and he'd spent much of that time almost alone. Nearby, Tadeo's mother still sat and Lupina remained on the ground, her empty face continuing to dribble the occasional tear onto Joana's skewered body over her lap. Apsinthos had told Dina to wait here, but the angel didn't know what they were waiting for, didn't know if the end was still possible. Tadeo was burning in Hell, as he was destined to, but it wasn't meant to happen like this, right? And if the end were really to come now — would it hurt? Or if it would be like falling asleep. Dina supposed it would come with the Son of God descending from Heaven, but there was nothing in the sky now, not even the silver birds. All the screams and explosions of earlier had simmered into a strange silence, where there were only crackles, buzzes of insects hungry for the dead, and some distant human voices. When he began to slump too much, Apsinthos called, 'Dina. Don't sleep now.' But he was half-dozing, thinking of soft things, of bed, of Heaven. Had it really been so bad? Uriel had been kind at times, offered him tea, warmed food, and the rooms were always so lush with plants. He never worried of death, never felt the bristle beside him of human suffering and family and love and bigotry. 'This is why I chose to end it,' he tried to tell himself. But Tadeo had known the evil of the world, far better than Dina, and he'd rejected apocalypse.

The demons on the winged horses arrived first; as they did, they saw the same desolation that Dina had. Sparse humans wandering, tanks tipped onto their sides, the gray clouds of burning, the bare bones of houses. When Baal landed the pegasus, Satan lifted his body so that he could see over the regent, and he felt his heart begin to drum slow, frightened. He clutched at the demon's shoulders, and he exhaled at the sight of it all. 'Am I too late?' No, he couldn't be. He was God. He was God. 'Is the anti-Christ dead?' No, he couldn't be. But where was he?

"There's Dina," Baal said, leading the horse deeper into the town, toward a crack in the Earth. "What the fuck happened here? Is Hell opening here too?" Hooves beat at the ground behind them, but they were slowing from their gallops. And all the demons quieted.

"Yes," Satan whispered tightly. It was true that Dina was up ahead, but there were bodies here too. One body in particular, laying limp in the arms of a young woman who was frozen, chest barely rising with gasps. The corpse must've died just hours earlier. If it weren't for all the open wounds, the blood on her clothing — Joana could have passed as sleeping. With her curls, her complexion, Satan saw her so much like Michael, the same as he had when he first noticed her beside the prince. It'd filled him with scorn then, but now there was a flicker of recognition, of pain.

Above, there was the whip of a breeze, an angel gliding down fast. Michael — he stumbled, lifting his hands to his head, grabbing his helmet, tossing it. "Joana—" left his mouth. "Joana!" The woman holding the corpse looked up slowly, her eyes distant, mascara forming streaks of black down her face, ash a coat that grayed her skin. "Joana." He lifted his hands, as if to grab her, but they froze in the air even when Lupina nudged her body toward the archangel weakly.

"She told me about you," said Lupina, voice raw and scratched. "Everything. She always used to talk to me about you. I didn't believe her for a long time—" She laughed, her voice hitching and breaking. "She said that you were an angel. That you tried to save her. She really loved you."

"No," Michael whispered in response, shaking his head, a sharp breath pulling into his mouth. "No, no, no, no—" His chest was rising, falling. All the weight of time was falling over him now, folding down onto everything he saw. He reached, touched her face, and a sob wrecked through him. 'Poor Joana. My poor Joana. My poor child.' He didn't care anymore to deny it. 'God, kill me. Kill me now for what I've done. I didn't do enough for her. Joana.' She looked so small dead, so young; she looked like when they'd first met. A little girl who stared at an angel without fear, who knew things far scarier, who'd reached for him when he tried to walk away for the first time.

"Angels killed her," Lupina said distantly. "They weren't armored like you."

"The Watchers," came Satan's voice from behind, and Michael felt his blood run cold. Slow, he turned his head, saw the devil climbing down Baal's horse, his expression like stone. "Azazel wanted revenge." One step forward, then another, another. "You killed his child, Michael. You killed all of their children."

"How did," fell from Michael's mouth hoarsely, "they know about her?"

Satan met his eyes. "I told them."

Chest tight, heart stopped. Michael's hands trembled, clenched into fists. Red, like blood, leaking into the edges of his sight. His whole body — growing a tremor of rage. He needed, more than anything, to lunge forward, to rip Satan's throat out. But he couldn't move. Couldn't even breathe. He could only stare at the devil who'd killed his daughter. "What," Michael whispered, "did you say?"

Dina lifted his head, then climbed onto his feet. They had been ignoring him, he realized, something he should be used to.

However, when his gaze landed on Satan, anger lashed inside of him. The fallen rebel angel, still so beautiful, so perfect. Eyes narrowed, the young angel stepped forward, and he called Satan's attention. "You're looking," Dina said, "for the anti-Christ. But he's gone. The Leviathan cast the boy down."

Hesitating, Satan turned his face away from Michael. He answered in monotone, "You're lying." Thousands of years, the devil hadn't failed. He had maintained Babylons, he had killed every anti-Christ. He had rot the world in human evil to maintain it. "Tell me where he is."

"Look at me," Michael interjected, rage shaking his voice. "Lucifer." He screamed "Look at me!"

The devil refused.

"Look at *her*!" His voice broke, stripped raw and bleeding. "The Lord rebuke you! You're responsible for all of this. For evil, for death, for pain. I will burn you myself for the rest of eternity. I don't care if I must destroy my own hands to hold you under the flames. I want every second of the burn to feel like the first. I want you to realize God was right. He was always right. You're a heartless beast. You're a monster. You deserved everything God ever did to you!"

A rage twisted in deep, so guttural that Satan almost choked. His entire body twitched hot, and a snarl built in the back of his throat. But hissing interrupted. He'd thought, initially, it was another angel flying downward, but then he heard Baal shout for him to move, and he felt heat at his back, and he watched his shadow start to trail far from him. Slow, Satan inhaled, body tensing. Rigid, he turned his face, still hearing Baal's shouts though he could no longer see him, just sense his movement from the distant thumps of the horse. A star, right before him, as there was a star right behind Dina. It was of the same grotesqueness and fire as Apsinthos, and it held hundreds of mouths, but it held no eyes.

"Satan!" Baal, trying to make his way around the star on the horse, then abandoning it, but he wasn't quick enough.

The light, the star, swallowed him.

CHAPTER 43

The screams of the devil were not unlike the howls of agony in Hell. However long Satan had attempted to differentiate himself from every other angel, demon, living thing — when he burned, he sounded as horrible and bloodcurdling, raw, as everything else. The perfect favorite of God, humbled by suffering. His shrieks were tinged with rasps, and through the flames, all those who saw Satan witnessed his skin reddening then growing wet, dark — flogged. Mere shadow now, the devil sunk into the fire that swelled larger, larger. Baal hurried to Satan, to the sphere of fire that had just consumed the devil, but Michael watched, his eyes cold. Then the flames began shaping into something slimmer, taller. A mouth opened wide in what was becoming a face, a head. Limbs tore out of its sides, and hair fluttered down like the rays of the sun. It was only once the screams stopped that the body settled, then turned downward — a giant flaming figure above the buildings, standing among the other stars. All those there saw that it was Lucifer.

Lucifer, burning as bright as morning, as great as a god.

"Satan," Michael breathed, lifting his body, reaching for his sword. The sun-angel lowered the top half of his body slowly, his face the size of two or three angels standing over each other, and his expression was unreadable as great hands of fire curled against the cement of the street. Ruins surrounded him, demons and angels surrounded him. 'Like when I first saw you.' And Michael's heart clenched, but not with love. Wrath — to know that even now, transformed into this enormous burning god — Satan still had the gift of beauty. 'When you're the most horrible, grotesque thing ever created.'

In contrast, Baal stared adoringly, compelled to approach and kiss his god. 'Sweet Satan.' The one he'd fallen from paradise for. 'There you are.'

Far away, the prince Uriel startled. Where had he, Uriel, been all this time? Well, the same place he'd been during the war for Heaven and during the flood — a library. This time, however, it was in ruins and in a language he didn't know well. A few humans had come in and out since he'd made refuge here, but they didn't bother him, except to ask for reassurances that Uriel was ill-equipped to give. And he'd been too busy, concerned with trying to decipher as many texts as he could before the world ended. Really, it was the first time he'd delved so deeply into humanity's thoughts. Some were interesting; 'I'll only give them that.' But he found himself lingering on a few romance novels, then some old folk tale collections.

Staring at the illustration of a princess and her beloved, he'd felt his heart turn. 'Dina had loved these more than anything.' And he'd never bothered to ask why, to really understand. 'But I understand it now, Dina. I do.' His face had warmed at the poetry. 'If I'd let myself listen to you, or let myself feel anything for you, maybe none of this would have happened. And maybe I would have earlier realized what is so obvious now: I haven't loved. For billions of years, I haven't loved. I only thought that I did. Kimah must have known this, too. One day, I had grown to love grieving him, rather than loving him.'

Uriel knew now that he deserved all of Kimah's resentment, and he knew he deserved Dina's rage.

But when he heard a rumble outside, and screams, Uriel looked across the quiet library with shelves toppled to the ground, flooding the tiles with pages. Over the heads of huddled humans, he saw a window. And he breathed out shakily. 'Kimah,' Uriel thought, then he hurried to cross the building, toward the exit — every human scattering out of his way. Uriel peered out to examine what he'd seen through the glass. Some streets down, a figure of fire loomed over the buildings. At his head, a star like a halo. The same star that had called itself Kimah before Uriel abandoned the war. However, lifting his gaze even higher, Uriel noticed a swarm. Angels, but not armored. The Watchers, hesitating among the clouds.

And in that same tendon of the sky, Kokabiel stopped suddenly, all the Watchers above, not quite to the empty void of space above. 'Kimah,' he thought too. Craning his neck back, a thousand voices suddenly rushed at Kokabiel, but they all said the same thing. 'Kimah.' He whispered, "Wait," and when no one heard him, he had to shout, "*All of you!*" It was so urgent, coherent, that it almost didn't sound like Kokabiel quite at all. The lucidity turned Baraqiel's head first, of course, and it was only through seeing him that Kokabiel was able to grit out —"The stars— Wait—"

Holding Samyaza's hand, Azazel stopped as well, turned his head, fluttered his wings to remain in place. "You told us that the stars made room for us, and the Earth is a wasteland." He nodded his head at Rosier, on Danel's back, and Armoni, fluttering clipped wings and latching onto Samyaza. "We shouldn't put ourselves in the Leviathan's way."

"Then don't," Kokabiel suddenly giggled, "but I think I will."

Meanwhile, Dina was staring up at the beast of Lucifer, eyes wide, breath harshly coming in and out of his mouth. He stepped back just as Apsinthos hissed, 'Kimah has given his body to Satan—' Then, Apsinthos addressed him: 'Kimah! It's too late to intervene with the end times.'

'It's not my body,' Kimah replied. 'I'm split among trillions of stars. Like you, Apsinthos. I have no single body left. All I've given him is fire.' And from fire, came flesh.

For Satan: it was liberation. Liberation — at last — from a body. How long had it been since the devil had felt this? Lifetimes. His eyes saw God, though he'd refused to see Him at the Throne. He saw Him now, better than he ever had. And when he saw Him, a slow, churning wrath began to build within. Satan grunted, and when he turned to Apsinthos, the anger only swelled until all the fire that composed him scorched his vision. But the screech of the Leviathan was near. The end was near.

Michael only watched, then reached to touch Lupina's arm, trying to urge her to take a step back, silently asking her to take Joana's body somewhere, too. 'Everything is going to end now.' Joana's love should spend her last seconds not knowing that, in a safer place, away from this. Lupina nodded, then went to wheel Tadeo's mother away with them, and Michael shakily stood. His armor might protect him from the flames, but his sword would be useless against it, against him, Satan. 'How to kill a star?' Michael wondered.

"I know," Kokabiel whispered now to Baraqiel, "how to kill a star." In response, Baraqiel furrowed his brow, almost in irritation, and the angel of the star's mouth twitched. 'You are never going to forgive me?' he thought. 'You are never going to forgive me.' All he'd done was force Baraqiel to sleep with a woman; all he'd done was sleep with several humans right in front of him. "Aha," he laughed breathlessly. "I still love you," he said plainly, "Bara." 'The last thing I'll love,' he promised. 'First thing I loved.' "Don't stop me," Kokabiel said next, and the fallen angel of light tilted his head. "I know it's against your nature, but you must let me burn out."

Dina stumbled backward, heart a hammer against his ribs, then told Apsinthos, 'We're done here, aren't we? We need to leave. They want to destroy you. I love you. I don't want you to be hurt.'

'This is just one body of many,' Apsinthos reassured, 'though one of the few I have complete control over. Even if they destroy me, it will change nothing.' Even still, the star obeyed, creeping backward and higher.

Satan had just lowered himself onto the ground, on his hands and feet like an animal. Then, his crawl began fast; he plunged through everything on the road — the toppled vehicles, the debris. Closer and closer, he sped toward Apsinthos, but before he could reach him, the Leviathan's shrieks sounded again. Turning his head, eyes wide and burning like dual suns, Satan caught the sea serpent just as it bulleted in his direction from its hiding place behind houses on another street. It threw itself against the devil, and together, they crashed into a building and an abandoned tank. Satan raised a blazing arm, scratched it against the head of the Leviathan, and his mouth went ajar with light and a shout of fury.

Unlike Satan's body, a sword, Michael knew, could cut through the sea monster. But, again, he didn't move. Even after Lupina had made it elsewhere, the weight of Joana's corpse lingered. 'I did this for you.' But she was dead. And God had said it would all be over after the apocalypse; Michael would be dead, free from every painful second of living. He could see, from the corner of his eye, angels. But all of the world was muffled. He was hearing Joana still. His legs were rooted to the Earth she loved so much, that she would have rejected Heaven a thousand times for.

On the contrary, Baal shouted for the demons to raise their weapons. "Kill the Leviathan!" he barked, hurrying back to get on his horse, to lead it away from so close to the battle, swerving it just in time before the Leviathan crushed the road where he'd been standing. Baal pulled on the reins, bringing the winged stallion up into the air, and as soon as he was approaching the height of the Leviathan's head, he lifted a shotgun that'd been attached to the horse's armor with a single hand, pressed on the trigger. The bullet passed straight through, and then so did the next, and the one after that. The legion of demons all followed, and a rush of gunshots chased the sea monster.

Uriel, meanwhile, landed stealthily in a crouch on top of a building nearby. "Kimah—?" His heart thudded hard in his chest at what was *not* Kimah, what was Satan in every feature of his face; and yet, he felt something there, a sensation like it was his own body standing on that road and fighting the Leviathan. "Kimah...?" Then, Uriel noticed Dina, who was retreating the same as Apsinthos and ducking his head to avoid any stray bullets. His mouth opened, closed, opened: he was yelling at Apsinthos to leave with him somewhere safer. But then, the archangel heard even more noise, raised his head, saw a few more angels descending, hovering. Watchers.

Satan was still screaming in all his fury, pummeling the

Leviathan who coiled itself around his limbs, even with bullets tearing hundreds of small, dot-wounds to bleed from. It screeched in the face of Satan, matching his yells, refusing to surrender. When a red-haired angel fell from the sky, the devil didn't notice. It wasn't until he heard the smash of something colliding with a hovering star nearby that he turned his golden face. Body flared, howls halting for a second.

After the plunge, Kokabiel had felt a second of peace, and then, as he sunk into the star — an unbearable scorch. His mouth opened in pain, and yet, he couldn't scream, the fire bursting his lungs first, then his throat. 'This is the pain you've told me of.' All the stars. For all other things, the stars never agreed, whispered to Kokabiel conflicting truths, expressed their different dreams — but they shared the same pains. Long ago, he'd learned to recognize some voices; he knew them from their wordplay, the desires they expressed the most. To silence all the other voices, to hear only one, to know everything, to have the truth for the first time — he did this. Spreading thin, picked apart by the flames. 'Kokabiel.' Was that his voice or another's? 'Kokabiel.' His thoughts, like his flesh, were pulling, stretched out into time, far into the dim vacuum above.

'Baraqiel,' he'd always called to him in Heaven after the war, 'the stars told me—' He wanted to tell him what he saw now, wanted him to know all the truth. How to kill a star. How to kill God. Kokabiel drowned in it — the truth.

Above, Baraqiel jolted, and though Danel grabbed at his arm, he stopped himself on his own. Azazel asked what was happening, his heart stuttering and caving in, but Baraqiel said nothing. The blaze was beautiful, all the fire more magnificent than God, in that moment. 'Koka.' How stupid he'd been. 'You burn as bright as I always felt you did.' He grimaced deep and a choke fell from his mouth. 'I loved you because you were dangerous, because you were like fire, but I ran from you when it started to burn.' The star they all witnessed grew brighter, as if Kokabiel had turned into its fuel before, suddenly, it swerved one way, then the other. Briefly, Baraqiel thought he saw Kokabiel's face, his eyes, in the mass of fire-flesh that composed the star before it lurched toward Apsinthos with a thousand mouths opening, closing around the blaze of the most wicked sun.

Dina screamed at this, barely managing to beat his wings to throw himself far from the stars. As he did, he stumbled onto a wall, not far from Michael. He watched, heard, Apsinthos roar and struggle against the star Kokabiel had managed to manipulate, but as he was bit into, chunks of his body tore off, flares whipping out like wings from them both. Frantic, horrified, Dina turned to Michael, called, "What are you doing?! Aren't you supposed to bring about the apocalypse? For good! For the greater good!" Tears gathering, starting to stumble down his face, the young angel pleaded: "End this, Michael! End it, please!" But the chief prince's eyes were dark, cruel on him. And Dina shuddered. 'Maybe Tadeo was right. The world ended a long time ago, and it's this place that is Hell.'

Apsinthos' sight began to slip, all the suicidal intent that he'd had came to a grinding halt. Ferociously, he fought back; he resisted the growing darkness, the sudden drowsiness, and Apsinthos forced himself to grow brighter, to bite back. As he did, the star of Kokabiel shuddered, began to dim itself and shrivel.

Satan, in the hold of the Leviathan, watched: the darkening, weakened star backing away, close to the ground. Kokabiel, almost certainly dead now. But Apsinthos was also noticeably less bright and smaller, his spherical body now misshapen. With renewed vigor, Satan tore the Leviathan off of him, just enough for him to immediately crawl over the ground in a burning, terrifying panic, vision narrowing to tunnel around Apsinthos. He had to crush him, in his hands; he had to *eat* him. He had to do it now.

Nearby, Baal cursed, trying to reload as fast as he could to help his fellow demons prevent the Leviathan from reaching Satan. As he worked, he saw Michael, 'stupid fucking Michael,' with Dina by his side. And, breath catching, clenching his teeth in anger, he turned the gun. Knowing that Michael's armor would protect him — Baal opted for Dina.

Jolting, Michael heard the boom, then looked over to see the young angel thrown back, crash against a wall. The bullet had gone through his mouth, tearing little of his lips but decimating his teeth, the base of his skull. Instinctively, Michael tried to reach for him, but then he stopped, and oddly, he remembered where he was, what was happening. He looked at who'd done it as Dina jerked, clutching at a throat now covered in blood. 'Baal.'

Dina, shaking, eyes wide, choked up, though he could still breathe — angels could not die, angels could not die, though Dina had just seen one burn up. 'Why won't the world end?' What had he done wrong? Why wasn't God satisfied? Why couldn't He put them out of this suffering? A mercy kill? Wasn't God merciful? Warily, he looked up at the one who'd made him do all of this.

But the devil didn't reach Apsinthos in time. The Leviathan wrapped itself around Satan and, in a final effort, flung its own body with Satan's into the crack in the Earth. Nails and fingers of flames clawed at the Earth as Satan was pulled toward Hell.

Watching it happen, Michael held his sword and thought, 'Goodbye, Satan. Burn. For everything you've done.' He didn't react, didn't even move, when the devil thrashed, managed to pull some of his body above the gash in the ground and reach out. Fire stretching over the pavement, toward Michael. The prince didn't move, met Satan's terrified face. The devil's fingertips touched Michael's armor — his chest, over his heart.

'Michael—' Satan's voice, but in the chief prince's head, and Michael's breath hitched in a cold, furious terror. 'Michael.' Shuddering, the archangel saw another face in his mind, suddenly. God. 'Eden.' Petals crushed beneath a naked body, darkened by blood. A bed of flowers. 'The Lord's hands.' And pain, a terrible pain. 'I never told you. I never told you that you were right. This is all because of you.' Dying, the devil finally confessed. 'He told me that I was made for Him and made for this.' This? 'Do you know now?' A twist of his stomach, and Michael did see it. 'Do you understand now?' It hurt. 'I thought I'd die.'

Satan was jerked back, and the sensations stopped, but the ghost of them lingered on Michael, in his body, in his core. God, the Father. His hands. His jealousy. He had seen love among angels, then tried to correct it, using Lucifer's body. Violently now, the

Leviathan wrenched the devil back, and silent now, the serpent dragged Satan back into the ravine. 'It was my fault.' The Lord had told the truth. 'It was my love that caused this, every second of this.' But not his love alone. The punishment for love; God's punishment for love.

And, in unison, the demons screamed for their ruler. Baal abandoned his horse again, tried to fly down in time, though there wasn't anything he could do. Worst of all, the crack was trembling, starting to close around Satan.

Finally, Michael moved — numbly, hearing nothing but the dull thumps of his own heart. He beat his wings, threw himself forward, and yelled out in anguish, suddenly. In confusion. Lifting his sword, he reached the Leviathan to slice, hard, strongly, beneath its head. Screeching, the serpent revolted but refused to release Satan from its hold. Its skull folded forward, away from the rest of its body, in death, black blood gushing out, but the head fell with the devil, the gash in the Earth closing around them both.

The chief prince, cold, shaking. 'Lucifer?'

CHAPTER 44

In Hell, Tadeo saw Christ, arms spread but not lifted enough to hang from a cross — instead, as if he'd just stepped down and was still finding his balance. His face was as it was in every painting that Tadeo had ever seen, but he was far more beautiful, almost angelic. He blazed even among all the hellfire that embraced his body, that almost seemed an extension of it, of him. The Son of God. Though Tadeo could no longer feel the scorch of the flames, he felt a sudden new pain, a churning ache in whatever was left of his heart and a sense of familiarity. It was the same as he'd felt when he saw Joana dead, his uncle dead, Dante dead, his father dead. Like he'd known Jesus' crucifixion not as a Messiah's sacrifice but as the murder of an old friend.

Careful, the anti-Christ set a foot down onto the same flames that were embracing him, and then he began to trek forward, step by step. He shouldn't be able to move — he was in a sea of fire — and yet he did. Tadeo approached the glorious Son of God with many years' worth of questions trailing down his back like broken wings on a fallen angel. None of them were reaching his mouth now, however much he remembered them in perfect clarity. What were Jesus' last words? What did he eat? Did he really walk on water? Did he turn bread into meat? Did his followers taste the golden flavor of blood when he handed them wine?

The face of Jesus, however, looked less brilliant each second. His mouth began to sag, as did his eyes, then his very skin. The shine on him seemed too red, and his limbs seemed too long. His torso was too thin, and his clothing faded as if burning away. An ugliness bloomed. Grotesqueness tore apart the face of Christ until it appeared he was screaming and that his body was pulled in every direction, every organ of his stretched until they ripped. His blood spilled out in pulses, like he were a mangled heart. And his monstrosity itself, all that incarnated agony, dribbled down; he could have been a wilted flower, doubled over. Finally, Tadeo saw that there were more limbs on him than a human must have: two pairs of wings, as well as more heads than a human ever carried — four total.

Though the anti-Christ opened his mouth first, it was the decaying Satan who spoke. "You remind me," his voice was a whispered rasp, "of a man from Nazareth. They told me he was born in Bethlehem, in a manger, because there was no room for his mother and father in the inn. When he was young, they wrote, he performed miracles, and he taught his rabbis. When I heard that he claimed himself to be the Son of God, I sought him out, and I asked him to prove to me that he could do what it was written the Messiah would do. He didn't. I asked him to step down from the crucifix, but he didn't. Did he resurrect? I can't say. But whether he was a Messiah — that I can tell you." Satan's horrifically burned, disfigured body shifted. "Whether he died a Son of God or not, I think we have made him one. Christ is a Messiah only for as long as we believe him to be."

Tadeo, quietly, said, "You're a liar, Satan."

Satan, lowly, gutturally, answered, "You're the bastard of a liar."

"Parents raise their children; you're not my parent." Tadeo wondered how he might look like now — if as terrifying as the devil or as the human man he'd been on the surface before being dragged down to Hell or as the young girl he'd been when he died. "I have a father, and he died because of the horrible, horrible world. And I have a mother, who is waiting for me."

The devil replied, "You were damned. You will burn here forever."

"When humans burn," Tadeo answered, shakier, "all the nerves of pain in us eventually wither, and we're left feeling nothing. And I think that's happened to me. I fell, and I screamed, and I screamed," 'crying and begging and kicking and choking on the boiling blood in my throat,' "until I couldn't feel it anymore. Even if that hadn't happened yet, there is no pain you can't accustom to. And no matter how much it hurts, I'll return to Earth."

"The wicked Earth that killed everything you ever loved?"

"I can't," Tadeo snapped now, "argue with you about why I won't destroy the world, despite what it's done to me. There's no reason to it, no logic. An argument won't do justice to it. But I have known happiness despite, and I have seen kindness, and I don't *care* if it isn't everywhere I look. I don't *care* if all the good in the world only remains in the love that I *know* is there between me and my family who remain, between me and those I've lost. I don't care if the good in the world is nothing but a warmth in my chest. For the sake of one, I wouldn't kill a billion. I can't do it. It's not the right thing to do."

"Right according to who?"

"To *me!*" Tadeo shouted. "*To me!*"

Satan snarled now: "It's my world! It's my wickedness! The world is all wickedness, and I know because it's mine. Because you didn't obey me, you have made everything worse." 'Obey?' Tadeo couldn't remember when Satan ever gave him an order that needed to be obeyed. "You will be destroyed forever when God reaches to crush you. And I will have to pick up the pieces of this rotten world. I will have to make it all right again. Because of you. Because of you!" His voice pitched higher, thinner. "I must return. I will mend it all. They will all listen to me. They must. If they don't, I will make them."

"You're a stupid fallen angel," Tadeo grunted. "Don't you realize it? You're not a God, devil. A God doesn't get cast down to Hell."

"I know now why God punishes His children. I understand now."

"You know nothing," said Tadeo. "Look around you! We've lost!" He saw the devil's horrible faces flare. "But we're not dead, or destroyed. I'll return to Earth, and if it's true that you can help it, then I'll take you with me. I don't care if you're the devil or if I'm your child. Even if I hate you more than anything—" He gasped for a breath of the fire, but it felt like nothing. "If you will only tell me the truth—"

"In Rome, you were born." Satan shifted again, but his body was too mangled to read his emotions well, and his voice was hollow. "The first anti-Christ, I've always said, was the Emperor Nero. He committed atrocities, and I stood hidden behind him. Because I was jealous of God and His child, I coupled with the emperor, and we had you, the Beast part of you. Nero died to madness, and I tried to raise our child, but though it was as beautiful as me, it began to morph into a monster that attacked the servants and the slaves. When a prophecy reached me of a Beast and of an anti-Christ, I held my child down and burned it until it was ash. To save this world of mine, I did it — even if it killed a part of me inside as well. But a few decades passed, then I heard of a monster, and I realized I would have to murder my child that was born again, that would continue to resurrect.

"I spent the next two thousand years chasing down every anti-Christ with a Beast inside, and I tempted them by making them believe I wanted to end the world alongside them. Once I had their trust, I would burn them. It's slow. There must be... so much trust. Or else I would have killed them all much easier. I would have killed you. But here you are." Satan tilted his enormous, disgusting head. "Not an emperor, not a king, in this life. You are not special; you're not the first to hesitate, and you're not the first to come from destitution. But you're the first to try to save the Earth, instead. Why?"

Tadeo blinked once, then a few more times. "I don't believe you." 'I wanted to end the world, too,' he almost said. 'I rose from the dead with so much rage that I was almost blinded by vengeance.' But a girl had appeared to him in an alleyway, pressed a gun to his back, told him he had a responsibility.

"Don't believe me, then," said Satan. "I don't need your faith."

"You need my faith more than anything," said Tadeo. "Or else you wouldn't talk to me." He allowed his eyes to shut just so that he wouldn't have to stare at the devil's body anymore. "What happened to your beauty?"

"This is what I am beneath it, ever since I fell from Heaven."

"Why did you fall?"

Satan, suddenly, laughed. "I can't say that I remember."

"I've heard that it's because of your vanity."

"That makes sense to me," the devil continued to joke. "I would cast someone down from paradise for vanity, as well."

"It doesn't bother you that you act like Him?" Tadeo wasn't sure where such a jab had come from inside him. He supposed that he'd come, without even realizing it, to a revelation, about God and about his own religion. The word itself, religion, no longer felt adequate for what he felt. This was something else, belief rooted in disbelief, the truth found for him in a lie. Tadeo saw God in his pain, never in his joy. To him, all the suffering was proof of God. Love was proof that God could die. Tadeo could still taste Dante's alcohol in his lips. He could feel Joana's shoulder that he often leaned against.

"I'm greater than Him, worse than Him."

Tadeo couldn't be sure what that meant, how greater and worse could ever mean the same. But he'd been told to love God, to fear Him — all his life. The Lord is good; the Lord is cruel.

"Tell me," said the devil, stiffer, "how you plan to save what's left of the Earth. You will still eventually die, and your successor may not make trees grow for the people. All the water is poisoned, and the stars have fallen from the sky."

Tadeo admitted: "I don't know."

"I can save the world for us demons but humans will not survive long on it anymore. Maybe it is best for you to slaughter the remnants of humanity, then yourself, to stop everything once and for all."

"Isn't there another way?" Tadeo asked quietly. "Isn't there another way to stop this? Can't we confront God?" He opened his eyes again, finally. "If you think yourself so powerful, then why not face Him?" Satan was quiet, and Tadeo decided, then, to say what he'd felt earlier: "I can tell you why I'm different. It's because someone told me I had a responsibility to our people. Even if they looked at me with scorn, I had a responsibility to meet them with grace. It's the right thing to do. And what I think is right and good is larger than myself; it's larger than God. Isn't that what you wanted to be?"

"There's nothing rational about you."

"There's nothing rational about love," confessed Tadeo. "Haven't you ever loved someone, devil?"

CHAPTER 45

The chief prince fell to his knees. 'A bed of flowers. Eden. God, our Father.' Those had been the devil's thoughts, inside of Michael. That had been the devil's pain, lodged deep and gutting him open to spill wickedness out of his own body. Yet Satan was gone now, dead like Joana, dragged enormous and bright into a wound in the Earth. With a glance behind him, Michael saw streaks of redness where she'd been, disappearing around a corner of a toppled building. Where were all the humans? Gone? Had Christ returned and raised them to Heaven? Had the second coming of the Son come and gone? Maybe they had all left, and God had chosen for Michael to remain on Earth to rot alone.

But he was not alone; almost, he didn't hear the steps coming up behind him. He almost didn't feel when talons grabbed Michael by the back of his neck, wrenched him onto his armored feet. Then, with a growl, Baal shoved the prince, spat at his face, "I'll fucking kill you." Throaty, stuttering in all its rage. "I'll fucking kill you." Over and over.

"Baal," Michael said, slowly, wondering if he'd ever addressed him like this, "it was Satan who wanted to come here, who thought himself capable of fighting stars and God—"

"Fuck you," said Baal, then pushed him once more, and the saint took just another step back, taking the blow. "All of this is *because of you,* because he made the mistake of loving you. And you fucked it all up. You were a coward. You cut his wings off without being asked to. You're worse than God—"

Immediately, Michael yelled out to cut him off, threw himself forward to shove the other back — but Baal beat his wings to stop the momentum and keep himself from crashing into anything behind him. Even still, the regent of Hell wheezed, a splatter of blood left his mouth. Michael's mere shove had been strong enough to break bones, muscle.

Nearby, Dina lay with his mouth still mangled and, twitching, turned his head slowly to eye Apsinthos, now a dim-star, half-shriveled. 'Apsinthos,' he thought desperately. 'Dear Apsinthos. Forgive me. I love you. Forgive me. This body of yours is hurt. We're both hurt.'

'Dina,' came Apsinthos' rumbling voice soon after. 'Don't listen to them.' The angel was about to ask who, but it wasn't long before a choir of beating wings came toward him.

"Dina!" Azazel called a second later. "Stop this. Now." Arms came around Dina next, around his throat in a headlock. Frantically, he reached to claw at the arms just as Samyaza's grunt sounded by his ear. "Dina— Look at me!"

But Dina refused, eyes wide, panicked, searching for Apsinthos even when a few other Watchers dropped into the street before him, obstructing his view of the great star. He tried to speak, but all it did was release a gurgling noise as blood splattered down his mangled mouth. "Hhgh," was all he could manage, and so he kicked and continued to scratch. 'Apsinthos, is it over? Can it be over?'

Armoni stumbled over, coming to stand beside Azazel, and he said, "Dina, you're being used."

'I don't care,' Dina was crying out in his head, 'I want to be used. I want to be manipulated. I would do anything to be wanted enough to hurt and use.' Azazel and Armoni continued to shout at him to open his eyes, but Dina's were wide open. If he could shriek, he'd say: 'None of you understand, none of you could ever understand.' He continued to look for him, Apsinthos, in desperation. It couldn't have all been for nothing. He had to end all of the world now more than ever. It was all so terrible. His heart hurt so terribly. The pit of his stomach twisted so tight he thought he'd rip inside.

On a rooftop, Uriel still stood, watching. Though he maintained his gaze on Dina, thrashing and gurgling on his blood, he heard Baal and Michael's brawl continue.

"He's *gone!*" Baal was snarling, but his voice cracked and broke. "Lucifer is gone now because of *you!* I don't care what happens to me. I'll kill you. I'll kill you over and over for the rest of eternity."

Michael breathed out, "There's nothing I could have done—" His sword finally slipped from his hands, clanged to the ground.

"You didn't even *try!*" And when Baal tackled Michael, the saint didn't try to dodge. He allowed the demon to ram him into the side of a car, then reach for his helmet and tear it off of him to fling far from them. Michael even raised his hand to stop any demon or stray angel from intervening, and he looked at Baal's panting face — shuttering between anger and a childish sadness. It made the demon hesitate for a second, but his hand still curled into a fist. He punched Michael's face hard, using his other hand to keep him pressed against the car, then he struck the chief prince again, again.

'Lucifer.' Fiery and enormous and brilliant Lucifer, tempting anyone to fall to their knees. To pray. 'I spent every day since the fall telling myself I'd killed you.' He coughed out blood, his skin swelling and darkening with each punch. 'God told me that you were dead. I believed Him because I wanted that lie. It was easier to believe you dead than changed.' There should be rage in Michael, wrath at how he had been misled by the Lord, but his chest ached raw. Instead, such guilt flooded him that it was as if he'd committed the horrible evil on Lucifer's body. 'I am responsible.' This was his sin, as much as God's. Michael had done nothing. 'I saw the hollowed corpse of the angel I loved, and I kissed his limp, tortured body. I didn't listen to you. I didn't trust you.' Satan had rebelled, violently, horrifically; Michael had fought him down. 'I broke you, too. I handed you to Him.' He'd worshiped God, all that He had done. He'd worshiped a rape.

Baal dropped his fist, and his eyes were reddened, wet beads slipping down his scarred face, but then he threw Michael aside, to the ground by his abandoned sword. Over the clang of armor, Baal said, "You'll take his place in Hell." Gasping, trembling, eyes wide and frantic. "I'll save him, and I'll have you burn in his place."

Michael wanted to beg, 'Do it, please,' but he heard the devil in his head, whispering, '*You God-damned martyr,*' still trying to sacrifice himself instead of facing what he'd done. "Baal——" but he couldn't force any other words out.

Sighing, Uriel had realized that no one was going to finish the job with Apsinthos, and so he called, 'Kimah.' And he met silence. 'I know that you listen.' Anxious crinkling in his chest, the prince tilted his face to see a great sphere of a thousand mouths, descending slow to hover beside him. Kimah, who'd offered some of his fire to Satan before he'd been defeated. 'You're beautiful,' Uriel said, then smiled sadly. It hurt his cheeks to do it; he'd not smiled for billions of years, except for rare moments with Dina, when he wouldn't be able to smother his fondness, his pity, in private. 'I think that I understand now why you've come to hate me. Everything that I thought I did for you, I did for me. And I bowed to the Lord who did this to you.' Swallowing hard. 'I'm not asking for you to forgive me.'

'I cannot,' said Kimah, 'absolve you.'

'I'm not looking for you to absolve me,' Uriel said, but a softer joy continued tugging at his lips; he'd long become so unfamiliar to happiness. 'I'm asking for you to help me.'

'You saw what happened to Kokabiel.'

'I did.'

'It won't kill him. Apsinthos cannot be killed. There are pieces of him scattered across a trillion stars.'

'I'm doing it for Dina,' confessed Uriel, turning back to the youngest, most beautiful angel. 'Look at him. He's fallen so deep into the lies of that star that he can't remember who he is. But I know what that is like, Kimah — to follow hate out of hopelessness. Even if it's only temporary, to break him out of the spell — Dina must watch this star die.' If Lucifer had killed God during the war for Heaven, even if just for a moment — Uriel might have run away with him. Maybe that was wishful thinking. Angel of hindsight.

Kimah said: 'I don't want to destroy you.'

'Nothing can ever be destroyed. I won't really be gone, Kimah. I will be with you, even if you can't hear me. For an eternity — if you can remember — I couldn't speak, but I was still with you'

'I might have grown to despise you,' Kimah replied, 'but I never stopped loving you either, Uri.' Then he approached.

On the street, Dina was still writhing, refusing every word that all those around him tried to offer. It wasn't until he was suddenly punched hard against his stomach that he jolted, looked up. Azazel and Armoni were still standing before him, but it was Baraqiel who'd just driven his fist into Dina's abdomen, then another time. Dina spluttered out more blood before Azazel quickly put a hand on Baraqiel, telling him to stop. But the mournful angel of light struck harder before other Watchers had to grapple and pull him back. It hadn't helped; Dina just continued kicking, banging both his arms against Samyaza's hold in hysteria. In every direction, he whipped his head around, only incidentally catching a figure in a nearby roof walking toward a star. First, he believed it was just one of the demons, but when he looked back, he noticed their stern gaze. Familiar. 'Uriel?'

Michael watched brightness bloom over the ground he was thrown over, and he lifted his chin at the same time that Baal did. In the dark, reddened sky, there was a star, and just as it began to swell, a few ripples across its fiery body opened. A thousand eyes of every size revealed themselves all over its shape, and a hundred mouths parted to pant like an animal and bear an infinite amount of teeth. An angel must've thrown themselves into the sun, how Koka-biel had, but who? Who?

Breath hitching, Dina saw how the enormous star above had a few eyes on him, and he shook his body against the Watchers some more. 'Uriel.' He had seen that gaze in all those thousands of years that he'd run into the prince in his own home, in the libraries, in the kitchen, in the bathing area, in the dark, by candlelight, reading. 'I convinced myself that you liked me, secretly, that you didn't mind me. And then I realized that your affection was another mere story of mine, one of my fairy tales. What are you doing now, Uriel?' Dina shook his head. 'Don't do it.' He wanted to scream. 'Don't do it! Don't do it!' Kicking, thrashing, sobbing. 'Don't hurt him, Uriel!' Then, he turned to Apsinthos. 'Devour me! Please! Kill me for you!'

Apsinthos inched back, but like all stars, he was slow. 'Kimah,' he called. 'What are you doing? It's all almost over. And this won't stop me.'

'This has never been about you,' said Uri-Kimah before rushing forward, mouths opening wide. Apsinthos revolted the second that Uri-Kimah reached him with his teeth, and Apsinthos flared erratically and threw his body back, then forward, then away. But Uri-Kimah was relentless and fast, tearing into Apsinthos' body with bite after bite, chasing wherever Apsinthos tried to nudge himself to safety. The wicked star's glow grew even darker than it had been, and when it was like candlelight, Dina broke through all the broken bones in his jaw to scream at the clash incoherently.

It did nothing. It wasn't long before Apsinthos began to die out, graying as he disappeared into the mouth of Uri-Kimah. But the last of Uriel was soon to follow. Each eye rippled over the great star began to shut, slow, sleepily, and the size of Kimah shrunk in a soft, calm decrescendo along with his brightness. Kimah's weakened body fell to hover close to the center of the street. Michael and Baal both hurried away in the same direction. At the other side, the Watchers, too, scrambled to get far from the remains of half a lover, burning quietly still.

As this occurred, Samyaza lost his grip, and Dina broke away. 'Uriel.' He tore his wings out from his back, beat them, threw into the disarray to disappear into it. 'Uriel.' Uriel had always glared at him when Apsinthos had bombarded Dina with affection. He should hate Uriel, now more than ever, but he didn't, couldn't. 'No book I ever read had the words for how I felt about you. And there are no words now for what I've done.' The new Heaven after the apocalypse was supposed to be worth all the suffering. Worth all the blood of children on his hands. Worth murdering his own friends, loved ones. Uriel, angel of wisdom, had just looked Dina in the eyes and burnt up. 'Why didn't you help me? Why didn't you want to return to paradise? Why?'

CHAPTER 46

'It's what I wanted,' Rosier thought emptily, the weight of Asmodeus' severed arm in his sling making his entire body slouch. 'It's what I wanted,' he told himself again. But revenge is not justice, it's surprise. Revenge was breaking the cycle, gaining the upper hand, with an exhilarated thrill. But it isn't justice, not on its own. And then, it's nothing but this emptiness. In the wreckage of the world, the fallen angel of fruit could only stare at the closed crack in the ground where his old friend had disappeared to. Sweet Lucifer, golden head in Rosier's lap, fluttering his violet wings absentmindedly, asking if God dreams. Of course God dreams. What does He dream? This, all of this. 'Asmodeus would laugh whenever he caught me coddling you, Lucifer. He said we raised you well.'

Slow, the demon of fruit slipped down from the back of Danel, who turned back at him curiously; he'd remained latched onto Danel's back, too numb to involve himself with Dina. Michael remained doubled over with a bloodied face and pressed to a vehicle, not far from the one he'd been beaten against by Baal. And the regent of Hell in question was standing firmer beside Michael, panting for breath, some blood still in his mouth. Rosier's eyes trailed down both of their bodies, found the chief prince's sword, laying lonesome in the rubble.

Michael felt the ebbing tremble in his body — a new clarity blooming, solid, stabilizing. When he looked to Baal again, he noted a wincing face: broken ribs or terror. 'It's not your fault he's gone,' he wanted to tell Baal. 'It's mine.' But that was just more self-sacrifice, and Satan had snapped at Michael for it, and if Satan was just a memory now, Michael was compelled to pay respects, to listen, to obey him, for once. "Baal," Michael tried, low, grunting it. "Baal." Joana's death lingered still, but what she'd pleaded the prince to do was have mercy, not forgive. And to see that wretched souls are still souls, that there are no good people, no bad people. Satan had tried to stop the world from ending; if he'd succeeded, Joana would be alive.

"If," Baal began gravely, "you don't want me to order my demons to slaughter you with the fires of the stars right now, then you should hand yourself over to me without a fight." He turned over with a limp, taking a step back, seemingly quite prepared to return to fighting. "I meant what I said. I'll have you take his place. I don't care what I have to do. I'll make you suffer everything that Satan has tenfold."

Hesitating, the prince straightened, shifted away from the car he'd been leaning on. He said, strongly: "There will be no war between the angels and demons anymore." Immediately, Baal quirked a brow, and there was a rumble of noise from the angels and the demons alike. "There will be no more war." None at all. "But I won't hand myself over to you."

Baal jabbed: "What the fuck are you saying? Are you willingly going to save Satan with us?"

'Save,' Michael echoed in his head. 'Like I promised I would once.' "I'm going to kill God. You're going to help me."

Far from them, not far from a river running red — Dina landed across a wide road with a stumble. His wings folded back into himself, and he shuddered, and he gripped his top as if he were a human suffering a heart attack. All around him, discarded cars stood empty, and there was nothing but a few wandering animals and human bodies. When he raised his face — he noticed a house cat with a collar, fur matted and dark, face pressed into the open, fly-infested gash of a human. Stomach twisting, Dina took a step back, though he should be far, far used to this sight by now.

But it had been so easy, just some hours ago, to justify every face of death with the promise of salvation, of paradise, of the return to the past. He had told himself every scream and cry was a brick on the road to a Heaven he'd been born too late to know. Without real-izing, he'd begun to ask if this road could ever be worth it, could a new Heaven ever make up for this brutality. And he'd realized, perhaps more crucially, that those who'd known the old Heaven, the place before sin, were not standing beside Dina, fighting for it. 'Uriel wanted the apocalypse stopped more than anything.' Had all things really been better before sin? How had Satan invented sin? Had he pulled it out of his body like he had the Beast? Or had he seen it, somewhere, named it?

The cat continued to eat the corpse, and Dina listened to the hiss of hot breeze, and he listened to the heart-beatings of the stars above. Apsinthos might speak to him again soon, but he thought of Tadeo, who'd fed the people like the cat now ate. 'You wouldn't end the world, Tadeo, even if you have every reason to.' Was he really in Hell now, burning for refusing God's will of the end? Slowly, Dina looked to the river. 'I know where Hell is.' It was a short trip if he flew. 'I'll know where to look for them.' Dina didn't doubt the demons would come looking for Satan soon, but he could still heal in a way they couldn't. Painfully, Dina shut his eyes, and he heard Azazel's shouting in his head. He remembered Uriel, in his library, touching his head.

Then, Dina heard neighing, turned, and he opened his eyes to see a winged horse, one of those angelic, armored ones that the demons had stolen. It must've run off in the chaos, the same as Dina. As it nibbled on some browned grass, he noticed it carried large saddlebags on its flanks, including an open one that hinted at onyx-black demon armor. He approached slow, and he immediately deciphered the shape of a helmet, a chest piece. It would do, wouldn't it?

In the center of town, Baal said. "Kill God? *Kill God?*"

Michael replied, "There's nothing we can do but that."

"Even Satan couldn't kill God," Baal snapped. "He knew that was impossible. And I don't give a shit whether God lives another day or another billion years. The only thing I care about is saving Satan."

"We can't save him," Michael insisted, "unless God is dead."

Someone's throat cleared, calling Michael's attention, and the prince turned swiftly, but the one who'd made the noise was none other than a demon with broken horns. Rosier — carefully holding Michael's sword with both hands, offering it up at him. His eyes seemed tired, and his hands trembled. "If you're to kill God, you'll need this," the stout demon whispered.

Instantly, Baal's gaze softened. "Rosier... Where have you been?"

Rosier hesitated as Michael carefully took his sword's handle. "Baal," he began, then didn't answer the question. "You should listen to Michael." The regent scoffed. "Please. The hellfire is what killed Asmodeus. Satan may be already dead and so is that boy. So many, so many are already dead..." Just as Rosier's voice trembled, Armoni hurried to stand behind him, laying his hand on the fruit demon's back comfortingly, and Azazel stepped forward as well, looking at his old friend Rosier pitifully. He didn't touch him, however, as he looked at Michael and drew in a slow breath.

Heart thumping too quick, Azazel glanced at Samyaza, whose face twitched and twitched, who was trying to reach for Azazel's hand, who took his fingers and squeezed them. They could run, still, to the stars, away from all of this. 'But as the world flooded, we spoke of killing God, didn't we?' And so the leader of the Watchers sighed, and Azazel said, "We will come with you too."

Baal blinked twice. "What?"

Azazel stared; he wanted to say, 'Because Lucifer is not God, and I'm not Lucifer. I don't run away.'

And as if Baal had heard the thought, he laughed. He looked at Samyaza, then at Azazel, then at Michael. "What the fuck are we doing here? You still haven't explained how we can kill God, Michael. Or are you asking for suicide?"

In Hell, Tadeo and Satan had long stopped speaking, burning in silence, wondering if the rest of time would be spent like this. There was nothing recognizable in the flames except for each other, except for perhaps those dark silhouettes below in the shape of people — the worst of souls, realizing all the horrible things they'd done on Earth. And though Tadeo was able to walk, Satan was nearly paralyzed, his many limbs feeling like they were bolted far from him to some distant walls. 'Have you ever loved someone?' the boy had asked. And Satan had wanted to snarl, 'I've loved. I love more than anything that's ever lived.' But that thought didn't settle right. Nothing of how Satan had felt suddenly felt right. 'I've loved.' He tried to remember when he had. He tried to remember what it felt like to love.

On Earth, Michael said, "Satan tried to strike God down from His Throne during the war. I stopped him." He realized now why Rosier had handed him the sword, what he meant by it, and he turned to give him a look in thanks, but Rosier was in Armoni's arms now, face solemn and empty. "I don't know what would have happened if I hadn't taken this sword back from him." He faced Baal again, and he stiffly added, "You said that Satan failed to kill God, but he failed because of me. And I won't fight for God ever again." For Lucifer, if not for himself. 'You're not the Lucifer I fell in love with, but I kissed you, and I felt you, and I loved you — whoever you are. Lucifer, Satan, devil. Live and die a million more times — my heart will follow.'

"What about that Dina?" Baal suddenly said. "What about the other archangels?"

"The other archangels don't believe in God much more," Michael answered truthfully; he had been the one who insisted they follow God's will even when they didn't want to. He would have to spend an eternity trying to make it up to them, as well. He had another eternity set aside for Satan, and yet another for Joana. Michael had long accepted his death because there was nothing ahead of him, and now there was almost too much. "Baal," he called again. "Please. Do it for Lucifer."

Baal was quiet, and he looked back at his demons, who stared at him, too, with conflicted faces and uncomfortable shifts, then he turned to Rosier again. Visibly, the regent clenched and unclenched his jaw before he licked up the last of the dried blood on his bottom lip. Lowering his voice to almost a private hiss, he said, "I don't trust you." Then, however, he surrendered, "For Lucifer, I'll try it. But the second that I see that we're wasting time, I'll feed you to God myself."

"I won't stop you," Michael promised.

Nearby, Azazel turned to his Watchers, and he said to them, "For our human loves, for our children, for everything that ever happened to us. And because of what we became — beasts like what we bore on Earth."

"Well," grumbled Danel, "the one leading us to the stars is gone, so perhaps suicide is our best option indeed." And Baraqiel twitched beside him. Some laughed low, bitterly. A small moment of peace.

When Dina arrived at the coast, he wore stolen armor — the helmet, chest plate, and some coverings for his arms that the pegasus had carried on its saddles. And now the angel reeled in his wings as he began to walk through what had once been a sea but had gone dry. He had swam through the shallows here with two young men — one the anti-Christ and one a soldier — but now he walked through dry sand and between some suffocated fish. Here, like at the road, there were some hints of humanity long gone — garbage, abandoned beach chairs and umbrellas, though very few human bodies. Dina continued walking until he saw the sea floor dip and the narrow, rocky mouths that lead into the underwater caves. They didn't look so terrible when it wasn't pitch dark, though the red light of a setting apocalyptic sun didn't make the descent into Hell look very inviting either.

Dina didn't hesitate to start crawling through it, even moving quickly. Though hellfire had erupted out of so many gashes into Hell, this one was dark and not particularly hot. It must have spat out its fire long ago, but once Dina traveled deep into it, the heat began to rise slow, as if he were sitting in a furnace. 'Will I survive long enough in Hell to find them? Satan. Tadeo.' Dina didn't want to die, but he'd come this far. Heart stinging in fear, Dina watched as flames swelled at the end of the tunnel, and before he could even begin his thoughts of retreat, his hand slipped, and he plunged into the inferno.

Silent still, Tadeo and Satan soon heard a new screaming nearby. Neither of them reacted much, assuming an angel, demon, or human had fallen inside and was burning alive brutally. But the screaming didn't stop, it continued for many seconds, far longer than it would take for someone to burn to ash. And so Tadeo, tiredly, lifted his head, and Satan managed to do the same, terrible body twisting. There was a flash nearby of something, like a glass shard beneath the sun. The devil called out to it: "Who's there?"

The voice was still wailing in agony, but then it forced out, "Follow me!" Dina's words, broken and wet. "Follow me out! Tadeo! Lucifer!"

"Dina?" Tadeo called, but a burst of anger almost made him growl like a Beast. "Fuck you! Fuck you for everything that you've done!"

Dina said, "If you follow me, I can get you out of here— Please hurry— Please—"

Satan replied: "I can't move."

"Please," Dina was still begging, and the shape of him began to bloom from the flames. "Please." His legs were gone, finishing in burnt stumps at his thighs but the rest of him remained, hidden beneath demonic armor however much hellfire raged.

Tadeo hesitated, then he finally looked down at himself, and he saw a monster. "I can cut you free, Satan." The devil didn't reply. "But — you must promise to kill God."

"I've always wanted to kill God," snapped Satan.

Tadeo shook his head. "Kill Him entirely. Kill the God in Heaven, and kill the God on Earth." Kill the God in the devil's head. "Promise it to me."

Satan still argued: "There will always be a God. He cannot die.

He wishes He could die." But the second that those words left the devil's mouth, he twitched again, and then he laughed, deep, happily. "That is what He wants, isn't it? All God has ever wanted is to die."

CHAPTER 47

As angels and demons rose to Heaven, they oversaw the burning Earth — sick, hungry, dead, and war-torn; the dim light of a black sun loomed, a red moon on the horizon hummed, and the low-hanging stars were quiet.

Within the ruins of paradise, however, nobody waited for them. Raphael was directing the half-dozen angels crowded by him toward the north, and when they said that Metatron had sent them to the center, the angel of healing groaned and waved a hand dismissively. "Don't listen to him," he advised. One angel reminded Raphael, though without much sincerity, that the Lord, their God, had ordered them to heed Metatron's words. "He's always told you to heed me, as well — so make your choice." Quietly, the angels smiled, and they headed north to continue the hasty reconstruction. Raphael, gripping his staff with both hands, could only sigh at that; he'd spent much of his life tired but never had he felt this much exhaustion, not even in the aftermath of the first war. He couldn't remember the last time he'd rested his itching eyes or even his trembling knees.

"Raphael." As if sensing the healer angel's pain, Gabriel landed beside him with ruffled wings and stepped closer, one hand falling onto Raphael's arm, squeezing firmly. "You must rest, brother."

"Where have you been?" Raphael replied, voice tighter, his brows furrowing enough to form a crease on his forehead. He turned and saw Gabriel out of his armor as all the angels were now, with a flower in his hair again and a distant glaze over his eyes, lips parted slightly. "Tell me— Tell me where you've been."

"I was looking for Mary," Gabriel confessed softly, and Raphael felt a familiar sinking feeling in his chest.

"Gabriel," he began tensely.

"I was thinking about," Gabriel went on speaking anyway, tilting his head to gaze down a street with the remnants of a stone monument scattered over it, their laws broken, "how I was the only one who ever visited her. She was in a house, but you never went to see her, and neither did Uriel, Michael, or even Metatron. And we always talked about the same things, brother. I apologized for what I did to her, and she would tell me that I did nothing wrong. That I had asked, not demanded, her to carry the son of God. She could have rejected it. But is that true? I could have said no to God, too, whenever He forced me do what I didn't want, but I believed he'd never hurt me. Coercion is larger than a question. And I think that if Mary were really here, really in Heaven all this time, she would have spit in my face. Why would God do that to a girl? Break her once, break her again on a crucifix."

Raphael quietly said, "We tried to tell you long ago, but you didn't listen—"

"I do think Mary left the Earth behind, but she's not here," Gabriel murmured, a sad smile fluttering the ends of his lips upward. "Somewhere else. One day, we should leave too." When Raphael frowned, he added, "One day, if you can ever bear living for your own wellbeing and not that of others, beloved brother."

Outside paradise, the chief prince Michael broke through the veil between the earthly and divine, and he settled onto where clouds turned cobble, trailing toward pearl gates. Leading the way, Michael saw that the gates were closed, locked, and immediately grabbed the bars, gritted his teeth. Groaning low, he stepped forward, pushing hard. And before the demons or Watchers could catch up to him, he'd already forced open the gates into Heaven. A shuddering pant fell from his mouth. Then, he met the city he'd left in ruins with its destroyers behind him and the Watchers who had been corrupted not on Earth but in this Heaven. Baal and Azazel moved closer behind Michael, looking at the city with an almost equal amount of disdain but Azazel's gaze was crueler, for Baal could hardly recognize this as a place he'd ever lived in.

Azazel lowly said, "We should have gone directly to God."

"The angels will help us," Michael said.

"Even after all of this?" Baal chuckled and gestured vaguely at the destruction.

Without answering, Michael marched forward, listening to the footsteps of everyone who followed. And as he walked, he saw angels lift their heads, step away from their homes, set down what they did. He'd expected to see loathing, but they eyed Michael more careful than they'd ever seemed, trying to decipher him. Anxiously, they noticed the demons, but they remained quiet except for murmurs passed between them. Michael raised a steadying hand to them, ordering them to be patient, to not run, without words.

"Michael?" It was Raphael, beside Gabriel; they looked down the road at them from the foot of the Fountain of Life, the younger one holding the arm of the healer. "What are you doing?"

Hesitating, Michael looked to all the other angels who'd gathered to watch their chief prince, and he addressed them, first: "The time has come for God to face what He has done. He is the one who allowed the war for Heaven, who allowed for the birth of evil." There were some sharp breaths, but the prince continued, "When all the devastation in Heaven and Earth enrages you, angels — you must remember who is the father of it all. There is only one Creator, and He created sin. If it wasn't Him, then He is no creator, and He is no God. And we ought not to worship someone who is just like us. But now, we must war against God for every transgression He has wrought upon us. He has made us all suffer — tortures, deaths, violations — and we have taken it all instead of turning to him and saying, 'Give me one reason to worship you! Why should we pray to someone as foul, as wicked, as the one who created suffering.' We turn on God today not like we did in the war for

Heaven; we turn because He is the evil we so claimed to detest. He is the Beast! He harms us, toys with us. This jealous God punishes us for daring to love anyone more than Him!"

Suddenly, a furious voice called: "Michael!" And Metatron dropped down onto the golden roads, face twisted. "You couldn't protect Heaven, and now you join the demons in destroying it?"

"You can have your Heaven" Michael said, "that you've always wanted for men, Metatron. Stay here. I and the angels will go to God to count our grievances for the rest of eternity." Then, the prince looked to Gabriel, Raphael, and said, "Come with us." To all the angels, after that: "Come with us!"

"Don't listen to him!" Metatron shouted. "He's long been corrupted by the devil!"

Baal shifted; he remembered the devil, in a moment like this. Lucifer, standing on the fountain, shouting, 'Why do I worship this God? Imagine no God.' A paradise for the angels, Satan had asked for. Opening his mouth, the regent wanted to parrot all of what Satan had once said. Instead, he only found himself whispering: "Why worship this God?" None of them had ever received an answer. And the angels closest to Baal lifted their heads curiously, a few remembering who had asked this question first. One turned to the other, whispering, 'If we built this Heaven,' 'If we don't ask the fruits, the flowers, that we have grown to worship us?', 'If we don't demand to the towers and bridges we've built to sing our praises forever?', 'If God is so all-powerful,' but 'He cannot serve Himself a drink,' 'cannot sing for Himself or even wash His own feet.' Why worship this God? These murmurs turned Metatron's attention to the gathered angels, and he grunted.

"Stop this," Metatron snarled. "Return to the apocalypse. End all the wars if you so want evil to be defeated."

Turning away from him, Michael tensed, then he noticed Phanuel, stepping up behind Metatron. Their eyes met, brief. "The first war," the prince confessed, "was for love. And God ignited it. Because of love between us, God committed the greatest evil on His own angels. He violated our bodies. He took our tongues. God demanded violence because He could not have love like we do."

Raphael tried again, "Michael, we tried to speak to the Lord — Gabriel and I." Gabriel nodded, but then he smiled a little, happier and sadder than he'd ever been. "You're not saying we should try to fight Him, are you? With demons and Watchers—" But he noticeably flinched when he saw Samyaza, and when Gabriel touched his hand, Raphael's entire face twisted in a grimace.

Azazel noticed how Samyaza' gaze flickered, as well — another rare awakening in him. And he frowned, then solemnly said, " Michael. Let us meet with God.

Michael hesitated, but he supposed he'd said enough. "Let us confront our Lord." Rolling his shoulders, he straightened himself to stand proud, like he'd done in his youth. 'Pride, again.' The prince wondered if this is how Satan felt when his shame fell away — the ability to lift his chin and say, 'Yes, I'm a sinner. I'm unforgivable. I will never be loved again. I'm a traitor to God and to nature, and I reject this body, and I will burn in Hell happy but liberated from the chains of Heavens.' "Angels, if you will, come with us to kill the one who is responsible for every second of this suffering. Come with us to demand answers, to know the peace we haven't known for hundreds of millions of years." Some of the crowd shifted, and though Metatron started looking around himself, telling the angels to stay where they were, the other archangels intervened.

"Follow Michael," Raphael ordered.

"Yes," Gabriel agreed, his face still a picture of sadness and joy. "Follow Michael."

"No," Metatron began, and he tried to grab at Raphael before another angel swept in, so quick he was a blur. "Agh!" The old man was seized from the back, a long sword pressed to the front of his throat, digging into the skin. "Phanuel—?" Metatron choked out.

"Michael," Phanuel called; though he'd spoken to the prince for many, many years now, the break of his muteness to all those around was so sudden that every listener jolted. "Go. Everyone — go."

Eyes wide, Michael wanted to tell Phanuel that he was right, and that he didn't want to do this without him, and that he was sorry for what he'd said, and that he was grateful that Phanuel had spent so long beside him despite knowing the truth of God and of Michael.

"Thank you," was all Michael could manage before he, shakily, pointed his sword upward and told everyone to follow. The angels still hesitated, but once Raphael and Gabriel flew toward the army of an angel, demons, Watchers, the rest of Heaven followed with them.

On Earth, as soon as Tadeo reached the surface, he was able to transform back into his human likeness, and he spluttered fire out of his mouth, crawling desperately onto the drained sea, shaking, trembling, watching as Dina dragged his torso toward a minuscule puddle that he flopped weakly on top of. However much the angel was responsible for the apocalypse thus far, Tadeo couldn't help a pinch of pity seeing him like that, trying to heal himself with a puddle that wasn't cooperating. Grunting, then, Tadeo moved closer, then he put his hand on Dina's back, and he said, "Let me heal you. Dina—"

Dina said, "Wait— Where is Satan—?"

His answer came instantly. Behind them, the rocks that formed the entrance into Hell rumbled, then began to crack, split, fall away. The giant of fire and light that Satan had become forced his way onto the surface; his hair flowed like the rays of a sun again, and his entire body was only in the vague shape of an angel with horns on his head, four wings on his back, three other faces — one like an ox, one like an eagle, another like a lion. But Tadeo hadn't been there for Lucifer's transfiguration, and so he looked up in horror, wonder, mouth reeling in air harshly. "Lucifer," he whispered. This was the angels as he'd always imagined them — cosmic, beautiful, powerful.

Lifting his body high, eyes widening, Satan whispered, "They want to kill God. All of them. Angels, demons, Watchers."

Dina whispered, "But that can't be done. That can't be done."

"I'll kill Him," said Satan, his voice booming and singing, elegant and terrifying. "I'll be the one to do it."

"Satan!" Dina called helplessly, but the four wings of light ripping out of Satan's back beat once, twice, lifting himself slow like a god ascending. "Don't do it! Don't try!" Tadeo pressed his hand harder on Dina's back, trying to force him to stay still. "Stop!" But Satan flapped his wings another few times, the wind of each strike cast a storm of sand onto Tadeo and Dina, who both ducked their heads, shut their eyes momentarily. But Tadeo managed to look up in time to watch Lucifer, Satan, the great devil, disappearing into the sky. Some stars trailed behind him — slow-moving, flesh-y, flaming spheres pushing beside the clouds, leaving the Earth naked to whatever war was going to cast a rain of blood down onto the Earth.

And as Michael led the way past the bright firmament, past the cosmos, past the ceiling of the universe, he felt himself morph into what he'd been when he cast Satan down — a creature of wings, flames, armor, chains, sword. Strength itself, however weak of will he'd always been. Yet, he was not afraid; for the first time in eternity, he was not going to be weak. He was not going to obey his Father. The demons, as they rose, had to shut their eyes, as they were soulless husks of what'd they once been, but even blind, they pointed weapons. Swords, firearms, spears. Every weapon across all of history — angel and human alike — raised to direct themselves at the Throne of God, enormous, impossible. Golden and silver and sapphire and ruby and jade — the seat and the Father Himself. Bright, darkness, every hue, every shape. He was shaped like crops, like harvest, and like the wilt of starvation. As if He were drought.

"God," said Michael. "Surrender your Throne. For all the wickedness that you are responsible for — surrender."

"Michael," the Lord answered in a hundred voices — low and high, airy and throaty. The Creator of all things, calm and angry. A hand lifted from the armrest, turned, offered a palm, holding a world, another world, a trillion stars, faces, eyes, wings. The beginning and the end, in the fingertips of God. "Do what you came here to do." The Lord turned His hand back to the armrest of his Throne, and He sat still.

Baal blindly whispered, "What is He doing?"

Azazel answered: "He's not doing anything." He was wings, six pairs, but Michael didn't look to him.

If Michael could breathe, he would. He would reel in all the air in the entire world in the hopes that it would settle his heart, but there was no air in the space above space. There were only misshapen lights, the sensation of other beings around him, the feeling of being watched, of not being alone. Even the chief prince couldn't see accurately, he could only feel before God. He lifted his sword, and he felt himself trembling. He heard his Father's firm voice in his heart, telling him that Lucifer had died because Michael had loved him, and his voice saying that Michael was dirtied, and all the angels were sinners because of him. But he remembered everything Satan had suffered, what he'd witnessed and what he hadn't. He thought of a young girl, so far from God, fighting on the Earth the Lord had made with wars He was so removed from, so meaningless to him and devastating to her. Michael's own cowardice infuriated him now; how dare he have kneeled for cruelty? When he flew to God — yelling in rage — all the others followed.

Tadeo, meanwhile, pulled on the clothes of a corpse a little after he arrived home from a beastly run, then he bundled the naked man in a blanket he'd found, kissed his forehead for dignity, then stumbled away. Behind him, Dina walked, also in the clothing of the dead. The anti-Christ had healed the angel with a touch of his hand, and Dina had remained silent since. The town was destroyed, and though Tadeo would have liked to sit and mourn, he found himself saying, "Maybe I'm lucky, Dina, to have only ever known ruins most of my life, ruins of a place they tell me used to be beautiful, prosperous." He walked past the burnt cars, and he knew that it wasn't the first time he'd seen that, nor the first time he'd seen abandoned buildings, nor the first time he'd seen bodies. It never got easier to see it, but he could soothe himself a little easier, know how to handle the pain. "Because I know that we can still be happy among ruins. There can still be a life worth living after apocalypse."

Ahead, they finally saw humanity. Not many, but a few people huddled, and Tadeo jogged on ahead, leaving Dina behind to watch as the boy shouted happily for his remaining family, all having prayed for his safety. Lupina was there, as well, brightening up weakly, and sitting with some of Joana's youngest siblings, a few neighbors, an old man who clapped his hands and cheered. Children threw fists into the air and hollered in victory.

'Victory?' Dina thought that this couldn't be victory. Everything was gone — homes, history, lives. But they were cheering a small victory. Among ruins, still daring to be happy and to live.

A voice in his head: 'Dina.' Apsinthos. 'Dina, listen to me.' The angel shut his eyes, and he listened to the distant sound of barking, the sound of a world refusing to die. 'Dina!' Urgent, panicked. 'I'm still alive. So are you. It's not over.' But Dina didn't answer, hearing survivors shout in joy at the sight of Tadeo, kissing his cheeks. Apsinthos' voice was fading. Dina didn't call it back.

The Lord took every hit, every shot, unmoving when Michael flew the highest of them all, raised his sword, brought it down. Slow — cutting through a dark void of a crown, an inverted halo, and slicing downward, splitting their God. But as the prince did, his hundred eyes widened, and he saw. He heard, behind him, angels and demons and Watchers. Their voices, all trampled over one another, a stampede of their thoughts, their sensations — all rushing Michael at once. 'Michael.' 'Michael.' 'Michael.' Chants of death. He saw: a thousands Michaels, a thousand Lucifers, a thousand Earths, Watchers, demons, in every direction. Mirrors, everywhere that he looked. He saw: infinite wars, occurring alongside them now. The war for Heaven, the war for Earth, and now the war for Heaven and Earth. In every time, every second, it was all occurring. Eternal; infinite; forever. The never-ending cycle of this story. It will all end, to begin again.

The worlds began folding into one another and Michael was thrown back by the weight of every world folding over one another, on top of all of God's warring creations. He funneled them closer to Him, shrinking the forever expanding walls around them. And as the prince fell, he crashed into Baal, and he looked at him, saw his eyes partly opened, blood pouring down them. Michael wanted to grab his arm, urge him to shut his eyes, to keep alive right beside him. Everyone needed to live. Even Baal. Azazel called out to Michael that they were all going to be crushed, but he didn't call for retreat, and neither did Michael, and neither did Baal. And when it seemed the crush was going to collapse all of time around them in a burst of fire, they saw what they feared — bright flames, rushing out of the floor a million suns away. But it was not the eruption of a universe beginning again.

'Lucifer.'

'Lucifer!'

'Devil!'

Beating his flaming wings and clawing at nothing, Satan climbed rapidly, all the demons opening their eyes despite the danger, cheering for their king who'd escaped Hell. 'Of course he did,' Michael thought with all the pride and joy he'd ever felt. 'You were inevitable.' Satan, king of Hell, father of sin, mother of evil, the god of nothing against the god of everything. He reached them, and he rose before everyone, and he looked, briefly, to Michael, Baal, then to all those others he knew. Rosier, Azazel. Several stars began to rise with him, and they surrounded their Father now. When Satan turned, slow, he faced God, met Him as a child. Obedient, adoring.

'I know,' thought Lucifer, 'how to kill you.' And he surged forward, toward Him, watching every other Lucifer of every other world do the same with him. Every sensation, every thought, every emotion anyone had ever felt — he breathed it in, swallowed it down. The Lord was still split apart by Michael's sword, and when Satan reached Him, he took the split, and he began to pull Him apart, more, more, light raying out of Him of scorching brightness, of every other light. It rushed all the others, many who covered their bodies with their arms, who screamed in pain.

For all those still in Heaven, they noticed the bright dome that caged Heaven beginning to tear, as well, and the light leaking down hot to sizzle on the streets. Angels all began to scurry, hurrying into their homes. Phanuel remained with Metatron, looking up and shutting his eyes to find peace.

For all those on Earth, nothing had changed. Dina continued to watch as Tadeo comforted the humans, kneeling by where they sat. They were laughing, in shock and in relief, traded jokes, though sometimes trembling, about what they'd witnessed. And Tadeo told them that though they'd all suffered great tragedy, they were still alive, and they must respect the dead by continuing to live.

"Our life is lent to us," Tadeo was saying, voice gentle, "and we'll have to give it back when the time comes, return it as honestly as we came into it. And we spend so much more time dead than alive, so let us cherish the few years we have so that we pass on, we have a lot of stories to tell. Well, we might have plenty already, but I'm trying to cheer us up." The people laughed, and Dina felt himself almost smile. Then, Joana's youngest brother frankly told Tadeo that he was hungry, and Tadeo paused, then chuckled. "Let's get some food then." He planted his hands on his knees, lifted himself to stand, raised his hands, only to pause. Tadeo had prayed so much of his life, hoping for good to win, and he wanted to pray still, but not now. He looked back at the child.

Tadeo waved the boy over, and when he noticed a few other children scattered about, he gestured for them too.

"Come, come," he said. "Let's all do it together." Within a minute, eleven children had all scurried over, including some that had been hiding behind rubble and cars, simply watching; two of them being a young girl with her toddler brother. They organized themselves around Tadeo patiently, excitedly. "Show your hands like me." And they did, planting them before themselves at a patch of grass with some stray, surviving flowers, and a half-collapsed prickly pear cactus without fruits or flowers. "Imagine it, want it. Imagine you're a saint, and you're making miracles."

Slow, the ground before them sprouting greener, rising higher. The cactus' damaged side bloomed anew, flowers unfurling from its head, then curling apart to reveal fruits. But the miracle continued as the children awed. More cacti grew beside the original, and some flowers, some trees, the kind that Tadeo had known all his life. And breathing out slow, Tadeo shut his eyes, his heart settling in his chest. Life gasped awake all around him and fought through concrete and rocks and underground infrastructure to grow. All the older humans, and nearby Dina, watched all of it return to the surface of Earth after bombardment and razing and death. And they watched it begin to overrun every building. Green and green, swallowing them in a flood. When it began to climb up their bodies — they allowed it. Dina did as well, wondering if Apsinthos was still calling him. He was no longer listening. Flowers grew by his bare feet, roped around his legs, and Dina watched it happen with burning eyes. Joana's brother reached for the fruits of the cacti, first.

Satan felt the burn of God tearing apart but knew better. The Lord was not a creature on a chair, and He was not in the sky, and He was not below. Inside every angel, demon, human. He had been in Christ; He had been in Judas; He had been on the crucifix and nailing Himself to it. God, killing Himself. Torturing Himself. God, on Earth, as Christ. Christ, without a memory of His life as God, only knowing the Lord is His Father and that he can feel Him in a way that no one can. Christ, a man of Nazareth, born on Earth; a God without the memory of being God, trying to find meaning through being small, mortal. Where had God found meaning — in love or in suicide? Had it been suffering that had taught God meaning? Or had it been love? Another man, a betrayer? A human mother? A human father?

The light would burn them all, would kill them all, but Lucifer persisted. The demons and the angels and the Watchers were all burning, and they seemed to understand what was about to happen. But they told Satan, "Kill God!"

Baal called out: "End it, Lucifer!" 'My love, Lucifer. I told you that it wouldn't all be for nothing.'

Michael called out: "Kill God!" 'Forgive me. Beloved Lucifer.'

Azazel tried to shield himself from the blast with his arms, but what he saw in between was Samyaza, grabbing him, trying to save him the pain. "No— Samyaza—" The light swallowed him, and Azazel begged Satan, "Kill Him, Lucifer! Please!"

God shattered into three, and the burst of light, like at the beginning of time, swallowed them all.

On Earth, the end was gentler. Dark green, quiet in between the sound of children rustling the leaves.

CHAPTER 48

In Heaven, an angel sat at a riverbank, and he ran his fingers through his golden hair, though his skin was warmly dark. Over a great stone, he laid on his belly, staring down at his reflection in the crystalline waters, devoid of fish. His eyelashes cradled dual stars, and his lips were wonderfully plump, and his figure held softness and toughness in all the proper places. From his mouth, a wordless song seeped. No clothes hid him, for he had no shame, but chains of gold and gem were strung all over his sweet throat, his limbs, his waist, hips. In paradise, there were no laws, for all the living are kind and do not ever harm without permission. And the angel of beauty is proud, but it isn't pride without kindness, empathy.

"Beloved Lucifer," called a lover, and the most beautiful angel in paradise sighed dramatically, setting his hands on the damp rock, arching his back as he lifted himself. A tough angel of a different kind of beauty — broadness, strength — with dark curls approached, then settled beside Lucifer, strong hand coming over the beautiful one's fingers. "Why have you hid from me? Don't you know that I spend every second apart from you in grief?" His other hand came to rest on the lean back of the blonde to tease jewelry into chiming, but Lucifer looked away and turned up his nose with a huff. "Oh, tell me what is the matter."

"I," began the grievances of angel Lucifer, "don't like how you parade me around to the others. I'm the most beautiful angel that has ever been born of this paradise, but, Michael, I don't belong to you." Even still, Lucifer tilted his face, then lifted a hand to plant over the chest of the angel of strength, soft in its ease and lovely. "Kiss me."

Ever obedient, Michael leaned closer to the brilliant face of Lucifer as the younger one rearranged himself to sit with his stretched legs pressed together and to the side, toes dipping into the river current that went nowhere. Michael found Lucifer's soft mouth and claimed it, soft yet earnest. Their lips pressed and dragged, beginning to move in hunger. Within the most beautiful angel's core, he felt the familiar twist of love tangling his stomach and heart together, as if to build a knot that only this lover could reach inside to disentangle. But Michael's hands went for Lucifer's waist instead, gripped him securely. Careful, Michael set a foot down, then lifted his body and Lucifer's. His kisses didn't dare falter, not even when he raised the beautiful one high enough that his feet dangled above the ground. As if Lucifer were flying. Or as if they were falling, mouths interlocked. Michael and Lucifer kissing, falling together, never sparing a glance away from each other to watch Heaven fade into the horizon.

'If we could fall together, I want you to land over me. Break me, my bones. Love begs for pain. To be held too tight, to cry out as if hurting, to bruise beneath puckered lips. Love demands a grave; come lie in it with me. Angel, choose death over eternal life. Turn away from creating and kill us both.'

"Mm," Michael said against Lucifer.

And Lucifer tilted his face away now, though not struggling in Michael's grasp, and said, "Do you see now? You kiss me like my mouth is only yours."

"Forgive me," pleaded Michael. "But I can't bring myself to let you go. You were the one that taught me. This, this love. Or should I call it worship? Be it either, I'd leave my Father's house with nothing but desire for you on my back to come to know more. I carry you already on my shoulders even when you're not with me. How can I offer myself to you?" His breath lapped warm against Lucifer's mouth; their fronts pressed flush together, warm, naked. "How can I be yours, if you will not be mine?"

At that, Lucifer's lips twisted into a scheming smile, then he heard leaves shake and footsteps crunching.

Swiveling his gaze over Lucifer's shoulder, Michael grunted, "Baal," to the golden-haired one's laughing delight.

As Baal approached, his robes dragged along the ground, and he tilted his head to peck a kiss at Lucifer's jaw, utterly ignoring Michael. "Lucifer, my love, you didn't say you'd bring Michael." His wings were already revealed, in their great darkness — folding, unfolding anxiously. When Baal brushed his lips toward Lucifer's upper cheek, Michael's grip squeezed the angel of beauty's body in a flame of jealousy, but Lucifer smiled brighter.

"He hunted me, Baal," said Lucifer. "And now he's caught me. What could I do?"

Michael, delicately, set the most beautiful one down, then he murmured, "Lucifer, I've told you about Baal."

"Hm, you see, you see?" Lucifer elegantly stepped away but not without tapping the angel of strength's mouth with an index. "You always tell me what I can or cannot do. Why should I listen? I like you better when you're the one listening, and when you win me new jewels to wear. Won't you win me some more? Don't I deserve it?" Michael made yet another noise of disapproval just as Baal wrapped both arms around Lucifer's hips from behind then brought his face to Lucifer's neck, kissing and nuzzling. "Baal seems to think so."

"Leave, Michael," Baal said, trailing up his mouth and nibbling on Lucifer's ear to spur out a sharp breath.

"Now, now," Lucifer chided, "Michael doesn't have to leave." He took one of Baal's hands, then guided it to trail down his body, to the area between his legs. "He likes to watch. Don't you, Michael?" A soft cry slipped from his mouth as Baal began to work his fingers — slow, then firmer. Warming with each flick of Baal's wrist, Lucifer body bloomed with arousal. And he shivered as Michael's gaze trailed up and down his body. "You can touch too, Michael." When the angel of strength glowered, Lucifer chuckled. "Come. Kiss me again."

Michael hesitated but not long; he stepped forward and, though Baal tensed, he leaned in to take Lucifer's mouth again. One of Michael's hands, too, touched the beautiful angel's stomach, lightly ran his fingers up to his chest, then gripped the back of Lucifer's throat.

The angel of beauty's voice broke with a cry into Michael's rough, scraping kiss as Baal adjusted to press two fingers into Lucifer's heat. Crushed between the two, Lucifer couldn't be happier, and he teased, "You see, Michael, I'm meant to be shared." And when Michael's irritation pressed further into his mouth, Lucifer moaned, languid and high, again for them, the both of them. "Lay me down," he breathed between his pleasure. "On the flowers." Nearby, a crowd of them formed a petal bed of blues, whites, yellows, pinks. "Lay me there."

Soon, he thrashed against the larger angels, and so they relented. Michael and Baal brought Lucifer to his bed of flowers, watched as his hair sprawled over the leaves, and he hummed, calling them down to devour him in kisses, in bites. Encouragingly, Lucifer ran his hand through their curls and stroked their bodies, and when he shivered, he realized the pit of his stomach was terribly empty.

"Let me drink," Lucifer ordered. "Fill my mouth with you." Offering his face, he allowed Baal to slide hardened love past his lips, into his very throat, and begin to rock forward. Michael's hands, meanwhile, found Lucifer's rear, his thighs. Taking a second of eternity to coat his own fingers in the wet of his mouth, Michael then prodded. The angel of beauty's perfect entrance welcomed him, and it was as if digging into the body of a fruit. Like Baal, Michael thrust, coaxing an opening that was already eager and impatient. Choking on sweetness, Lucifer moaned, and he arched his back once more, rolling his hips back against Michael. Not deep enough, he was saying. Not cruel enough. Twist it, like a knife. Love demands blood.

When Michael returned his hand to his own body, he used his

other to grip Lucifer's hip. He guided the pretty angel onto his side, held him there, then guided his weeping arousal to push past the tight gate into paradise. Slow, he pressed on, feeling how he widened him, how a flower unfurled, how a burrow shut around a seed. Lucifer shook in bliss, and he twitched and groaned with his mouth full. The first rut forward made him twitch, and when the ruts continued, rolling into him like tides — he shook. His core burned, and the coiled tightness tore open from his belly to where the strongest prince offered himself. Michael asking to be owned by someone, having left his Father's house, looking to be wanted and commanded.

A low, guttural noise rumbled from Baal's throat, and Lucifer felt the angel of flight comb back his hair, then hold his face tenderly as he continued. The salt of the Earth — procuring from him, a gift to feed the most beautiful angel. Nothing but jewels, salt, and honey are to bother Lucifer; he must be spoiled. Spoiled until he rot, but it would be a beautiful rot.

'Love me,' he wanted to say to them. 'Love me until I can't walk, and I must be carried everywhere we go. Hold me between your bodies, and love me until I forget if I've ever felt anything else.' This body of his wasn't made to be empty; it was made to be shaped. Delight — shuddering Lucifer's body, 'Beg for me, every time. Pray to me.' He tried to stop those thoughts. 'Worship me.' But he couldn't. And Michael and Baal murmured prayers as they drove into him like swords into a victim.

"Mm," the angel of beauty continued to moan, and he saw brightness, then felt pleasantness raking its claws up his body. Death tore out of himself in tight, wet finish. And Baal and Michael were quick to follow, spilling into both mouths of the angel, then lowering to kiss him everywhere again, praising him, adoring him, the most beautiful angel in Heaven, in all of life, of all creations. The favorite. Their favorite. The favorite of no one else.

As Lucifer laid with them, eyes on the golden sky, he held the both of them to his chest, running his fingers through their hair once more; eventually, he tried to tilt their tired heads to make them kiss for him. They scowled, refused. But Lucifer maintained a light, sweet smile.

After this — the three returned to the city of angels, where there were preparations to celebrate the birth of a new star somewhere. Several colorful homes, at either side of the road, were pressed to each other, so close that it could have been that there were merely infinitely long houses trailing in every direction, only occasionally intruded on by amphitheaters, bathhouses, galleries. Walking far ahead of Baal and Michael on the crowded golden pathway — Lucifer watched plants travel alongside him — migrating fungi, wandering trees that left fruits in their wake. The beautiful angel plucked one off the ground swiftly, then made his way over with a hum to a certain figure sitting on a stone bench by a plaza. "Rosier!" Lucifer chirped over the chatter of all the hundred angels bustling about. "Brother, how are you?"

Rosier, an angel of fruit; he was working through a basket of pomegranates when he startled and lifted his head. His friend, Asmodeus, was asleep with his head draped over one of Rosier's shoulders. "Oh. I'm well, I'm well. How are you?" His voice shook, but then he smiled gently, almost shyly, and the tall angel beside him grunted, shifted in his dreaming.

Dropping the fruit into Rosier's basket, Lucifer smiled. "Well. We always are." And when the angel of fruit stared up at him with a quietly pensive gaze, Lucifer added, "If you'd let me, I want to deliver fruits with you again."

At that, Rosier laughed, though softly. "Really? But aren't you busy? I thought you were going to lead the celebration for the new star with your songs."

"Mm, but I have to go get my timbrel and...." His voice trailed, and he blinked, trying to remember.

"Pipes," offered Asmodeus, though his eyes remained shut.

Just as Rosier began demanding to know how long his friend had been pretending to sleep, Lucifer stepped away, turning back to his lovers who hated each other, but he noticed a fountain, and two angels standing before it.

One was dark-haired, his face speckled, his hair enshrouded by veil. "Excuse me," Dina was begging. The one before him tilted his head — his almond eyes widened, his feathery hair cascading down his shoulders. Phanuel. "But I wanted to ask you for forgiveness," Dina said. "I realized it. I realized it just recently— I asked God for forgiveness for a pain that I inflicted on you. That is why I never felt forgiven. It was you that I should have asked. It was you who I should have made amends with. Phanuel, I stole your rings— During the war in Heaven, I had your rings. I was a thief."

The angel of forgiveness stared, and he whispered that he'd forgiven Dina long ago.

"Dina," Lucifer called, then tried, "What—" The youngest angel twisted around, eyes far too wide, reddened with sadness, knowing. And before the angel of beauty could speak more, there was the sound of an angel clearing their throat. Hesitating, Lucifer turned his head another direction, and he saw now Azazel, down the road, where Michael and Baal should have been. He still carried a hole in his heart and smeared white paint on his face.

'You never desired to go back,' Lucifer thought at the Watcher. 'Nostalgia never made a fool of you, how it did me.' When he looked to the youngest angel again, his eyes darkening, his brows furrowing, his lips pressing thin — all the angels who'd been crowded around and preparing for the birth of a star faded into the eternal brightness of the new Heaven. Rosier was gone, as was Asmodeus, and Phanuel disappeared as well. The plants melted into the glow, then so did the last remnants of a golden street and a fountain and stone bench.

Lucifer laughed — low.

Any second now, Azazel with his bleeding heart and Dina with his frightened face would disappear like all the others. No great bang nor screams of death. Without noise, they'd drown in the light.

But he surrendered: 'We cannot return.' His shoulders shook as he continued to giggle, more and more miserably. 'We cannot return. It can never be like before. It will never be like before.' He hadn't even remembered Heaven well enough to recreate it accurately. He'd missed flying, but he forgot how to do it now. He hadn't been an angel for what had felt like, what surely were, lifetimes. But what was he, if not an angel? Where was he?

CHAPTER 49

Tadeo woke somewhere green, his body scarred and still bleeding. He lifted his head at the sound of buzzing — some insects whizzing by. Too, he saw trees, but not any type that he could recognize, and he noticed some birds, many of which he couldn't quite make out either. Some had familiar calls, some sounded entirely new. In the distance, he heard the rumble of an animal. Again, this one was unfamiliar. Instinct made his hand twitch for a weapon, but he had nothing on him except his typical clothes, also slightly different.

"Hello?" he called out, then he climbed onto trembling legs. "Hello?"

Despite how dense this place was with trees, flowers, fruits, almost falling over him — Tadeo felt no claustrophobia, nor fear. He dragged a foot forward, felt himself bump into a scurrying rodent, then another animal he couldn't recognize. Polite, he apologized to them. 'The last thing I remember was trying to make fruits for the survivors.' Well, he'd certainly succeeded — if he was alive and this wasn't some afterlife that he'd accidentally slipped into. The thought of potentially being dead annoyed him. He had people to protect, and he had more of loving and being-loved to experience. Suddenly, he almost laughed. 'How ridiculous am I?' But there was so much left unfinished, as there always would be. He had taught the children miracles, but he was not done doing it. The world never ends; there is no return; there is just one tree ahead, then another.

A *clink* sounded beneath his shoe, and he looked to see coins, some meager money but money nonetheless, in the soil like ruins. Familiar silver, never to remove its teeth from this world, however new it seemed. This new Earth, which was not quite new at all.

Soon after he'd begun trudging through the grass, trying not to crush any of the hundred creatures by his legs, he heard a sound, something human. 'Tadeo?' Is that what they were saying? Oddly, he remembered the first time he'd been able to answer to that name, the first time he'd returned home after his resurrection. His family had asked him to respond to another title, the one of a young girl, and he'd insisted, heart in his mouth, that his name was Tadeo, that he was someone new. Eventually, they must've stopped believing Tadeo was another person than that girl who died. He always prayed for that, that they had come to accept him, however imperfectly. But, now, he was perking up at his name, warm and confused and frightened. 'Tadeo, that's my name. It's Tadeo.'

He wasn't sure whose voice it was, in the distance, or if they were even really saying his name. Yet —

'Dante? Joana?' Or was that his father's tired rumble? Or was that even his mother? Tadeo's walking quickened, then his feet propelled him into a run, shoving branches out of his way. "Wait!" he called to them, and he felt himself begin to smile, to laugh happily at realizing who the voices belonged to. The dead and the living — all before him. "Tell me where you are!" he called helplessly. He would find them. 'Dante, Joana, mother, father. Everyone.' "I'll find you whether you tell me or not!" Tadeo jumped; he waved a hand, hoping they'd see him, tears swelling in his eyes. "I love you! I'll find you! Stay there!"

THE FINAL INTERLUDE

He dreamt: of the past, for some time. Lucifer tried to recall every detail of it, and he realized that he'd had quite the modest birth if nostalgia was an honest prophet. The archangel Raphael had been there, and Lucifer had met Asmodeus soon thereafter. When Lucifer saw himself for the first time, he had asked who it was, and then he'd said that this was too much beauty for an angel to carry. He had been right, in the end. For many slow, monotonous years, his greatest concern had been finding a purpose that wasn't imprisoned to a body. God had held his chin and told Lucifer he was ripe for love. One day, Lucifer had stood and burst into a song of worship, and the angel Michael had seen him and said that there had never been an angel as fine as him. He'd grown vain, and the Lord berated him, and Lucifer had traded God's love for an angel's love. The greatest sin was to love. He was groomed to be beautiful and to be beautiful to break. He was raped by God and told no one. Had almost forgotten about it, over the centuries.

The Lord tore him open, and when he looked down, he never stopped bleeding. Why should he have told anyone? It belonged to him, like a heart — the rape; it was his to carry and hear the echoing beat of. Michael then betrayed him, and Baal fell with the demons. He dragged others down. An angel named Rosier. Asmodeus. An angel named Gemory, and one named Moloch. There were so many names that he confused them, and he had to shut his eyes and start the dream over again. He remembered Azazel and Samyaza, and he remembered telling Azazel never to become like him. There, too, had been emperor once. A Christ on a crucifix. There was once a young human boy named Cain, whom he'd cherished more than anything. He remembered Eve, her anger at him, and his pity for her. He remembered, and he remembered. And he slept often.

Lucifer began to understand why God had done it, all of it. He grew tired of being alone and dreamt of love, of kisses and praise, and he began to ask himself if he was really alone or if he had wandered away from the others long ago, without realizing it. He wasn't God; he couldn't be. Where was he? Who was he?

All he could do was lay on what was like a cloud and stare off and keep trying to recall. Sweet nostalgia twisted it, lengthened the good times, dwindled the bad. When Lucifer didn't waste away with what was, he thought of what could have been — with Michael, and if not with Michael, then with Baal. He'd curl up on his cloud — this bored, pretty, and vain god — and continue with the fantasies of embraces and lips molding to each other, equal and perfect and soft and rough when he wanted it. How nice it would be to rest, then perhaps, one day, rise to walk toward the end of the light and search for whatever existed outside of this. Whoever existed.

When that day comes, I think it will be like being born again.

Perhaps I have misled you. I'm an angel still, still have the desire in me to be a messenger. But I speak for myself. I tell the truth, but I offer you no comfort. I don't know what it was all for. I don't know why God ever did this to me. I know that He is dead, and that He sought death in wretchedness. Suffering is all that the almighty could never have, suffering and forbiddenness. But He is not gone. He is pieces. He is me; He is you; but He is dead.

And I ask myself once more if I'm alone until I feel soft eyes watching me. I ask myself if I'm God, again. I ask myself over and over, waiting for an answer. I feel something past the horizon. The humans felt it, felt it better than angels did. Angels with God right before them never had a need to ask if there was anything more, and so it was the humans who reached out to it, the world beyond, and perhaps something had reached back.

Then, I feel someone, coming up behind me, pressing and curling his body against my own. I don't open my eyes. I don't need to. There are voices now, thousands of them, nearby — familiar. If they see us, they'll see us so close that they'll think us one, one god. How much I have grown to hate, but I know still to love. It lingers the greatest in my memory. I love you. How do I love you? This is how. With the beginning and the end born from these bodies, the promise of what has happened and suffering of our present. It is not right to be alone, my friend, my beloved friend. Eternities let us sleep, twisted together. For some time, let us rest. Creation can wait for another day.

As we slumber, the others will see us. They'll ask if this is what it means to be God. I won't answer. And they'll ask if I still worship. I'll tell them I do.

I do worship myself; I worship my love. The only God is love.

ABOUT THE AUTHOR

Standing Figure of a Youth,
Giovanni Battista Tiepolo

rafael nicolás is an author of queer fiction. He likes marigolds.

www.ingramcontent.com/pod-product-compliance
Lightning Source LLC
Chambersburg PA
CBHW061034310726
48969CB00004B/947

9 798999 325133